W9-CQF-411

Moby Dx

A Novel of Silicon Valley

Dan Seligson

With warm regards
Dan

Melvillean Press

Palo Alto
2014

This is a work of fiction set in an almost-real world. Names, characters, places, and incidents either are the product of the author's imagination or are used fictitiously, and any resemblance to actual persons, living or dead, companies, events, or locales is entirely coincidental.

Moby Dx: A Novel of Silicon Valley
Dan Seligson 1954 -

ISBN
978-1-941207-01-7 pdf ebook
978-1-941207-02-4 kindle/mobi
978-1-941207-03-1 epub
978-1-941207-06-2 softbound

Printing 03

1741 Middlefield Rd., Palo Alto, CA 94301

Cover by Elisabeth Ajtay
Book design by Melvillean Press
Author photo by Scott R. Kline
Logo Design in Chapter 124 by William E. Keene

In Token of My Appreciation
for her inspiration,
this book is inscribed to

Judith T. Seligson

In Memoriam

William E. Keene
1956-2013

My feelings at the moment ... were prompted by that glorious principle inherent in all heroic natures—the strong-rooted determination to have the biggest share of the pudding or go without any of it.

Typee: A Peep at Polynesian Life
Herman Melville

Contents

VOLUME 1 MAX EBB

VOLUME 2 GENORMAX

VOLUME 3 GENORMX

VOLUME 4 MAX IS OUT

VOLUME 5 N_{MAX}

VOLUME 6 MAXED OUT

Volume 1

Max Ebb

Prologue

... it is an ever-fixed mark
That looks on tempests and is never shaken;
It is the star to every wandering bark,
Whose worth's unknown, although his height be taken.

\- *Sonnet 116,* William Shakespeare

TO THE long-suffering returning from exodus, Silicon Valley is the land flowing with milk and money. It is the mecca of would-be entrepreneurs making their hajj. It is the Fountain of Youth to those remaking their careers. It is tne cosa vera, the genuine article, the real McCoy, the true cloth, the ne plus ultra, the veritable North Star to those venturing forth into the world of startup companies. It is no longer a place much driven by silicon, but would you rather we auctioned naming rights to the highest corporate bidder?

For decades, through thick and thin, through the 1970s birth of biotech, through DRAM- and EPROM-dumping and the near-death experience of the early 1980s, through the Asian Flu of the 1990s, through Wall Street's infatuation with the dotcoms, and even through the Lesser Depression, about a third of all venture capital invested worldwide has originated in Silicon Valley.

There is so much startup fever in these towns that ██████ is working on a vaccine to prevent it, and middle schoolers are figuring out how to transmit it. Taking a page from John-Hennessy-of-Stanford's playbook, the school districts require that every child, upon enrolling in kindergarten, sign a contract with the teachers' union permitting the latter to buy up to ten percent of any qualified offering in which the former is a cofounder. The schools have great science labs and no sports facilities, so high school students must assign all their invention rights to the Sports Boosters.

Instead of dance parties, there are hackathons. The balloon-tying clowns on urban street corners have been pushed aside by millennial buskers who perform feats of coding 3-D printers powered by stationary unicyclists. Parents worry that their high schoolers' uncontracted liaisons might lead to procreation—shorthand for product creation—and downstream litigation. The nerds are so revered there that the jocks feign Asperger syndrome just to get a date. On Halloween you'll see more girls dressed up as Sheryl Sandberg than Batwoman, and more boys as Hank Rearden than the Man of Steel. It's a place where mooning doesn't mean teenage pranks or moping, but going to the moon, and maybe further, and not metaphorically. It's where PARC is neither a typo nor a Francophile's garden, but the birthplace of the GUI and the laser printer. Cupcake and Ice Cream Sandwich are ten-foot-high sculptures commemorating software releases, and so is Jelly Bean. Over forty different languages are spoken in the homes there, and that doesn't include PHP, R and Ruby, HTML, Verilog, or Hadoop, or dead languages like COBOL. Cakes are delivered by drones, crime is illegal, MOOCs and Tor are POR, thirty is the new fifty, and the singularity is around the corner, always around the corner.

At a fountain on California Avenue in Palo Alto, legend has it that Bill Hewlett and David Packard added grape Kool-Aid to the water supply—in an engineer's idea of a bacchanal—and danced there naked on the night they sold their first oscillators to Walt Disney. To this day, street urchins stop cars at the intersection of University and Emerson, imploring "Drink the Kool-Aid, ma'am," and offering glass vials with a milliliter of putative purple holy water from the same said fountain, while across the avenue, Cassandras and end-of-the-worlders holding placards chant "Don't drink the Kool-Aid!" over, and over, and over.

On the street where Steve Jobs lived, pilgrims come from halfway around the world—and they'd come from further if they could—to take selfies in front of his slate-roofed former residence.

LOOK around, and what do you see? Thousands and thousands of mortal souls fixed in startup reveries. All of which is to say that if in Melville's time Nantucket was no Illinois, neither is Silicon Valley in this one. Silicon Valley is the Nantucket of entrepreneurs.

MOBY DX

A Novel of Silicon Valley

CHAPTER 1 BEGINNINGS

I WAS DOE, Baby Jane Doe, in Delivery. I'm Rani at home. I'm Dorani on the dotted line. I'm lucky in life and Lakshmi in the lab. Call me Lakshmi, Dorani Lakshmi Stein, born in Baltimore, January 22, 1984. I've lived the tale I'm about to tell you. Every bit of it is true. What I didn't experience firsthand, I've learned from others who did. What they couldn't tell me, I've imagined.

MY mother had come to Hopkins for its MD/PhD program after an impressive undergraduate showing at the Indian Institute of Science in Bangalore. She was in her second unhappy year of medical school. Well, she was happy to have met Isador Stein and won her parents' approval to marry him. But she was discovering that her professional love was scientific research and not the practice of medicine. The burden of acquiring a medical education she no longer wanted was proving unbearable.

In the first moments of January 22, my mother concluded a twenty-four-hour shift during her clerkship in Women's Health. While she dreamt of sleep and prepared to walk out into one of the coldest nights in the history of our Monumental City, the attending physician in Ob/Gyn, another Bangalorean, said, "Naija, stand in on a real delivery?"

Thinking about it now makes me remember those days as a skinny thing when I asked, "Amma, tell me about the night I was born?" In her candy-sweet voice she unwound the tale, sprinkling in the rhyming timing of Tamilian English *Vinglish* she never lost.

"It came to pass that I was watching as a beautiful young wisp of a woman—she couldn't have been more than twenty years old—was rushed into Delivery, already in labor. She had jet-black hair, and the deep, dark skin of my people, and the brown eyes, of course. Immediately, there were problems. She did seem to be term, but she was uncommunicative. Not in a medically serious way, but she said very little. She wasn't one of ours. I mean, we were not expecting her. No one on our staff had seen her before. She was not in our medical records. She hadn't been receiving prenatal care from us. She was all alone and she identified no next of kin.

"The labor was not going well; she was so petite, too petite. She nodded her approval for us to do a C-section. It had to be done stat. Maybe it would have happened anyway, but when the chief resident opened her up, some of the amniotic fluid around the baby got into her blood, the mom's blood. The baby was fine and had an out-of-the-box APGAR score of 8 that was soon followed by a 10, but all of a sudden the mother began to have severe trouble breathing. Her blood pressure dropped. Then her heart stopped. We couldn't save her."

"Tell me more, Ammaji, please." I would nuzzle up against her buttery soft skin, warm and so comforting.

"Rani," she would say to me, "I am trying to spare you!"

"Amma, please?"

She sighed, knowing that there was no escape. "Amniotic fluid had leaked into her bloodstream and it made her clot up. An embolism, a big one, lodged in her heart. She turned blue and had convulsions. It was awful, more awful than I can tell you. Watching that young woman vooman, watching that girl-child suffer, then vanish in moments...." She always stopped here, to gather composure before she finished with my favorite part of the legend.

"She was the darkest cinnamon little Tamil girl, like me. A beautiful baby. Seeing the mother die in front of me—my medical career ended right there. I did not have the stomach for more of that. But, I loved that infant from the moment I saw her. I knew that I was going to find a way to keep her, and I did, kid."

Not long after, my mother dropped out of the MD program. She would finish her PhD in immunology on schedule in three more years. Later she gave birth to my little sister, Dhaya.

CHAPTER 1 BEGINNINGS

THREE months into my colicky infancy, my mother—and my father, too—might have been having second thoughts about the wisdom of that adoption. After the colic passed, I had colds, and ear infections that kept on giving, and diarrheas my mother had thought she'd left behind on the subcontinent. A fast-moving virus produced a faster-moving fever, and then a seizure, the one and only, that was over before my poor mother could think about calling for help.

Cat is admitted into Woman's Cave in Kipling's tale because he soothes Baby, putting his crying to an end and giving Woman some peace. Not in our house. Neither cat nor dog, nor TV show, nor music, nor my father's warm hairiness, neither bottle nor binky, would satisfy or calm me. Until my seventh month, only my mother's breast would do. By that time, the midsummer humidity and the daytime highs were both in the low nineties and everyone in the mid-Atlantics was on edge, hoping for a break in the weather.

While my mother slept, and while the TV was tuned to the summer Olympics in Los Angeles, my father watched as I crawled around on the floor, noisy and unhappy, a condition he had almost gotten used to. I was restless, always in motion, leaning on a wall for a moment, then unsatisfied, scrambling to another place, trying to sit up without the wall, falling over, crying on impact, moving some more. Applause and national anthems occasionally held my attention, but that was fleeting. As for the events on-screen, I might look at the swimmers or the runners, and then look away. The pole-vaulters seemed to get me, my father said. He noticed me gazing at them, quieter than I had ever been, and then I was back to my usual disconsolate self, until something happened.

The something was Greg Louganis. My father noticed it when, in the tower prelims, Louganis—the greatest diver of his era—dropped from ten metres and made a hole in the water through which he slipped without a splash. I sat up by myself. No wall. I squealed with joy. I smiled, sat still, and never looked back. My mother, when she woke, hardly recognized her cheerful child.

My father made tapes of the tower and the springboard, the men's and the women's, the prelims, and then the semis and the head-bonking finals. For years I watched and re-watched Wendy Wyland, Sylvie Bernier, and the others with the kind of dedication that only a child can give, absorbing details of Louganis's Buddha-like calm or Michelle Mitchell's steely nerves that must have stood me in good stead later. The VHS cassettes were augmented by videos from dual meets and national championships, and then the next Olympics in Seoul.

My happiest early memories are of standing at the top of the stairs in a tiny bathing suit and goggles when my father walked through the front door after work. With my toes curled over the edge of a step and my head tucked between arms pointed straight overhead, he hoisted me up, flipped me halfway around, and carried me head first to the ground floor, all the time repeating variations on, "Point your toes, Lakshmileh," or "Stretch it out, little one." Then, another flip onto my feet, and his applause, and my mother's if she was home. I would take a bow, and with much ceremony my father would put an old math Olympiad medal around my neck. Joy, Dear Reader. Joy, unalloyed. There was something about the leap, the power, and the grace of diving, the beautiful bodies, the wetness, the intensity of it. Divers are comfortable with themselves. I may have admired them for that from the start.

Before I could swim I was tumbling, and when I could swim I began diving with the Retrievers, a club named after the mascot of the University of Maryland, Baltimore County. I kept at it all the way through my freshman year in college.

MY mom was to give a keynote at the Annual Meeting and Science Innovation Exposition of the AAAS—that's the American Association for the Advancement of Science—one year when it was held in Baltimore. The annual meeting is a science circus, delivering the full panoply, from the anatomy of ancient ammonoids, to policy or politics, all the way to the swift retreat—that's the redshift or z—of the remotest objects in the cosmos. The meeting is part celebration and part public outreach, bringing together the makers—the Stephen Jay Goulds and the John Holdrens and the Ginger Mascarpones—and the moochers—the journalists and teachers and the science-loving public. For most of a week every winter, there are meetings and lectures and demonstrations, some targeted for AAAS officialdom, some for educated nonspecialists, and some for laypeople and children.

Our own home was its own circus. My mother's professional colleagues from around the globe were frequent overnight guests. In my pajamas, I shared cereal with many Nobelists-in-the-making, also in their pjs. Even more frequent were visitors for whom my mother cooked dinners and planned parties, where conversation ranged from lymphocytes to mast cells—in other words, all immunology, all the time. Not true. Not true. My father had his own non-overlapping cast of computer scientists, mathematicians, and artists, and he always drove the conversation into political territory.

While himself not a child of the Great Depression, he says he is an honorary member of the Association for Adult Children of Children of the Depression. He speaks as if he'd lived through it—its days of six cents per pound ground beef, and people too poor to buy it—so deeply ingrained in him are his own long-gone parents' own experiences. He would fit right in among the card-carrying Communists of the 1930s if they were still around.

While other kids were taking winter breaks in Bermuda, he took me on a tour of Works Progress Administration projects from the McKissick Museum in Columbia, South Carolina, to the Merritt Parkway in Connecticut. We didn't need a holiday to go see Camp David; that was done one Saturday before I was ten. When we all went west in my eleventh summer, be sure we saw the Griffith Observatory in Los Angeles and the Timberline Lodge at Mount Hood, and heard Isador Stein's lectures and those of the tour guides, too, on the wonders of the WPA. In fact, I was so conditioned to the presence of that agency that it wasn't until the Great Recession hit, and we needed it again, that I learned it had been shuttered. So much for the conventional wisdom that all government agencies live forever.

We were not skiers, so it was easy to find time one Presidents' Week to chill in the Deep South. Not only were we dragged through the cities of Civil Rights Era fame, but we also made a pilgrimage to Hale County, Alabama, site of James Agee's poetic prose and Walker Evans' photographs of sharecropper poverty, courtesy of that other Depression stalwart, the Farm Securities Administration. On the West Coast trip, driving from Los Angeles to Portland, Oregon, we detoured off the spectacular Pacific Coast Highway in San Luis Obispo County to visit Nipomo, where Dorothea Lange, working for the selfsame agency, took the photo she captioned *Migrant Mother*, the photo that became an icon of the Depression. We must have been the only visitors in years.

My mother, whose political conversation was limited to issues of fairness in medicine, made up a narrative about that picture. "Rani. That woman could be Sikh, don't you think? One of her children must be sick, too. I'll bet she's waiting to see a doctor. She looks worried. She has no money to pay, but what's she going to do? She can barely feed them on what her husband makes picking peas. Look at their clothes, Rani. What does that make you think?" We had a cheap, framed reproduction of *Migrant Mother* hanging in a hallway at home. All of which is to say that my father has the conscience of a liberal and he imprinted me and my sister with it like so many ducklings.

By the time of that AAAS meeting, I was twelvish and could be counted on not to throw a tantrum or make a scene, and on a good day my parents would say they were even a little bit optimistic that I would not grow up to be a beggar or a criminal, so they said they would take a chance and bring me along to see my mother perform before an adulatory crowd. The Vice President, Al Gore, was speaking the same day. My parents thought it would be enriching for me, they said, if I heard him too, and thus I got a day off from school and spent it with a bunch of grown-ups, many of whom I had already met at home. I thought it was no big deal.

Gore did get my attention, and at the special reception for him, the plenary speakers, and some very select others, I managed to get his. I was trying to balance my Mad Libs, spiral notebook, plastic case full of pencils and sharpeners, plate of tiny chocolatey desserts with colored glazes artfully applied, and plastic champagne glass of sparkling apple cider. Right in front of the Vice President, I tripped on my own leather shoes—my parents wouldn't let me wear my favorite pink tennies—and made the scene after all. I will never forget how he reached down and offered a hand to pull me up. He was a big man, smelled better than my dad, and had a surprisingly friendly face. "Well, hello there. You didn't have to work so hard to introduce yourself. I'm Al Gore. What's your name?"

My parents looked terrified and were about to intercede with apologies, but once I was back on my feet, all those cordial handshakes and conversations at home served me well. "Excuse me, Mr. Vice President. It's an honor to meet you," I said. Then, *sotto voce* for his ears only, "I am so clumsy. My parents are going to kill me." And back to normal volume, I announced, "Please call me Lakshmi, sir." Then Gore, seeing my parents, stepped forward to introduce himself and make them prouder (of me) than they had ever been. Camera shutters were clicking away. A film crew moved in.

"Call me Al, Lakshmi," he said. "And what did you think of today's proceedings?"

"Mr. Vice President, I agree with your remarks about the importance of government support for science. The need for scientific advances only grows as billions of people in the developing world enter the middle class." It sounded erudite, but all I was doing was stitching together snippets of what I'd heard during the day. "If America is going to maintain its leadership in the world, it must lead in science. America cannot stand pat." My father had always broken out in hysterics whenever he used that Nixon-era line, and my little speech had the same effect on everyone within earshot. Departing from the wooden scripting he'd been given, the VP's big face melted into real laughter. He whistled and slapped his thigh before he put his arm around me. He pulled me close beside him for the photo op, which made the first page of the *Baltimore Sun* and page three of the *New York Times* and some local-color segments on the evening news broadcasts.

It was a big deal after all. Al Gore and I were pen pals through the next general election cycle, and I became a regular at the AAAS Annual Meeting. I took a week off from school each January or February, and my parents traded off shuttling and chaperoning responsibilities year to year when we traveled to Seattle, Anaheim, San Francisco, Philly, DC, or Boston. It was at these events that I developed my journeyman's appreciation for the full gamut of contemporary science. I heard and even met so many of its practitioners, just as I did at my own house, that I lost any sense that the best, even the greatest, were different from me. My mother was my mother, and I never completely appreciated what she'd accomplished. I wasn't going to be a scientist just because my mother was one, nor because my father was, either. What finally inspired me to become a scientist was the troupe of young beauties, the crop of women who had grown up after the gender barrier had been cracked open. They were mostly chemists and biologists, so much so it was even a cliché, but a few were physicists and engineers. In my mind I tried on their different lab coats, assessing the fit of each.

THE last AAAS meeting I attended was in Denver. I no longer needed (nor would accept) a chaperone, and went instead with my high school boyfriend. He wanted to turn it into a ski boondoggle, so we had some words over that. I shouldn't have gone at all. Princeton was too demanding. My diving coach was unhappy with me for missing so many days of practice. I couldn't give myself to the meeting and leave my own thoughts and work behind. The whole experience had an unexpected effect on me that began during a session on new developments in DNA sequencing. Ginger Mascarpone was the featured speaker. I'd heard of her, and heard she was riveting—that's why I was there—but had never seen her. She was a theoretical physicist showered with honors and awards, and had devoted herself to the most abstruse foundations of the theory of time. Then she pivoted, as they say, and focused thereafter on molecular biology. Rumor had it there were suicides in the aftermath. The laurels kept on coming, from institutions in her new discipline and more yet from the former ones.

The meeting room was SRO, which didn't surprise me, given the publicity that had surrounded her since she had flipped. When she got up to speak, her strawberry blonde hair flowed over the shoulders of her tailored linen jacket. She wore a simple gold necklace, weighted down by a pendant of uncut cinnabar. Her black V-neck blouse, probably sleeveless, plunged (discreetly) in parallel, but revealed at its base the slightest, slightest hint of her bare abdomen. Her linen slacks fit perfectly over legs we imagined were equally perfect. The audience moaned. Her beauty, her worth—there was no other word for it—overcame me. I was blinded; I had to hold up my arms to cut down whatever it was she radiated. My boyfriend shuddered and put his head down, covering it with his hands as if in despair. Something went liquid inside me. My swoon was mirrored by everyone else in the room, too. Everyone.

Her talk rocked us on another level. The deceptively simple way she used her command of atomic physics and thermodynamics to explain the origins of life. Her lucid explanations of which problems would fall in the next few years, and which ones could be made to do so in the few that followed—if only some brave souls could be convinced to try their hands at them, or if the crippling cost of research could be reduced. She made me want to grow up to be like her, but she was different from me, from everyone. How could so much virtue exist in the world? That I understood. That it could exist in one person? That I couldn't understand. Did she create virtue? Was her worth consistent with the Marxist theory of value my father believed in? Or had she lucked into it, some princely windfall that she—no more and no less than anyone else—didn't deserve, yet still held fast to?

Before that moment, I had never, at least not consciously, wanted to kiss a girl. All that changed with the arrival on the podium of the iridescent fusion of Jodie Foster and Richard Feynman. Jodie? Sure, we all get that. But why Feynman? If I'd said Einstein, you'd be thinking of the white-haired grandfather figure on a bicycle, and that image wouldn't convey the juiciness of Ms. Mascarpone. Feynman, about whom more later, was as much rock star as physicist, the sexiest man at Caltech.

Ginger Mascarpone made only the rarest of public appearances, each the subject of myth and legend. Still, one sighting was enough to awaken me. I broke up with my boyfriend that day. When I went back to Princeton, I quit diving, got serious about school, and started thinking about going out with some girls.

CHAPTER 2 THERE WAS BLOOD

At first I did it for love, then I did it for a friend, and then for money. I wasn't doing anything at all when it ended in darkness and blood. Working for Max Frood, being in his sphere, there was no other word for it than love. Then I began to help a mutual friend, and that led to a business, or a business idea, really, but one with money in it. Along the way, the love hit its sell-by date and then there was blood. All that's left of Max is this story.

There's been legal action by Frood Metal, Inc., so while I'll be as complete as I can, I must abide by the terms of the TRO, the Temporary Restraining Order.

CHAPTER 3 THE LUCKY STRIKE

Driving a Harvester full of ten-cent gas in Depression-era Keota, in Keokuk County, Iowa, and responsible for every last detail of the corn in the southeast quadrangle of his family's farm while studying hard at school, Jenk Orrix had time for little else. Still, every day he managed to hurl a few dozen baseballs through the tire swing. Twenty-first Century Reader, let me clarify. There weren't a few dozen baseballs. There was one baseball and a hay bale for a backstop. He threw the ball through the tire swing sixty feet six inches away. Then he walked to retrieve the ball, and then back to the mound where he wound up and threw again.

There wasn't enough money for him to go to university, until the Hawkeyes' Coach Otto Vogel saw him fire once and only once at the State High School Spring Tournament championship game. Although the matchup was being played on the university's diamond in Iowa City, Coach Vogel had been unable to free himself of pressing obligations until late in the ninth inning, just as Jenk wound up on a 1-2 count and unbottled a sinking sliding streak of mystifying lightning that pretzeled the batter and gave the Eagles their victory.

Jenk always called it the lucky strike. He'd made nine Ks that day, so there was no luck in the actual fact of his mechanics or the missile's dynamics. He believed, as he told everyone, including me, that without that one pitch, without the simple act of it being observed, an act that upset some equilibrium in the cosmos, he would have stayed at home with his sisters in their threadbare but better-than-seed-bag dresses. Only a year later they were forced off their original Homestead Act property when his father, in an act of desperation born of humiliation, was thrown in jail for threatening to hang a judge who was ruling on its foreclosure. Life was a grindstone for them until war broke out in Europe, and then here in the US of A, and the biggest stimulus program that ever was—some would call it a bubble—swept over the land. But with that one pitch, with the chance he got because of it, Jenk became an engineer, an inventor, an entrepreneur, a captain of industry, and the father of another.

CHAPTER 4 EXITS

IN THE spring of 2010, Travie McCoy and Bruno Mars captured the sentiment of the moment, crooning of billionaires and of longing, of celebrity and fortune and Forbes. And even if they hadn't, teenagers would have absorbed the message from the world of money, money, money all around them: The so-called meritocracy we live in is a ranked and rated, one-dimensional society where money is the adult scorecard.

The way startups are turned into money is through exits. Whether you're the founding entrepreneur, an investor, or an early employee, there's almost no chance you'll end up a billionaire, but it does happen.

If you're an early-stage investor, the most likely outcome on any one investment is that you'll lose your money, although there's a small chance that you might make more on it than you lose on all the others, and an even smaller chance that you'll make much, much more.

If you're an entrepreneur or employee, if you're lucky, you'll find that you worked ungodly hours for a below-average salary for a very long time. You will have sat and cried alone; alone because you gave up your social life in pursuit of your dream, or more often, someone else's. Alone because you can't talk to anyone else because your obsession is, ultimately, boring to them, even if it's momentarily entrancing. There is, however, a remote chance you might make a few years' salary as a bonus, and an even remoter chance that you might make a fortune.

A venture-backed startup company generates money for the investors and stockholders in one of two different ways. One, a private offering, amounts to a merger with or acquisition by another company. The other, a public offering, is the sale of a company to the public, that is, to you and me.

If you're selling your company's shares to the public, first you must register those shares with the SEC and demonstrate conformance to a host of regulations too numerous to mention, all of them intended to ensure good governance and transparency. Then you must find buyers for the shares, a process usually involving large fees paid to bankers, and then you go to Wall Street and ring the bell when the shares are first sold. Given that public markets define a small company as one worth $250 million to $2 billion, you're well past the startup stage if you're selling to the public. All the more reason that it's every entrepreneur's dream to do it. Intel raised $6.8 million in 1971. Genentech raised $35 million and Apple Computer raised about $100 million in 1980. Netscape raised $140 million in 1995. Millennium Pharmaceuticals, $57 million in 1996. Amazon, $144 million in 1997. Genentech, $1.94 billion in its second IPO—itself a contradiction in terms—in 1999. Google raised $2.7 billion in 2005, and Facebook raised almost $16 billion in 2012. Whether the investors buying these shares do well or poorly is another matter.

There are many more variations in the world of mergers and acquisitions, again, too numerous to mention. The main idea is that in contrast to what I've just described, wherein a small percentage of shares is offered to each of many different public buyers, in M&A the transaction is with just one buyer. There may be nuances that creep in, such as a transfer of the assets only and not the people, or of the IP, the intellectual property, and not the physical assets, but the main idea remains the same; materially everything becomes the property of one or a very small number of companies, trusts, or other entities. These deals can be great for the seller, like Life Technologies' purchase of Ion Torrent for $725 million in 2010, or Yahoo's of Tumblr in 2013 for $1.1 billion, HP's of Autonomy for $10.2 billion, or Facebook's 2014 acquisition of WhatsApp for nearly $20 billion. Whether the buyers do well is, again, another matter.

There is one kind of exit that is somewhere in between these two, and that's the *private,* not public, market sale of a small number of shares. Lacking the transparency required of public offerings, this secondary market activity is restricted to qualified investors, which is a technical term meaning investors who are supposed to be able to lose it all without a whimper. Trades like this have been very rare since the 1920s, when buyers were fleeced buying fraudulently touted entities. About these purchases, I have these words in Latin, *caveat emptor*, and then this final one in English, Groupon.

CHAPTER 5 THE INTERNSHIP

SEVENTY SUMMERS after the lucky strike, I was a Princeton undergrad and a summer intern at Jay Orrix's Sandbox Institute. Jenk's son Jay founded it and then funded it with exit proceeds of his first company, Agrigene, $600 million worth of well-told dream that failed to deliver on its promise. There had also been one tangential but commercially important discovery, a serendipitous insight that became fructuse, or Fruct2, the revolutionary fat-burning sweetener used in 2Sweet brand products, whose salacious slogan, "Fruct2: Without it, you're fruct!" was plastered wherever eyeballs might see it. Sadly for Agrigene's investors, the commercial significance was for a customer. Under the research contract, the company received a single milestone payment for the discovery, not ongoing royalties. That infusion allowed the young company to keep moving forward without having to raise cash. "Your first deal is your worst deal, but it's also your best deal," Jay said, shrugging off thoughts of what might have been. The institute had no ostensible purpose and was, as the name implied, Jay Orrix's sandbox.

Undergrads like me wanted summer jobs, paid or unpaid internships, to test out a field of study with no more commitment than the time spent, to learn something, to get outside our own social fish bowls, to make, we hoped, a little money, and to polish our résumés for grad school. Should we work on a vaccine production line in Valley Forge or in a mouse lab in Maine? Should we delve deep into the basic science of molecular biology, or moby as it's known in the vernacular, or should we try to translate the findings at moby's frontier, pushing them over the boundary between science and medicine? And then there were startups, too. A summer startup gig might lead to stock options and riches later, or more likely nothing at all except for war stories and bragging rights.

I'm often asked why that two-syllable portmanteau, moby, has survived selection. But it's a lost story. Horace Freeland Judson, the great chronicler of molecular biology, was a Hopkins colleague of my mother and a frequent dinner guest at our house. He texted me long ago, "Moby! I've found it, finally. An explanation that is wondrous, but these 140 characters are too few to contain it! TTYL." And then, like Fermat, he took the secret to his grave.

François Jacob said to me, "*Sais pas. Mais, pourquoi utiliser huit lorsque deux suffit?*" Fred Sanger told me the same, "Why use eight [syllables] when two will do?" And then there are the other possibilities. Mobio? Yuck.

Mobi—with a hard /I/ and without the 'o'—sounds like the phoneme amputee it is. When the 'i' is pronounced /E/, as in shriek, that sounds OK, but to make it American, you'd spell it like Americans already do. *Ergo*, moby. Time to stop this blubbering.

Jay had left Princeton with some fanfare a decade earlier, settling in New Hampshire because it was home and "I like the politics and the pizza," he said. He established himself as one of Portsmouth's rising stars in biotech. Among those few, only he could claim to be an entrepreneur playing on the national stage. Even though his institute wasn't a startup, it would get me within reach of a capital-P player, and who knew where that would lead? I applied there and got the job.

CHAPTER 6 THE CONVERSATION

I TALK TO my mother every day. It's part of my pact with her. I never laid on the guilt about her moving halfway around the world from me, and she did whatever she could to make me feel close.

"Rani, so what is it you're doing in that sandbox of yours?" she asked me, Skyping from Bangalore.

"Well, it's not what I thought it would be," I said. "Jay says I'm his TA."

"Who is this Jay, Rani? I thought you were working for Dr. Orrix schmorrix."

"Yes, Ammaji. Jay Orrix. Jay is Dr. Orrix, Ammaji."

"Oh, I see. First name basis. Make sure you are polite, Rani. You are just a little bit of spice in his life. What about his wife? Know your place. Know your space, Rani." Her head bobbled at this and she smiled at the old jokes we shared.

"Yes, Ammaji."

"And TA, Rani. Do you work side by side and hand him instruments, or do setups? What do you do all day, Rani?"

"Amma. I wish, Amma. I'm just a gofer. A fancy gofer, but just a gofer."

"Yes, I had a gofer years ago when I was Lab Director. She would go shopping or schlepping for all the little things I forgot. What a big help she was."

"Amma, we don't go anywhere anymore, or at least not now. It means I look things up for him and write short reports and make lots of slides for him. You know, Amma. PowerPoint. I am a PowerPoint biologist now."

"I thought you were a molecular biologist, Rani. Do you have a project to show, Rani? Results of your own, Rani?"

"No, Amma. No, I don't, Amma. I am learning a lot, Amma. He says I am very fast and thorough. I like what I'm doing now. But you are right, I do need my own things, and I want to get back to the lab. Jay will give me good recommendations, so I think it's OK, Amma."

"Rani, you look so skinny. Are you eating enough, Thangama, my golden child?"

"Yes, Ammaji. Yes, Amma. I'm working hard, that's all. I'm eating plenty. And it's fun, really. I'm going to be giving a little presentation for him, and we're going to work on it on his boat over the weekend."

"Oh, Rani! Very exciting. But is it really proper, Chellam, my dear? He's married, isn't he?"

"Amma! Such a dirty mind. Yes, he's married. But the wife, she's not here."

"Wife? Not there? Trouble and strife?"

"No Amma! Why do you even suggest that? What a gossip you are. She's away, filming a movie. I'll be staying in a room with Lucy, their eleven-year old daughter. His parents are here. It's his parents' boat; very grand, you know, a super yacht. It's called the *Lucky Strike.*"

"Tobacco money, honey? Rani, now you'll be the dirty one. *Ha!*"

"No, Amma. The name of the boat, umh, is some kind of family totem. I'll tell you more about it after the weekend."

"Yes, Rani, but what do you know about boats, Rani? How can you be helpful?"

"Oh, Amma! It's a ship. There's a captain and a staff to run the boat, and a chef, too. They even have the crew chew your food for you."

"Oh, Rani. You kid me too much! How much of this is true?"

"Amma, I will chew my own food. But everything else? All true. All true." We pause for a moment. Time's up. "And I'm sorry, Amma, but I have to go now to get ready for the weekend. Sorry I didn't get to see Appa."

"He's flying to Mumbai, doll. He sends his love from above. But you missed your sister. Don't you have time to talk with her?"

"After the weekend. Not now, Amma. I promise, next week. You make sure she is studying hard, will you? Tell her I'm looking at her grades online."

"Yes, Ranita. Yes, I will. Be safe, Rani. I know you will be polite and make us proud. Bye-bye."

We both waved to each other and clicked the iconic red telephone icon to end the call.

CHAPTER 7 THE *LUCKY STRIKE*

IN 1614, Adriaen Block sailed into Long Island Sound from its southwest entrance by the Isle of the Manhattoes. He became the first European to enter those waters, to see the great bays of the Housatonic and Connecticut Rivers and the small pink granite Thimble Islands. Continuing his northeast journey through the rocky narrows now called the Race and into not-quite-oceanic waters beyond, he discovered and mapped the ten-square-mile pork chop of an island that now bears his name. He also named Narragansett Bay and Rhode Island, completing an epic journey on a forty-five-foot vessel before abandoning it on Cape Cod and sailing home to Amsterdam.

At 7:00 a.m. Saturday, I met Jay and his eleven-year-old twins at a small airfield south of Portsmouth. His single-engine Mooney M20K was warmed up and they were waiting for me to step in and shut the door. An hour later we landed at Tweed in East Haven, Connecticut. From there a driver shuttled us to Moby's Dock, a private wharf where Jay's parents and his parents' boat, the one-hundred-thirty-five-foot *Lucky Strike*, were ready to go. The Thimbles were only a stone's throw further east. The captain, Captain Nick, set us off in that direction while I was given a tour of the out-of-scale luxury of the carriage class.

To imagine a boat like this, start with a luxury apartment whose air conditioning rivals that of a Four Seasons hotel, then crank up the scale of opulence a notch and you're close. Everything is designed, as in Designer-designed. You can like it or not, but these boats are kept in a constant state of readiness for the Concours d'Elegance. The theme for the fore and aft exterior sun decks was white leather with teaky trim, teak on all the floors, brightly varnished mahogany on the handrails, and lots of chrome. The interior was Palm Beach boardroom, mixing robin's-egg blue with rosewood and unending stretches of glass. How the crew kept the glass free of any signs of ever having been near the sea is a secret never to be divulged. On three decks there were six staterooms, a galley, storage for food, drinking water, fishing rods, spare engine and compressor hardware, toys of all sorts and for all ages, and accommodations for Captain Nick and her crew of five, as well as three yellow kittens, Sassafras, Aloysius, and Sandy, each the color of summer corn.

Every crew member had been selected for her or his social graces as well as for more utilitarian qualities. Their roles, after all, were largely social. They had to get along with each other in close quarters and for long periods of time, and then they had to entertain the owners and their guests. One had raced sailboats around the globe and was particularly handy in rough weather, in the dark, and with a knife. He'd also been a nanny and was the one usually found taking care of the smallest children. Another had been a commercial fisherman in Alaska and for a while busked as a magician. One was there to please the eyes of men. She, Sheri, was a heckuva free diver and underwater hunter. The chef, famous among guests for her ceviche and other variations on raw fish, had worked as sous-chef to big names in New York and Kyoto, in between bar fights and short stays in prison. Taxon was a West Indian who drove Jay's elderly parents when they were on shore, otherwise acting as their personal valet. And finally, Nicole, the captain, was a third-generation captain who'd once been a big boat pilot in Piraeus.

CHAPTER 8 POT ISLAND

WE CAME to a stop off of Pot Island. Disbelieving Reader, I am not making this up. It's a real place. With supreme confidence belying his youth, Lucy's twin brother Jason went overboard in an overpowered sixteen-foot RIB, a rigid inflatable boat, on a mission to retrieve Jay's longtime friend Vladik, who would join us for the weekend as we made for Block's eponymous island.

Pot Island is typical of the Thimbles; a granitic lump, about an eighth acre of which sits above the high tide line. Inland it is partially covered with mosses and spruce and maple. Its smooth pink rock is exposed at the water's edge, sloping steeply. Maximum elevation is ten feet.

In the four hundred years since Block's visit, the inhabitants and owners, if Man can be said to own any land, have gouged out four faux beaches for easy access. Quarrying of the famed Stony Creek pink granite, used in the base of the Statue of Liberty, the lower exterior of Grand Central Station, and Grant's Tomb, all in Manhattan, South Station in Boston, and the Battle Monument at West Point, and elsewhere, continues to take place nearby on the mainland.

There were five houses on the island; two owned by hedge-fund managers, one a Yale faculty member, and one a trust-fund baby. Originally summer homes without proper insulation or power for even a New England spring or fall, they were, one by one, being upgraded in scale and opulence. Only the fifth remained the simple retreat of the previous generations. It was this modest 900-square-foot, one-story residence where Vladik came to get away from it all. At one time such a bungalow was called a trophy home, symbolic of the owner's triumph elsewhere. But the game had changed, as it had changed everywhere thanks to the concentration of wealth in this second gilded age. Now, such a bungalow was called a teardown.

I took a break from the tour and watched Jason as he beached the boat on the southeast landing. Vladik hopped in, carrying what looked like a heavily laden bike messenger's bag over his shoulder, a long duffel in one hand, and a black rifle in the other. Moments later, they had returned, and Vladik climbed a ladder onto the *Lucky Strike*. From the second deck, a crane arm rotated outward, lowering a halyard to Jason, who secured it to a stainless steel shackle polished to the bright sheen I'd already come to recognize as regulation on the yacht. Then he too climbed the ladder and the RIB was hoisted out of the water. Captain Nick put the engines in gear, and thirty minutes after boarding the *Lucky Strike* at Moby's Dock, we were steaming, that's a nautical term, for the Race and Block Island.

CHAPTER 9 ROBERT HOOKE, FRS

AT THE dawn of modern science, that is, in the time of Newton, science was natural philosophy and there were no walls between biology and physics. Robert Hooke published the first detailed drawings of organisms viewed under a microscope, coined the word "cell," speculated about the mechanisms of memory, made some cogent interpretations of fossils, elucidated the fundamental nature of springs, helped Boyle discover the basic laws of gases, and got within an RCH of scooping Newton on the inverse square law of gravitation. Gradually, specialization forced the physical and natural sciences apart, although Nature was not aware of it. Still, the history of biology has been punctuated by contRIButions from physicists, and not just through the application of discoveries like the X-ray or NMR, that is, nuclear magnetic resonance.

CHAPTER 10 VLADIK

An ex-lover still calls him Vladimir, but in all the years since I first met him on the *Lucky Strike*, I've never heard anyone else call him anything but Vladik, unless Arianna's unique pronunciation "Vladique" qualifies as an altogether different name. Well, occasionally Vladi. And Vova, too.

He and Jay go way back, back to when their age was but a single digit, when they met at a chess tournament about halfway between their respective residences: Jay's in New Hampshire and Vladik's in New Jersey. Despite the differences that are so obvious now, that is, financial means, political leanings, temperament, gregariousness, physical assets, love of the outdoors, and attitudes about spicy foods, differences that might prohibit them in today's polarized America from even knowing each other, back when they were nine years old, the binding agent that held them was their mutual aversion to the chess tournaments their fathers required them to attend. It didn't matter to them at all what they did when they played hooky together, as long as it got them out beyond the walls of those dreary halls.

Their first adventure, launched within hours of having met, began by escaping the gaze of their chaperones. Then they hitchhiked from Pittsfield to Portsmouth. The driver of the VW minibus who picked them up was heading south on Route 7, and then by felicitous circumstance was headed east on I-90 for a while, but only as far as Blandford. The boys were holding a cardboard sign. On one side were the tournament's offset-printed event details, and on the other were the words "Portsmouth or Bust!" hand-printed as neatly as boys of their age were able to manage with a fat black felt-tipped marker. While on the Interstate shoulder, having reasoned that there was more traffic on the roadway where it was illegal to stand than on the on-ramps where it was legal, young Vladik hoisted the handwritten sign while Jay entreated the state's Volvo-driving brie eaters—Jay's words—with waving arms. The first car to stop was licensed to the Massachusetts State Police. The boys' heads reached somewhere between belt and armpit of the Rabelaisian trooper who left the vehicle to talk to them. Wide, easy smile and cowboy good looks aside, his calf-height black leather boots and black leather belt holstering radio, billy club, Chemical Mace, and semi-automatic handgun, and the martial gray-blue stripe down the side of his trousers, all left Vladik frozen with fear. He had been conditioned by five years, admittedly a period during much of which he hadn't any memory, of living under the surveillance state—more on which later—but Jay was conditioned to live free or die. This legend of theirs, which was unfolded to me that first weekend we all spent together, exemplified one of their key differences, albeit one that didn't get in the way of friendship; Jay was like the beautiful blonde who never played the part of victim because she knew she wouldn't get the speeding ticket. Jay, leaning in, so charmed those beefy officers—whose individual tonnage was nearly twice that of the two protagonists combined—with his natural generosity and a confidence that could never be emulated that before long, both boys and men were headed for the New Hampshire state line, but not without first stopping at Friendly's in Amesbury for a dinner of outsize proportions, finished off with a banana split, for each, of equally outsize proportions, and a sharing of family photos that had been warmed, moistened, and made raggedy in back-pocket wallets. In an age before minute-by-minute tracking of an officer's whereabouts was a matter of course, or even possible given the primitive radios they were carrying, the troopers called patrolling friends on the New Hampshire side of the line and received permission to drive the boys all the way to Jay's parents' estate in the d'Anconia Gnotch suburb of Portsmouth. Jay offered to host the policemen and their own children on a weekend of good clean American gun worship, and then the two agents of the State of Massachusetts drove off. Thus began Jay's and Vladik's life together.

The Orrix family was always expansive and inclusive. After saying to Jay's mother, "K, with a k, just a k," by way of explaining his last name, Vladik immediately received from her—Jenk the patriarch was away and couldn't object to the fact that Jay had so brazenly violated his edict to participate in the chess tournament—an open invitation to visit and stay, and this was hours before the ritual hazing—as if the day's events were not evidence enough of high spirits—in Jenk's neuron-stimulating electrified lounge chair.

Before Vladik was sent by Greyhound bus back to New Jersey, Jay introduced him to Zelda. Zelda's Lago di Garda was and remains a brick furnace cum pizzeria of unique construction that drew a crowd every day of the year. The fifty-eight-inch tall, bottle-blonde proprietress had hand-fed Jay his first bite of Neapolitan crust before he was three, as she had thousands of other children in a ritual not unlike communion in the atheistic little town about which she would say with a mixture of *ka-ching!*-stoked glee, sarcasm, and disgust, "Where the women trade gold, the men make their own steel, and the children lack compassion."

The wood-fired furnace was an inverted paraboloid of revolution rising four stories from the subterrane before climbing skyward in a cooling tower that would have stirred the imagination of Thomas Edison. At each of nineteen access ports, architects of pizza—master chefs she had imported from the Italian lake country, Naples, Staten Island, and other havens of the doughman's artistry—prepared pizza for Zelda's customers in a most personal and intimate manner, and shoved them into the heat on thirty-inch-wide wooden paddles of New Hampshire timber. Locally sourced, organically produced, and individually prepared, the leptocrustean creations towered over mere pizza, and the demand for them fully occupied the abutting railway siding. Zelda was a maker of pizza.

She took one look at the nine-year-old Vladik and said, "You're not one of them, are you?"

"I'm a guest, a friend, if that's what you mean."

"*Fina boychik*," she said, and rubbed him on the back.

Jay and Vladik saw each other on vacations long and short. Sometimes they grew apart, but always they found their way back. Vladik's family could never have afforded the travel, in either its scope or style, that Jay and his family undertook. Yet, every year, at least once a year, thanks to Orrix generosity, he was off with them to some exotic place, most often exploring nature under the tutelage of Jenk, who seemed to know every plant and animal by name; Latin name, common name, and often first name. Jenk particularly liked the southern oceans, with their atolls, reefs, and abundant brown-skinned natives willing to fawn all over the guests, and for the opportunities for getting into clear, often deep water. Vladik loved being in the water. Jay preferred to be on top of it. He hated, too, being tied down to anyone's schedule, even his own family's. Often, it was only the release valve of Vladik's listening that calmed Jay down enough to keep the Orrix family party from disintegrating.

While Jay was more interested in physical materials and their exothermic combinations, Vladik drifted toward code. He was LISPing at eight, and he had learned to program all the early home computers: TRS-80, Commodore 64, Apple II. As a sop to his father's interest in games and puzzles, he wrote programs for board games. To improve performance, he dove into the machine's own language, exploitations of which made him pretty famous in the small group of people who cared about machine backgammon. The drive for performance led next to an obsession with the microprocessors at the heart of it, and there he ran up against the fact that the best computers you could buy deployed chips that were already two years old. There was nothing to be done about that except to rage against the manufacturers.

Vladik switched gears and became absorbed in the nuances of compression and cryptography, and in the summer of his fifteenth year, he got a paid job optimizing code for one of his mother's colleagues at Bell Labs. "Ah, monopoly profits," Vladik used to say, before he began a riff on all the ways monopoly worked for and against us. Later that same year, Intel came out with its breakthrough 80386 32-bit processor. There were no sockets for it to call home. "What I could have done in backgammon tournaments if only I had a computer with that engine!" he told me.

Jay and Vladik reached the age of majority. The two had made explosives in the family's basement lab, had lived to tell of it, and had retained all their fingers and toes and both eyes and ears, too. They had grown plants of religious significance and isolated from them interesting molecules which became the starting materials for the synthesis of controlled substances which they then assayed—grading themselves favorably on the results. They both had held jobs of some significance in Orrix Enterprises, although neither of them showed any continuing interest in Jenk's agriculture products.

That spring, Vladik wrote a letter to Intel's founders, Bob Noyce and Gordon Moore, explaining what a great showcase his software would make for their so-called i386, and he provided detail on exactly how to prototype such a machine, suggesting that Intel should hire him in the following summer and provide him with the chips, a prototyping system, and electronic testing hardware to pull it off. He wrote, with boyish glee, "even if the first users of this hardware are only nutty hobbyists whose aim is to compute all the names of God, more serious parties will soon recognize that, with a little logic gluing them together, these inexpensive and innocent-looking boards are the components of a parallel supercomputer that will be able to compete with the multi-million dollar machines from the likes of Cray. Beware the killer micros!"

At the end of the letter, he also mused on the fact that without a competitor for this generation of chips, Intel's monopoly would allow it to "rule the world for the next fifteen years." Noyce believed that, sure enough, but what struck him most was that the kid's ideas about compiler optimization were as advanced as the company's. Intel hired him as a summer intern to work on exactly that. There was no protocol for employing a boy twenty-six hundred miles from home, so while they put him up in the same Santa Clara residences where Intel housed the college-age summer interns, Human Relations recruited a dream team of older and more experienced employees who would introduce him around the company and show him much more than the other interns would ever see. They were also to invite him to dinner, take him to baseball games in San Francisco and Oakland, guide him on tours of Bay Area, and make sure he was occupied, well-fed, and drug-free.

"I flew in to Silicon Valley's airport, San Jose International, SJC, around noon on a Friday. My program didn't start until the following afternoon, so my host drove me directly to a condo complex called the Oakwood and there showed me my furnished one-bedroom home for the summer. 'Get some sleep. We have a busy schedule for you this weekend,' she said, handing me an agenda that stretched out for the next seven days. I would have gotten quite a bit of sleep that night, but for the thin wall and the pounding it took as my neighbors slammed each other up against it for what seemed like a very long time. I had never heard anything like it. In the morning, I saw the two men on the balcony, clean-shaven and tidily dressed, enjoying their newspaper and coffee, occasionally stroking each other's hands, before departing the Oakwood in matching Camrys. The veil was lifting from my eyes. A cliché, I know, but that's what it felt like. They were as much a part of my education as what I picked up at Intel.

"At 3 p.m. that same Saturday, the summer solstice, Bob Noyce—himself!—picked me up and drove to San Francisco where we were going to have a picnic dinner beside the Golden Gate before heading off to see the 9:30 showing of *Beach Blanket Babylon.* With time to burn and both of us wanting to avoid the commercialism of Fisherman's Wharf, he drove straight to the Presidio, parking near the South Tower of the Golden Gate Bridge. We watched surfers and windsurfers and sea lions ride the breaking swell there. Then the wind got light, as it does when the sun drops toward the horizon and the wind machine shuts down, and we began to walk under the bridge and out to Baker Beach to watch the sunset. You can't do that anymore, but you could do it then. He told me about jumping off of buildings, and of flying jets, and of some other exploits, and as we walked, we happened upon a couple of guys dragging a sculpture. Bob asked me, 'Is he carrying a cross?' But it wasn't a cross; it was a man, an eight- or nine-foot wood sculpture of a man. They were looking for a place to prop it up, after which they were going to light it on fire.

"We talked to them, listening to their tale—which was none too clear, something about love lost and suffering—of why they were doing this, as we helped them find kindling and put it in place. Bob even lit the thing with his already-lit cigarette.

"People love fire, especially fire at night, and from all over the beach, and even the hillside above the beach, the grateful came over to share the light and the heat and to participate in the spontaneous little community that formed. Burning Man! Incredible. My first full day in California."

"What's Burning Man?" I asked, still very young in that Orrigenal summer when I first heard this story. Vladik didn't tell me then.

Noyce had lunch with him a couple of times after that, in the unassuming class-free company cafeteria, in the small section set aside for smokers. The elder told the younger about his own youth, in Iowa, and of hunger, and of doing something wonderful, and of the deadening effect inherited wealth had on the spirit.

There was no precedent for retaining Vladik, a promising high school student, after ten weeks. So, even though he had laid down the strategy for the next several years of compiler development for the world's most widely used microprocessors, and even though he wanted to stay, his managers tried to convince him that he'd be best served by completing high school and college. They promised him work the next summer and sent him back to Summit, New Jersey.

Vladik returned, had to return, but not to school.

When Vladik called Jay and told him he was about to quit high school, Jay told Jenk and Jenk made a visit, his first ever, to Vladik's home. With the full heft of his CEO-ness, Jenk tried to persuade him to find another way. "Look, son, you're going to be the valedictorian of your class. I couldn't buy that honor for my own kids." No logic or reason of Jenk's, or of Vladik's own distinguished parents, or of their even more distinguished friends, could overturn his determination to quit. Vanechka, his mother, cried. His father, Yuli, shouted, and wanted to hit him, but he wasn't the hitting type, or to lock him up and force him to continue at school, but he wasn't the incarcerating type, so, after shouting, he cried, too.

With a little of the money he had earned at Intel, Vladik took the high school equivalency exams, receiving perfect scores on all five of them. Then he began a period of itinerancy.

Bucket list in hand, he took Noyce's advice and did something wonderful, or tried to. He lived for months in Bali. He fell in love with a Danish girl, traveled with her through South Asia, married her, separated, and filed for divorce by mutual consent, all in the same year. Hanging from a wing of his own design, he caught afternoon updrafts off the slopes in Chamonix and then floated up and around the Alps until daylight ran out. He read a lot. Each adventure began with an incandescent glow, later dulled to compact fluorescence, and then flickered out. When enthusiasm had flagged altogether or money ran out, he solved software problems for a fee before starting the next adventure. He never starved. "Not a high bar for happiness," he said.

Thinking that maybe wonderfulness wouldn't be found at the end of a list of entertainments, he made a new list, this one consisting of serious things, problems he hoped to make a dent in. Then, as he had sought out Intel because he had recognized that his interests and their needs overlapped, he selected his next employer on the presumption that they'd be interested in that dent, too, if he could make it. After a short stint trying to make the world safe for compressed music, he decided that wasn't a big enough idea, and another short and unsatisfying stint looking for signs for extraterrestrial intelligence—willfully kept under wraps by the DOD, he thought—in streams of data coming off of radio telescopes, he decided to take a break from deciding exactly where satisfaction lay, accepting employment instead at a big place where there were lots of problems to solve. And so he was hired at ITSy, International Technology Systems, or as he liked to call it, the itsy bitsy machine company. Today a global leader in technology by almost any standard, it was still small enough in those days that his mentor told him, with a straight face, and in what proved to be an understatement, "In five years you'll know everyone of significance here."

"By a decade, at least, I was the youngest in my group, and the only one of them not to have at least a master's degree," he said. "They were all physicists, optical engineers, chemists and chemical engineers, trying to overcome diffraction in photolithography masks, you know, master images that are used to make chips."

I barely knew.

"My job was to improve some old computer codes used to translate chip designs into physical masks used on the line. They were all we had, but they were not working, and we knew the codes were not working because there were all these lithographically induced chip failures. 'Find what's wrong,' I was told, and I was handed this big blue book called *Principles of Optics*, or simply 'Born and Wolf,' after its authors."

I think he was waiting for me to say something, but all I could muster was, "I've seen it on shelves."

"Yeah, most people see it on the shelf but have never opened it. Whoever wrote what I'd become responsible for fixing hadn't opened it either. Or maybe they had, but they had had too few computing resources to implement what Born and Wolf taught. I read some introductory chapters and then the chapters on diffraction. The physics wasn't hard, even though the equations were intimidating. There were hairy integrals that accounted for all the different wavelengths of light, and all the different angles at which it would be incident, and for the phases and the bending and all that. The old code had made too many approximations because it would have been too expensive, compute-wise, to do it right. I drew a flow chart explaining what we had to do, and what was not being done in the company's code, and how the change might improve things for a bunch of designers and manufacturing engineers, and make our products better at lower cost. Our group decided to do a little test, which required me to prototype the software for an idealized case. It worked great, and then the whole thing was taken away from us because we were a research group and we'd done our piece. They needed some industrial-strength solution, and we could never have given it to them." He paused. "I can talk about this stuff forever, but why I am telling you this now?"

"You were explaining how you got from being a high school dropout to being a PhD in physics."

"Right. That mask work was the most satisfying thing I'd ever done. Some, that is, other people at ITSy, were out of joint, and I was, we were—there's no 'I' in team, remember?— assigned to help them. They really cared, because those errors cost them, us, a lot of money. They were impatient. They were counting on me, us. I liked that. I'd never felt it before. And, I picked up the optics very quickly. That little bit of wizardry was equivalent to a master's thesis. It was noticed, you might say, and I became known as a troubleshooter, because I could learn a new field and deduce what needed to be done. In the case of the masks, like the compiler before, I didn't do the work; I just showed everyone else how to do the work. You could say, I wrote the program that they followed.

"Within a year I was living on a plane, assistant to the Vice President of R&D, traveling around with her all over North America, Europe, and Asia. I got exposed to the full range of our manufacturing, and our partnerships, and our products, and I learned about the financials and licensing. ITSy was my Harvard and my jail. My Harvard, obviously, but my jail, too, because of the golden handcuffs. I wasn't spending much of my salary, and it had gone up alarmingly, and the company made matching grants in tax-protected savings programs, and these appreciated at double-digit rates in those days. It was a lot to walk away from, even though the torpid pace of that big corporation made me think I might want to be part of something smaller and faster. And, just getting out of the job I was in, even staying at ITSy, was going to be a step down to something lesser."

"Why lesser?"

"I was a minister without portfolio. All the people I worked with at these meetings were VPs and directors, and twenty years older, too. They operated groups with hundreds, even thousands, of employees. I had never operated anything, except maybe a mouse and a keyboard. I wasn't going to make a lateral move into one of their positions. I was going down, for a while at least.

"I also realized, though, that I'd become assimilated by the Borg. I'd suppressed too much of my bucket-list mentality and become an organization man, and I needed to take a step back. I asked to be reassigned to a research group, so I could write some papers and maybe find an institution that would grant me a degree. All of a sudden, I wanted a degree. And, I wanted to have some management responsibility. The veep very much wanted me to stay by her side," he smiled suggestively here, "and she suggested something else." Pausing, shaking his head as if lost in reveries he wouldn't share, he then said of the veep, "That woman, Ulya Khoslovsky, had everything: the brains, the legs, the smile, the grace, the ambition, the job, the city apartment; everything except a life. I was the missing piece that she thought would give her a life. She was fifteen years older than me, but looked only five, maybe.

"Anyway, using her academic connections, which were very strong because of all the money ITSy pumped into the labs of individual professors, departmental initiatives, and industry consortia, she would help me find, she said, a collaboration that would result in me getting a PhD, assuming I could pass the oral exam at NYU. After that was done, she'd release me to get the ops experience I wanted. This route would be slower, but it would give us both half of what we wanted. I'd be delaying my operations experience but getting the degree, and she'd be getting only part of my time, but for longer.

"Three years later, I had completed "On the Inversion of Nonlinear Forward Models of Submicron Complementary Metal-Oxide-Semiconductor Processes by Machine Learning," and was holding a PhD in mathematical physics from the Courant Institute at NYU, and in another year I was running a group of ten. While my relationship with Ulya was falling apart, if only because she was always up in the air, my team was cranking out software tools for circuit designers. Valuable to the company—that making of software widgets for the widget makers—but kind of boring. Jay, though, has never let me get too bored."

When Vladik arrived in Maynard, Massachusetts, to work for ITSy, Jay was in his third year at Harvard, barely half an hour away. They'd seen little of each other in the few years before, but once they began living near each other again, their friendship expanded. Business was never something he and Vladik had shared an interest in. Jay had learned about it at the dinner table and on the knee. Vladik's parents, while employed by the phone company, regarded the corporation as something like a Soviet state enterprise, but one whose pasted-on smiling face was sometimes persuasively sincere, and they passed their skepticism on to him. So Jay watched in amazement as his friend completed one year and then five years at ITSy, and at his chameleonic transformation into a suit, and not just by wearing the clothes—fine, ultra lightweight, silk-wool blended and made to measure in Hong Kong—but by a transformation of the soul. Vladik was educated, or re-educated, into the wonders of the commercial world. It was Jay who first said, "ITSy's your Harvard, dude!"

When Vladik discovered that he was an entrepreneur stuck in a big company, he remade his bucket list again, this time organized around new ventures. He pitched lots of bad ideas, and ones way ahead of their time, and was always met with the same lukewarm encouragement: "Keep trying." He could have left, but those handcuffs were binding.

Around that time, the two young men found their professional interests beginning to overlap. Vladik kept his day job but became an advisor to Jay's new company, Agrigene, conceived to create optimal breeds of corn through the power of genomics. There were machine learning problems lurking beneath the surface of what they were trying to achieve, and Vladik, as he had many times before, laid out the strategy for their elucidation, and helped hire the people who would get it done. Ten years after he started at ITSy, Vladik retired on Agrigene's IPO.

Genomics and machine learning, or deep learning as it had come to be called in some circles, had mostly dropped off his radar in the few years that followed, but Jay had planned this weekend to put them back on it.

CHAPTER 11 ORRIGEN

AT MIDMORNING and max ebb we hit the Race—the 7.5-mile eastern venturi of Long Island Sound through which nearly thirty million cubic feet of water flow back and forth every twelve hours—and left

Valiant Rock to starboard. Only an hour earlier I'd learned that starboard meant "on your right as you're looking forward." There was little wind, but three-foot standing waves had built up as the water ran fast over boulders and complicated hard-rock topography hundreds of feet below us.

A summer Saturday, there were dozens of boats angling for a piece of the northeastward migration of striped bass. There were dark-skinned working-class men in the most modest of open aluminum-hulled skiffs, boats incapable of surviving a significant turn of the weather. There were fiberglass center-console fishing boats, some with sleek flush-mounted hardware designed to minimize the possibility of snagging a fishing line during a cast or a recovery. Their better-heeled and usually lighter-skinned owners were sometimes accompanied by a wife, a pretty girl, or a child. There were also full-cabined cruisers of forty or even fifty-five feet, with racks of well-maintained rods and reels leaning against a three-story scaffolding topped with an expensively instrumented perch I learned to call a "flying bridge." And there were commercial fishing boats, some with crowded decks of paying passengers, and some with decks piled high with nets and lobster traps; all showing rust and use and insufficient maintenance.

There were also sailboats of all sizes coming and going, some freighters, some ferries, larger commercial fishing boats, yachts, and the occasional super yacht en route to somewhere. The places and the names—Fisher's Island, Montauk, Stonington, Newport, Cuttyhunk, Martha's Vineyard, Cape Cod—each had a unique appeal. For every vacationer or sailor or merchant seaman, there was a set of sounds or sights or circumstances evoking memories and feelings of discovery or awe. I, in the fresh air on the foredeck while everyone else was in the HVAC'd splendor of the *Lucky Strike*'s enclosed quarters, was collecting these experiences for the first time and would never forget them.

We made it through the Race, not that there had been any doubt, and entered those not-quite-oceanic waters of Block Island Sound. The wind became light and the sea flattened out before us. Sailboats rocked but made no way, their sails flapping as we ran by them at twenty knots. Low-lying clouds moved in on us and we slowed, soon to a crawl, as we were enveloped in gray gloom. The cold upwelling ocean waters hit the warm and damp summer air, making wet murky haze all around. I'd learn eventually that the same thing happened in San Francisco, but on a much larger and more regular scale. When visibility shrank to a boat length, we stopped.

You could hear foghorns going off on the mainland and from the rocky or pointy corners of Block Island. There was nothing to see. The boat's radar would have sufficed, but Jay had something else in mind.

While Lucy, his daughter, watched TV below decks, and his parents had a late breakfast in their stateroom, and the chef prepared tea and Portuguese soda bread with brandy, Jay and Vladik and I lounged and talked in the glass enclosure of the main deck. Jason had his feet up and half listened. If and when the weather cooperated, the sun would burn off the soupiness by the late morning, and then we'd go sit out on the aft sun deck and wait for the sight of Block Island emerging from the gray murk.

Among the seemingly unconnected things that Jay had had me working on all summer, I was tracking down the résumés of academic faculty from San Diego to St. Petersburg, Russia. They were thought leaders in genomics, of course, and agriculture, of course, but also in large-scale bioreactors, fast-cycle hybridization, micromachines, thermodynamics, economics of energy markets, and liquid fuels.

In each category, Jay had a set of questions he wanted me to answer and attributes he wanted me to characterize. Were they affiliated with the leading large companies, or the hottest small companies in their fields? Who were their students and where were they employed or when were they graduating? Did their networks of friends overlap with his, or with each other's? What patents had they filed, and who had licensed them? Instead of making a movie, in which case he'd have been both producer and director, he was producing, as financier, and then would direct, as CEO, a new venture of some kind.

Vladik said, "I'm looking forward to getting in the water. Lakshmi, do you dive?"

"Yes, but I haven't in more than a year."

"You can get some diving in later, but let me tell you about this idea I'm trying to shape," Jay said. It's not so much that Jay was all business, but he was all himself. His moods, his interests, drove every moment you spent with him. His agenda was in his head and was occasionally shared.

Looking back all these years and watching myself among the two men, I'm surprised I wasn't even more deferential. I was silent, waiting for the bristles on Vladik's back to flatten, and for Jay to begin.

"Energy, you know, is the mother of all markets. Look at the largest companies in the world. Look at the increasing demand coming from China and India, not to mention Korea, Brazil, and Russia. Imagine Africa someday. Energy is where we have to focus genomics. If we can own the IP that helps us grow our own fuel more efficiently than anyone else, we'll have the mother of all exits."

He went on to explain in detail how the Exxons of the world had had to invest billions upon billions, and harness governments to fight their wars, in order to get control of production of a commodity. Sure, there were differences between the sweet crude of Maracaibo and sulfur-rich barrels from Canada, and the extraction costs varied enormously between Bahrain and Bakersfield, but at root, the products were the same. He followed with a lesson in the history of exploration and refinement and distribution.

He did not say, as Nobel Prize-winning chemist and discoverer of c60—buckminsterfullerene, aka the buckyball—Rick Smalley had said in a talk I heard at Princeton, his alma mater, during my freshman year, "Cheap, clean energy is the world's most important problem amenable to a technical solution."

Jay's take on the fact that there was an insatiable hunger for liquid fuels was different. "The next wave of genetic engineering is going to allow us to redesign life so we can make more money from it." His work might be good for mankind, but that was incidental.

"But, the problem with energy as a startup market, is that it takes too much money. You'll see the venture guys go running after it in the next few years, but I think most of them will fail because of the capital. They'll exhaust the capacity of their own investors. There will be new investment models, and maybe they'll find a way to pull later-stage investors into the deals."

My head swam amid all the new terms, but Jay was magnetic. Every few sentences he'd insert a comment like, "Isn't that fantastic?" into his soliloquy, and with his boyish smile, even if you didn't really understand what he was talking about, you felt you had to say yes, or project some flat but not too flat affect back at him, to get him to release you from his gaze.

"I think we can be huge, but without requiring all that money. Intel owns a $30 or $40 billion business in microprocessors, not because other companies can't make them, or can't make them better." Jay threw a look at Vladik, a coded compressed message that hinted at the lessons the two had shared over the years, and one that carried more content than the words he took time to say out loud. "If you look at all the elements that go into a computing solution, microprocessors are just one layer in a tall stack of layers. There's the operating system, there are compute boxes, there's hardware that goes in boxes or connects to other boxes, there are applications, there's purchasing, there's training. Intel gets their billions because they own one of the layers of one of the most widely used computing solutions. Their IP, awarded patents by the US Patent and Trademark Office and protected by the American judicial system, and by parallel structures in other jurisdictions, connects layers in the stack in a way no one else is allowed to do without Intel's permission. They do really have a great solution, even if it's not exactly Pangloss's solution. There's so much inertia to change in the other layers of the stack that they're almost impossible to displace.

"Intel's position would be even better if they didn't actually have to build the factories, which cost billions, and make the processors themselves. If they could just license the IP to someone else and collect a royalty, yes, that would be better. Then they'd be almost like a software company whose marginal costs of production are nearly zero. A software company that controls a layer in the stack might be even more profitable than Intel. That would be Microsoft. Are there going to be software layers of the energy solution stack? Can there be proprietary products that every energy producer or every energy consumer has to use, so we get huge volume and monopoly pricing?" He laughed and then continued, "I mean proprietary pricing? Lakshmi's been my research librarian, and Vladik, I want you to help me put a team together."

"Let me guess," Vladik said. "You mean to pull together a team to make new genes, insert them in your GMO corn, and get best-in-class conversion efficiency into biofuels. And you'll call it CornFuelIx, right?"

"No, we'll call it Orrigeneometrix. Isn't that great?" He waited for all of us to say, "Yeah, Jay, that's great!" but none of us did, because it was too awful. First, the name was all about Jay and not the enterprise. Second, it could have been the world record holder in the category "Most Uninformative Suffix."

"Jay, why not truncate at Orrigen?" I said.

"Even Darwin would have liked it," Vladik said.

"You're right. You're right! That's great! I'm glad you like the name I thought of."

Still, we weren't thinking that much about the name, anyway, much as when I someday receive a proposal of marriage, I don't expect the first thing I'm going to reflect on will be the cake.

Jay moved ahead, asking Vladik, "Can you work on this now? Think of Lakshmi as your assistant for," and he paused to look at me, "Lakshmi, how many more weeks will you be working with us?"

"Six."

"So, Vladik, you two can get a lot started in the next six weeks. I'm not expecting you to play an operating role here, just to help me set things in motion, interview some people, set up some systems. You know I don't like doing that."

Vladik later told me that he had wanted to ask Jay about equity, rather than just nod as if there was nothing more to discuss. He had been about to do it when another memory overwhelmed him and he decided to wait. Once upon a time, when he was only a green teenage consultant, he had spent most of a day trying to get a hiring manager's attention about payment for his first week's work, and the guy kept avoiding him. Having failed with subtlety, he tried a direct approach. "Heh, Mike, can we have a few minutes to talk about this?" Mike, the manager, had been uncharacteristically formal that day, even wearing a suit. "Vladik. We're trying to get out of here at 4 o'clock today, so we can make it to Nassim's funeral." Nassim, one of the staff, had been fatally electrocuted while working late and alone a few days earlier, a fact known to everyone but Vladik. The embarrassment he felt always came rushing back to him whenever he had to open a conversation about his comp.

CHAPTER 12 GOLDEN, NOT EMERALD

THE FOG had begun to dissipate and you could see yellow sunlight streaking through its canopy. Visibility had become a few hundred yards. Portuguese soda bread, and juice and tea and coffee and water appeared on the bar in the lounge. Jay's parents were moving around. Diesel generators had been on all the time, but now the engines were fired up too and Captain Nick put them in gear. We were moving.

The clearing was fastest in front of us, to the east, where a glow grew golden. I followed Vladik onto the bow to have a better look at what was coming. In the small bubble of our visibility, we could see that we were no longer alone, although what we were heading for remained featureless opalescence and black sea.

And then, maybe because I blinked, or looked away for just a moment, or because it happened suddenly, the wall of blankness gave way to an island in full color, topped with blue sky all the way to the heavens. Surf broke at the base of auric dunes. Emerald trees glistened in the sunlit moisture of the departed haze. To the north, the isle's sandy spit thinned to water and the water to nothingness, and the bluffs to the south did the same, the water on either side perfect parentheses packaging Block Island. Was I Dorothy, about to reach her malachite city at last—Oz, but golden?

We closed the gap to a promontory, a breakwater, a man-made pile of rocks terminated with scaffolding that offered a light and a horn sounding off for boats miles away and enshrouded in the mist. Two points define a line, and a red buoy, "2," made one with the tower, "4." As far as the eye could see along that imaginary infinity, sailboat after yacht after fishing boat after cruiser after cruise ship, having come from all the mainland harbors within one hundred miles, and some even from France or New Zealand, converged on the island. The sea, the Sound, was black beneath us.

Mast tops poked out above the trees as if they belonged to ships on shore, but they rocked back and forth inexplicably. Then I got it; the rock pile marked a cut through the lowest dunes. Their low bulk hid a bay behind them and the hulls afloat in it. We joined the parade as it entered the Great Salt Pond, or New Harbor as some called it, although it hadn't been new for a hundred years. On the sandy shore, fishermen and swimmers, waders and sunbathers and six year olds raised their heads to watch and to gawk at our extravagance. They waved their hands at us in greeting, and at everyone passing through, and we did the same.

There must have been a thousand, maybe two thousand boats in that well-protected basin. Jason pointed out the prominent features on land and sea: a house owned by a media magnate, a peninsula confiscated in a drug bust and repurposed as a bird sanctuary, a white tent set out for weddings, tidal flats rich with quahogs and oysters, an old Coast Guard lifesaving station given a new life as a clubhouse. We passed a gray tug that looked like it had been decommissioned from the Mothball Fleet. It sprayed rainbows from fat firehoses. The week of the Fourth of July is a party in the pond. Friends came from the mainland, rafting up, two, three, even six hulls deep. Mostly it's powerboat next to powerboat and sailboat next to sail, because it's only so far that polarization can be depolarized even in Oz, but there were occasional mixed-marriage breachings of convention. Swimmers swam, kayakers kayaked, paddlers paddled on surfboards, and the smallest of sailboats tacked and jibed around.

We were, at that moment, in a great channel, flanked by all the variety in motion and under anchor. Docks lined the shore at the back of the bay. We avoided them. The tug had been given a wide berth by other boats, so we dropped two hooks right near it.

Jason appeared to be racing, readying the crane to lower his RIB into the water. But who was he racing? Unhesitant, I dropped my shorts at my feet and threw my blouse off, too. I wore a swimsuit beneath my street clothes, so *Ha!* Then I went flying upstairs to the third deck. Boats were moored nearby to port, but not to starboard. I wiped the chrome railing dry on the starboard side, then climbed on it, faced outward from the *Lucky Strike*, and came to balance with my arms and hands over my head. Slowly, I swung them down and back, bending at the knees as I did, keeping my chest upright and my chin raised. Then I exploded skyward, stiff upper limbs swinging, lowers extending, and feet pushing so I was high and away from the boat's edge, left with just the slightest angular momentum. Tension in one long strand of flexing muscle from extremity to extremity pulled my legs up, and I began rotating backward. For a moment I was a plank, horizontal, arms out beside me. Looking back, I could see the boat then, all eyes on deck watching me as my head fell below my feet and I began the thirty-foot plunge to the water. Vladik locked eyes with me and shot a smile my way, so I splayed my arms and legs like a clown, heard the on-board laughter, regrouped, lined up all my parts, pointed them, stretched and lengthened to slow the rotation, and then made like a gannet for the water. Although I hadn't been off a ten-metre tower in more than a year, it all felt very familiar and very good. I beat Jason and everyone else into the seventy-degree Great Salt Pond.

When I surfaced, Jay yelled to me, laughing like a caricature of a cartoon character, "Nice bikini!"

"Tankini," I said, as I swam to the boat ladder and climbed it.

CHAPTER 13 SPEARING

When Vladik had asked me if I was a diver, we weren't yet speaking the same language. He meant free or breath-hold diving, sometimes just for fun, but usually hunting for food.

Murky Long Island Sound near Pot Island had great hiding places for bass and bluefish, but the visibility was never more than a few feet. Block Island's waters were among the clearest on the East Coast north of the Carolinas, usually with visibility, or in the jargon, viz, near twenty and sometimes thirty feet. Bait collects there, as it does at any coastal feature, drawing larger fish toward it like a magnet. "Big fish eat little fish," says the proverb. If you knew where to look, on a summer's day you could find a camouflage-sandy flat fluke, a fat black tautog among the rocks, a gray stingray with three-foot wings and an eight-foot barbed tail, schools of bluefish traveling fast, or schools of striper, some more than fifty inches and as many pounds, circling slowly near the bottom, looking for something, maybe lobster, but they don't tell us what. There are thick clusters of spiny dogfish less than four feet long. And then there are harmless twenty-foot basking sharks, and not-so-harmless threshers and makos. One reliable source says he saw a hammerhead in the pond in the 1960s. The great whites live nearby but don't inhabit or visit the immediate waters.

Jay's bait for Vladik was not only a few days on the *Lucky Strike* and its first-class service, but also spearing. Prime fishing spots were taken by the rod and reelers among the twenty thousand other island visitors on that Fourth of July weekend. We would have to pick our time and place very well if we were going to be in the water and avoid their hooks.

Vladik said he was so old that he'd been trained by the local Indians. He was, in fact, barely a decade older than I, so it wasn't the Indians—long since eradicated—who had trained him, but other locals, or imports who had become locals, lured by the surfing, the fishing, the drinking, the off-season quiet, or the air of the nineteenth century that pervades Block Island. These devotees taught him how to fish the Block, and the secret, he said, with cryptic antecedents, was the same as Willie Keeler's, "Hit 'em," meaning the fish, "where they," meaning the fishermen, "ain't."

Not many hours later, my phone vibrated enough to wake me while leaving Lucy undisturbed. Tentacles of dawn suggested themselves but had not yet crept over the horizon when Jason, Vladik, and I put on wetsuits and loaded up the RIB with snorkels, masks, fins, dive floats and flags, float lines, fish stringers, three Chekhov spear guns, a Froodblade for each of us to strap to a neoprene-sheathed calf, weight belts, water, bottles of 2Sweet electrolyte replacement, some foodish goo, and a big cooler half-filled with ice to preserve our catch. Jason, the little pisher who handled the boat like a pro, lit up the outboard, and it was still before first light when we were scudding along on flat water. We weren't alone, of course. There were a few other early risers.

Vladik directed us to a secluded spot whose coordinates I'm not permitted to disclose. The water was shallow and two-foot waves almost washed us onto rocks, making conditions just tough enough that all the bigger boats stayed away. There were two smaller craft supporting divers. One belonged to a thick-necked owner of prodigious lungs, an infamous hunter of fish that had grown fat in deep, federally protected waters. Another belonged to a glamorous ballerina and cable channel celebrity. Both boats had their white-striped red flags flying, and divers were in the water, as it was light enough, if not after sunrise, to hunt without (much) fear of accidentally being shot by another diver.

Vladik held two guns and then we both rolled overboard backward. He loaded one, handed it over, and said, "Don't shoot me, please." We could have anchored and all gone in together, but Jason wanted to stay with the boat.

Big boulders broke the surface. Only twelve feet deep, we could easily see the rocks, sea stars, and baitfish below, even through the sand washed back and forth under wave action. "Try to settle on the bottom and wait," Vladik told me. "There are fish here. Patience does it."

Yes. Fish everywhere. We'd dropped into a school of small striped bass, all six to ten pounds, twenty-five to thirty inches long, hundreds of them—silvery streaks slowly circling around. Vladik moved in shallower water, where he signaled that there were bigger fish. The viz was worse, though. I would be satisfied with something smaller. I tried to calm my heart, relax, take a deep, deep breath, and plunge, but when I did, all I found down there was a place the fish had been. I had disturbed them. My observation pushed them away, as in some gedanken experiment in elementary quantum mechanics. The game was, as it usually is, to observe without creating a disturbance, and then shoot.

As I was figuring all this out, Vladik swam by me on his way back to the RIB. There were two much bigger stripers, maybe forty inches long, secured to his float. "I'm going to dump these with Jason, and then come back to help you."

His return was reassuring, although I was worried about putting a spear in him. My breathing slowed. On the bottom, with Vladik alongside, I wasn't fidgeting like before, and the fish reappeared after the initial disturbance, circling again. I felt like my lungs were going to explode, making me want to quit and freshen them up top. Somehow, I found more air and more calm within. I waited longer. The surface was close and I knew I could go up at any time. The stripers were by now coming right up to me, six, even three feet away. I tracked them with my gun and finally decided my moment had come. Looking down the length of the spear, keeping it trained on my target's head as it swam, I pulled the trigger and *wham!* A sharp metallic zing traveled in the water as the stainless steel spear pierced the striper's bony gill plate and out its side. It went wild, flopping and trying to get away. The spear was on a short, tough line, its other end secured to the gun. Ten pounds of muscle and bone yanked and fought and swam away and up and to and fro and made crazy knots of everything, while I made a few hard kicks and was then breathing delicious marine air, watching the rising sun paint the bluffs red. I was puzzled, though, about how to conclude what I'd started.

Vladik's gun twanged a moment later and he brought his third fish to rest under water, removed it from the line, and strung it up on his float, all so quickly done I couldn't comprehend it. Vladik the Impaler. Technically, at that moment, he was Vladik the Poacher, inasmuch as the legal limit was two fish per day. I'll leave it as an exercise to you, Agile Reader, to do the math and see that no agent of the Rhode Island's Department of Environmental Management would find us, collectively, in violation.

"Heh, Lakshmi!" he yelled. "Let's swap guns and I'll clean up your catch." I was happy to oblige. With his snorkel back in his mouth, he pulled my line in until the spear itself was in his hand. Walking his hand up the shaft, all the time keeping pressure on its barb so my trophy couldn't get away, he then reached for the animal's head. When Vladik put his thumb in one fish eye and his middle finger of the same hand in the other, the fish calmed down. Vladik grabbed the Froodblade strapped to his ankle and stove it hard into the piscean skull, stirring it around in the brains for good measure until the end came. The RIB had meanwhile motored up so close that Vladik tossed my one fish in, and we scrambled over the pontoon while Jason pulled in floats, guns, and Vladik's number three.

Jason led us back to the *Lucky Strike*. Our outboard motor whined like an enraged sewing machine. As I would come to learn, Vladik's favorite joke form was the Russian reversal; for instance, "Soviet Communism is a perfect expression of man's inhumanity to man. American Capitalism is just the reverse." And so he shouted over the engine noise, mocking an accent he'd often heard but had never had, "In America, we spear striped fish. In Soviet Russia, striped fish spears you!"

The chef would be happy to have fresh *M. saxatilis* on the table that evening and for her larder later. With three of us in the RIB, we could have brought home six, but four legal ones would make the ship's chef happy. No need to be greedy. It was not even two hours after sunrise when we pulled back up alongside the *Lucky Strike* with our haul. We took hot freshwater showers and the chef had breakfast ready for us when we were clean, dry, and clothed.

CHAPTER 14 SPOUSE HUNTING

LUCY AND Jay were engrossed in *Grand Theft Auto: San Andreas*. I was listening to the Orrix family history as told by Jenk. White tablecloths had been laid out and German porcelain was being placed on them in preparation for lunch when Vladik asked Jason to bring him ashore. "Secret mission," was all he told us, but Jay knew something was up.

"Do something impulsive, will you?" Jay blasted, laughing, as if it was the funniest joke.

"Just looking," Vladik answered.

From the Boat Basin where Jason docked, and harbor launches did the same, Vladik walked into town. He passed the Oar and cut left across a field of gravel and mud, heading for the red mansard roof of the Narragansett Inn. At the back of it, he saw cooks taking a break by the screen door, sweat pouring off them like they were farm animals, and there he skirted the building, walked down the manicured lawn, and passed Dead Eye Dick's and Fishworks—yes, Local Reader, it was still there then. Walking toward town, he left behind the Block Island Maritime Institute, then the Hog Pen, Block Island Marine, and stacks of kayaks for rent, all before he crossed the bridge at Trim Pond and climbed a short rise to the police station and the Volunteer Fire Station, where hung banners advertising a post-parade picnic. He jogged right there, and looked up to see an osprey nesting on a telephone pole by the Block Island Power Company. The garage of the Department of Transportation and then the Depot were next, followed by another garage and Island Hardware.

When Connecticut Avenue teed off to the right, Vladik came upon a real estate office, one occupying the first floor of a two-story house sheathed in cedar shakes weathered to gray. Like every other business and like almost every other residence, it displayed a drooping American flag. Under the portico formed by the open balcony of the upper floor and taped to the inside of the street-level windows were color xeroxes of all the "For Sale" listings, advertising a "Recent Price Drop." or "Just Offered." or "Great Views," or "Access to Town." or "Remote from Town." or "Great Rental." or even better, "Sub-Dividable." After his relationship with Ulya the veep had disintegrated, and especially since the Agrigene IPO, he had been thinking about buying a house on the Block. He poked his head in the door. A woman on the real estate office phone seemed to be talking about rentals. Cupping her hand over the mouthpiece, she whispered to Vladik that she'd be free in a moment, but Vladik just waved, nodding to inform her he'd be back.

Island Outfitters and Dive Shop caught his eye only a few more steps toward town, and he couldn't pass by without a look-see. Kyra, a gentle, chestnut-haired beauty who was also the owner, presided over SCUBA regulators you could depend on for your life and fashionable watches you could depend on for your lifestyle. There was also a display case, a mini-museum of artifacts she and her fiancé had plucked off of wrecks in the deeps and shallows nearby. She explained the major pieces, after which he bought and paid for a fresh set of power bands for his gun and a broad-brimmed straw hat to keep away the broiling sun.

There was a right turn and a left, and then he passed a church on Chapel Street, after which he found another real estate office behind the Island Free Library. It had pretty much the same set of color xeroxes as the first one, but this time they were pinned to a board in a glass case hung on the outside of the house, and nobody was home inside the house. The nearby candy shops and ice creameries didn't interest him, nor did the moped rentals or the pizzeria. If there'd been carrot cake for sale, maybe he would have taken a stab with his fork at that, but the carrot cake lady had been sent to prison and her old shop had become an art gallery. There's a rhythm to retail on Block Island. Wait long enough, and every storefront will eventually become an art gallery, a surf shop, a real estate office, or a café—but probably not another carrot cake shop.

Still painted carrot orange, the building was the only freestanding one on the street. During the brief period when it was neither an art gallery, nor a real estate office, nor a surf shop, it had been, truly, believe it or not, the Carrot Cake Shop. "Only carrot cake?" Vladik remembered asking.

"Yes, only carrot cake."

"No chocolate cake?"

"No, only carrot cake."

"No lemon cake, ginger cake, coffee cake, or pineapple upside-down cake?"

"No."

"No pies?"

"No."

Vladik pondered this, looking around the shop, which, although tiny, seemed large when he took it in that all that was for sale, really and truly, was carrot cake. There were only two tables for sitting and eating. He had been alone in the store, and two seemed more than adequate. Maybe they sold whole cakes, too. There were none on display, so it was a little hard to tell.

Vladik recalled imagining the rich cream-cheese icing and the texture of shredded carrot sliding by his tongue on a bed of sugar and fat. "OK," he finally got around to deciding, "I'll have a piece of carrot cake."

"Sorry, we're out," she had said.

That kind of thing happens on Block Island, and some people will try to persuade you that it's part of the charm. That it's the very reason you leave the hustle and bustle of the city. Whether you agree or not, the carrot cake lady went to prison, not for failing to stock and serve the only item she served, but for fraud. More about fraud later.

By the year of our visit on the *Lucky Strike*, the building housing what used to be the Carrot Cake Shop had become Art Block. The olive-skinned young proprietress was, by Vladik's guess, about thirty. Her hair was pulled back in a bun, black and thick. Her smile was bright and open. She spoke with an ineluctable accent, maybe French, maybe Arabic or Israeli. Paisley. She was dressed in paisley, flowing yards of lightweight paisley, draping and wrapping her, a look most unusual for the mostly white Block Island. Azure blue Capri pants. Gold bangles. No wedding ring. And there was a sophistication about her, too, as if she could have been Vladik's art history professor, or the empress of a fallen kingdom in the Middle East, and yet with European eyes, deep shining pools of limpid blue.

What he saw in her shop was not for day visitors. There were no painted driftwood picture frames, no planter boxes decorated with bright blue broken tile, no affordable pottery. Everything there was capital-A Art, one-of-a-kind, handpicked in Miami or New York or Milan. There were no prices. Nothing was for sale. And that made an infinitely compelling pitch of scarcity. 'You can't have it,' she was telling you. All but one of the pieces belonged to her clients. She was selling you an idea, not the art object itself. You would be buying her taste, a relationship with her, maybe a very long relationship. The gallery was her showcase, her portfolio, built to land new clients. If you were a hedgie or a movie star, or a corporate executive, or a thirty-year-old retired entrepreneur, and if you wanted to find the art pieces that said something about you, or that you wanted people to think said something about you, or the sculpture that you would have wanted if only you knew what you wanted, then what Arianna had on display at Art Block told you that she could guide you to answers and purchases you had only gotten wrong before. If she landed two new clients over the summer, she'd have done what she wanted.

Vladik didn't know what to say to this exotic woman, but he knew he had to say something, so in his native Russian, he asked her name.

"That's a new line," she answered in Farsi.

"Vladimir, with emphasis on the second syllable, like Lolita," he said, bowing to her slightly, arms at his side. Then, less formally, "Vladik."

"Arianna," she said, offering her hand in a scene that might have come out of *War and Peace*.

They talked for a few moments about a suggestively erotic sculpture—"Onyx, carved in Italy"—about a figurine that could have been her—"In my youth"—about when she opened the store—"This is my first season"—and about his visit—"I came on a friend's boat." Not wanting to overstay his welcome, or to give himself time to say something stupid, he said instead, "I hope I will see you again."

"I hope so, too."

He turned to leave, and after taking a step to the door, heard her say, giggling, "and I like your hat," referring to the straw sun shade that had been dangling from his left hand as they spoke. His only comeback was a smile of the smitten, she told me years later.

As he headed back to the docks, he walked into yet another real estate office, chatted with an agent, and was soon taken on a tour of several properties. By the end of the afternoon, he had a signed contract to buy an older house on several acres of the island's south-facing bluffs.

From the Boat Basin, he hired a launch to motor out to the *Lucky Strike*. "I bought a piece of the Block!" He told them all about the house, the land, its siting, its feng shui, and the price negotiation with the owner over the phone. He told them everything about his purchase, everything except the chance meeting with Arianna that had precipitated it.

CHAPTER 15 HARVARD

WE COULDN'T stay at anchor through the night. The Great Salt Pond is protected from direct assault by the ocean in almost every direction, and even on the windiest days, hurricanes aside, there's rarely more than a foot of chop. The exception is fifteen degrees west of magnetic north, the bearing of the cut through the dunes. Only once every couple of years does the wind blow hard from that way, but when it does, the waves slide in through the channel and build up like the liver of a force-fed goose. Then, although Elmore Leonard says never use this exact phrase, all hell breaks loose. In four-foot seas, every boat in the harbor is at risk, either of being smashed against the docks or another boat it's tied up against, or of swinging into others swinging crazily, or of breaking free from its anchor entirely, whereupon it would become a fast-moving multi-ton trash maker.

Captain Nicole had been keeping her eye on the radar and her ear to the National Weather Service radio, hoping that the complex of storm systems from the northeast and the southwest wouldn't combine to produce the dangerous north-northwest gale. At three in the morning, though, she decided that with so many boats, and so much drunkenness and unpreparedness, she needed to protect her ship and get out to the safety of the open sea. She woke the crew and they weighed anchor. They did it so stealthily that none of us on board would even have been aware of it, but Jenk was up anyway, walking his deck for no reason other than something he couldn't fathom was keeping sleep at arm's length. And Vladik and Jay were still going at it, continuing a conversation begun in Pittsfield more than twenty years earlier, one they had no plans to ever end. And the bucking of the boat as she left the channel and the tolling of the gong on red "2" woke me, and that led me to the bar on mid-deck.

When I joined my boss and his friend, Vladik had just then agreed to help out with Orrigen for the summer, but insisted that after those few months he'd only take a seat on the company's board. I had been conscripted for the project and assigned to be Vladik's assistant, but I wasn't quite sure what that meant. Vladik would explain someday.

"Vladik, Lakshmi," Jay said, "there's something I have to tell you both." Jay knew what we didn't. Orrigen was on a collision course with an old friend of his, and if we were to come out all right after the battle, we'd better know something about that friend before we went in.

When Jay was a student at Harvard, he had shared a freshman dorm with a boy named Max Frood. "According to close readers of the facebook,"—and, Fair Reader, we had this conversation before Facebook—"by the accounts of most of the nymphs I knew, Max was the best-looking freshman boy in the Yard." On high cheekbones, his skin was pale, pink-tinted and silky smooth, his lips rosy and plump. His brown-black hair flowed back in an impressive mane that received and required no maintenance. No jock, he didn't have about him the characteristic airs of the high-testosterone crowd. He had a feminine beauty to him, very youthful, and with no beard potential, as if he were only fifteen.

"He kept a picture of him and his mother on his desk. He was probably thirteen in it. The two of them were on the beach somewhere, Marco Island I think he said, both beaming. I never once saw Max as happy at Harvard. There was no mistaking the fact that he was her son. She was a ..."

Jay paused with the pursed lips of an 'm' frozen in place, as if he was going to use that revolting four letter word, MILF. Did he see me about to judge him? I don't know, but then his lips relaxed and he finished the sentence, "a beaut, too, and a very young mother."

"Max told me," Jay continued, "he'd taken a lot of shit for his good looks. Even in his senior year of high school, someone would mistake him for a girl, maybe innocently, maybe to provoke him. He got ribbed at Harvard because he looked exactly like a Roman bust of Hera or Aphrodite, I can't remember, in the Sackler Museum. There was no end to that after someone draped one of his red knit shirts over it. But the girls dug his looks. They wanted to mother him. If he'd had an easy personality to match, he'd have been getting laid by sophomores!" Jay laughed big, guffawing chest-shaking laughter, and Vladik was swept up in it. My own was more nervous. I had just finished being a sophomore.

At first Max and Jay had been competitive friends, as high-achieving private school boys at colleges like Harvard are wont to be. How could they not have been competitive, two eccentric, brilliant science majors? "It was weird, though, that we'd been assigned as roommates. Don't you think?" Jay asked us, inviting us to say, "Yes, Jay, that's so weird," although it seemed not very weird, and we were uncomfortable as we waited for him to go on. "Was it chance, or had higher powers, you know, like the psychologists who reviewed all the room assignments, been playing a prank?" To Jay, it was as if Federer had drawn Nadal in the first round of the French Open. It seemed not right that one of them was going to lose so early in the tournament. The game was still on when they decided to live together and were assigned to Al Gore's old suite in Dunster House.

"I know Al Gore," I said. This was Jay's spiel and there was no interrupting him. I got as much attention for my remark as one of the crew got when she walked by while trying not to disturb us; that is, none.

"At the Dartmouth game, Max was in the end zone bleachers and was introduced to a particularly choice Emerson College coed, my cousin's nineteen-year old roommate, Joosey. Her name is Josey, but we called her Joosey." Jay's went wide, and he began sucking on his lips as if he was about to dig into something succulent.

"She was an actress, blond, ravishing, and nearly a clone of Max's mom in that photo he had on his desk. She was there like we all were, to get sloshed and picked up. Like I said, Max was beautiful, and they were drunk. He had on his easy side that day, and she was his for the taking. After the 6-5 victory, the two of them got lost in the stadium's warrens. After all the fans had left, and while hiding from the stadium cleaners, the two of them found a sufficiently private spot behind a concrete column, and he kissed her. Then he clumsily felt her up, and she reached beneath his belt, and then he not-so-clumsily lifted her skirt…I can't describe this soft-core in front of you!"

"Don't worry about me. I've heard better."

"This is not prurience. If you don't know this, you'll never understand Max, and if you don't understand Max, you won't be able to do what I'm asking you to do for Orrigen."

"Don't hold back on my account."

"But will you still respect me in the morning?"

"If it's a good story, yes."

Confident that he had the goods, and freed by me to deliver them, no subtlety of the intimacies Max shared behind that column with the girl who would briefly become Jay's first wife was withheld.

Then he continued. Max invited her to a Dunster mixer the night before the upcoming Princeton game. It wasn't the first such invitation she had received."

The week went by. On the cool Friday evening, the air was filled with the smell of dry leaves that Max would never forget, and the prospect of cozying up to Joosey must have been all too appealing. He came back to his rooms to get ready for too much drinking, and there he found Jay in bed with the very girl, his prospective date. The widely circulated account of that interruption, and Jay's animated telling of them are too lurid and cinematic for me to convey well, but they included something about the appearance of galloping as she braced herself against the wall; lubricating raspberry Jell-O shots tossed back and thrown across the room; Joosey turning to see what had made the front door slam; breasts swinging in a great arc as they fell free of Jay's hands; and Jay's curly hair and joyful face peeking around her bare torso to see Max in a fury. The encounter in the stadium had not actually made Joosey Max's girlfriend but he thought he'd staked out territory that Jay should have respected. Eros thwarted emerged enraged, and from that moment, the competition between the two young men turned not so friendly.

Jay explained that Max then found another place to live and began a vindictive campaign of behind-the-scenes character assassination aimed at him. It backfired. No one cared about Jay cuckolding him. Everyone had his or her own life to lead and pain to endure. "What was his problem?" or "Get over it" was all the sympathy he elicited. Max earned a reputation for backstabbing that he couldn't shake.

In the winter, a student reported that Max had been copying results from yet another student's lab notebook, and while the Code of Conduct Board didn't sanction him, because there was enough ambiguity that they couldn't be absolutely certain that the results he was copying weren't actually his in the first place, there was an investigation and it stained him. His circle of friends narrowed further and he transferred out of Harvard at the end of that sophomore year, obtaining his undergraduate degree from the National University of Singapore. NUS provided him with about as much geographical separation as he could find, and that's what he wanted.

"Max is a genius." Jay said. "I know he's got some IP right in the middle of what Orrigen will be doing. You might be navigating the gray area around it."

That's where Jay left off. He was wrong, though. We didn't need to know the play-by-play of Max or Jay fucking Joosey to prepare Orrigen's future. But he was right, too. Without understanding that scene, you can't understand Max Frood.

CHAPTER 16 SINGAPORE

SINGAPORE SEEMED like a great choice, at first. The tiny island nation was at the inception of a multi-decade technology-building effort, so they treated all the expatriated scientists and students like they were celebrities. It was a creation myth, and everyone who could wield a hammer, if only on paper, could build a part of history.

Max's uncoupling with Joosey marked the end of his youth. During his years in Southeast Asia, his mother's photos—and dreams of finding her replacement—were put in a drawer, the romantic Caravaggio boy faded away, and what or who emerged had a rapacious appetite for nameless sex and a notable capacity to dismiss the interior life of the people around him.

Max distracted his ravaged psyche while advancing the island's genesis story. Always having a better idea about how things should be done, he was soon sought after, even though a lowly undergraduate, for his creative genius.

Singapore was and remains, though, a place of very strict rules and hierarchy. It's an economic miracle, but an Asian miracle, quite authoritarian by Western standards, if not by Asian standards. Bans on chewing gum. No smoking. No laughing. No whoring. Just joking, Disbelieving Reader, about those last two. But, boring gambling. Caning! Firmly enforced accounting procedures, unless you're a Party official.

Max was a bit too loose with his interpretation of reimbursable expenses. Party elders, exercising power through the Institute of Science Technology and Engineering Research, took away some of his privileges, excluded him from participation in the highest-level planning sessions, and encouraged him to focus on finishing his degree, all of which led to his characterization of them as sinister Fucking Idiots.

He had trouble getting dates, too. Too exotic. Too extreme. More than three-quarters of the students were Chinese. Prime Minister Lee Kuan Yew's perorations on how to breed for a great society might have led the girls to Max for his IQ, but those slim Singaporean nationals, all lovely, upright, and well-educated, whose pasts had demanded obeisance to everyone older, richer, or more powerful, seemed to have been sent a message about him. If they were adventurous and ready to leave the country with Max, then maybe they'd consider dating him. If they were hoping to have a prosperous life in Singapore, they would just stay away.

Daughters of Indian potentates were headed for arranged marriages when they returned to their princely estates. They would titter among themselves about his eccentricities and his brilliance, but they wouldn't be seen alone with any young man.

The Eurasian girls, the mixed-race beauties at the top rung on the ladder of elitism didn't even notice him. His ersatz appeal was hidden below a sartorial affront to their tastes. He was not someone they could bring home to meet the parents.

There were some Caucasians. The Americans, a handful, or maybe only half a handful, were all transients there for a junior year abroad. They were away from home and wanted to live on chocolate rather than Max's vanilla. The Europeans, there to put down an anchor in Asia, included him in their partying and weekend traveling to beaches and cities from Hong Kong to Saigon and West Timor. More sophisticated than the Americans, they'd discovered that the overbuilt real estate market created great off-campus housing. He joined a group of them who lived in fabulous residences on Pasir Panjang Road.

For a while he honed the French he'd learned—at his mother's breast—on a girl he dated, but he was too quirky for her and her kind. Delphine was a type, the daughter of a Swiss banker seconded to Singapore. Riveted by fashion runways, fluent in a couple of Germanic and several Romance languages, and learning Mandarin, her sights were set on the kind of guy who'd be jetting to his own *Lucky Strike*, rather than on a scientific whiz kid who didn't own a suit. And after Delphine there were Gitta, Susann, and Chloe, and with none of them could he crack the code.

About that suit, it was a point of contention for the elders, too. If it sounds like a gross generalization to say that Asians love uniforms more than Americans, how far from the truth is it? Conformism, Confucianism, and *Wa*—the concept of group harmony—all lead to at least the occasional wearing of uniforms that demonstrate group solidarity. Uniforms had been as commonplace as postal workers and policemen in the United States, but they broadcast too much conventionality for the '60s, and their use went into decline. Japan's manufacturing success brought uniforms back to our attention in the '80s and '90s, but they had been ubiquitous in Asia's leading companies before. Now workers, managers, and owners were proud to wear the company colors. At SINISTER, whose emergence from landfill was a historic event being recorded and celebrated at every opportunity, the uniform was a dark suit with a dark tie over a white shirt. Max wouldn't wear it. His uniform was a pair of khaki pants with shredded cuffs, a red shirt half tucked in, and a Boston Red Sox baseball cap sometimes worn bill back. In those days, before he'd gotten fat, he did accept one deviation, shorts. The Institute could not have him in their group photos. He was an embarrassment to their sense of their own accomplishment.

At first he was invited to the photo shoots, and with a grimace, photographers hid him behind others as much as possible. When elders reviewed the pictures, they found everything about him offensive, but his cap, which he had refused to remove, was intolerable. In the age before digital retouching, a skilled technician in the darkroom could manipulate a negative or a print to fix an errant head, but the elders wanted to make a point. They insisted that the photo shoot be repeated, and that Max attend, but that he be excluded if he didn't conform. They hoped that pressure would do the trick. They hoped that he would be shamed into doing the right thing by being singled out as the cause of everyone having to spend time and money on a second attempt to do something that should have and could have been done right the first time. Their hopes were dashed on the rocks of his response. "I prefer not to," he said.

Even in the yearbook of the National University of Singapore, the institution granting his degree, he is absent from all individual and group portraits. The only photo of him is one where he is coming out of the water after an expedition with the Dive Club. He was wearing the right kind of suit for that.

The growing ostracism from officialdom drove him further into his work. He hardly needed any encouragement there. Ultimately, and to the chagrin of some administrators and the delight of his curriculum advisor, he won the Best Undergraduate Thesis Award in the School of Science. A condensed version of it would eventually be published in *Physical Review Letters*, the hot American journal for short physics papers.

Studies aside, he found Asia beyond Singapore had other charms, in particular, and not necessarily in this order, exotic diving, legal gambling, and a vibrant sex trade.

Max's Caucasian friends at NUS were always talking about getting away for the weekend to Kuala Lumpur. KL has long been an import center for trafficking, so there was a greater variety of girls there than in Singapore. They, my downtrodden yellow- and brown-skinned soul sisters, are brought in from every country in South and Southeast Asia. Young and younger, and not just girls. The NUS boys raved on and on about the selection. There was no gambling to speak of, though, and Max was generally satisfied by the Chinese and Malay girls for hire he found only minutes away in town. Unless he could persuade those boys to go diving on Pulau This or Pulau That, a trip to Malaysia held no allure. Macau, on the other hand, that would be worth the effort.

CHAPTER 17 MACAU

THE THREE-NIGHT weekend just before the Chinese New Year in Macau was going to be a boys trip, not like the overnights across the causeway into the Kingdom of Rhizobia, or the trips to Bali or the weeklong jaunts to the Gilis. Macau was a boys' trip because it was just too seamy. The NUS ladies thought that everywhere they turned there'd be love for sale, with the trappings, too—for instance the sex tourists, the girls from all over the world to service them, the pretty boys to fill in the gaps, the inescapable signs of trafficking, not to mention the gambling, narcotics, and every other nihilistic pursuit of some male fantasy in an Asian Las Vegas wannabe. In the cheap hotels they could afford, there would have been no respite, and the girls just didn't want a part of it, they said, until they changed their minds. The young men, boys really, painted pictures of the elaborate festivities that the girls shouldn't deny themselves, and of the city's other charms, like the pastel churches built 400 years earlier under Portuguese rule or the modernist apartment buildings from the 1930s.

Then the girls found some discounts that made a stay at the historic Hotel Lisboa affordable. They decided to go along, but only on the condition that the boys—whom they knew would be gambling and maybe worse—keep their distance. The NUS ladies would meet up with the boys in Macau only for the shuttle back to the airport.

The boys decided on the Hotel Holiday, away from the high-priced waterfront, choosing to sleep cheap and bet dear, and travel by foot and taxi to the old-world piazzas where the elegant casinos were found. Having flown in late and avoided gruelish airplane food, they planned on finding dinner along their walk toward the city center where a lazy doubleheader of gambling and whoring awaited them.

For Max, it was more like a hockey game, scoring a hat trick but spending time in the penalty box for brawling. Also, there was no poker. How could he have missed that there was no poker?

On the crest of a little hill in the Santo Antonio district, a hole-in-the-wall ceremoniously called Maître Jacques beckoned Max in particular, whose appetite for anything French left him always on the prowl. Jacques presided over his six linoleum-covered tables, crowded so close together that his customers had to turn sideways to navigate between the chairs. Jock, as his clients called him, had emigrated when his family was young, believing that they all had to be fluent in Mandarin and the ways of the Chinese in order to survive in the coming millennium. For his wife, that would be no problem, as she was Macanese, and for his children, the magic of the human brain would take over if they were immersed. For him alone it would be hard. He brought along years of restauranteur experience, and he maintained at his little place the highest standards of French cuisine. One of those was simply to enjoy eating. When Max and his two friends walked in, Jock was carrying on two conversations with guests at different tables, and throughout the course of Max's meal, one departing guest after another came to give Jock a kiss on both cheeks, and to kiss his wife, the sous chef, too. Committed to the best raw materials, he'd found no alternative to importing them from France. Wine, oysters, cheeses, of course, and the goose liver for his signature fois gras. Two hours after the boys arrived, they had filled up on Alsatian wine, bacon-dusted greens, foie gras, lapin chasseur with mushrooms and shallots served in a large cast-iron pot, and several samplings of other dishes, and fat slices of Jock's wife's bread to go with them. Their bellies expanded beyond comfort, begging to leave, they accepted Jock's offering of a small bag of his colorful macarons, and then said goodnight. By then it was very late, midnight, but the casino never sleeps.

One stood out among the others, its mango façade and gaudy lights calling them. When the three boys went inside, they were greeted by a parade of Chinese and light-skinned Southeast Asian girls, and a small crowd of Chinese, Japanese, and other Asian men observing the girls march back and forth on a seventy-yard course through the hotel casino's basement shops—a fruit stand, several clothing stores, a pharmacy, a jeweler, a photography studio, one specializing in fine Chinese ceramics, and another in cookies, cans of soda, and condoms. The girls were all very well made up, teetering in fuck me pumps and almost vacuum-packed into tight dresses. They chattered with each other like so many schoolgirls as they gamboled back and forth. The men gathered at one end of the track and the girls walked up to within a yard of them, beckoning the Asians with fingers and words, trying to make eye contact, while not so much as glancing at Max and his Caucasian friends. Occasionally, one girl walked off with one of the men toward the elevators just beyond the entrance to the gambling halls where Max and his friends soon disappeared.

On the first floor were only slots. Up a short curved flight of stairs were the much larger, round moneymaking halls of the casino, the ones full of blackjack tables. How could he have missed that there was no poker? His two friends sat down at tables with 25 Hong Kong dollar minimums. He knew the rules well enough, but he'd never been serious about playing blackjack for money, and he needed a plan. He walked around the room, calculating odds, and constructing *ab initio* the rudiments of a card counting system and working out the casino's methods.

The tables with the lowest minimum sat seven, and all the others sat nine. A Chinese, Macanese, Filipino, Burmese, Javanese, Balinese, or Malaysian banker or dealer in white shirt and black vest would be seated on one side. That first night, the dealers were women, all sporting one of two regulation haircuts, the flip or the ponytail. A lockable rack of chips was immediately in front of each dealer, the shoe from which she dealt to her left. Opposite her, written on the green cloth, were the numbers one to nine, ascending from each banker's left, a chair in front of each number. The number five, directly in front of the dealer, was given the widest berth at the table, one and nine the least. Minimums in the main hall ran from 25 HKD to 500 HKD.

Through the clouds of smoke, Max saw families and friends stuck together, often dominating a table. If he had wanted to play 25 HKD blackjack he could have played alone, but three-dollar minimums were not for him. Instead, he played alone among strangers.

Dotting the floor were various casino staff. Men, mostly men, in red jackets were observers, and men, mostly men, in blue were their supervisors. They milled around, talked, pointed out noteworthy and maybe suspicious or questionable behavior to one another, and laughed while doing so. Armed men in paramilitary outfits smiled at customers, but moved around the floor much less freely, as if they had very precisely defined territory to cover. In tan jackets were food servers and gofers for Mr. Red. Yellow jackets were worn by the lowest of the low, presentable untouchables who swept and took out the trash. The men in black were the floor managers—the best looking, the most gregarious, with the best English—in constant motion, training their underlings and dispositioning problems too big for Mr. Blue.

Ringing the main room of the hall were bars, fast food and elegant restaurants, cashiers behind cages, and members-only clubs, each one guarded by a pretty Chinese girl dressed in some shade of red. In these VIP rooms were tables for special guests and players with deeper pockets. And then there were smaller open-access rooms to accommodate the overflow on the busiest nights—like those in the build-up to the New Year—although night was a term with little meaning where there were no windows and activity went uninterrupted around the clock.

Seating himself in position three with about 4,000 HKD of chips at a table with 250 HKD minimums, Max was sandwiched by the young and the old, the casually dressed and the formal, mostly men but a few women, too. The cards went with him. To the strains of classical Muzak and beneath the lights of the crystal chandeliers, he won more money faster than he had any right to. A little crowd built to watch. Red supervisor and then blue supervisor joined, and even Mr. Black, the floor manager. Max was offered drinks, but all he accepted was water as he played quietly and intensely.

When he had amassed 20,000 HKD early in the morning of what was his first night in Macau, he pushed his chair away from the table to retrieve his friends and grab a taxi back to the Hotel Holiday. Stepping through the crowd, Mr. Black's manager, the casino manager, introduced herself. "I Wuang Wenqian, but you caw me Wendy, OK, O D2?" She was an indomitable fifty-nine inches in her heels.

Max looked at her, trying to break the cipher, perplexed.

"Wenqian rike Wendy in Engrish," she said. "Wuang Wenqian is two doubr-u. Make me doubr-u squaled."

Max still needed a little help.

"Too hald to say. Too many syrrabres. D is shote fo W."

"And just two instead of squared?"

She winked at him, poked him in the gut, and said, "You got it! You think it ridicurous, but why use six when two wir do?" and she let out a belly laugh bigger than you would have thought her frame could summon.

"You come wit me. I have gift fo you." Max could no more refuse D2's order than he could have stopped envying Jay Orrix or wanting one of those hookers he'd seen on parade, so he followed her across the round hall, down the curved staircase, and into the subterranean parade grounds. "You pletty boy, but you rike girr, eh?"

Max nodded and smiled while his friends from NUS looked on in astonishment. She led him to the track turnaround, a spot at the crossroads of corridors and shopping, beginning to fill with foot traffic of merchants opening their stores in the very early morning. One by one, the girls, many of whom he'd seen hours earlier, approached to within a few feet of Wendy and Max, turned all the way around once, smiled to leave exactly eight teeth showing, turned halfway around again, and walked away. "Which one you rike?" D2 asked.

He pointed to several, commenting on legs or face, and favoring not-too-obvious makeup.

"OK, I take care of it. Send you flends home and come wi me."

Max told the other boys to meet him at this same spot at six o'clock that evening if he didn't catch up with them before, and then he followed Wendy up a flight of marble stairs to one of the grand entrances of the hotel, past museum-quality examples of red-glazed porcelain, fourteenth-century bronzes, rough hewn jade, and carved malachite. She stopped before an ornately decorated entry, marked by a sign that read Macau Golden Group and guarded by another of those pretty girls in yet another shade of red, seated behind a bow-front desk. Black granite, mirrors, gold-painted mouldings of floral designs, half-metre yellow limestone tiles trimmed in smaller white ones and even smaller gold ones, were all elements of a formal design that led to two elevators under arched entries finished with the same attention to detail.

Wendy handed him a set of keys. "You lest now. Pray betta rata. Someone they to hep you. OK?" Then the doors to the elevator on the right opened, and in it were two of the parade girls he'd commented on favorably. D2 gestured and Max walked in. "You no rike. You ret me know. OK?" Max obliged and went in.

The elevator was on the corner of the building, its curved window-glass exterior mimicking the rounded features of nearby apartments and office buildings in the international style. Although pointed away from the water, its glass enclosure provided the best views of any hoist in the joint and some of the best views in the entire hotel. The girls spoke no English.

When they arrived at their twelfth-floor suite, one of them took a seat on the couch by the window, picked up the room phone, and began a conversation as if she were at home. The other waved Max into the bathroom, speaking in a language he didn't understand, and indicating that he was to shower, and in particular to wash himself aggressively between his legs and under his armpits. He obeyed and was barely wet when Number Two girl, naked, climbed into the shower with him and gave him a hand.

Job over, wrapped in white terrycloth robes, the two of them returned to the sofa where Number One girl was still talking away. She paid no attention at all to Max, as if she were his bored girlfriend, but occasionally used her free hand as a fan as if she were overheated. Then she undid the top two buttons of her blouse. D2 later said that Max took his cue from her and undid a few more buttons, for which he was granted the slightest hint of a grateful smile, and then slid his hand inside to explore her breasts, after which she half turned away, inviting him to remove her bra altogether, never hesitating a second in her vigorous phone call. The game was for Number One to ignore Max while he tried to seduce her and for him to play One's role for Number Two. Gradually Max had One undressed down to stockings and pumps. He was on his knees in front of her spread legs, and Two in her open white terry was behind him, pressing her flesh, arms wrapped around him and well positioned to work him up. Whether One was having an actual conversation or merely acting a part, Max never found out, but when he had stripped her of her stockings and elicited the first recognizable sounds of stimulation, faked or otherwise, he took the receiver from her hand and returned it to its cradle. The three of them repaired to the bed where Max was fucked to sleep in a hail of short little fake cries and moans of ecstasy. The girls showered, dressed, tidied the room, and left.

D2 was born in Chengdu in 1955 and came of age during a period of organized brutality and mass suffering that left no one unchanged. She conformed to survive, unlike her parents. Her diligence as a laborer and her unforgiving hectoring of others earned her a coveted bed of straw in a loft above the pigs' quarters. By candlelight, she read everything she could, and in particular, mathematics. She was in and out of the Red Guard before puberty. Her habits as an enforcer made her a natural drill sergeant and then she was made one formally, too. At eighteen she joined the Party and the Army, and married another young idealist of the same last name. By nineteen she was a mother. The husband's career was fast-tracked into climbing Communist Party ranks and he disappeared from her life. With no parents and no husband, the demands of taking care of the toddling Wuang Huizong did not jibe with her job. She led, at that time, a training program for People's Liberation Army drill teams, and she traveled all over China. She asked to be reassigned to a unit bound to Chengdu, preferably one that better suited her more mathematically inclined self. It was then that she entered the Army's Security Apparatus.

In Security, D2 acquired basic skills in computer science, cryptography, and espionage. Survival in the Cultural Revolution had been her on-the-job training in management and business administration. She led a burgeoning effort in international corporate espionage, and dreamt up a bigger role for herself, one she was able to sell to her superiors.

She and young Huizong moved to Macau. By day and night she was a fearless, fear-inducing, and charming rising executive in the gambling and prostitution businesses, with some dabbling in trafficking girls, narcotics, and organs. Her casino clients were entranced by her Napoleonic personality. In the hour-after-hour conversations, in the year-upon-year they would spend with her, she acquired nearly bombproof English and an education in businesses from aeronautics to zeolites, all in exchange for a few free drinks, nicer rooms, and strange pussy she doled out as if it were Halloween candy. By day and night she also ran a group of undercover PLA agents, male and female, who made important contacts with the same—or at least the same sort of—easily compromised businessmen traveling through, sampling what Macau had to offer.

Like mother, like daughter: Huizong was a natural at everything mathematical. When Max and friends made their Macau trip, Huizong was in her first year at Tsinghua University in Beijing. It would be another five years before she and her mother were again able to live close to one another.

Max's clothes had been laundered and were in a neat pile beside his bed when he awoke late in the afternoon. He began reflecting on Number One's bored-vixen role-playing and how it had tantalized him, and left him satisfied like no other whoring he'd ever had. D2 had picked up the tab for them. The girls were a gift, but they were worth a tip. He knew that. The thought had nagged at him, but he wanted the gift to be pure, unadulterated by any payments. He'd feigned sleep when they got up to leave, just so he wouldn't have to tip them.

His friends had returned from the Hotel Holiday and were back at the pickup spot when Max went there at six. They exchanged notes, and Max promised to see what he could do about getting them a room at the casino hotel. After he retrieved his chips from the cage, Wendy appeared as if she'd been notified. She comped the boys a room to share, not in the Macau Golden Group, but nice enough, and then she shooed them away. She showed Max to a private clubroom off the main hall. There were only three tables, with minimums of 1,500, 5,000, and 10,000 HKD. All tables were being played. Along the wall were food platters from the hotel's best restaurants, an open bar, and pretty girls to look at. Private bathrooms obviated the last reason a guest might ever need to leave.

Sitting at the 1,500 HKD table, Max was immediately, stunningly aggressive. Aggressive and on fire. Of course he'd been brought there to lose, but luck was against the casino that night. D2 came by, congratulating him, and encouraging him to bet more, bet more. He moved to the 5,000 HKD table. D2 let his friends in to watch as he weathered downpours and soaked up sunshine, as the hours rolled by, as strains built up. Through the hot and the not, he amassed a pile of chips worth about 100,000 HKD, and he was no longer tired, he was drained. He begged to be released from the table, his head full of percentages and odds and some simple tricks that might not qualify as card counting. His two numbered girls were back in his suite and they tried to service him again, but he was crisped. The girlfriend experience they'd offered the night before was not working for him the second time around, and he wanted sleep, only sleep. They asked for a tip anyway, and he handed them about 200 HKD each in chips. Taking it from him, One dug her fingernails so deep into his palm that he squealed, "Fuck me!" as it gushed red. "You pig," she whispered loudly at him. From the bedside, she swept a handful of chips into her little purse, the other did the same, and they left Max to tend to his wounds.

The flight home wasn't until the next day. He was worn out, deep in the black, and wanted to go home. The other boys from NUS were still enjoying the largesse the casino had shown them. What they hadn't spent on girls they had lost at the tables. A couple more meals, a night's sleep, and they'd be at the airport the next day. Max decided to cash his chips in and play out the clock with them, but D2 had other ideas.

Max had done too well and she needed to recover some of his winnings. She spoke to him beside the cashier. "I have gift fo you," and she handed him keys to a larger suite. "And this time, girrs speak Engrish. You have nice dinner in city and come back lata," she said.

It would be convenient, Dear Reader, if it had been the Year of the Pig, because then some of the stranger aspects of what I'm about to tell you would seem slightly more plausible. Alas, it was not, and if I told you otherwise, it would be too easy to prove false. Then you'd question the veracity of other elements of this tale, and possibly reject it, reject even *me* as only fiction.

Max warmed to the girls waiting for him. Wendy's idea of "speak Engrish" was not exactly his, but they could converse in more monosyllables than "You pig!" and that was an improvement.

"Handsome boy. I no fuck you. Rike fucking girr."

"You know girr rike this?" Max said as he yanked her hand onto his package.

"I stirr no fuck you. You sprit me rike a chicken!"

He let them lead him on a tour of some of the Chinese New Year decorations, and then they found him a magnificent Portuguese-French restaurant. As they headed back to the hotel, they wandered into a district where the celebratory decorations were sold, along with masks and costumes for the celebrants. In a costumery there were animal masks for all the creatures of the Chinese Zodiac, pig included, and not just masks, but also tails smooth and furry, long and short.

When the hotel guards walked into his room much later that evening, their excuse was that guests had called Hotel Security, complaining of loud and insistent animal-like squealing emanating from Max's suite. They claimed to have knocked and entered only after receiving no answer. Max—wearing his pig mask and nothing else but a squiggly tail drooping down the crack of his ass—was backed against one of the luxurious fabric-covered walls and was being fellated by a goatess on her knees, naked except for a brassiere. Beside her, leaning in to the wall, stood Mrs. Pig, in whose bush Max seemed to have lost most of his right hand, and in his ass she seemed to have lost most of her left. Squealing and shouting, oblivious to everything around them, they might have missed the knocking on the door, if indeed the guards did knock.

Their appearance took the edge off of Max's enjoyment, and soon the girls had dressed and left for the night.

When Max went to retrieve his chips and exchange them for cash the next morning, D2 was there again. She was holding a videocassette. In perfect English that chilled and caught him by surprise, she said, "It's very embarrassing, Mr. Frood."

"You're blackmailing me?"

"Too many people know. They'll say what they want. It's not my decision."

"All of it?"

"I can buy silence for you and leave you 4,000 HKD, just like you came in with. It's a good deal for you. You had girls, you had food, drinks, the hotel, fun. It's a good deal for you!"

"Fuck me," and he slid his chips to her.

She took no offense, but she pushed them back to him. "You go play and lose them all. It will look better to your friends." Then she slid over the tape and 4,000 HKD. Max returned to his members-only room and sat at the 10,000 HKD table. There he promptly went broke before his friends and their open mouths. Shrugging it off, he told them as they walked to the Hotel Lisboa to meet up with the NUS ladies, "Heh, it was a good deal for me. I had girls. I had food and drinks. I had the hotel. I had fun. And I still have what I came in with. It was a good deal for me!"

On the shuttle to the airport, the girls carried bags full of animal masks to give as gifts to their friends back home, and they talked non-stop about the visual and culinary delights, the art, the shopping, and how they had altogether avoided the cesspool of smut they'd been expecting. They felt indebted to the boys for persuading them to come along and witness the celebration. As a gesture of gratitude, they gave masks to the three boys, delivering a little speech with each. On Max they placed the mask of the metal pig, a zodiacal variant that comes around every sixty years. The mask was indistinguishable from the one he'd been wearing when the hotel guards walked in.

"Max," one of the girls said, "you are Metal Pig. According to legend, he runs from discord, has an army of friends, and loves big parties. Metal Pig is virtuous, loves justice, and is always straightforward with words. He is sometimes stubborn, but always persistent and self-reliant. We see at least half of that in you, Max." Then, to the sounds of clapping and laughter, and while embracing him, she placed the mask of Metal Pig on him. Max himself was speechless.

CHAPTER 18 THE GILIS

VERAWATI KATAWIJAYA had escaped the life of a kitchen galley lackey in East Java. With a broad chef's knife she cut a rapist's act short, and then she took his wallet home. Its contents bought her a satay cart on the streets of Surabaya, and then a Nasi Goreng shop in Perth. There she met Murray, and with the extra liquidity provided by his hashish import/export business, the two of them opened Wet Dreams, the second beachfront bungalow on Gili Trawangan. Murray blacked out and drowned a few feet below the surface of the Apnean Sea as he performed an ill-advised stunt involving hyperventilation. Vera became the sole empressaria of a small but promising business at the beginning of a tourism and construction boom that has slowed only for the few months following the 2002 Bali bombings in Kuta.

Nusa Tenggara Barat is one of Indonesia's twenty-eight provinces, part of the island chain east of Java. Its westernmost island is Lombok, and west of that is the province of Bali. The Gilis—and there are three of them, Trawangan, Meno, and Air—are wooded atolls (or barely more than that) a few square miles in area, a couple of miles off Lombok's northwest coast. The surrounding waters are clear as crystal, with seventy-five feet of visibility on a typical day, and ninety on the best of them in the dry season that lasts from April or May until November. As the beaches disappear beneath that transparent sea, they impart to it a palette of turquoises that deepens shade by shade until the shelf falls off abruptly at about fifteen feet. From a great distance offshore, a visitor would see the green fronds of coconut and banana trees waving in the trade winds, then a line of white sand, then the pastel hues, all floating in the deep blue of the 85 °F sea. Gili Trawangan, the largest and furthest island from Lombok, bears the shape of a pregnant kidney, its baby bump on the eastern shore just south of center. For those who care about coincidences, if you picked up Gili Trawangan and dropped it halfway around the world onto Great Salt Pond on Block Island, the fit would be nearly perfect.

Vera's new chosen home had been a penal colony and agricultural development that failed the objectives of local governments and business interests. Circa 1980, a few of the participating families remained to fish and farm on their own. The island, the sea and teeming life below its surface, and a few traditional sailboats were the sum total of Gili T.

On a tip or a hunch, some adventurous tourists—not Hartmann-toting, not Louis Vuitton-carrying, and not Abercrombie and Fitch-packing tourists, but intrepid pot-smoking travelers—made their way to Gili Trawangan, stayed as guests in the homes of some resident families, and from there spread the news of an undiscovered, hard-to-get-to dive idyll. The spreading dynamics were not unlike that of the AIDS virus, involving exchange of bodily fluids—often in the case of the Gili news and always in the case of AIDS—and reliance on airplane travel for rapid crossing of national borders. With the perspicacity of the best Silicon Valley venture capitalists, Vera and Murray sensed the opportunity at first whiff. She sold off her Perth establishment to buy land from the original families, a member of which told me later, "Boss, if I knew what it would become, I wouldn't have sold so cheap back then. But who knew?"

Traveling with a herd of twelve NUS foreigners, Max's first spring break began with a flight of three hours from Singapore to Ngurah Rai International Airport, south of Denpasar on Bali, then a taxi ride of ninety minutes or so to Padangbai, a midnight-departing five-hour ferry trip across forty miles of the Bali Sea to Lembar on Lombok, a three-hour drive to Bangsal, and a boat ride of under thirty minutes to Gili Trawangan. There the travelers deposited themselves four to a bungalow at Vera's Wet Dreams and looked east across the half-mile channel to Gili Meno. From beneath the waters, blue coral glowed neon bright. No dentist's office aquarium was ever so enticing. It was paradise, one of many, but paradise. "Fuckin' 'Donesia!" became Max's all-time favorite maxim.

THERE were strawberry daiquiris and mojitos and straight margaritas, or just cold Bintani pilsner, served on the deck of his bungalow while he dangled two feet in the tiled pool that had been built to encourage mingling among guests. It worked. There was much mingling, and not just with the guests. Vera took to Max and installed him in Bungalow Zero, normally reserved for special friends.

A mile walk clockwise along the beach and they watched the sun set over volcanic Mount Agung on Bali. A walk out from under the palms and toward the beach less than a hundred yards away and they saw the sun rise over Mount Rinjani on Lombok. A walk straight into the water led them to world-class snorkeling in the reefs. A short ride on Indonesia's equivalent of a Grand Banks dory with outriggers gave them world-class fishing of every kind from the shallows to the deeps. Indian, French, Indonesian, and other East Asian meals were offered up as the infrastructure for delivering fresh ingredients for western tourists was gradually put in place.

Vera Katawijaya recognized that Max was different; neither hippie tourist nor luxury-seeker. She listened rapt while he explained, well, anything. She had never met anyone so serious about the books he read, his projects at university, or the workings of nature. She was serious, too, and he made her feel serious. She liked that.

And he recognized that she was a diamond among the palms; as luscious as any Gaugin fruit, as ambitious as any Harvard coed, and as efficient as any military officer. He reveled in the night-black coils of her hair, hair threaded with fresh flowers, hair brushed straight, braided, and bunned, or hair that fell all the way down to her inviting round rump. He reveled in her natural, uninhibited self.

His girlish-goddess good looks were like none she had ever seen, and she teased him by threading her own frangipani in his curls. Making love to Max on the mattress where she'd stashed the remains of Murray-the-hash-dealer's fortune, Vera realized that she had always missed the sight of feminine beauty in the heat of sex. Max responded too, throwing himself into the vermillion crack of her cocoa bottom with a new frenzy. But nothing she did or could do completely satisfied him, and she sensed it, pragmatist that she was, even though she had begun to love him.

Vera took care of Max in every conceivable way, and when she wasn't up to it anymore, she procured others who were: middle-aged European or North American ladies who needed a good ride with no strings attached, or younger ones on a long rite of passage who needed some extra cash to extend said passage another week or more. There were no imported professionals at the time. They came later, and by then, Max wasn't interested. As for local girls, it wasn't that kind of place.

Max made one other visit there during his two years in Singapore. He hired an Indonesian who taught him to use a slingshot of a spear in the reefy shallows, never going much beyond the shelf where it dropped off sharply. Still, he shot enough one- or two-pound fish that he didn't have to sneak in

Vera's back door. She would grill them and serve them to guests at teatime when they returned to their rooms to shower, fuck, sleep, read, write, or recuperate before going back out on the esplanade, as the five-mile walk—without even a footpath in most places—around the island's periphery was known, for a night of eating, drinking, dancing, and forgetting.

There were big reef fish, but he never saw the hundred-pound humphead wrasse that were said to come in to the coral. He didn't have the gear or the technique or the strength to land one, even if he managed to shoot it. He was disappointed that he didn't see any, though.

He overheard SCUBA divers reporting schools of the toughest game fish in the area, maybe in the world—the dogtooth tuna. Spotting a school of those in these waters, or watching someone land one, would be a once-in-a-lifetime experience. Max booked a ride on a charter boat and went out with a SCUBA group the next day. He snorkeled on the surface and watched them swim among pelagic fish more than sixty feet down. They saw everything—reef sharks, Spanish mackerel, barracuda, marlin—except doggies.

That night he told Vera—who at the time was using her weight to sink as deeply as possible onto his cock while the large amplitude orbital mechanics of her hips put pressure on every pressure-sensitive contact point in the vicinity—that he wanted the Gilis to be his second home. "Tha's got the nicest arse of anybody. It's the nicest, nicest woman's arse as is!" he said, quoting from *Lady Chatterley's Lover* just to hear it said properly in context. And then, "Tell me how to be in business with you and I'll find the cash."

"Max. Shhh. Shhh. Just be here. Shhh." Lips and tongues explored each other while her breasts bumped him, and for a moment he returned to that sex spot in his mind, that Platonic ideal of sex, pure and untrammeled, where there was nothing but the here and now, nothing but his partner. So lost there was he in his tropical paradise of sensuality, in his mind's eye Vera had become Miriam, his mother. And after the celestial moment when his champagne flowed and flowed and Vera pulled him so tight against her that they almost fused, a bolt of electricity brought him back to earth when he discovered he was in bed with a slippery brown mama and not his smoking white *maman*, smoking.

Side by side in bed, they talked about Max's ultimate return. Would he provide her capital to grow? Would they start a new venture? Would he join her or be the remote partner? Was it pure fantasy, like a shipboard romance?

"We'll do something together, make something new together. I don't know what," she said.

He said that when he retired (and he was only twenty-something at the time) he wanted to return and stay forever. The next day, forgetting his copy of *Catch-22* at Vera's bedside, he began the trek back to Singapore. He wouldn't be in Fuckin' 'Donesia again for several years.

CHAPTER 19
THE ÉCOLE NORMALE SUPÉRIEURE

RATHER THAN return to the US to get his PhD, Max took advantage of his mother's heritage and his good French and obtained a fellowship at an applied physics lab within the École Normale Supérieure in Paris, the Laboratoire Pierre Aigrain. Alas, he found more Fucking Idiots. The French even had their own special way of saying it, a con fini. He applied the term without caution, particularly to the students who surrounded him. And they had a term for him, a *crack*, a term of admiration mixed with contempt. They were undecided whether he was also a *polar*, roughly equivalent to the American term nerd. When he was most insulting, consensus had it that he was a *polar*.

The girls from France's elite classes, whether the academic elite at the ENS or the simply chic at the Sorbonne or the Université Paris Descartes, were tantalizing fauna for him, and for them, he was a disappointing toy. Generic Cheri or Sophi or Marie found him lacking, they told him, in *philosophie* at the bars and *savoir-faire* between the sheets, even after the education Vera had given him. That they may have been insulted by the fact that—as he told me later—"I could give a fuck in a flying baguette" about their vaunted local heroine status as *normaliennes*, he would have to guess. He thought the young men—generic Pierre, Philippe, Michel—were fops, with their scarves and berets, twenty-nine-inch waists, confidence in securing a future no matter how mediocre their minds full of Marxist discourse, and the whatever-it-was with the girls that he so lacked. What he did like, in addition to the world-class assemblage of laser and condensed-matter physicists, was the food and the gambling. And there were some other things, too.

If Max was good at one thing more than any other, it was problem selection, the art of knowing where to find gold in scientific research and its application.

It's a conundrum, or at least it's odd, that the world would need more trained scientists than there are worthy problems for them to solve. Example: when Prof. A strikes pay dirt, many others jump in immediately. Ms. B may have her tools trained on something else, just a few degrees off course of A, but they're not yielding results, so she asks, "Can I make them work where A is working?" "Can I put my grad student B* on it and be an early mover?" Variations on questions like this come up all the time, and if the course correction is small and the cost of graduate students is low, B hops on A's bandwagon. When Dr. C sees this, C* is thrown into the ring immediately. This is not objectively bad. It's good to the extent that ideas that work draw the talent to advance them. It's good in that A's findings are tested right away, and if they're flawed, exposed. It's bad to the extent that ideas that are hard to explore get abandoned to fads. Max sensed earlier than most where the fads were going to be, and he achieved pioneering first results in several fields.

The history of twentieth-century biology is full of physicists, dating back to the 1920s and the emerging quantitative study of the effects of radiation on matter, living or not. Their work on the genetics of viruses and in discovering the molecular structure of DNA was pivotal. So, in the early 1990s it was not exactly news that physicists had discovered biology. But, there was a seismic shift underway because DNA, the centerpiece of moby, was being cracked open with ever better tools. Physicists had played a part in that, through instrument design, methods of data analysis, even at the bench, or as theorists. And if, Fair Reader, you are puzzled by the notion of a theoretical biology, please be reminded that the discovery of the structure of DNA in 1953 was a theoretical prediction based on very much incomplete evidence, evidence that would not be forthcoming from crystallographers for another decade or so.

Richard Feynman, one of the two folkloric figures in modern physics history, famously lectured in 1959 on what is now called nanotechnology in a talk entitled, "There's Plenty of Room at the Bottom," or less enigmatically, "Tiny Machines." In doing so he inspired generations of scientists and engineers to miniaturize everything under the sun, from motors to laboratories to books. Even before college, Max knew of that talk, as he'd seen clips of Feynman on TV, riveting the world with his simple hypothesis of the space shuttle *Challenger*'s demise. Feynman's influence was fermenting slowly. In

Paris, Max's own ideas bloomed within him.

Moby was hot in Paris. Who woulda thunk it, in this epoch when French leadership in the world is limited to single-handed sailboat racing and afternoon sex? But it was. Of course it was. Louis Pasteur, the father of microbiology, had made Paris a center of biological science in the nineteenth century, and while the blush of his glory may have faded, it was not at all forgotten. Max, hungry and eclectic as he was, took advantage of the fact that much of Parisian academic life is concentrated in the 5th arrondissement, around the neighborhoods of the Montagne Sainte-Geneviève. He heard François Jacob give his final course on cellular genetics at the Collège de France. He sat in when leading figures in biology lectured at the Sorbonne or his own ENS. Gradually he built up an understanding that moby had moved beyond knowing the structure and gross function of DNA, and was aiming its sights on what it encoded.

Our own DNA is a molecular message, a giant polymer of inheritance defined by two intertwining backbones—the famed double helix. Each chain is made of millions upon millions of identical monomers; sugars—the (pentagonal) deoxyriboses—linked one to the next by a (circular) phosphate group. Why are they helical? A linear polymer will form a helix unless, *unless* the angle formed by three adjacent monomers is zero, an unusual occurrence. Absent that, more and more twist accumulates with the addition of more monomers, until a turn of the screw is completed, and then repeated, thus forming a helix. Hanging off of each and every identical sugar is one of four different molecules, the nitrogen-bearing bases adenine, cytosine, guanine, and thymine. Those are usually denoted by the first letter of each, e.g., GATTACA as in the movie of the same name. The two filaments of sugar-phosphate backbone wind in helical harmony together, and the base of each deoxyribose on one fiber binds with the base of the corresponding sugar on the other.

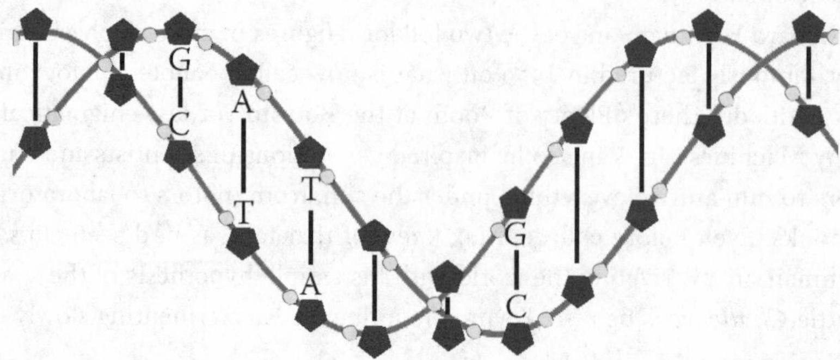

A wonder of nature—and one of the insights of James Dewey Watson and Francis Crick that led to the most important discovery in biology since Darwin—is that G pairs preferentially with C, and A with T. Before the structure of DNA was known, it was the biochemist Erwin Chargaff who had made the observation, immortalized as Chargaff's Rule, that G and C appear in equal quantities, and A and T as well, but only Watson and Crick explained why the rule holds. The G-C and A-T pairings make the marriage of DNA's two strands particularly regular, energetically favored, and therefore stable. G and C, and A and T are complementary, so the two strings are complementary; know one and you know the other. Split the double helix, and you're left with two templates. When complemented, the two are exact copies of each other. Division leads to reproduction. The form of DNA, the complementarity of the bases, leads to the function of replication.

The sequence of bases in the incomprehensibly long, doubly helical biomolecules is unique to us as individuals and yet common to each of the trillions of cells within us. According to the sequence hypothesis, first formulated by Crick, the sequence determines the proteins that give us form, function, and uniqueness. Stability is more than a nice-to-have. Without it, there would be no reproduction, and no life as we know it.

And yet, the complementarity is only a preference, not an absolute. Occasionally, where a C should have been, a T will sneak into place in the interstices of the windings, increasing the potential energy, but not so much as to be disallowed altogether. When the helix splits and the replication enzymes go to work, the result, owing to the much-favored complementarity, will be two different DNAs, one a mutant form of the other with an A in one spot where its parent had a G. But I digress.

Frederick Sanger, at the Laboratory for Molecular Biology in Cambridge, England, had developed a method to find the actual sequence of bases in a fragment of DNA hundreds of bases long. Within a few years, David Botstein, then at MIT, and three others scattered around the US, described a strategy to combine the information from sequences of shorter fragments and obtain the complete three-billion-base DNA sequence of a human. Their work inspired others, per the principle of faddism, to get involved. By the time Max was in Paris, there was a movement, which is just a particularly enduring fad, involving dozens of lab directors to marshal the resources—the money, the talent, equipment, the space to put it in, and above all, again, the money—to sequence the entire human genome.

One of the many beautiful truths of DNA is that it's a string of almost identical components. To sequence the mind-bogglingly-long human genome is the same challenge, sort of, as sequencing a short stretch of DNA with only thirty bases, but about a hundred million times more expensive. Those thirty would have cost about ten bucks when Max was in Paris. The scientists began to realize that sequencing could be thought of as a manufacturing process, and manufacturing principles like scale and efficiency should be brought to bear. He heard visiting lecturers from other parts of Europe, the UK, the US, and Japan explain that waste and expense could be squeezed out of the process in many different ways.

Max's chemistry was weak, and his biology weaker, so he often felt that listening in was no more than a hobby. He was enthralled by the promise of modern biology, but he was at a loss as to how he could be part of it. Eventually he came to realize that miniaturization was one of the keys to wringing out the inefficiencies and reducing the costs of sequencing. He connected that with Feynman's observation that there's plenty of room at the bottom, and he made his first career-defining choice: to focus his research on the applied physics of miniaturizing the machines of DNA sequencing.

CHAPTER 20 SELF-DISCOVERY

MAX WAS still youthful-looking and slim in those days. The smart and short brown beard he'd grown gave him the air of a very French psychiatrist, partially masking his slightly feminine good looks. It didn't hide his vivacious blue eyes. OK, his eyebrows were positively scary when he forgot to have them waxed off to almost imperceptibility, and he was a bit too serious, and his humor was lost on most, but physically, he was very attractive to women, and yet he made himself unattractive to women. Always sure to reinforce everyone's sense of his own brilliance, as a *crack* he was for the most part considered deserving of the credit he demanded for himself, even in the rarefied atmosphere of the École Normale. With women though, it was not just that he pumped himself up; he pushed them down. He dismissed them. They noticed. Even Max, not a pioneer of self-awareness, came to recognize that he treated women badly, and that it was a problem for him if he aimed to participate in the French national sport.

It was a long dawn, the awakening of Max's homosexuality. All those moments of intimacy with Miriam formed layers of resistance that nagging dissatisfaction only slowly dissolved. Never mind whether he could live with himself once he was aware. His mother had left him wanting more of her: more of her unabiding appreciation of him, more wriggling into the slippery slice between her legs, more disappearing from the world and the haunting feelings about a collision with his father. No other girl could give him that, he was learning. What would satisfy him?

At Harvard he had been oblivious to the lesbian cabals of self-discovery, or to the attention certain distinguished faculty showered on the prettier undergraduate boys, or how the leather-shod roughnecks in the Square spent Sundays when they weren't prinking beside their manicured and chromed rides. In Singapore, homosexuality was as illegal as chewing gum, which of course didn't mean it wasn't there, just that it was buried deep in the closets.

In France, sex doesn't sell, because it's free! In the Jardin du Luxembourg, at the tables around the Place de la Contrescarpe, in the crowds thronging the Champs-Élysée as the Tour de France charged into the city, and everywhere he went, he began to see public displays of affection between openly gay couples from all walks of life. Gayness. Gay sex. Anus! It repulsed him. It intrigued him. It scared him that it intrigued him.

In his work, Max had a very low threshold for action. Most people see a problem, and they wait and wait and wait until there is no avoiding doing something about it. They procrastinate. They find excuses. They delay. Max saw a problem and he immediately tried to fix it, and he usually succeeded. He'd go to the library to do the research. He'd call six friends and corral them into spending the weekend at the bench. He'd stay up all night working alone if no one would join him. Almost nothing got in his way.

"*Una forza della natura*," said visiting Professoressa Serena Fraguglia.

When it came to sexuality, the great equalizer, Max was stumped. He knew there was a problem, but what to do?

CHAPTER 21 TROUVILLE

After Macau, where he intuited the rudiments of blackjack strategy, Max read *Beat the Dealer* and became a devoted card counter. There being very little casino poker in Europe at that time, the skills he had developed at that American game remained wasted until he returned home. To basic card counting he added some of his own homegrown count-dependent odds calculations, along the lines of what has become known as EV, or effective value, and these he called, in Parisian fashion, *la méthode*. When combined with a constant patter that seemed inconsistent with the concentration needed for counting, with some feints that confused casino managers who were tossing card counters as soon as they were detected, la méthode always returned him to Paris with a fat wallet. But blackjack is not poker, where a big pot or a chump move by another player can make your weekend. It's a game of statistics and slow accretion of winnings. That worked well for Max, as he was tireless. He might have preferred the hand-to-hand combat of taking money from fools, but he did what was practical.

He needed the money. His stipend paid for necessities, but socializing cost far more than that would support. His fellow students were from families of pharmaceutical executives, bankers extraordinaire, senior managers at Petro This and Petro That, or their families had money and no explanation of where it came from. Drinks and eating out, weekends dining at a beach resort at Hyères, skiing with his research group at Chamonix, all were dear. And prostitutes cost, too.

Max paid for all of this, and more, with his gambling winnings. The Casino d'Enghien-les-Bains outside of Paris would have been the most convenient, but Max couldn't conform to their dress code. Instead, like most weekend gamblers, he made his way to Normandy, home of 1066, 1944, and all that.

Like Minneapolis and St. Paul, the twin cities of Deauville and Trouville are separated by water, and neither one of them is Las Vegas. But the Minnesota simile works for those vacation spots, as they are as white as Wonderbread, and the class difference between them is wider than the Rive Touques. Deauville is relentlessly polite and upscale, filled with luxury goods merchants you could find in Jackson Hole or Miami. It is flat, and its streets appear to have been laid out according to a plan. Trouville is organic, takes all comers, seats them on the sidewalk, and feeds them *les fruits de mer*: steaming pots of mussels ready to be hand-dipped into sauce meunière, sauces provençale, or some local variety; metre-wide round platters of ice covered with a shellfish extravaganza—several varieties each of crab, lobster, oyster, mussel, and scallop—all served in seaside air redolent of a fresh fish market, which it is. Instead of the brand outlets, you find artists in their own shops selling wood carvings of mermaids, wine shops with fare so unusual the owner hates to part with it, dance clubs with live music, and a social ladder that begins at least two rungs below Deauville's, whose lowest is "two homes." And there were the meandering alleyways on the steeply sloping hillside where late at night you might meet anyone and anything could happen.

At Deauville, like at Enghien-les-Bains outside of Paris, Max was turned away at the casino door for dress code violations. Trouville, more forgiving, welcomed any wretched refuse that had washed up on Normandy's shores. He saw past the oh-so-dreary gaming floor, Reno to Deauville's Tahoe, outlasting one dealer after another, fifty hands an hour at a table with FF 50 minimums and FF 2500 maximums. Later, as he refined his skills, and in particular when he could play two hands simultaneously, the floor managers would have liked to exclude him, *le loup americain*, as he became known, but there was no way. All they could do was offer him drinks, meals, and vouchers at nearby hotels, while holding out hope that his discipline would break down.

Max could count on returning home most weekends with FF 10,000, and that was after services rendered by working girls. At the time, only a few years after the collapse of the Iron Curtain and all that went with it, young women from the USSwere—a pun, Dear Reader, a black-spirited pun of the times—rushed abroad, trying to make six French francs. There was no shortage of trim and hustling beauties with poor prospects and a pragmatic outlook. He'd learned his lesson and paid them in full. A whore was less troublesome for him than a girlfriend, a real person he couldn't escape from after premature infatuation. Since society looked down on hookers as a class, Max could look down on them without some nagging concern that he might have a problem with women in general. He had no post-transactional cognitive dissonance—no asking "why am I here?"—after fifty minutes with one or two of them, knowing that they'd be gone in ten more. Back in Paris, the cash would keep for a few weeks. And when it wasn't Trouville, it was Nice, or Menton, or Monte Carlo. He didn't want to be too regular a regular anywhere.

In Nice, an Algerian gigolo made him an offer he didn't refuse and Max had his first taste of male. It was furtive at the start, with the young man pressing rough up against him, sending bolts of lightning through his pants, and then his tighty whities. Swept away by the aroma of the boy's armpits, the texture of small firm nipples in his mouth, and the electric currents of his bunghole being lubricated, Max could only whisper, "*Capote. La capote.*" There was fiddling with a foil packet. Max's head bobbled on swallowed cock after he had condomized and caressed it.

Spinning Max around, the boy pulled up close, crushing Max's face into the sidewalk, radiating heat as he pierced him, bursting, and tearing at Max's muscled breasts with desperate urgency. The screaming, ass-up, face-down packing of man on Max left him in a nasty disequilibrium of self-loathing, alienation, bliss, and the sense of being home at last. But there was no more asking, "Why am I here?" and he knew he'd be back for more.

CHAPTER 22 EVADING AUTHORITY

ONE OF Dario Javaheri's daughters told me, thirty-some years after the fact, that her father had seen the writing on the wall long before Khomeini returned to Tehran. The tenuous peace that prosperous Jews had made with secular Persians would evaporate. His wife's parents were committed to stay. His parents, may their memory be a blessing, were still buried in the rubble of the 1968 earthquake.

Packing as many diamonds, other gemstones, and finished goods as they could into whatever hiding spaces suppressed-indignity would permit, and it permitted many, Dario, his wife Vida, and all but his eldest child prepared to flee. Dario let his beard grow unkempt. Vida and the girls didn't wash their hair.

On a cloudy day in December 1978, they bid their farewells behind closed doors. Then their driver took them to Qazvin, Zanjan, and after 600 kilometres, to Tabriz where they had dinner at a home of their longtime family friends, the Javans. There they switched cars, drivers, and clothes, hoping that the colorless worn-out attire they'd put on might let the hawk's eye seek out richer prey. In the middle of the night they left for the Turkish border another 300 kilometres to the northwest. The little girls slept. Dario and Vida were silent. They passed Marand and the turn-off to Qarah Zia od Din before dawn. A little light came over the horizon behind them when they drove through Maku and stopped in Bazargan.

With their counterfeit Turkish passports, well worth the glorious rubies that had paid for them, Dario and Vida, each carrying a sleeping child, stepped outside into freezing but clear air. Their driver loaded two modest suitcases into a taxi headed for the border less than two kilometres uphill. Unceremoniously, without so much as waking, or appearing to wake the girls, they survived passport control. From there they walked through the iron gates into Turkey where they found a rusted minibus of a taxi to make the final forty-minute drive to Doğubayazit. In the privacy of the little van, Dario and Vida could finally look at each other, eyes wide, eyes wet, embracing, clasping two of their daughters, and cry, and gaze as Dylan said it best, upon the chimes of something something. Two days later, with all the loot disgorged or otherwise removed, they were in Ankara, where they bought proper clothes for their flight to Paris.

Dario's sister, also named Vida, had, in the service of Rezā Shāh Pahlavi, emigrated to Paris a few years earlier with her husband, Arsalan, then the Vice President for European Affairs of Petrochemical Industries, Ltd. There they raised their two girls and made the home-away-from-home for Dario's eldest, who attended a Catholic day school with her cousins and other daughters of France's business elite.

Themselves children of the wealthiest jewelry merchant in Iran, Dario and his sister had been educated in England and France. Dario had raised his own young family in the same multilingual mode, speaking three languages at home in Tehran from the moment the first baby, Arianna, was born.

In Paris, Dario and Vida bought a big house in the 19th arrondissement and opened a small storefront on the Boulevard Saint-Germain in the 6th. Arsalan had assimilated into France's industrial boardrooms and was saddened but unharmed by the collapse of Pahlavi Petro. The two families, French-speaking, well-employed, and optimistically matriculated, were safe and sound while they worried about those left behind. Together they watched on TV and wept as their home country went to the dogs.

CHAPTER 23 LE COUR AUX ERNESTS

ARIANNA'S UPBRINGING as the child of two expatriated families was neither French nor Persian, neither secular nor religious, neither liberal nor conservative, neither political nor apolitical. It was all of those. She soaked up the cultural bouillabaisse of Paris, finding some meaning in every tangy drop. She painted, and drew, and sculpted, but only imitating. She knew she was not an artist.

As a student at the Sorbonne, she became a skilled interpreter of art and literature, moving into critique and analysis and away from creative effort. There were a couple of college semesters abroad in Italy and Japan, and then a summer in Santa Fe, absorbing the desert and its influence on ancient and modern artists. She was courted aggressively—and to no effect—by alpha males of all ages. In her fourth year, she became an assistant to Nicolas Poussin scholar Jacques Thuillier, in whose private library were found handwritten margin notes about *'levée du voile,'* and other apparent references to how her fresh eyes opened even his experienced ones to the wonders of the *Corpus Pussinianum*. She became first a copy editor and then a contributing editor to the influential *Revue de l'Art*, a plum position facilitated by Prof. Thuillier's status as one of its founding members. The world-renowned professor and collector then anointed her Assistant Conseil for what has become recognized as his seminal catalog of the master's early work exhibited at the Feigen Gallery in New York.

She had no room in her life for men who were not as earnest about their own work as she was about hers. The social climbers, family-made men, older men looking for a pretty protégé, and boys on a quest—they bored her. Her parents were worried that she was too serious.

The Sorbonne was located a few minutes' walk to the north of Max's lab at the ENS. But as she was an art history major, most of her classes were at the Institut d'Art et d'Archéologie located by the Rue Michelet entrance to the Jardin du Luxembourg, equally close, but to the west of the ENS. All of which is to say, they spent much of their days, for years, only moments away from each other, and they had seen each other, but had never spoken or met eyes.

On one of those days—it was a gray fall afternoon, she told me—in her fifth and final year, she left her father's shop on the Boulevard Saint-Germain not far from her daytime haunts, stepped out onto the street without looking at what was coming, and almost collided with Max. He was returning to his lab after attending a seminar at the UFR Biomédicale, walking fast with his head down and buried in a book. Without appearing to take any notice of her at all, he got out of her way and kept on going, not only in the same direction, but headed for nearly the same place, she knew, because she'd seen him so many times in her neighborhood. And when she had seen him, he had always been absorbed in conversation with old men whom she was pretty certain were as distinguished in their fields as Prof. Thuillier was in his. (She was right about that, and found out later that his companions on the boulevards had been Abragam, de Gennes, Monod, and others.)

After the near collision, so engrossed was he that she took it as an affront and then bumped into him accidentally on purpose. When he said, "*Pardon*" without so much as making eye contact and then continued on, she struck up a conversation he could not escape.

Max was startled. She wasn't coming on to him, but she wasn't treating him like an untouchable either. His clothes didn't put her off. *Incroyable*! What he didn't know was that his apparent intense involvement with his own work turned her on, reflecting as it did a male image of her own self, someone she already loved. *Merveilleuse*! And she didn't know it then, but she'd disrupted a pattern of prejudice and behavior in him, and room was being made in his life for a real woman.

Max was cautious, reluctant to get entangled in a relationship with someone whose opinions and feelings he'd have to endure, and maybe even respond to. He had so much to hide from her, too, or to abandon. A fervid trip to Marseille did not achieve its mission of burning out desire for those crazy, delicious couplings with boys who looked like the androgynous ancient goddess he had been in the years before his beard. So he went slowly with her, a ridiculous pace for two experienced twenty-somethings in Paris. So many afternoon meals at the Café Aix on Rue Mouffetard, and no afternoon meals at Arianna's Temple of Y. There was no precedent for such a progression.

As far as she knew, he worked when he wasn't with her, gambling trips aside. And from what she overheard about him, his work was leading to stardom. The slower he went, the more reserve he showed, the longer he held off giving even the slightest hint of sexual interest, the stronger was her own sense that this man was not only her spiritual soul brother, but her life's partner.

She was naïve, but she wasn't bluffing. He read her hand down to the suits, and it only restrained him more. He wouldn't seduce her. She itched with heat as winter descended on the city. She plotted her own seductions, wearing fabrics so sheer he could see, well, everything—her dark raspberry nipples, the divot of her navel, and even the outline of a curly hair belonging to what he later learned was an espresso delta. And when seeing didn't push him over the edge, she found occasions to brush her sweetest parts against him. The smell of her should have been enough to overwhelm him, but he didn't succumb to, or even nip at temptation. She had never been so forward with a man. Her friends said they had never been so forward either, nor so unsuccessful. "Is he really worth it?" they ridiculed.

Going home to her parents' house after her often-late-into-the-evening but platonic visits with him, she'd bathe, scratching that itch with the spray head of the hand shower, turning up the water pressure to the max, or if she couldn't find the *petite mort* that way, kneeling under the bath's faucet so the full force of its flow ran down onto her pubic bone and over her clitoris and between her lower lips, helping nature along if necessary with a nubbly rubber toy she'd bought at *la vibroutique* on Rue Gay-Lussac, rasping herself with fury till she almost fainted, then recovered, gasping, surprised at herself, and in need of another shower.

Meanwhile, Max took covert trips to one beloved casino alleyway after another, each time making futile resolutions that it would be the last. He was human and had no disease, just desire, and as Turing taught us in yet another important lesson of his life, there's very little explaining, much less controlling that. The trips were an irritation to Arianna even before their first kiss. She didn't know what to call this "thing" of theirs. Max didn't want to call it anything, although she had gotten under his skin with the way she said his name, "Maax." And he did want to peel her clothes off, or rather, for her to peel her own clothes off and drop herself on him so he could absolve himself of any responsibility. He hoped she would seduce him, and take the blame if the "thing" failed. About the trips; she dreamt of beach resorts, a romantic cinematic scarf holding her hair in place and flying free behind her, and a perfect setting for *la séduction*. Max said simply, "I go gambling alone," and she didn't have any traction to pull herself into the adventure.

In recognition of the special demands of her contributions to his catalog and journal, Dr. Thuillier arranged for her to have a private office near his own in the great Mesopotamia-invoking Institut. Of the Art Nouveau period and designed by Paul Bigot, it was all red brick in bas-relief, friezes from Sèvres freezing gryphons flying, horses in battle, chalices worthy of Napoleon, and topped with a fortress-like parapet on the roof. Though her window was not on Rue Michelet and did not look up towards the Jardin du Luxembourg—she was only a student after all—she could see the Fontaine de l'Observatoire, surrounded by affectionate couples and small children when the weather was fine. There was also a ground-glass window in the door. Of all this she was very proud and optimistic. She envisioned after-hours abandonment on a desk in the little room, and she asked Max to visit her there, but it wasn't until much later that he first came by. And when he did, all doors had been thrown open to officials, architects, engineers, and surveyors examining and measuring every square centimetre of the building about to be named a national historic monument. In other words, there was no privacy.

Instead, they would rendezvous at Café Juliette, Café Les Ursulines, Café Les Arts, Café La Méthode, and every other Chez Quelque Choses nearby. Occasionally she showed up unannounced at the ENS lab.

In mid-February, months after their first encounter, after a late lunch at Café Delmas—too late for him he said, but intoxicating for her, not only because of the three inches of freshly fallen snow and the quiet, but also because of the litre carafe of Médoc that had accompanied the meal, she taking more than her share—they stopped to part in the Cour aux Ernests, the courtyard of the ENS. Its centerpiece was a round pool, maybe twenty, twenty-five feet across, in which for more than a century have swum red carp—they were the Ernests. A pump sprayed water skyward to make a little fountain. Set back a few feet were four arcs of short trees and low hedges, with gaps between them so visitors could reach the pool from any of four directions. And set back further were benches and chairs and tables, summoning images of Jean Paul Sartre sitting with Simone de Beauvoir. And a few feet further back, more hedges, and trees reaching to the rooftops of the four-story rectangle of buildings that framed the quad. And all of it was painted in fragile flakes of white cold. Only the pool, which melted the falling crystals, appeared as before.

The frosty coating was thin, covering only the branch tops. Their brown barky bottoms remained as they always were. And so each elongated feature became a pair of stripes. One was white, flat, and ghostly, but brighter than the sky. The other, below it, locked onto the first by the physicality of the limb itself, was shadowy, and darker than the gloaming. Branches branching like alveoli, they were visible in the finest detail in the barrenness of winter. Under the gray light of dusk, Paris' winter sounds were deadened in frozen fluffy softness. The spot's romantic associations mixed with the wine and the moment, and Arianna kissed Max without warning. Her breathing became slow and shallow, and she could sense the same within him, the arrival of awareness and opportunity, and of tentatively adjusting to delicious intimacy with a new lover. At such a moment, she could continue with a hunger that might scare him off, or pull back and wait.

She pulled back, bit her lower lip, embarrassed, fearful that maybe she'd offended him, and said only, "Maax." He was biting his lip, too, saying nothing, until he took her hand.

"Let me show you something, something special to me," he said.

CHAPTER 24 MLLE AMPÈRE

Entering the administrative offices along the quad, Max led Arianna left along a corridor and then right to wide stairs spiraling downward. They came upon a broad landing that had become a common room—Kfêt it was called, a pun resonating with functionality (café), entertainment (fête), and nerdiness (FET)—for the *normaliens et normaliennes*; the upper floors of the same building were the students' residences, and so they didn't simply study there, they lived there. Students, several of whom Max tutored, were hard at work playing foosball, pinball, and billiards, pulling espressos or beer on tap, or lounging on foam couches. They shouted greetings and invitations to Max and Arianna as they swept by.

Another level down was the bottom, but it led to a hallway lined with windowless offices and one entrance to a passageway, set apart by windowed eye-level portals on swinging steel double doors.

“A tunnel,” he answered to her questioning look. Indeed, a network of them connected the buildings of the ENS, giving refuge from the winter for Parisians not inclined to put up with it, and during the war—which in France means only World War II—refuge from the Luftwaffe. Underneath Rue Erasme, Max and Arianna walked in silence in the passageway’s cold fluorescent lighting.

Admiring the ceramic tiles, feeling them with her hand, she said, “It’s the Metro, Maax.”

“Yes, like the Metro, but dingier.”

“And narrower.”

They were all alone. She waited for him to push her against the wall and take her there, to make a decision and do it. But he waited for her seduction.

“The air in here is different, Maax,” she said. “Different from the outside. Different even from the building.”

“Yes. It’s uncirculated, warmer.”

“Dead?”

“No, not dead. Alive with ancient physics history,” Max said.

They passed by junctions and forks. In some places the ceiling closed in so low that they could touch it, and at others it was four or five metres overhead. They were in an unmarked maze but Max knew every turn. One person walked by. He and Max exchanged hellos without stopping, and the fellow’s kind eyes met Arianna’s.

"That’s Cohen-Tannoudji. Nobel Prize someday. For sure." Max whispered to her. It was another confirmation for her that Max kept the best company.

“Maax. Don’t people get lost down here?” she said. “I’m expecting to see decaying bodies.”

“The ones who never found their way out?”

“Yes. It’s creepy, don’t you think?” and she shivered.

He didn’t answer, but squeezed her hand and led her through another set of tunnel portals and they came out, not into daylight, but into what was obviously at least a building.

They had arrived at the subbasement of the five Laboratoires de Physique on Rue Lhomond, the research home of France's most selective university, and of Max's Laboratoire Pierre Aigrain. She soaked up images of peeling paint, nasty bathrooms, unfinished concrete, asbestos insulation wrapped over exposed heat pipes, copper tubing, electrical cabling, and strewn pell-mell, tanks of cryogenic fluids on wheels. The subbasement, Max explained, housed the laboratories for those experiments needing an extra special degree of isolation from the vibration of Paris' moving parts. Again, there were windowless entrances, and because of the snow and the season, and being so far below the beaten path, not a soul, just a hum of machines that Max said were vacuum pumps.

"How far have we walked Maax?"

"Three hundred metres maybe."

"It feels like we're kilometres from civilization."

The tunnel had been comfortable enough in their coats, but in the lab basements, the heat was too much, so they shed them.

There were a few carts holding racks of glass or electronic instruments, each parked beneath signs from the Fire Marshall informing the residents that the halls must be kept clear of obstructions. Posters of experimental findings were taped on the plaster walls for the benefit of visiting committees.

Max opened one of the doors with a key, switched on the light, and let the door spring closed behind them. They both heard the latch click. Putting her coat down, and doing the same with his, Arianna then pressed herself up against his still youthful and firm body, applying the second kiss, French. At first, she felt his mouth take her tongue, but with resistance. Then it softened, accepting, warming, giving in to the moment. His hand wrapped behind her, its fingers finding their way into the cleft of her buttocks, her skirt barely a veil. He pulled her toward him, his mouth taking her tongue deeper, his stiffness scratching at her, before pushing her back.

She was frightened, but she saw he was grinning, not angry. "Really, I wanted to show you something." Turning her around and pointing to a table supporting a centuries-old apparatus enclosed in a table-sized glass box, he said, "Ampère, André-Marie Ampère was the father of electromagnetic theory." The instrument was all brass and copper and wood (of almost the same color), lovingly handmade and cared for. Max tactfully reminded her of how Ampère's law quantitatively connected the forces of electricity and magnetism. "Can you imagine having a fundamental law of nature, an equation, named after you? Every science and engineering student would learn about your work. They'd all remember your name and pass it on. You'd become immortal. Ampère is immortal."

Arianna, who had tried hard over the months to pry some intimacy from him, held back her impulses to kiss him again, and looked into the window, the window into himself that he opened for her.

"What's it doing here, Maax?"

"Its home is the Collège de France, where it's been for decades, on display, but just a display. I've been asked to revitalize it and make it a working exhibit, so this piece of history, one Ampère made with his own hands in his lab on the Rue des Fossés Saint-Victor, is mine for now."

He activated a hoist on the ceiling, lifting the glass above the instrument. "Air currents would have reduced the precision of the measurement, so the case isolates the setup from them. Ampère was the best of the French experimenters in his day."

Max tried to show her the pieces and how they worked. She bumped the table and a part of the mechanism swung back and forth like a pendulum.

"I didn't break anything did I?" she asked.

"No. No," he said, and then guided her hand to a rocking switch with four contacts on one side and four on the other.

"It looks like a big bug."

Max grinned and said, "When Ampère moved this one like so," and he rotated her hand forward until the contacts made a metallic click. Without finishing his thought, he shouted, "Watch out!" and let go of her.

Arianna, already spooked by the thought of corpses in the corridors, was scared another halfway to death, and jumped back into him. He wrapped her in his arms, and leaned her back, looking into her face with a devil's smile she had never seen.

"Just kidding."

The game, the trick, made her furious, but that look of his made him even more appealing to her. And it was the turning point for him. For the first time, he took the lead, exploring beneath her clothes. But then he stopped, and again placing her hand where it had been on Ampère's apparatus he said, "Now where was I? Oh, yes, when you close this," and they closed it, "current from a huge battery flowed through these two conductors, generating minute magnetic fields around each one. I'll show you in a minute. Those fields pushed or pulled feebly on the moving charges in them. This one stays in place and this one swings in or out a very, very small distance."

He let go of her hand to point out how the pendulumized widget she had knocked loose was connected to a thin vertical thread held taught at both ends. "When the pendulum swings in or out, the connection causes the fiber to twist. See this mirror?" He drew her attention to a miniscule mirror attached to the filament.

"Ampère focused a beam of light on the mirror, and he could see its reflection on a screen at the other side of his lab. The mirror rotates when the force between the wires pushes or pulls on the swinging conductor, and then the reflection on the screen moves across the room. Ampère calibrated his instrument so that he knew how strong a force produced how much deflection. He could infer from the motions the force of deflection produced by the currents and the fields they induced."

"You're in love, Maax," Arianna said.

"I am?" he said. And then, "I am," and paused. "The idea for that twisting fiber, the torsion balance; there's so much history in that. Coulomb's measurement of the inverse square law of electric charges, and Cavendish's measurement of Newton's gravitational constant."

He went on to explain to Arianna—herself falling further in love and anxious for him to get on with the first item on her agenda—that the instrument had once been powered by a six-foot high battery developed by the École Polytechnique in a day when the study of electricity was so new that Ampère would have been stuck without it. Max compared the effort to produce that cell to modern-day efforts to produce a particle accelerator, a project of such scope it could only be taken on by a state. The voltage source had since been replaced by a solid-state power supply, but all the connections to it were original. He waxed on about how Ampère had designed his tools so that he could reverse the direction of all the currents and the associated motions, eliminating a class of systematic errors that would have swamped the miniscule signal he was hunting.

Using a peculiar phrase, Max said, "Ampère chopped the signal," and paused. He was going to elaborate, perhaps explaining what he meant, when he stopped and watched Arianna blush. She might have asked him to go on, but she wanted no more delays before the main event.

He changed course. "This is breathtaking for me," Max told her. "The foundations of one of the greatest accomplishments in all human history were laid right here, on this stuff. Not in this room, but by Ampère, turning this knob. Touch it," and he put her hand on the brass knob that had once controlled the voltage from the battery but now controlled it from the power supply. "That is history. You touched Ampère. Can you feel the electricity flowing through you?"

Arianna was crying as she leaned back to kiss him again, and this time their mouths joined fully, he giving in to the moment she had long been ready for. Her tears did not bother him, did not make him push away. Together they fashioned a bed out of two overcoats. She began to undress herself, but Max said, "Don't." Kneeling down, he pushed his head between her legs, able to feel her tightly wound short hairs and her lips through the tissue of skirt and scant undies. Reaching up with both hands, grasping her glutes, he pulled her into his face, before tearing the underthings to the floor. She stepped out of them and bent forward to brace herself against the wall. When Max put his nose under the tent, she exhaled, "Maaxi," while he licked her and flicked her. "You taste like oranges," he said. She gurgled and bore down on his lips and teeth and tongue.

When it was all over, and the lights were out, in a room so obscure they could hide away undetected in it any hour of any day, and they were huddled together, brains awash in bonding hormones, blissed out on a pile of their own clothes, and covered with a black sheet whose given purpose in life was to shield an experimenter's eyes from stray light, Max and Arianna each had a hand on the other's leg, caressing and admiring its shape from knee to waist. Arianna had never been so happy with a man. She wanted to sing, to shout, to hug, to cry, to bite him, and fuck him again, again. But that might have been too much, too soon, and she worried about overwhelming Max, who had been so reticent. He, whether he compared her to Miriam or Vera, or a man on a dark street, said only that she was "lovely and delicious."

Then, in low whispers, they both said, "We should go." Lights went on, and they were dressed, and the disarray was re-arrayed, and before opening the door, she said, "Maaxi? I am happy. *Merci*," and kissed him, letting him drink her, long and slow enough for her to feel the restraightening of his cock and the loosening of her own loins, and they pulled each other in close enough to hump dry. He cupped her crotch and said, "Take care of Mlle Ampère," and let it go at that.

When she was gone, finally, many hours after the start of that late lunch, I can imagine Max saying to himself, maybe out loud, "You are a Fucking Idiot!"

CHAPTER 25 THE TUTELAGE

THE OTHER Javaheris didn't welcome Max as unabashedly as Arianna. Those clothes! But the ionizing brilliance that surrounded him, the range of his scientific interests, his ability to paint visions of a better future through applied science, and his apparent joy at being with Arianna won them over eventually.

Her uncle Arsalan saw something else in Max, something generative. He saw Max as a source of ideas that could be harnessed to an industrial empire. Max's distinctly American originality and impatience was lacking in French business, so having him on your team could give you a certain competitive advantage, if he controlled himself. Arsalan envisioned Max as Directeur Laboratoire, pumping out new products and processes that gave him, Arsalan, the winning formula. When it was clear that the boy was going to be his son-in-law, or his nephew-by-marriage, he began to take Max under his wing and introduce him to the world of business.

The two talked for hours, time after time, about nuances of petroleum refinement, and nuclear fuel cycles, and agribusiness. Arsalan dragged Max to meetings and showed him how decisions are made at the nexus of expertise and private relationships. One could trump the other at any moment, and you could never know in advance which would win. It was always better to stack the deck. Max would have almost unsurpassable credentials. Being from one of *les grandes écoles* would set him up for the best possible private relationships, too. But the degree would only set him up. He would have to exercise those relationships and develop the skills and the will to nurture a network, a social network. A young man for whom everyone was a *con fini* was not a good candidate for this. And then, again, there was the matter of his clothes.

In France, fashion is as important to everyday life—and that means business life too—as afternoon sex. He was, literally, unpresentable. Max didn't have it in his genes. He must have had the repressor gene for fashion. Whatever Arianna taught him about the national sport, Arsalan tried to teach him about grooming and dress, but it was a no-go. Max simply wouldn't cooperate. He hated the idea of conformance, even though his rigid non-conformance was a kind of conformance to his own standard that everyone sooner or later expected him to conform to. As for an explanation to lion-hearted Arsalan, all he could offer was "I would prefer not to," a phrase that Arsalan thought befitting of a dumb brute, not the kind of man he would like his niece marry.

Son-in-law or not, Arsalan concluded after some time that Max was destined to be a business failure in France. Most definitely, he was not a big company guy. Maybe, and only maybe, he was a small company guy, an entrepreneur. But in France, that class of character *n'existe pas*. Entrepreneuring is a sucker's game there. Between the vestiges of the guild system that keeps newcomers out and the financial burdens imposed on all companies large and small, not to mention the missing infrastructure for funding new ventures, emerging companies face even longer odds than in the US. Therefore, being an entrepreneur is for outcasts, the socially inept, the unconnected, and the unambitious, much the same as being a government bureaucrat in America—a characterization common among financially successful people. So, if Max were to go that route, the startup route, he'd be going back to the US, and probably to Silicon Valley, where being a company founder or CEO confers the same social status as a movie director has in Hollywood, or as once upon a time bequeathed a whaling captain in New Bedford.

Arsalan counseled him. "Paris is no Silicon Valley, son. Take your academic job, wherever it is. Stay close to people in industry so you understand what counts, but develop your ideas in your lab. Use it as a sandbox and make your inventions there. If you go to Boston, our friend Ali Javan at MIT will show you how it's done. I know investors and company builders who will help you get your ideas into the market. You can get rich doing this, very rich, once you find the levers and their keepers. It will take time. I know you can do it, but don't give up your day job for any one of them."

And this became Max's template.

CHAPTER 26 MAX'S DISEASE

I'VE SPENT enough time watching and listening to Max and those who know him to know he thought he had a disease—wanting to fuck men. But his disease was that he thought he had a disease. Arianna's tang was no cure for him. The only cure for him would have been coming clean about what ailed him, and that wouldn't have cured him of his desire for men. If Arianna were up to it, their relationship might even have survived coming clean. He liked her. He may even have loved her. He loved her pussy, Mlle Ampère. He heralded it, saluted it, toasted it, stuffed it, drank from it in noisy gulps, fed it fresh fruit and vegetables, ate brownies from it, and wrote bad poetry to it. And the doing so did exactly nothing to slake his hunger for cock and every other part of man. There's the rub.

CHAPTER 27 TIME TO GO

MAX KNEW Arsalan was right about going back to the US, and the need was greater than even Arsalan imagined. The physical realization of his ideas was held back by the absence of the right kind of facilities in Paris. To move forward and become the pioneering big-swinging dick he felt was his due, he had to be working at a university where they had a MEMS lab, and maybe even a semiconductor lab. Microelectromechanical systems, the generic name for many tiny machines, were often built using the same materials and techniques of miniaturization and of mass production used for semiconductor integrated circuits. Max conceived his sequencers as MEMS devices.

After the epiphany that had set him on this course, Max had holed up in his ENS office trying to imagine how to miniaturize the instruments of capillary electrophoresis that were the standard of the day. Nothing came to him except a casual reference that one of the biologists had made. Loosely translated, she said, "A cell is like no beaker of stuff. It's too full."

Some people call the place Shallow Alto. I guess I know why. It rhymes. But Palo Alto is deep, deep, deep when it comes to thirteen-year-olds per square mile doing original research in astrophysics. One of the explanations is the flow of extraordinary invited speakers through the public school classrooms. A decade after he left France, Max was one of those speakers.

In handwritten notes for a talk on the history of his early work that he gave to a Gunn High School biotechnology class, he described how "Over and over, this message echoed in my head, a koan I couldn't escape. Gradually the cloak around its meaning unraveled. If there was more chemistry going on in a cell than any beaker could manage, then chemistry that did work in a beaker could certainly be done in a cell, and even in something simpler. A droplet is simpler than a cell. The chemistries of DNA sequencing can be done in a beaker. *Ergo*, we can hope to do DNA sequencing in a cell-sized drop. But how do you hold such a thing? With tweezers? In a depression on a glass slide? Maybe those would be possible, but why not put the little proto-cell in an immiscible fluid matrix and apply the principles of hydraulics for transport?"

What he meant was that since oil and water don't mix, and the reactions of DNA sequencing take place in water, a droplet—or a picobeaker in Max's phraseology—full of sequencing chemistry would remain stable in oil, the fluid matrix he mentioned. In a channel etched in a MEMS device, the droplet-bearing oil would move forward or back depending on the pressure applied at the channel's end; imagine pushing on a piece of dry spaghetti in a straw. The tiny spheroids would move along with the matrix. Genius! Max is a genius.

Max's concept depended on valves to switch the matrix to one of several different channels, and a method to merge drops on demand, and more. He would have fun inventing these things, he told Arsalan, as they didn't exist at the time, and he thought he already knew enough to begin work on them, so that's where he started his experimental program.

Water droplets in oil form an emulsion, an emulsion is a colloid, and Paris was thick in colloidal chemists and physicists. Max spent many hours talking to leading scholars there. Academics in Paris gave no thought to patents in those days. Arsalan had advised Max about their importance. The conversations led to notebooks full of ideas about surfactants, van der Waals forces, Reynolds numbers, and more, and the books became the basis for his patent applications when he returned to the US.

Max intuited what Prof. John G. King would later tell him at MIT, "A good physicist makes a lot of mistakes quickly." He understood that he must take an appointment where there was an already-operating MEMS lab, because without it, without even a simple one, he would waste time traveling, deal with loads of soul-numbing bureaucracy, be subject to someone's whims or failures, and become a second-rate figure, not—as he intended—the best in the field. That's what would happen to him in Paris, and why he had to go back to the States where he hadn't lived for the better part of a decade, and where he'd felt forced to leave when he did. Every day away from the position, and placement he didn't yet have, felt like a day lost.

CHAPTER 28 THE COURTSHIP

ARIANNA KNEW all about why he would be returning to the US. She knew, too, she would follow him. "I went to lycée on Rue Saint-Jacques," she told me, "and after that I walked across the street to the Sorbonne. Then, I was curator at the Musée only blocks away after graduating. I could have spent my entire life within a few steps of Montagne Sainte-Geneviève, only to die watching my grandchildren in the Jardin du Luxembourg, and be buried beside Mme Curie in the Panthéon." She winked at me and laughed, conveying the unlikelihood that those hallowed catacombs would be her final resting place. After a moment, she went on. "I wanted more. I didn't know whether I would follow as Ms. Frood, that's all, and we didn't talk about it."

The Javaheris had come to enjoy Max's intensity and they were looking forward to a wedding, even if their daughter would live across the Atlantic. That crossing was easy—farther, but easy—compared to the journeys they'd been forced to make before. Max was always on his best behavior around them, entertaining them, showing appreciation for their generosity, trying to please them, teasing them.

He sat between Dario and Arianna, reclining at a snaking ensemble of tables seating thirty. All of the extended family had wanted to see the prospective husband at his first Passover Seder. Full of wine, confident he could get away with almost anything, Max said, "Dario, your eyes." Dario and both Vidas had Arianna's eyes, radiant blue ones you'd never expect to see among Iran's Sephardic Jews. "You might have been hanged as spies."

"Yes. That was coming. But they look good on my daughter, don't they?"

"Like your best sapphires."

Dario gave an approving nod. Other conversation stopped.

"I'll bet you one of those that there's Europe in your blood," Max said.

"You couldn't afford it if you lost." A few laughed quietly. "But you're right. A French banker, a Jew of course, was swept off his feet by one of our beauties in 1638. He never went home. There were a few others then, and other Askenazim have married in over time."

"Dayenu!" Max said, echoing the famous song from the Haggadah he had learned just that night. And the whole table erupted in joy.

Dario slapped him on the shoulder. "*Cherchez les femmes*, Son. *Cherchez les femmes*. We're the children. What about you, Max? Where do you come from?"

"My story is lost before 1830 or so, in Pittsburgh. From there, it's Roman Catholic all the way. I don't know much about them. My mother was French. But you knew that. She was a lapsed Catholic and didn't practice. I can't even say I'm an ex-Catholic. I was never anything."

"He's postlapsarian, Papa," Arianna added. Side conversations broke out as guests tried to understand her meaning.

"Ah, my Catholic-educated art historian," Dario said. "And what do you want for your children, Max?"

Arianna cut in abruptly. "Papa!" And that was that.

MAX was open about his gambling, and they were at least a little impressed, although as uncomprehending as Arianna about why she never accompanied him. Her mothers, the two wise Vidas, expressed to her some worry that there was a secret he didn't want revealed. That possibility worked away at the veneer of their good feelings about an impending marriage.

His homoerotic self, of course, he kept in the closet. Life had been simpler for him when there was no one to keep secrets from. There were a lot of moving parts, as he liked to say.

Arianna finished her bachelor's degree a year before Max was to finish his doctorate. Professor Thuillier placed Arianna in a position as assistant curator at the Musée du Luxembourg. Max finished up his work on miniaturizing the componentry of DNA sequencing instruments and applied for teaching jobs at several of the first-tier universities that had made major investments in semiconductor processing research. When Arianna stopped in to see him, women in his lab remarked to her that Max had been kinder to them since the romance had begun.

Max and Arianna were in Paris already, so they needn't have gone anywhere for a lover's getaway, but they got away anyway. They travelled around in a Fiat Tipo that he'd bought with gambling money; they visited caves, vineyards, rugged beaches, battlefields, castles, cathedrals, museums, small hotels, and everywhere else but casinos.

They stayed away from casinos. He claimed that having her there would be too much of a distraction to his concentration. "It's not fun, really, it's work," he said.

She suggested that they go so that she could see, and he wouldn't even need to gamble. "Just a weekend in Deauville would be fun, wouldn't it? I love Normandy. The beaches with their briny air? You could pay Mlle Ampère a special visit and we could wrap ourselves in sheets, eat in, eat out, stroll on the boardwalk. It would be delicious wouldn't it?"

"No, it wouldn't," although the thought of her electrified gash had taken the edge off his hostility for a moment.

When her pleading began to morph into something more like a demand, he answered, "Absolutely not!"

The force of his obstinacy hit her like a brick, and he too was surprised by it. He'd rather he'd said, "I'd prefer not to," but in the face of her repeated request, he didn't know what else to do. Saying yes seemed not to have been considered.

They barely spoke for a week. He burrowed into the lab and kept to himself. The secrets that might be revealed on a trip to one of his haunts were so dark that he was prepared to give her up, to find a way to hate her if he had to, rather than give in to her request. He didn't call her before he left for Deauville.

Arianna disappeared into her texts and took comfort in family. She accompanied her little sisters, now finishing at the lycée, to cafes and on walks. Before this, she'd been too busy with school or Max, ignoring them. Now she could see them and how they needed her. She cried to her two mamas. They tried to console, but also, because the idea of that secret bothered them, they probed a little. "Why haven't we met his family, Arianna?"

"He's an orphan, *Mamman*," she reminded them. She called them both *Mamman*.

To their cries of sadness for him, Arianna explained what little she knew at the time.

"I ask, but he's secretive. His parents are gone and he's estranged from the aunt who took him in. He gets angry when I ask him. A little bit like now. There are conversations he just won't have."

Aunt Vida said, "A marriage is long, if you're lucky, *chérie*. Secrets corrode the bond. It doesn't matter who has the secret. The bond holds both of you."

"He's a nice boy, Arianna, but maybe he should see a psychiatrist," said her mother, the other Vida.

"I think so," Arianna said. "A Froodian, maybe. Do you want to bring that up?" She wore a smile worthy of a thousand kisses, and they all laughed till they cried.

In private the Vidas agreed, "How they get out of this first quarrel will be an omen."

CHAPTER 29 DEAUVILLE

THEY, THE Vidas, were not happy when Arianna announced a few days later that she no longer cared about having casino privileges and would put the whole affair, the fight with Max, behind her. She said she didn't need an apology from him. She decided to show up at the lab and act like nothing had happened.

He wasn't there. He had left without a word and yes, he was due back for a meeting the following Monday, but no one knew more than that. More hurt.

Of all the casinos in France, Trouville was his favorite and Deauville was his favorite to hate. It was to him the most luxurious, the most expensive, the most pretentious, and had the fewest like-minded men and places to meet them. To his professional colleagues, Arianna, or whoever would listen, he vented about the charming Anglo-Norman architecture and the manicured boardwalks.

"It's a gambling theme park, phony to its bones. They paper over all the criminality and seediness that drives gambling. And people buy it! That's the worst joke." With his arms waving and his face animated, he would conclude with a shout, "*Family friendly gambling, if ever there was an oxymoron, that has to be it!*" How much of his rancor was resentment over the fact that he was excluded, he never let on.

Max had gone to Trouville on a mission to cool off and to make a real stake. Returning to the US to start a company, unless he had the backing of the two men he expected to be his fathers-in-law—and he didn't want to count on that, no matter what he'd been told—he'd need money of his own. He'd need money of his own in any case if he wanted autonomy. Usually satisfied with winning ten thousand francs, this time he dreamt of winning more than ten times that.

When he returned from Normandy, Max told Arianna all about his trip. Later, much later, she concluded that his tale was as much lie as it was truth. She and I, aided by some old-fashioned shoe-leather detective work, pieced together our own version of events.

La mèthode had proven to produce winnings of a little less than one percent per hand, averaged over hundreds of hands. At Trouville's tables, with their FF 2500 limits, that translated into something like a thousand francs an hour. Even playing around the clock for two days, he couldn't expect to take in hundreds of thousands. But he had a plan.

His accumulated savings amounted to almost FF 90,000, or about $16,000. Combining half of that with what he figured he could get for the Fiat Tipo, if he needed to sell it, he'd have FF 75,000, enough to protect him against some long unfavorable odds, enough for him to eat better and stay in better rooms. He had a lot of things planned for that long weekend, among them being fucked harder and by better, more expensive fuckers.

Max went at it for a few hours, experimented with playing two hands at once, and after adding another FF 10,000 of winnings to his bank, he decided to sell the car, for insurance. Placing a call on the hotel phone, he sold the car for FF 30,000, a real bargain for someone. At around two o'clock on a Thursday morning he crossed the Rive Touques and pulled into a quiet parking lot beside a marina, only yards away from a wall of buildings painted with the greeting *Bienvenue à Deauville*. Two guys from the nearby port city of Le Havre, two guys who never would have made it through Security in post-911 America, were waiting for him as he drove up. He left the car running while they inspected it. As he stood outside, one of them was behind the wheel and the other handed him a wad of bills. He counted it and found FF 20,000. "Heh," Max said, "It's light."

"*Putain de merde*!" said the seated one while the other walked around to the passenger side. Reaching in to the still-open car, Max grabbed the driver, who then yanked on the door handle, bringing fast-moving sheet metal into the meat of Max's arm. Max howled and recoiled, the door slammed shut, and the car squealed away, leaving Max groaning and bleeding.

Psychically bruised and physically wounded, he needed sleep and nourishment. On the five-minute walk back to his hotel room, he picked up a couple of girls to join him, bringing him very close to a line of infidelity he hadn't crossed since he'd taken up with Arianna. Guys, yes. Girls, no. At the door, too exhausted, too conflicted, he sent them away. They wanted to be paid just for the effort of getting there. He tried again to send them away. They pummeled him and took FF 5,000, a ridiculous sum for their trouble, but generous, considering they could have taken it all. He slept as if he were dead.

When he awoke, daylight was already fading. This struggle with Arianna and within himself had left him more upset than he had at first recognized. Then came the two assaults. Max needed to put all of it aside. The neon-lit brasseries beckoned, but he settled for a baguette rustique at a pâtisserie, and taking what cash and chips he had, he meandered through side streets and eventually back to the casino and its tables.

His counting was better than it had been the day before—if it had been only a day before—and he made fewer mistakes that gamblers in stress tend to make. Playing two hands again, by Friday's dawn he had won back the FF 15,000 he had lost to the tramps and the cheats, and another FF 10,000. The casino managers expected that *le loup americain* would be eating their lunch all the long weekend to come, but when he left that morning he changed his chips at the *caisse*, and that was the last they saw of him.

Max was only warming up. At Deauville, they played tables with FF 12,000 maximums. He needed to play those to meet his goal. After a breakfast feast of langoustines, winkles, whelks, and coquilles St. Jacques at a table beside *le marché de mer*, Max slept until the shops reopened at three in the afternoon. Then he entered a men's boutique along the Rue de Quelque Chose and bought dark trousers, a black sport coat, black socks, leather shoes, a white shirt, and a Hermèsish tie. He had the shopkeeper fashion a Windsor for him. Then, placing his familiar khakis, red polo, and tennies in a bag emblazoned with the store's logo, he left them all in the store "for a few hours," and wore his new kit out the door.

He never broke the FF 500,000 dealer's bank at Casino Deauville, but he had dented it, and in honor of that, he'd was offered every legal amenity. Along with water and the simplest of meals brought tableside, he accepted a seaview-suite on the third floor of the Normandy Barrière next door. Casino staff packed up his belongings and checked him out of his Trouville room, before collecting the bag of clothes waiting for him at the boutique. They brought all of it, although there was not much, to the Normandy.

Playing two hands, chattering away as if it were the most casual and normal of behavior for him, he was, by the end, drained, depleted, exhausted, fried, baked, dry, and empty. All his mental resourcefulness was dedicated to winning. The lab, his position in the US, and Arianna, especially his squabbles with Arianna, all might have been on Mars. He played for twenty-four hours and needed sleep even more than food before he could play another hand.

He awoke in the early evening Saturday. His side ached where he'd been whacked by the girls as they'd fleeced him in Trouville. He peed a little blood. Kidney damage. Room Service delivered a selection of fish terrine, smoked salmon, offerings from the local charcuterie, baguettes, and coffee, which he did not drink. Vaguely aware he was supposed to be in Paris for a late-morning meeting on Monday, he nodded off again. On his next waking, in the middle of the night, after peeing clear, after another meal, he began feeling refreshed, even invigorated. To cross that line with Arianna, to unbind himself from her, he went looking for a girl. As he headed for the elevator, a former resident of some former Soviet republic exited a room, entered the hallway, and a deal was struck. Then he found he wasn't ready for the task. She fluffed him up and sucked him bravely, but he went noodle limp and they both gave up. *Hiring that girl was a bad idea. I'll get a boy next time.* He paid her fee of FF 1600, but because he hadn't really had her, hadn't owned her and boned her, he didn't tip her. That was a gross affront. In her mind, she hadn't been paid at all, and that's what she told her pimp.

Max played for another twelve hours on Sunday and walked out of the casino with FF 375,000 being held for him. He felt triumphant. True, he no longer had a car, but he could buy a car. He was thinking about what he would tell Arianna. What had happened to his car? Would he emphasize his humiliation, or tell her that he'd sold the car to build up his stake? And the bruises where the car door had hit him, did they even need an explanation? He'd tell her that he'd been roughed up for no reason and that would appeal to her maternal instincts. He missed *Maman*, Miriam. He missed Arianna, and he imagined the reconciliation with her, but now he was ready for that boy.

The boy appeared in the hotel elevator as if on cue. Max paid, not hinting at the pile of cash he had in his bag. After the spanking, hair pulling, and vigourous banging, Max relaxed in the glow of having flown free and away, his face buried in the hotel's plush pillow, his own juice pooled and warm beneath him, the click at the door didn't arouse his attention. Then there was the sound of several people rushing into the room and he was overwhelmed. One used another pillow to push his head into the bed. Others grabbed his arms and legs and held him spread-eagle. He couldn't even thrash, and his shouts, his screams were mostly unheard. "Now you'll feel what it's like to get fucked and not get paid," he heard the girl say. She spread him, removed a dribbling condom with her gloved hand, and shoved a greased billy club a foot deep in his ass. She gave his torso two good twhacks. A few more and she might have burst his already tenderized kidneys, but she stopped at two. Then she pounded, outright falanga'd the balls of his feet, and shoved the billy home one more time.

Her pimp said, "Turn over before we're out the door and you won't leave this hotel alive." Emptying his clothes of the few thousand francs he had in his pockets, they expressed their disgust at finding so little by spitting on him, and as quickly as they'd come in, they were gone.

They needn't have worried about Max turning over soon. The pain—a hideous flaring into his lower legs, a vicious variety of pain usually reserved for victims of secret police, drug cartels, or stateless terrorists—immobilized him. Humiliated, weeping, desperately alone, without even a thought of revenge, he lay there. After a while he was able to pull the billy from its sheath between his cheeks, being careful not to tear more flesh in the doing. Leaving shit smears on the carpet, his legs nearly buckled when he put weight on his feet, but he managed to get to the shower by skillful use of a chair as a walker. Bad as it was, the pain abated to nine on a scale of ten and continued to diminish. As it lessened, he began to feel the ache in his side. He'd see blood in his pee again later.

He woke early Monday morning and dressed in his regular kit. On his own power, hobbling but without improvised mechanical aid, he walked out of the hotel. A taxi drove him a hundred yards from the Normandy to the casino. It waited while he cashed out, and then drove him the short distance to the train station. In the two hours of travel to Gare Saint-Lazare in Paris, and for the first time in days, days that must have seemed like an eternity, he began wrapping his mind around work in advance of his meeting. He rode the Metro from the station to Place Monge, coming aboveground there, and again hiring a car to take him the final two thousand feet to the laboratories on Rue Lhomond. Having achieved their intent of leaving him with no scars, his abusers had done him a favor; he didn't have to explain away any bruises or open wounds. No one would know anything about his damaged kidneys. He'd tell everybody he'd cut his feet on beach glass and make light of what had happened.

He blamed Arianna for everything. If she hadn't nagged him about the casino, he wouldn't have been so angry with her, he would have remained faithful and wouldn't have hired the Latvian or whatever she was, she wouldn't have lied to the pimp, and Max wouldn't have been set up, beaten up, raped, and robbed. And he wanted the comfort of Arianna, too, and that's why he'd taken some moments Sunday, in the immediate aftermath of his misery, to go to the Bijouterie Nymphéa on Rue Désiré Le Hoc in Deauville, and buy her a vintage but classy little ruby on a gold band.

CHAPTER 30 A MODEST PROPOSAL

THREE DAYS after Arianna had turned up at the Laboratoire Pierre Aigrain and found Max gone, she got a call. He was home, injured but OK. He'd been in an accident, he said. He promised to clear the air and tell her everything when they next met. She flooded him with questions he wouldn't answer and with sympathy he could accept. She shouldered the full burden of responsibility for pressuring him about the casino. He accepted that, too, but didn't reciprocate. She had hoped he would. She was surprised at his callousness, but she was sincere expressing regret.

She went to his apartment for the long-awaited resolution and epoch-making make-up sex. Max was tender and sweet with Arianna, and she more so with him. She held his hand while he told her a story, a piece of fiction, in minute detail.

"First of all, everything I did, I did only for you, for us. I didn't want to depend so much on your family for getting started in the US. I thought if I played carefully, I could come back to you with FF 500,000 in my pocket, and that would be a wonderful beginning.

"Anyway, I drove to Deauville with most of what I had saved, and then I sold the car so I would have a decent stake to start with. I had FF 60,000 then.

"I was cautious in two ways, too many ways, at first. I was so worried about losing what I'd already built that I bet too little. I was winning, but only slowly. By 4 a.m. I needed sleep. I went to bed to rest up for a long stretch of serious poker. I wanted to call you, to hear your lovely voice and make up, and get your backing, but we were … you know, I just couldn't, and it was too early for you, so I didn't.

"It was after noon when I woke up. That was a great sign. I'd slept well and my head was clear. I knew it was going to be a big day for us. I could feel you reassuring me, and I wanted to please you and for you to be proud of me. I had FF 70,000 with me when I was washed and back on the floor at six. I played like a machine for ten hours. I don't know where I got the strength to keep going, but I did. There was nothing heroic about it, no giant pots, just steady playing, winning, and building. I drew a crowd. It kept changing because no one else had my stamina. I saw some of the same faces coming back to watch through the night, and then into the morning. My stacks of chips grew. After I reached FF 200,000—"

"200,000! Oh Maaxi! Really?"

"Yes, and that was just the beginning. After I reached 200,000, I had the casino put half the chips in their vault. A rack like mine would have scared away the small fry who came to play. I didn't need all that money and the temptation to overbid in front of me.

"The gods were with me. I didn't have any long losing runs and I never lost my confidence. One fish after another showed up and let me clean him out."

"What's a fish, Maaxi?"

"A chump. A loser. A *con fini*. A tourist who doesn't know how to play." He saw she was satisfied with the answer, and then continued. "So, I was emptying their pockets into mine, one after another, but I started to feel tired. I made a few mistakes, but ones only I noticed. The errors made me think I had to sleep or crank up on coffee. I left the tables and went to bed. Then I had the coffee and played some more."

"Oh, Maaxi, you were so patient. I didn't know you had so much self-control!"

"You don't know me at these tables. I'm a different person in the casinos. You wouldn't recognize me.

"The bank was holding FF 300,000 when I went back to my room. The casino upgraded me, just to keep me playing. I slept the sleep of the innocent, ordered room service, and went out to the floor again, this time for bigger stakes.

"I wanted to get out of there and back to Paris for my meeting. At first I'd planned to buy another car in Deauville and drive it home, but then because it wasn't going as fast as I'd hoped, I gave up on that decided to buy one when I got back to Paris.

"Then I started to feel like I was protected, like I couldn't make a mistake. I mean, like it wasn't possible for me to make a mistake. I made some good bluffs on some stupid Americans with too much money, and all of a sudden, I was up FF 500,000 and it wasn't even time for drinks yet."

"Oh, Maaxi. You're a genius!"

"I don't know about that. But I was done. Half a million francs was my goal. I'd met it, so it was time to quit. Without any fanfare, I just got up. No one was expecting it, but I just got up, cashed in my chips, and checked out. The casino managers encircled me, offering food, drinks, better rooms, even prostitutes."

"*Non!*"

"*Mais si!* Then I left the casino and began to rethink this idea of buying a car in Paris or Deauville. You can always find cheap cars for sale near the casino. People are desperate to raise a stake."

"Like you were?"

"I wasn't desperate." Max did not like being thought of as desperate. "I already had cash. But yes, I sold the Fiat there. So I walked around the neighborhood, looking for *À Vendre* signs stuck in the window, or for someone hawking a car right there on the street."

"Hawking, Maax?"

"Selling, that's all. I had been walking for only a few minutes and then decided it wasn't a good idea to buy a car that way, so headed back to the front of the hotel to get a taxi, when some guys, I don't even know how many, threw a cloth bag over my head, grabbed the bag with my money out of my hands and shoved me into a van or a truck, I don't know what."

"*Non!*"

"*Oui!* They held my face down on the floor so I couldn't even yell, while one of them drove just a little and then stopped again. Then they pulled me halfway out, legs first, and began beating the soles of my feet right through the shoes. I thought I was in a movie. I thought I was going to die at first, but they didn't want to beat me to death, they just wanted to torture me. I didn't know what it was about. I still don't know what it was about. And then there were some phone calls and they stopped. I couldn't understand the language they were speaking, Turkish maybe, and my ears heard only the rushing of blood in my feet. Then they pushed me out of the car and drove off. All over. *C'était fini.*"

Arianna shook as she clasped him and whimpered.

"Maybe I should have fought harder."

"I don't know, Maax. I don't know. I'm just glad you're alive and well, or sort of well." She pulled him toward her and kissed him. After a moment, he pushed her away.

"And look at this." He pulled stacks of bills that totaled FF 375,000. "I had this hidden in my jacket, so it wasn't in the bag they took. I still won!"

"Oh Maax. I'm not sure I'd call this winning."

He asked her to turn off the lights, to give his feet a little rest. Then he returned her kisses and they undressed each other.

Lying in bed she asked, "And what did you tell the police?"

"There was nothing I could tell them. I saw nothing. I didn't even bother going to them. I won and it's best forgotten."

Max hoped that the reconciliation and not-even-half-truth telling was over with that dismissal. Mlle Ampère might have been satisfied, but not Arianna. The air Max had promised to clear for her remained cloudy. She loved him more than ever, and yet he frightened her, too. "What am I going to tell my family?" she asked him. "You've lost your car, you're walking like an old man, you're involved with criminals."

"I am not *involved* with criminals!" he said. "Some criminals beat me up. There's a difference." He paused, maybe to gather his thoughts.

"Tell them I bought a new car after winning big in Normandy, and that we're getting married." He handed her the small box from Nymphéa, the jewelry store in Deauville. "They won't ask about anything else."

When she confided so many details to me later, she said, "I thought, 'Is that all there is to a proposal'?" Breathless at his audacity and the perfection of the red ruby against her pale bronze skin, and delighted that they would be getting married, Arianna was at first paralyzed. Then she grabbed him by the chest hairs, and he yelped at the tug on his tenderized torso. "What's that?" she asked.

"Nothing. Nothing," Max lied.

She wriggled herself up to him on the bed, kissing his neck and eyes and ears and lips. When she ground the newly minted Mme Ampère against him, cocking her hips forward to ease onto him, he pled exhaustion. "He'd asked me to marry him, in his own idiosyncratic way, and he was pulling back only a moment later. He'd never withdrawn in the thick of it before."

CHAPTER 31 FUCKIN' 'DONESIA

MAX FROOD and Arianna Javaheri were married in Paris in the spring. Her first preference for honeymooning, the Dalmatian Coast, was ruled out by war, her second, Iran, by the militants, and her third, the Aegean's Kyklades by Max who said he had a better idea.

"I know an isle where a mild wind blows.
Few tourists. Only the diving purist goes.
Quite over-canopied with banana trees,
Fresh coconut milk, and a few monkeys."

Max and Vera Katawijaya had exchanged only a few letters in the years since he had left Southeast Asia. She had struggled with *Catch-22* but proudly wrote to him of finishing it, asking, "What is it with 'Where are the Snowdens of yesteryear?'" Max sent her *Lady Chatterley's Lover*, and she wrote back in a letter, "Are you my game keeper?" He was not.

She knew he was in Paris, and he knew she had expanded Wet Dreams from six to sixteen bungalows—seven and seventeen if you included Bungalow Zero—but neither of them was much good at writing about their inner selves. It came therefore as a surprise to Vera that Max had settled down in marriage, a fact he disclosed to her in his fax requesting a week's accommodations at Wet Dreams on Gili Trawangan.

Before arriving on Lombok, Max and Arianna toured Bali, making up for in the exotic what she had missed in the archeologically significant in the Kyklades. She bought batik sarongs as gifts for her mothers and sisters, and old rosewood carvings for the someplace she and Max would be living in soon.

Max's description of the islands had prepared Arianna well enough, but what came as the second biggest surprise to *him* was the growth. It could no longer be said that there were beachfront bungalows anywhere on the island's east side. Every property had had its beach separated from living quarters by the bricked esplanade supporting the foot, bike, and wagon traffic that got heavier by the day. As the tourists came, so came the boat traffic carrying them and their food, fuels, fresh water, telecom equipment, t-shirts, sunglasses, medicine men, money changers, dive gear, fishing gear, furniture, flatware, glassware, paper products, lumber, concrete, and plumbing—for starters—and the locals who would deliver all the services at third world prices. And with the locals came a mosque, and amplified prayers and community announcements blasting from the minarets. Blast fishing, the use of explosives to kill schools of fish and provide meals ready-to-grill for the ravenous western guests, had already put the fish stocks in decline. So, like coals to Newcastle, fish were being imported to the islands.

The biggest surprise for Max was Vera's girls. Maxime, fivish, could have been the fruit of Max's last visit from NUS. Putu, a splendid Balinese girl, looked to be about twenty, and was not Vera's daughter, but a gofer of the first order with unrestricted access and unlimited resourcefulness. Like Maxime, she shared Vera's private quarters.

Arianna and Max dangled their feet in the pool waters from Bungalow Zero, snorkeled, swam, walked, ate, made love, and slept soundly until the roosters and the mullahs roused them. She was manicured and pedicured and ayurvedically massaged by Swedish hippies in dreadlocks. She took the local psilocybin mushrooms that had been dried until they were blue and the consistency of cardboard. She avoided the sometimes-fatal local moonshine tainted with methanol. She smoked the imported hashish. There were no police on the island, and if there were laws, they were for the proprietors and not the tourists.

Arianna asked Vera, "How did you choose such a beautiful French name for your daughter?"

Vera omitted many facts when she answered, "We Indonesians like western nicknames. Her given name is Gema, and Maxime was favored by Murray, my ex." When Arianna inquired about Murray, Vera left out the dates, steering her away from the truth, leaving Arianna to infer that he had been the father before he died.

"Tragic. I'm sorry," Arianna said, and let the subject go. In their few days together, Arianna and Vera walked the esplanade hand in hand like little girls, laughed at Max's obsessions, and cried like old friends on parting. Vera did everything she could to protect Max, and his new wife left without the slightest suspicion that Vera had preceded her.

To Max, Vera said, "We *did* make something new together. You wouldn't have wanted to know, would you?"

"No." After a long pause he said, "I should do something for her."

"She doesn't need help now. She may need it later. Promise me you'll be there then, for whatever."

"Western schools?"

"I don't know, but that's what I'm thinking."

CHAPTER 32 CAMBRIDGE

THE NEWLY wed couple arrived in Cambridge, Massachusetts on a muggy July day about six weeks before the fall semester was to make Greater Boston home to a quarter of a million students again. Max's doctoral thesis described the sequencing lab-on-a-chip, all the technological innovations that would go into it, some prototyped components, and the application of the innovations to other disciplines. The work had convinced the search committee of MIT's Department of Electrical Engineering and Computer Science that Max was ready for an academic appointment without fire-testing as a post-doctoral fellow.

His job was to complement their ongoing work in MEMS and quickly establish MIT as the leader in droplets. He'd been given a year's grace before a teaching load would cut into his time for research. The Institute had also asked him to be a charter member of the Singapore-MIT Alliance being formed at that time, expecting that as a graduate of NUS he would be an especially capable ambassador. Max had agreed, but only reluctantly. Having since learned that he had a daughter, a secret second family only a thousand miles from Singapore, he came to realize that the Alliance would give him a good excuse to see her.

Arianna would meanwhile set up a temporary home for them in MIT's married graduate student housing while she looked for more gracious accommodations and began to prep for the LSAT.

Cambridge in July was quiet compared to how it would be only two months later. The heat and humidity wore everyone down. With so few undergraduates around, every day was as sleepy as a Sunday morning. Not so for Dr. and Mrs. Frood.

They were still honeymooners. Between the obligations and anxieties of establishing themselves in this new place, they explored and sampled broadly. There were day trips to Crane's Beach in Ipswich on Boston's North Shore. There they walked, to the limits set by Max's still-recovering feet, in sand and clear cooling ocean, and on the trails, all the time yakking lovers' yak and observing birds in that natural sanctuary. They took overnights to Cape Cod and the twin islands of its underbelly. There were evenings in Lenox, listening to music under the stars. And there were lunches by the boathouse along the Charles River. It wasn't Paris, but it was romantic. As the peak of summer passed in August, there was an occasional breath of fall in the air, and fall is Cambridge's greatest season, every year a new triumph of hope over experience. That's just the slightly cynical me, Dear Reader. It's great there, really, and hope, really, hope is the best aphrodisiac, the best prophylactic, the best parent, and the best all-purpose motivator.

Arianna and Max found married student housing more satisfying than they had expected. Arianna quickly met French-speaking and Farsi-speaking couples, and pairs like hers with one immigrant spouse, and others who spoke only English or weren't married at all, but were serious thinkers or hilariously entertaining, and from them she learned what people like her needed to know: what's the best route to the consulate, and where to find real pomegranate soup, and what's it like to be married to an MIT professor. Max found something too, unexpected: relief from Arianna. Even though she was a fresh bride and at her prime, and he performed all the marital duties with pleasure, he preferred to be alone or to work most of the time, sometimes dreaming of gambling and often dreaming of men. Leaving her to the care and attention of others, he could get away.

"I missed him, and I tried to accept him—after all, I'd fallen in love with him because of his obsessions about work—but I had hoped he'd change for me, silly me. I wasn't bored or lonely," she explained.

When she first suggested that they stay in married student housing rather than look for their own apartment, or even a house that they could afford thanks to her family money, she worried that he would be his all-too-frequently-dismissive self and tell her it was a bad idea. He surprised her with, "Great idea!" but there was something about his reaction, a crack in the poker façade, a barely perceptible lack of contraction in the Oribicularis oculi, small muscles of the eyes that respond to genuine joy, that made her think he'd already decided it for them and was simply happy to have been spared the confrontation.

"Max gave no signs of being either happy or sad," Arianna explained, referring to his return to the US, the place she thought of as his home. The roots, or many of them, that he might have held on to were broken. He had only one friend from Harvard and none he ever mentioned from childhood.

In the first years, he told her that his mind's eye held only one recollection of his father. Rhetorically, Arianna asked me, "And how surprising was that, since the man died when the boy was only three?" What remained for Max was a single cloudy recurrent memory of his father running toward him. Was it in excitement? Max didn't know. "On the first few occasions when I got him to talk about it, his attention then turned inward, as if he were trying to retrieve or make sense of another image that was just one too many neural firings removed, and there the conversation faded out."

He had loved Miriam, his ultimate MILF, to the point of impregnation, and he missed her affections. He had never found, with any other woman, the same satisfaction. He had been empowered by her cries of joy—rapid and guttural, breathy cries, like a wild animal in full flight. They were the most artless, the most affecting he'd ever heard, as the scrapes of her nails were the most unaffected he'd ever felt. Returning, or trying as he had to return to his own womb, was not in the realm of the possible with anyone else. He knew what it meant when they said you can't go home again. He'd gotten closer than most men ever had.

Arianna came within a short hair of Miriam's standard. She made life exciting, discovering corners of MIT's maziness where they could have a dalliance française, and he never failed to indulge her. The greatest risk, she thought, was always that she would attract attention with her shouts and cries and screams. And her fists pounding on the walls. And her feet stomping on the ground. Even at 2:30 a.m. she had to worry that they'd be discovered—coupling and woven together near heat pipes coughing in a basement corridor—by some freshman on his or her way back to campus dorms after fun-filled hours of checking a graded calculus problem set against the teaching assistant's answers posted along the walls of those infinite corridors.

Max wanted nothing beyond that from a woman, except that she would not complicate his life. Max told someone later, and that someone later told me, "Fucking whores was like shooting fish in a barrel, unsporting. But at least they go home. At least I can pay them to go home." And of course, Arianna brought complications and responsibilities along with all her charms.

Miriam, too, had been full of complications. She would have been jealous of Arianna. But mothers know things and maybe she'd seen through his cover to his real self. She might have guessed that the pretense of marriage wouldn't last, and that no woman would ever truly win him away from her.

Max tried to forget Miriam, forget his father, forget the cheating scandal that led to his departure from Harvard, forget the traumatizing loss of Joosey to Jay, forget gambling, and forget his closeted needs, and to live as if he came from nowhere. By external appearances, he did a good job of it for a while.

Arianna missed her immense and immensely close family. She was not twice exiled, but she was twice moved far from what she knew. Some friends of her parents had children who had come to live in Boston, and some friends of her parents had moved there themselves. For the first year, she and Max had more invitations to dinners and brunches than they could accept. The great Ali Javan, Professor of Physics, inventor of the helium-neon laser, and her father's and uncle's childhood friend, opened his arms to them. There were professors of nuclear engineering, authors, political exiles, and middle managers and executives of multinational corporations. Max found something interesting in all these people, once, but not twice. He bled them for all he could learn right away and that was that. He preferred not to see them again. Where Max found some new fact, Arianna found friendships, and with these new friends she took excursions to the farmers- and outdoor markets where she preferred to shop, conversing, maybe haggling with the merchants about their cheeses and fruit. The sounds and smells reminded her of France, where she'd spent most of her life. Her memories of Tehran had faded, becoming as pale as watercolors held up against the saturated oils of the City of Lights. She hoped that law school would be a big extended family of a kind, and she promised her parents she'd join Hillel. In the meantime, she joined the Iranian Association and the French Cultural Center and wondered to herself why she had decided to study law.

CHAPTER 33 THE LAB STARTUP

A NEW YOUNG faculty member will either start from scratch or be the junior partner to someone else who is willing, for whatever reason, and there is always a reason, to give them part of their lab. Max was starting from scratch. He hadn't even looked around to see if a senior faculty member wanted him along. He simply asked for space and a startup grant to hire some associates and buy some equipment. He didn't need much; the MTL, the Microsystems Technology Lab, where he planned to build his devices was one of the best-outfitted semiconductor processing lines at any university in the world.

Max's appointment was in EECS, where they designed circuits and developed manufacturing technologies to make them, invented and analyzed systems of power generation, studied neuroscience, wrote software, wrote software to write software, and collaborated extensively within and without EECS boundaries. He thought of himself as an applied physicist and he fit right in, until he didn't.

The MTL—which was to be the foundry in which he'd forge the next generations of MEMS devices he dreamt of—had rules. The rules specified, among other things, the operating conditions of the millions of dollars worth of well-maintained, carefully controlled machines that were shared by hundreds of MIT staff and students. Contamination in a diffusion furnace, for instance, would transform the dozens of man-years worth of work cooking inside it, usually not the work of the individual responsible for the contamination, into trash. Hence, the rules, and the implications for Max he had failed to appreciate before he showed up. His inventiveness in silicon MEMS pushed the limits of those rules. A sputterer deposits micronish layers of material—silicon dioxide or niobium, for example—from a hunk of it called a target onto some other surface usually called a substrate; in Max's case, silicon or glass. After one late night when he was discovered dismantling a sputterer to replace its target with one of his own unsanctioned composition and design, he was denied further physical access to the MTL, and only retained rights to use it as a service, putting him back in a position only slightly better than the one he'd been in back in Paris.

"Fucking Idiots!" Arianna painted the scene after he returned from the committee hearing on the matter. "I can't work this way. They're gonna kill me with their fucking rules."

What Max sought was a lab of tabletop experiments, free of the rules of an entrenched power. Each experiment would be the principality of a single experimenter. Max would be king, absolute monarch in a universe containing everything needed for his NGM, the next generation in MEMS technology. "If we break stuff, we'll break stuff. We'll fix it or get new stuff, but we won't be hamstrung by a bunch of gray old bureaucrats protecting their turf," he told Arianna. He envisioned having a team, at first small, of students and post-docs and visiting faculty who would together have the set of skills needed to apply NGM to a broad range of different applications. If he himself didn't have the domain knowledge needed for his junior partners to make progress on a hard problem that he'd selected, then in his vision, when his group was big enough and had achieved critical mass, someone else would have it, and he would mentor the one in need. He wanted to get to point where his whole job would be problem selection, motivation, and getting rich starting companies.

There was a problem. The NGM technology didn't exist, and after having been booted out of MTL, his job of inventing it would be that much harder. Overcoming that little obstacle became his goal.

There were others at MIT who found the MTL a little too rigid for their taste, even if they understood why it had to be run that way. Many smaller labs had one or two pieces of the equipment that MTL was full of. Max went on a walking tour to discover them, learn what their scientists and engineers had learned, and hear what they had to say about his challenge. They turned out to be iconoclasts of a stripe he'd never seen; scientists who'd gone against the conventional wisdom and been proven right, but who had never sought to build empires. To them, the fact that he'd been tossed by MTL was a badge of honor.

He heard things from them like, "MTL is overkill. For what you're doing, their cleanliness and precision is unnecessary." And, "You need flexibility more than anything else." Also, "I know where you can get your hands on surplus gear that will do your job."

Physics Professor John G. King invited Max into his paper-filled office shortly after the MTL hearing. King's pedigree went back all the way to Jerrold Zacharias at MIT's Radiation Laboratory where radar was perfected during

World War II. King had worked closely with Zacharias on the invention of the second. That's not a typo. The modern second—9,192,631,770 oscillations of a cesium atom—is based on atomic clocks developed by Zacharias at RLE, the successor to the Rad Lab, in the early 1950s. But those were simple days. He filed his patent application after public disclosure of the invention and it was ultimately declared invalid, although the commercialization was a success. That would (almost) never happen today.

"Max explained what he was trying to do and asked for my thoughts on it," Emeritus Professor King told me when I called him in Maine nearly twenty years after the fact. "I told him to make a lot of mistakes quickly. Max sat silently, looking at me quite seriously, waiting for something more from me, maybe, trying to absorb my message, which I think he already understood. Then he thanked me for my time, winked at me as if we shared a joke on someone, got up from his chair, and left. I never saw him again."

"Sir?" I asked as we were about to hang up. "What about your experiment?"

"You mean my charge experiment?"

"Yes, that one. Why didn't you ever publish?" I was referring to what was often considered the most precise experiment ever done, a null measurement of the imbalance between the charge, q, on the electron and the proton, in which King had shown it to be indistinguishable from zero to within a few parts in 10^{23},

$$\left|1 - q_e/q_p\right| \leq 0.00000000000000000000005$$

but the work was never published and remained barely more than a legend.

"Because I didn't find anything! Believe me, everyone would have heard about it if there'd been a signal. Anyway, it's long been superseded with even better unpublished results, 10^{27}, maybe. And there's an atomic interferometry group out of Stanford—Taxovich I think—who's going to beat that, too."

"Those are incredible numbers, sir. Thank you very much," and that was the end of the call.

I did a little homework. At Stanford it's Kasevich. Taxovich is someone else.

GIFTS of used equipment that no longer had any value to the semiconductor industry were delivered to MIT's receiving docks from warehouses around New England, from Texas, and from California. In basement machine shops along corridors Arianna had first shown him, Max used lathes and mills to replace missing components, and made non-faculty friends there who would do it better for him next time around. He knew when everything ordered was supposed to arrive, and he demanded that suppliers update their estimates weekly. If a shipment date began to slip, he'd get on the phone and begin harrying whoever picked up, telling them that what he was doing was so important they would compromise national security if they didn't beat their commitments to him. He took on two graduate students, one in EECS who would help with valve design, and one from biology who would bring the sequencing expertise. Then he put them both to work setting up the lab, for which they were ill-prepared but eager to learn. Max taught them. He wanted no excuses for why they wouldn't be up and running their first experiments before the New Year.

In different departments, in seminars about his work, he'd convey a rich brew of possibilities about where this technology might be used. He enlisted collaborators across the spectrum of the Institute's science and engineering departments. There were those in EECS who were already saying, "I told you so," referring to the sputtering incident, and he irritated a wide range of others, including those who were slow and therefore jealous of his rising starrishness, and those who were rigorous and therefore offended by what they thought of as juvenile glibness, and those whose first priority was not themselves and who therefore recognized that his value to the Institute was limited because he could never lead prima donnas or the masses. But by and large he convinced his EECS selection committee that they'd chosen well.

Volume 2

Genormax

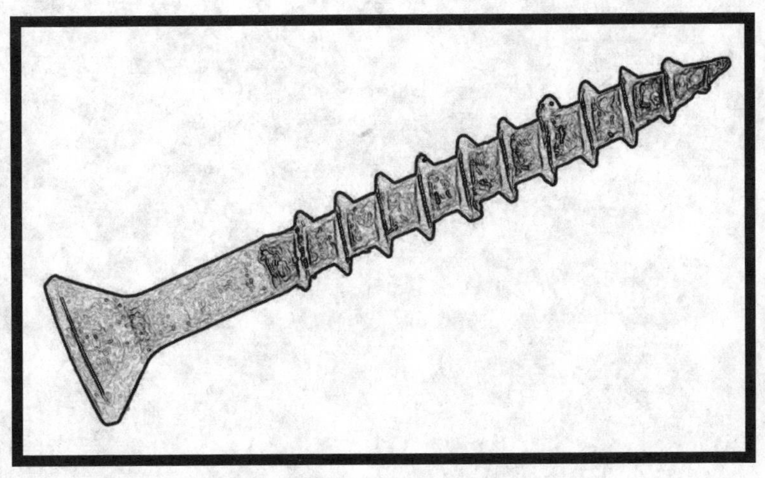

CHAPTER 34 THE COMPANY STARTUP

FROM PARIS, Uncle Arsalan wrote a letter to an Armenian friend in Cambridge, asking him to give an audience to his young "son-in-law." The friend's first name was so, well, awkward to pronounce, and his last name so long that everyone knew him only as Armen. A successful biotech entrepreneur, Armen had become an independent financier. He knew Arsalan from his own émigré days in Paris, when the two discussed oil strategy and choices in women. Armen was the opposite of glib. He looked for leadership. He often said to his young CEOs, "It's great if you can have strategy and character, but if you can only have one, let it be character."

Uncle Arsalan suggested to Max that it would be wise if he wore a suit to this meeting, but he had little hope Max would hear him.

Max walked over to Kendall Square and flipped through a printed set of PowerPoint slides he used for academic audiences. It was a hodgepodge of scientific results, assertions about the ease of achieving more, and thinly researched claims of commercial potential. Max was a terrific scientific presenter, as long as he stayed on task. He seemed to have been born with professorial authority. He was a poor business presenter, sharing with Jay Orrix the premature ejaculation of "Isn't that great?" And so he was always a beat or more out of rhythm with the audience's thoughts and emotions, and many beats ahead of their readiness to sigh or shout in ecstasy, "Yes, that's great!"

Max wasn't sure exactly what to request of Armen. He hoped Armen would tell him. Indeed, Armen did. Maybe it was the clothes, or evidence of narcissism, but Armen saw right away that Max lacked the character to be a CEO. He could also tell right away that Max was one of a kind and should be heard out.

He was aware, as Max had told him, that ideas about lab-on-a-chip, or LOC, had been around since the 1950s when the integrated circuit was invented and people saw the analogy between electron fluids and material fluids. It had been another twenty years, though, before Stephen Clark Terry made the first "instrument," a miniature gas chromatograph for air analysis. After another twenty years of mostly academic research, where were the products? Armen told me, "I wondered if Max's arrival in my office was a sign. Given the Defense Department's heavy funding of LOC in response to worries about bioterrorism, and a growing interest from the uber-rich human genome sequencers, and Max's innovations—maybe this was the moment."

"Are these your ideas or MIT's?" Armen asked Max.

"All these are mine," and then added, overly proud, "I do my best thinking in microchannels." If he was hoping for some applause from Armen, he didn't get it. Armen only looked on, his face immobile. Max continued, "The École gave us free reign over the commercial use of everything we did. And some of this I did on my own."

"In America, there's no such thing as 'on your own' when you work for MIT. It's good that your lab isn't set up yet. The Institute will own every one of your ideas from the moment you turn on the power, and maybe even before." He paused for a second, "For sure, even before. Have you met with TLO yet?"

"TLO?"

"Technology Licensing Office."

Armen paused, absorbing Max's inexperience, and thinking, "He's young. He's young." To Max, he said, "Here's what I think. These ideas are fascinating, really fascinating, but it's early. You haven't built even two copies of any of your prototypes, and it's not clear to me from your presentation whether you want to build a platform company to sell technology and general-purpose instruments, or to build a sequencing company, a vertical application of your core droplet technology. So,"

"Sequencing company," Max interjected.

"Well, that's interesting. So," he continued, "let me try to find a CEO who would take this on and sort it out with you and me. You know, it's an enormous risk for someone. He or she could waste three years easily, even five, before discovering that your ideas are flawed in some little way that no one today can see. You believe it will work, and you inspire trust, but that's not enough. Some technical problems cannot be solved before the money runs out, never mind the market. Anyway, that will be my due diligence, to find out if there is such a person. If there is, then the three of us can incorporate a new company, a NewCo, and I'll find you eighteen months of financing after you and he put together a five-year plan." Max remained motionless.

"You'll be the Chief Scientific Advisor. You'll assign all of your existing IP, all of it, to NewCo, and you'll agree to lean on TLO to license all of your MIT inventions to the company. It will take some doing to get the licenses, but with your commitment to lean on them, and with noncompete clauses in your invention assignment agreement with the company, we should be OK.

OK? You'll get 5 percent of the equity in the company."

"Max was composed, Lakshmi, but his shallow breathing told me he was tense, and maybe ready to explode," Armen told me. Then he went on.

"5 percent? That seems pretty small."

"Max, the investors will take 60 percent. The operating CEO and cofounder needs to get 10 percent and we will set aside 20 percent for the first employees." That leaves 10 percent for you and me to split as non-operating cofounders."

Max had done everything he could, for as long as he could, to avoid thinking about Jay Orrix, but once Max had become focused on sequencing instruments, he couldn't escape news of his old roommate's doings. Agigrene, Jay's first company, was discussed in the press and the subject of rumors. Max sensed that Jay owned a lot more than 5 percent of Agrigene, but he hadn't yet thought through how that had happened.

"And the CEO will get 10 percent?" Max asked, trying not to whine.

"He'll be there all day, every day. He'll build the company. Operating guys always get more. They're indispensible. Ideas are cheap, and most of them no good. The team, our team, will determine which are good and which are not. We have to be careful not to waste their time making them test too many ideas. Us, we are just accessories. Sometimes very valuable accessories." He laughed. "Sometimes nothing more than baubles. We'll have to prove our value. Are we diamonds or paste?"

"Yeah, but 5 percent? And after dilution?" Still not whining, but clearly disappointed at the way the system worked. "After dilution, what will we have?"

"For what we've put in, we'll be well rewarded if it's successful, and we'll get nothing if it's not. There's a natural order of things here, Max, a delicate balance. Investors have to see the potential for return balanced against the risk of the endeavor; otherwise they'll put their money into something else that *does* balance.

"This one is risky, whether we create a better sequencing mousetrap to compete against Applied Biosystems, or we launch a platform technology into a brave new world. Your patent applications haven't even been written. Then they must be issued and tested by the courts. We don't know how that will go.

"And the team members, they have to get paid market rates. We may be setting aside a little too much equity, but we're in boom times, and to get the best people you have to pay them. The whole pie has to add up to 100 percent, so we can only get what's left over after the market has spoken. Would you rather work here full time, as Chief Technical Officer?"

Max shook his head and said, "No, I want to give academia a shot. I just thought ..." and he didn't finish the sentence. To himself alone, he must have said, *I'm going to make some new rules for this game.* To Armen, he said, "I guess it's 5 percent."

Then Max asked, "And what about my consultant's fee?"

Armen paused. He was impressed at the Max's tenacious negotiating, but put off by the greed. "We won't have money to pay you a consulting fee until the next round of financing. We need to conserve cash wherever we can." They stared, taking the measure of each other through the windows of their souls.

It was Internet bubble time in America. Freshly minted capital was seeking new opportunities as immense profits were being taken on dotcoms. Aggressive liquidity was the term coined in those days to describe the hot money moving around, seeking yield in a world where the United States Treasury paid only 6.5 percent interest risk-free. Shortly after the New Year, Tiny Machines Inc., a Delaware corporation, was formed to introduce a new LOC platform technology, and $6 million was raised for the first round of investment, the Series A. Max had lost the battle to focus the company on building a sequencing instrument. Armen and the new CEO believed that large-scale exploration of the genome would be coming to an end before any new product from Tiny would come to market. After much bruising discussion, Max capitulated to their preferences. The new CEO was Armen's son, Papken.

CHAPTER 35 HLS

LIKE MOST first-year Harvard Law School students, Arianna didn't know more than any recent college graduate would about torts, property, contracts, criminal law, or civil procedure. In fact, she knew almost nothing. America being a foreign country to her, she was even more ignorant than most. But, she'd had life and travel experiences, and professional experience as an editor and a curator, and as a receptionist in a family friend's law office during that first year in the States and also at her father's jewelry store while still in lycée, so she knew at least a little something of the world besides classroom striving for grades. And, she was married to an income-making guy, and she had family money to fall back on. She didn't succumb to the many sources of panic that plague the first-year students at HLS.

Her marriage and her apartment at MIT put an uncomfortable distance between her and her classmates. Max didn't demand much, but she was bound to him and so formed only weak bonds to them. Two miles, the distance from MIT to the law school, seems like not a great distance to travel, but it was enough that she couldn't bring her friends home for lunch. She did all she could to mix with them, in spite of their different trajectories. She spent long hours in the library, observing who was coming and going and with whom. She put names with faces in the Harkness Commons dining hall. She formed a study group with four others from her subsection, crying with them over grades, internship rejections, and social snubs, and celebrating with them over grades, internship acceptances, and social victories. She volunteered at the *Harvard Journal of Law & Gender*, and at the Harvard Immigration and Refugee Clinic. But she did not love these pursuits.

She told me, "I felt like I was impersonating a stock character—dutiful wife, eager law student, glamorous immigrant, grieving émigré—that someone, I don't know, Max, my parents, maybe even I expected to me play. Whatever it was, I couldn't do it."

Against everyone's advice, she left Max in Cambridge and went home to Paris for the summer, living with her parents and her younger sisters, and trying to regain her sense of self. On TV, she watched with them as Tehran's students flamed up in protest, and she watched with them as the NASDAQ bubble inflated and money continued to grow on trees in America. She worked in her father's jewelry store again, for the first time in many years. She was reminded of how much she liked to talk to clients about what they bought, and how she could help them find their own preferences. She walked museums and browsed galleries. She strolled among the tourists and artists, acquiring from the latter little paintings and etchings after much discussion of their lives. She modeled for a sculptor. He later shipped her a bronze casting.

Did she miss Max? She didn't even know. She missed something. That she knew.

She returned to Cambridge with the conviction that she should mix more art into her law.

CHAPTER 36 THE SINGAPORE-MIT ALLIANCE

When Arianna flew to Paris, Max flew to Europe, too, but for the purpose of continuing on to Singapore through London. He had worked diligently as a member of the Alliance startup team, and had been able to stay in Cambridge all the while. The mission of the Alliance was one of the products of Max's effort. He knew Singapore and was not fooled by pablum from executives or bureaucrats who had never worked there. Max was instrumental in emphasizing the importance of economic development and research collaborations for Singapore on the receiving end. He was skeptical that MIT would gain anything from the program. He didn't get in the way of such discussions and planning, but he ignored them as much as he could.

On the economic development side, Max considered himself an expert, now that he had cofounded Tiny Machines, and this grand view of himself was reinforced at every turn. With the dotcom bubble still building in the western world and the Asian financial crisis leaving Singapore and its neighbors badly hit, people like Max were viewed as white knights who could turn those affected economies around. Old School faculty, that is, professors who devoted themselves to teaching and research, were almost ignored when young studs like Max showed up with their high-finance familiarity and their talk of get-rich possibilities. In Singapore, his aura was even more powerful, although some had not forgotten his intransigence vis-à-vis dress code.

John King, however, reminded him, "An expert is only someone more than fifty miles from home and carrying slides, or these days, a laptop."

"I'll keep a lid on it while I'm there," Max told Prof. King. "They've billed me as a technopreneur. I can't dissuade them of that. My slide deck shows them how I went from some ideas developed in France about genomics and miniaturization into a venture-funded startup that's going to be worth a billion dollars. Then we'll brainstorm the possibilities for startups and big companies in the new economy—not the desktop economy, but the mobile and robotics one. I don't have the answers there, but I can lead the workshop and they'll all think it's great."

"They"—scientific group leaders from NUS and the Nanyang Technological University—did. After presenting exactly what he had described to King, during which time Max was magnanimous and gracious and focused, he spent two more days having short meetings with state and university officials, company officers, faculty, and post-docs, many of whom wanted nothing more than to touch the hem of his garment. Then there was a break, and he began a workshop on research collaborations at MIT, requiring that he deliver reasonable renditions of presentations he'd collected from twenty-something MIT scientists and engineers. Those slide decks ranged over biomechanics and biomaterials, optoelectronics, reactor engineering and transport phenomena, semiconductor processes and process equipment, design for manufacturability, computational biology, DNA sequencing technologies, and of course, his own MEMS. Few people could have delivered such diverse material, and even fewer could have handled the Q&A. He received quite the standing ovation when it was over. Max kept a photograph taken at the conclusion as monument to his rehabilitation. It was of him—tattered and faded clothes, baseball hat, and all—and the blue-suited Singaporean Alliance Director, arms draped comfortably over each other's shoulders, beaming togetherness.

More one-on-ones followed for the next two days, until Vera and Maxime flew to Singapore to meet him.

READER, you might think that I'm about to tell you a tale of infidelity to Arianna, and if that's what you're hoping for, you'll be disappointed. True, Max and Vera shared a suite, but he slept on a foldout sofa bed in the living room while she and Maxime shared the king-size bed. The infidelity was a matter of disclosure.

The purpose of their trip was Maxime's introduction to the big city of Singapore. Her parents, Max and Vera, thought she should be going to boarding school by middle school if not sooner, and they wanted her to have as much off-island experience as possible before then.

The adults kept it light, spending time in butterfly forests, parks, and open areas as much as possible, except when they needed to eat, when they repaired to the dense shopping districts where the world's best street food was for sale. Maxime had been to Mataram on Lombok and to Denpasar in Bali, so she knew a little something of the sights and sounds, but she had never stayed in a hotel as nice as Max's Mandarin Oriental. "I could get used to this," she told them.

Maxime called Max "Max," and was told that he was "Momma's old friend." It would be many years before she connected the dots that made her skin color the biologic average of Vera's browned pumpkin and his pale pink.

She appeared destined to become a great Eurasian beauty.

The three of them returned to the Gilis together, cutting out the ferry, and instead flying from Denpasar to Mataram. Still, it was a very long trip.

Again, the growth shocked him. The coral that had once shone like blue lights in the water had been bleached to white, the result of a large-scale coral die-off that had its origins who knew where. Ocean acidification, El Niño, global warming, blast fishing, cyanide fishing, overfishing, boat traffic, human traffic, pollution; you name it, there was someone who would say with certainty that *it* was to blame.

The first SCUBA instructors had set up shop. The first Italian restaurant. The first western-style hotel. The esplanade was no longer just a joke of an idea. Where it wasn't bricked-over, there was a worn path on dirt or sand. New dirt paths penetrated the island. There were hundreds of tourist guests every night, and hundreds of year-round local residents, even some year-round western residents. A trash problem had surfaced.

Vera had opened a locavorian fish restaurant where her chefs grilled, curried with pineapple, broiled, pan fried, deep fried in coconut oil, decorated with chutneys, or served raw the freshest offerings she could find. When the fishermen could not supply her, her girl Putu would hunt the big pelagic fish herself, and had never yet failed to bring home a trophy to provide Maxime's—that was the name of the restaurant—with a delicacy unavailable elsewhere. She had assembled a collection of thin wetsuits and sophisticated spearguns—long, heavy guns for deep water—which she offered to share with Max whenever he was ready. He donned the wetsuit, but couldn't dive to those depths, so the gun sat on the shelf and he dropped down, maybe to twenty feet, to watch her tough elegance from above.

After five days, Max shoved off for Bangsal, Mataram, Denpasar, Singapore, London, and finally for Boston. Max and Maxime had had some time to hang together, swimming, skipping rocks, and telling stories. When they walked together, and she found a shell, or a crab, or spotted a bird, he asked her to make up a story about it. With a light touch, he introduced her to natural history. Vera and Max had talked about a new hotel they would launch together. Vera had Max's assurance that he would pay for Maxime's private school, somewhere. Late at night, after Maxime was asleep, he had heard Vera and Putu and their ecstasies together.

THE Alliance wanted more of Max than he could or wanted to give, but he made the long journey annually, and on each trip he arranged a rendezvous with Vera and Maxime, either there in Singapore, or over the causeway into Rhizobia, or in Bali, or on their paradisiacal turf, Gili Trawangan.

CHAPTER 37 NATURAL BORN LEADERS

MY FATHER told me that there are three kinds of soldiers. "The first kind does everything he's ordered to do. Him you should put in the infantry. The second kind is the natural born leader. Make him your general. The third kind thinks he's a natural born leader. Him you should shoot." Max thought he was a natural born leader.

CHAPTER 38 GOING PUBLIC

AGRIGENE WENT public just before Tiny Machines raised their first financing and issued their first shares; Series A shares they were called. It was that kind of time. All you needed was a fantasy. Max badmouthed Jay to Armen, saying that Jay was a shameless self-promoter and hadn't accomplished anything. "All he's done is take other people's technology and wrap it up for sale. There's nothing new there!"

Agrigene's line was that the genome of everyday crops contained secrets of pest resistance, carbon fixation rate, taste, or pharmaceutical value, and that this moment in history, the final years of the millennium, was the modern-day gold rush. Once the genes were discovered, patented, and owned, it would be over, and those who held the secrets would be as rich as Rockefeller. Scarcity increased the investors' anxiety and made them impulsive, that is, imprudent.

Jay Orrix was one of the early believers in this optimistic view—in particular the part about how FOMO, fear of missing out, would make buyers impulsive. His PhD thesis—finished only six years after he left high school—on mapping complex plant genomes was completed in the lab of Harvard biologists who had helped build moby from the ground up. The thesis was the foundation for a cover article in *Nature*. The Haldane Medical Research Institute tempted him with a ten-year Principal Investigator grant, offering him the kind of freedom only afforded to Nobel laureates, IBM Fellows, or other distinguished scientists who'd made it big in industry. And what was that kind of freedom? Three things, all of them autonomy: think what you choose, operate as you choose, spend as you choose.

The John Burdon Sanderson Haldane Medical Research Institute, or HMRI colloquially, was famous, or infamous, for the restrictions it placed on its Principal Investigators vis-à-vis their consulting and commercializing activities. Jack Haldane was a mid-twentieth-century English biochemist and geneticist strongly partial to Karl Marx. His inherited wealth became the cornerstone of the most richly endowed private research institute in the UK. Global in its reach and British in its administration, the institute founded in his name demanded that its investigators focus on research and not on its commercial exploitation. In addition to political leanings favoring the common good over individual riches, the institute's policies were born of the observation that many a fine scientist had become only a mediocre businessman, with dire or tragic consequences for the productivity of the former. Also, they believed, or recognized, or both, that the conflict of interest battle that inevitably arises when a research scientist is directing his or her research with the commercial implications in mind is usually won by the commercial side—again, with consequences for research quality and productivity. Principals were asked to make a bargain: give up prospect of riches in exchange for a protected, ivory-tower research experience with unparalleled job security. Some PIs had tried to have it both ways, retaining all the privileges and exploiting the commercial potential to the max. They had learned to navigate the gray areas of HMRI's policies or to secretly evade them. HMRI rewrote its policies to eliminate more and more gray area. Navigators had to make up their minds. Evaders were fired when they were found out.

Jay took the position for just long enough that it burnished his résumé, and then he resigned rather publicly to found Agrigene. Almost no one ever walked away from an HMRI grant. Doing so brought much attention to his venture.

He incorporated the company in Delaware, the company-friendly state, designed a logo, and sketched a business plan. That cost pocket change. He seeded it with some of his inheritance, and then asked his family and Vladik—who had cash to put to work while getting paid like an executive and living as his boss Ulya Khoslovsky's boy toy—for more. All told, he found a few million dollars. Hiring a few of his college and grad school friends, he outfitted a lab in the least expensive space he could find near Kendall Square, hired some technicians and an office manager, printed business cards for everyone, hung a large neon sign on the outside of the building, gave away white, button-down, oxford cloth shirts embroidered with the company logo on the pocket, became the darling of a sage biotech investor and the mentee of his favorite CEOs, and negotiated some multi-million-dollar research contracts with Fortune 500 companies.

Could Agrigene accomplish what it set out to do for these companies? Who knew? But since no one else was promising to deliver these secrets of the genome, and the risk of missing out on them was so huge, and the amounts were, as one pharma CEO said, "less than the cost of cutting the grass in front of corporate headquarters," who could say no? Scarcity and narrative enabled Agrigene's growth.

Jay was able to do all this while giving away very little of the company's equity. His family didn't negotiate tough terms. Vladik didn't negotiate at all. The research contracts paid for themselves with enough to spare so that Agrigene could fund some of its own R&D, pulling itself up by its own bootstraps.

Jay was a natural born leader, in a goofy kind of way. He wanted smart and talented people around him, but he didn't need many other natural leaders on his staff. Company direction was something he synthesized from the distillates of meetings with advisors, conversations over lunch, and everything he read. It's often the case that a startup team will have—to use an expression full of double meanings, inconsistencies, and racial biases—too many chiefs and too few Indians. Jay seemed to know, instinctively, that he didn't need many or any other chiefs, every one of whom who would demand a lot of stock. Indians would get paltry handouts and be happy about it.

A year after he had incorporated, he owned 70 percent of a company that was taking in $5 million a year in research contracts and burning all of it. To fuel growth he'd have to spend more on the company's internal research, its IR&D, yet he couldn't expand fast enough. Offering his research partners an opportunity to buy a share of the company when they renewed their existing contracts, he raised $10 million in exchange for a quarter of the company. With the additional cash he hired forty more people and started several new IR&D programs, attracting bigger research contracts, government grants, and offers to buy more equity. By the end of the third year, even though he had not a single product in field-testing anywhere, nor a concrete lead on a product like that, Agrigene went public, raising $40 million. That left Jay owning 32 percent of a publicly traded company worth $140 million, a company gearing up to lose $10 million per year and hoping against hope for a scientific breakthrough.

Any hopes Tiny Machines might have had for going public three years after *its* founding were dashed by the bursting of that Ponzi-less Ponzi scheme called the Internet bubble. By that time, a dream alone was no longer good enough.

CHAPTER 39 CHIEF SCIENTIFIC ADVISOR

A VENTURE-FUNDED STARTUP like Tiny would typically have a scientific cofounder in an operating position, and that person would carry the title of CEO or CTO. The Chief Technology Officer would drive the technical progress of the company—which was where nearly all its gold would be spent—as well as provide other members of the staff with engineering and scientific input on strategy, milestone setting, partnerships, funding, grant getting, financial planning, regulatory matters, and anything else anyone else—from Chairman of the Board to Chief Bottle Washer—felt required his or her wisdom. Without a CTO, or someone performing those functions but without that title, Tinyesque companies would be as adrift as the ancient mariner in the doldrums, unpowered and undirected.

Max did not hold the title and did not perform the functions. He was the Chief Scientific Advisor. When doing the research for this book, I asked Armen what he had intended for Max in the role of CSA. He began with a wink, as if to let me know that he knew that I knew, or suspected, that CSA was as meaningless as Genomics Evangelist, or some other made-up title. "First of all, Lakshmi, I wasn't sure that Max knew the meaning of POR." Then he stopped and said nothing, filling the room with silence for so long that I realized he was waiting me for finish his own explication.

I began. "You mean he didn't understand that the acronym means plan-of-record, or he didn't understand that POR informs everything, from what you're going to do today to what you're doing to over the next three years, if you can look out that far."

"I wasn't sure about the former and I was certain about the latter," Armen said, "The role I constructed for Max was to help the company, principally through Papken the CEO, to execute its POR by getting us out of tough binds, and to give us his perspective—and the guy is a genius, seriously—on what was developing outside the company. When operating staff, who were there all day every day, were stuck or needed vision beyond their means, that's when I wanted Max to turn on his headlights. If he had to call in other experts, then that was fine, so long as he got us good solutions."

Armen stopped again. I didn't know where he wanted me to go, and I waited, but again, he outlasted me, and I forced myself to come up with something, in the form of a question. "Sometimes being stuck, as you say, was an urgent thing, sometimes a long-term strategic problem?"

"Right. And to do the job well, Max had to know the details of the strategy and the operations of the company so that his advice was well targeted. In general, an advisor must be a very good listener and yet know the right moment to offer an opinion. When asking a question, I expected him to be educating my team, not merely collecting information for his personal interest. These guys," and here Armen waved his hands as if to encompass the set of all possible advisors. And he caught my eye before continuing, "and gals are, with rare exceptions, people who've become conditioned to believe they are *very* important. Max was not rare in that sense. And that made one final aspect of his responsibility very difficult for him to learn. Papken and I, we the company, expected to be very respectful of the team's time. Tiny was not a casual endeavor for team members; it was their life and livelihood."

When Armen stopped this time, I didn't hesitate. "And Max wasn't too good in meetings."

"All of our work was conducted in meetings!" Armen's voice rose, in agitation, as if I had hit him in a tender spot. In an apparent effort to calm himself, he began to recite what sounded like the intro to some course on meeting culture that he'd taught to teams in his many companies. "But what is a meeting? It is a planned gathering of two or more people that has a stated purpose and a schedule, spelled out in an agenda. The purpose might be simply to renew an acquaintance over cake and tea. More often, it is to reinforce the values of the group or to solve a particular problem. Whether you are getting together with friends for a party, conferring with coworkers at the lab, or reviewing progress with investors, you want to have that agenda nailed down in advance so you know how to prepare, and so you know that everyone else is equally prepared to be prepared. Whether or not you think I've overstated it about the party, you get the idea. If we don't stick to the agenda, we won't accomplish whatever we're trying to accomplish. There's a reason why that matters. We are trying, collectively, to do something, to meet an objective, maybe an objective spelled out in the POR. If we didn't care about getting it done, then we should have done something better with our time. But we do care. However compulsive this may sound, its really just about self- and mutual respect."

Well warmed up, Armen did not pause long this time. "In the second year of operations at Tiny Machines, we set aside the first Thursday afternoon of every month for a comprehensive program review that included Max. For two hours he listened to the presentations. Then Papken arranged for him to attend problem-solving meetings with some senior staff, and he finished the afternoon in a thirty-minute meeting with the two of us. In that last session, we expected him to give us his appraisal of the overall scientific progress and make recommendations for what to do next.

"A program review with him in the room was shambolic, if there is such a word. He was disruptive and capricious. He drove the meeting off the agenda, wherever the hell he wanted it. The staff got impatient, and then resentful. He behaved as if the only purpose of the meeting was his entertainment, or to be more charitable, his education. If he wanted to learn something, he'd grill everyone there. If he wanted to talk about something, he'd just start talking. Ideas about applications or new technical approaches sprang from his head like sparks from a Roman candle. He'd derail someone's presentations by suggesting alternative approaches, some of them impractical, most of them headed off away from the project itself, some of them transparent attempts to further his goals and not the company's. He would suggest new initiatives, oblivious to the fact that the POR had to be respected. It can change, but only in a controlled process, lest the company veer off course. Am I making this clear enough?"

Armen's tone as avuncular, and I was grateful that he was carefully going over old ground instead of saying to me, "Well, what can I tell you that you don't already know?" I needed to hear someone else's firsthand experience, so I nodded, trying not to interrupt his flow.

"You're probably thinking, 'Gosh Armen, why didn't Papken just tell him to table it and stick to the agenda?' Well, we did manage him, eventually. In the meantime, Max's stature, as cofounder, as Assistant Professor at MIT, and as inventor of the company's core technology, made it difficult enough for the others to stand up to him. Compounding it, he had heard that he was brilliant too many times, and while it was true, he probably overweighted its significance.

"If he hadn't thought of an idea himself, how could it be a good idea?" Armen asked rhetorically. "He had a pathological case of not-invented-here syndrome. He crushed the open debate so essential for us to move forward. Think about how that plays out. One of my engineers has an idea about a particular technical problem, but she knows that Max will piss on it, excuse me Lakshmi, because she's seen his NIH at work, so she says nothing, and an opportunity to make progress is lost. The staff began to have their own shadow meetings to get things done, and the official one became a masquerade, all phoniness."

Between the half-day he spent at the company on those Thursday afternoons and the hours he spent thinking about its problems, Max's time commitment to Tiny Machines was about one day a month. Nevertheless, he thought of it as his company, and he projected that sense of ownership to everyone all the time, implicitly diminishing their contributions. The projected ownership made him even more difficult to challenge.

Armen and Papken tried to coach him, but Max was uncoachable. After three months, they abandoned the program reviews with Max. Instead, Papken gave him a short version of the managers' presentations while Armen observed and occasionally interjected. Max spent more time in the problem-solving sessions with staff. Engineers and scientists were instructed to speak freely, to learn what they could, but to avoid taking direction from him. The POR would be sacrosanct, until it was changed by Papken in a transparent, open manner. The revised agenda for Max's visits was time-consuming for Papken and Armen, but it worked. Max's talents were harnessed and his destructive tendencies neutered.

"Chief Scientific Advisor was a bullshit title, excuse me again, Lakshmi. It meant whatever Papken and I wanted it to mean. We could have called him Special Advisor to the CEO for all that it mattered. The new arrangement was a demotion for Max as far as we were concerned, but to our *enfant terrible* it was a promotion. He was happy to be spending more time in closed-door discussions with us. You could see on his face that he believed the private office was where the real decisions were made, where the chess pieces of strategy were moved. But he was wrong. It all happened out on the floor, in real-time, and we adjusted the strategy accordingly. Look no further than that shadow program review. Our managers found the meeting Papken and I held ineffective, so they held their own until we were smart enough to codify it and make it the official review. You can run a small company with decisions made in the executive's office, or you can run it so that decisions are made in broad sunlight. Companies with transparent processes have better growth prospects."

CHAPTER 40 TLA

THE only thing to fear is the agency so secret it has no TLA.

- General ████████, Unacknowledged Security Agency

NATION, YOU will have noticed that this history uses three-letter acronyms, or TLAS, with abandon. Have a peek in the tent. They're the lingua franca, the insider's jargon. We, my colleagues and I, my fellow citizens and I, use them to simplify, not to obfuscate: USA, JFK, NFL, and NSFW—ok, that's four, but you get the idea. Robert Norton Noyce, in one of those lunchtime conversations, told the teenage Vladik to avoid jargon with the uninitiated, yet TLAS were everywhere in Noyce's company. The Programmable Logic Operation became the PLO and the Onboard Microprocessor Group became OMG. After Noyce's death in 1990, his company named its newest building RNB in his honor.

CHAPTER 41 THE TLO AND BAYH-DOLE

MAX'S EMPLOYMENT contract with MIT included an assignment agreement stipulating that all his (new) inventions, patented or otherwise, were Institute property. Agreements like that are standard practice across the US, in the profit and not-for-profit world alike. If you take a salary, or some other compensation, you hand over the inventions. That's the bargain.

What varied from institution to institution was how the assignee, let's say MIT or IBM, would reward the inventor if the assignee made money from the innovation. Some companies paid researchers a fixed fee, maybe $1000, for every filed patent. They based this practice on the belief that you could never know in advance which patents were worth more than others. These companies bought, sold, or licensed patents by the piece or by the pound, although the unit price would vary based on the perceived quality of the inventor. Another school of thought said that inventors should be paid a royalty, a portion of the revenue earned by the practice of their brainchild. Since the invention was never the entire product, it was exceedingly difficult, some would say impossible, to determine how much of product revenue was the result of the patented contribution. Still, some companies made the effort to estimate that contribution, and then to pay a fraction of it as a royalty to the inventor. For universities the choice was simpler. The universities—not themselves in the business of making products or services—licensed assigned intellectual property to companies and received fees—often but not always royalties—in exchange. The university then shared the fees with the inventors.

MIT's Technology Licensing Office is in charge of this "business." It oversees filing of patents and their prosecution—prosecution being a fancy name for haggling with the USPTO—the United States Patent and Trademark Office, over patentability. The TLO also markets the inventions to companies large and small, negotiates contracts, recovers fees, distributes payments to inventors, and fulfills part of MIT's mission for technology transfer. In round numbers, a staff of forty oversaw three hundred patent filings in a recent year, the product of several years' effort. In each of those years, approximately $700 million was spent on research and $16 million on legal fees. That same year, the Institute, as it is sometimes known, received about $150 million in licensing revenue.

MIT's nonprofit status under section 501(c)(3) of the IRS tax code confers special "public service" responsibilities on it. The Institute takes in money from grants, tuition, licensing fees and investments, but it pays no taxes. As one MIT grad I know says, "Niish!" True, the Institute is expensive to operate and it graduates thousands while advancing research and development in many fields. It has need-blind admissions and enrollment, a public museum, dozens of education programs for kids of all ages, and has been a pioneer in putting course material online for all to see and use. And there are flaws, but it is as fine a meritocracy as we have in this country. Data rules MIT, and MIT sets an example of how "it" should be done. But as a nonprofit, it has an implicit social contract with the rest of us, and the obligations or boundaries of that contract are continually being explored.

During World War II, Vannevar Bush—who at various times in his career had been: an MIT student, master's thesis advisor of Claude Shannon, the father of information theory, Dean of MIT's School of Engineering, and Vice President of the MIT Corporation—was chairman of the National Defense Resources Committee, a Federal agency he proposed and which FDR approved in a fifteen-minute meeting in 1940. In 1945, Bush wrote a report entitled *Science: The Endless Frontier*, in which he encouraged increased government support for research and the creation of the NSF, the National Science Foundation. This was the beginning of the idea of technology transfer.

The country's need for science had outstripped the federal government's ability to conduct the research, so the report recommended that the government should pay for research to be done at universities and elsewhere. Commercializing the research results turned out to be difficult because the government, having paid for the research, owned it, yet there was no federal infrastructure for getting it out to society as a whole, short of just giving it away, which everyone thought was a wasted opportunity. Why would giving it away be a wasted opportunity? It's counterintuitive, but companies are loath to invest in something if everyone else can do it, too. As Yogi Berra said about some popular restaurant, "Nobody goes there anymore. It's too crowded." Muse, Gentle Reader, on that scarcity Jay played so well.

Jerry Weisner, who would become President of MIT in the 1970s, was Science Advisor to JFK in 1963 when he advocated finding better ways to license the federally funded results back to the universities where the research originated. In 1980, Congress passed the Bayh-Dole Act, giving universities ownership of federally funded research conducted under their auspices. Bayh-Dole made possible the technology transfer that Vannevar Bush envisioned. It was the means by which Max's research results, paid for with NSF grants, ended up being MIT property and then licensed by TLO to Tiny Machines.

MIT, the owner of research results paid for with federal money, and the beneficiary of many other tax breaks granted on the basis of its social contract, charged TLO with returning the inventions to the public. At least three constituencies had to be considered and balanced. First, there were the licensees—corporations—who would demand exclusive licenses that would enable an effective monopoly and the greatest profitability. They would assert that only with exclusivity could they recover the costs of commercialization. The second constituency was the private individual—the citizen—who would prefer lower prices and broader availability, both consistent with non-exclusive licensing policies. The third constituency was the MIT Corporation, which sought the greatest possible revenue from the licenses in order to offset the annual burden on its endowment.

And what did Max Frood have to say of TLO? "Fucking Idiots!" As in most tense relationships, the feelings were mutual.

CHAPTER 42 INTELLECTUAL PROPERTY

IP IS a term encompassing ideas, methods, data, and other intangibles. For some types, let's say patents, trademarks, and copyrights, the owner of said IP discloses the property to the public in exchange for certain privileges codified in and enforceable under the prevailing governing law. For other types, let's say trade secrets, the owner does everything within her, his, or its means to keep the IP from leaking out into public view. Once public, the trade secret owner has no protection other than contractual rights it might or might not have established with the leaker.

In biotech, life sciences, pharma, or healthcare, whatever you want to call it, IP is among the most important assets a company has. A patent is a right to exclude others, for a period of years, from using a disclosed invention that passes certain tests of novelty or newness, usefulness, and non-obviousness. A granted United States patent on the composition of a molecule that is an effective Rx, a prescription drug, might give the owner ten or more years of monopoly pricing power worth billions of dollars, and therefore justify hundreds of millions of dollars of research, marketing, and legal investment to harvest it. But if that molecular composition is known and in the public domain, then a company manufacturing and marketing it successfully will soon find competitors doing the same, killing pricing power and driving profits to the bone. In biotech, one reason the legal protections of IP are considered so important is that the costs of discovering an interesting molecule and validating its efficacy through long human trials are very, very high, but the costs of copying the molecule once it's been proven effective are very low. Biotech entrepreneurs seeking capital are turned away at the door if they can't show the IP, or the route to the IP that will protect the investor.

Other fields are different. Consider a social-networking company, like, let's say, Silicon Valley darling LinkedIn. When it launched in 2003 there was approximately nothing that distinguished it from several other companies focused on business relationships. One of those competitors, Plaxo, had been cofounded a year earlier by Napster cofounder Sean Parker, and therefore had at least as much startup jam as Reid Hoffman's LinkedIn, Mr. Hoffman having been COO and then EVP at PayPal in its early days. Over time, the set of features and the user experience LinkedIn offered became more attractive than Plaxo's, driving faster growth. The growth made it more likely you'd find your colleagues on LinkedIn, further increasing its relative merit.

And thus spun up a virtuous cyclone of utility that attracted users, and more users created greater utility, and so on and so on. This is a winner-takes-all world, with all the unintended consequences, conflicts of interest, denials, fraud, and skullduggery worthy of the prize.

LinkedIn has patents, but its most valuable IP is not in that realm, but in trade secrets, closely guarded proprietary information, the database of customer information, and the self-proclaimed or algorithmically intuited bonds between individuals. Imagine that a competitor cloned the site and its features, launching ClonedIn without any users. It would be worth nothing and no one would go there because the value of the site lies in the database users, the customers—the actual network of real people connecting, messaging, and discovering each other. It does not lie in ClonedIn's potential to have such a network. You, the user, become part of someone else's experience of the product, like it or not, and hence the meme, *If you're not paying for it, you are the product.*

As Max had explained to Arianna about Ampère, to have an equation or an idea named after you is a special tribute. Bob Noyce is almost forgotten among people younger than me, but Gordon Moore, the other Intel cofounder, lives forever because of his law describing the exponential rate of decline of the cost per function of semiconductors. Andy Grove—Intel's most important non-founder—said of Moore's Law, "I wish I'd said that."

Bob Metcalfe, co-inventor of Ethernet and founder of 3Com, wrote in 1980 that the value of a network is proportional to the square of the number of users. He was trying to make quantitative and predictive the network effect, the observed fact that bigger networks are disproportionately better than smaller ones. His message came to be known as Metcalfe's Law in 1993. With an equation named after him, he became immortal, and he probably should be, but not for that. The law is wrong, or so explains mathematician Andrew Odlyzko in *Metcalfe's Law is Wrong*. Andrew hired Vladik's mother at Bell Labs.

Patent-reliant biotech becomes more like database-reliant social networking when the data tape called DNA is involved. A patient's sequences are easily determined with a test that gets cheaper by the day, but the interpretation of test results depends on having—as a basis for comparison—similar data from thousands or millions of other people, so it's the database that's valuable. Winner-take-all economics will rule.

The race to get patentable IP in biotech, as in software and other fields, has overwhelmed the patent office and led to issued patents that are obvious and not novel, and therefore should never have been granted. Gene patents, patents on naturally occurring gene sequences, fall into that category. Unmodified but isolated genomic DNA is not an invention, and no patent protection should be granted to claimants who say otherwise. SCOTUS, the Supreme Court of the United States, seems to agree. Fortunately for Jay and Agrigene, the IPO came fifteen years before SCOTUS ruled that the genes Agrigene set off to discover were not patentable inventions. Had the ruling come first, there would have been no scarcity, no FOMO, and no gold rush for the fortunate.

Separately, there are inventors seeking the inventon [sic], the atom of patentability, the smallest invention that will pass USPTO scrutiny. That's incrementalization, not invention, and not non-obvious. At the other extreme is the attempt to get patents for broad or general ideas, often not original and not so well formed in the mind of the inventor as to constitute—as required by law—a definite and permanent idea of the complete and operative invention. Those are the prophetic or land-grab patents, and many have slipped through. They're all getting their comeuppance.

Another IP battlefield in biotech is in Dx, diagnostics. Simply stated, a Dx is an observed correlation between something and patient health. As a concrete example, let's say that something is hematocrit, the percentage of blood volume made up of red blood cells, in which case low hematocrit correlates with anemia. There are many causes of anemia, but that's for another book. Is measuring hematocrit an original idea? It was in 1927 when Maxwell Wintrobe, née Weintraub—then a twenty-six-year-old Assistant Professor of Medicine at Tulane, later founding Chairman of Medicine at the University of Utah in 1943, and recipient of the first-ever extramural research grant by the NIH—dreamt up a new and easy way to measure it, and then went on to establish correlations between observations and medical conditions. Today, an application claiming hematocrit as an invention shouldn't pass USPTO scrutiny. A new means of counting the red blood cells and assessing their volume, or an original or novel interpretation of the measurement might satisfy USPTO examiners.

Applications wouldn't, or shouldn't get through if the purported invention is merely the observation of a law of nature. That's why diagnostics company executives, lawyers, investors, healthcare administrators, doctors, insurers, and regulators are up in arms about the recent case of Supreme Court case, *Mayo Collaborative Services v. Prometheus Laboratories Inc.*

Prometheus's patent claimed "observed correlations between blood test results and patient health." After many millions were spent, SCOTUS denied Prometheus, asserting that laws of nature belong to the world. The company, SCOTUS ruled, could not lay claim to underlying laws of nature and rent-seek the rest of us. To do so would be tantamount to patenting the practice of medicine. The patent had been granted by USPTO, and SCOTUS struck it down. For some, meaning Prometheus and other Dx companies that had built businesses assuming patent protections would remain in place, it meant the sky was falling. For others, meaning doctors who wanted to practice good medicine with as little interference as possible, it meant the sky was clearing. Why had the patent ever been granted? Again, another book, but the reasons can probably be reduced to nothing more than fear, uncertainty, and doubt, aka FUD. The jargon of biotech had overwhelmed the patent examiners. At the same time, officials of USPTO were under pressure from powerful small-government interests, and the examiners were under pressure from the officials to grant patents.

Can you see where this is going? The structure of a naturally occurring molecule, for instance the base sequence of a gene, is a law of nature. Therefore, patent claims on that structure will ultimately be denied.

CHAPTER 43
COHEN-BOYER, AKA THE PATENT

I AM TOO young to remember when there was no commerce on the Internet. There was no commerce because there was no commerce. The Internet was, supposedly, too free and beautiful to be ruined by commerce. Then one day there was Amazon, and well, who wants an Internet without Amazon?

You may be too young to remember the time before biologists thought about starting companies, or working for companies. OK, maybe there were a few of them, but so few that they formed a set of measure zero. Until Cohen-Boyer, if you were a graduate student in the biological sciences, your plan was to get an academic appointment or work for the NIH. The biologist's world didn't flip as fast as the Internet user's world flipped after Amazon, but it did flip. Along with the flip came a loss of innocence, kind of like free agency in major league baseball.

In 1956 Arthur "I never met a dull enzyme" Kornberg, having been catalytic in building a great biochemistry department at Washington University in St. Louis, discovered the polymerase that assembles DNA's double helix from its constituent building blocks, the nucleotides. In 1959, just before the announcement that he had won the Nobel Prize, he and many of his Wash U colleagues moved to found a new department of biochemistry at Stanford.

In 1971 Paul Berg, whom Kornberg had recruited eighteen years earlier, and who had made the move to Stanford with him, spliced some bacterial virus and *E. coli* bacterial genes into a monkey virus. The product was called rDNA, recombinant DNA. In 1974, Herb Boyer and Stanley Cohen, from UCSF and Stanford, respectively, filed a patent describing their own methods for making and using rDNA, methods that harness the molecular machinery of microorganisms to make products like human growth hormone, products that had been very difficult to obtain otherwise. HGH, for instance, had been available only from cadavers until Boyer's company began making it.

Those were carefree days, the 1970s, or so the graybeards might tell you over beer or lunch or both. They'll begin talking about an enchanted place called Asilomar and then mumble to each other about Dionysus, the Beast, human sacrifice, and twelve-step programs. Fearing then they've already said too much, or just had too much to drink, they'll shut themselves off to anyone who wasn't there. Something must have happened; something dark, something worthy of a Pynchon novel, but no one is talking. Remember, those were the years when Roman Polanski could have sex with a drugged 13-year-old (girl) at Jack Nicolson's home, and be remembered instead for *Chinatown*. It was a more forgiving world.

Six years after filing, and four years after Boyer had cofounded Genentech to commercialize the fruits of the filing, the application had worked its way through the patent system. It finally issued two weeks before the passage of Bayh-Dole and a few days before the King of Sweden draped the medal for the Nobel Prize in Chemistry over Paul Berg's neck. The Patent, and yes, it deserves capitalization because it's monumental, earned the parent institutions $255 million over its lifetime. *That's* IP! Neither Cohen nor Boyer received a share of the fees, but Boyer did appear on the cover of the March 9, 1981, edition of *Time*.

CHAPTER 44 THE BIOTECH EXPLOSION

FOR BIOLOGISTS, there followed a palpable change in attitudes about the meaning of life and life's pursuits. Once a home for ivory-tower-loving academics, biology became, in words Hunter S. Thompson used to describe the TV industry, "a long plastic hallway where thieves and pimps run free and good men die like dogs, for no good reason." I exaggerate, of course.

The Patent drove the flip, but there were many factors energizing the explosion of biotechnology innovation and commercialization of that period. Bayh-Dole, which connected the inventor and the licensing agent, was a big part of it. So was the controversial nonexclusive licensing strategy for The Patent that emerged from Stanford's incarnation of MIT's TLO, that is, OTL, the Office of Technology Licensing. That brainchild-of-many ensured that many companies—some of them large and established, some of them small and just taking off—could use recombinant DNA.

There were companies connected to the same family tree that birthed Cohen-Boyer. There was Genentech, of course, Boyer's company, emphasizing not only genetics but engineering and technology in the name itself, implying the scaling up of laboratory processes, making them routine, and using them to produce products. Then there was DNAX, founded in 1980 by Arthur Kornberg, Paul Berg, Charles Yanofsky, and Alex Zaffaroni. Zaffaroni, already president of Syntex Pharmaceuticals and founder of Alza, went on to fund or cofound a diverse family of other companies including Affymax, Affymetrix, Symmyx, SurroMed, Alexza, Perlegen, and Maxygen.

Cetus wasn't obviously of the same lineage. Cofounded in 1971 by Nobel Prize-winning Berkeley physicist Don Glaser, Cetus was an emerging biotech company when it saw how the Cohen-Boyer methods, and others, were going to be transformational. Its pivot, where pivot is a trendy word meant to suggest that your management team is agile and flexible—even if it had been working on the wrong thing as recently as the day before—led Cetus to many things, including the largest IPO to date in 1981, and polymerase chain reaction, or PCR.

PCR, the 1983 invention of Nobelist Kary Mullis, is a procedure for making many identical copies of a strand of DNA. It depends entirely on DNA polymerases like the one Kornberg discovered. It has been ubiquitous and inescapable in the world of sequencing. Cetus sold off its PCR portfolio to the Swiss pharma company Hoffman-La Roche for $300 million. Before the original patents expired, Roche was earning as much as $350 million annually in royalty payments.

CHAPTER 45 THE ARTS LAW SOCIETY

MAX'S SOUL churned. Every autumn there'd be a day when the smell of dried leaves on cool night air brought back a decade-old trauma of walking in on Jay and Joosey, conjured images and sensation with shocking vividness, and he'd be consumed with rage he couldn't direct at or share with Arianna. When the fury abated, he'd still be watching over his shoulder as if the neural firings could creep up on him from behind. And then there was the closeted self-loathing he couldn't share with her, and the lies he told her when he'd been out with the loathed loving boys. And yet, on occasion, he said he loved her. She, more than anyone since Miriam, accepted him. He basked in the acceptance while pushing her away, resenting her, and acting cruelly under the influence of his untreated PTSD.

By the time of her second year in law school, and while he was in his third year on the faculty of MIT, Arianna and Max embraced their work and not much else. Max kept his distance, unwilling and unable to give back the love she had to give him. She hoped for a return to what she remembered as better days. When they did (on rare occasions) embrace each other, he was dry lipped.

We are always alone, even in the mad embrace of love. Most of us dream of melding together in those moments, but whatever Max dreamt, to her he was as cool as old dishwater and remote as a quasar. He was not the melding type. His soul was separate, had never been one with hers, and she had not quite caught up to knowing this.

"When he said he loved me, I believed him." Arianna told me.

Arianna had never been completely sure why she'd decided to go to law school. She liked the practical side of life, working in her father's store, cooking in her mother's kitchen. When she thought of a career in art history, that ivory tower in her mind was an abbey, fruitless and juiceless, and not like what she imagined for herself. It was the Vidas who first suggested she study law, painting a picture for her of a woman with a craft, an independent woman.

Returning from Paris with her conviction to mix more art into life and law, she was surprised to find so many artists in class, and so much love of art and art business in Cambridge and Boston. At the Fogg Museum she put her hands on Rembrandt's actual etchings, the 350-year-old originals marking the various stages of his engraving. At the Gardner Museum, an 800-year-old plate transfixed her. A couple gazed outward from a distant Persia, tranquil and glazed in iridescence. It reminded her of what she'd left behind and the serenity she hadn't grasped with love, with Max, with life. Thirty-somethings, even twenty-somethings with money, the *nouveau riches* of the Internet were emboldening gallery entrepreneurs to enlarge their old or open new spaces. Artists were being encouraged to produce more ambitious pieces for their more ambitious benefactors. Anything on paper or canvas, cut into stone, shaped out of plastics or clay, even art on video became collectible. Sales meant property and property meant law, *ba da bing!* Among Arianna's friends she was always the first to connect the artist's or the legal dots. She fantasized about an Arts Law Society, and her friends encouraged her to become its founding president. They didn't know what Arts Law meant, but it sounded very Harvard to them.

Homemade food, and especially pho and ramen and ciopino and fejoiada in January and February when the cold and the short days drove everyone indoors, were so central to the first Arts Law Society meetings that its membership growth almost outpaced the Shut-In-and-Fretting Society's. Large monthly social gatherings built around potluck dinners and slide shows of exotic collections and visitors and discussions of tax code or IP law lobbying became so popular that they garnered faculty attention and participation. Arianna was at the center of it all, a slender, dark-haired, dark-skinned beauty, smoldering, and usually without a date.

CHAPTER 46 THE GENOMICS BUBBLE

WHEN WATSON and Crick discovered the physical structure of DNA in 1953, they may have dreamt that in some far-off day, future generations of human beings would know the coded message that is our genome. Many, many obstacles stood in the way of genomic medicine. Each would take a decade or decades to overcome. In 1975, Frederick Sanger hurdled over a big one when he described a method for determining the sequence of DNA fragments. He received his second Nobel Prize in Chemistry for that wizardry, sharing the stage with Paul Berg and Wally Gilbert in 1980. Gilbert—a Harvard physicist turned molecular biologist—and his student

Allan Maxam developed the second practical protocol, one that was more widely used at first. Eventually, refinements to Sanger's made it the preferred one.

Linkage maps illustrate the relative positions of genetic markers. Tools of classical genetics, they were first deployed more than a century ago—by Alfred Sturtevant, a student of pioneering geneticist Thomas Hunt Morgan—to locate genes on the chromosomes of fruit flies. In 1955, Seymour Benzer, a physicist turned geneticist, extended the method to map the positions of mutations within a single gene, providing the first evidence of its divisibility. His medium was the genome of a bacteriophage—a bacterial virus—a few tens of kilobases long.

A trick is a something you pull out of your hat to solve a problem. A technique is that same trick as written about by others. A method is a very widely used technique. A program is a plan to use a method on a very large problem. In a landmark 1980 paper, David Botstein, Mark Skolnick, and others described a program for creating a linkage map of the entire three-gigabase human genome, showing the way forward to a detailed map, if only moby and sequencing ever became cheap enough.

In December 1984, Botstein and others met in Alta, Utah to figure out if DNA sequencing methods were sensitive enough to detect mutations in the survivors of Hiroshima and Nagasaki, and in the survivors' children, too. Sensitivity and cost are often two facets of the same question. What's my sensitivity to something at the price I'm willing to pay? If I were willing to pay ten times as much, would I get better sensitivity? Sometimes yes. At Alta, the participants concluded that the methods were still too coarse and the costs too high. For five days they racked their brains while skiing as they thought about how to overcome the limitations. They inspired each other so profoundly that they came up with solutions they realized might make the Botstein-Skolnick map possible in their own lifetimes. Four years later, one of them wrote a paper about it and called the program the HGP, the Human Genome Project. Over the next few years, billions of dollars were committed.

No one outside of biology had heard of genomics in the early 1990s. A few companies were founded and some made money on the tale being told about how genomics would transform scientific and medical understanding. Max became aware of its scale and scope, inspiring him to move into MEMS research. In the late '90s, Jay's Agrigene went public on the story. Dozens more companies were started to capitalize on the discoveries to be made, that is, to harvest the money that was to be made.

There was competition. There was intrigue. There was scandal. There was the Internet, and there was Wall Street, and the bubble of dotcoms. That drove billions into these companies, creating a genomics bubble alongside the dotcoms. There was also a schedule. Scientists knew how much sequencing was to be done and how much sequence each lab could produce in a day, so they knew when they would have results to show the public. The news media knew it too. The folktale got taller and taller. Some readers inferred—perhaps they wanted to believe—that much of medicine would be solved once the human genome was finally sequenced. Even some scientists were fooled. Certainly the public was fooled.

By late 1999, as investors began to get wind of the genomics bonanza, there was tremendous scarcity of investment opportunity. FOMO left investors willing to pay, and I can say this now, ridiculous prices for companies that were already public, like Agrigene. Investors were multiply-orgasmic as they bought Internet stocks that went sky-high and then sold them to buy genomics stocks that went sky-high the following year. Jay, probably having a few orgasms of his own, was all of a sudden worth $500 million. When he sold stock, the *New York Times* covered it.

Max was beside himself. When the air cooled and the leaves dried and the scent of an October evening brought back memories of crystal clarity, memories of walking in on Jay and Joosey, Max's sense of failure peaked in the face of Jay's success. He vented to Arianna. "I am living in graduate student housing and Jay is buying properties from Sotheby's! He is probably buying a boat, the fucker!" He pulled his hair. He tore his clothes. "That Fucking Idiot!" Tiny Machines was perking along, but not public and could not benefit from the bubble. "If only we'd been earlier. If only they'd listened to me. If only I owned more of the company."

Arianna wanted to be sympathetic, no matter how he estranged her. She knew how to fake it, and she tried, but he was aloof. "He would barely look at me," she said. "I didn't understand why. I didn't understand him at all, then."

He found his outlet in work, and when that wasn't enough, he found the gay sex bars and mob-sponsored poker in Boston, and gambling under the auspices of the Indian tribes in Massachusetts and Connecticut.

The greater fool theory says that I buy my stock today because I know there's a fool bigger than me ready to buy it at a higher price tomorrow. On a finite planet, the pool of fools will be exhausted, eventually. For the Internet and the genomics bubbles, eventually came on March 10, 2000. After that, the IPO window—through which Max had hoped Tiny Machines would exit and parachute in golden splendor to the bank—became only a narrow little slit.

CHAPTER 47 THE SHARK HAS PRETTY TEETH

ARIANNA DESCRIBED to me the events of a long weekend vacation she and Max spent on Block Island right after the Labor Day madness. They could have instead just zipped down to Woods Hole and jumped on the short ferry across Vineyard Sound to Martha's (Vineyard). It hardly seemed worth it to make the larger effort, but Block promised something besides just vacation; it promised time travel. Arianna loved combing the galleries, talking to the artists who staffed them, or the owners whose friends filled them. The relationship buyers had with the artists there was intimate, reminding her of walks along the Seine, conversing with painters and sculptors. Following wine and smoked bluefish at an opening, she'd visit one of the creators at his or her home. Arianna's family felt extended.

Max hated Block Island. "There's nothing to do here," he told Arianna at the end of their bike tour around the island. He wanted casinos, or at least a floating poker game, or spearfishing. After carrot cake at a little shop, she walked off to explore her favorite places and he tried to rent some dive gear and scope out the spearing scene. He learned that the stripers had migrated away for the season, and the visibility wasn't good enough for fluke, and renting all the gear would be tough anyway, and and and, so he gave up and wandered over to the commercial fishing docks. He was pointed toward the charter boats, and after interviewing some of the captains he secured a spot on a sharker for the next morning. To Max, the captain's exceptional competence showed through layers of weather-beaten, sun-browned, unshaven jowls, and a belly grown fat. He cleaned up the boat and its gear after the morning's clients left. Hating almost everyone else around him, the captain, aka Sharky, was someone Max recognized as kin. A small wooden plaque was nailed beside the instrument cluster at the helm. It read, "They call it Tourist Season. Why can't we shoot 'em?"

Predawn the next morning, Max was on the *Sharkings* when it left the harbor and headed toward feeding grounds off Montauk to the southwest. A father and his tween daughter hung out near the transom. They admired the early light as they drank cocoa from a thermos and chatted with the mate.

Up on the flying bridge, it wasn't long before Max and the captain were trading stories about sex and gambling. Max told old stories. Sharky lamented the difficulties in procuring for his clients. Max didn't care and didn't let on. "It's a drinker's paradise, but not a hooker's. Girls are so easy here, a hooker's got no takers," he said. "Some of the rich guys bring 'em along on their megayachts. Ukrainians or skinny Asians with balloon tits. They look ridiculous on land. You aren't here a couple a weeks, you won't even see 'em." He paused as Max stroked his chin and winked at him. "But you know, sometimes, the girls who come here just to work for the summer, sometimes they work the night shift too. Sometimes." Then he shrugged, open palms up, as if to say he had no leads.

"No contacts at all?" Max asked, baiting the captain.

Sharky wrote a number on a piece of paper, folded it, and handed it to Max. "I'd be careful. Just because she's wearing a "Hottie" t-shirt and says "Da," she's maybe not meaning what you think. You could offend some little Polish girl and end up, you know," and he laughed, "shark meat!"

Short-fin makos and blue sharks had been reported from the Montauk shore. They fed on schools of bluefish, and the bluefish fed on smaller baitfish. Sharky had his binos out, looking for frenzy on the surface. The sun at his back left him with ideal visibility. "What's the height of this bridge over the water?" Max asked him.

"Standing up, maybe twenty-six feet."

"That makes the distance to the horizon, let me see, one point two two times the square root of twenty-six, uh, a little less than six miles. Visibility's got to be, what do you think?" Max said.

Sharky explained to me when I caught up with him at Vladik's recently. "The visibility was more than four times that, 'cause I could see the lights on the Jamestown Bridge when we left New Harbor. It was a razor-sharp morning, one I could have remembered for that alone, not to mention everything that happened afterward, but I would have remembered it just for that one comment. Been running charters for over thirty-five years now, and never once heard anything like that from anyone."

The mate threw chopped-up mackerel and bluefish carcasses overboard. Their smells wafted up to where Max sat with the captain, adding to the sting of salt in the air. Whole mackerel, fourteen inches long, oily, and green-black, were strung through with hooks, ready to drop into the water when the fish finder signaled with a *boink!* that the boat was over schools of bait.

"I can't believe they're going to kill those wonderful fish, Dad," the girl said.

"We're here to witness it, honey. If we take some pictures and publish them, then maybe fewer people will come out to do it next time."

"I think we should just look at them."

Max's eyes rolled back into his head. "Fucking Idiots!" he said to Sharky. "If they don't want to be here, why are they here?"

"They pay with green money. I just want everyone to have a good time. It's easier for me if they don't actually want to hunt."

"As long as they don't kill my buzz. But they're killin' my buzz."

"Patience, Boss. We'll be on fish in a couple of minutes."

They worked several schools, seeing stiff gray fins feeding, but weren't able to latch onto anything. Then it hit.

The mate cried, "Waahoo!" and Max echoed it. Two hundred yards of fluorescent monofilament flared out of the reel, so fast that the clicking sound of the pawls made one continuous sound of buzzing. The daughter backed up against her dad, afraid and horrified.

"Tension the fuckin' line," Sharky shouted to the mate while he maneuvered the boat, following the shark out to sea. Max, with help from the mate, worked the shark in all the way to the stainless steel leader, and then the mako dragged the line out again one or two hundred yards, and the cycle repeated itself a couple of more times. "Max held the rod alone, without a break. He was drenched in sweat and looked like he might have a heart attack," the captain told me.

After about two hours of that, the shark began to slow down and show signs of giving in—swimming on its side, vainly pumping once or twice with its big tailfin, but mostly just floating near the surface. The boat listed to port as everyone on board ran over to the gunwale where the gray head was now so close they could see the hook piercing the flesh around its jawbone and the remains of the bait trailing in the water.

Exhausted, Max still didn't want any help. The mate warned, "Don't bring that shark broadside until it's completely worn down!"

"I think we're all right. This one's spent," Sharky replied for everyone to hear. And then, "Heh. Heh. Careful now. We don't want any of our blood in the water," he whispered in Max's ear.

"What's the length on that one?"

"Eight feet."

The mate lassoed the mako's tail while Sharky sank his Froodgaff into its mouth, stabilizing it, readying it so he could remove the hook and release the shark to its waters. Max unhooked the leader from the line, put the rod away, and then accepted the gaff from Sharky, who for the first time connected the name dots between his gaff and his client.

Sharky went to work with his hook-removal gadget, urging Max to keep pressure on the mouth with the gaff, and ordering the mate, "Raise the tail! Raise the tail!" The ammoniated smell of urine, the shark's smell, poured into Max's face, stinging his eyes and making him gag.

"*I'm* fucking spent," Max breathed heavily.

"Nice fish. Maybe two hundred fifty pounds."

"What's the record?"

"Ten eighty."

"Ten fucking eighty? Oh shit." Max look dejected. The fight had been so hard, and yet he wouldn't win a prize.

While the *Sharkings*'s diesels idled and the soporific shark lay idle in the water, the girl and her dad chattered on. "The shark has pretty teeth, Dad. I'm glad they're going to release him." She wept over its suffering. And then she said it again, and again, almost chanting the same words and thoughts.

Max wanted serenity. "For crying out loud, it's not even ten yet. Will you shut up?" he said to them. They jumped back to the furthest corner of the boat to get away from him.

Sharky was having a hard time, struggling with the extraction tool to get a purchase on the hook and pull it through the mako's jaw, leader and all. For an instant, the mate released pressure on the tail, letting it fall. The captain yelled, "Get back! Get back!" before the clients even recognized that there was new danger. Suddenly, with energy no one suspected it had, the fish drove its tail hard down into the water, forcing its head up and over the gunwale, and from there it twisted, looking Max in the eye. Max dropped the gaff overboard. If the mate hadn't instinctively started pulling in on the tail, the shark might have just fallen back with a splash, and the worst of it would have been the girl's screaming and the clatter of rods and beers falling to the deck as everyone scattered. But the mate did instinctively pull up on the tail line, and between that and the shark's twisting, all of a sudden there was a very much exhausted but still breathing shark lying still and quiet on the deck.

"Get forward. Get forward, now!" the captain ordered, hoping Max, the mate, the father, and the daughter moved to safety before the shark found any more energy. "That thing gets an idea in its head … you don't want to be near it." Sharky pulled his handgun from its shoulder holster and prepared to shoot the beast. As Max made his move to get away, and with what he ever after described as malignity, the shark's eye scanned. It locked on Max's, and then with the very reserves of energy Sharky warned it might yet have, the mako flopped its tail on the deck. With a blinding thrust, its jaw of pearly-whites moved forward far enough to slash Max's right leg to the tibia. Then it collapsed, undeniably and reliably dead.

The girl's howling now went off the charts. Max fainted—and who wouldn't have? He hit the deck hard on his way down, bringing up a hematoma the size of an egg over his left temple and a smaller one on the other side. What followed might have been chaos, but Sharky and his mate had rehearsed for moments such as these, and lived through them, so it was more minuet than mosh pit. The mate put the boat on a heading back toward Montauk and then used the VHF radio to inform the Coast Guard of the medical emergency. "You guys got an EMT in place at Montauk?"

"Roger that."

The mate then went aft to assist. Sharky had already brought Max back to consciousness with smelling salts and ripped his trousers away to get a clear visual on the gash. It was clean. Ghastly but clean, long, running nearly the full length of his shin, along the muscles, not tearing across them. There were no torn arteries so the bleeding only looked awful. It was not catastrophic. The captain wrapped the wound with a clean bandage, sans tourniquet, shot Max full of morphine, and told the mate to order a helicopter evacuation.

Arianna was walking along the beach and had no cell coverage when the call came in from Sharky, who informed her voicemail that Max was a champion sharker, but there'd been an accident. When she got the message, she learned that Max was OK, and they'd be back at Block Island before dark, not before lunch. She reached Sharky while Max was being given stitch fifty-seven of eighty-three, and Sharky made her feel as good as she might. The doctor's report was much as Sharky saw right away—a deep laceration without neurological damage. Arianna spoke to Max, who actually said he loved her! "It made me think there was still hope," she told me.

I imagine, knowing Max as I have come to, that having confessed, or admitted, or stated his love, he then lobbed recrimination after recrimination at himself, beginning with "What the fuck am I doing?" The answer would have been that he was totally dependent on her, and he would have known it. At that moment, it was the love of a baby for his mama, not a lover's love for his mate. It made him hate himself all the more.

He regained his composure on the boat ride back to Block Island. The sea was calm. Even so, Sharky went slowly so as not to bump his patient.

When they arrived, dozens of locals and the newspaper photographer were there to watch as he stepped off on crutches. The picture in the *Block Island Times* highlighted the two small eggplants of contusion on his brow. Was he a hero for catching this big if not record shark, or a fool for getting so close to death's jaws? *I'm fucking neither. That mate is a Fucking Idiot*, Max thought. The captain thought the same.

The daughter got her minutes of fame, recounting every detail to a reporter, especially Max's fainting and the way his head bounced, and bounced, and then bounced again off the planks. *Fucking little bare-twat idiot*, he thought as he hugged Arianna sheepishly and as Arianna cried.

Sharky thought Max was a bit of a Fucking Idiot himself. Seeing Arianna, he guessed Max didn't need a girl after all, so Sharky offered to connect him to a poker game. Max, though, was too depleted and drug-slowed. Playing would have made him the fish, and he preferred to be the shark. He asked for a rain check, "In case I ever come back to this godforsaken island," aka Sharky's home.

Arianna ordered an anchovy pizza from a local shop and brought it back to their hotel room along with some pilsners. Max drifted off to sleep and her mind wandered over the dream of her own gallery on Block Island, and a family, too. At 10:45 the next morning, while Max hobbled, she wheeled their bike onto the ninety-eight ton *M.V. Anna C* bound for the Port of Galilee in Narragansett. Little more than an hour later, Max grimaced his way off the ferry and she rolled the tandem beside him. He waited with the bicycle and the gear while she walked to the car, drove it back to pick him up, loaded it, and began the drive home to Cambridge.

CHAPTER 48 MAXCENTRISM

MAX WAS unfazed and his career unaffected by the accident and his slow recovery. He may have been limping like an amputee, but he was also building a reputation in the Institute as someone who was unafraid to take on hard problems. He promised students and postdocs exciting results if they could make the grade. That was the big if. He knew he could make the grade, so the responsibility for failure would always be on them. There was a grant from NSF and several applications in the channel. The team had grown to six, including Max.

They worked on every aspect of droplet MEMS: the materials they were made of, their physical design and geometry, fluids to flow through them, methods of actuation, means of manufacturing them. Each new innovation was translated into an invention disclosure and filed with TLO, where Max made an enemy of himself by insisting that each one be submitted as a new patent application.

TLO wanted the next Cohen-Boyer, the next new thing, the big platform technology that would generate millions in licensing revenue and burnish MIT's public-service image. Small filings would probably never generate enough revenue to cover their costs. Max let everyone know he thought TLO was staffed by Fucking Idiots. "They're lazy and mediocre. Paper pushers. They're not motivated to serve me!" he railed to Arianna.

Max's thinking obeyed a logic others came to call maxcentrism. To capitalize on the productivity of his lab, Tiny Machines would have to license every one of his new inventions. The inventors would get a slice of the up-front licensing fee as well as royalties and other fees later, call the whole thing $\$_{fees}$, equal to the fees divided by the number of inventors, *n*. If there were *N* licenses, then Max's share was

$$\$_{Max} = \sum_{i=1}^{N} (\$_{fees}/n)_i$$

The big Greek letter is a compact way of saying, "add up $\$_{fees}/n$ for each of the N individual instances." The principle of maxcentrism was a refinement on the playground game of "heads I win, tails you lose." Max did best when more inventions were filed and licenses issued—hence his insistence on filing many individual patents rather than lumping them together—and the number of inventors on each license was as small as possible; in other words, one. Max was meticulous in maintaining his invention notebooks, competing with his own students for priority dates, and keeping them off the list of inventors unless there was absolutely no dispute that they'd made a contribution so large they'd fight him over it. Students are generally not in a position to fight their advisors, being so dependent on them for recommendations and financial support. He may have maximized his revenue, but he burned a lot of young people, young people who later said they felt like chess pieces in his game.

Armen and Papken were none too thrilled with this strategy either, as it racked up Tiny Machines' licensing costs to TLO and their own legal fees and promised to hurt their revenues in the future. Max had a conflict of interest here. The fewer patents he filed and subsequently licensed to Tiny Machines on terms least favorable to MIT, the better for Tiny Machines, and inasmuch as he was a Tiny Machines shareholder, the better for him if Tiny Machines became successful. On the other hand, the more patents he filed and the more favorable the licensing terms to MIT, the better for him personally, but the worse for Tiny Machines. His equity in Tiny would only be worth something if it was successful, but he'd get a portion of the annual licensing fees as long Tiny held the license, profitable or not. He acted behind the scenes to help TLO negotiate against his own company, extracting terms particularly favorable to MIT and himself. As he felt he had been screwed out of his rightful slice of Tiny Machines equity, thanks to Armen's control of the investors and his son the CEO, these maneuverings were, to him, just leveling of the playing field.

And he was frustrated with the Armenians for other reasons, too. Papken had been very thorough in putting in place a version of big-company decision-making, although lean and without all the overhead. Big companies tend to make decisions very slowly, and that doesn't work for small companies that must to be particularly agile. On the other hand, those practices, when done right, keep the entire enterprise well attuned to what's going on and why, and in particular, why things change when they change. Meetings, memos, and announcements reinforce the mission and the message. Decisions are not entirely top down nor bottom up. They're a synthesis. Properly executed, these processes protect the company from tyranny and imprudent change. Max hated the structure, the processes, the rules, the inertia. He wanted to decide what the company would do. He wanted to make those decisions with Armen and Papken over dinner and fine wine, or in the sauna, or in a dark room with a bare light bulb while wearing a green eyeshade. He didn't want to have to convince a board, or a team. He wanted to be the decider, and was frustrated, sometimes enraged, that he'd been outmaneuvered at Tiny Machines. They'd made him an advisor, but they didn't take his advice. He thought of himself as *the* executive and wanted his advice to be law.

CHAPTER 49 THE NONCOMPETE CLAUSE

IF THERE was one term in his Tiny contract that made Max feel warm and fuzzy, it was the noncompete clause. The Armenians had wanted a land grab, covering all aspects of droplet MEMS hardware and applications, or from another perspective, every aspect of Max's research program at MIT. Had Max conceded, he would not have been able to consult for other companies at all, much less kick off a new competitor to Tiny. "I knew it stank," Armen told me. "I thought I had him boxed in. Then he decided to fight me to the death over it."

Max told Armen that he was walking away from the deal if that term stayed. "I didn't believe him when he left my office that day. When I didn't hear from him for almost a week, I called. He didn't answer the phone. After two weeks, I rang Arianna. She explained that Max was around and healthy, and that he'd mentioned nothing about Tiny, and knew of no reason why he wasn't getting back to me. I asked her to have him swing by, or at least call, and she agreed. I didn't hear from him. I was starting to get worried because there was a schedule, milestones I had to meet for the other investors, and it was falling apart. Pretty soon I was going to have to tell them the deal was dead. I always had kept Max believing that the deal was risky and we weren't sure if we wanted to do it. Heck, Lakshmi, Max is Max, maxcentric, I know, and you know, but so generative, so inspiring. Tiny was important to our plans, a cornerstone of our hopes. Lose it? No way. But if we'd shown how important it was to us, he'd have renegotiated every term in the contract, including investor equity.

"I called Arsalan, who did succeed in reaching Max. Unreasonable. He told Arsalan that Papken and I were being unreasonable. Arsalan sided with Max, although he kept that from him. My old friend went on to tell me that Max had one term, nonnegotiable, and if we gave it to him, he'd sign. He wanted to keep the sequencing applications for himself, no noncompete, and we could have the rest. If we couldn't deliver on it, he'd find another firm to back him. We caved. It was a land grab after all. We felt like we'd won.

"This whole process had eaten up almost all of the slack in the schedule, and if we were going to get the deal done by December 31, which was important because of tax consequences, we had to move very quickly. I had set up an escrow account to hold the other parties' money just for that reason. Several versions of the terms were faxed and emailed back and forth, and on the last day but one, we came to an agreement. I called Max and invited him to dinner that night so that we could celebrate and sign the papers. That would have given us a few hours the next the morning to take care of the very final details and wire the money from escrow to Tiny. He said he was working late, had made commitments to his students, and while he'd be short on sleep, he could meet me at 7:30 a.m. on the morning of the 31st. I ordered fruit and some pastries. Max was late. A cold snap was headed our way and the temperature, already below freezing, was dropping. My secretaries had come in to help me, and they were anxious to go home to their families for the long weekend. The lawyers were charging me holiday rates, and complaining about the drive to Killington, and how if they didn't get on the road soon they'd end up driving alone while their wives and kids left to beat the crush of traffic heading to Vermont. We were hemorrhaging cash, on edge, and waiting, for him. At 8:00, Max showed up, cheerful and unapologetic."

"Armen, I'm not sure I've ever heard Max apologize."

Armen acknowledged me with a nod. "When I put the final set of documents in front of him to initial and sign, he riffled through them to find the noncompete clause we'd agreed to. 'You have to get rid of this for all applications,' he told me.

"I couldn't believe it. Papken and the lawyers, they couldn't believe it. But we had nothing in writing from him confirming his acceptance of the term. He had agreed verbally to the changes, only verbally. On the phone, he'd tell us to strike this or add that, dictating whole clauses. Here was this piece of shit, excuse me, Lakshmi, dressed like a turd, going back on his word at absolutely the last minute. I'd made promises to investors. We were there to sing the national anthem and shout 'Play ball!' He had read me and *played* me when I didn't think he had. I had to fold. We struck the noncompete for applications from the contract. That left him free to do what he wanted. He didn't even smile. He talked a little about the Celtics and the Super Bowl, stuffed an apricot Danish in his mouth, drank a glass of orange juice, wrapped a raspberry strudel in a napkin, shook my hand, and left."

"Par, Armen," I said. "Par."

CHAPTER 50 BIOCOMPUTING

THE MEMS hardware would require years of effort before Max could focus on how its applications were going to change his career. He began to muse on designs in the opiate-soaked euphoria of the first few days after the shark bite.

He could, being Max, open up new areas. He could start new companies. He could consult for others. Genomics was ripe for every one of these, and other scientists were already showing the way. He had focused since Paris on the materials issues, as that felt like the shortest hop from his general physics background into the world of miniaturization. But he was a physicist and could learn anything. "I'm not chopped liver!" was a phrase Max used when he wasn't getting enough approbation from his interlocutor. He probably said it to himself, bolstering his own spirits when doubt crept in to his thoughts about what he could accomplish.

The bursting of the genomics bubble didn't mean to Max that genomics was dead, only that Jay had been ridiculously lucky and there were a lot of stupid investors who had made him überrich. There was a future there, Max believed. Although he was barely thirty, few physicists of his age or stature ever became biologists. They had too many responsibilities, too many preconceptions, and too few hours strapped to a bench, pipette in hand, mulling over the basics on weekends with their fellow lab rats. There was a new term coming into vogue—biocomputing. Michael Lewis mentioned it in his book about Jim Clark, *The New New Thing.* Jim had had this dream of creating a Department of Biocomputing, one that would rival in productivity its world-renowned Department of Electrical Engineering. Max thought the term suited him. He set out to become a biocomputer scientist, whatever that meant.

Max, physicist turned biocomputer scientist, or biocomputing engineer, or whatever, thinking about droplet MEMS in moby and genetics, channeled Feynman again and asked himself this question: What is the limit? That's the way a physicist thinks. What is the limit? What happens when you take your thinking about the world to the end of what you know? What can you do that has never been done before? Can you do something with your instruments at their limits that everyone has always wanted to do but never pulled off or never dared to try?

MEMS, with or without droplets, is all about miniaturization. But what were the limits of it? Could you look at the moby of a single cell? Could you handle one molecule at a time? Max couldn't see that the answer was no, and so concluded that it must be yes. Around the time Arianna graduated from law school, he began to expand his career into the arena of the single cell and the single-molecule.

CHAPTER 51 THE EPIC FAIL

Venture capitalists will stop at nothing to copy success.

-Eugene Kleiner, cofounder Fairchild Semiconductor and Kleiner Perkins

TOLSTOY WROTE that all successful startups are similar, but all failed startups fail in their own unique way. In Silicon Valley the cultural ethos teaches that you only learn from the experience of failure, or put another way, that failure is its own success and deserves a badge of honor. Another teaching is "Go big or home." The two together brew some epic fails.

Candescent Technologies Corp. was a 1990s-era company in San Jose dedicated to building a newfangled flat panel display that would displace the omnipresent liquid crystal display. At the time of its founding, LCDs were pathetic by today's standards. They were dim, their contrast was poor, the color was bad compared to TV, they didn't show detail well, they had poor off-angle viewing, they were lousy for video, they were power-hungry, and they were expensive. Alas, they were the only solution for laptops. Put one on a desktop? No way. There were no slab-o-glass tablets or phones in those days. If you wanted a really good computer display, you'd buy a sixty-pound cathode ray tube driven by an energy-slurping electron gun. Candescent's technology put millions of very, very small electron guns behind a sheet of glass and *voilà!* The ultimate flat panel display, marrying decades-old TV technology and the manufacturing methods of the semiconductor industry. As it had passed by Tiny Machines, the IPO window of the Internet boom passed by Candescent. By the time their patents were sold to a Japanese company for $11 million and there was an empty 300,000-square-foot plant on San Ignacio Road, they had spent nearly $500 million. There was nothing else to show. Epic! Why did they fail? They underestimated the resourcefulness of the companies already in the business of making LCDs.

Webvan Group Inc. wove a romance about how the Internet was going to transform grocery shopping. Moving quickly in the hot atmosphere before the Internet bubble burst, they described a future for VCs that—just as can happen in physics or biology research—was faddist and made the venture guys want to harness their careers, or rather, their investors' money to that future. After an IPO at the veritable peak of orgasmic enthusiasm in November 1999—an IPO that raised $375 million, following $400 million of venture investing, and another $400 million or so afterward—and a total of $1.2 billion spent, the company filed for Chapter 11 bankruptcy in July 2001. Epic! Why did they fail? They were not retailers and they made bad assumptions about customers' buying habits.

Perlegen Sciences Inc. was spun-out of Affymetrix, a moderately successful biotech components company in 2000. The idea was brilliant, they say. They would use Affymetrix's technology to find the genes associated with disease and sell or license the IP to pharma companies who would in turn bring the drugs targeting these genes to market. After approximately $250 million raised, and grants, contract research, and possibly revenue totaling tens of millions more, the company folded because the scientists found that few genes have a strong effect on disease. They discovered what there was to discover, but what they discovered wasn't valuable. Epic! Why did they fail? Biology did not cooperate with the business plan.

No history of the epic fail would be complete without a mention of photovoltaics and optical semiconductors—although, sadly, there is insufficient space here to discuss the fantasies of the latter—both hoisted on their own petards when they tried to dethrone silicon from its primacy. Copper indium gallium selenide, CIGS, is a compound semiconductor that was promoted as an alternative to silicon for solar power generation. A trio of CIGS companies—Nanosolar, MiaSolé, and Solyndra—raised not quite $2 billion, and their assets were ultimately sold at auction for pennies on the dollar, a phrase masking howls of outrage. What happened? They didn't account for the fact that Chinese manufacturers of traditional solar panels would be willing to lose billions of dollars, selling below cost, in order to hang on to their share of the market.

These failures are all measured by the amount of money burned. There are other kinds of failure.

CHAPTER 52 BEING PREGNANT

While Arianna's classmates interviewed for clerkships on the Supreme Court, or associate positions at Skadden or Weil or Goldman, or planned to work for the social good in immigration law, her Arts Law Society had already become her career. She was a practice of one, advising Harvard's wealthy alumni on managing their art portfolios. She looked forward to graduation and the bar exam, because when they were behind her she would no longer have to divide her time between classes and work. She could just work, for herself. She had rented a small office on Brattle Street, put out a shingle that said, "Javaheri Art Advisors" and would soon hire an assistant to help her manage the small stuff. She was not at all worried about what was to come, professionally, because she was already a professional.

What she was worried about was Max and their marital unit, and it showed. She had wilted and withered under Max's inattention. She had lost weight and her curves with it. Her face was pale and drawn. Her breasts were shrunken. Her hair had lost its sheen. Her gorgeous smile was almost never seen.

Arianna would not be the first woman who mistook her own desire to have a child for the glue that would keep her marriage together. Max was lukewarm—which for him was hot—about the idea. Some months were set aside to let the effects of birth control subside, and in the summer after her graduation, at the apex of her fertility calendar, Arianna and Max came together again.

Wound around him, she knew him, but he was new. "Change is the only aphrodisiac," she remembered hearing somewhere. That pent-up energy of strange sex with a fresh purpose made her grasp for him on a Saturday afternoon, and socket him with her sheath as she had done only years before in an underground laboratory. She was giddy and teary. She whispered affections to him in three languages. They lay around on sheets damp with their sweat, the sun still amber through the shades, as afternoon became evening. He napped and she ordered Chinese takeout from Central Square. She so wanted to believe he was there with her. Max, on the other hand, was repulsed by the closeness she demanded of him, and trying his best not to show it. He could not be aroused again, but he was as sweet as he ever could be.

He could not be aroused again for the rest of the summer, but she missed a period. "I missed a period, *Mamman*!" she shouted over the phone to her aunt.

"It's too soon to get excited, but I'm excited too! Look, honey, don't tell anyone else. It's bad luck."

"I know, *Mamman*. I won't even tell Max."

Vida was silent on the other end of the line. Then she said, "Arsalan and I will be there next month. We can see whether there's something to celebrate. OK?"

The conversation dwindled down to details of flight numbers and arrivals and departures and hotels, concluding with a mutual "I love you" and a click.

Reviewing her schedule of calls and deciding she was free if she wanted to be, Arianna pulled her purse from the desk drawer, asked her busily typing assistant if she could get her anything in the Square, and then walked casually over to CVS, buying gum and three different pregnancy test kits. "I'm preggie!" she shouted to herself in the bathroom mirror, and then she called her Ob/Gyn. Later that night she told Max.

VIDA and Arsalan had planned a long trip to the US, spending two weeks in Boston and two weeks in Los Angeles. Arsalan had business and they both had friends everywhere. The well-established Persian community in Beverly Hills was ready to greet them with planned party after planned party. A bat mitzvah in the next generation was the draw. And then they'd be spending Rosh Hashanah with others in the extended family, returning directly to Paris a few days later. In Boston, the scheduled entertainment would be more muted, but Armen had something planned one night and Max had agreed to at least one social event at his and Arianna's apartment.

On the morning before Vida and Arslan's arrival, Arianna had her first ultrasound. Max had not been there, as he was off on some mission—"Mission critical to some MEMS thing," he said, "and long-planned,"—whose details he wouldn't disclose to her. Dr. Arnoon coated her belly with a thin, cool gel and scanned the transducer back and forth over her abdomen. "It all looks normal," she said. "Now, let's look for that heartbeat, shall we?"

She rotated a few knobs clockwise to zoom in, and then began to scan more slowly. Only her technician was in the room. Dark and quiet were everywhere. Arianna lay back, eyes closed, relaxing, not a worry at all, and dreamt of the baby. Dr. Arnoon broke the silence. "Well, there's a heartbeat!" The technician clapped and yelped. Arianna stifled happy sniffles. Then Dr. Arnoon said, "And there's a second!" Then they all yipped and laughed. The doctor and tech congratulated Arianna while her teardrops flowed, they held hands and thanked whoever there was to thank for the gift, the bountiful gift.

"Only two?" Arianna asked with the radiant grin of old.

"Just two. Two sacs. Two heartbeats. Beautiful. See you in two weeks."

VIDA and Arsalan walked through security at Logan International Airport, dark-skinned, slim, and with French elegance, and when they spotted

Arianna waiting for them, Vida nearly ululated with joy, then broke into a run until she reached her almost-daughter and took her in her arms. "There's two, *Mamman*, there's two," Arianna said. Vida was uncomprehending until Arianna reached into her purse and pulled out a grainy black-and-white ultrasound image. There were two little sacs, and within each, a spot, a beating heart. They clasped again and wept.

Even Max's coolness was cracked by the news. He kissed Arianna, which happened even less frequently than they made love, and they made love, too, that night, after they'd put her relatives in a boutique hotel in Kendall Square. He was on his best behavior for this visit, putting aside any resonating irritations about Armen that Arsalan's presence may have provoked. He cooked, and then he ordered food in. He and Arianna took her relatives out to Boston's finest and coarsest. Max was gregarious. He was attentive to Arianna. He was everything he was not normally.

Arianna was buoyant, afloat. Her smile had come back. Color had returned. Her shape was filling in. She took her almost-parents everywhere, too, touring Harvard and the other squares and the trains, and north to the beaches. Everywhere she went she told her friends about the twins and received the most overjoyed hugs of congratulation. Vida told her she'd need help at home and they'd need a bigger place. "Yes, *Mamman*, of course. I'm working. I'm going to keep working. We have money. We had money before. We'll be fine." Vida hinted that she shouldn't share the news with so many people. She thought Arianna knew why, but she couldn't bear to tell her; she couldn't bear to say it aloud.

ARIANNA and Max parked, although Vida and Arsalan told them they shouldn't have bothered. It had been a wonderful few weeks, especially with Max transformed, although Arianna didn't let on much about how these weeks were different. Extending their closeness to the last possible moment, the four of them said their goodbyes at the gate as Arsalan and Vida boarded UA 175 to Los Angeles. Max and Arianna watched like children as the plane taxied and was wheels up at 8:14 a.m. The tangy Cambridge morning, the smells of the Charles River and the grass, and the hopefulness like a second spring left no doubt why students from all over the world wanted to be there.

With the effects of the falanga almost gone, and the wounds of the shark attack fully healed, Max was able to run beside Arianna on their way to the car. Even though it was rush hour, she made her 8:45 appointment. Max introduced himself to Dr. Arnoon and the technician. This time, the technician performed the ultrasound, spreading the gel out onto Arianna's belly. Max watched, poking his head among the knobs and nodding at their settings. The tech set about her business with the usual banter and then was strangely quiet. Max studied the two fetal blobs on the monitor, trying to spot the telltale pulsing.

The tech left the exam room to get Dr. Arnoon, only to find her and everyone else huddled around the TV in the waiting room. A plane had crashed into the North Tower of the World Trade Center. Then Dr. Arnoon walked back to the ultrasound room as if this were a day like any other day. Taking the transducer in hand, she scanned Arianna methodically but found no heartbeat. Shouting came from outside the door, from the waiting room. "Arianna," the doctor said, "have you had any bleeding?"

"Maybe just a spot, this morning."

Arnoon, taking her hand, said, "Arianna, Max," she said, "they're gone."

"What do you mean, gone?" Arianna asked.

"No heartbeat. The twins have died, Arianna. I'm so sorry."

Her mind seemed to float free of her body, she told me much later. Looking down at herself, she wondered *who is this woman and why is she here? What does "gone" mean?* "Max, how can they be gone?" Hands clasped hers, and she thought of Vida's gentle warnings, and then passed out.

When she came to, Max wasn't the Max who'd come into the room with her. He was the aloof Max who wanted to leave. He knew he had to stay, though. She was not the same woman, either. Where was that girl? An overbearing sadness suffused every joint and every pore. Hope had just been killed. "Max, I need you Max," she said. Max was there but not there. He could not emote. He was inside himself. He bit his tongue. He wanted to tell her that not so much had been lost. But he knew it wasn't true. His hope about something living had been aroused in a way it hadn't been in years. He couldn't find words to say to her that weren't trite. He wanted to be alone and gone. He didn't want to, couldn't give himself to her suffering. He hated himself for his coldness.

They left the room together, wondering how to find a way out of the hellhole they'd found themselves in so suddenly. The waiting room was packed with patients and doctors and nurses huddled around the TV. Mothers with small children had pulled their children away, distracting them as much as they could. Arianna and Max crowded their heads in to see what was so interesting. "For those of you who have just joined, you are seeing the South

Tower of the World Trade Center burning. The North Tower has collapsed after American Airlines Flight 11 crashed into it at 8:46. United Airlines Flight 175 bound for Los Angeles flew into the South Tower at 9:03." Arianna fainted again as the South Tower fell in on itself. Max sat down and hung his head between his hands.

CHAPTER 53 STAYING PREGNANT

URBAN CAMBRIDGE was preternaturally quiet in the first week after 9/11. Arianna felt that all of America mourned with her. A hundred calls came in from friends who knew—about Vida and Arsalan or the miscarriage—and friends who didn't. Each call began with choking grief and ended with puffy eyes and a slack face. She felt like a mouse in an owl's shadow. She slept whenever she didn't have to be up, but soon city noises came back to near normal, and Arianna walked across Cambridge and made her first appearance in her office. She became increasingly impatient with Max.

The twins had sprung in him a hope he had not felt since youth, a hope for happiness. He had expected to be a distant parent, but from the first heartbeats, he had bonded with those rapidly-dividing twins-in-the-making and imagined scenes of blissful parenting. Those fantasies died along with the little lives, and he had retreated to a convenient message; something only a few weeks in the making couldn't amount to such a big loss for his wife, and less for him. She didn't talk to him for three days after he first told her how she should feel.

Arsalan had been the only father figure Max had ever known, and Max's denial engine had to work overtime to keep up. Her relatives' remains were never found, but a funeral with much keening was held in Paris six weeks later when Arianna was strong enough to travel. When they returned, he worked and disappeared to she didn't know where, and when he was home, she threw shoes at him or just slept.

A grant application to the NIH received a favorable score and would be funded. Max added another postdoc and a graduate student. He started a research program to study DNA one molecule at a time.

The year died in November. Leaves, all brown, were on the ground. Branches, all bare, were grey spikes in the air. She soaked in the autumnal morbidity. She attended the minyan service at the Tremont Street Shul, walked around cemeteries, explored crypts in the Old North Church, and read obituaries.

She (and Max) made the first of several visits to Ground Zero in Manhattan. No need to hide her grief in those pursuits. They made her feel at home. That helped. Arianna's energy, maybe even her spirits, began to improve. She and Max tried again, this time without that crazy aphrodisiac of the strange. She missed a period, and at her sixth week, she miscarried again.

On the phone with her family in Paris, she continued mourning the loss of Vida and Arsalan. But she couldn't bear to ask her parents, her sisters, and her cousins, all of who had lost so much, to comfort her about the twins. Max was the only one she felt entitled to draw on, and he was useless. "Useless!" she shouted at him, or into empty space when he wasn't there to hear.

"You're so smart, so brilliant. Why don't you figure out what's going on?" she spat, not quite over dinner, because they no longer actually dined together, but they were in the same kitchen eating at the same time, standing up.

"What do the blood tests say?" he asked. He had adopted a professorial tone whenever he was challenged. It was the way he dealt with stress.

"I don't know what they say. What do you mean, what do they say. They say I'm healthy."

"What's your ANA?" Max asked her.

When Arianna told me of this scene years later, she interrupted the flow to explain that elevated levels of antinuclear antibodies were seen in some patients with autoimmune disease, but I knew that, and I begged her to continue.

"ANA? What, do you think I have lupus? I don't have an ANA."

"Look, if Arnoon didn't measure it, you don't know whether you do or you don't." They'd lost the ability to converse without every sentence escalating the tension. "And no, I don't think you have lupus, you're not showing the signs, but a high ANA could be associated with antiphospholipid syndrome, and that's been implicated in clotting disorders." He stopped there, but Arianna shot a look at him that meant, "So?"

He continued, "Those fetal capillaries are tiny. A little clotting could be its end. Miscarriage. Kaput."

"I hate the way you talk to me. One minute so condescending. The next a despicable attempt at humor. And you tell me it's my ANA. You think it's my problem? What do your blood tests show?"

"I haven't had any blood tests."

"And why not? And why not!" Arianna shouted at him.

She stopped her story again. "Oh Lakshmi, the way he rolled at his eyes at me then, like I was an idiot. For a moment, he shook his head, taking a long time to decide how to answer me before saying, 'Just get your ANA. I've been farther along in pregnancies than this.'"

"You what?" Arianna said to Max.

"I've gotten a woman pregnant. Past the first trimester."

"Then what? She carried to term?"

"One to term. The other one, she died."

"Oh Maax!" Her mood and tone shifted. "I'm so sorry." She tried to embrace him.

He wouldn't let her near, pushing her away. "One minute you're like a viper and the next you want to mother me?"

Arianna, angry again, starting to wonder who it might have been, dug at him with questions. "Two! I've gotten a woman pregnant. There's a half-truth if ever I heard it. A Harvard girl, was it, or were they?"

"No, not a Harvard girl."

"From before that, high school?"

For a long time, he wouldn't answer. Then he said, "Maxime."

"Maxime? Who's Maxime?"

"Vera and Maxime."

"Vera's Maxime? That little girl? You're the father? How could I be so stupid? You fucked me on our honeymoon on the same bed you fathered that girl? You pig."

Max, without so much as a fauxpology, tried only to explain that he had not known about Maxime until they arrived on Gili Trawangan. Arianna wasn't having any of it.

"Your secrets dissolve the little we have still holding us together," she said. "I treated Vera like a sister, and she was a lover of yours? How demeaning that she would have that knowledge and I wouldn't. I'm your *wife!* How could you do that to me? Were you fucking Vera, too, while we were there? I wasn't enough? Couldn't get enough from me?"

"Now you're hysterical. I had a fling with Vera years—"

Arianna cut him off. "Is that why you're still going to Bali, so you can fuck Vera and have another child, while I'm here *barren*? I'm your second family, not even your first."

"I shouldn't even dignify that with an answer, but I will, with one word. *No!*" His shout shook the room. "I had an affair with Vera years before I met you. Is that not allowed? Maybe I should have told you, OK. Maybe I shouldn't have booked us at Wet Dreams, but we were on that little island, and I would have seen Vera anyway, and you would have too. And we both would have met that little Eurasian girl who seems to be my daughter. I told you I didn't know of her beforehand, and I assure you I wasn't thinking about either of them while I was in bed with you."

"You were probably thinking about Putu."

"Will you stop it? I haven't been with another woman since I met you. I promised I wouldn't, and I have every intention of keeping that promise. So stop. You're hurting yourself more than you're hurting me with this assault."

"We need help, Max."

"I don't do therapy."

"And why not?"

"I don't know. I just don't do it."

Arianna decided she could wait him out.

"It's a Froodian thing," he offered.

"Meaning what?"

"My mother, she was against it. Said it was useless. Worse than useless."

"Profound wisdom acquired at your mother's breast, then."

"Something like that."

Max clammed up, and Arianna, too, until the image of the second girl rose up again in her mind.

"What about the one who died?"

Max was stone cold and wouldn't answer.

"Not a Harvard girl. Another Indonesian? A French girl?"

Max shook his head.

"Then who? Then who?" Arianna told me she shouted at him, beating on his chest as his silence built. She was crazy with rage—almost as if he'd been unfaithful—that he had these corrosive secrets. The Vidas has warned her. She and Max had known each other for over six years, and to be hearing of so much for the first time, just then, made her want to tear him open to find what else was there inside. She was also hoping that maybe he'd show some tenderness, some sympathy, or just fight back a little and subdue her physically. But Max wasn't talking. Only much later would Arianna learn that the second woman was his own mother.

DR. Arnoon tested Arianna for ANA and a genetic condition called Factor V Leiden that had also been implicated in clotting disorders and first-trimester miscarriages. Arianna had a moderately elevated ANA, although not elevated enough to worry about or to make Dr. Arnoon think that it was the cause of the two miscarriages. She was also heterozygous for Factor V Leiden.

It's moby's central dogma that every protein has its origin in a gene, and every protein variation in a genetic mutation. The simplest form of mutation is called a SNP, a single-nucleotide polymorphism, and it involves nothing more than a change of a single nucleotide, that is, an A, C, G, or T, in the sequence of nucleotides that defines the gene.

Factor V is one of the proteins that clot blood. The F5 gene, the one that codes for the protein Factor V, can admit SNPS and produce a variant called Factor V Leiden. Proteins come and go in response to your body's own need-driven signaling processes. The FVL form resists degradation and therefore results in increased clotting.

You get two copies of every gene, one from your father and one from your mother. If they're the same, for any given gene, you're homozygous. If they're different, you're heterozygous. Individuals who are homozygous for FVL are one hundred times more prone to dangerous clots than individuals carrying the normal, the wild-type F5. Heterozygous individuals carrying one copy of the FVL variant are four times more prone to these clots, and pregnant women who are heterozygous for FVL have a slightly elevated chance of miscarriage.

Arianna was the ping-pong ball in a game between Arnoon and Max.

"There are no treatments other than mindfulness and counseling, Arianna"

"You mean I'm supposed to accept this? It can't be. I can't be," she moaned in Arnoon's office.

"Sure," Max told her, "your ANA is not so high, but it's not normal. If it were high, they'd look for the antiphospholipids and if they found them they'd recommend heparin injections to reduce clotting. Yeah, your Factor V by itself is probably not responsible, but I'll bet in combination with your elevated ANA, it's the thing. I'd have you on heparin." Arianna was apoplectic at his audacity, as if he could make these medical decisions for her, or could just read a few papers and come up with the answer. She couldn't stand being in the apartment with him, and so went for a walk in the rain of that warm January.

"There's a study across the river I could enroll you in," Arnoon told her when she explained Max's view. "Mitigation of pregnancy-associated risk for venous thromboembolism and pregnancy outcome in women heterozygous for factor V Leiden. Not very likely to do much for you."

"Placebo effect, Dr. Arnoon."

"Maybe just that. Two self-administered sub-cu shots of heparin."

"That's not bad."

"Daily, for the duration."

Arianna did the numbers. "Thirty-nine weeks, times seven days, twice a day, that's sixty-three plus two hundred ten is two hundred seventy-three, times two, is five hundred forty-six. I have to give myself over five hundred shots! You're kidding me."

"Almost six hundred. For your safety, we'll need you to continue the injections for two weeks after delivery."

She fainted when she gave herself the first shot, but long before she went to delivery, expectant, but not really believing it was going to come out all right, she'd become a pro.

Max was very proud of himself. He wasn't the problem. He was the solution!

The boy was named Arsalan, in honor of Arianna's deceased uncle. The world was being made right for her family. Her parents and sisters and cousins came from France and the UK and all over the US. Max fainted at the bris, but Arianna had expected that.

CHAPTER 54 THE INSTITUTE SCREW

The Institute Screw is a left-handed thread, three-foot-long aluminum wood screw. It is a useless, obtuse piece of sculpture. Claes Oldenburg would approve. It is a priceless honor to be on the receiving end of the annual MIT award to "whoever on the faculty or staff is most deserving." A priceless honor? Or was it an irony-rich bit of mockery given to the worst teacher on campus, the one who most screwed over his or her class.

Max thought he received it for his exemplary role filling in for an ailing member of the team teaching Circuits and Systems. What the students were thinking was never revealed.

CHAPTER 55
INBORN ERRORS OF METABOLISM

METABOLISM IS the cell's art of making and breaking molecules. Enzymes—metabolic proteins with highly specific functions—grab hold of a particular kind of molecule and position it for interaction with another kind that will bond to it or prepare it for bonding with yet another. That's all in the service of building the special entities that cells need to go about their business, or breaking down those larger molecules that have served their purpose and are no longer needed. As with Factor V, if the genes that make the proteins are mutated, then the essential enzymes are not made and the cell doesn't function properly, usually with fatal consequences for the organism. As with Factor V, being homo- or heterozygous in the mutation makes all the difference. Inborn errors of metabolism—a term coined in 1908 by the physician Archibald Garrod who studied a metabolic disease called alkaptonuria and its genetics—arise when a child is homozygous in the mutation of the gene of an important metabolic protein.

How does a child become homozygous in that gene? Each parent contributes one copy of the gene, mutated or not, to either egg or sperm, so both must be carriers. If the disease is not fatal or severely debilitating, then a parent may be homozygous, but usually both parents are only heterozygous in the mutation and the chance that egg or sperm will be carrying is a coin toss. The fertilized egg has a one-in-four chance of being homozygous according to the rules of Mendelian genetics.

There are hundreds of these diseases. All are rare, the most common occurring only once in several thousand births. They become more common in closed societies. In one such disease, Tay-Sachs disease, the newborn is missing hexosaminidase A, an enzyme that breaks down molecules found in cell membranes of the brain. Absent the enzyme, phospholipids build up, wreaking developmental havoc and causing early death. In Asia, the disease is almost unknown. Among Ashkenazi Jews, about one adult in thirty is a carrier, so there's about a one-in-nine-hundred chance that both parents in a child-bearing couple will be carriers, and of the children from those pairings, about one in four would be homozygous. That is, Tay-Sachs can be expected in about one in thirty-six hundred Ashkenazi live births. Carrier screening reduces this in practice to about one in forty thousand.

CHAPTER 56 TAY-SACHS

ARIANNA'S LAW practice had come to include an associate and a paralegal, as well as her office administrator, aka her secretary. Arianna's vitality had returned, and the blooming pressure of young motherhood had amplified it. When Little Arsalan, as he was called, was born, the office staff picked up all of her responsibilities for three months while Arianna enjoyed life for the first time in years.

Max was transformed, at least with the boy. "Endlessly fascinating," was the way Max described their son. Also, "a screaming, sometimes-sleeping bag of shit." It was doting, Max-style, the way the man strapped the boy to his chest and strolled all over Cambridge, over the bridges into Boston, and back. Some of his tenderness leaked through to Arianna. After all, it was she that had brought him this joy. But still, she said that Max had never been as warm with her as he was with Little Arsalan.

She returned to work, carrying the infant in his car seat carrier cum nest when the city was shoveling out from the biggest one-day snowfall in its history. The dark-haired little boy thrived there, and elsewhere, growing brighter and more active by the day, offering some new trick or movement to the world and the adults who hovered over him.

April showers brought even more showers in May, and while Arianna's parents were visiting from France, her blue-eyed mother was the first to notice that the young namesake was starting to withdraw. Vida shook his favorite tambourine in front of him. Instead of a smile and a squawk, his response was a look of surprise and fear. She had returned to France by the time Arianna took him in to see the pediatrician, Dr. Arnoon, the Ob/Gyn's husband.

He didn't like the signs, and though he could divine no explanation as to why Arianna—whom he (mistakenly) thought of as a Sephardic Jew—in a union with Max—whom he had no reason to think of as anything but a bread-white melting pot American ex-Catholic—would give birth to a boy with Tay-Sachs, he pulled out his ophthalmoscope, held it up to the strangely still child's eye, and saw the telltale cherry-red spot on the retina.

He masked his concern and ordered a panel of blood tests, if only to have time to compose himself. Through his wife—who had flouted the privacy conventions of HIPAA, the Health Information Portability and Accountability Act of 1996—and through Arianna's first months as his patient, he knew the case all too well. As for the suffering she was about to endure, he couldn't bear to have it start that day. He needed time and confirmation. Arianna carried Little Arsalan off to the phlebotomist, where after a lot of his screaming and her crying, they drew blood from his heel and sent it to the lab to check for kidney and liver function, blood sugar, red and white cell count, and specifically for activity of hexosaminidase A, the quantitative metabolic measure that defines Tay-Sachs.

She was keening again, inconsolable. Dr. Arnoon had called to tell her that the diagnosis was infantile-onset Tay-Sachs. Metabolic activity was very low and the prognosis poor, six months at most.

"Four centuries ago an Askenazi Jew marries into your family, and you're carrying Tay-Sachs. That's not impossible. But how can I be carrying Tay-Sachs?" Max said, starting out with denial. He *did not* want to be part of the problem. "That's crazy. My mother was an anti-Semite." Then, trying to be funny, he offered, "Mommy's baby, Daddy's *maybe*?" Arianna was not amused.

Max, fatally ignorant of his family history, wondered whether one of his great-great-grandmothers might or might not have been from an Orthodox village near Minsk or Pinsk, from there spirited off beyond the Pale after a pogrom, and then raised as a servant or married off if pretty enough, her seed diluted sixteen times before it got to Max, and never a hint that he might be carrying Tay-Sachs. And if not, then was his Catholic mother Miriam Straus a convert, or a descendant of one? Either way, Max was carrying. The genetic screens he got after the fact were conclusive on that, and that there was Northern European Jewishness in his bloodline. There were few people living who might have known that history, and he didn't want to talk to them. He began making plans to sequence his own genome, on a machine of his own design if necessary. For the time being, he knew what he had to know.

For four months, the family watched helplessly as Little Arsalan deteriorated. Arianna hired a partner to shoulder the load at work. She pushed her child in a stroller along the river, telling him about the buildings and their history and the seasons and how they change the look of everything. She pushed him in the day and the night. She carried him to the zoo and the museums, cramming as much experience as she could into that tiny frame, every day more isolated from her, in what remained of his too-short life. As much as she suffered, she wanted only to bear his suffering.

Max walked with his son as he slept, feeling the gentle breathing, and then the congested breathing; the rising and falling rhythm of the innocent's life.

Arianna and Max watched the breath go out of the little boy at home, saying together, unscripted, "*Mais où sont les neiges d'antan?*"

Where *are* the snows of yesteryear?

They buried the boy beneath a little stone on Block Island—not Max's first choice, but he had no better idea, and no fight in him.

Arianna needed Max, and she would have consoled him if he had let her. But he was conditioned against giving or getting help. He could not share his grief with Arianna, the grief at losing the only one he'd loved since Miriam; the only one he'd felt able to give himself to; the only one whose needs he'd catered to. He went about his work as before, in the lab all day, on the phone or computer all night, traveling, spread thin on many collaborations, often secretive.

She tried to draw him out. In a gesture harking back to sweet times in Paris, she showed up unannounced at his lab. "You're stalking me," he said when they were seated in his office.

She held her face in her hands and wept.

There, then, the marriage ended for her. She had loved Max, or loved the man she thought he was, given him everything she had to give, and he could not reciprocate. Whatever the excuses, whatever facts he'd told her about his past and how those were supposed to suffice as justifications, she no longer cared. She'd rather be single than lonely in marriage.

"I want a divorce," she said.

"I love you."

"That thing you call love? It's too one-sided for me. I need more."

"I need you."

"I need you too, but what do you give me?"

Silence.

She moved out. Her lawyer filed Complaint for Divorce papers citing an irretrievable breakdown of marriage. Max would not sign them. The lawyers, their conduits for all communication after his refusal, finished the transaction. A judge issued a divorce decree. The parties retained their own businesses and income. The furniture was given away. Arianna changed her name back to Javaheri and moved to Block Island. Max went west, accepting a position long before offered to him at the Haldane Institute.

CHAPTER 57 THE I

The dotcom bubble had been very, very good to the endowment of Jack Haldane's Medical Research Institute under the leadership of the Oxonian Qasima Zipp. Qasima was the eldest daughter of the maharani of the princely state of Mayapore and her husband Stefan Zipperkopf, a German-Jewish alpinist who had been the sole survivor of a late '30s British climbing expedition in the eastern Himaaalya [sic]. He stayed for the duration (of the war), finding refuge in the royal household where the then-young maharajkumari was smitten with his fabulous body and his encyclopedic knowledge of Gilbert and Sullivan in the original.

Qasima was tutored at the family's Calcutta residence in maths, Marxism, and genetics by a family friend, Jack Haldane himself. At the age of nine, slow to recover from some generic enteric disease, Jack personally nursed her back to health with a concoction from his own kitchen, something he called "my primordial chicken soup." Jack later encouraged the girl to finish her education in England. She never gave up repaying her indebtedness.

Eventually taking a first in maths at Oxford, she devoted herself to computing, and especially mundane computing problems like payrolls and banking. Soon she found herself sitting on a sprawling empire of small but royally profitable companies automating very boring tasks normally assigned to large teams of clerks. These she rolled up and sold as a package for nearly a billion pounds sterling back in 1984 when that was a lot of money.

Her considerable share of the proceeds she then gifted in their entirety to her mentor's institute, overwhelming its previous endowment, in exchange for a lifetime position as Director and Chairman of the Board. Her business experience and no-nonsense attitude led to extensive pruning of quaint projects that had lost or perhaps never had their way, and a slow convergence on a mission she believed Jack would have wanted. Biomedical research for the public domain, that's what they'd concentrate on. She found the niche and navigated it with discipline, an unusual feat for not-for-profits of the day.

Qasima had no qualms about making money. She liked to make money, and she was exceptionally good at it. She felt the Institute's scholars, though, should be focused on research.

Recombinant DNA might have been invented in the UK if science were all that mattered. But more than just science is behind innovation, and the Institute found itself supporting more and more researchers outside Britain.

Qasima began to meditate on the idea of an Institute Research Center, a place where investigators could pursue their investigations free of all other obligations. She divined that Northern California had all the special fuels needed to make the I, as it had come to be known, *the* benchmark in biomedicine. Long before HMRI had the money to build a new research campus, and long before the dotcom boom shot real estate prices one more sphere closer to space, and long before the commute from the Pacific Coast to Silicon Valley became a commonplace and therefore a parking lot, Qasima bought several large farms on the Pacific side of the Santa Cruz Mountains that divide the San Francisco Peninsula. She gave away a large tract as a sop to the Land Trust. The remainder became Lobitos Farm—thirteen hundred acres of developable land overlooking the rolling foothills descending to the ocean. Forty minutes away was Sand Hill Road, the world headquarters of venture capital.

She continued to dabble in software enterprises, as a hobby. After the first Internet browser was developed in the US, she realized a new bonanza was in the making. Increasing the risk profile of the endowment by a few ticks, she bought slices of pre-IPO financings in Yahoo and Amazon, riding them up to improbable heights before unloading them in favor of similar deals for eBay, ARM Holdings, Chemdex, Millenium, CuraGen, MicroUnity and alas, Webvan. It was a time when you forgot how to lose money. With uncanny timing, the I was out of the market by March 1, 2000, and sitting on two billion dollars of new capital ready for investment in Lobitos Farm. They broke ground within a year and planned to occupy the campus two years after that. The Institute had been courting Max for some time when he finally said he'd like to accept their offer.

CHAPTER 58 CREATIVE DESTRUCTION

MAX'S CLOSEST associate in the Alliance left Singapore to become president of the Royal University of Rhizobia. His departure coincided with the end of the MIT academic year as Max was preparing to move out west. That move signaled the conclusion of Max's alliance with the Alliance. The powers wanted to show their gratitude and honor him with Max Frood Day as the opening event of his friend's gala going-away party. Almost a year had passed since Max had last seen Maxime, and more than two since he'd last been in the Gilis. The stars were aligned for a visit to see his daughter, and to fly business class at someone else's expense.

His belongings, including his mud-caked Outback, were en route to California when Max boarded a flight from Boston Logan to JFK, where he would pick up Singapore Airlines SQ25 and fly, by way of Frankfurt, all the way to Changi Airport on the other side of the world. Three weeks later he would touch down in San Francisco and take up his new position at the I.

THE outrigger from Bangsal landed on Gili Trawangan, and once again Max was shocked by the accelerating growth. Maxime and Vera greeted him at the beach, a beach piled high with ten-kilo bags of ready-to-mix concrete that had been off-loaded by hand from other boats. As fast the bags were bucket-brigaded onto dongsols—wagons pulled by ponies—more boats arrived carrying more concrete. On the hard-surfaced esplanade, standing beside the dongsols that would carry the bags to construction sites, Max bought Italian gelato from a pushcart and handed it to Maxime. Italian gelato on Gili Trawangan? Where there had been one scuba training center, there were now six. Where there had been one Italian restaurant, now there were four, and French, and Spanish, and Croatian. Where the jungle had run right up against the esplanade, punctuated by a few shops, it had become mostly wall-to-wall shops. Where the esplanade had been footsteps in the sand, there was new brick. The most luxurious hotel had been replaced by another one more luxurious yet. And the coral was dead in many places; white calcium-rich husks were broken and lying on the seabed. And the turtles were disappearing. Inland footpaths were getting bricked over, leading the adventurer to bungalow after resort after cottage and then on to restaurants and businesses serving the locals who were seeking work there rather on Lombok with their families, because on Gili T you could earn three dollars a day. And everywhere there was trash.

A new island experience was being created while the old one was being destroyed.

CHAPTER 59 THE TINY MACHINES IPO

THE FEELINGS of humiliation and animal rage that had come along every year or so in Boston couldn't overtake Max in California. A perfect confluence of leaves dying and wind rustling, and early closing in of night was the recipe for resurfacing memories of Joosey riding Jay. In California, the climate just didn't make that weather. Max was happy to have left Greater Boston behind.

He lived in a dilapidated farmhouse near the Lobitos Farm campus. His beaten feet were back to normal health, and most days he rode a bicycle to the lab over trails or just plain overland. Technically, formally, the routes he found were off-limits. The groundskeepers took great pride in their work. Rather than have everyone tear up the turf in every direction, they tried to herd all foot and bike traffic onto a few more heavily worn areas. When Max couldn't talk sense to them, daring them to go to the Director and complain about her new and highly prized Principal, he concluded they were Fucking Idiots and he ignored them.

The I gave him an almost inexhaustible budget, a pharma-level salary, and ten years job security. With his reputation growing, particularly with Tiny Machines' IPO that first autumn, the I was the perfect home for him to expand and rebuild. Tiny had hired several of his MIT group, Max had invited only a few of the others to make the move with him, and some of those declined. Strange as it may seem, not everyone relished the isolation of the Lobitos Farm campus, or the tough daily commute if they chose to live near civilization. As his first postdocs moved on to permanent positions, there was soon no one around who had lived through the tumult and suffering of Max's final years in Cambridge.

An IPO is a big deal and Max made a big deal of Tiny's to all his colleagues at both institutes. He flew back to New York City on one of the underwriter's private jets, and everyone heard repeatedly and in great detail of the catering, the wonderful design, the fabulous materials, the meticulous cabinetry, the attentiveness and competence of the crew in their formal regalia of starched white shirts, service pins, hats, and even military flying medals, the extravagance of four passengers flying east on 13,000 pounds of jet fuel, and, of course, how his clothes were a big Fuck You! to everyone else involved, who themselves treated the experience reverentially.

The stock, trading as TNYM, was considered pricey in the post-bubble environment when profits, or at least revenue, or something more than PowerPoint anyway, was required. The company did have revenue, and a growth story that was all about how the HGP was not the end of the line, but only the beginning of a Cambrian explosion of innovation in research and medicine.

The narrative was also about IP, and how the company's early patents were so broad that they and the gladiatorial litigators defending them would keep competition out.

Max and Armen and Papken and some of the key executives were there, all better dressed than Max, cheering, ready for their moment of fame when they rang the bell at NASDAQ, opening the stock for trading to and by the public. The offering was neither over- nor under-subscribed, so trading was flat at the IPO price of $13. There was no wild run-up to $52 as everyone might have hoped during the not-easily-forgotten times when every new offering quadrupled on the opening. The price fluctuated slightly as noon came and went, eventually closing slightly down at $12.75. Volume was unimpressive.

Max had received 200,000 shares of an original four million, giving him 5 percent, or $2.55 million on paper on the end of that first day of trading. Over the years, nine million more shares had been issued and sold to investors, diluting Max's founding ownership to 1.538 percent, a number he was heard to recite to at least two more decimal points, and with not a little bitterness. Of the dilutive shares, he had been granted another block as options, but less than half the size of the first one.

TNYM slowly lost value, hitting $9.80 on the day when the lockup on Max's shares expired. He sold all 200,000 of his startup shares—three times the average daily trading volume—through a Wall Street trader who shorted TNYM in his own account and leaked the news to others. The short selling and the founder's evident loss of confidence in the company's future cratered TYNM, causing it to fall 30 percent before his entire block moved. Max took away $1,666,000, an amount he thought both paltry and fantastic. Gloating over his triumph, he was untroubled that his loose lips and impetuous selling had produced a $38 million loss (on paper) for the other investors and a weakening of the company's financial position.

Armen and Papken, consummate gentlemen, scaled back Max's consulting relationship, asking for only enough of his time to keep his noncompete clause in force. With Homeric dedication, they adopted the phrase, "Oh, we're big fans of Max Frood." They listened attentively to the deals he pitched; following up with enough due diligence to collect valuable competitive information, but steering clear of any investment or involvement with him. Their reflexive response when asked what they thought of his pitches was "We think it's too early. Why don't you keep us posted about any developments?" They hid their contempt and Max never caught on. Armen had loved Arsalan like a brother, and the one thing he did not regret about Arslan's passing was that he did not have to share his son-in-law's betrayal with him.

CHAPTER 60
SEQUENCING WOULD BE FREEISH

WITHIN A year, Max's group at the I regained its numbers—after the move from MIT had weakened it—and was back at a headcount of ten, headed for twenty as fast as he could pull it off. Max's dreams of fame and fortune depended on a brew of genomics technologies and their application to medicine.

He was forever on the phone, in meetings, or at conferences, recruiting talent and spinning up his flywheel of understanding about the upcoming transformation. He needed to master all the DNA sequencing technologies, developing intuition about what made them work and why. The laws that dictated how much faster, cheaper, and better the processes could become were unknown, but he and his staff could figure that out themselves.

A stream of visitors was brought through the lab, MDs and PhD biologists who had become specialists, key opinion leaders in their fields over decades of research. They came for a few hours, or days, or even weeks, educating and being educated. In Max's final years at MIT, the published results of collaborations had rained attention on quiet, mousy scientists who had never before been interviewed by *New York Times* reporters. This was the *quid pro quo* that delivered. They, the invisible experts, would share their insights with him. Then, with chutzpah, he and his team would find innovative ways to solve long-standing problems in the field by applying either Tiny Machines technology that had not yet reached commercialization or still-emerging and proprietary technology from the Frood Group. The published results would advance everyone's careers, thereby inviting deeper collaborations and new ones with people who read the journals. He was spinning a virtuous circle. There was a promise, if not in writing, that the other parties might get rich like Max, too, even if Max's riches were more fiction than fact.

An international consensus emerged that the fundamental obstacles to advancing genomic medicine beyond the lab and into the clinic were the costs and speed of sequencing. Yes, there was far too little scientific understanding about the role of DNA in disease, but that would be remedied if the price tag for sequencing were to fall, driving down the budget for experiments that would lead to the scientific understanding.

The rewards for making a breakthrough in that technology were colossal, and you had to look no further than the $500 million budget request of the NHGRI to see it. The National Human Genome Research Institute funded a substantial fraction of all sequencing. Groups large and small—in corporations, academia, and not-for-profit research centers—were trying one scheme after another, pushing all the possible dimensions of improvements, hoping to strike it big. They were striving, even if they didn't all recognize it at the time, toward a world in which sequencing would be free, or nearly free.

As Max tried to figure out how he, in his small lab within the not-for-profit universe of HMRI, could advance a field where his competitors' spending dwarfed his own, he ruled out many possibilities. Some were just bad ideas and would never work. Some were about improving an existing technology and could only be pulled off with a large-scale development team of dozens of engineers, chemists, packaging specialists, and computer scientists. There were moonshots that stood a chance of working, but would require at least $100 million and venture capital backing. Then, there were a few remaining ideas, each one like a holy grail that stood out from the rest. A small team with a modest amount of money could tackle them. If they worked, they'd change sequencing forever, and whoever brought them across the line would at least be recognized by national academies of science and engineering, and perhaps even by Stockholm.

The one idea Max decided to go after in his lab was something he called pore genomics. Imagine coaxing a single strand of DNA into a tiny hole that was not so big that the DNA would slip through it, as if it were in free fall, and not so small that the DNA would stick in it without budging. Through this goldilocks pore, the DNA would be pulled in a controlled manner. Surrounding the tiny orifice would be a sensor that read, somehow, the nucleotide sequence, the GATTACA, sliding by on its way through.

There were reasons why sequencing a lone strand of DNA was desirable. For one, a motherhood argument, it required the minimum amount of starting material. For another, it eliminated sources of error that stemmed from making millions of copies of a molecule—each copying step error-prone—as was required for even the most contemporary sequencing methods. And, to quote Max, "Single molecule allows you to bypass those fucking PCR royalties to Roche," because PCR is needed to make those millions of copies.

Then there were arguments about speed and system simplicity, both favoring one-molecule sequencing over traditional methods. Taken together, all the justifications for single-molecule sequencing made it look very attractive in theory. In theory, there's no difference between theory and practice, but in practice, there is.

Max was sure he'd be able to do it, single-molecule sequencing through a pore. He had already filed the invention disclosure and started the attorneys writing the patent, although he'd not yet made or tried anything. He had even incorporated the company, Porenomics, that would license the technology through the I's answer to the TLO, the TTO, the Technology Transfer Office. He owned 100 percent of Porenomics. When the time came, he'd give up equity to investors and the operating team members, but starting from 100 percent, he felt sure he would end up with a lot more than 1.538 percent this time around.

Qasima and her lawyers would someday opine on his ownership, he knew, but he put off ruminating on that one. Rules were for little people. "Rules," he said to me in a moment of boasting, "do not apply to me."

CHAPTER 61 THE COMING SINGULARITY

SANGER'S SEQUENCING protocol was laborious and physically cumbersome, employing a two-hundred-year-old method, electrophoresis, to move cleverly prepared DNA fragments of different lengths down a track in such a way that the shorter ones moved faster and farther, and a one-hundred-year-old method, autoradiography, to mark how far down the track the various pieces traveled. His gel electrophoresis apparatus was neither large nor small compared to other lab equipment, that is, it was bigger than a church mouse and smaller than an X-ray crystallography setup. After the fragment separation was completed, the scientist would examine the gel track and systematically, painstakingly translate the autoradiographic spots into a meaningful sequence of Cs, Gs, Ts, and As.

If one experiment took a day and succeeded in finding the order in a single strand a hundred nucleotides long, then the process of sequencing the three billion bases of the human genome would take some combination of a very long time, a lot of people, a lot of equipment, or a lot of lab space, and in every case, oodles of money.

At the Alta meeting in 1984, George Church—a Harvard geneticist who had just completed his PhD under Wally Gilbert—began thinking about parallelism: how to sequence many strands at the same time in the same physical apparatus. By 1994, there were commercial instruments that would sequence thirty-six samples in parallel, yielding 400 or 600 bases for each sample, taking about a day to do it, and using light sources, optics, sensitive detectors, and computers to read the gels. That's roughly 18,000 bases per day. Using the most naïve and optimistic analysis that ignored the need for redundancy or machine maintenance, sequencing the entire human genome in this way would require 170,000 machine days, or 500 machine years. In addition to parallelizing within a sequencer, a lab could buy many sequencers. If it was impractical for a lab to own and operate five hundred instruments, several labs could run one hundred each, and together they could get it done in a year. In practice, the solution demanded far more sequencing than called for by the naïve analysis, if only for statistical reasons beyond the scope of this history. It also required software and analytic innovations, usually called bioinformatics. That mouthful of a term is the science of using computers to understand biology. Launched as a field by Margaret Dayhoff in 1962, who died at fifty-seven in the year before I was born. Modern bioinformatics permitted the GATTACA-like strings from all the different gels to be stitched together into twenty-three humongous strings, one for each human chromosome. But still, machine-level parallelism was the key innovation. The HGP was completed over several years, distributing the work over many different labs, at a cost of several hundred million dollars.

Sequencing innovation was just getting started, though. Jonathan Rothberg brought parallelism to a new level in 2005, ushering in an era of synonymous terms: next generation sequencing (NGS), high-throughput sequencing (HTS), and massively parallel sequencing (MPS). Abandoning electrophoresis but making more advanced use of optics, sensitive electronics, and the devilishly named enzyme luciferase, Rothberg's instrument, dubbed 454, sequenced tens of thousands of different strands in parallel. Solexa, another company that went on to be more successful than 454, used even more parallelism. George Church threw his hat into the ring with his own scheme, called the Polonator. The cost of sequencing a whole human genome had come down to only $10 million in 2005, but that reduction wasn't enough to advance the practice of medicine. The ecosystem of patients, doctors, and payers take it as given that the cost of a widely used diagnostic test must be under $1000. Whole-genome sequencing, improving fast as it was, was on track to hit that $1000 target in about 2050.

After 2007, the economies of scale brought on by the increased demand for sequencing, as well as continuous improvements by the biggest companies striving to stay ahead of their competitors, and provocation by upstarts trying to muscle their way into the multi-billion-dollar per year market, all caused the rate of improvement to increase to what can only be called unprecedented levels. By the end of the decade, twenty thousand dollars would buy a genome, and the $1000 genome was imminent. As usual, those with a conflict of interest play fast and furious with the numbers, sometimes referring only to the reagents that feed the machines, occasionally to the amortized capital, less frequently to the labor and overhead, and almost never to the cost of making sense of it. That's the analysis and presentation to the patient by an expert in genomics medicine. And there's the difference between cost and price, too.

Back in the mid-aughts, there was no end in sight to increases in parallelism, speed improvements, and simplifications that would bring the price tag down, nor is there yet. What Max preached was that if sequencing wasn't yet actually free, it would be free soon enough, and you had to plan for it. There was a firm analogy with Moore's Law from the semiconductor world. The price of transistors halves, or they halve in size or their speed doubles, every eighteen months. The exponential decline had been in place for forty years or more. Electronics companies had learned, like Wayne Gretzky, to plan for what was coming. The change transforming genomics was even more dramatic, if less steady and predictable. Max told his group that they should be asking themselves the following questions: What could we do if sequencing were free? How would it change medicine? How would it change the things we're doing now? What opportunities would it create? How would it help me to get rich?

A SINGULARITY is a discontinuity, a kind of mathematical explosion, a kind of infinity. A denominator goes to zero, so the quotient blows up. If the cost of sequencing goes to zero, what goes to infinity? The number of experiments you can do for a dollar blows up. The amount of information you can get for a dollar blows up. The collapsing cost of sequencing implies a coming singularity.

Gene Amdahl is an American physicist and engineer who developed computers for IBM and later Amdahl Corporation. Amdahl's Law, a topic covered in every computer science class, quantifies the law of diminishing returns. An *infinite improvement*, *p*, in a module of a computer program doubles, only *doubles!* the program's speed, *S*, if the program spends half its time, *f*, in the unimproved module. More generally, Amdahl wrote;

$$S \leq \frac{p}{1 + f \times (p - 1)}$$

The infinite speedup removes one bottleneck and another takes its place. In practice, the only singularities are adverse.

Everyone in Silicon Valley sees a singularity coming. The herding is called the rapture of the geeks.

Chapter 62 The Material Gene

Not since the days of Robert Hooke has biology been physics. Without a hint of criticism, it's fair to say that physics as practiced has been much more quantitative than biology. Yet, even in physics there's a discovery period, sometimes a very long period, when the endeavor is all about "stamp collecting," that is, meticulous observation of what's out there. The first astronomers had to look to the heavens and record its changes before they could try to create a predictive model of planetary motion. There's another difference between biology and physics, at least historically. Physics has been focused on identifying the essential similarities, the universalities among the objects investigated. This encourages simplifying assumptions. For instance, if a physicist were to embark on a study of elephants, he or she might begin with the assumption that the elephant is a uniform and homogeneous sphere. Biology, on the other hand, has more often dedicated itself to identifying the differences among the objects of its investigation, as Darwin did with the finches of the Galapagos.

By the end of the nineteenth century, physics had become so adept at the quantitative explanation of celestial motions, the flow of heat and fluids, the interrelationship between electricity and magnetism, and almost everything but the very, very smallest of things, that there was serious but wrongheaded talk about physics being a closed book.

In 1900, Max Karl Ernst Ludwig Planck may have told his then seven-year old son, "Ach du Lieber! I've made the greatest discovery in physics since Newton!" Did he mean that he'd found the quantum? No, although he made that discovery in the same year. What he meant was that his study of thermodynamics, statistics, gases, and Maxwell's equations of electrodynamics had given him the first-ever glimpse of the intimate connections between mechanics and radiation. That quantum he invented, the preposterous constant h, was but a mathematical trick until 1905. Twenty-six-year-old Albert Einstein wrote then that the light waves of classical theory actually came in bundles, or particles, or quanta, and that Planck's h connected the energy, E, and the frequency, ν, of their vibration by means of the simple relation, $E=h\nu$. Hardly anyone believed him. Then, in 1913, the twenty-seven-year-old Dane Niels Henrik David Bohr, realizing that h could be thought of as angular momentum, l, wrote of a model hydrogen atom in which its electron's l could only assume specific discrete or quantized values such that

$$l \times (2\pi/h) = \pm\ 0,1,2,\ldots$$

and so forth. Bohr's model was a spectacular success, explaining the origin of previously inexplicable observations made nearly thirty years before, but hardly anyone over the age of thirty could grok it.

By the 1920s physics was in the midst of the revolution known as quantum mechanics. Biology had moved little beyond the descriptive phase. Morphology was about the shapes of living things. Taxonomy was a system for naming them based on morphology. Physiology was an attempt to explain that a kidney was a filter or that a heart was a pump, but without the mathematical framework that James Watt applied to his steam-driven pumps. And evolution, the profound conceptual triumph of Darwin, was utterly lacking in quantitative underpinning.

An exception was Mendel's genetics breakthrough published in 1865. It came about because Mendel believed that meaningful conclusions could only be obtained by tediously counting and classifying the results of his breeding experiments; that is, by being very quantitative. Although his subject was biology, his methods were those of a physicist, a quantitative scientist, a more mathematical scientist. Yes, Learned Reader, I know there have been aspersions cast at the integrity of his work because of statistical anomalies that may or may not have been uncovered seventy years later, but who doubts today that Mendel got us on the right track?

Writing about physics as if it's the only quantitative science is overly simplistic, even egotistic. Physics and physicists don't own quantitative analysis. They may have brought it to a refined state. They may have even invented it. But quantitative, mathematical thinking is a frame of mind, an approach, more than it is subject matter. I shouldn't be talking about physics and biology. I should be talking about the more mathematical sciences and the less mathematical sciences. Astronomy, physics, chemistry, computer science, statistics, and all of the subspecialties and interdisciplinary sisters like materials science, geology, quantum computing, physiological neuroscience, and combinatorial chemistry; these are the more mathematical sciences. Everything else, that's the less mathematical sciences. What's happened in the 150 years since Mendel, very gradually until the 1930s, and much more rapidly since, is that the subject matter of biology has been taken on, even attacked, by the physicists, and by chemists like the inestimable Linus Pauling, and by mathematicians like John von Neumann, J.B.S. Haldane, and R.A. Fisher, and computer scientists too numerous to mention. Biology has become a more mathematical science.

In 1927, the American geneticist Hermann Muller, who by that time was already an alumnus of Morgan's "Fly Room" at Columbia University, determined conclusively that X-rays can produce mutations in *Drosophila melanogaster*, aka the common fruit fly. We have to learn these things; they're not given to us by a higher power. Muller warned of the dangers of radiation. Yet again, something to be learned. Whether she was paying attention or not, the warnings were too late for two-time Nobelist and radiation physics pioneer Marie Curie, who succumbed in 1934 to disease born of bone marrow damage she probably incurred while inadequately shielded from her own experiments.

The language of the new ideas itself must be created, the new words made by hand. "Genetics" is not one Mendel had. Seven years after he published, the word "genetics" was coined by the English biologist William Bateson, and given to mean the study of heredity. "Gene" was not a noun Bateson knew; Mendel described factors. "Gene" came from the Danish biologist Wilhelm Johannsen in 1905. Decades later, it was adopted into common usage. And "photon," that conceptual sprite we throw off today as easily as "uh," was conceived in 1926 by the great American chemist Gilbert N. Lewis. In a letter[1] to the editor of the British journal *Nature*, he reviewed the arc of Planck's suggestion, Einstein's insights, and twenty years of subsequent experimental science, observing that light's "remarkable abruptness and singleness," its

1 *Nature*, Vol. 118, Part 2, December 18, 1926, page 874-875.

particulateness, demanded a name of its own, so he proposed "photon." It stuck.

At first, the meaning of "gene" wasn't understood as anything like what we think of today. Those early genes had no materiality. Were they a thing or a process? Could they be localized or were they diffuse? Was the gene a molecule, or molecules, or something else? No one knew. Muller became an advocate of the materiality of the gene.

Travel in time to 1927. The world was roaring back after the Great War. Babe Ruth had hit sixty home runs and the Phillies had finished last, again. Muller found that X-rays produce mutations in flies and Gil Lewis had just given a name to the light quantum. The confluence of these ideas led Muller and others, many of them physicists, to develop the "target theory," stating that particulate x-radiation transforms material genes, the targets, one photon at a time. It's a theory full of simplifying, elephantine approximations. But it's one that predicts that the gene is a thing, a thing about the size of a molecule.

Muller went to Berlin in 1932, to work with Russian geneticist Nikolai Timofeeff-Ressovsky. Between there and Copenhagen, he met Bohr and Max Delbrück.

Max Delbrück, a German theoretical physicist, a disciple of, if not actually trained by Niels Bohr, is the quintessential physicist-turned-biologist. In the 1920s he had studied theoretical physics in Göttingen under Max Born. After failing the oral examination for his doctorate on his first attempt, he finished up in 1930 when he was twenty-four.

Bohr was by that time the patriarch of the Copenhagen School, a name given to the place and to a particular interpretation of quantum mechanics. The best of the young prewar physicists, Delbrück among them, visited Copenhagen to be immersed in the thinking of Einstein, Dirac, Schrödinger, Oppenheimer, Heisenberg, Pauli, Fermi and others as they and their ideas and Danish beauties flowed through. Bohr didn't so much teach as he did influence by talking openly about the issues. His own father was a prominent physiologist, and so the son had learned to appreciate biology and medicine at the family table. Some of Bohr's knowledge of and interest in biology and medicine rubbed off on Delbrück, in particular at the 1932 lecture called "Light and Life," he delivered at the International Congress on Light Therapy in Copenhagen. Coming off the success of his theory of complementarity, which states that a complete understanding of light or matter demands that you look at it as both wave and particle, Bohr asked questions about whether physics-as-we-know-it can explain biology, or whether a new physical understanding is required.

After attending the Congress on Light Therapy, Delbrück returned to Berlin and his position under Lise Meitner at the Kaiser Wilhelm Institute of Chemistry. Meitner was the co-discoverer of nuclear fission and the first to recognize that the energy of Einstein's $E=mc^2$ is locked up in the nucleus. After the Reischtag fire in 1933, Hitler's Nazi Party began driving Jewish scientists, their relatives, and their sympathizers out of academia. Max Born, Leó Szilárd, Eugene Wigner, Emmy Noether, Richard Courant, and the model for Dr. Strangelove all fled from Gottingen alone, and that doesn't begin to capture the magnitude of the exodus that included Albert Einstein. In 1934, inspired by Bohr's "Light and Life" and his collegial style, and by the desire to keep his own "internally exiled" colleagues connected, Delbrück began a series of informal gatherings, a salon of theoretical physicists, geneticists, biochemists, specialists in photosynthesis, and one zoologist. Among them was Timofeeff-Ressovsky, with whom Muller had worked with less than two years before, and Karl Zimmer, a radiation physicist who had refined X-ray dosimetry in biological samples. Also in Berlin at the time was Barbara McClintock, the American Nobel Prize-winning geneticist who, in her research on maize, was the first to use radiation-induced mutagenesis as a tool. Berlin was a happening place for radiation and genetics.

The zoologist was Vladimir Nabokov, insulated in Russian-émigré Berlin, and cut off by choice from German society. His friend Timofeeff-Ressovsky invited him to Delbrück's club on the pretext that solipsism was a curable disease and that the lepid evenings would brighten his spirits. Drinking too-sweet Riesling Beerenauslese at the end of the evening with the guests and host, the novelist said, in English because his German was bad and the rest of them but one spoke no Russian, "Light and life," referring to the title of Bohr's address, "they go together like beets and borscht. Mind if I lift that line?"

In 1935, Delbrück, Zimmer, and their Russian colleague published "On the Nature of Gene Mutation and Gene Structure," usually referred to today as the 3MP, or the Three-Man Paper. Improving upon the target theory using Zimmer's quantitative measurements, and relying on mutation phenomena known to Timofeeff-Ressovsky, and on their interpretation by Delbrück using physical principles, the three made this statement: "we view the gene as an assemblage of atoms within which a mutation can proceed as a rearrangement of atoms or disassociation of bonds."[2] The gene was pronounced a molecule. Although their paper appeared in an obscure low impact journal, the authors made sure it was widely distributed to influential readers in Europe and the US. It traveled to Enrico Fermi and colleagues in the Physics Department at the University of Rome, where in 1937 a young MD, Salvatore Luria, extended the 3MP's findings to bacteria.

I heard it said somewhere at Princeton that you go to war with the army you have. Delbrück, or anyone, might have preferred to ask, "How does my brain work?" Or "What is life?" Or "How does a human develop from a fertilized egg?" But a scientist doesn't get to choose the problems that his or her generation has the tools to solve. In the 1930s, you could do little more than stamp collecting in those fields. If you wanted to be quantitative, you needed to think small, hoping that you could build up an understanding that would someday allow you or your students' students to tackle, quantitatively, something big, like embryology.

On a fellowship from the Rockefeller Foundation, Delbrück left Germany in 1937 for Caltech, determined to study drosophila genetics with Morgan who had moved there from Columbia. Flies are small and cheap, and they reproduce quickly, making them everything a primate is not, and hence, good for experimentation. But Delbrück concluded that even *D. melanogaster* was too complex. He needed a simpler organism, one that better satisfied the elephantine approximations necessary to make progress. This led him to bacteria and bacteriophages. "Phage" has its roots in the Greek verb "to devour," and bacteriophages were mysterious bacteria-devouring viruses. At the time, they had never been seen under any microscope. Delbrück's hunch was that the life cycle of the bacteria they infected would leave behind unmistakable clues about their own, and that would lead to, well, something. Where it led, immediately, was to the founding of bacterial genetics, an important next step in materializing the gene.

Luria, having already fled Italy by bicycle in 1938, and determined to collaborate with Delbrück, came to the US in 1940 on a Rockefeller fellowship. They met in the company of Pauli and Fermi at an American Physical Society meeting in Philadelphia and began working together from various labs and offices they inhabited at Columbia, Caltech, Cold Spring Harbor on the north shore of Long Island, the University of Indiana at Bloomington, and

2 As translated by Brandon Fogel in *Creating a Physical Biology*, Sloan and Fogel, University of Chicago Press, 2011, p. 268.

Vanderbilt University in Nashville. In 1943 they published results showing that bacterial resistance to viral infection arose because of spontaneous mutations, not in response to selection. This answered a longstanding question in genetics and evolution: Are mutations random and subject to natural selection, or are they directed adaptations of the organism in response to its environment, that is are they Lamarckian? The Luria-Delbrück experiment ruled in favor of Darwin, and won them the 1969 Nobel Prize for Physiology or Medicine.

Delbrück had learned to ask questions that could be answered quantitatively. That he pipetted into petri dishes, and kept time with a stopwatch, and wrote of "broth" in his papers, did not make the pursuit any less fun or any less real science in the greatest tradition than if he had been shooting atomic beams in high vacuum chambers and using oscilloscopes to measure signals on time scales of microseconds.

His training and character positioned him to share and to lead, and through both roles, to build a new "Copenhagen School," this time called the American Phage Group, focused on the nature of the gene. Delbrück's status as the young colleague of the graying eminences of quantum mechanics surely made it permissible for impressionable young physics minds to study phage, but even without that, the "nature of the gene" was very much cutting edge. Later he wrote, "if it be true that the essence of life is the accumulation of experience through the generations, then ... the key problem of biology from the physicist's point of view is how living matter manages to record and perpetuate its existence." The 3MP, the Luria-Delbrück experiment, the Phage Group, and his bohemian camping trips in the desert were working examples of the thinking he imposed on the practice of biology, genetics, and phage science. Teach a man to play cards and he'll surely find a fish, or something, as someone once said.

The 3MP, and Delbrück in particular, was lionized in Erwin Schrödinger's 1943 lectures *What is Life?*, a popularization of early biophysics and materialization of the gene. Schrödinger was one of the geniuses that had brought quantum mechanics into being with his famous wave equation

$$\mathrm{i}\frac{h}{2\pi}\frac{\partial}{\partial \mathrm{t}}\psi = H\psi$$

He read the 3MP in 1940 and was impressed. Max Perutz, the Nobel Prize-winning father of hemoglobin's molecular structure, later wrote of *What is Life?*, and I paraphrase, "All that's right in it is not original and all that's original was known to be wrong at the time." Nevertheless, Schrödinger's deified status was such that *What is Life?* motivated and influenced many more people than would have known Delbrück's name if their only access to him had been through the 3MP. Among them was one of Perutz's students, Francis Crick, a physicist who read *What is Life?* and came away believing molecular, that is material, explanations of genetics were imminent. And thus another physicist became a molecular biologist, ultimately the leading one of his day.

In 1947, James Dewey Watson—also inspired by Schrödinger's book—received a BSc from the University of Indiana's department of zoology—the department of Alfred Kinsey, the Kinsey of the *Sexual Behavior in the Human Male* (1948) and *Sexual Behavior in the Human Female* (1953)—and enrolled in the same university's biology department to do graduate studies on the structure of the gene with Hermann Muller. He finished as one of Luria's students. At twenty-two, he completed his PhD thesis on the application of the target theory and the 3MP to bacteriophage. Later, he would become a close colleague of Max Delbrück, and through that link, Delbrück became the first American to hear the news of Watson and Crick's 1953 deciphering of the molecular structure of inheritance.

In this elephantine approximation of a history of science, one which omits all the contributions from brilliant but less-recognized individuals, one which leaves out errors and dead ends and the myriad subtleties that make it impossible to schedule a discovery, there is a path that leads from Röntgen to Planck to Einstein to Bohr to Lewis to Muller to Delbrück and Schrödinger, and from there to Watson and Crick.

One thing has led to another these seventy-something years since Delbrück first went to Caltech to study flies. Qualitative explanations in biology have become acceptable only as stepping-stones toward quantitative ones, and not just in genetics, but also in embryology, neuroscience, and even immunology. At Princeton, Botstein—again Botstein!—and William Bialek reimagined the undergraduate science curriculum. To practice this new biology, they said, you must have the problem-solving viewpoint of a physical scientist and the phenomenological understanding of a natural scientist. The guinea pigs for this experiment in education were Princeton undergrads, for instance, yours truly.

CHAPTER 63 ORRIGEN STORY

JAY DIDN'T want to let Vladik know how much money he was prepared to put into Orrigen. He wanted Vladik to figure out how much was needed, and then tell him he couldn't have it all. But gradually Vladik ascertained that Jay had $6 million ready to put in, and more later, too. He leaked that to me, and it helped both of us figure out how fast Orrigen could be moved along.

The key idea behind Orrigen was a bacterial model for corn. Remember, Orrigen's mission was to discover genes that gave the plant particularly desirable properties for energy markets. No experiment in the field could move faster than the life cycle of the crop. It would have been prohibitively time-consuming and expensive if for every one of the hundreds of thousands of genes the company wanted to test, Orrigen had to grow corn in a field for six months, harvest it, and then dry-distill the kernels to isobutanol. Jay sought a short life-cycle model, an organism, e.g., a bacterium, which would tell him secrets about long life-cycle corn, but in much less time. Jay had been meeting with biologists at the Ames Center for Maize Genomics, hoping to license some breakthrough IP. They'd learned to insert genes of interest into a modified gut bacterium, *E. kerneli* (Ames), which would selectively express the kernel's carbohydrates in sufficient quantity that they could be distilled to the desired end products. The model system had been calibrated so that its measured distillation efficiencies accurately predicted those in field-grown corn. This promised to short-circuit a decade's worth of work that would have cost tens of millions of dollars.

Jay's dream involved mechanizing, and to every extent possible miniaturizing the task of manufacturing strings of genetic material per recommendations of the company's optimization software, inserting them into a small population of *E. kerneli*, waiting thirty-six hours for the bacteria to multiply and express the ensemble of carbohydrates, harvesting the carbohydrates, fermenting them, and then measuring the overall efficiency. Then they'd take the most promising gene sequences, feed those back into the computer that was driving the gene synthesis at the top of the loop, and generate a new set of genes somewhat more likely to yield improved conversion efficiency.

"It's directed evolution," Jay told me when we were back at the Sandbox.

"If I may differ, Jay. Directed evolution would involve using selective pressure to cull the best ones. What you're proposing requires us to do the cull-ing based on isobutanol yields. That's some sweet protein engineering, but not DE."

"We'll call it DE anyway. It sounds better, and only you will care." How true.

Orrigen promised to be one of the biggest protein engineering projects ever attempted. Jay had submitted a provisional patent application on the process, but the most valuable IP was going to be sequences of the best genes themselves, and the patents for those could be filed only later, after they'd been discovered.

A manual process to do all this would be too laborious and demand too much hardware. Imagine all the techs, petri dishes, pipettes, DNA synthesizers, sequencers, incubators, fermenters, and calorimeters you'd need. There were far too many steps here and too many different genes to sample. Jay was focused on lab-on-a-chip to scale down the hardware and to scale up the number of genes that could be tested. He had some of the expertise already at his institute, but he was going to need more, and of a different caliber. He also knew he was going to have to work around Max Frood's IP at Tiny Machines.

My job was to sketch out some LOC concepts and compare them. How did each stack up against Tiny's claims? Should bacteria and reagents and by-products flow through the chip like water through a hose, or should they be enclosed in microreactors, and should those micro-reactors be floating Tiny-style droplets, or should they be stationary? Were some designs bigger than others, and what did that mean for cost? How many genes could be tested on a single chip, and over what period of time?

I read the Tiny Machines patents, Tiny's publicly available patent applications, and the examiners' reports. The early patents, the ones with broadest claims, were the ones we kept bumping into. They'd never been tested in courts so we didn't know how they'd withstand a challenge, if we challenged them.

A patent is a sanctioned monopoly to license an invention in exchange for the obligation to disclose it. Companies infringe patents all the time, hoping to get away with it as along as possible, and expecting to pay a license fee when the assignee—the patent owner, not necessarily the inventor—finally catches up with them. If we built our instrument while infringing Tiny Machines' early patents, would they sue us and would they win? If they won, could we live with the consequences, or would we just expire? I say we, because I was by then an employee and stockholder in Orrigen.

I thought the whole prospect of LOC was too complicated. It would be two years before we were up and running with a chip we could rely on. We'd be better off with robots, generating data in less than six months. [Note to the patient comp lit major: when you read "robot" here, do not think C3PO, but rather, something closer to a mechanized pipette on a track above an array of thousands of smallish test-tubes.] Robotic handlers would save us labor costs and reduce our vulnerability to human error, even if we didn't get all the advantages of miniaturization, and we'd be getting information eighteen months sooner. That had to be worth something, didn't it? That's what I advocated in my final report when I went back to Princeton at the end of the summer.

Jay's initial plan to hire a bunch of people in the summer had been changed. There were too many uncertainties about how the company was going to operate, so we still didn't know what kinds of positions to staff. Vladik put out job descriptions for a Director of Moby and for that rare and prized crossbreed of biologist and computer scientist, the bioinformatician, who was particularly adept at making sense of gigabyte streams of biomolecular sequence data. We'd need those folks in any case, and Jay had a list, of course, of people he thought we should talk to. We had an office manager already because the Institute had an office manager. Vladik agreed to continue working fulltime until we hired a COO, perhaps by the end of the year.

VLADIK and I became good friends, thrown together as we were on this thought experiment of Jay's, and both of us away from home.

As Jay had told reporters, when asked why he hadn't stayed close to one of the centers of biotech, he returned to the Portsmouth area for the pizza. Every week he hosted a dinner at Zelda's for the entire Sandbox Institute staff, bringing his twins Lucy and Jason—when they weren't at camp—or his wife—when she deigned. And Boston was close enough when he needed to be there.

On our first dinner there, Zelda greeted Vladik like her long-lost son. Before he had a chance to introduce me, she pinched my cheek and said, "You look different, too. Do you have compassion, honey?"

It was a rhetorical question, and I pinched her cheek in return, a kind of secret handshake I'd learned from my paternal grandmother. Zelda must have been going on seventy, but still had the vigor to terrorize customers and staff.

Jay, controlling Jay, made the selections when we were there in the group. Otherwise, there were several ordering processes, from online to decorate-your-own, but Vladik and I preferred to choose from Zelda's standard formulations described on the tomato- and hot-oil-resistant menu at the table. The mighty pies did not disappoint. Delivered on large aluminum trays, our sausage-and-eggplant or our all-anchovy pizzas ran with oil that gleamed. Dots of Manchester Brand mozzarella melted into a chunky puree of light and fresh handmade tomato sauce. The thin crusts were sliced through, not randomly, but not orderly.

"There's too much order in this town as it is. I bring a little chaos into your life, like it or not," Zelda told us when she stopped by to discover what Vladik had been doing for the previous decade.

Night after night we worked our way through the menu, arriving finally at Pizza Rockefeller, an oyster-topped extravaganza.

"Don't you love the way they slide, so slippery down the throat?" Vladik asked. I thought this was the first step in his inevitable hit on me, and I wondered how I was going to feel about it, was even kind of looking forward to it, my still-developing and unresolved sexual preferences being what they were. He was only enjoying the food, as it turned out.

He was away for a couple of days at a time almost every week, usually having to do with the purchase of his house on Block Island or the sale of the one on Pot Island in Connecticut. In between nights at Lago di Garda and his nights away, we watched a hundred episodes of *Seinfeld* in a common room at the Sandbox, and sometimes we made a long drive to foodie Portland. On one such evening, he described a dinner and promised he'd make it for me before the summer was out.

"I learned to blanche tomatoes from one of the greatest characters in modern mathematics. He was a frequent visitor to Bell Labs in the '70s and '80s, an MIT professor working on a book called *The History of Computing in the Twentieth Century*. His name was Gian-Carlo Rota, and although he was already extremely famous as both a combinatorialist and a philosopher, he was a friend and professional colleague of the much younger mathematician who ran my mother's cryptography group, Andy Odlyzko. One of the lab directors would host large dinner parties—Rota loved company, almost as if he was afraid to be alone—at which Rota would sometimes cook in the director's modern kitchen. I'm told that Claude Shannon was there once before Alzheimer's took him away, but I don't remember him. I met John Tukey, who invented the word "bit," and Hamming, cofounder of the Association of

Computing Machinery. Once we had Shockley and Brattain, but never Bardeen. Dennis Ritchie was a regular—and he got me a job at Bell Labs in the summer before I went to Intel. And, of course, Metropolis, co-author of that book, and Ulam once. You know Ulam and Metropolis invented the Monte Carlo method with von Neumann, right? I'll never forget that. Gods. These were Gods, Lakshmi."

Dear Reader, if it's any consolation, with few exceptions, I didn't know who Vladik was talking about either. He was on a roll.

"My family was swept up into the mix by our association with my mother's boss, and over the years we became friends with Rota, and he became my first mentor.

"I remember the smell of his cologne and the texture of his big overcoat brushing my face as he embraced me like no other stranger did. Inside the warmed house, glowing with sunshine-yellow light in the days before these awful compact fluorescents," and Vladik gestured to lights that weren't in the car we were driving back from Portland, "or with fading sunshine on those long summer nights, twenty or so guests milling about—only a few of them kids,"

As Vladik painted the picture for me in the dark car, I thought he was describing a scene of growing up at my own home.

"Rota insisted that I help him make his signature tomato sauce. We called it *sugo bella rota*. He began from scratch, with whole tomatoes, hence the blanching.

"He kept himself well lubricated with red wine, and carried on a conversation with me—which was really with himself because I understood nothing—about phenomenology. I remember two things he said. The first is 'nothing nothings.' I had no idea what it meant. I looked it up. It's Heidegger. I still have no idea what it means, but it does help me get to sleep. It has become my mantra. The other he taught me when I was not yet old enough to appreciate it, maybe thirteen; he leaned over to me beside the stove and said close to my ear, guarding against that possibility that someone would walk in and overhear this great life lesson of Gian-Carlo Rota. "'Vladik, you must appreciate nuances in life. Touching a lover is not at all the same thing as touching a doorknob.'"

"Good advice. Was he always that deep?" I asked.

"Always." Vladik paused. I thought he might move his hand from the knob of the gearshift to the knob of my knee, but he did not. Instead, he continued. "Eventually large sauté pans were filled with our creation, and it would be my responsibility to peel and press the garlic he added just before serving. My special pleasure was carrying the serving dishes into the dining room while he sang Verdi and Mozart. The taste of garlic was sharp when we forked the spaghetti through the sauce and the hard, course-grated Parmigiano-Reggiano and into our mouths."

On our final night in Portsmouth, Vladik made me the famed *sugo* in the kitchenette at the Sandbox Institute. Again, he didn't hit on me. The next day, the two of us went to Block Island to close out the summer the way we had begun it.

VLADIK had rented a cottage for us on an east side bluff. We had too many margaritas. I snuggled up to him as he lay on the floor. He draped his arm over me. Putting his nose in the crook of my neck, he breathed me in deeply and said,

I know a beach where the eelgrass blows,
Where potheads smoke while shedding summer clothes,
Near over-toppling dunes and rich black pine,
Their wrinkled roses, and their turpentine.

Then he paused and said one more word, "beetles," before continuing, "I've been working on that all summer, but don't quite have it."

I thought this was his long-awaited come on, so I dared to say, "How about, 'let's wrinkle noses, and my body's thine'?"

In his heaviest mock-Russian accent, he offered, "Intoxicating Lakshmi, all summer I have waited for the right moment. Each time you pass me, there has been something I wanted to say to you, that I can say only to you." I pressed even closer, waiting, when he said in his normal voice, "Of my many vices, adultery is no longer one of them."

"Adultery!"

"Well, this wouldn't exactly be adultery, but it would feel that way, and I know the feeling."

I slugged and tickled him in punishment for his teasing. He did not tickle me back. He told me there was a woman, and that I would meet her that weekend. He told me about his year-long first marriage, but avoided the second almost-marriage, steering the talk to other things, especially work and fish. For the first time, he asked me about my family.

"My father was a normal bearded Jewish Princeton prodigy before he met my mother. He had never wanted anything more than an academic post in computer science, preferably in the northeast corridor, and that's the track he was on. She derailed him. Something about the exotic East," and my voice trailed off.

"And they met?"

"On a bus. Lived in the same neighborhood off the Hopkins campus. They found themselves standing next to each other, he holding a strap and she, barely tall enough to reach the strap, holding onto one of the posts. He said that the smell of her cardamom skin wafted up and he became a different person. Love at first sniff. It triggered something in him. He was so head over heels for her that I'm surprised he didn't scare her away. But, what do we know about other people's courtships?"

"Nothing, nothing," Vladik said.

"She fell hard, too. And within a year they were married. He says he would have lived in India if she wanted, but I don't think so. He's so steeped in Americana, he would have missed the cultural references too much. It's not safe to let him drive because he gets distracted by the story behind every telephone pole."

"And your mother?"

"My mother came here to be here, not to go home. So we lived here like Tamilian Jews, and there are no Tamilian Jews that I know of—"

"Maybe not, but the Indians are the new Jews anyway. Big family events, embarrassing uncles, fat aunts, scholars, artists, argumentative, driven. Right?"

"And you think we're different from the Chinese in all of that?"

"I think you're less insular than the Chinese. More inclusive. Gregarious. Always wanting to go beyond the boundaries of your own clan. Funnier—"

"And we don't mix meat and dairy."

"See? Funnier. Am I off base?"

"Funnier, I'll give you that. Anyway, we visited India every year while we were little. Once in a while, like a family joke, my father would bring up the possibility of staying, but I wanted to be in Baltimore, Amma wanted to be in Baltimore, and he wasn't going to sway us. My little sister, though, she loved India, or maybe she loved being doted on by all the aunties and uncles. Gradually, my parents hatched a plan to move back there when I went off to college. For two years now, they've been in Bangalore. He's some kind of guru-in-residence at a software company, and Amma's running the Department of Immunology at the institute where she started out, and helping my sister to survive her teens."

"It's not so easy to be at college without your family to lean on."

"I feel like I've lost a limb."

We were silent for a moment.

"They live in this enclave called Palm Meadows. Gated, guarded, groomed. It's in Bangalore, but is not Bangalore, if you know what I mean. Like Beverly Hills and only ten minutes from Bangalore?"

"Never been to Beverly Hills," Vladik said.

"Well, me either. But Palm Meadows is full of monster houses, maybe 5,000 square feet, on 6,000-square-foot lots, with travertine floors and rain-forest hardwoods you can't even import to this country. And the servants, and the amenities. It's dope. There's a clubhouse, you know, a restaurant-and-pool thingy, so plush that South Indian directors shoot films there. My mother's decision. My father would have wanted to live in the 'hood. It's all we can do to keep him from walking around the house in a dhoti."

We slept together that night, narrator and harpooner, like silver spoons, nested, but individually bagged to prevent tarnishing. I liked his scraggly hair. He made me feel safe. It was as if we were beginning a voyage together, even though this was the end of the voyage as we knew it.

He spent a lot of time that weekend, he said, with his real estate agent and lawyers, working on the closing of the house sale. Eventually I learned that he had also been sneaking in brief encounters with the woman, Arianna. He did not spend a lot of time shaving. He arrived the clean-shaven man I had met at the beginning of the summer, and he left with three days of stubble.

She was on her way out the front door of his newly acquired old house when we arrived to have a look at the property. He introduced her as his friend. She was so exotic! She made my own Tamilian genetics and Russian Jewish upbringing seem positively Anglo.

It was quiet out there on their property, his property. Not desolate but empty, like from another century. There were acres and more endless acres of land, some of it cleared and some of it covered in thick black-berried bushes. A good place to have big dogs and little kids. He was going to move out there in the fall. He wanted to live in the place before he had it demolished and built something new.

That weekend, much more than the one at the beginning of the summer, I fell in love with Block Island. My summer over, I returned to Princeton.

When Vladik hesitated about hiring a COO, Jay did it himself. "Vladik," he said, "they're like razor blades. Disposable. Undifferentiated if not interchangeable. You're worrying too much about the brand." Vladik knew that Jay was half kidding, but no more than half. Jay wanted nothing more than a brain to listen to him and a body to get things done. There had been a time when there were titles CEO and maybe COO, and CFO, and that was it. Now there was CSO, CTO, CMO, CIO, CBO, CRO, and even CΘO. Everyone wanted to be C-level, so with the inflation in usage came a devaluation of the currency. It was headed down even further.

The new COO came on board. He and Vladik hired academic consultants who flew in from all over the US and Europe. They brainstormed and whiteboarded and flipcharted until they were exhausted or bored or exasperated. Gradually the COO took more and more of the responsibilities, but Vladik continued to run the meetings, keeping control of the message and the task of summarizing the key ideas. The consultants offered their recent graduate students and post-docs as full-time employees. Gradually the mix of attendees included more employees than consultants, and then it began to feel like a company.

As Jay had intimated on the *Lucky Strike*, funding an energy company was not for the fainthearted, or even the super-rich—and Jay was not yet super-rich. Once you have an energy technology that works, you have to build copy after copy of it, with real stuff that costs money. As the bazaar grows, so grow the capital investments, and the size and number of existing competitors you have to displace, requiring all that much more money for advertising, positioning, and lobbying, not to mention the time needed to convert the participants. Energy may be the mother of all markets, but it's got inertia and is slow to change. You might as well call it the mother of all money pits.

Jay knew this, and understood that his $6 million, even if he extended it to $20 million, was barely enough to get Orrigen started, just started. He'd need to raise a lot more, like $50 million more, to show tantalizing results to a proper suitor who would buy him out.

When Vladik left at the end of the year, the plan he and Jay and the COO had laid out was this: They'd take my advice and try to prove that (what Jay deemed) directed evolution was useful for making these new fuels, using automation but not LOC miniaturization. There were decisions ahead about what equipment they'd buy and what services they'd contract, but any way they skinned it, the budgets for this were about $3 million for the first year. At the same time, Jay would run a skunkworks to miniaturize the process and have a lab-on-a-chip made at a foundry or at someone's academic lab. Within twelve months they'd have an ugly but persuasive prototype working, and that would cost them as much as $1 million dollars. Meanwhile, Jay would try to drum up $50 million of venture capital on terms he liked. There'd be day-long quarterly board meetings to monitor and direct the process, with a three-day retreat at the end of the following year when everybody, consultants included, would get together and make a decision about the direction the company would take. The outcome would rest heavily on what Jay found from the venture guys; yes, mostly guys. In the end, Jay would make a decision, but he would make it look like an inevitable conclusion based on the discussions of that hullabaloo.

CHAPTER 64 THE UZHE

RIGHT AWAY, Max began having the usual trouble with TTO, the same trouble he'd had with TLO at MIT. What's patentable? What's the Institute patent strategy? How did these collide with Max's habits? His patent applications were too speculative, or prophetic as he preferred to say, covering everything that might come to pass. The United States Patent and Trademark Office in Alexandria issued some broad patents like those, but when the patents were challenged in the courts, they failed there. The prophetic patents were too full of all-too-obvious extensions of common practice, or they lacked sufficient disclosure to meet the examiner's written description test for the patent claims. It was common knowledge that you could use Sanger sequencing to look at a gene, so was there a novel or inventive step if the filing claimed to apply a new sequencing method to identify that gene? Max said yes. TTO said no. The lawyers took whichever side they were paid to take. Max wanted a longer list to beef up his CV, and more individual licenses to beef up his checkbook. TTO felt that weak patents increased their expenses and exposure to litigation. They had to work harder to stay in place. Was it all worth it? Did these filings support science and its translation to practice and commerce, or was their sole function to generate attorneys' fees plus fear, uncertainty, and doubt?

Larisa Sertantiy, Armen's daughter and Max's IP counsel since the founding of Tiny Machines, said "File 'em and let the courts sort it out later." But it wasn't the lawyers' money, and it wasn't Max's either. It was the I's. Rich as the I was, its offices all operated on a POR and a budget, and Max was blowing TTO's. Sure, the I would try to recover their legal fees in various payments from the licensees, but there were no guarantees that filed patent applications would ever generate license fees.

Plus, Max was disliked at the same time he was revered. At first he was unctuous— "transparently insincere," others labeled it—and then mean and dismissive at the first sign he wasn't treated like a yogi. He had clout because Qasima had sought him for so long—and Principals had a lot of clout anyway—but he abused it. The battle with the TTO was over professionalism, courtesy, and transparency. Later, Nathalia Nguyen-Berry, TTO's director said in an interview with the Grey Lady's reporter, "He was like Leona Helmsley, treating everyone as if they existed only to carry his water. I think he was cowardly, operating undercover where tracks were hidden and you could only hope to trace the sources of influence in a decision. Within a year, we all knew he was trouble and wished he'd go back to MIT. He was a vicious s.o.b."

The idyllic setting in the hills didn't guarantee that the I would be an idyllic place to work, and Max was seeing to it that it wasn't. The fractious battles of the lowlands were being repeated.

CHAPTER 65 GENORMX INC. — SCENE I OF V

PORENOMICS' ODD ring was outside Max's audible range. "I'm terrible with names," he said. It did not escape Dykkur Ph'eer's, though. Dykkur was Max's attorney at Ph'eer, Dowd, and Sertantiy. A sycophant, Dykkur was also one of those guys Max listened to, sometimes.

"It sounds like a management consultancy for the porn industry," he said, scratching his bullet head during one of his thrice-annual visits to West Coast clients.

"Well, your head looks like a dinosaur dick."

Dykkur was also out West for a post-chemo residual disease scan at the Institute's Center for Synchrotron Health. He'd been assured his once-heartthrob flow would grow back, and he was well paid for the insults.

He slid Max a list of alternatives that his firm had paid yet another consultancy to suggest. Each worse than the next, there was Seqeon and Doublyndra and Pore Tech and DNAture and Genomarse, even Froodonics and Froodonix. Genormx, though, sounded big, sounded kind of fun, sounded like something you knew but didn't know. It sounded good. Max wanted one slight change, and the company became Genormax.

As for the Fucking Idiots in TTO? They weren't going to get in the way of Max moving forward on Genormax. The big idea, the new, new thing, was that sequencing was going to transform medicine, and it had already begun to happen on a small scale at places like Myriad Genetics. Max liked to preach and mix metaphors on the subject.

"Myriad is just one island in a huge sea of testing. Someday, there will be dozens, and then hundreds of islands. They'll get so close to each other that you'll hop from one to the other. Wherever you were going, you'll be able to walk across the sea of testing without falling in the drink. With these new molecular diagnostics, you'll be able to walk on water." For those who didn't yet believe he walked on water, this argument was supposed to persuade them he'd be able to do it soon enough.

Genormax was going to be the centerpiece of this new kind of medicine by cutting the cost of sequencing faster and further than had ever been done before. Then, using its own instruments, it would develop and commercialize molecular diagnostics that were better or cheaper than anything on the market. Max had set a goal of sequencing the entire genome for $100 in ten minutes within five years of funding. The goal seemed audacious at the time, but not too audacious.

"You can't lose if you meet that goal, can you?" he would say to doubters.

"If it rained gold pieces, we'd all hold out our hands," said the first VCs who heard him pitch.

Max knew that the HMRI-funded results he might be able to show within the next few years would make for only a thin story, short on details and confirmations. His hope was that on the strength of the Frood brand after the Tiny IPO, he would be able to raise a decent pile of cash for the new entity anyway. If all the dominoes fell in order, Genormax would complete the development and owe only minimal royalties to the I; minimal because only a few patents would be licensed from there. The crucial innovations needed to commercialize the pore sequencer would come from the company.

The names of his students and postdocs look like they came from a documentary about a Congressional investigation on the paucity of "Americans" in graduate education today. I can't help that. This is not a joke.

The Shanghainese Mo Xiulan, or Nico, was so gorgeous she could have been a Hollywood starlet, but not one in China. She wasn't beautiful enough to meet the standard there. Accepting that it was so, she let her high IQ and self-discipline take her through a doctorate in the School of Life Sciences at

Tsinghua University in Beijing.

There was only one reason for living away from everything she loved in urban China, in particular her husband and young child. Max Frood had all but promised he would put her in a top role in one of his companies. From there, she'd return to China with the imprimatur of having cofounded—it was that impression he left with her—a Silicon Valley venture-funded biotech company. And with that internationally recognizable stamp, she could return home to start a new biotech or investment company. She could become a professor in a business school or a school of science. Max Frood was her launching pad.

Her glamour and allure remained. On any given day, she might be wearing haute couture, or spandex that showcased her dancer's legs. Both stunned. One of the graduate students, on his first day in the lab and therefore the first day he had seen her, tripped over his own feet, opening his skull on a resin-impregnated quarried-sandstone countertop. One of the admins was unable to take her eyes off Nico as the two of them walked by each other, the admin cracking her neck at the extreme of rotation. She was out of work for four weeks and in a neck brace for another twelve. Other coworkers, male and female, took to wearing blinders so they weren't distracted when they were near her. Max instructed Nico to start work on controlling DNA's motion through the pore.

Very few Tibetans ever found their way into the stratosphere of biomedical research. Rinchen Gyadastang was one of them. His grandparents, exiled with His Holiness the Dalai Lama in 1959, had made their life's work public service to Tibetans everywhere, and so had his parents, and so had he. As a boy in Los Angeles, he joined the Tibetan Scientific Society, or TS2 as they refer to it, and began developing science and math course materials for Tibetan Schools in Exile. At UCLA he did research in the physics of complex systems with a focus on macromolecules. From there he went to Oxford on a Rhodes, receiving his DPhil for experimental work in the biophysics of molecular motors. That's where he met Qasima on one of her bimonthly shuttles between Oxbridge and the Santa Cruz Mountains. She thought he'd be a great asset for Max's pore genomics work. Max concurred. And so it was that the monkish Tibetan found himself at Lobitos Farm, trying to develop a method for identifying bases as a strand of DNA was pulled through a tiny orifice. As always, he was in touch with his worldwide community in exile, mentoring them and giving money when he could.

Max told both postdocs he'd let their grants expire if they didn't get some fundable results within two years, and he'd be the sole arbiter of whether they were fundable. After that pronouncement, as if to increase everyone's agitation, he put two experienced graduate students, Xue Feng—she called herself Fanny—from Hong Kong and Miyuki Schwartz from Tsukuba, to work on the same problems, independently of the postdocs. "There's no team in the I," he reminded them. Another of his maxims.

CHAPTER 66 MARY-CLAIRE KING

For approximately $3600, a diagnostics company headquartered in Utah will determine whether you are carrying some particularly pernicious inherited mutations in the genes called BRCA1 and BRCA2. These mutations increase the likelihood for developing BReast and ovarian CAncers, and so are called susceptibility genes. The price is significantly higher than other genetic tests. A karyotype, a test characterizing the number and visual quality of chromosomes, is about $500 and so is a test for Fragile X, a cognitive impairment syndrome. A panel assaying forty inborn errors of metabolism is $60. Whatever differences exist in technology and application between BRCA and the lower-cost tests, the price difference is all about volume and competition, and in the case of BRCA there's been no competition since the test was introduced in the late 1990s. However, if the BRCA findings may be lifesaving and can't be obtained any other way, and you and your insurers are up to it, then you can be like more than a hundred thousand women who send their blood samples to Myriad Genetics every year.

In 1972, Janet Rowley showed that certain leukemias and lymphomas could be traced to genetic mutations that sometimes develop in white blood cells. That was the beginning of cancer genetics. In 1990, Mary-Claire King, a mathematician-turned-biologist, announced the discovery of a RING, a really interesting new gene, a cancer susceptibility gene on the long arm of chromosome 17 in a region called 17q21. After a seventeen-year pursuit, she and her team had shown to the standards of peer-reviewed publications that somewhere in that RING were anomalies found almost exclusively in women with early-onset familial breast cancer. It was a landmark finding because it confirmed the then-very-controversial idea of a heritable predisposition to cancer. And for a complex disease expected to involve many genetic and environmental factors, to have found an almost monogenic dependence (in the population that has it) was remarkable. A year later, King named this gene BRCA1.

In genetics-speak, the opposite of complex disease is Mendelian disease. For Mendelian disease it's true that if you have the gene, you'll get the disease, and if you have the disease you have the gene. There are exceptions—like the Woody Guthrie's Huntington's Chorea, for which an excess of the trinucleotide CAG on the fourth chromosome, at 4p16.3 is decisive—but most diseases are not Mendelian. BRCA1 is not Mendelian for breast cancer. Carriers are much more likely to develop somatic mutations that lead to the disease, but "much more likely" is not the same as certainty.

In Thomas Kuhn's The Structure of Scientific Revolutions, there's a before and there's an after. After the paradigm shift—that is, a profound new finding or a new interpretation of old ones—the scientist's worldview shifts. If not a paradigm shift, King's discovery of BRCA1 let loose a big ripple in the fabric of understood disease and genetics. It also led to a race to nail down the precise location of BRCA1 and to discover the gene's sequence. While her work confirmed that a gene was there, the discovery alone did not yet have predictive power. Without the gene sequence itself, you couldn't test someone's blood and tell whether he or she the bad-acting variants, nor could you predict whether they were going to develop breast, ovarian tumor, pancreatic, prostate, or even uterine cancers.

CHAPTER 67 MYRIAD

KING'S EPIC paper in the journal SCIENCE started the race to track down BRCA1 and commercialize it as a diagnostic or prognostic test. Less than six months after its publication, Mark Skolnick, of that 1980 genome mapping paper with David Botstein, and Wally Gilbert, the Nobelist, cofounded Myriad Genetics in Salt Lake City, Utah. In 1994, Skolnick, still at the University of Utah, and leading an international team of forty, became the first to clone BRCA1. Myriad filed a patent for the gene and some of its mutant forms. Myriad went on to clone another important gene, BRCA2. In 1996 they introduced BRACAnalysis, a predictive test of hereditary breast and ovarian cancers.

Back in those days, twenty years after Sanger but still more than a decade before modern high-throughput sequencing, all those sequencing and linkage analysis tasks were very difficult. Efficiency, using your discoveries to the fullest, buys time or money, and gets you to the most important and patentable discoveries first. Efficiency was one of Skolnick's great strengths.

But will it save your life to know that you are carrying the BRCA1 and BRCA2 mutations? Will it even be useful? This is not the black and white of Mendelian disease. There are hundreds of different mutations on those genes. This is a gray scale in many dimensions. The answer is buried somewhere in statistics and the complement of variants you carry. Interpreting the finding depends on knowing the outcomes of many women harboring those BRCA variations. How did their sisters and mothers fare? After a cancer in one breast, what happened to the other one five years later? What about her ovaries? At what age was the onset? What effect did chemo and radiation therapy have? Were they smokers? When did they have children? Combining your test results and your answers to all these questions and more, along with the myriad details of your own BRCA, and sifting these through the findings from thousands upon thousands of other patients, BRACAnalysis informs prognosis and helps you and your doctor plot a course of action, a course of action which might include a prophylactic lopping off of two healthy breasts for fear of what might happen if you let them be. That's harsh, but taking a step back, would you rather say "Farewell Angelina" or "Bye-bye, boobs?"

This tale illustrates the fact that the discovery of the gene sequence is just the beginning of the challenge in making good medicine from King's discovery. There's always the hope that a noxious and newly discovered gene will help pharmaceutical companies develop new drugs to fight the products and processes that the gene makes or enables. If that's the case, then we all know how regulatory agencies like the FDA, the Food and Drug Administration, intervene to ensure that a drug is safe and effective. Effective really means that the positive effect it has or may have outweighs the negative effect it has. All drugs have side effects, negative effects, so the positive effect has to be big enough in a large-enough percentage of the target population to warrant its use.

What if it's a test? There are no side effects to measurement, so why not just do it? One part of the answer is cost and the other is liability.

If one woman in 1000 carried threatening BRCA mutations, and if all women were given the $3600 test, there'd be a social burden of $3.6 million for the identification of one woman whose life might be extended as a result of the findings. Even if, as a result of interventions taken in response to the finding, every such woman lived six years more than she otherwise might have, that cost, $600,000 per year of life saved is considered twelve times too high for society to bear. That forces Myriad to find subpopulations in which the likelihood of carrying the mutations is much higher, and that group is Ashkenazi Jews. For these women—and remember, my father Isador Stein is an Ashkenazi Jew, so this hits close to home—about one in twelve is carrying the mutations. For most other healthy women, the insurers say the HER, the health economic research, doesn't pencil out. Those insurers are the ultimate regulators of healthcare, everywhere, but certainly in the USA. Other regulators, for instance the College of American Pathologists or the Centers for Medicare & Medicaid Services, but very rarely the FDA, intervene only to certify that a test offered for sale exceeds agreed-upon standards or best practices that confirm its statistical significance.

Liability comes into play because it's not really true that the measurement has no side effects. The doctor and patient are going to embark on a course of therapy based on the findings, and the therapy is probably irreversible and may have life-altering consequences, so the findings themselves had better be statistically significant; otherwise, *tag!* you're the defendant. If you might be the defendant someday, you want to have very good insurance against such lawsuits. Insurance costs money, and that fact acts to even further narrow the population to whom it makes sense to give the assay in the first place.

What all this means is that before the diagnostics company, Myriad in this case, can offer their product, they must collect samples from many, certainly hundreds, typically thousands, of patients. Then they combine these with patient health and therapeutic records and family histories, correlate those findings with outcomes, and come up with a set of rules, a logical or mathematical model, a simplification of reality that more or less accurately predicts the known outcomes using the observed inputs. They'll refine the rules in a process called "tweaking" until its prediction accuracy meets whatever standard the biostatistician has specified. Biostatisticians are like priests who sprinkle holy water. Until scientific findings have been dampened with it, the results are missing an essential blessing.

After the blessing, the predictive algorithm is ready for validation against another dataset of diagnostic results and patient records and outcomes, a dataset that was not used to develop it. Ideally, the equations will accurately predict the known outcomes for this cohort, too. If it doesn't, then it's dismissed as "too brittle." After a lot of finger-pointing, head-scratching, garment-rending, and flesh-tearing, and after more data collection, at great expense of time and money, and after having given the competition an opportunity to be first to market, and possibly after removal of the biostatistician or the CEO, the model is tweaked until it works well on both the training set and a test set.

Linear regression is sometimes taught in high school algebra. Given a set of observations, that is, a first dataset or training set, with controlled inputs $\{input_i\}$ and measured outputs $\{output_i\}$, and an equation, like this,

$$output_i = A \times input_i + B$$

simple methods exist for finding the two constants A and B that "best" fit the observations. If, when applied to a second dataset or test set of input/output pairs, the predicted outputs are "close" to the actual outputs, the model is deemed to be good. A diagnostics company does exactly the same thing, except that there are many input variables rather than only one, the variables may be qualitative, not quantitative; the relationships between input and output may be nonlinear; there may be important time dependences; the data is expensive and time consuming to collect; instead of linear regression the methods are called nonlinear regression, neural networks, machine learning, or even something else; and breasts and lives and loves are riding on the quality of the insight-giving model.

For a diagnostic of complex disease, the genetic test itself is only a small part of what's required to deliver quality medical care. The moby may have been *avant-garde* and expensive in the days of Myriad's founding, but in today's world, one on the verge of sequencing an entire 3,000,000,000-base human genome for $1000, the cost of sequencing the 100,000-base BRCA1 is miniscule. Further, there are dozens of commercial labs and thousands of academic labs that could perform the sequencing, and publicly available software that could help read the sequence. But that information won't get you very far without all the patient studies, replete with patient records. Myriad, and the other so-called molecular diagnostics companies, the MDx companies, are really data warehouses using moby to help with acquisition. The moby has become generic, and the next generation of these companies may not even bother to collect samples or process them themselves. Rather, they might dedicate themselves to analyzing data sent to them by central labs already servicing hospitals and clinics. Those central labs have become very efficient at transporting samples from the site of collection, be it hospital bedside or clinic exam room, to the lab itself. The MDx company will control the big databases on which the analysis is based. As in social media, their product is you, or your friends and family. Software eats everything, as the adage goes, and it will eat a lot of medicine, too.

DEAR Reader, you might have asked along the way, "How did Myriad patent naturally occurring sequences like BRCA1 and BRCA2 or its mutations?" The answer is that mistakes were made. Only years later were they corrected, or partially corrected, thanks to the unanimous decision by SCOTUS in *Association of Molecular Pathology v. Myriad.* The ruling states that naturally occurring sequences of genomic DNA are not patentable, and then it muddies the waters by introducing the notion that naturally occurring sequences of CDNA are patentable. But the ruling changes little for Myriad in the commercial sphere. Why? Myriad has patented methods of diagnostic analysis that it will use—along with fear, uncertainty, and doubt in time-honored tradition—to protect its market dominance for as long as it can.

That Myriad was able to make those diagnostic inventions while protected by gene patents that have since been declared invalid, and that they sued their competitors aggressively during that period, that's a different matter. The company's founders were brilliant, but the founders and shareholders and their heirs were lucky that bad law gave them nearly twenty years of monopoly during which time they built a tough-to-defeat empire.

After the events of Orrigen and Genormx, and after the invalidating of gene patents, Vladik and I had a chance to talk about the company. "Myriad is like modern Russia, built on a pile of lies," he said.

"That's harsh. They had the law on their side at the time."

"But they sued like they had virtue on their side."

"That's the American way. They had corporate virtue on their side. The CEO says, 'If we didn't do it, some angry shareholder would come after us for fiduciary irresponsibility.'"

"*Bozhe moi.* 'They made me do it.' Self-serving bullshit. So who rights this wrong now?"

"No one. They're the winners in the new meritocracy, the robber barons redux."

"Robber barons says it all, doesn't it?"

"In the new Newspeak, yes.

The losers of those battles before *AMP v. Myriad* are pissed. They were right all along, and forced out of the business. All they have to show for it is a moral victory, and that's cold comfort while the Myriad fortunes stand. But the only undoing of bad law is the making of good law. The consequences of the bad remain for a long time. Remember that thing called slavery?

And for other companies pursuing other genetic markers, now that sequencing is nearly free, and it's agreed that the genes are not patentable, there should be big power shifts ahead in molecular diagnostics.

Back in the day, Myriad might have had to invent special moby techniques to extract precisely the right DNA fragment, thus permitting them to devote the minimum cost or effort to sequencing. They would file the patent and hope USPTO would look kindly on it based on that moby. Now anyone can order chemistries ready-made to extract the chromosomal regions of interest and sequence them with an instrument not much bigger than a desktop computer. The ante, the barrier to entry, has been lowered to almost zero, making it much harder, maybe impossible, to protect, using patents, any sequence within the genome, any more than you can protect a mathematical result, or a natural law.

How then can an inventor or a company protect one of nature's genes? Keep it a trade secret. If it's not that hard to find then the secret may not be a secret for long. And, if it remains a secret, its value is limited because what patient wants to be treated on the basis of secret findings? That's not scientific medicine. That's witchcraft.

The database of test results can be protected, though. The database and the rules of analysis, the algorithms, are trade secrets, constantly evolving, never to be patented, and expensive to reproduce. Myriad earned many billions in revenues over the years before *AMP v. Myriad*. The data they collected in the process, invaluable to the analysis of each and every new sample, becomes the barrier to entry for new competitors. The quality of service, the relationships with customers—that is, insurers, hospitals, drug companies, physicians, and patients—differentiates them from a new company starting from scratch with none of that; LinkedIn as compared to ClonedIn, again. The innovation is not in the moby. It's in the user experience, or the UX as software aficionados would say. As MDx drifts toward the software business, UX becomes an-all-the-more-appropriate term.

The researcher who first discovers a gene will be heralded, but will not become rich, nor will his or her host institution. The finding must be published to be useful, and there will be no patents for it. If the researchers once had dreams, as Max had, of reaping fat fees or thick sheaves of founder's equity in exchange for licensing rights, those dreams will need recalibration. The rewards will go to the commercial entities that spend far more than the cost of discovery in the service of assembling the protectable database and customer-facing UX. The specialized technical skills of the researcher are not so valuable in building those businesses.

In the case of Myriad, which compiled its database enabled by rulings that have since been overturned, and patents soon to expire anyway, the database still confers a competitive advantage. How long that advantage will stand is not known.

Following the Summer of Snowden—when revelations about the surveillance state proved that no company holding your data records can protect them from unwarranted search and seizure—some communications companies are figuring out how to provide services without warehousing the data. MDx companies should do the same. If you are the product, and you *are* the product for the diagnostics company that use your records as part of the analysis of the next paying customer's sample, do you want your data warehoused with parties that you know are going to give it up to the NSA after the application of only the slightest bit of pressure?

CHAPTER 68 CLINICAL CHEMISTRY

Centuries ago, doctors first began to quantitatively analyze precious bodily fluids, counting blood cells per unit volume, categorizing that count by type, measuring concentrations of electrically important sodium and potassium ions, or measuring molecular by-products of metabolism, e.g., serum creatinine, which serves as a marker of kidney health. Struggles persisted between vitalists, like Frankenstein's creator Mary Shelley, who believed that life's molecules were empowered by a higher life force and could not be properly analyzed in a test-tube, and mechanists like René Descartes or Hermann von Helmholtz, mostly chemists or physiologists who believed that life reduced to physical principles and chemical properties alone. Findings in German, Austrian, Swedish, and British labs, where researchers systematically sought pathologic changes in chemical makeup of bodily fluids to guide diagnosis and therapy, migrated slowly to the diagnostic toolkit of a few physicians. In 1843, the words "klinisch-chemischen laboratorium," or clinical chemical laboratory, appeared in print for the first time, and in 1895, the University of Pennsylvania opened the first laboratory of clinical medicine in America. It was called the Laboratory of Clinical Medicine.

There followed decades of scientific development, construction of facilities, training of physicians, and often-futile attempts to retrain those physicians hanging on to the old ways where intuition rather than quantification was the principle tool of diagnosis. Forty years in the desert usually, but not always, suffices to rid society of old habits. Even late into the twentieth century, results from clinical labs were tossed if they didn't confirm the physician's intuition. As quality improved, where quality meant day-to-day consistency and calibration between different laboratories and establishment of the range of normal, more physicians were swayed. And for all those who felt too little testing was going on, there were others who felt that taking oral histories and sharing face time with patients had given way to overreliance on test results. But go to any hospital today and you will see nurses and doctors carrying sheets of paper detailing patients' lab results for batteries of standard and patient-specific tests. They've become entirely dependent on the labs, much as a surgeon is fully dependent on her scalpel, or an internist on his stethoscope.

And those labs? They're shrinking. Once upon a time they were barely a closet. Then they occupied floors of hospitals or hundreds of thousands of square feet in centralized facilities servicing many hospitals. On Palo Alto's University Avenue you can find a miniaturized and automated version of such a lab. This "wellness center" from Theranos is installed in a drug store. It is the product of a decade's work initiated by Elizabeth Holmes when she quit Stanford at nineteen. Hundreds of the tests offered by traditional labs are or will soon be available at a disruptive price, delivering a favorably disruptive user experience, and their reliability certified by the usual fleet of regulators.

CHAPTER 69 THE ARC

PHYSICISTS LOVE universality, a fancy name given to the mathematization of generalizations, and here I'm overgeneralizing. To them, the phase transitions of magnets can be made to look mathematically identical to the percolation of water through loosely packed coffee grounds. The very notion sends thrills through them, the physicists. What does the equation tell them, they ask, if the same one describes such disparate phenomena? At a minimum, it's telling them that after having solved the problem in the first instance, they've also solved it in the second, or as Feynman tautologized, the same equations have the same solutions.

The relationship between advisor and student—and in this case postdocs fall into the category of student—follows a universal curve. At first, particularly for a graduate student, the Principal Investigator is revered. Why not? The PI has amassed seemingly measureless resources and has a dozen or more people working for her. She seems to know answers to all the questions, has time to hobnob with esteemed visitors, and to reflect on problems she might want to work on in the future, and yet, she is never seen holding a pipette. She is a thinker! She is a doer! More than that, she gets things done for her. She is a lord. The new graduate student says to anyone who will listen, "I am but a grateful vassal. Oh, PI! Pour water into my vessel that I may carry it for you. Fill me with your wisdom. My PI will get me my next job. Someday I will be one of her spiritual children, and my students her grandchildren, all carrying the imprint of having been in her group. The PI will proudly point to my bench or my papers and take credit for what I've accomplished, thereby acknowledging the value of what I have done. I will owe her everything."

Within two years, the student will have a new take on things. The PI is not a good listener, so the student's own ideas are suppressed in favor of the PI's. Yet, the PI's range of activities, once seen as marvelous, will be seen as the reason the PI is not a good listener. She has a broad understanding of the grand implications of the work, but little understanding of the challenges of getting it done. The PI is not listening because she has nothing to offer about the details. "Oh, the details are easy," says the PI. "Next presentation, please," says the PI at Group Meeting, the biweekly review the PI uses to find out what is going on in her own lab. The student thinks the PI has something like ADHD, hopping from project to project, avoiding some in which she's lost interest and focusing hard on others she thinks are cool. To her friends, including the other students and postdocs, the student says, "The PI is good at getting credit, but we do all the work. The PI doesn't even know what work to do. She has bad pipetting technique, anyway. She'd never get any publishable results. Her ideas aren't even that good. I am a serf, and not so happy about it anymore." She grinds out the next two years of indentured service. In her darkest moments, she imagines herself strapped to the bench by a twenty-first-century restraint, with feed bags—designed for hands-free operation so she won't miss a beat with her samples—conveyed on rails above her head, their arrival timed (for maximum productivity) to her cycles of metabolism, alertness, and fertility. Her resentment builds because she knows that the PI will take all the credit at the end, even though the student is now working on her own idea, which the PI dissed for a long time but has finally recognized as worthy and claims as hers.

In her final year, she reflects on the PI's contribution and says to herself, "In all this time, in all of our meetings, at most only once was the PI ahead of me on understanding my experiments." The student now divides her time between writing up her results for her thesis, writing up her results for publication, writing a grant application for the PI, helping a new graduate student and a new postdoc plan out new and different experimental programs, writing a grant application that will fund her as a postdoc, wondering whether she wants to continue as a postdoc or go into industry, and worrying about where she'll be working in her next position. She is particularly resentful of the PI's critiques and pickiness about style in the manuscript for publication. Her critiques of the PI have become personal and sound like a discourse on income inequality. To her, students are the oppressed class, and the PI is The Man, with her $190,000 salary and her three-, four-, and five thousand dollar a day consulting fees, and paid-for boondoggles in Hawaii or Snowbird or Prague, and occasional stock payouts when a company she is advising gets liquid. The pie is getting smaller and the PI has a big slice only because she is older. At the student's moments of peak agony, she is so furious she must avoid the PI so as not to say what she feels, because she is beholden to the PI for her beneficent letter of support.

She is passing through a scientific adolescence. When a few years have passed, she will come back to the PI's lab, have beers and cake, celebrate a paper, a grant, an appointment, a marriage, or a child. The young students will look up with some reverence to her no-longer-adolescent self, an intellectual heir or "daughter" of the PI, and all will be forgiven, and most forgotten.

And all of what I've just said is universal. Although your mileage may vary, universal is universal. For Max's students, the lows were lower, but the great results produced within the Frood Group made the highs higher and the cakes bigger. His students got jobs and his favorite students got great jobs. Maybe the exception to universality was that not all was forgiven.

Volume 3

Genormx

CHAPTER 70 THE TWO INNOVATIONS

TWO YEARS after Max's arrival, the Frood Group had become largest at the I, a force of nature spreading out beyond the control of Qasima or anyone else. The group had taken more than 10 percent of all the lab space at Lobitos Farm, and was still growing. The staff of twenty-five could not be supported on Max's generous I-funding alone. Government money had been applied for and some had been awarded. A grant from the Ginger Mascarpone Foundation paid for one of his lines of work, and he had applications pipelined into all the leading private money pools. Max established an easy internal review process for spending decisions. The group was awash in the stuff of bioengineering: computers, reagents and equipment, and with the stuff his researchers made the advances that justified additional funding from the same and from other agencies.

Beyond the walls of Lobitos Farm, there were groups working on pore sequencing in Europe and the US, and even in Asia. Naturally occurring channels in cell membranes were proteins, so most scientists accepted as fact that those macromolecules would be central to pore sequencing. There had already been a few billion years of evolutionary development on them, and there was much to learn by their study, if only they would give up their secrets. Of course, the proteins observed in nature had evolved to solve a different problem.

Max started two initiatives to find an optimal pore. One was based on directed evolution and the second surveyed the landscape of viral proteins. Viral ones made sense to him—although most practitioners investigated cellular products—because viruses had evolved to inject DNA through cell membranes. Directed evolution was so much in favor that it was hardly a coincidence that he and his old roommate Jay Orrix had both decided to use it to attack their respective problems. Even though Nico, the postdoc, had all of Tiny Machines' instruments and IP available to her, she decided to throw robotics and human labor at the problem rather than build a Tiny-style LOC. Faced with a similar problem back at Orrigen, I had recommended exactly the same brute-force assault. Although Max had tried to keep the two approaches separate—believing, he said, that publish or perish competition among his staff would be healthy for the group—Nico and the grad student, Xue (Fanny) Feng, ignored him in favor of sharing solutions to common challenges. Fanny devised and built a testing platform, and with it she identified several promising viral proteins that they could use to start the DE process. The young women openly if not brazenly ignored Max's directive. Max was, in the end, practical, and too busy to micromanage their work. If they failed, he'd abandon them both. If they succeeded, he'd claim credit.

In parallel with optimal pore design, Genormax needed an innovation in sensing, or base-calling. Only a fool, Max explained, would separate detection challenges from those of moving—transmigrating, in the jargon—that DNA molecule through the hole; the two problems were too intertwined. Transit time would play a part, a very big part he insisted, in choosing the preferred sense technique. Max was pleased that the rest of the world was determined to build a sensor optimized for rapid transmigration, because that kept them "locked down at the wrong watering hole," in his phraseology. He said that a raft of better sensing solutions would be available to whoever managed to slow transmigration, as Nico and Fanny were intent on doing. That left Rinchen, the other postdoc, and Miyuki, the other graduate student, to work on practical means of base detection.

The prevailing view was that the pore's ability to conduct electricity would depend on which of the four bases A, C, G, or T was in it, and that by hooking up some sensitive electronics you could detect each base on a transmigrating string as it slipped through. A slower moving molecule would give you more time to 'see' the change in conduction, improving the signal and reducing the error of measurement. That's why Max was so insistent on slowing down the DNA's passage through the little aperture. He was also contrarian in his view of conductance and how it would vary.

High speed conductance-sensing of a million pores on a single substrate would require that something like a computer memory be embedded in a futuristic LOC derived from Tiny IP. While conceived to serve the dual purposes of making Max a fortune and delivering the best performance to Genormax's putative customers, the estimated $50 million development cost of the new LOC put it outside what any early stage company could afford. If Tiny Machines was going to be the platform, Max needed another approach.

Physicists know about scattering. Ernest Rutherford was already a Nobelist in 1911 when he scattered helium nuclei off of gold atoms, divining in the analysis that an atom is a tiny planetoid, a result that led to Bohr's model and beyond. In 1912, Max von Laue demonstrated X-ray diffraction in crystals. Taking his work a step further, the elder, William Henry, and the younger, William Lawrence Bragg diffracted X-rays off rock salt in 1913, interpreted the pattern, and determined the structure. For their efforts, Laue won the Nobel Prize in Physics in 1914 and the Braggs did the same in 1915. Without X-ray crystallography we would be almost blind to crystal structure, and certainly to the structures of DNA and hemoglobin that were revealed in the Cavendish Laboratory where Bragg the Younger was Director. Scattering electrons off atoms and imaging them is electron microscopy, patented in 1931 by Laue's student Leó Szilárd. He was also the physicist who first described a neutron chain reaction and later went on to persuade Einstein to persuade FDR to start what became the Manhattan Project. In the 1950's, Szilárd converted to moby.

Max felt in his physicist bones that scattering might be the key to detection, and that a modified SEM, a scanning electron microscope, could be used to discriminate one type of nucleotide from the other. The idea was that the SEM's thin beam of electrons focused on the pore would scatter subject to the electron densities of the different molecular structures of each base migrating through. Rinchen and Miyuki ended up working together, following the lead of Nico and Fanny. There were too many large and small tasks to get right, and too many possibilities for getting something wrong. The mission was out of reach for one person.

There were, for example, lengthy molecular orbital calculations to estimate how the scattering would change as the beam drifted off the pore and as the molecule was pulled through it, or as it rotated around; each effect averaging and reducing the signal that might differentiate the four base types. Methods like these were widely used in the more mathematical sciences to pull signals from noise, so the team learned them, adapted them to this problem, and then coded them up. There were sample handling platforms called stages to be built, much of that work drawing on what Nico and Fanny had already done. Not long into their effort, they realized that they were a team of four, not two teams of two or four teams of one. Max's belief, his very loud and humiliating assertion that everything they were trying to do was "easy as a Macau escort," was his dream, not their reality.

In retrospect, it's all easy to see that Max had chosen a path optimized for his future royalty streams, not for HMRI's glory, and not for the advancement of science. At the time, he alone understood the road he was headed down, and it didn't look dark to him. At first he jeopardized the careers of his students and postdocs. Later, he'd be jeopardizing the careers of many people who worked in his companies, and also, whether you find them sympathetic or not, the fortunes of his investors. But that's in retrospect.

Nico and Fanny and Miyuki and Rinchen weren't terribly concerned about the commercial potential. They were concerned about the publication potential, which they all believed to be very high. Unlike most others in the Frood Group, they were able to work together, and that was its own reward. They became the Beam Team, a silly name that only increased their enjoyment of it. For two years they plugged away at optimizing the pores and developing an e-beam detection system. One got married. A married one had a baby. There were boyfriends and girlfriends who came and went. They worked late nights and weekends. They made and shared meals and tears. The experimental program lagged, and then it leapt, and then it lagged. Visitors came and went, from Tokyo, Shanghai, Beijing, Shenzhen, Singapore, Berlin, London, Cambridge, Menlo Park, Paris, Moscow, Seattle, DC, Cambridge, San Diego, Tel Aviv, and more.

Max dropped by weekly. But the four of them were so spun up, so much a team, he was an outsider and couldn't contribute much. He set aggressive goals, but he couldn't help them get there except by spending money or lending his name to a grant or a special appeal for funds to the powers at the Institute. There was a lesson there, which his students learned, but he did not; part-time contributions usually amount to nothing if part-time is less than most of the time. Even Max, with his IQ in the stratosphere, couldn't be a technical contributor while spread so thin you could see through him. Delbrück said, in Bangalore of all places, that you can't afford to work one day a week on an important problem, even if you are Feynman.

Two years into it, after having solved problems in synthetic chemistry, lipid bilayer engineering, electron beam steering, photomultiplier noise statistics, signal deconvolution and many more exotic disciplines, a pore protein had been engineered. Through it the Beam Team dragged a single strand of well characterized bacterial DNA, and accurately detected its every base with a modified but off-the-shelf SEM. Patents were filed, manuscripts prepared, and champagne was poured, and then poured again, although champagne was not the drink of the mostly Asian Frood Group, so many tea bags were dipped, too.

Some technical problems remained, and those were left for Genormax to solve. The goal of sequencing a whole human genome for $100 in ten minutes was targeted for five years off, and it seemed at least that far away. The prototype they'd made had a single pore, but they'd need to have 10,000 or even 100,000 pores on a single substrate, and they'd need to figure out how to load thousands of DNA strands into those pores. They envisioned a 1000-

fold speedup their detection and computation five years into the future, multiplexing to keep up with the pore parallelism. The required 100,000-fold improvement seemed quite out of reach. The team knew very little about repeatability and reliability, both of which would be very important. Better protein engineering was required, too, but of exactly what sort, they weren't sure. And there were commercial questions which drove technical questions, none of which they addressed, even when Max hijacked a weekly meeting to discuss them.

CHAPTER 71 REPUTATIONS AND RESIDENCES

IN THE months leading up to the demonstration of the prototype, Max was busy explaining his dream to investors. The picture he painted was vague, necessarily vague because the prototype didn't exist, and the technology it embodied had not been licensed to Genormax. Nor was there a team in place to make it come true. The future he described had to be particularly grand to make up for these not-so-small deficiencies. The narrative was all about macro trends in moby, clinical chemistry, computing, and medicine, and how they were going to converge in one giant transformation, or "cluster fuck of the status quo," as Max put it.

He began with Armen, who listened patiently, with interest, asked mildly probing questions, and having decided what he was going to say before having begun the meeting, said, "I really think it's too early Max. Why don't you let me know when things are a little further along?"

Max was perplexed. He thought Armen loved him. So he Skyped Dykkur Ph'eer in Boston and asked him to decode the message. Without telling Max that he lived in a bubble, Dykkur explained that Max's block sale of Tiny Machines stock was a cardinal sin in Armen's eyes.

"You stabbed him in the back, hit 'em blow below the belt, blind-sided him, sucker-punched him, cheated on him, cuckold—"

"OK! I get it."

"Then you should be happy that Armen hasn't blackballed you with other investors," Dykkur concluded.

"Those guys were fucking me all along, so too bad if they can't take a joke," Max replied.

Dykkur encouraged him to make reparations. "Just keep him informed and don't ask him for money. Those assholes like to give free advice, so ask him for advice."

"I do need a team, though. I need someone who is going to run this whole thing for me."

"That's the tradeoff. If you come to your investors with a CEO, or even better, with a team, then they think you're ready to make money. But on the other hand, they think the founders are going to run out of gas and will need to be fired later, or maybe sooner. So when you bring them a team you're bringing them a," and here Dykurr made air quotes with his fingers, "founders problem."

"But you just told me they *wanted* the managers."

"They're schizophrenic. Whatever you have, they want something else. Perfect for them would be for you to show up with a management team ready to work for free and then walk away politely when the VCs no longer have any use for them."

Max interrupted. "That's likely."

"Right. Not."

"And you're sure I've got to give up control from the beginning?"

"From the beginning." Dykkur picked up his discourse. "Investors, what they really want from a guy like you? Demonstrated willingness to bend over and grease up."

Max winced.

Dykkur continued, "Someone like you, an academic, not an entrepreneur."

"What the fuck do you mean, not an entrepreneur? And HMRI is not an academic institution, it's a foundation."

"A distinction without a difference here, Max. You have to know, the word is out on you already. Entrepreneurial is not the same as entrepreneur."

"Who said that?"

"Attorney client privilege, Max."

"Fuck you. Whatever."

"For entrepreneurial academics, the investors want to bring in their own management team from the start, people they trust. With them controlling the narrative, you'll get credit for having dumped a pile of lab notebooks on their laps, and not much else. Then they can cut you a very very thin slice of pie."

"This is Tiny Machines all over again," Max cried. "But this time, I've incorporated already. I've got staff ready to jump in. We're way further along."

"Incorporation is worth a few hundred bucks. Unless you are ready to quit HMRI and build the team yourself, take on the responsibility and the risk, it's going to play out like it did before. That doesn't seem like you, going all in. Are you ready to quit HMRI?"

Max scrunched up his face as if Dykkur was out of his mind. "No, that's not for me. Too risky!"

"Then you can expect single digit equity."

"Low single digits last time around. The fuckers."

"Then I think you have to find someone other than Armen, or give Armen a blowjob. Then high single digit equity."

"Not my thing," Max deadpanned.

"Mid single-digits, then. Well, it should be your thing. Everybody needs to know how to give good head in this business, or at least be ready to pay for someone else to give good head."

"I didn't think he'd have taken it so personally," Max confided. "It's just business, isn't it?"

"Yes, and that sale hurt their ability to do business. They could give a rat's ass about whether you were ever liquid, but when you sold that stock, and your broker shorted it, you destroyed all the deals Papken had queued up." Dykkur paused rather than finish and explain out loud what a bone-headed, selfish, shortsighted move it was.

"OK, OK, OK!" and Max paused too. "I get it. I'll invite him to the demo and I'll line up other investors."

Max had become pretty well known. His reputation as a bold problem solver in bioengineering, burnished by his HMRI appointment and his now quite long string of publications and grant awards, did give him some cred among investors, some of whom sought him out for their brain trusts. Armen had been very discreet, very gentlemanly, avuncular even, in keeping Max's shortcomings to himself, so the Max the world knew was the Boy Genius, the scientific founder of Tiny Machines. His contract with HMRI permitted him to consult a few days a month, and he'd been gradually filling out his calendar with meetings on Sand Hill Road. He had thought, or believed, or hoped he was above having to grub about for capital.

A third of all venture capital invested originates on Sand Hill Road in Menlo Park. There is no greater concentration of VCs anywhere, and the locals would have you believe they invented the business. But Melville wrote in 1851, "People in Nantucket invest their money in whaling vessels, the same way that you do yours in approved state stocks bringing in good interest." And, no less a VC pioneer than Arthur Rock told someone who told someone that some queen sent her explorer over the edge of the world, offering him a piece of the return for his sweat. And is the time-honored tradition of rape and pillage in wartime not but a precursor of the same? Of course venture capital wasn't invented in Silicon Valley, but its VCs have shaped the game.

Today, Sand Hill Road is a place and also a figure of speech, referring to all the venture firms in Menlo Park and Palo Alto, including those on palm-lined University Avenue in Palo Alto or in a Stanford-owned business park near PARC, Xerox's famed Palo Alto Research Center.

THE drive from Lobitos Farm to prime real estate on Sand Hill takes about forty minutes; most of it in low gears on switchbacked roads. Skyline is a ridge road dividing the heavily populated Mid-Peninsula Silicon Valley from the rural, forested rolling hills that run down to the ocean. On the westward ocean-facing side of Skyline, there are only a few houses along Lobitos Creek Road as it climbs to the ridge. In their yards you might see rusting RVs, a 1969 Dodge Dart jacked-up and unshod, loud barking dogs on chains, and occasional signs that read "Make my day but don't make me shoot you." Descending eastward from the crest into what some consider the center of the known universe, or at least civilization, are expansive estates with views of San Francisco Bay and the sometimes-snow-covered East Bay Hills, horse properties in cleared glens, and even icons of American architecture priced like van Gogh's. These were the homes of rock stars, Fortune 500 CEOs, Olympic champions, Stanford professors cashing in, and Silicon Valley VCs. In more modest homes, occupants grew pot or cooked meth for a living. Those winding roads, with redwoods on one side and cliffs on the other, might be potholed or might be freshly paved, but would sport almost as many bicycles as cars, except on weekends, when two wheelers always outnumbered the cars.

As Max discovered the gay nightlife in Mountain View and high-stakes floating poker games in Woodside, where he took money from rich guys who thought they were clever until they met him, he found more and more reasons to make the drive over the hill and into the valley. A year into his stay at the I, and ninety days after he'd gotten a DUI on a late night drive back to the I, he had bought himself a condo in Menlo Park. By the time he went out to raise money for Genormax, he was splitting his time evenly between his mountain home and his valley *pied-à-terre.*

ARTIST in Residence: You can take the artist from his garret—although never the garret from the artist—and give him a stipend so he can paint with a quiet stomach. That works, unless he needs an empty stomach to paint.

Poet in Residence: Take the poet from her cave beside the pond and give her a room of her own. Away from her inspirations, can she write? History must be the judge.

An Entrepreneur in Residence is not an entrepreneur while in residence. The EIR is a paid gig for an experienced entrepreneur with a successful endeavor behind her. While bathed in sunlight and sitting in her antiseptic office, a Bluetooth earpiece connecting her to phone or music, she is meant to help a VC firm manage a stable of less experienced entrepreneurs, to be an analyst of deals flowing through their queues, and to brew her new, new thing before leaving the residence to give birth to it with the firm's blessing.

After his conversation with Dykkur, Max decided that what he needed was an EIR, probably among those employed by Intuition Ventures, Pernicious Planet Absolute Return Partnership, Guzman, as the firm ABG was as usually known, or Venus NV. These firms had begun to pay him to review deals, to critique pitches, and even to participate in occasional strategy sessions where the partners got together to envision the future. They preferred to form new companies themselves, building the team without a "founders problem." They also looked to Max for ideas and trends that one of their EIRS could spin into gold. He was being considered for a retained appointment, a position on one of their advisory boards.

CHAPTER 72 3000 SAND HILL ROAD

ON A glorious Northern California winter day, the blue sky unflecked by a single cloud, the sun shining blindingly, the air 67 °F, a lunchtime ritual unfolded. By a roundabout at 3000 Sand Hill Road—the epicenter of venture capital—dozens of partners, associates, analysts, secretaries, and supplicants waited in line by trucks that brought in food from the corners of the world.

Max's favorite eating in all of Silicon Valley was Sameer's Samosas, but he would sample Zamir's Zupwagen, Crepe Là Là, Consuela's All Mex No Tex, or Moshe's Mobile Sushis. He might even try Dim Sum Things, or sample a newcomer's free offerings. Never sated, he found room to finish off lunch with a tasty goody from Little Sumpin,' Dangerous Yogurt Yo!, or Vinnie's Very Good Gelato, and he always complemented dessert with a hand-pressed doppio from the Javamobile.

The slender frame of Max's youth had stayed with him through NUS and France. In Cambridge, the delta of his upper body became a rectangle. In California, the upper body delta reappeared, but had reversed direction.

Sameer did offer the best samosas money could buy. Their fried wrappers were light and crisp. Oil from GMO avocados had been engineered to a smoke point temperature ten degrees Fahrenheit higher than nature's best, so frying time was short and oil penetration a minimum. The hot vats were his family's custom-made designs built on the carcasses of discarded furnaces from a semiconductor industry grown long-in-the-tooth. Combined with his sister Sameera's combinations of pistachios, potatoes, artisanal vegetables, and homegrown spices, infused with fruit or her whimsy of the day, and smeared with a schmeer of selected chutney or yoghurty raita, Sameer's samosa was a savory delicacy. Sameer's girth was still years ahead of Max's.

He greeted and laughed and taunted and teased and flirted and thanked from behind the serving portals of his truck. "Hi, friend. It's so nice to see you again. Where have you been hiding? You're looking healthy, my friend."

The furnace heat, although diminished by ceramic bricks recovered from NASA's dustbins, kept the truck hotter than Kansas in July on the best days, and like the atmosphere of Venus on the worst. Stripped as naked as the Food Police or Sameera would allow, Sameer's pirate-black hair pulled back in a pony tail, his bushy beard combed to a mock-evil point, Sameer was a beloved fixture at the roundabout for ninety minutes on most weekdays. He also delivered delicious, ripping pain and came like a whale when Max met him at the empty kegs behind Moby Dick's near Castro Street in Mountain View.

The circling food wagons created a community and occasionally a carnival atmosphere very different from the one within the buildings. Inside, there was nary a sound but the hum of air conditioners or the swoosh of a glass door in motion. Inside, of course, there was no mixing between firms. Outside, the cubicle walls were down. You could share thoughts, if not your IP, with your buddies or girlfriends from the other firms. Sameer was not the only one flirting at lunch time. It was customary to use the waiting line's density to advantage, taking a chance to rub against your secret flame, exchange pheromones, get some feedback, gauge the potential for reciprocity, and blame it on some oaf's clumsiness if it wasn't well received.

Max made several useful sexual, gambling and professional contacts in line among the trucks, promoting himself or exploiting his obvious friendship with Sameer to ingratiate himself with others. If only he had worn Business Casual instead of his Goodwill Usual, he could have hidden better and gotten a lot more action, but alas, he was Max, always Max, straight through to the end.

CHAPTER 73 THE FINANCING

MAX MET Carmie by the trucks on her first day as Guzman's new EIR. He'd listened to a pitch at Intuition in the morning and was grabbing lunch before heading back to the I. With his male gaze on her bodacious breasts, he figured she must be a new mom.

"Carmella Kahn," she said.

"Max Frood," he said. "My pleasure."

"It smells like the *souk*," signaling that she'd been in close quarters before and that physical contact didn't frighten her. They launched into a mildly competitive but mostly genuinely engaging discussion about where they've traveled, where the crowds were thickest, where the street food was best. Then conversation turned to more serious topics.

"Yeah, I had the baby twelve weeks ago, and I feel like I need something else to do. I'm back sooner than I thought I would be. What do you do here?"

"I eat!"

"Literally very funny. *Ha!* I can see that. But what else?"

"Oh, I advise a bunch of these clowns about biotech and physics. Not much physics entrepreneuring these days, but it comes up. I also run a lab at HMRI over the hill," he said, pointing toward the forest. "I'm incubating something. Not my first."

"I ran an orphan drug startup before the baby came. We sold that, my husband and I. Guzman wants us to try again for them. I guess that makes me a clown." They bumped phones and she promised to find time to meet with him.

The deal that Carmie struck with Max four months later was not exactly what he had hoped for, but it was going to net him more than the 1.538 percent he'd ended up with at Tiny. "You were wrong, Dykkur! And Fuckin' A, they lost my 'a,'" Max began the phone call with his lawyer.

"Max, you gotta give me a little more context."

"My 'a'. Genormax is going back to Genormx."

"You called me at 3 a.m. to tell me that?" Dykkur asked.

"Oh. And a double-digit slice of the pie! You were wrong about that, by one of Carmie's red cunt hairs, but wrong."

"We'll see about that after the next round. Good night, Max."

Genormx would use the Frood Group IP on pores and e-beam detection. The company would abandon the diagnostics plan because that depended on too many other things going right. Their focus would be to scale up the prototype, package it in tastefully painted sheet metal, and sell a few instruments before unloading the entire company on one of the three large sequencing companies.

Max would chair the Scientific Advisory Board and commit all of his consulting time to Genormx. Nico and Rinchen would join the company as the core of the technical team. Whatever cofounder's status Max may have promised or intimated to Nico before she signed on at the I, when time came to sign on the dotted line, Max told her she had misunderstood. Maybe the graduate students would come along after they got their degrees.

Carmie would be the CEO and cofounder. She and her husband, Kozmo, would run the executive office, taking responsibility for finance, operations, marketing and business development. Later, when the company grew, they'd split up the responsibilities and add more bodies.

She'd been able to pull together a syndicate of investors on a set of investment terms she dictated. Armen was in for $4 million, Intuition for $8 million, and Guzman for $12 million. The first tranche of $8 million would come in at the beginning, and the remainder within twenty-four months if the company hit certain performance milestones.

The cap table, the ownership pie, assigned 66 percent to the investors, 15 percent to Carmie and Kozmo together, 12 percent to Max, and 7 percent to the rest of the team. The team's slice was thin and should have been 9, and dilution from the next round would only thin that slice, but there were no team members in the negotiation, and the other parties were fixated on their numbers. Max's 12 percent was more than Dykkur had forecast, but he felt fleeced anyway.

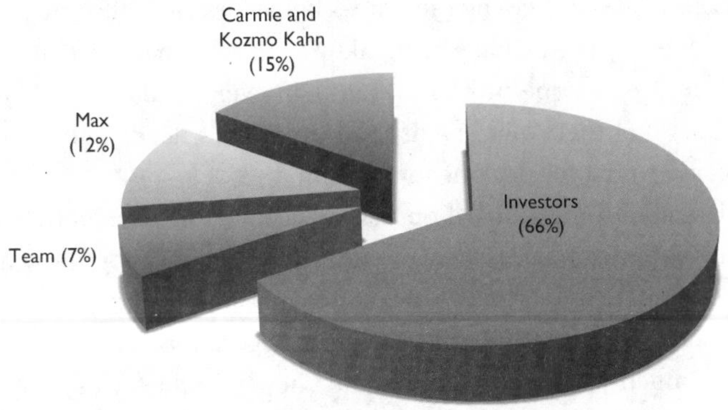

Still, in addition to his equity ownership, he would be double-dipping in the returns through his share of royalties and other fees on the IP licensed through TTO. From the shadows, he'd instructed the office to negotiate very hard with Kozmo and get a 5 percent royalty rate. That hurt the long-term prospects for Genormx and its investors and employees, but was particularly good for him.

Here's the arithmetic on that. Royalties are computed as a fraction of a company's revenue, its top line. Even for the most successful and profitable of companies, 5 percent off the top line would be very damaging to its profit, its bottom line. Suppose a company earns $20 profit for every $100 in revenue. Remove $5 from the top line, without changing anything else, and its profit would become $15. Its profit would be reduced by $5 out of $20, or 25 percent. Typically, a company's share price is a multiple of its profit. Thus a 5 percent royalty delivers a 25 percent blow to the equities. Max was maximizing his total return, the sum of his royalty stream and his equity appreciation. Only Max could have done this. That was his prerogative and he took it, even if it meant screwing all the other stakeholders.

As for his 12 percent, Carmie thought he should get 10 and he thought he should be getting 50 percent. "I invented this! It's mine, all mine!" According to Carmie, he really did rant as he paced around the room pushing chairs into walls, waving his arms and glaring through fierce eyebrows at anyone who would listen.

According to Dykkur, "He was immune to every argument about every industry norm. 'They're all idiots, Fucking Idiots! What do I care about what everyone else does? They're all wrong. Wrong, I tell you, wrong!'"

As I try to make sense of the accounts from all sources, the move to California marked a singular change in Max's behavior. The cause might have been the death of Little Arsalan, the breakup with Arianna, the Tiny IPO, or the move itself. He became more focused than ever on his needs. And the fact that others had their own needs, and everyone's needs had to be balanced, appeared to matter not one iota to him.

Max had wanted to be a board observer. Carmie, forewarned by Armen, blocked him. Max, again, was furious, ranting and raving about how he had started a company before, about how he was not just the technologist but also the brilliant strategist and the toughest negotiator, how his thinking would add so much value because of all he knew of industry development, and that without him in board meetings, decisions would be too slow in the making because they'd have to go back to him for vetting anyway. If he wasn't on the Board, he said, he wouldn't give his IP, his time, and his name to Genormx.

Carmie listened to him and called his bluff. Max had been so sure this deal was going to close that he had stopped pursuing any other funding. Without her, he would have nothing. When she played his own trick on him, and didn't return calls for two weeks, he caved. With him on his heels, she argued that the team needed a couple percentage points more equity. Threatening to let the whole deal collapse, she drove him down to a 10 percent stake that made the numbers work. He responded by sticking his own shiv in her, and in the company, when he proposed appointing a board member to represent his interests.

Dyk was a lawyer, experienced in biotech deals. He was also a pompous ass, and Max's local gambling buddy. He interviewed well, his résumé checked out in the due diligence calls, and he was OK'd by Armen, Carmie and Kozmo Kahn, Guzman, and Intuition's rep on the Board, any one of whom could still have vetoed that appointment.

"Dyk Schmalis is," in the words of Dykkur Ph'eer who knew him and had seen him in action, "a pettifogger and a prick. Max gets Dyk these board positions, and then takes all his money from him playing poker. Max loves Dyk. But he's not someone you want on your board." Dykkur, conveying those sentiments to Vladik several years later, slowed his speech and said, "He's *Old School*," in a ponderous voice, echoing his Norse ancestors, maybe. "He's always right. Dunning-Kruger? You know what I mean?"

Vladik did not know what he meant.

"I mean, the fool doth think he is wise." And then Dykkur shivered.

Carmie said later, "When you were on the other side of the table from

Max, you never knew how much he was just trying to terrorize you or wear you down, and how much he really cared about the extreme positions he took. He was a toxic negotiator. But we put up with him because of his star power. He was sexy in a weird way. He had an allure, in spite of himself, and in spite of his clothes and his bulk. We got him down to reasonable numbers, but it was exhausting and demoralizing. It's easy enough to forgive Albert Einstein for his foibles. He was less than the greatest parent that ever was, as a case in point. But Max," and she paused, "Max was six months or maybe a year ahead of everyone else. Not that much. And he wasn't a magician."

Then Carmie took me off on a discussion about the meaninglessness of being first. "I think the patent system was intended to prevent copying of non-obvious inventions, but so many ideas are in the zeitgeist that first-to-file is an arbitrary distinction."

"You're saying that if I file on invention X, and three months later you file the same invention without having seen mine, then no matter how clever X may look to the patent examiner, the fact that I filed independently is proof that X—."

"Was in the zeitgeist," Carmie said, finishing my thought, "and no one should be rewarded for the distinction of being first to write down something that belongs to all of us, even if there was an inventive step."

"Many people would make the same inventive step. You're saying invention has become commoditized?"

"I'm not sure I would take it that far, but yes, many people will take the same inventive step independently. Carver Mead invented the microprocessor at Caltech long before Ted Hoff did at Intel—"

"I've heard of Ted Hoff. Who's Carver Mead?"

She tried not to show her disappointment. "Carver codified VLSI design and wrote the book on it, among other things. Gordon Moore endowed a chair for him at Caltech, if you need more than my say-so that he's certifiable. Long before it could be made, he described a chip with programmable logic and memory. And it wasn't obvious to many people. But by the time it could be made, it was obvious, and not because he had said something about it years before. The inventive step was doing it."

"And that deserves to be rewarded," I chimed in.

"Yes. Max wanted to get rewards for being first to recognize what was in the zeitgeist. He didn't change the world. He just wanted us to treat him as if he did."

Carmie sounds too good to be real, but there are surprisingly many terrific execs out there. She was just an exemplar of the species. That she was able to get Armen to participate, against his earlier commitment never to invest in Max again, was testament to the confidence she engendered. Hard working and insightful, but not smug about what she knew or how she'd acquired her experience. Firm and direct, yet gentle in her delivery. Focused on the problem not the personal, she was open to personal conversation when the moment was right; for instance, she and Nico found common ground as young mothers. She left you loving her, but not flirting with her. Armen and the other investors were prone to calling her "beloved daughter" when she delivered beyond their expectations at board meetings, which she did often.

CHAPTER 74 THE ROYAL SCHOOL FOR GIRLS

At least one visit to see Maxime, annually. That was Max's promise to himself, and to Vera. And he more than kept it. The President of the Royal University, Max's former associate from the Alliance, had persuaded Her Highness that whole-genome sequencing of the royals was a critical next step in modernizing her own healthcare, and that Max Frood was the man to supervise the sequencing and the analysis. And so began Max's association with the Queen.

Maxime was admitted to the Royal School for Girls in Rhizobia in the sixth grade. A lush green campus mixing Oxbridge exteriors and modernist interiors, the school drew girls from plutocratic families all over South and Southeast Asia. Maxime was the odd one, her parents having, relatively-speaking, no means at all. But she had met the monarch.

The school's head mistress held parent conferences throughout the year. Verawati Katawijaya's scheduled meeting fell in the height of the monsoon. She left the seething but competent Putu in charge of Wet Dreams, and then flew into Changi. There she met her former lover, Max, who always made arrangements to be working at the university at the same time. After a few days together during the week, Max, Vera, and Maxime would take a long weekend in Hong Kong or one of the other metropoli in that corner of the world.

Putu hated everything about those trips because she didn't trust Max further than she could throw him. She knew her lover's flame for him was still lit. All that time together and out of her reach left too many moments for trouble to brew into a storm.

Sometimes, he and Vera returned to Gili T together. New high-powered speedboats had come online. Dual-hulled and multi-engined, they traveled directly from Bali to Gili Trawangan in as little as two hours. Max was looking forward to plunging through the Bali Sea on one of those, as he was looking forward to indulging himself in as many ways as possible, and that included pondering over the facts of "Frood's Law."

Max believed that the number of dive schools on Gili Trawangan was a marker of island maturation—"Its state function," or, "Its index of self-destruction," as he would say—and one much easier to measure than other candidates like pounds of trash per day, overnight visits, kilowatt hours, reported robberies, or those collected by the Bureau of Econometrics, if there had been a Bureau of Econometrics. Tacked to the wall above the desk in Vera's Wet Dreams office was piece of quadrille A4 paper. Frood's Law was written at the top in his hand, and a pair of axes was labeled "Time" and "#." On the horizontal time axis, Max had written 1990, 1995 and so forth all the way to 2015, and the on the vertical axis he had written 5, 10, all the way through to 50. Individual points representing the number of schools at a particular date were plotted as he or Maxime had acquired the data. Collectively, the points appeared not as an exponential rising upwards from the left, as Max had initially expected to see, but as something much more interesting to explain to Maxime. Years of exponential growth were followed by years of approximately linear growth, and Max was anxious to see if the latest data point showed hints of slowing down. His curve should eventually form a classic sigmoid, an s-shape characteristic of most bounded growth processes, but the number of dive schools hadn't yet rolled over and begun to plateau.

MAX and Maxime had a relationship, awkward but real. His efforts to connect with her over Frood's Law led to discussions about growth in general, and what fed or limited it, and methods of quantifying it, and equations that represent it, and so on. What he gave her on those infrequent visits, she took and found expression for in her classroom projects. The head mistress, who may have surmised that the famous Dr. Frood was more than a family friend who occasionally gave lectures at the School for Girls, told Vera that Maxime was an outstanding and probing intellect and should be thinking about going to college in the United States.

Over dinner on their last night in Rhizobia, Vera recited the head mistress' remarks to Max. Max told her about his conversation with Maxime about a field study they had begun the year before on Gili T, and how she had interested her classmates in doing a similar one in Rhizobia. The two parents shared that rare satisfaction of believing, not that they knew what they were doing, but had done something good for their child.

Vera almost cried with happiness, and she wiped the nascent tears away from the large whites of her brown eyes. Max held her hand. Ensconced in five-star splendor, away from their homes, away from jealous Putu and from Sameer who didn't care enough, they both lost all sense. After more than a decade since Max's days at NUS, they found their way back into the same bed. The beginning, as beginnings always are, was impassioned, blinding, feverish with rippings and tearings, pressings and suckings, and as the minutes ticked away, Max's face buried in the cleft between her breasts, Vera's hips in big ellipses, their minds began to stray far from the moment, far from the bed, far from each other, and they both grasped that there *was* no going back. And yet, neither could bear to disappoint the other. They did love each other. Hiding the cracks in their ardor, both proceeded with the greatest of care and consideration, selflessly fucking each other's brains out. Prepared to fake it with heroic fervor, Max and Vera finally yielded to unforgettable, this-is-really-the-last-time orgasms.

"Where are the Snowdens of yesteryear, Max?"

"Gone, Vera. Gone."

"I love you, Max. You know that?"

"Yes, I know that Vera. I love you, too."

Max didn't travel back to the Gilis with Vera as planned. Earlier that day, a courier from the Ginger Mascarpone Foundation had informed him of an urgent need to return home in a week. There would have been time for a short stop in the Gilis, especially with the new fast boats, but the sense of loss he felt overwhelmed him, and he must have known it would only be worse on Gili Trawangan.

When Vera returned, Putu knew that something had happened. Vera was at first aloof, and then too loving. "That fucking Max. I'll have his head on a pike," she said to no one.

CHAPTER 75 JULIA NOLASTNAME

After that fateful AAAS meeting, after the summer at Orrigen, after my junior year when I spent the summer at Myriad Genetics, and after graduating from Princeton, I shunned the advice of everyone I respected. Instead of leaving to broaden my horizons, I decided to stay at Princeton for graduate school. Reed Aackted, my advisor, voiced his opposition most vehemently, but wouldn't stand in the way of my admission. Anticipating a sliver of the improvements soon to come in sequencing, we had mapped out a big program to study entropy in the vaginal microbiome. Of course he wanted me to stay, to carry forward that NIH grant I'd co-authored. But at the same time, he said, "You have to go out West. You need to see the way it's done in other shops. Come back when you get a faculty appointment." So why did I stay?

Julia.

By the time I was making that decision, I had stopped thinking I might want to be with a boy ever again. Julia, who has asked that I not use her last name, had come to Princeton as a first year graduate student when I was a senior. She had a pedigree from Hollywood, a bachelor's degree in molecular and cell biology from Berkeley, and a master's degree in cunnilingus from Oakland. A more determined lesbian than I had been, she explored places I didn't know I had, and she took me places I'd never been. I became her slave—that's an exaggeration, although it felt that way at first—and I wasn't ready to give her up for some abstraction of broadening on the West Coast.

I also got back on the boards, the diving boards.

CHAPTER 76 LGTBQ

The Ginger Mascarpone Foundation hosts an annual conference so selective and exclusive that its dates, location, and agenda are kept secret until a week before the event. The lucky few, the Chosen, are notified of their invitations by the arrival of a courier bearing conference swag and a key to an encrypted email message. The message contains airline e-tickets for three—the Chosen and two guests of his or her choosing—details about local transportation to the conference hotel, and the topic of the talk invitee is expected to prepare. All expenses are paid by the Foundation. The little that's predictable about this pop-up conference is that it always takes place during what proves later to be the worst winter weather of the year in Chicago, and that it is always held in a location south of the Mason-Dixon line and north of the Tropic of Cancer, or in the mirroring latitudes of the southern hemisphere. Also predictable is that there will be surprise announcements, memorable talks, and career-changing conversations. Ginger's list of chosen people was developed by the Choosing, an even more selective group of regulars. Max was one of them until, well, he never told me why, but maybe he decided he was too important to participate at all.

I met Max at the conference with no name in the year it popped up at a resort enclave on the southwest coast of Florida. The white sand beaches and semi-tropical weather—the highs were in the low 80s—were a relief from bone chilling New Jersey. Upon arriving at the hotel with my advisor and with Julia, we were outdone by the organizers' attempts to hide the event's whereabouts from prying eyes. We first found ourselves in front of the bright pink posters of the Southeast Regional LGTBQ Confab and its perky, pierced staff. That looked inviting, too. When we finally found the right ballroom, I told whoever would listen that our nameless conference should have been called Linkage-maps, Genomics, T-cells, B-cells, and Quarks, and the name stuck.

The Chosen were all medalists in something. They had abundant honorary degrees and fan clubs, too. Their guests included spouses, mates, students, academic colleagues, children, friendly journalists, and business allies. Graduate students like me, like I was, took every chance to meet the Chosen and prepare the way for job interviews one or two or even four years in the future.

Ginger was inexplicably detained and did not show up for the Ginger Mascarpone Cocktail Hour on the first evening. Everyone else was there, and that's where I first met Max. He didn't laugh at my modest LGTBQ joke, but he was infectious about the prospects for Genormx and the millions he was going to make. It was intoxicating to hear him talk irreverently about the giants in the field and about the range of projects he had started. He made it sound like he was an absolute factory for startups. He had entrepreneuring all figured out, and had put the pipeline together to pump ideas and students into one startup after another. Princeton seemed antediluvian after I had spent five minutes with him.

Max's address to the conference was about the revolution in diagnostics made possible by the exponentially falling costs of sequencing. This was still a new story. A few dreamers believed it. Even fewer comprehended how far sequencing had come since the nine- or ten-figure genome of the millennium and how far it would go. Almost no one had seen the charts showing sequencing improvements outpacing Moore's Law. Max reviewed all the sequencing technologies and compared them for their potential, not just for where they were at that one moment in time. He spelled out which ones were going to thrive and which were going to be dead and gone in a few years. He hinted that he'd had a breakthrough with pores. That sent the journalists scurrying into the halls to use their phones. He talked about the coming revolution in diagnostics, the irrelevance of the FDA, how these diagnostics would lead to personalized drugs, and on and on. It was brilliant, although superficial, self-aggrandizing, etc., and just what the conference organizers wanted from him. I decided I had to go to California and finish my PhD with him, and the thought of Julia didn't cross my mind until later.

I DON'T look bad in a bikini; a side effect of my lifetime of diving, I guess. I've even been told I look great in one, but it's not really for me to say. I just know that I don't look bad, and I'm not at all embarrassed to be seen in one, Brazilian or no Brazilian. It wasn't summer, though, so I wore a black and aqua, short sleeve, cropped neoprene rash guard top to complement an aqua and black bikini bottom; very becoming I thought.

Max, well, OK, this is not about Max in a bikini. Max was thick everywhere, carrying a lot of flesh. He looked a bit like a wine barrel, wider in the middle than at the top. An athlete long-gone from training, but not gone from the training table, he did not look good in a bathing suit. And yet, during the two-hour mid-afternoon break, after his talk had wowed us all, he put on a way-too-small black Speedo and showed off a not-so-happy trail. He played touch football on the beach with a contingent of students and postdocs, running just-noticeably lopsided because of the aftereffects of the falanga in Deauville, but playing. No other "adults" played.

He made excessive not-entirely-necessary contact with the girls, and with the guys, too. It was noticed. He didn't let on that it was noticed, just laughing it all off as if there was no motive and it was all in the course of the game. In his expression, you could not read what you expected to read, that is, the smirking look that said, "I know that you know that I know that I was groping and not just tagging you." It wasn't there at all. And yet, the affect was not flat. He was dangerously deceptive or he was innocent. I gave him the benefit of the doubt and used our game to find a way into his lab.

"A few summers ago I learned something about your Tiny Machines patents." What was I supposed to say next? "The work you're doing now is really exciting," I told him as we walked back to the hotel and got ready for the late afternoon sessions.

"You look great in that bikini."

I laughed out loud. "Is that what you say to all the graduate students?"

"No, just the ones who look great in bikinis."

"How do I get you to talk about work?"

"Tell me about your work."

"Haplotypes as eigenvectors in the genetics of the vaginal microbiome, but some things are not working as—"

"Yeah, that can be stinky business."

I tried not to laugh, and failed. He showed not a hint of pleasure at having got me.

"They're great people at Princeton, but," and I waved my hands while trying to find the right word, "they're all too theoretical for me. I don't want to be an academic. I shouldn't have stayed there after my bachelor's. I like to build things. I want to finish my degree with you." And then I paused. "*Ouch*! I guess I wasn't very subtle about that was I?"

"No. Not too subtle. Let's get out of here for dinner and we can talk about it."

"You mean like just you and me? A date?"

"Not a date, but yes, just you and me." Pregnant pause. "If you want to have a real conversation, we can't do it here." Now he waved his arms, suggesting all the possibilities for intrusion. "There's my room and there's a restaurant. The food here is awful. I don't think it would look good if you came up to my suite."

"There's my room," I suggested, trying to get a rise out of him.

"*Ha!*"

"We could just walk on the beach."

"And we'll still have to eat the same food."

"Don't you have other people you have to talk to?"

"I know what everyone else is doing."

"OK, dinner."

"I'll meet you out front after the talks end."

"I'll need another half hour to clean up."

"This is not a date."

"I'll still need another half hour to clean up."

Julia—girlfriend, roommate, and lab partner—and Reed, my advisor, were talking together when I told them I wouldn't join them for dinner. "I'm going on a *date* with Max Frood!" I batted my lashes at Julia.

Reed's eyes went wide, but then he shrugged. Hand stroking his beard he said, "Well, I guess we'll make do. Don't let him take your wooden nickels from you. He's a gambler." I gave Julia a kiss and ran off.

MAX met me at the front of the hotel, wearing his signature red knit shirt in need of laundering, khaki pants in need of hemming, and tennies in need of replacing. Max, the slouchy scholar, epitomized a trend of dressing deviant to signal status. From what I'd seen in two days, he had more pairs of tennies than he had red shirts. I was wearing a clingy black knit dress, not too short. Simple gold dangles on my ears and three gold bangles on my wrists. I wore low heels so I wouldn't be taller than him. "You're dressed for a date," he said.

"I'm just dressed in case I meet a cute girl." If he was going to insist this wasn't a date, I thought I'd take a step out. Max looked a little stung, and then he did something inexplicable with his eyes. Maybe it was a wink. When I'd winked at Julia, she and I knew exactly what it meant. It meant, "I'll see *you* later, cutie." I had no idea what his tic meant, so I winked back, smiled like the Cheshire Cat, and we started talking science. His phone buzzed with incoming texts. He ignored them, but not the rarer messages that came in with a sonorous blip. For those, he worked his thumbs vigorously and then returned the phone to his pocket.

"I'll get it, and dinner," he said, in the taxi and long before we arrived. Some flash of doubt must have creased my face. "You can eat French, right?"

Max gave me just enough details of his life in France to explain why he we were driving twenty minutes. "I miss the food," summed it up. "Gourmand, gourmet, but not effete, I make no excuse that I like to eat," he said, patting his belly. "My only vice," he chuckled. He chuckled but I flinched. There was something transparently insincere about the way he said it. Was it irony for me to see through, or a distortion he believed? I felt uneasy, not knowing how to read him. Then we got back to the science, and I forgot about the exchange for many years.

The incoming texts buzzed and blipped at a steady pace through the ride.

"Do you know about, cfDNA, cell-free DNA?" he asked.

I looked at him but did not answer.

"When a cell dies, everything inside it spills out into the bloodstream, or eventually gets in there." I was still looking kind of stupid, I guess, so he went on, in full professorial mode.

"Until Watson and Crick determined the structure, not everyone believed that DNA was *the* genetic material. Oswald Avery had demonstrated it back in 1944, but no one read his paper and the world wasn't ready to be convinced. All the emphasis was on proteins, and DNA was a stupid molecule. I mean, that's a ridiculous thing to say, but I think Watson said it, referring to the way DNA was thought of by most scientists; that it wasn't the genetic carrier, just a kind of backbone. Its function was incomprehensible. In 1948, these French guys, Mandel and Métais found DNA in blood. I don't even know what they said it was doing there, but since most people thought DNA was a stupid molecule, no one really looked into it until a long time after we learned about the double helix."

I was following him, so I picked up the thread. "The DNA is there because the cells die and their guts scatter into the blood, right? Organelles, chromosomes, fluids?" I looked at Max and got a poker face. Taking that as a yes, I continued. "All that stuff will get metabolized pretty quickly. But then it's replenished by the other cells that are dying, so there's an equilibrium and that's what you're measuring."

This implied the application of the simplest differential equation that ever was. I could visualize my high school physics teacher writing about capacitors on the blackboard, and then so many teachers after that. Same equations, same solutions, Feynman said.

"OK. There's a rate of cell death and an exponential decay rate, so what you measure is the product of those."

Max's face revealed nothing. Was he thinking, "nice bikini," or "trying to impress me?" or simply "nice."

"We're here," he said.

The taxi stopped at Maître Dix. An exceptionally handsome and fit young man opened the door for me. He wore a deep blue Hawaiian shirt decorated with red herons, yellow palm trees, and salt-rimmed margaritas. The attire was a bit incongruous for the maître d' of a fancy French restaurant, but who was I to judge?

"Your date is very elegant, Dr. Frood. I see you are dressed like a schlub as usual."

I knew nothing of Max's personal life since the late 1980s, but I knew a thing or two about body language and hiding feelings behind a curtain or propriety. For a moment, memory played back days of listening to my father's old 45s. Ricky Nelson's Travelin' Man came to mind. Was Max the kind of guy who owned the heart of at least one lovely boy in every port?

"Haha. Lakshmi, this is Dixon Mock. Dix, this young woman is going to be a great scientist, please be respectful. For now, she's going to be my student, right?" Max said, flapping those bushy eyebrows at me incomprehensibly.

"Well, I am sure you will have something to teach her."

Was he flirting with Max or with me? I wasn't paying too much attention. I had returned to thinking about my equations and hoping I wouldn't say something stupid.

Dix seated us at a table by the window with a panoramic view of the pier and Tarpon Bay. The owner's tri-deck superyacht, also called *Maître Dix*, was tied fast to the pier, all lit up, very quiet and elegant.

Max waved Dix away, "Give us a few minutes." Then he said to me, "Why don't you keep going?"

"What's the concentration?" I asked, meaning how much DNA is there in the blood?

"One thousand genome equivalents per millilitre of blood."

"*Yikes*! That's um, uh, a big number. But it's the product of all the cells in your body. What, like ten trillion? But how many are dying per second? Red blood cells live for like what, a hundred twenty days? But other cells can't turn over that fast. So what, ten times that on average? Three years. That's 10^8 seconds. That makes the cell death rate 10^5 per second. You've got five litres of blood. 10^5 per second divided by $5*10^6$ millilitres, that's $2*10^{-2}$ cells per mille per second times the time constant, τ, equals 1000. So τ is $5*10^4$ seconds. Twelve or fifteen hours. Seems too long. What did I do wrong?"

"You had one too many factors of 10^3 going from litres to millilitre."

I blushed as red as I can blush. At least he was following closely.

"10^5 per second divided by $5*10^3$ gives you τ of fifty seconds, which is too short," he said. "The right number is in between the two. Good. Better than not bad. Good."

Margaritas looking like the ones on Dix's shirt arrived. We hadn't ordered, but the meal was on.

And then I began to think about how I'd behaved. I hadn't been such a showoff since I couldn't remember when. With Vladik? No. Vladik didn't make me want to be that way. Vladik was more about being thoughtful and having penetrating insights. With Max, I had to be first, couldn't be anything but first. It was something he brought out in me.

I don't remember the clichéd choice of oyster appetizers, or the wine with its embossed bottle, or the lemon sorbet to clean my palate before the *poisson,* or the cheese and fruit or the sweet wine to go with them. Dear Reader, I don't remember, so I'm transcribing text from the *prix fixe* menu on heavy card stock I took home as a souvenir.

What I do remember—besides the blipping of his phone that seemed to take priority over everything, and the large number of insanely good-looking men, mostly dark and Latin, lean and well-dressed in tight-butt show-off trou or comfy linen pants, age group eighteen to forty-eight, noisily carousing at the bar—is hearing about how someone had detected fetal DNA in the circulating blood of a pregnant woman, and how he was trying to use that to diagnose fetal abnormalities without amniocentesis. That same researcher also speculated that in organ transplant recipients there should be DNA from the donor in the circulating blood of the recipient.

Max wanted to get into this, this thing with cfDNA. He was effervescent as he explained his vision of transformation, about how this was going to be an earth-shaking breakthrough in diagnostics, and it all depended on sequencing being free.

He said that there were some other groups racing to solve the fetal diagnostics problem. "I've spoken to everyone giving it a shot, including a couple here at the conference. They're all focused on PCR, not sequencing."

"They won't have the signal will they?"

"It's worse than that, … "

"Excuse me, Max," Dix said. "So sorry to interrupt." He refilled our water glasses from an oversize, lovingly detailed, penis-shaped decanter that he gripped about its erect shank, balancing the torque with his palm beneath its glass scrotum. Red veins of solid glass running lengthwise gave his fingers purchase. When he caught my eyes admiring the bulbous head he said, "Individually blown, of course. And makes a great bong, too," showing me a ground glass port where you could insert a pipe head.

They were not expecting it when I asked to handle it myself. After giving the mushrooming detail of its fat round glans an appreciative touch, I made as if I was about to slurp it up, and then handed it back. "Nicely done, but too much of a mouthful for me, and not my thing anyway," as I shook my head in disapproval.

After a pause while they re-evaluated me, Dix said, "But will you be having coffee or dessert, or maybe a plate of fruit and cheeses?"

Max looked at me, gesturing with his hands for me to go first. Since dinner was on him, I ordered a café macchiato and the cheeses with fruit. Max didn't want anything more, saying only, incomprehensibly, "I need to leave room for more later."

I brought us back to fetal diagnostics. "Max, what's that you were saying or about to say about the other groups?"

"Never mind. Sequencing is just going to blow every other method out of the water."

From what I knew about the scientists Max wanted me to go up against, the competition would be formidable, and victory only possible if they stuck with PCR.

Changing the subject, Max asked, "How are your hands?"

"In the lab?"

"Yes, in the lab. I've already seen how that you handled that other thing."

"My mother trained me. Do you mind if I boast?"

Max nodded.

"Naija Stein does not give praise lightly, and less so to her children. She told me I have magic, masterful hands. But I didn't want to become her kind of immunologist, raising mice by the thousands and then killing them softly with squeak sounds."

"I don't do rodents," he said.

Dinner was over. Dix brought my things and then the check.

"So look. I've got the funding if you want to move out to California and work on cell-free DNA. Reed will have to approve the change of research plan, and Botstein will have to approve the remote residence. Princeton will be the degree-granting institution because HMRI doesn't do that, but we will supplement your measly NIH grant."

"Fellowship from NSF, and it's pretty good," I corrected him.

"Well, NSF is very nice. Congratulations. I'm not surprised." He paused for a second to let it seep in that I'd scored a point, and then he went on with a speech I guess he'd given before. "We'll supplement it anyway. HMRI is just different. I'll sit on your thesis committee—"

I got an incoming text from Julia. "Ginger Mascarpone!" with an accompanying photo of my girlfriend sitting side by side with the legend.

"Max," I said. "Look at this," and I handed him the phone.

"Now I'm doubly glad we're not there. I can't stand walking around the dead bodies after that sapphic genius has passed by."

"I am sorry I missed her. She's a hero to me." I told him about when I'd seen her once before.

"And here you've had to dine with chopped liver," he said with a spark of petulance. Leaving no room for me to pray before other idols, Max took up the thread where I had cut him off.

"I'll sit on your thesis committee. That's what I do for all the other graduate students in the lab. You're going to have to travel back and forth, probably quarterly or so, to keep Princeton up to speed and happy. You don't want them to forget you. Work on the margins and you're marginalized. But this field is wide, wide open right now. You're going to be able to invent the future. It's gonna be great, really."

Another incoming text I showed Max. "She was smashed."

He asked if he could take my phone. I nodded. He texted Julia. "A bombed blond shell of her former self?"

"Have you been waiting to use that line?" she texted to us.

Max typed back, "Yes, MF"

I WAS giddy happy, and a little drunk myself, and also overcome by Max's aura. Most of what I knew about Max was about his MEMS patents, and we'd talked about those. We both had confidentiality agreements preventing us from going very deep. The rest of what I knew about him, or I thought I knew about him, well, it hadn't come up. Should I have just blurted all that stuff out, full disclosure like?

I flashed back to the *Lucky Strike* weekend, visualizing Jay and Joosey together. Jay's description was so luscious I wanted to be him. But in my mind's eye I also saw Max's shock. I sympathized, but without knowing anything of how those moments haunted and drove him still. Then I flashed forward to playing Jay to Julia's Joosey within the hour. Luscious Julia. Ginger Mascarpone or not, she was going to be pissed.

Max, chivalrous, opened the door to the taxi, gesturing for me to get in first and then closed it behind me. He walked around to the other side and told the cab driver to take me back to the hotel, handed him cash, and leaning in the driver's window said to me, "Nice night. I'm meeting some friends here. I'll be flying out early in the morning. Sleep it off and write to me when you get back to Princeton, OK?"

That surprised me. I thought he'd make a pass at me on the way home, and I had wondered how I would suppress it, or if I would, and how we'd keep the conversation going, somehow, through the fog of all that wine and food.

But to be left alone, that was weird. I guess if I were going to be working for him, Laks with Max, I shouldn't be seen snuggling with him in a taxi, but I did want to snuggle right now. "Julia!" I imagined her golden-toned self stretched out long and lithe for me. Then I remembered my upcoming move to California and what that was going to mean to her. I had to open up to her before opening her up.

Max walked away. As the taxi left the curb, I turned to watch him. He was talking to Dixon Mock who had his arm around Max's ample butt. Dix' hand rested comfortably in Max's back pocket. They were ambling over to the crowded bar of beautiful men.

CHAPTER 77 ON THE BEACH

Gambling would have been Max's first choice to complete the evening, but the Seminole Casinos were too far away if he was going to make an early morning flight. The only in-town gambling was for gifts, not cash. He'd tried that once before. Gambling for gifts reminded him of taking a shower with a raincoat on, and he'd done that just to be sure it was as disappointing at it sounded. So the only alternative was an evening of dancing in the bar and debauchery in the shadows with the handsomest Cubans, Haitians, Dominicans, Trinidadians, and other well-muscled imports in ribbed tank tops that Dix could round up.

Their skin was tawny and taut, their hips slim, the house music was loud, and the dance floor crowded. The DJ mixed lambada with Ry Cooder, drawing on yards of vinyl and years of experience. When the beat called for it, he flamed jets of propane above everyone's heads, adding heat to an already hot night, in that hottest February in memory. Meanwhile, Chicago froze solid. A few women of every color were peppered into the crowd; dates, singles, escorts, professionals. Half of the men were stripped to the waist, six-packs and eight-packs, mostly shaven, glistening with perspiration and oil. The women dropped their shawls, revealing scanty tubes, tanks, halters, and crop tops, or finding other ways to expose shoulders and belly and let them cool as much as they could cool.

Max didn't so much dance as get down. Far away from everyone in his professional life, Max shuffled and hopped. He was uninhibited, and that's what made him a good dancer. He pushed his belly up against anyone nearby, forcing a reaction, escalating the energy until, until something broke the tension. Then he backed away laughing, not acknowledging that there'd been any extraordinary forwardness. Pushback was no insult, just a message he received easily. Did he enjoy this more with the men or the women? He grabbed crotch. He found a way to look up many skirts and down a lot of cleavage, and to touch both without inviting slaps or angry boyfriends. Laughter peaked around him, loud belly laughing, and wild whooping, like cowboys or Middle Eastern celebrants, particularly when he grabbed a woman's scarf and paraded around like a queen. Dixon Mock's description of that evening fit no experience I ever had with Max.

And this was just in the light of the bar. Who knew exactly what went on in the shadows behind it, the private rooms, the very dark and not-so-private rooms? They stank of sweat and sex. There were beanbags the size of queen mattresses for partners to spread out on. A voice admonished, "Don't you go trippin on somebody's ass." Max, or anyone, would guide himself in like a bat to avoid the bodies, listening for sounds of flesh on naugahyde, flesh on flesh, deep grunts, or the occasional higher pitched squeal of a woman, and sharp slaps. "That's all you need to know," Dix told me.

THE poorly ventilated rooms were too hot for their purpose. At about midnight, the last dining guest had gone home. The bar crowd had thinned to Max's paid or invited guests—a few boys and one lady, each the subject of a blipping text he'd received during our dinner. With a signal from Dix, they all made their way across the parking lot to the beach and the boat. The waning moon shone bright and high over the horizon. The air was still and warm, nearly 80 °F, and the waters invited. After so much alcohol, and some pot, and a few snorts of heavily stepped-on cocaine, Max was too high to think better of wading into the bay. He kicked shoes off and rolled pants up. Others did the same, or disrobed entirely. Someone carried all the detritus to the boat. There was more shouting and howling with pleasure, splashing in the warm water that was cool and refreshing against their hot skin. "Jesus Mary fucking God!" Max had sliced his bare foot on something in the water. "Shit!" "Mierda!" "Ah la puta!" Every variation on that theme came in staccato succession as one after another hurt themselves too. The nicks were mostly small to non-existent, and not bothersome enough to shut down the action.

The group repaired to the beach where the lady leapt onto Max, wrapping her arms around his neck and her legs around his waist. He fell forward as she kissed him and they landed in a heap in the sand. Max's khakis were only half off while she squawked at his penetration. Dix finished removing those pants in need of hemming and then he invited one after another of the guests to take turns making their mark on Max's hairy fat ass. Max bleated like a sheep at first, but after a while the screeches became only low grunts. Eventually the lady wiggled out from under him, strapped one on and pegged Max before heading home to her kids. Dix rested Max's face on a pillow and the men kept on cycling through. Dix brought him water and beer, and a Reuben on corn rye, but without Thousand Island dressing. Max hated Thousand Island dressing.

At 2 a.m. maybe, Dix told Max it was time for a boat ride. That's when he gave up on trying to make the 6 a.m. flight from Fort Meyers to SFO. "Change my flight, will you Dix?" he asked. After a shower on *Maître Dix*, he wrapped himself in a clean bathrobe and seated himself on the deck. He watched the play of the moon shining on the water, the lights on land and the navigation markers and the few other boats coming or going. On her knees in front of him, a staff girl put a small bandage on the cut on his left foot. He brushed off her offer to give him a blow job. He was wasted. "Bring me some socks, will ya, please." She brought them. Then he got up and walked to his stateroom. The boat was a floating disco, motoring slowly out through the channel and into the Gulf of Mexico while beautiful boys and girls danced, a mirrored ball flashed lights onto the deck and the water, and drinks and food were served by equally beautiful but uniformed youths.

Alone in bed, Max didn't know what he hated more. He hated needing anything, anything at all, so succumbing to his need for sex disgusted him. He hated wanting men. He hated being, in the inimitable phrasing that once appeared in *Harper's Magazine*, condemned to a permanent niggardom among men. He hated having to think that someone he knew might have seen him, or that someone in the club might have snapped a picture of him, exposing him unintentionally or blackmailing him. That made him scared, so scared he almost puked. He hated feeling scared. He wanted to be a fortress, impregnable. Island Max, all Max, only Max, no dependencies. He hated being reflective. He hated this moment and all moments like it. There was one more complex of images and thoughts that came to him before he fell asleep, a mingling of images of Joosey and his mother Miriam, and of Jay, and how much he hated Jay.

He woke to broad daylight in the late morning. The sun filtered through the curtains, shimmering off his silk sheets. "Bless the Lord," he said when he discovered he was alone. Max's clothes were ironed and in a neat pile beside him. His foot ached like he'd driven a nail through it. The boat was back at the pier and everyone but Dix had gone home, or wherever those folks go. He wanted to slip back into the hotel when no one was around, and in particular he didn't want to see me, so he timed his return for the middle of the afternoon session. The lunch crew at the restaurant made him a little breakfast, and then Dix called a taxi.

The timing wasn't perfect. I had bailed on the first few talks of that session, leaving lunch to do the noon ride with Julia. Then both of us decided we should keep up appearances, and while walking past escalators that headed to the hotel's main floor, I saw Max—can't miss that red shirt—enter the lobby through the revolving door. Quite the partier, I thought, and kept on walking to the ballroom where Reed was prognosticating on what paleogenomics would someday tell us about migrations of modern humans out of Africa. Later in the afternoon, I learned Max had checked out.

CHAPTER 78 THE INFECTION

He jacked into the Internet and let Carmie and key folks in the lab know that he had decided to return a day late. There were no critical meetings to attend, so he didn't have to endure the sour email phrasing or later the facial expressions of displeasure from colleagues forced to accommodate, again, his ever-changing schedule. There was an email message from me in his inbox, thanking him for the evening and letting him know that I was going to move ahead with the plans we'd discussed. There was no need for him to reply to it, and he didn't.

He used days like this to unplug from his usual sources of news and ideas, and just think, ruminating on the possible and the worthy. He was looking forward to that, and he would have gotten around to it if only the pain in his foot had subsided. Swallowing as much ibuprofen as he thought his kidneys could handle, he then checked out of the conference hotel. A taxi drove him to RSW airport, an hour away, and there he checked in to a lesser hotel, but one more convenient for the early departure the next morning.

He explained to the bellman, "I must have really tied it on last night. I am shot," by way of asking him to carry one light bag up to this room. It was an effort just to get into bed. The pain in his foot was now pounding in his head, "but maybe that's a hangover," he thought. His belly made it difficult to see the bottom of his foot, and he was too tired to prop it up and examine it in the mirror over the dresser. It was only the late afternoon, and all he could do before settling in for more sleep was to take more ibuprofen and arrange for a 4:30 a.m. wakeup call.

That call came, arousing him from a dream of psychedelic intensity. It was a parboiling sort of nightmare, one that horrified but not so much that it woke him up. It was something about being consumed by ants, but he couldn't remember, and didn't want to remember much of it. He was soaked through with sweat.

A shower was all he had time for, and he had to be quick about it. Sliding his legs over the bed and onto the floor, it hurt like hell to put pressure on that left leg. The falanga had been worse. He could deal with this. He took the time to look at the wound in a mirror. The slice was blackened at its edges, but not enlarged. The foot was swollen and tender, and his ankle wobbly. Still too early to call in and make an appointment at his clinic in Palo Alto, he made a mental note to do that from the air, and to drop in to Urgent Care without an appointment if he had to.

The shower felt good, but his foot ached, and someone was boring a hole in his head, or so it seemed. His clothes were pretty fresh, having worn them so little the day before. His left tennie would only fit when the laces were loosened. The bellman got his things and let Max lean on him as he limped to the elevator. He hadn't eaten since breakfast the day before.

THE conference had one more day to go, but Max was not the only one leaving early and headed out through RSW. Checking in for the Chicago leg of the journey home, Max couldn't avoid them altogether. He tried to keep conversations to a minimum by saying that he was ill, and it took no persuasion. "You look flushed, Max." "Get some rest, Max." "Inspiring talk, Dr. Frood." "LGTBQ is a burnout. I'm fried, too." "Do you have a fever, Max?" "Sleep it off, Max." "Great conference, again. I don't know how they do it." He leaned on one of his colleagues as she boarded. Then he took his business-class window seat and fell asleep again.

The dream returned with more intensity this time, enough to wake him up somewhere over Tennessee, panting, startled, and very thirsty. His breathing was rapid and shallow. He was scared. Pulling up the left pant leg of his khakis. His lower leg was black from his foot to just above his ankle, and red streaks radiated upwards. "Gang Fucking Grene!" he said to no one but himself. He'd be lucky not to lose that foot. The blackened flesh had no feeling, as if anaesthetized, and was like wood to the touch. The reddened leg was warm and his forehead was hot. There was no one in the seat next to him, no one to ask to reach overhead and push the flight attendant's call button. He had to do it himself and he was barely able. By then the dream of being consumed was coming back to him while he was awake. He shit in his pants.

When the flight attendant came, all Max could do was lift the pants leg and show her the streaks while smiling wanly, his face coated with sweat. Next he heard her call on the intercom for a doctor, but no one responded. Later she said he looked at her very strangely when she sat down and introduced herself. Her name was Miriam.

"He couldn't focus. It was like he thought he knew me but couldn't place my face, and if only I were in sharper focus it would help."

Like all flight attendants, she was trained in CPR and could use a defibrillator, but she was no EMT. She called MedAire, an inflight emergency assistance provider to help her make decisions about what to do next. After describing Max's condition, Reggie at their Global Response Center told her, "It's probably necrotizing fasciitis. You need to get down. He could be dead, umh, uh, let's see, what's your local time?"

Miriam told him it was 7:15.

"He could be dead by 8:15. Unless you're prepared to deliver intravenous antibiotics, there's nothing else you can do in the air." Miriam relayed this to the captain, who radioed Nashville, asking permission to make an emergency landing. MedAire called LifeFlight, preparing them to carry Max the final few miles to the hospital. Then the captain went on the intercom and made this announcement:

"We have a life-threatening medical emergency on board and are going to make an unscheduled stop in Nashville. We have begun descending and you will soon be experiencing an unusually sudden cabin pressure increase. All passengers, please take your seats, put your seatbelts on, and move your seatbacks and tray tables to their full upright positions. Flight attendants, please prepare for landing. Again, passengers, we apologize for the inconvenience to your flight plans, but please bear with us while we attend to this matter. When the patient is evacuated on the ground, we will do our best to reschedule missed connections in Chicago and answer your questions. Thank you for your patience and understanding."

The plane dropped down steeply and was on the ground in ten minutes, fifteen minutes after Max hit the call button. A helicopter waited on the runway. In two minutes they were airborne and making the eight-mile journey to Vanderbilt Hospital at one hundred fifty miles per hour. In radio contact with the team on the ground, the flight doctor confirmed that the patient needed immediate surgery, and the EMT relayed Max's vital signs to doctors and nurses in the operating room being prepared. She set an IV in his right arm and began delivering a cocktail of vancomycin, clindamycin, and gentamicin.

In Max's wallet was his California driver's license, a health plan card from Blue Shield of California, and two HMRI business cards; his and that of Qasima Zipp, Director and Chairman of the Board. They notified BSCA. Qasima's number was in the UK, and the phones on the helicopter weren't set up to make international calls. Someone else would take care of that one later.

In four minutes they were landing on the SkyPort atop Vanderbilt University Hospital. In two more Max was being whisked into the operating room.

His leg was black nearly to the knee. He was delirious, shocky, and no longer competent to make medical decisions for himself. The surgeons felt that the only question was whether to take the leg off above the knee or below. Below the knee, the risk of spreading infection was much higher. Above the knee, the shock and awe when he woke would be all that much greater. But leave the leg on, and he'd be septic and probably dead by 8:15, just like MedAire had said. Every moment's delay only increased the possibility of an even more bitter outcome.

CHAPTER 79 THE SURGERY

Angus Elphinstone, the anesthesiologist, slipped a central line through Max's aorta by way of his neck and began dripping propofol, saline and more antibiotics. By the time he had taken his hands off the tangle of tubes, Max was out. The circulating nurse, Anita Singh, covered all but his left leg with heated blankets, then tested saws and organized tools. The scrub nurse, Ms. Mandlangbayan, slipped a thin elastic sleeve over the exposed lower left leg and wrapped a sterile tourniquet high on his thigh to reduce blood flow and bleeding during surgery. Then she inserted a Foley catheter into his penis, and holding his foot almost vertically, waited in place for the show to begin.

When Dr. Rajni Klitenik entered the room, a sulfurous blast of gas from the wound overwhelmed the smell of surgery-grade Ultrableach that normally dominated the OR. Her second, Dr. Kali Chandrasekharan, eyed Elphinstone who signaled that Max's blood gases were hinting at sepsis and it was time to move with a special urgency. Chopin nocturnes played, metal clicked and clacked against metal. There was no chatter, per Klitenik's order.

Klitenik and Chandrasekharan were almost eye-to-eye as the latter sketched circumferentially on Max's leg, preparing for a big flap in the front that could be folded rearward, leaving the scar in the back. Under the spell of the nocturne's broken chords and emotional energy, Klitenik made the first incision about halfway between the iliac crest of his hip and the top of his knee, cutting through skin, subcutaneous tissue, and fascia. Working her way around the leg, she found Hunter's Canal carrying the femoral artery, vein, and branches of the nerve. Using it as a reference point, she continued incising all the way through the muscles and to the bone. She cut and tied off the saphenous vein, electro-cauterizing other gossamer-thin ones as she worked. Hands moved in and out, supporting the leg, repositioning it for her, sopping up blood, delivering forceps and scalpels, or applying them as needed. Only subtle communication through gestures, the learned practice of thousands of surgeries done together, guided this plastic and reconstructive surgery team.

Gobs of Max's yellow fat wobbled and glimmered in the mercury lights. If Chandrasehkaran's morning sickness had not gotten the better of her, the smells of gangrene alone would not have led her to shout out "Bowl!" and Ms. Singh would not have held one while the nauseated surgeon vomited into it. Recovering, she displaced the major structures to one side while Dr. Klitenik reached in, transecting and dissecting muscle, elevating the quadriceps, separating it and holding it back with large retractors to expose several inches of bone.

If the Bastille had been stormed by citoyens on two-stroke dirt bikes, the sounds would have been similar—enraged, unsynchronized, and unstoppable—to the bone saw Ms. Mandlangbayan handed to Klitenik. Its oscillating motor never failed to put everyone on edge, but she was quick, steadily applying pressure as she worked her way through the femur and as Singh sprayed saline on it for cooling. In moments, she was done. After more dissection, the femoral nerve, the superficial femoral artery, the femoral vein—ultra-wide at thirteen millimetres in diameter—lying deep within the leg, and finally the sciatic nerve were all cut and sutured with polypropylene.

Chandrasekharan used her index finger to push the sciatic nerve at least five centimetres into the red meat of his leg, where it had no chance of tethering to the flap.

With the amputation complete, Ms. Singh took away the stockinet-covered left leg and marked it for dirty disposal. All five team members eyed the vital statistics monitor, observing the signs of imminent renal failure, maybe worse. On the instructions of Klitenik, Mandlangbayan gave him an extra dose of epinephrine to support his falling vascular pressure, hoping that would be enough to let him keep the kidneys, even if they were damaged.

Chandrasekharan filed rough edges of the exposed end of the femur and then drilled four holes into it, preparing it as an anchor for muscles she'd sew on top for protection. Using a technique developed in Sweden, a hollow titanium sleeve, threaded inside and out, was inserted into the marrow-filled medullar cavity of his severed femur. Six months later, after his wound had healed and osseointegration of the sleeve was complete, surgeons would open Max up again, pierce the healed flesh with a solid titanium bolt, and thread it into the sleeve. The exposed fixture in the residuum of his leg would be the anchor for any prosthesis he wanted to attach, far stronger and more trouble-free than the cups and straps or other paraphernalia that had been used for centuries.

Mandlangbayan released the tourniquet, achieving hemostasis by electrocautery and ligation of small vessels. They washed away debris and sawdust, and then Klitenik folded the adductor up and over the end of the bone with its titanium fixture, securing it with the catgut sutures she'd woven through the holes. Then she did the same with the hamstring, always focused on keeping the femur centered in the muscle mass.

The flaps of skin were placed, and they began the process of closing. Like fine dressmakers, they tested the pieces for fit, measuring twice and cutting only once, then sewed up fascia, leaving room for a couple of drains she'd inserted into the raw stump, hoping any residual bacteria could be coaxed out, and finally sewed and trimmed and made her final stitch.

Years of experience had ritualized the process of covering the wound with gauzes of different shapes, protecting it well and compressing it without inducing any skin damage. A wide elastic bandage was wrapped around the now white stump, diagonally to avoid constriction. And they were done, twenty-seven minutes after Klitenik made her first cut.

CHAPTER 80 THE WAKEUP CALL

There had been half a dozen people from LGTBQ on that flight. Within moments of the evacuation they all knew that Max was the evacuee. One of them had gone to school with an MD at Vanderbilt—someone who was up to her eyeballs in genome wide association studies and therefore likely to know of Max—so she was called and asked to look in on him. Each of the researchers and journalists on the plane made calls or sent texts and emails to close associates in their networks outside the fuselage, and from those associates the fanning out went further, informing dozens and then hundreds of people that there'd been some crisis and Max was in the hospital in Nashville. No one had any more details yet.

The Critical Care Team was providing the critical care, but without next of kin, with Qasima's office in Oxford closed for the day, with Armen—whom Max had identified as an emergency contact on documents filed with the insurers—not picking up the phone in Boston, there wasn't much to do except wait for Max to wake up.

Dr. Amrita Amritamoorthi, the Max and Manny Delbrück Professor of Biophysics and Director of the Vanderbilt Center of Human Genetics Research, was on campus that afternoon when she got the call. By the time she finally was free of commitments, she should have gone home for sit-down dinner with her girls and her husband, but this stuff about life and death took precedence for her, even over that. Her family would have to understand. Besides, they had probably seen the spot on WTVF about the emergency landing, and for Amrita to be visiting the victim would make her famous by association. She called home to let them know.

She located Max in the ICU. After showing her university credentials to the Care Team and explaining that she was a friend of a friend, she gowned up and sat by his side for what she thought might be a very long night.

Dr. Amritamoorthi was not idle while she waited. She Googled Max and found that he was a superstar, and tangentially in her own field. With good sleuthing skills and the modest social networks of the day she made a list of twenty people whom she thought should know about this. Then she Skyped Qasima in the UK, introduced herself, explained what she knew of the situation, and turned her head as Qasima wept. Then she passed the list she'd compiled to Qasima, who of course had her own.

Other than returning the call to her friend who'd been on the plane, Dr. Amritamoorthi didn't feel comfortable informing others. She stayed focused on being the first person he would see when he woke. Her friend had no such reserve, sending out a news update to more than one hundred people who'd been at LGTBQ. The news radiated outward from there and soon a thousand people knew that a tragedy had befallen Max Frood.

When Max did wake, around dinnertime, he was greeted by strangers bearing bad news they didn't deliver. He had been out of his mind from the "Gang Fucking Grene" moment, and he had only the most fragile grasp of those garbled morning thoughts. No longer delirious, but in a stupor of morphine, he asked for food and went back to sleep.

Dr. Amritamoorthi overheard Max's doctors as they came and went. His serum creatinine was 6.3 mg/dl, not 0.9 mg/dl as it should have been. The fix was in on his kidneys. "That's ominous," she found herself saying to the walls.

A few hours later Max woke again and Dr. Amritamoorthi was able to introduce herself. She explained that she was a friend of a friend, but Max didn't recognize the name of the friend. When the Care Team reviewed what they knew had happened, and Dr. Amritamoorthi translated that into scientific English, Max passed out. The Care Team coaxed him back and fed him clear liquids.

Max's mind was black inside. His island dream, his dream of being an island, would not be real anytime soon. He hated this, this dependence on so many people, this public exposure.

He asked for his phone. Blackberry Messenger showed him that there were dozens of texts, and too many voicemails to sort through, although he could guess what each one was about by the caller's number. He called Dixon Mock.

"Max, I've been worried about you. I wondered why you ..."

Max interrupted, "You don't know the half of it. Is everyone alright?"

"What do you mean, alright? What's wrong with you?"

"You know, on the beach, those cuts we got? Is everyone who got cut alright?"

"Yeah. I mean, I think so. No one told me anything. Is everything alright with you?"

"No. Fuck no. I lost my fucking leg above the fucking knee. No, I'm not all fucking right."

Dix was silent on the other end of the line. Max didn't want sympathy from him, but he could feel it coming over the cellular network: waves of sympathy riding up from Florida. It was a wakeup call for him. Sympathy was just another form of pity. He didn't want pity. He wanted to be a fortress, impregnable, indomitable. His dream of Island Max demanded that he suppress any message that made him look pitiful. So, whatever he may have felt, that moment was the last time Max ever expressed any bitterness about his leg. Max turned the conversation around.

"Heh, I'm lucky to be alive, Dix. Lucky to be alive. I guess they're all lucky too. We're all lucky."

Amrita, uncomfortable intruding and listening to Max's half of the conversation, but feeling like she was in the middle of someone's religious awakening, was agape.

Dixon Mock, confused by the rapid turnaround, embarrassed by his inability to find the words when Max needed them, said the only true thing he could think of, and that was exactly what Max wanted him to say, "Max, I'm glad you're alive, too. You're one of a kind, one of a kind."

When Max went back to sleep, Amrita returned home, promising to check in on him daily, by phone if not always in person. She knew, from his creatinine, that this was not going to be a short stay.

QASIMA and Dix were there by the next day, Armen the following, and Carmie with her baby the one after that. Sameer was on the same flight. Max was almost happy that they came. Dyk and Dykkur, the maxophants, did not come. They Skyped. He was happy they did not come. There was only so much of their fawning he could take. They would never have known when to leave. They'd remind him of whatever it was they didn't know he was doing on the beach, and how it led to his hospitalization. Flowers, food, cards, calls, and thousands of email messages flowed in from all over the world. He ignored almost all of it, and those he answered, he answered with the aim of suppressing sympathy. "I'm fine. Wear beach shoes. MF."

The one person Max really wanted to see was Hugh, the legman. Hugh came down from MIT and showed off his latest devices. Max was being dialyzed by then. Hugh gave Max hope, and hope is good.

THE leg improved fast. When the dressings were changed, nurses and doctors got their first chance to see the wound. They oohed at the reduced swelling and the rapid healing of the flap, and dragged in medical students to view the artistry of Dr. Klitenik's stitching. Dr. Amritamoorthi brought in PhD candidates to meet this hero whom she believed was a direct spiritual descendent of Max Delbrück, Vanderbilt's most famous faculty member ever.

But Max was a mess. Though he could focus his mind and had the concentration of a blue-crystal addict after losing his source, his kidneys had only gotten worse. His skin was taut and edematous from the litres of retained water. Between the shock-induced low blood pressure and the nephrotoxic antibiotic gentamicin, and the mild but permanent damage from beatings he'd received at the hands of angry prostitutes, and some bad luck, he was close to renal failure.

Gentamicin had been the right choice by the EMT. Cultures grown from his erstwhile leg turned up *Proteus* spp., a somewhat vague categorization of multiple Gram-negative bacteria for which that old and inexpensive antibiotic was the ticket. The good news was that *Proteus* didn't turn up in what was left of Max, so three days after surgery they stopped the gentamicin. He hoped, they all hoped, that taking him off it would put an end to the short seizures he'd had at least daily. It did. The dizziness and the abdominal cramps all went away too. The subjective tinnitus that made him think he was in a tunnel fronting the ocean? That didn't end. But the really bad news was that he hadn't made any urine the entire time, and his creatinine had risen to 8.0 mg/dl. He was carrying so much water in his blood he was at risk of heart failure. With every extra milligram per decilitre, the kidneys were being asked to do more and more, yet they needed R&R. There were no drugs that would solve the problem of the electrolyte imbalances, the buildup of urea and other crap, and no urine. That's why they'd had to dialyze him, aggressively.

For five days, eight hours a day, the arterial catheter in Max's arm carried his blood to a filter, aka an artificial kidney, in a rack with pumps and knobs and dials. There the blood was scrubbed of the byproducts of metabolism, the electrolyte imbalance was restored, the excess water was removed one molecule at a time, and his new improved blood was returned to him. The dialysis hangover hit Max hard, leaving him with barely enough energy to sit up in bed. His muscles cramped. His head ached. He was nauseated. The edema came down, and so did his creatine, like clockwork, 1 mg/dl each day. His temperature began to rise, worrying everyone about healthcare-associated infection, and then it passed. On day three, he made urine for the first time. He cried. Amritamoorthi cried. The nurses saw suffering every day, but even they felt he'd been dealt a low blow, several low blows. After Amritamoorthi had educated them about the most illustrious physicist in Vanderbilt's history, Delbrück, that other Max whose own long line of intellectual ancestry went back all the way to Röntgen, and whose mantle she herself carried, they cried, too.

After day five, when the creatine was 3.0 mg/dl, the nephrologist declared, "Enough, already. You're going to keep that original equipment and we're going to get you stabilized and on your way home."

His clothes had been washed. Dr. Amritamoorthi had even offered to buy him some new and fresh ones. Max declined. He did accept her offer of help getting to the airport. Seventeen days after he was admitted, she and her daughters and her husband wheeled him out into the corridor, down the elevator and into fresh air. There she and her family stood by while he was loaded into a wheelchair-enabled van, and she accompanied him to the airport, through security, God only knows how, and all the way to his seat on the plane, taking every opportunity to tell onlookers and attendants what a very important and saintly person was this Dr. Max Frood.

CHAPTER 81 NOT DEAD YET

I DIDN'T GET the message, and I don't know how I missed it. It must have been self-absorption, Julia, and devotion to laying the groundwork for my move. That move was a fait accompli as far as I was concerned. All that needed doing was the details, and I had my arms around the details. That Max didn't reply to my messages was worrisome, but he was busy; he had dozens of people working for him, he had those companies, and speaking engagements, and other responsibilities. I was only a mouse, and easy to forget about.

Finally, after a week, I called the main number at HMRI, and that's when I learned, at least superficially, what had happened. Like everyone else, I was stunned. I had gone through a tunnel and come out the other side into a different world, one with a peg-leg Max. With his khakis on, who would know the difference? Still, for him, the adjustment must have been beyond my ability to find the words. But if anyone thought that cataclysm would make Max soften or slow down, they were wrong, and maybe even disappointed.

"The thing is," Max explained to me from his hospital room in Nashville two days after the dialysis ended, "the one person feeling least miserable about the amputation is the amputee. He's already gotten over it. The rest of you are scared shitless that it might happen to you, and then you're going to have to get over it. Hugh! Look at fuckin' Hugh." And then he paused. "I really shouldn't speak to you like that." That was the closest I ever heard Max apologize for anything, anytime, ever. He backtracked. "Look at Hugh! He got up and changed the world. I'll do the same. The same!"

I was silent, but had questions weighing on me. Paramount among them were: "Hugh?" and "Does the offer still stand?" Then, reading me, he said, "Heh, my offer still stands. Kenneth, my assistant, will help you with the paperwork. When you need me to sign something I'll sign something. If Reed needs to talk to me, let me know and I'll call him."

He paused, waiting for me, but I still couldn't find words, so he continued, "Cheer up! I'm the one cheating death. I'm going to be finer than frog's hair. I'd leave today, but they have me tied to these bags of God knows what, so it will be another week, and my kidneys aren't liking it too much so they're watching me for that, too. Really, you don't want to hear about this. About that paperwork, it's a formality. Make believe it's already done and get yourself to California in a month. Kenneth can arrange housing on the Farm for you for as long as you want."

I didn't know exactly what he saw in me, but he was making it easy to become his protégé, and I was dumbfounded that he had space in his head for any of this so soon after the incident. I hadn't yet caught up with his optimism, so all I could do was try my best to sound like I had.

Carmie met him at SFO a week later. He made her wipe away her tears. "You're projecting, Carmie. Projecting onto your baby, that she'll have an accident and you'll have to watch." he said. "Fuggetaboutit. Humans adapt. We're great at it."

She hadn't seen him funny and upbeat before. He was almost vulnerable, and at his most charming ever.

"You know what was absolutely the worst part of this whole experience? Realizing I was going to lose it. That sucked. OK, and then waking up and finding out I'd lost it. That sucked, too. But by then it was done. Over. Everything's just getting better now. I'm not going to let this slow me down. Part of my therapy is to be a bigger bad ass than ever, so watch out!"

Later she told me, "He wasn't kidding."

"I haven't sorted it all out yet," Max said. "All the logistics. Sameer will get me some help at home, and a driver. It's definitely not so convenient living out there in Appalachia"—referring to the rural west slopes of the Santa Cruz Mountains—"and having the company and my place here in the Valley. But I'll adapt. I'll adapt!"

He could not console her when she broke down again, pushing the wheelchair. Island Max was not capable of giving consolation. Missing the gene or something.

"The finality of it. The brutality. The disfigurement." Carmie shook her head and rocked in silence.

"The horror! The horror! I know. But if I don't care, why do you care? Anyway, when I get my leg, you'll hardly notice. I'm not disabled. That leg was busted and it had to go. And what am I going to do if I don't go on like before? Rail against a lousy microbe? Crusade to improve First Aid? Heh, you're the one whose supposed to perk me up. I want more stock if I'm going to have to do any more of this."

At the end of my interview of her, Carmie said, "I'll tell you Lakshmi, I was envisioning some philosophical embitterment, his back erect, and a peacoat, maybe a cloak, if he had a cloak, dramatically sweeping the scene. Then in a deep voice and over-delivered lines, he'd say something poetic about retribution and grand schemes. But he made me laugh instead. He had me amazed at his resilience and good nature, and with new hope about the power of the human spirit. Put that together with what happened later." I could tell she had at least a few more words in her, so I waited until they were ready to come out. "There's never been someone as mercurial as Max Frood."

THE Institute had provided Max with a special van to accommodate his wheelchair, so Carmie said her goodbyes at the airport. Sameer's brother, Issahaq, drove him over the hill to Lobitos Farm where he was greeted like a returning warrior by the entire staff. "I shall return!" he shouted, although he already had returned. Everyone knew what he meant.

"This is just a little setback. I am not dead yet!" He laughed and made everyone else laugh. "Technology will make me stronger and better than I was before. To science and to technology and to Medicine!" He raised his arms to cheers and loud applause. As with Carmie, there were tears of joy and surprise, too. He had relieved them of their need to grieve.

Champagne was poured and Qasima offered a toast, lamenting Max's bad luck and honoring his fortitude and commitment to HMRI's mission. Elegant hors d'oeuvres were served by tattooed ladies, pierced twenty-something lovelies in black and white uniforms. The students snuck away with the left-over food, as it would make excellent fuel later that same night. A few faculty stood around gossiping while the trays and carts were taken to the kitchens, and finally, Qasima and Max shook hands, signifying that HMRI was fully staffed and back to normal again.

Max made an appearance at his lab, if only to remind everyone to keep on working and inform them that he'd be in close contact with the usual suite of text, email, chat, online video, and phone. "I'm staying on this side of the hill for the next six weeks at least, so you'd better get used to seeing me around more than ever," he told them.

The full recommended recovery period for osseointegration was twelve months. After six, he would fly to Sweden where the real pros in the field worked. They would give him the baddest stud on the planet. Hugh would set him up with the latest and greatest prosthesis, whether money could buy it or not. According to the Swedes, he'd have another six months of gradually increasing the load on it until he was able to put his full body weight on the android limb. "I'm not waiting any fucking year!" was his response to their schedule. He expected though, to be spending fewer overnights at his apartment in Menlo Park for a while. He informed his team, "Until I can walk out of here easily, you're stuck with me." His colleagues and students were looking forward to having more of his attention. They believed it would be good for all of them.

That plan hit its first pothole when he learned how inconvenient it was to travel in a wheelchair. Issahaq couldn't drive that van like Max drove his Outback. Sliding the van's tail through the hairpins was out of the question. And the doctors wanted to see him in clinic more frequently at the Palo Alto Medical Foundation, PAMF, than he'd counted on. At first there were twice-weekly visits to the bloodsuckers in the chemistry lab, tracking his slowly recovering kidney function. By the time he had convinced the system to save him a trip and have the blood draws done at Lobitos Farm, the frequency was cut to weekly, on the same schedule as his stump check, where they kept an eye on secondary infections from the surgery and drainage, too. And they also wanted him in physical therapy daily—to which Max said "NFW"—to keep his strength up and restore sensation to the leg. NFW or not, there were too many long daytrips and much time-consuming and inefficient shuttling between clinics in the Valley. He was missing Sameer and his lunches at 3000 Sand Hill Road.

Progress was initially slow, but before long, he was terrorizingly swift and devious on crutches, staying overnight in Menlo Park, visiting some of the floating poker games, hosting a small one himself, and returning back to form, if still staying away from Moby Dick's.

CHAPTER 82 ARRIVALS

I MEANT TO read a pile of books about Silicon Valley before I left Princeton, but all I managed was the one at the top of my list; Ellen Ullman's *The Bug.* A guy's life unravels, in part over a bug in a piece of software, and (spoiler alert) he kills himself. Her punkish lesbian character was attractive. The book was better, more literary than I expected, and I learned something about obsessions and human decency, and but not so much about Silicon Valley *per se.*

I finished it as we touched down at SFO mid-morning. Spring hadn't quite arrived in Princeton, but from what I could see through the airplane's scratched windows, it had been in force for a month already in California's cradle of innovation.

Max wasn't feeling reborn though. His kidneys had stopped improving, and it was affecting his mood. Plus, he was hearing cicadas, lots and lots of cicadas, and he couldn't concentrate the way he used to. We had them in Princeton that spring before I worked for Jay. We're so removed from nature that it was thrilling to hear their ninety-decibel thrum. When we tired of it, we went inside or closed the windows. I didn't like the thought of having that sound follow me around everywhere and all the time. Max felt the same way, but for him, there was no escaping it.

He was cranky instead of ecstatic when the physical therapists fitted his custom ergonomic crutches. Standing on them for the first time, he felt his world wobble and he had more trouble balancing than he thought he should. The orthopedist and nurses and techs and physical therapists were encouraging, but Max thought he detected surprise at how much trouble he was having. He needed patience, like he needed a lot of things.

I, on the other hand, was feeling great. Julia and I had broken up, true, but there I was in California, the Garden of Eden. The refrain of Woody Guthrie lyrics played in my head, almost as difficult to displace as the cicadas in Max's. My father, who'd made me listen to Dust Bowl ballads on long car rides, was happy when I told him. He said, "My parents would have been happy, too, Rani," while I wished for some relief.

Max had another appointment at PAMF that morning. Issahaq had driven the Maxmobile from Palo Alto to meet me at SFO while Max got serviced at the clinic. He had parked so he could help me with my luggage. Dressed in salwar kameez, loose fitting vest, knit cap, and thick beard, that is, looking every bit like a Pakistani terrorist, Security would have given him a cavity exam if given a chance. But he wanted to go no further than the baggage carousels. He was sweet, had a huge white smile, spoke perfect colloquial English, and had the manners of a butler to go with it. If everyone could have looked past his intentionally provocative clothing, he'd have been just another guy meeting his Indian nerd girlfriend, or maybe his lesbian sister.

As the two of us drove the van south to collect Max, a text from him told us we'd need to kill some time. He didn't want us watching him in physical therapy, so we went looking for food at the shopping center across the street from the clinic.

Issahaq swore in Urdu at the packs of kids who'd left the neighboring high school campus in search of lunch. There were cool black kids mooching cash or another kid's teriyaki chicken over rice, girls with bare bellies or bare shoulders or see-through yoga pants who got lunch for free, bros in sports shorts paying for it, kids waiting for their friends' leftovers, kids who ran in front of moving cars while swinging white plastic bags of candy or fabric bags emblazoned with the words "Who is John Galt?", even-more-privileged kids of the IPO'd and IPO'ing eating at white-tablecloth establishments where they have standing reservations, and an army of Asian kids poring over their books. They walked every which way over the parking lot or filled every table and seat to be had. What Zac Efron was doing there, huddling over a trig and analytic geometry textbook with a Muslim girl wearing a headscarf, I was never able to confirm, but I was told that he'd been hired as her private tutor because, "He's cute."

Failing to find a parking place, and almost being run over by two girls in a Porsche singing *a cappella* out the windows at the top of their lungs, Issahaq texted Sameer in search of some critical intel. Then he bolted out on to Embarcadero Road. At the light at El Camino he went left, heading south a few blocks for the satellite office of Ph'eer, Dowd, and Sertantiy.

A caravan of parked lunch trucks awaited us and dozens of other devotees who knew quality, or those who would rather eat standing up in the parking lot than risk their lives crossing that thoroughfare by foot. Issahaq was a little disappointed that I didn't buy lunch from one of his family's trucks. A converted Airstream caught my attention, as in front of it a dozen eye-catching women were waiting patiently. On its original aluminum cowl there was an eight-inch high banner of pink paint running all the way around. A band of small LEDs, arrayed twelve rows high and all the way around, too, partially covered it. Driven by some nifty electronics within, it could, in principle, put up any message the truck's proprietor desired. "Eat Pussy Not Cow" ... "Eat Pussy Not Cow" ... "Eat Pussy Not Cow" ... tickered around endlessly in a pulsating infinity of color, protesting one thing and offering another, interrupted only by virtuoso, almost pyrotechnic displays of LED graphic art, sometimes abstract, sometimes representational, and defying belief that so much realism could be conveyed with so few lights. This was someone's instrument and they played it, from somewhere, with ardor and genius. The door opened, a smiling and apparently satisfied woman left, another entered, the door closed. There were no overt prohibitions against men, but maybe there was a code I hadn't yet deciphered. To eat or be eaten, that was another code to be deciphered. Tempting though it was, my first day on the job ... I wasn't ready for it. There's always another day, and the call of Flo's Saigon Pho Real was too strong.

She gave me a steaming bowl, a ceramic bowl, not a styrofoam throwaway, of rice noodles in ox knuckle broth, two slices of beef, one of pork, three fried shrimp, a pile of bean sprouts, sliced Serrano chilies, cilantro, ginger, garlic, scallions, and a quarter of lime to squeeze into the mix. While I was eating, Flo made me a divine and high-joltage Vietnamese coffee, dripped slowly onto ice with sweet condensed milk and served in a clear glass. Just like that, I'd become a devotee of trucked food. The long familiar slurring slang "roach coach," no longer applied. "Gourmet valet" would have been more like it. When we finished, I handed Fay the dirty dishes and it was finally time to pick up Max.

An entourage of attendants was with him, carrying the crutches. He was strapped into his wheelchair, which he was coming to hate, while they rolled him into the van. *I'm the invalid I was not supposed to be,* his eyes said. *I don't want to be seen this way, all sweaty and worn out.*

He was quiet at first as we headed up Sand Hill Road, eating from the box of samosas Issahaq had picked up for him, and knocking back a can of soda. Crossing Interstate 280 and passing SLAC, the Stanford Linear Accelerator Center, we turned right onto smaller roads and were soon passing by what looked like a Japanese village, vineyards, and monstrous mansions of both good and garish design. Then we turned uphill through five miles of redwood forests I'd heard about but never seen, crested on Skyline Boulevard, went through an invisible wall that marked the entry to a much wetter and cooler climate, and began the steeper, windier road that eventually landed us at Lobitos Farm.

Max raced his motorized chair like a gocart down the corridors, banging into only a few racks of rats and chemicals and books and other rolling storage that shouldn't have been there, without any damage being done. Then he did a hard left turn and entered his empire. There he had to navigate slowly because certain kinds of discipline he disrespected had been allowed to break down completely, and while I could walk from one end of the lab to the other without touching anything, it was only because I could twist my hips and shoulders to get by improbably placed obstacles. Max, on the other hand, pushed rolling equipment and chairs out of the way with hands or his good leg, and when I caught up with him, I did it for him. Along the way he introduced me, getting or giving the congratulatory handshake at each and every bench, explaining what was going on at each one, how it fit into the overall plan, and of course, saying a few words about what I'd be doing. Then we were in his office, a cul-de-sac.

Scientists from other labs got the news that he was on site, and they came over to say hi and cheer him on. He did get up now and then, to admiration and even applause, on crutches but standing nonetheless, just to show that he could, but the morning's exertions had worn him out.

What I would be doing was developing protocols for pulling DNA from blood, first catching up with developments elsewhere, as we'd talked about at Maître Dix, and then trying to outrun and outwit the rest of the world; that is to say, I was supposed to crush them. There were no postdocs working on this. There were no graduate students working on this. I'd get mentorship and advice where I could. Max would make introductions outside the I when I needed them, and that would be when it was time to acquire patient samples.

The west-facing labs were filled with afternoon sun that I at first mistook for the warm embrace of my mother. This clean, well-lighted, if not tidy place for kooks, genius kooks with streaks of Rube Goldberg's DNA running through them, was my new home. A few benchtops looked like they'd been ransacked. Other than those, every other square foot of counter or corner was packed with a work-in-progress. Brand new gear barely removed from boxes, hand-made and jury-rigged hardware to actuate pumps, exotic and not-so-exotic microscopes, shimmying agitators, magnetic stirrers, hot plates, glass-front refrigerators, laptops, thirty-inch monitors, robotic handlers, stacks of 96-well and 384-well plates, reagents in all sorts of bottles small and large, plastic and glass, clear and dark; all dispersed according to a plan neither chaotic nor orderly. And at the desks, or pipette-in-hand next to benches, huddled in groups or working alone, many of them with noise cancelling headphones, some in street clothes, some mud-spattered from a mountain bike ride, were Asians of every variety, a few Europeans, an African, and one token Caucasian American. Typical modern moby lab. I loved working for Max. I love-love-loved it, and I hadn't even started.

THE ransacked spaces had belonged to Nico and Rinchen. In the first few days of Max's rehab, they had moved out quickly, under what I was told was surveillance by Institute lawyers. Their graduate students were still at work, pushing the frontier forward, subject to IP licensing and conflict of interest considerations that had everyone tied in knots. Those former postdocs were now trying to make the pore sequencing demonstration into something real and commercial at Genormx Inc., which had set up shop in East Palo Alto.

CHAPTER 83 GENORMX INC. – SCENE II OF IV

THE STRUGGLE of recovery took air out of Max's bubble and slowed him down. It deflected his attention from Genormx. Initially, Carmie worried that her company would suffer, but later, she opined that the postdocs were so good and so independent, and Max could be so disruptive, that the balance swung the other way. "They were better off without him. His absence allowed them to get off to the best possible start." This was the new normal throughout Max's empire. He had lost a step, with consequences both positive and negative.

While Carmie worked the investors and the strategy, and made sure everyone on the team knew what that strategy was, Kozmo took care of all the operational details. After employment contracts, healthcare plans, and IP assignment agreements were signed, after consulting relationships were formalized with advisors and members of the Board of Directors, after a letter of engagement was finalized with corporate counsel Molly Fugazy, and while Kozmo was polishing the licensing agreements with TTO, he also located and negotiated a contract for space they needed and space to grow into, all in a business park on the other side of the freeway.

There's little difference between the two sides of Caltrain's tracks in Palo Alto and Menlo Park. The tracks cut right through downtown Menlo and they separate downtown Palo Alto from Stanford. You drive, ride, or walk the underpasses and gated crossings. Except for the tragedies of accidents and suicides, the tracks are no demarcation at all.

Cross the highway, though, and you're in another country. Just northeast of Highway 101 is East Palo Alto, a three-square-mile tract of land without a single billionaire. Almost renamed Nairobi before most of you readers were born, a little finger of it called Whiskey Gulch jumped west of the freeway and used to sport Brazilian restaurants, a hip restaurant and dance bar called Club Afrique, latenight liquor stores, winos, gangs, and disproportionate violence. An affront to most of those on the favored side of the freeway, Whiskey Gulch's eccentricities were plowed under and then replaced with tall law offices and a swank Four Seasons Hotel. The northeast side, the real EPA, has retained some of its flare for danger and its welcome for the dispossessed. You'll know you're really there when you pass Las Adelitas and La Estralita Markets and Restaurant on your way to Genormx Inc.'s headquarters located near San Francisco Bay in a business park that could be in Anywhere, USA.

Carmie's strategic plan remained the same as it had been since the beginning. Get in and get out. That was the logic behind paring the diagnostics business from the plan; it was too different and therefore distracting. Few companies could be good at instrument building and also good at developing and selling diagnostics. It was probably true, too, she thought, that of the few companies that could be good at both, none were small, and none were startups. She called the original plan "Max's wet dream." Then she got everyone, except maybe Max, on board with the idea that developing a sequencing instrument was, again, a very different business from selling sequencers. Only multi-billion dollar companies with global manufacturing and reagent distribution could succeed at the latter, and then only if they had large teams devoted to (1) software tools for analysis of data streaming off the instruments and (2) applications of sequencing to real world problems in medicine. In short, this had ceased to be a game for startups. It would take a billion dollars or more to bring a new sequencer into a strong competitive position with the best already out there. Carmie didn't want Genormx to starve for cash while on the road to being best in class. She wanted to position it for sale—long before that billion dollars had been spent—to a company with a billion dollars it was prepared to invest in order to protect its present position. She hoped to get $300 million or maybe even $500 million from them, saving the big company years of development and dead ends, and justifying the fat purchase price.

That plan shouted for keeping the team lean. Had it been an academic exercise, the Beam Team postdocs could have learned how to scale a single-pore demo up to a first- or so-called Alpha-prototype with 10,000 pores. Maybe they could have learned how to package the Alpha so that with only slight modification, its follow-on, the Beta, could be distributed to major genomics centers for testing. But this was not an academic exercise.

The three firms of commercial import at that time were, flatly, not flat-footed. They had no intention of being scooped by startups like Genormx. There were half a dozen startups out there, all vying for the prize of being acquired. There were a few, too, so hubristic that they thought they'd win it all and take down one of the incumbents. Sequencing was an arms race where money bought speed and the possibility of being first-to-market. A company can still falter and founder even if it's won that race, and sometimes being first means being too early for your own good. The Kahns believed they understood customer requirements. Their own management experience and the strong financial syndicate behind them gave them good odds against faltering if they were first. For them, being first-to-market with a pore-based solution was nothing less than everything and the only thing.

Genormx had $8 million in the first tranche. The Kahns put it to use hiring an instrumentation consultancy, Packaged Systems, to help them build the Alpha. For $2 million, the firm of mechanical, electrical, optical, and hydraulic engineers signed up to take the Beam Team's forty-square-feet of table top experiment, rethink its intent from soup to nuts, and then fold it and reconstitute it into a slick looking box whose footprint was much less than ten square feet. Then, for another million dollars (*ka-ching!*) Genormx hired a microfabrication consultancy, Nottintel, to design a 10,000-pore version of the Beam Team's single-pore prototype. They were instructed to work from the Tiny Machines MEMS IP wherever possible. Nottintel would deliver chips with 100 and then 1000 pores, providing hardware to the Beam Team to use before the final one, the 10K Alpha, arrived twelve months after the start.

Taking into account the two hefty line-items in their budget, including early-completion bonuses, and after considering expenses for corporate and patent counsel, technology licensing fees, fire and safety insurance, workers' compensation insurance, directors' and officers' liability insurance, the lease, building improvements and maintenance, toxic waste disposal, Internet, phones and telecom, purchases of used lab benches and a few hundred thousand dollars of equipment, a monthly forecast of lab purchases, and salaries and healthcare and taxes for an office manager, the Kahns, Nico and Rinchen, a technician, and a bioinformatician, and making the unrealistic assumption that there would be no additional but unforeseen expenses, Genormx would have $600,000 left in the bank after twenty-four months. For all intents and purposes, that was equivalent to bankruptcy if they couldn't meet the milestones releasing the next $16 million infusion of cash.

Kozmo ran a weekly meeting with the Beam Team and the bioinformatician and representatives from the engineering consultancies. He had constructed a week-by-week schedule of milestones based on Carmie's POR. The meeting was used to review engineering progress against the schedule. When there was a miss, the schedule was changed, its consequences rippling through all the milestones still in the future. The Alpha was due at month fifteen, so a three-month slip to month eighteen could be tolerated, but not much more. If it looked like they would spend all of the $8 million before successfully delivering the Alpha, some painful decisions would have to be made.

The Beam Team was responsible for setting the technical requirements, transferring (to the consultants) all they'd learned in their years of effort leading up to the formation of Genormx, solving some key problems that had not been faced when working with a single pore in isolation, and keeping the consultants up to date on their latest findings in the lab.

One critical challenge they had to overcome was how to coax thousands upon thousands of strands of DNA into a field of pores. Parallelism was the centerpiece of cost reduction these new instruments were intended to provide. To achieve 10,000-fold parallelism with a chip containing 10,000 pores, one and exactly one strand of DNA had to penetrate each and every pore. If only a fraction were filled, it would be as if the chip had fewer than that many pores and its performance would be decreased accordingly. What they found was that they could fill only about 10 percent of them on the first, smaller-scale prototype parts Nottintel sent them. The DNA was in solution as it flowed over the sea of microscopic holes. If its concentration was very, very low, only a few percent of the pores would get filled. As Genormx engineers increased the concentration, the fill fraction increased too, but beyond a certain point, the strands stuck to each other, clogged a pore without entering it, and the fill fraction fell. Ten months following the funding, after untold late nights and weekends testing various conditions, and costly consulting with academic and commercial chemists, material scientists, rheologists, and specialists in fluids at low Reynolds number, the highest they achieved was 10 percent. Their newly developed theory of the subject said that they should only be able to achieve 9 percent. In other words, theory and experiment agreed, so it didn't look like they had much chance to achieve 100 percent fill factor. That was bad. Unless they solved it, or made up for the deficiency in some other way, they'd end up 90 percent shy of their design goal, a humiliating outcome.

Mirjam Sykes, a South African mechanical engineer and founder of Packaged Systems, was called in when her staff was stumped. Systems integrators are trained to look at all the contributing factors simultaneously. Her usual methods failed her, until the epiphany arrived. She concluded and made a convincing case that Genormx' commitment to the Tiny Machines IP was a crushing burden. Max had made that commitment in the beginning—systematically dismantling any suggestion of alternatives. Were his arguments well-founded or were they self-justifications that generated income for him? The IP did this in two ways, first through the patents licensed from the I—and from which revenue stream Max drank deeply—and second through the growth in Tiny's business which would ultimately accrue to him through stock appreciation and license revenue to MIT—from which stream he also drank deeply.

Armen, the Chairman of Tiny Machines, had his own conflict of interest—the prospect that his company would provide Genormx with IP and MEMS chips—but he told me later that his prime investment motivation was the belief that the new company would be a success on its merits and in its own right. "Max sold me, or *fooled* me for the second time. I don't think he ever considered the other MEMS platforms, but he convinced us that he had. Our own consultants, and Papken, who's of course not naïve about the difficulties, couldn't find the flaws in Max's logic when we started out. Maybe Max knew them himself. I think he did, but we'll never know, will we?" he said, shaking his head. "I went into this with greater confidence than I usually allow myself that I'd make 'tenex,'"—his phrasing—"this time around with him."

Max, forever the poker player, was calm on the outside, but Dyk's words—and Dyk was the conduit for Max's opinions—in the first Board meeting following Mirjam's report were, "Fire that lesbian Sykes!" By forcing the linkage to Tiny at the beginning, Max had backed his team into the decision to use electron scattering for detection. Now, if they abandoned Tiny, would the scattering decision stand up, or would they abandon that too? Their detection system was linked to their pore technology, so what then? What then could Max say was his? What about his royalties from Tiny? How could he remain the center of the Genormx technology universe if his two contributions were tossed out? He had to have been suffering from a bad case of NIH Syndrome.

There was another solution; double down on their existing plan. If they could only get DNA in 10 percent of the pores, maybe they should have ten times as many pores. That was the fix offered by the gals from Nottintel. Increasing the pore count ten times meant doing roughly the same to the chip area. Max found it heartening that there were reasons the chip would only have to be five-times larger. He also found it heartening that while the size increase would normally increase chip cost by an even larger amount, in this case because of the technology's tolerance for error, having to do with the low fill factor—"A nuance only a chip guy could love," Vladik told me—the cost would be only, *only*, 400 percent larger than forecast. Sure, this solution would eat up some of the profit margins, and sure, it would limit the long-term potential, but it would allow Genormx to stay on schedule, and being first was paramount.

Max used every bit of leverage he had, as Chair of the Scientific Advisory Board, as former advisor to the Beam Team, and as Board member Dyk Schmalis' sugar daddy, to have the decision swing where he favored it. He hectored them and schmoozed them. He appealed to their sycophancy and he argued from authority. He promised to behave. He tried to charm Carmie rather than browbeat her. He emphasized, for as long as anyone would listen to him, the possibility that moving away from Tiny would, or might force the company to take on more schedule risk than it could tolerate. He was a relentless lobbyist for his own interests.

Dyk made no new friends for himself. He let Francisquita Guzman and Intuition's Galena Radgloom know that he thought they were dumb cunts—or in in Francisquita's case, a dumb old dry cunt—because they couldn't see Max's genius. He tried to drive a wedge between Francisquita and Carmie, Carmie being on Guzman's payroll as an EIR. Intuition wanted nothing more to do with Genormx as long as Dyk was involved. The three ladies began a behind-the-scenes action to remove him.

When all the tooth-gnashing was done, Carmie presented the problem very simply to the Board. "Gentlemen and ladies, we are at a crisis. Our strategic plan has met an unexpected difficulty, an unknown unknown you might say. Stay the course we're on, and we'll fail for technical reasons. Abandon the Tiny IP and we take on too much schedule risk. Live with the low fill factor and increase chip size, and we'll give up some margin, but we'll have a product. The only other alternative is to give up, return the remaining cash on hand to the investors, and go find other work. If we can dispense with parliamentary procedure here for a moment, there's one other matter, though, one I'd like Galena to take up before we bring this to a vote."

Five minutes later, Carmie opened the door for Dyk as he exited the conference room and left the building without a word. Then she signaled to Max—ambling about the hallway pretty damned gracefully on L2, the name he'd given his robotic prosthesis—that he was wanted in the Board meeting. Sixteen months had passed since she first met him at 3000 Sand Hill Road. He had done more than lose a leg. He'd lost his youth, his health, and his good humor. His most common posture had become silent seething. And when had she last seen his visionary leadership or the flashes of jest or flirtation that she'd found so inspiring early on? She was driving an enterprise that he'd started, but whose weak underpinnings she was still discovering. She no longer trusted her founder. Now *that* was a founder problem. As Max brushed by her, he gave her the look, the one with eyebrows busy, signifying to her only that he misread the situation.

Kozmo, the engineering team, and a few advisors continued their nervous TV-watching and ping-pong-playing while waiting for a decision. Even Carmelita was there, napping the nap of the innocent in a portable car seat on the floor beside Kozmo.

Carmie informed Max that the Board had resolved to remove Dyk and replace him with someone of Galena Radgloom's choice.

"You've only got four now, what about a tie?"

"Galena will cast two votes today."

Max tried to look on with flat affect, but his teeth were clenched unnaturally. He breathed audibly through his nose, forcing himself to calm down, his chest and belly expanding slowly.

"Max," Carmie said, "we're giving you a choice. If you don't want to go forward without Dyk as your representative on the Board, you can resign from your advisory position effective immediately." She slid a document in front of him. "This is your resignation letter. You'll give up your unvested stock, 7.5 percent, and your claim to any royalties.

"There's risk going forward without you, but we'll take that into consideration when we vote on the proposal in front of us. Some here in this room think the chances of our success are greater without you. At this moment, I don't know how a vote would pencil out.

"If you decide to stay on, and if the Board votes in favor of continuing operations, the company will dissolve the Scientific Advisory Board." She slid another document in front of him. "We'll create a new Engineering Advisory Board. You will be invited to be a member of the EAB, but not its chairman. This second document is a new consulting agreement describing your role. The justification for the change is that we feel we are beyond the stage where basic science is determining. We need a different advisory structure, led by someone with commercial systems' engineering experience. The Board has resolved that Kozmo will lead a search committee to identify the EAB chairman."

Max seethed quietly. Carmie showed no signs of fear. Her voice like a bell was clear and firm as usual.

"Max, I know this a lot to absorb, but now is the time to decide. There will be no questions to the Board. We'll give you a minute to think it over, and then you must sign one of those documents. If you can't make a decision, we've made one for you," and then she slid a third document in front of him. "This is your termination letter, signed unanimously by the members of this Board," and sliding a fourth, "and the press release, too."

After Max had left the room, and the building, telling everyone that he was late for a physical therapy appointment in Palo Alto, and after the Board had voted unanimously, the Directors joined the staff beside the ping-pong table in the Common Room for an All Hands Meeting.

While cold beers, packaged teas, and sodas were unloaded from the fridge, and while trays of snacks from Costco were passed around, Carmie asked, "Will this hold me?" A moment later she was standing on the ping-pong table, open beer in hand, and addressing everyone with the confidence of a natural born leader.

"The company has just passed through its first crisis, and we've done so nobly. We, the Board are so impressed with all your efforts and accomplishments. The problem of low fill factor took us by surprise, and it shouldn't have. Let me tell you what we face and how we're going to attack it."

When she was done, and the new POR incorporating the recommendations from Nottintel was described, and Max's reduced role was announced and explained and swallowed with nary a sound, and the Board changes with not even that, there was applause, backslapping, and hugs. The new POR would send more money to Nottintel, leaving an even smaller cushion if the schedule slipped. That increased the pressure on everyone, but they would, as the cliché goes, live to fight another day.

Carmie had had to use all her own powers of persuasion to bring the Board members along. In the end, she had convinced them that the commitments to spend big piles of money, the next $16 million, were still in the future. "The team," she had said, "deserves the chance to deliver the first major milestone, as we promised them. We have so many obligations to Packaged Systems and Nottintel, and so many of our costs were front loaded," meaning that they'd already been incurred, "it doesn't cost us much to continue on and see. If they don't make it, and now it will be harder to make it, we can decide to wind down operations then. Max didn't provide the leadership we needed. He was an obstacle to bringing the necessary opinions forward. I hope that removing him from that position will be enough."

Everyone had been silent about Dyk.

CHAPTER 84 LOVE

OTHER THAN Orrigen's quarterly Board meetings, Vladik had disengaged from the company's business and was looking forward to resigning altogether. That business was exciting, but he was turning inward, preferring to stay on Block Island as much as possible and to focus his attention there. When a new round of financing came in, the investors would want to sweep away the amateurs, like Vladik, and put their own people in charge. He had prepared himself for that day.

Vladik spent three years building a new life with Arianna and a new house out on the bluffs. For people with a mainland clock, three years may sound like a long time to build a house, but everything takes longer and costs more when you're ten miles offshore. If experience said a project would take a month or cost a dollar on the mainland, then experience also said it would take months or cost dollars on Block Island, Rhode Island. See, three years was not so long after all. As for how long it takes to build a new life, well, even if there's love at first sight, it still takes time to weave two lives together. Island isolation, or cabin fever as it's sometimes known, often makes that clock tick faster than on the mainland, but neither Arianna nor Vladik was in any hurry.

A house is usually a custom creation in every way, beginning with its siting. Then there's layout and choice of materials, and after that it is built by hand under not-very-well-controlled working conditions. Vladik saved years and hundreds of thousands of dollars by going prefab.

Prefabrication of houses means different things to different people, from delivering a complete home on a truck—ready to drop onto a foundation, and not very practical on Block Island—to pre-cutting or pre-ordering all the parts and delivering them to the construction site in a very large box accompanied by a trained and experienced crew ready to assemble it. Vladik chose an ultra-modern design of only 800 square feet, a big railroad car of a house, seemingly made of glass, a dwelling that had won awards for energy efficiency. Then he had five of them delivered as kits, each sited as an arm radiating from a larger pentagonal hub at their center. A Block Island house is a boat on land. Connectors and windows had to be upgraded to withstand hurricanes and winter storms with their ninety-mile-an-hour winds. He increased the rust protection ratings on all the structural steel and paint, took special measures to eliminate galvanic corrosion of aluminum, and used wood and stainless steel wherever possible, all in the name of improving resistance to the brutal marine conditions the house would face. Nothing like it had ever been built there, and most residents wished it would go away, but the building met code and the design was generally recognized as pleasing if different from the weathered cedar exteriors that dominated the island. Vladik made one concession to convention; the cedar roof on the pentagon, contrasting old and new in a single structure. Since his compound could not be seen from the road, and only with great difficulty from the sea, and everything else was in order, its zoning and construction permits were approved, and the compound rose out of the ground. When the old house had been demolished and before he could sleep overnight in the new one, and when his coupledom with Arianna was still too nascent to share domiciles, he lived in the construction trailers on site, as did the crews who came and went.

Arianna had bought her own house, a non-descript place, but one to call home, close to her shop in town, and had settled into an island life of hectic summers. Those other three seasons, she traveled frequently; to Cambridge to be with her business partners, to New York to be with her clients, to Paris to be with her family, and to a spot in the Caribbean to get away from the windswept bleakness of winter on Block Island.

Vladik kept his distance but was almost always available. She did the same. There was never any doubt about their intent. They would be together. There were no other intimacies in their lives. They knew this. She was often in the trailer with him, and he was often in town with her, but they gave each other room to be alone, and could sense when it was needed. They got to know each other slowly.

Vladik told her about his earliest days, like a story from another century, his family's harrowing escape from the Soviet Union by steamer when he was five, arriving in Brooklyn's shipyards with his father and pregnant mother, living for a while with his aunt's family in Brighton Beach.

His uncle, Oleg, had been a boxer. He was a man who got things done, often by force, sometimes by too much force. Before fleeing he had spent five years in the gulag for hooliganism, and came back covered in tattoos, most of them obscene and obscured by his clothing. A young Vladik caught a glimpse of one on Oleg's forearm. It featured a bulldog, itself tattoo'd with a hammer and sickle, drooling, mounting a smiling girl who wore only fishnet stockings. Her black tresses flowed like those of Botticelli's Venus, and her naked breasts dangled just above a book of Party doctrine. The caption read, in Russian of course, "What's good for the Party is good for you."

Vladik made deliveries for him, sandwiches, he thought, to men at work. When he returned, with his pockets full of free ketchup he'd been instructed to collect from Burger King, he got a pat on the head, a dollar, and some kind words, like "*fina boychik*"—remnants of Yiddishisms that had survived three generations of Soviet oppression. Only years later did he figure out that criminality might be involved in those deliveries. He looked up to his older cousins, and was tight with the youngest, Lev. They were his family, sheltering him, his parents, his little sister who was born in Brooklyn, in their earliest and most vulnerable days, and showing him kindness after kindness thereafter. The floral wallpaper he came to think of as Old World. The erotic or violent prison tattoos on so many of the house's guests were shocking and intriguing. He owed them, and he loved them, their tough-guy ways notwithstanding. They were still in his life. When he was eight, he moved to New Jersey, what he called Real America, when his mother landed a crypto job at Bell Labs.

Arianna was very reticent about her immediate past. She let on that she'd once been Mrs. Max Frood, he let on that he knew something of him, and that was about it. The miscarriages and the boy who died were more interesting to both of them than the marriage itself. Vladik was not keen to talk about his first marriage or his protracted stay as the kept-boy of Dr. Ulya Khoslovsky. One day he asked Arianna, "If I promise not to ask you about your marriage, will you promise not ask me about my ... " and he stumbled, not being able to find a label for what it was he had with Ulya. Arianna didn't need a category. She was relieved and said, "Yes."

Not until Vladik excitedly told her about meeting Max at a conference in Boston did she realize that her present and former mates were in overlapping circles, and while Vladik did not ask, she then began to offer some details about her first marriage. Patience, Dear Reader, patience. We'll get to those events soon enough.

CHAPTER 85 THE MAKING OF D5

D2 LEFT Macau for Shanghai later in the year of Max's pig out. Even there she was still over 600 miles away from her beloved daughter, Huizong, but she had cut the distance in half, and that alone was worth something.

In booming China, there was an ever-greater demand for international real estate transactions. Turning her attentions to inbound capital, she was directly in the flow of naïve executives who needed, or felt they needed, to cut a deal and own a piece of China before the prices had gone to the moon or beyond. Her agency never denied her requests for more resources as she delivered an expanding web of espionage targets. What she collected—about marketing and pricing plans, regional and personnel expansions, research initiatives, manufacturing schedules, construction and operational blueprints, technical challenges experienced, leadership changes, logins and passwords, and more, much more—flowed from her PLA bosses to the National High-Tech Research Development Agency known as 863, and then on to state-owned-enterprises for the betterment of the kleptocrats, facilitating the greatest wealth transfer in history. All the while, she was building her business as a commercial real estate developer. On the rising tide of the biggest single city construction boom ever seen—as measured in additional square feet of usable space per year—with unlimited support of the Army—itself backed by the quasi-sovereign government of China and its bottomless supplies of capital made possible by negative real interest rates, excessive savings, and the one-child-per-family policy—D2 eventually laid claim to being D5, Wuang Wenqian, the Wealthiest Woman in the World. It was printed right there on her business card, and that made it true! Whether she owned what she appeared to own or whether it belonged to the People's Liberation Army, or the elite within the PLA, wasn't a question that came up. She lived like she owned it, but she lived relatively modestly.

HUIZONG moved to Shanghai after obtaining both a bachelor's and a master's degree in Computer Science at Tsinghua. She and her mother were happy to be living close to one another again. There the daughter took a job working for Army Agency Tao 61398, or simply Tao. A year later she became the founding engineer of APT, a faux software company fronting as a developer of deterrents to advanced persistent threats. APT's real mission was to attract the best and brightest software engineers, without a worry as to their PLA or Communist Party affiliation, and then deploy them on the task of coding the threats, not the deterrents.

Three years later, Huizong followed a boyfriend to Palo Alto and Stanford University. It was there that she joined the fledgling Slab Inc. during the development of its first handheld computers. As Slab's immigration lawyers untangled US law to get around a dearth of H1-B visas, Huizong untangled a heaping plate of spaghetti code on a project known internally as Bird. Then she removed a bottleneck that had throttled performance. When one of her managers recognized her by saying, "She rocks the Bird," the phrase morphed into Roxy Bird, and that was how she was known thereafter. On the strength of immediately demonstrated skill, and what her résumé claimed she had done at APT, she was promoted to Group Leader, Security.

She had a quirk—unusual among Slab employees, and Silicon Valley employees in general—that took some time to become evident. She never sought any growth or diversity in her career. It was widely acknowledged that she excelled as an engineer from the start. Where she was deficient, she found supplements. She attended classes in English as a second language and obtained an MBA at night. Then she excelled as a manager and as a mentor. But she didn't want to move up. When asked why, she replied simply, "I would prefer not to."

Five years into her American sojourn, Roxy Bird married the boyfriend and told her mother it was time for her to think about moving to California. D5 would be flooded with opportunities to spend or give away the great wealth she'd amassed, and she would also be close to a grandchild, if fortune cooperated.

On a dime, as if it had been planned, D5 became an overt fan of all things American. She began collecting American art, new and old. She made donations, large donations, to American NGOs. She began courting Chinese dissidents. Invoking the colloquialism "sea turtle" for Chinese who lived abroad and have returned home, she started the Shanghai Sea Turtle Shalong. A monthly meeting of artists and intellectuals held at one of her hotels, it was on alternate months devoted to (1) internationally hot issues like *habeas corpus*, freedom of speech, freedom of religion, and other human rights and (2) contemporary Chinese art and democracy. She invited renowned American politicians, intellectuals and journalists to visit and lecture on its themes. She received, for all her confrontational and objectively offensive behavior, only just enough backlash to quell any suspicion that this was state-sponsored activity. It goes without saying, I hope, that the guests at her Salon were rewarding and unsuspecting targets of espionage.

In Roxy Bird's seventh year, and after hundreds of millions of dollars of Slab failure, there came Slabloid, *the Glass Tabloid!* as the inescapable marketing campaign sang, in 4.2 inch and 9.7 inch formats. Eventually, they would become the world's most widely used mobile devices. She guaranteed device security, personally signing off on every hardware, firmware, and operating system release. Firmware had become her obsession. Every bit and byte she understood, and many she had crafted herself. Some were included without Slab Inc. being faintly aware of their existence. The prime exponent of that class was a piece of APT-designed firmalware, a rootkit of shim libraries creating a backdoor entry to device control.

In that same year, D5 began making preparations to spend time in America, not as a citizen, but as a businesswoman with long term interests and customers in the US, as a mother of a Slab Inc. engineer, and as grandmother of Amanda Bird, a US citizen born on the ship date of the first Slab42.

Among D5's target clients was a New York real estate developer seeking to expand by tapping into the booming residential property market in China. She partnered with Mr. Vyacheslav "Yoshi" Kocheryozhkin in acquiring suitable land and constructing there a thirty-six story block of condominiums for the burgeoning middle class, sitting atop three stories of enclosed and open-air shopping mall. That was followed by a much larger project consisting of six clones of the same structure.

In the course of their work together, she learned everything there was to know about him; from the brand of his shaving cream—which he'd once had Bloomingdale's fedex to him in Shanghai after discovering that he'd left his seventy-dollar four-ounce jar of it at his Upper East Side home—to the address of his wife's lover and yoga instructor, to the logon credentials of his Goldman Sachs brokerage account, and the name and contact details of the Persian art broker behind his fast-growing collection of European painting and sculpture, not to mention a complete inventory of that collection, including dates of acquisition, prices paid, and provenance.

ANTICIPATING her move to the US, D5 needed an art broker and advisor of her own. Rather than cold call Arianna, leaving a trail that would point to D5 knowing more than she should, she discreetly engaged Yoshi in a discussion about their respective art collections. She made admiring remarks about his, and steered him toward mentioning Arianna Javaheri by name. Behaving as if it would be a great favor to her, D5 asked Yoshi to introduce her to Ms. Javaheri, all of which had the effect of lulling him into the belief that D5 was indebted to him, making it all the easier for her to exploit him further, which she did.

CHAPTER 86 THE WEDDING

VLADIK'S HOUSE, or the house Vladik and Arianna called their house, was finished in their third summer together, the summer that they married. They had wanted a small, intimate wedding, believing that after the disasters of their first marriages it was better not to advertise the triumph of hope over experience. Their families thought otherwise. After those disasters, they believed you had to shout out to the whole universe that you were back!

The wedding was a raucous event with two hundred guests from all over the world and a hundred from Block Island. A Nor'easter had just blown through, leaving behind dazzling dry weather for three days while the two extended families discovered they were as well suited for each other as macaroni and cheese. The Russians and the Persians and the French and the rest of us savored the island on those hot September days. There was live music and dance around the clock. Not just the bride and groom, but unsuspecting guests were picked up by Russian strongmen and carried overhead in their chairs, often precariously, while others, if there were any still up at that time, laughed and applauded and joined in the dance. The food flowed as freely as the wine. Jay showed up on the *Lucky Strike* and ran an onboard outré-party. There were fireworks every night, and one extended rat-a-tat-tat of what sounded like automatic rifle fire, too, but to no ill effect.

We gathered together for one massive group photograph, carefully planned so that the golden glowing late afternoon sun made us look ruddier and healthier than we ever had. The photographer, a philosopher of the form, standing on scaffolding so we were looking up with the most flattering of elongated faces, kept his hand on the cable shutter release of the ancient view camera, choreographing us all into the field. Two assistants made last minute tilt and shift adjustments, and then focused the lens on the ground glass. When they achieved maximum sharpness, the photographer took one last look himself and signaled to us that we were in position. Two assistants closed the lens and wound its shutter. A third assistant slid the film holder into place. The slide covering the film was removed. "Everyone!" the photographer shouted. "Imagine the children!" Laughter. And we saw laughter in his face; a kindness that drew a special grace from each of us. For an instant, our best selves emerged. Imperceptibly, his thumb depressed the release, there was a click we could not hear, and it was over. Then, as if with nothing more than a gesture, we were all gone.

Gentle Reader, for those of you interested in this kind of detail, while Rhode Island law demands no blood test of the bride or groom, Arianna and Vladik were both carrier-tested for a host of recessive genetic diseases, the inborn errors of metabolism. While Arianna was of course positive for Tay-Sachs, Vladik was negative, and there would be no TSD in the next generation. Likewise for phenylketonuria and the others, their genetic markers were mismatched. The couple got the "All Clear" sign. There would be children.

CHAPTER 87 THE MOON AND BEYOND

AFTER THE honeymoon, or "the moon" as Vladik liked to say, in Turkey, traveling overland to Paris for another visit with Arianna's family, and returning to their Block Island home, they settled in together. Vladik tried to be helpful to her in work, but he needed his own projects.

Pissed-off at the island's awful Internet service, he helped create Mesh Block Island, a community-owned and operated Internet service provider. He was able to corral a hundred homeowners to put a weatherproof node of Wi-Fi hardware on their properties, those nodes becoming a virtual mesh of connectivity that nearly spanned the island. A microwave receiver with a direct line of site to the mainland fed the mesh. Two years into the experiment, the phone company tried to buy MBI back from the community, as MBI had destroyed their monopoly profits, but the community wanted more control over their Internet destiny. TPC retaliated by raising rates on the microwave link. Threats were made. Both sides lawyered up and there was after all of that a sale leaving the islanders with better Internet and a slightly more money in their pockets than they'd started with.

Arianna's business grew steadily, with only a temporary hiccup during the worst of the Great Recession when everyone, tycoons included, hoarded their wealth and hoped the sky didn't fall. When it didn't—a topic for another treatise and another author—the wealthiest began spending again, on art and their other pleasures. Outside the summer's high tourist season, Arianna helicoptered off island almost every week. Through referrals she was advising wealthier and wealthier New York City clients about what to buy and how to protect its appreciation from the bite of the IRS. She had even acquired an über-rich Chinese collector. Arianna was the founder and the rainmaker, bringing in new business, charming the wannabe connoisseurs, and letting her partners in Cambridge shoulder all the detail and dirty work.

Vladik fished, hunted deer and butterflies, tried to garden, mowed the lawn, learned Farsi and French, joined the volunteer organizations, and was, in short, bored. Forty, plus or minus, it was time for him to start a new career.

JAY showed up as he did once every season. He and Vladik talked late into the night, mostly about sequencing and Jay's belief that it was going to revolutionize medicine. "Parallelism is increasing so fast, the cost of sequencing is dropping like a stone. Faster than computer memory, even faster than disk storage. In a few years it's going to cost more to store the sequence data than to get it, and it will cost more than that to analyze it."

Vladik asked, "The law of diminishing returns? After a while it won't pay to keep reducing the cost of sequencing because all the auxiliary costs will mask it?"

"Well, yeah. But the cost of everything else is plummeting too as there's more demand. The economies of scale are working in the auxiliaries, too. We're a long way from hitting that point of diminishing returns."

"So sequencing, the totality of it, the storage and the analysis, will be free?"

"Are transistors free?"

"Transistors are so cheap they might as well be free, but you can't do anything with one transistor. You need thousands or hundreds of thousands of them working together to do anything interesting. And then the chip with all those transistors has to be packaged and put on a circuit board, and there are costs there."

"Sequencing a single base will be so cheap it might as well be free, but for any medically meaningful result, you'll need to sequence millions, maybe billions of bases. There will be a cost for that, but it will be small."

"Sequencing being free enables cost-effective diagnostics?"

"Right. This is going to remodel clinical laboratories and diagnostics. They're calling it MDx, for molecular diagnostics."

"But its really molecular biology diagnostics right? Moby Dx?"

Jay didn't hear or thought it was too weak a pun, so Vladik let it go.

"Cool. What are you going to do?"

Jay didn't answer at first.

"If sequencing is free, our directed evolution platform is powerful not just for synfuels, but for any complex optimization of gene products. The pharma guys? About to fall off their patent cliffs, and nothing in the pipelines? They'll grasp at anything right now. We've abandoned the whole fuels thing and have refocused Orrigen for acquisition by a drug company."

"Amazing."

Neither of them said anything for a while. Then Jay asked, "What are you going to do?"

Vladik, embarrassed that he didn't have an answer, gave him an awkward smile but no words.

"You're bored. I think you should jump in," Jay said.

"Jump in to what?"

"MDx. The field is wide open. Everything is changing"

"Starting with what?"

"Just jump in. Start reading the journals. Subscribe to some newsletters. Go to conferences. Figure out who you want to meet and I'll get the introductions for you. You won't need many. There are too many, not too few good ideas to chose from. Probably the biggest ones aren't even known yet. It could be you that figures it out."

"Draft in the MDx wake?"

"Meaning?"

"Ever seen a bicycle race? The Tour? Except in a breakaway, the sprinters, the ultimate winners, tuck in behind the leaders because that's where there's the least resistance, in their wake. Imagine you're one of those sprinters. When you're in that spot you can suss out what everyone is doing, who's really strong, who's hanging on by a thread. And you can do it because you're barely working, soft-pedaling but moving fast, dragged along with the crowd, the peloton. When the time is right, you make your move and jump ahead of the group."

"Right, unless someone else outmaneuvers you, but yeah, draft in the wake of MDx."

In his deepest voice and thickest Russian accent, Vladik said, "In America, you draft wake. In Soviet Union, wake drafts you!" Why that was funny, neither of them could have said, but they laughed like nine-year-olds, almost to tears. The old jokes are the best jokes, if only because they remind you of those old times, when things were simpler and maybe better.

CHAPTER 88
THE MOLECULARIZATION OF BIOLOGY

WARREN WEAVER was the first to use the term "molecular biology" in print, in a 1938 report to the Rockefeller Foundation where he was Director of the Natural Sciences Division. Weaver—later Claude Shannon's co-author on the landmark A Mathematical Theory of Communication—described "studies ... in a relatively new field ... in which delicate modern techniques are being used to investigate ever more minute details of certain life processes." He was referring to radiation physics applied to genetics and photosynthesis. Physical scientists had probed deep into the atom and revealed profound truths about the nature of earthly matter and even stars. Weaver believed that those physical methods—quantitative, precise, and requiring elaborate experimental hardware—would reveal profound truths about "certain life processes" if they were applied to the biologically important long-chain macromolecules. Biochemistry, studying the same molecules by more traditional means, was on a different path, and would not arrive at the same understanding on its own. The Division of Natural Sciences funded the early Luria-Delbrück collaborations. Oswald Avery, at the Rockefeller Institute for Medical Research, discovered that DNA was the molecule of inheritance, even if it wasn't widely accepted in 1944.

Biochemistry was the chemist's solution to biology. Life's processes, they thought, would be explained using the chemist's tools of reaction rates and equations in balance. In the six years following Avery, the biochemist Erwin Chargaff, elucidated the important and unexplained conclusion that of DNA's four bases, the As were always as abundant as the Ts, and the Gs were always as abundant as the Cs.

In 1953 Watson and Crick used Chargaff's rules, Rosalind Franklin's X-ray crystallography, and Crick's model of X-ray scattering from helices to explain the structure of DNA. Without any one of those three ingredients, there would have been no determination of structure.

After World War II, new institutions, funding methods, instruments, and results began to change the landscape of analytic biology, making it more molecular. Watson and Crick's paper—the most important paper in biology since when, Mendel?—is certainly moby, but what *is* that?

Francis Crick, the physics-trained biologist, said that moby is two things: (1) any attempt to explain biology in terms of atoms and molecules, and (2) the biology of the long chain macromolecular proteins and nucleic acids. The triumph of taking that abstraction called the gene and finding the structure of its material form in DNA led to a desire to make comparably crisp pairings of biological function and molecules.

Some wanted to go further. Jacques Monod, the French Nobelist who discovered the role of RNA in DNA replication said that the cell transcends chemistry. *Provocateur!* Chemistry and biochemistry have mostly been applied to systems in, near, or driving toward equilibrium. Thermodynamics, the language of much physical chemistry, is by definition the science of ensembles of atoms or molecules in equilibrium. A cell is nowhere near equilibrium. If it were, we wouldn't need food. Monod said to Horace Freeland Judson, "What is new in molecular biology is the recognition that the essential properties of living beings could be interpreted in terms of the structures of their macromolecules." Their precise shape—which gives rise to their enzymatic lock and key behavior—is written in the organism's DNA. The unique features of an individual's macromolecules are the source of the organism's individuality, as a macroscopic crystal of quartz owes its shape to its most fundamental sub-microscopic molecular structure.

Rinchen told me, "Biology is catalyst-driven, unlike most reactions in nature. Privileged reactions, low likelihood events, dominate. Chemistry, where statistics rules, wasn't built for biology. You can do moby without any chemistry at all, hypothesizing pathways, networks, and signaling, connecting phenotype and genotype. But the more important difference between biochemistry and molecular biology, one that's evolved—and you have to understand that the terms have evolved because look at what we've learned in this magnificent episode in intellectual history—is that molecular biology focuses on the genetic information contained in and transferred by the macromolecules, while biochemistry focuses on their binding and chemical processes. Get two of us in a room on this and we'll either have three opinions or a pollyannish agreement."

I asked Max about it. "People had dreams, and they were assembling the broad outlines of mechanisms—messenger RNAs and repressor proteins, for instance—while creating new methods and instruments, and then things got complicated. The details are really, really hard. There was tension between the geneticists and the biochemists, the former saying they didn't need the latter and the latter saying the former were glib. The Nobel Prize committee favored the biochemists, I think. I mean, why didn't they give it to Brenner and a second one to Crick, for the discovery of the triplet code in '61?" Max was referring to the fact that the fundamental unit of the genetic code is a triplet of DNA's bases. "Anyway, you need the biochemistry, because it's become a tool for doing stuff. When people learned enough of all that complicated shit to do something useful with it, like make human insulin, even if they didn't really know how human insulin worked, the dreams became commercialized. That was Cohen-Boyer. There were no companies formed after Crick-Brenner. It was too early. Now, every improvement in the lab becomes a business plan. So, you want my definition? Moby is the *thing*, all those things, inventions and what not, that made Cohen-Boyer possible."

My definition is that moby is the collection of results, methods, and teachings about genes and the proteins they make, and how a biological system operates in light of that. It assumes that an understanding of life's macromolecules is necessary and sufficient, and that the cell, being far from equilibrium, transcends chemistry. We don't yet have the equations or the models to describe the transcendent state, life.

CHAPTER 89 MOLECULAR DIAGNOSTICS

WHILE CLINICAL chemistry was advancing methods for flame spectrophotometry, or measuring metabolites of cocaine in a user's blood, or automating testing and data collection, the molecular biologists were advancing their case and their methods. Because of the remarkable cost reductions of sequencing, and because of the translation of genomics findings into the practice of medicine, and because the DNA samples originate in the same precious bodily fluids used by traditional clinical chemists, and because clinical chemistry had become so central to the practice of medicine, and because too many cooks spoil the broth, methods of diagnosis based on moby are converging with traditional clinical chemistry, and those methods are called molecular diagnostics, or moby dx. One way to monitor the trend is to watch as the established multi-billion dollar, multinational traditional clinical chemistry labs, like Quest Diagnostics and LabCorp, buy up the much smaller, regional genomics and molecular diagnostics ones.

CHAPTER 90 GENORMX, INC - SCENE III OF V

BEFORE THE clock and money had run out, and against all odds, the team actually delivered the Alpha. The instrument instantiating their dreams loaded 10,000 DNA fragments onto a chip of 100,000 pores. As the strings transmigrated through, the SEM momentarily placed its beam on a molecule in one pore for a fraction of a microsecond. The detectors, cooled to temperatures near absolute zero for maximum sensitivity, picked up the scattered electrons from the base in the pore and a computer recorded the signal. Then the SEM moved to the next pore, and so on, rastering back and forth across the rectangular array of pores until each had been interrogated. Having reached the end, the SEM rapidly moved its beam back to the first pore and started all over again. This took place in such a brief instant, and the transmigration had been slowed so much, and the synchronization of all these activities—more robotic than balletic, but still beautiful to the gals at Packaged Systems who'd designed it and the DIYers that observed it (and all experimentalists are DIYers at heart)—was so meticulously choreographed that the next base of the DNA fragment in each pore had moved into position and was ready for interrogation.

Computer software interpreted the detector signal, calling out its best guess among the choices of A, C, G, or T, and then appending that assignment to the string of called bases for a given pore. Having loaded DNA fragments of known sequence into the pores, they were able to determine that the system made the correct identification about 96 percent of the time. That wasn't good. Best in class was better than 99 percent, but it was better than their target of 95 percent for the Alpha. Someday, later, they'd have to beat 99 percent.

All this was great. The team was ecstatic.

The Board, although they did not show it and the team did not know it, had mixed feelings. Intuition Ventures wanted out and had expected the team to miss the deadline. Galena had brought in another very experienced Intuition partner as the fifth board member. She, Roberta Dickinson, soon turned negative, too, not because she had suffered Dyk's abuse and Max's manipulations, but because she thought the Board had chosen the wrong milestone for the Alpha, so it's success was a phantom. Their choice, she told them, had led the engineering team to make its own choices that would box it in and result, ultimately, eventually, in marketplace failure. The Board had relieved Max of leadership responsibility for the company's technology, but they continued to rely on him for strategic guidance about the sequencing industry.

"We need other voices in that strategy discussion, voices outside this little world. We're giving Max too much opportunity to shape our vision of the future."

Carmie responded, "We've made a bet that pores are going to be the next big advance, and we're positioned to be first. I don't see how bringing in other voices is going to change that."

Galena joined in. "Roberta and I agree that being first is all important, but there are other factors beside cost per base and read length shaping the industry, and we're not hearing them."

"Like?" Armen asked.

"Like fucking form factor," Roberta said. "Genormx is focused on instruments for the government sponsored genome center. There are how many of them? We should be designing for small labs, and the bedside. Will one of you tell me how you're going to miniaturize a SEM without turning this company into an electron optics shop?" Silence. Then she started again. "But you know what? This conversation I started is a rathole. If we continue down it, we'll never find our way out. You all know I think we should close up the operation and save ourselves the money and the headache, and possible embarrassment. Do I have a second on a motion to bring this to a vote?"

Galena seconded it but the motion was denied three to two.

Intuition Ventures had a commitment to fund the next tranche. They could have bought themselves out of it, another expensive option, and one with no upside. Furious and feeling trapped, Galena and Roberta committed themselves to someday taking Max's head for a trophy.

THE $16 million second tranche came in as promised. The team grew a little, although more on the computation side than the hardware engineering side. Carmie and the Board were very pleased with Packaged and Nottintel, and the new Engineering Advisory Committee's recommendation was to increase their contracts rather than build up the engineering expertise internally. It would be more expensive, but faster, and since the intent was to be first to market, speed mattered more than anything else.

CHAPTER 91 WHEN WORLDS COLLIDE

THERE ARE several good online publications dedicated to biotech and genomics innovations and applications. They aggregate press releases from the companies in the field, headline-making results from scientific and medical journals, the most interesting posts from hundreds of blogs written by anyone with a yen to get their message out, and conference notes written by their usually very knowledgeable staff. They send daily news feeds to subscribers based on their avowed preferences, and all the content is available by RSS. The best of them charge a hefty fee for their curation and the original content they create. Vladik was soon paying for it.

He took occasional advantage of Arianna's travel schedule to hitch a ride on her business trips to Cambridge, the East Coast center of All Things G, where G is for genomic. In the minds of the inhabitants, Cambridge was probably the center, without the East Coast qualifier, of All Things G, and maybe even the Center of All Things.

He didn't have a leg to stand on when it came to MDx and he knew it, so he thought it best to attend conferences and listen. He had learned to listen, rather than to show off, first from Noyce—who may have learned the skill from observing it honored in the breach by Shockley—and then at ITSy. Noyce, although his own thoughts were very highly sought after at the most rarefied reaches of industry and government, said very little when he spoke to Vladik, giving full attention to the sixteen-year old, and leaving an impression that Vladik tried to emulate forever after. At the MDx meetings, he sought settings where he could ask a few elementary questions without embarrassment, and then he'd sit better informed through some more conference sessions, and he'd iterate on that until he was worn out.

Gradually he came to believe that this emerging field was like every other one. There was an army of people who were expert at something, but very few who were expert at the range of things you needed to know to be a successful entrepreneur. The scientists had their science down, so they could educate you on the arcana. They'd be helpful in figuring out how to do something, but not what to do. The business types had their corner of the world, diagnostics in this case, and they told you that whatever they've learned in their area amounted to a universal truth. These guys, mostly guys, could recite the trends and the buzzwords, but they couldn't distill a finding from noisy data nor could they synthesize a new idea if their lives depended on it. Handsome, well-spoken, and brawny, they'd be helpful if you needed, let's say, to move a piano.

What was getting all the attention was whole-genome sequencing. It was easy to understand and explain in an article in the Newspaper of Record, the *Wall Street Journal*, or the *Los Angeles Times*. Everyone had by then learned that the price of semiconductors fell exponentially according to Moore's Law. The charts showing sequencing costs falling faster than Moore's Law looked good on the papers' pages.

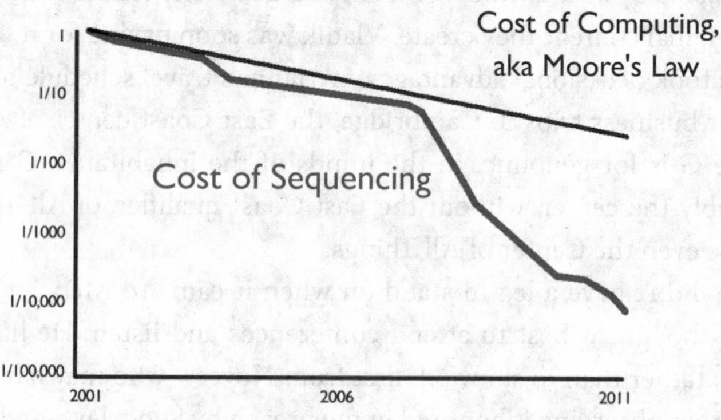

The sequencing companies promoted the achievement of besting Moore's Law. Fear of missing out drove their customers to frenzied spending. New companies dedicated to whole-genome sequencing sprouted up. Large companies formed new divisions devoted to WGS. There were new institutes for WGS, analytics for WGS, cloud computing and storage for WGS, books on WGS, reports on WGS, commissions on WGS, blogs and conferences for WGS; so many conferences. What was still missing-in-action was a medical rationale backed by health economic research. Individualized Medicine, the personalization of medicine, that is, the next step in using information about your own individual response to drugs, sometimes based on your genetics, was floated as the justification. In those days, when WGS cost over $20,000 and it took an entire medical school to analyze one person's genome, individualized medicine as the *raison d'être* for WGS was still many years off. An academic might not worry about such a gap, but an entrepreneur had better.

Vladik first met Max at a one-day individualized medicine conference in Boston's John Hancock Tower. Sponsored by several of the private research institutes, an investment bank, the law firm of Ph'eer, Dowd, and Sertantiy, and New England's largest HMO, Blue Comfort, the speaker list read like a history of the HGP. Max's name was not on it when Vladik had registered. Max was in Cambridge getting a hardware upgrade to his robotic leg, and giving a talk on MEMS developments to the research group of one of the conference organizers, Kupra Veraschaigina. A red-haired, high-voltage researcher who had filled his spot at EECS, Kupra pleaded with Max to delay his return to California for one day and to fill-in for another speaker who had cancelled. Not given to doing favors, Max agreed only on the condition that she eat dinner with him at Maison Robert, and pick up the tab, too. He had the slide deck ready to go and could have given it in his sleep.

Vladik was as surprised as anyone that François Jacob had fallen ill and Max had been slotted in. Of course, Vladik had a special interest in seeing this enigmatic figure who'd danced around the periphery of his life for several years.

Max talked about pore research done at the I and its impact on diagnostics, and he hinted at Genormx's intent. When he spoke of the big picture, the words from his mouth could have come from Jay. The metaphor about sequencing being free, that was Vladik's own! Not even Jay had said it.

With an unusual gait somewhat out of balance, and his hair thinning and his skin sagging, Max looked to Vladik—who was unaware of Max's accident or any of his ailments—a decade older than expected, that is, a decade older than Vladik. Max's spirit was upbeat, though, and as he departed the stage to thunderous applause, and that is no exaggeration, he was greeted by several men and women who had similarly odd gaits, almost bouncy, like they were hopping from foot to foot. One of them, no two of them, Vladik saw, had artificial hands. Then it dawned on him that this was the prosthetics team. All these people were amputees. Many, Max included, were walking around on some kind of robotic leg. Vladik had some catching up to do. Whatever his preconceptions may have been about Max, they were turned on their head in acknowledgment of the suffering that Max had endured.

Max's Wikipedia entry was modest, listing his academic background, which Vladik knew, his MIT appointment and the Tiny Machines IPO, about which Vladik knew, and his move to HMRI, about which Vladik did not know. Otherwise, it said that he'd lost his left leg in an accident, and that was it. Genormx, which Max had mentioned in the day's talk, was not in there yet. Vladik logged in like a good Wikipedian, clicked the Edit tab, and added the line, Genormx Inc., East Palo Alto, California, under the section heading "Corporate Affiliations." Then, as a reference, he cited the URL of the conference notice on which Max's name had been added to the speaker list. Was this "original research" and therefore prohibited by Wikipedia's policies? Vladik wasn't sure. He'd do some more homework on that later. It wasn't libelous anyway.

In the Hancock's sixtieth floor penthouse, Ph'eer, Dowd, and Sertantiy hosted an after party for the speakers, their friends, the organizers' invited guests, and a few guests like Vladik who had wanted to shake hands with Monod and had paid for access to the inner circle. On a moonless February night, in a city with only a few tall buildings, guests felt like they were orbiting the earth. Some pretty young things served drinks with LED cubes glowing blue in them. Other colored lights dangled and spun, but the glassed-in space was as dark as the night sky. A DJ kept a disco beat going and some other PYTs were dancing, trying to stir up some fun, a challenging task with that crowd.

Vladik, who was a nobody in this group, found Max, who was a demi-god, sitting informally on lush round ottomans along with Hugh Herr, another demi-god, both with their pants rolled up, explaining the intricacies of their bionic legs to a fascinated few.

Hugh had lost his legs to frostbite in a climbing accident as a teenager, alas. Then he'd turned his adversity into a virtue and began redesigning his body from the ground up. Vladik had heard about the adjustable length climbing legs, and how he would tune them to whatever the rock face demanded. Hugh had shown up at Harvard as a graduate student in biophysics. He was a teaching assistant in Physics 140, Physical Biology and Biological Physics, when Max took that course in his final semester. Max had stood out in the class, and Hugh—who had not been a part of the investigation into the supposed ethics violations—acknowledged Max's talent personally, with some sadness, when he left. The two exchanged a few email messages in the days before email was common, and then it got easier. Their correspondence was thin, but Max considered Hugh a friend, and the more-or-less annual exchanges kept them up-to-date on their blossoming careers.

Hugh was by this time at MIT, a bionics pioneer and evangelist in the best sense for people with disabilities. He was Dr. Feelgood for amputees, and it was his words to Max in the first few days after his surgery, along with Dr. Amritamoorthi's gentleness, and her transcoding of his doctors' message into plain English, that had helped him recover quickly.

They wore the same biomechatronic lower leg, an 'active ankle robot' as Hugh liked to call it, a prototype of carbon fiber, titanium, aluminum, and silicone, with several microcontrollers and even more sensors, and batteries to store energy that provided the context-dependent bounce that Vladik had observed in Max's step. Some of those sensors picked up depolarizations of the living-but-unattached nerve endings, sending them to actuators in the leg and foot. Hugh waxed on about how these robots were organic extensions of his body, and dreamt of making those extensions more and more intimate, someday connecting the actuators directly to the nerve endings. "We have only dysfunctional technology, not disabled people," he said.

Thank God for people like this, Vladik thought.

Max, whose amputation was above the knee, whereas Hugh's was below the knee, needed some other hardware. He was wearing one of Professor Herr's artificial knees, too.

That was the unlikely scene Vladik walked in on, and like the others watching, he crowded in close, asking questions and eventually introducing himself. It wasn't without some deliberation that he chose how he'd do it. Ruling out raising the topics of his careful analysis of the IP portfolio at Tiny, or the ins and outs of Max's former wife, or the vivid impression he held of Max's cuckolding as told by the cuckolder, he simply offered his hand, his name, and thanks for having given a great talk.

Hugh went home. Talk turned to work. Vladik was deferential. Max was unpretentious and receptive. Talk turned to politics and they found they hated the same people. They'd had an interesting first conversation, and Vladik's impression was Max would have wanted to continue if it hadn't been very late. They both left for their hotels.

Max made a stop along the way. The Hancock was nearly Ground Zero of the gay bar scene in Boston. He had some choices. His favorite, the Ramrod, was too far for him to travel on foot in that winter cold. Once he got in a cab, he knew he'd be done for the night. Instead he walked three minutes to Jacqueline's Cabaret, "Home of the CFNM Bachelorette Extravaginza!" Whatever happened there, suffice it to say that with all his limbs intact, he considered it another victory when he bid adieu to an all-male cast of three he'd come to know—after all, it was a school night—and took a cab to his hotel.

Late that same morning he boarded a flight to California.

CHAPTER 92 ARIANNA'S TALE

VLADIK WALKED to Copley Square, hopped on the Green Line, changed to the Red Line at Park Street Station, and four stops later arrived at Harvard Square. From there he walked to join Arianna at her regular hotel, the Charles. He knew she'd be asleep, so he entered the room as quietly as he could, only to find her awake, reading about parallel migrations of the plague and painting in Medieval Europe. He threw his clothes on the floor and crawled into bed with her, admiring her, brushing her hair with his hand.

"I am so lucky to be yours, just to be in your orbit," he said. "I never thought I would feel this way about anyone."

She wriggled closer so he could get his arms all around her. She purred, feline.

Having fallen within Max's aura Vladik felt that Max might be the key to helping him figure out what it meant to draft in the wake of MDx. Vladik was excited to tell her about his first encounter, and worried too.

He began with the evening and the nightclub atmosphere of the penthouse, trying to be suspenseful as he led up to finding these men showing off their legs. "One of them was a professor at MIT. That's Hugh. The other one is from California. His name is Max Frood," and there he stopped.

"Vladique, what did you say?"

"I said, nice talk, dude! He was incredible."

"No, I mean, did you say Maax is missing a leg? And, what did you say to him about us?"

"Yes, Max is an amputee, above the knee. About us, nothing. I said nothing. What do you think I'd tell him? I'm doing your wife?"

Arianna giggled while saying, "I'm not his wife, but I'm not sure he would agree." Not giggling, she said, "And this is too much, too many ideas at once. I wasn't ready for you to meet him. And then that tragedy. Poor Maax."

Vladik waited, hoping for an explanation, and got none. "What do you mean he wouldn't agree?"

"The divorce was contested, but finalized. The state decided. That's Massachusetts law."

Vladik said nothing.

"I don't know what's happened to Maax since he's been in California, but before then, he had only loved three women in his life, one he lost and should never have had, one he never attained, and one he had and let slip away."

"There's a juicy story you're going to tell me now?"

"Sometime. I feel bad for Maax, whether he hurt me or not, it doesn't matter. I don't," and she paused, stumbling for words, "I don't know what it is, I don't," and she paused again. "Thinking about him doesn't make me wish I could walk over and slap him in the face. Not anymore. I don't hate him. The last years of our marriage were so lonely and I needed him so much. I did hate Maax for that, but, uh," and she leaned over to kiss Vladik, "I have you. I can talk about him, about it, the marriage, now, or when you want, but not much right this minute. I want sleep. I guess he didn't offer how he happened to be missing that leg, did he?"

"No, and I was too polite to ask," and changing topics, Vladik continued, "and you have to tell me a little about these three women you dangled in front of me."

"I have lived with this knowledge for so long, I walk around as if you know it and we have decided not to talk about it. But you don't know it, do you? What has Jay told you?"

"I know some things, but not much. Who was the first?"

"His mother."

"You are kidding! Christ! He told you that?"

"Even Maax, and you don't know Maax, but even Maax, a man who doesn't want to tell you anything about himself, will tell his wife a few secrets after he's been through an ordeal like ours. Sometimes it only comes out in delirium, but things come out. And he'll lie. Oh, some of the lies he told me, but these things, Vladique, these things, they have to be true. Why would anyone ever tell a story like this about themselves if it weren't true?"

"How can I answer that, Arianna, since I don't know what you're talking about. I can't say anything except *Wow*! I can't believe there's that much I didn't know."

"You didn't want to know."

Arianna got up to go the bathroom and Vladik put on a bathrobe, taking a seat on the sofa. When she came back, he said, "And now that I'm mixed up with Max Frood, I want to know."

"Does that mean I can ask you about Ulya?" Arianna asked, knowing that she had to get something in exchange for her story.

"Yes, I'll tell you about Ulya, but I don't think *you* actually want to know."

"You're right, I don't, because I am pretty sure it's just embarrassing, and not interesting."

"Exactly."

Arianna sat in a lounge chair with her feet up beside him. "What do you mean you're mixed up with him?"

"I think Max is my domestique in this MDx thing I'm trying to do."

"Max doesn't do domestique. He only does the *maillot jaune*."

Vladik twitched and said, "We'll be using each other, then."

"When surfing the wave?"

"Drafting the wake, but maybe your way of saying it is better. Either way, I think I can complement Max somehow."

"After one conversation? It sounds like you're in love."

"He's a magician, one of those people who make the impossible happen."

"I know. Sadly, I know what you mean. I know exactly how you feel, caught in his tractor field. You don't see how he can hurt you yet, but he can. Something is broken inside him. I don't have room for much sympathy for my ex-husband, but he suffers."

"Other than having lost you, or thrown you away … You're the third one of those loves, right?"

"Yes, I'm the third," Arianna acknowledged.

"Other than having lost you, and his leg, how's he suffering? He gets around well on that robot of his, he's got an out-of-this-world appointment at some California institute, he's cofounded a publicly traded company."

"Vladique, how does he look? Does he look as good as you? He used to be beautiful. He used to look like an androgynous Roman god or goddess, with that Samson hair of his in a brown black flow. Sometimes, even usually, his face was as vibrant as Puck. Few men could have resisted him, and no woman, if it hadn't been for that affectless deadman's face he sometimes wore, the one that barely acknowledges your existence."

"I heard something about that. He's not beautiful anymore. He looks ten years older than me. He's fat in the middle, balding, his skin is loose and wrinkly. I'm not sure I can see through all that to the beauty beneath. But his face was lively. I saw the puckishness."

"So, Jay told you something about Hera?"

"Yes, about a sculpture, and being mocked for that, and about walking in on Jay and some girl they called Joosey. Was that really her name?"

"Maax called her Joosey. I don't know if that was her real name. She looked like his mother."

"You have seen Joosey?"

"He had a picture of her, of him with her, that he kept hidden, but only so he didn't have to see it, he wasn't hiding it from me."

"And his mother? What was she like?"

"I never met her. She was dead by the time I met Maax. He was an orphan. You don't know anything do you?"

"No, I don't. These details weren't on his Wikipedia page. Maybe I'll make some more edits."

"Vladi, you're kidding aren't you?"

"I'm kidding. I won't make any edits about this. So how old was he when she died?"

"Fourteen, I think, maybe fifteen. She died in childbirth carrying his child."

"Now you're kidding, right?"

"No, I am not kidding. And Joosey looked just like her. Dead ringer. Spitting image. Twin. He kept a picture of him with Miriam, Miriam was his mother, in a frame on his desk at work. Same composition as the one of him with Joosey."

"Joosey was number two, the unattained. And he loved her because, or at least because she was the perfect double of his deceased former lover, his mother," Vladik guessed aloud.

"*En effet.*"

"Jay told me that he didn't even know there was something going on between them."

"Maax thought otherwise. Jay's memory may be selective on that one. I don't know about him, I just know about men," Arianna said, and Vladik nodded, pursing his lips in sad acknowledgment of her truth telling.

"Max's anticipation for that evening with Joosey, the one they didn't have, was probably, no, definitely out of all proportion to what she had in mind. But that didn't matter. It was in his mind, and in there he had reunited with his mother."

"Jay wasn't just cuckolding him, he was fucking his mother, and killing the possibility of him, Maax, being with her again."

"He never tried to dress you up like her, did he?"

"And make me re-enact his past, or jump from a bell tower? No, that would have been rich, but it never happened. I think he had gotten over trying to find a replacement for her by the time we found each other," Arianna said.

"So, Jay casually kills this dream of his, and Max re-experiences her death, and goes kind of crazy. And he's an orphan ... wait, what happened to his father, and who was his guardian?"

"Max's father died when he was three. Max only told me about one memory he had. It must have been reinforced by things his mother told him, but he owned that memory. His parents had separated and then divorced. On his father's first visit after the divorce, Max sees himself rushing toward his father, and then the next image is his father bleeding out of his skull in their backyard."

"Does this story get any worse? Every kid whose parents are separated or divorced thinks it's his own fault, and now he thinks he's killed him, too?"

"Max does think he killed his father. Where he's undecided is whether it was intentional or not."

"Oy veh. Why would it have been intentional?"

"His mother? Domestic violence? The records may show something. I was never interested in looking them up."

"He was raised as the only child of a single parent, and who took over after she died? Where was the family?"

"The family! *Mon dieu!* All the vectors pointed to his stepmother, the woman his father married just before he died. It's complicated, and late, Vladique. Later, I can tell you everything I know."

Vladik must have looked at her like a puppy, because she continued. "The mother, and the step-mother were French. That's why he was in France when I met him, and why his own French was so good. But he never once, not ever, said anything about his mother's family. Anyway, his stepmother had become the CEO, the first non-family CEO of Frood Metal since 1832. Max moved in with her, and she tried to do everything for him; bring him into the family business, engage with him, etcetera, but he just wanted out, and got out. He never leaned on her for support, and he needed support."

"You mean he needed it after Joosey?"

"Yes, he was completely alone then. Traumatized. Mentally homeless."

"But to the rest of the Harvard world, it looked like some fraternal spat over a girl, no biggie," Vladik inferred.

"And as if draping his shirt over Hera's head wasn't enough, after the Jay and Joosey night, someone put horns on her, on Hera. They put the mark of the cuckold on her, so all of Harvard knew."

"It wasn't Jay, but he never forgave Jay."

"Of course not. Maax was a supremely sensitized adolescent and this was a major betrayal of the bro code. The shame of it, and the way he reacted to it, which made it a very big deal, the way he let his emotions get the better of him, unwinding his Harvard career, it still humiliates him, said it made him hate himself, or did when we were married. And Jay lives this disney-fied, non-stick, fairy tale of a life. It must have galled Maax even more than I knew."

"Is that the sun coming up?" Not waiting for anything more than a tired nod, Vladik asked, "You think that he'll overreact, again, if, or when, he finds out we're married."

"Vladique," she said, "Our was a contested divorce. He never agreed to it, but the courts forced him in to it. Massachusetts is a no-fault state. Fortunately, women are not property any more. Otherwise, I'd still be legally married to him."

They had by this time found their way onto the same couch, sitting close, wrapped in a blanket together. Vladik was shaking his head in disbelief at how tangled their lives were, and the possibility that Arianna's former marriage might thwart this new dream of his.

"I don't think you'd want to surprise him with it," Arianna went on. "The Joosey experience would re-inflate, *poof!* And when he was filled with that sense of humiliation rushing back, and then renewed because, well, it was actually happening again, not only remembering it again, I don't know what he'd do, but I don't want to be there."

"You don't think he'd get violent."

"I don't know what he'd do. I used to call him, to his face, *demi-homme, demi-cochon*, I was so furious sometimes. I could reason with him half the time, and the rest, well, I might as well have been talking to a pig."

"Very nice, Arianna, very nice. I'm not judging you, but very nice," Vladik said, laughing.

"Maybe you'll feel the same way after you've been married to him for five years."

"I'm not planning on marrying him, only drafting in his wake."

"You're going to have to be pretty close to him for that. You may pick up his smell. I'll be sure to tell you. But back to how he's going to react, you can't forget someone you've loved. When you tell him you're married to me, he'll remember. He loved me, even if he couldn't be with me because I had feelings and emotions and needs, because I'm human, and French, and Persian. He needs to be alone, but he also loves. He pushes love, friendship, affection, all of it away, in the name of having fewer obligations, all of them burdensome."

"So you think I shouldn't tell him."

"I don't know. The longer you wait, the more it looks like you're trying to hide it to get something from him. He smells exploitation like a cat smells mouse, even when it's not there."

"I should tell him next time we meet, or never?"

"Did I tell you that his mother was in prison when she died?"

"Stop it, will you?"

"OK, I'm kidding. They don't put you in prison for first time sexual abuse of your children, and she died during the pre-trial period."

CHAPTER 93 ORIGIN STORY

MAXWELL "MAX" Frood was born on April 1, 1970 in Pittsburgh, Pennsylvania, to Clerk Maxwell Frood and the sixteen-year-old former Miriam Straus. Mr. Frood was Chairman and CEO of privately held Frood Metal Inc., founded 1832, a diversified supplier of luxury (and mostly lethal) consumer products, including guns, jewelry, and knives. The parents divorced bitterly when he was three. The father died under mysterious circumstances on his first custody visit only weeks later. He is said to have tripped and fallen down the backyard steps of the mother's house, cracking his skull and suffering a fatal hemorrhage. Max lived with his mother until he was fourteen. There was money, but not plenty of money.

OF Rabbi Salomon Froodenberg's four children, his eldest, Maryam, was the archetype of the Hagaddah's wicked son, except that she was not a son. She had not always been like that. At the age of seven, when her first little sister was born, she was given the task of watching over the infant and tending to her every need except nursing. Maryam was sure that all of God's grace was revealed in that sweet smelling bundle of life. Less than two years later, when they buried the little one, the one whom the whole family and neighborhood watched over helplessly as she retreated from them, first in fear and then in listless isolation, Maryam decided there could not possibly be a god she would want to acknowledge. She refused to go to synagogue. Her maxim became, "What is this to me?" and she was never satisfied with the answers.

At sixteen she disappeared from Newport, Rhode Island, running into the wilderness with a *goyische* Pittsburgh smith. Her swain proved to be all chat and no anvil. Three years later, in 1829, she remained both childless and unmarried. Yoked day and night to his struggling shop, she once found the good-for-nothing, abusive, corn-liquor-drinking whoremonger instructing a paid girl in the art of hardening his soft steel. Maryam scared the girl off. With a red-hot bayonet fresh from the fire, she threatened him. "You can't gull me no longer you wanton ragamuffin. Git your limp dyk outta this shoppe and never piss in my forge again, or I'll cut your animalcule of a one-eyed rodent even shorter exceeding quick."

"Comely bitch! They have trials for women like you, they do!"

"You Fucking Idiot. It's witch trials. Now git."

He git.

By November of 1831, she employed three handsome journeyman smiths and four apprentices, all in the service of providing sharp tools to cooks, cavalry, and ship captains. On the fourth Thursday of that month, the entourage of Alexis de Tocqueville rattled through the City of Steel, and although in his own words "We stayed there but an instant, which I employed in writing a word or two to my father," that instant included a tour of Ms. Froodenberg's workshop—where she and her men ate turkey off the bone as if they were wild savages—and an equally instantaneous discovery of mutual attraction. For nearly three months Maryam ran her business by PMS, Pony Messenger Service, while accompanying him and acting as his cultural interpreter on the beaverish tail end of his journey through America.

He told her about the ill effects of aristocratic traditions on individuals and society at large. "Be wary," he said to her. "You have thrown off one kind of aristocrat, but your industrial revolution and its commerce bring a new kind into the world. If ever a permanent inequality of conditions penetrates your borders again, you can predict that it will come in on his shoulders."

"You worry too much, my love. Our laws are our own defense against just that. They give us the courage to seek prosperity, freedom to follow it up, the sense and habits to find it, and the assurance of reaping the benefit."

"Ah, Utopians! You're either busy giving birth to the future or busy burying the past. But like ghosts, the past will come back to haunt you if you dare to forget it," he sighed.

She failed to persuade him to write his historic memoir stateside, and he failed to persuade her to become Mme. de Tocqueville in France.

As he was about to board his Le Havre-bound sailing packet, he made one final appeal. "Mademoiselle of liberty. *J'ai du fièvre pour votre beavre.* You are my muse. My ideal. You are everything to me but my wife.

"I know a beach where the dune sand glows,

Pussywillow bending when the north wind blows,
A Norman castle you can call your home,
We'll sip caffe au lait and its white-brown foam."

And she said in return, "Among a democratic people, where there is no hereditary wealth, every one of us must work to earn a living. My labor, keeping those damn knives headed out the door, is held in high honor. The prejudice is not against, but in its favor. I can't live the liveried life of a noblewoman. And your life is too full of contradictions. You rail against yourself."

"My habits simulate true necessities. I shall not change them. You, born in this beaverish new world, are otherwise conditioned."

The little-bit-pregnant, Tay-Sachs-carrying Maryam Froodenberg returned to Pittsburgh and incorporated Frood Metal Works on the first day of March 1832. She set its "Do nothing, get nothing" policies into the founding documents. Valuing operations, that is, hands-on contributions, above all else, she said that if her child wouldn't work for the company, he or she didn't deserve any of its dividends. There would be no inheritance of equity. "You can't take it with you," is engraved on her gravestone. Nearly two centuries later, the maxim is emblazoned on the hip-worn picture-ID of every Frood Metal employee.

Clerk Frood, Max's father, had received more than a million dollars in dividends in the year before he died. In the years after, the company would provide only modest living and educational expenses for Max and Miriam, and only until he was twenty-one.

Equity may not have been inherited, but that recessive gene for Tay-Sachs, the one that had taken her infant sister, was passed generation to generation, improbably finding its way into the scion six times in succession. In the family that Maryam raised Catholic in honor of her second lover, the carriers went undetected until an unsuspecting Max married out.

IN school, young Max had trouble playing with others. He was also the victim of what today would be called bullying, maybe even hate crimes associated with his girlish good looks and long hair. Miriam and young Max left Pittsburgh for sunnier Florida, and then French-infused New Orleans, trying to find suitable circumstances for him. Everywhere he heard taunts, "Whatcha, some kinda freaky Froodenstein?" or "Heh, ya tooti Froody faggot!" The boys were cruel, and the girls crueler.

Shouts and incomprehensible cracking sounds at the Frood residence led a neighbor to call 911 on an undifferentiated Saturday. The police discovered a very pregnant Miriam *in flagrante delicto* in whalebone bodice, lounging on semen-stained pillows while holding a bullwhip. Fourteen-year-old Max's bound wrists were tethered to a ceiling bolt. He had large welts on his buttocks and legs, as did Miriam, but the police report noted that he expressed no complaint about his circumstances. The agent from Child Services said she had never seen such displays of grief as Max and Miriam poured out, in French, upon their forced separation. Neither had been forthcoming about the serious allegations of sexual misconduct on the part of the mother, but Child Services had their suspicions.

LUCIA Frood, née Straus, was Miriam's older sister, Max's aunt and step-mother, and Clerk's protégé. Her amorous relationship with Clerk had been the end of his marriage to Miriam and the source of its vitriol. Lucia married Clerk the day his divorce papers were finalized. She became CEO when Clerk died less than two weeks later. During the brief period while Child Services was trying to build a proper case against Miriam and provide suitable living arrangements for Max, Lucia stepped in as next of kin. An apoplectic Miriam went into early labor. The infant was stillborn and the mother died on the table. Max was despondent.

Lucia did her best to be parent and mother to teenage Max in Pittsburgh, still home to Frood Metal's corporate headquarters. He remained aloof. She tried to interest him in the 150-year-old enterprise, emphasizing the exclusivity of the club of seventh-generation family businesses he'd be entering, grooming him as she could, and putting him in position to assume Clerk's dividend-bearing equity. He sloughed off the opportunity as if it were no more interesting than a drunken parade in NOLA. She didn't believe, she told me, that she had ever discussed Maryam Froodenberg's Jewish roots with Max.

ALWAYS recognized as someone who thought different, and who was different, at least in the intolerant opinion of many children both older and younger, Max achieved notoriety as a stellar student. He was a high school senior when United States Senator Bennett Johnston moved forward a technology spending proposal to raise Louisiana from the swamps, so to speak.

Seeking broad-based support, he arranged several national conferences on semiconductors, synchrotrons, competitiveness, and such. He asked the senators of each state to nominate one high school representative to attend. Pennsylvania sent Max.

At the opening session featuring the Senator, Bob Noyce, and DARPA Director Bob Duncan, Max impressed Noyce with a question about the sensitivity of semiconductors to contaminants. "Couldn't you turn that on its head and use them as chemical sensors?" he asked. For that, Max ended up at dinner with the three big men and several directors of research at companies like IBM and AT&T. Noyce and Johnston soaked in reminiscences of soaking in the baths at Esalen, but Duncan told Max about a DARPA project he called stereo lithography.

"Not nanotechnology, not atom by atom, but drop by drop assembly. We can't know the limits of what you'll be able to print someday. But imagine our men and women in space who need a spare part." Duncan had directed guidance and control system engineering for the Apollo program. "Instead of bringing a complete storehouse with them, they'll print the one they want when they need it."

Then Duncan asked Max, "What would you want to print?"

"A human heart," Max replied.

Before Max's freshman year at Harvard, he spent the summer as an intern at a DARPA lab devoted to what would now be called 3D printing. The experience left Max with an interest he would come back to.

He was admitted to Harvard, about which much has been said earlier. And like his tossing off of the family business, he tossed off the efforts and kindnesses of Lucia, breaking contact with her when he went to France, and never re-establishing it.

Decades later, he was printing anatomically correct body sculptures, still dreaming of his human heart, and following the advances. When he came back from LGTBQ one leg short and with kidneys that threatened to fail, he got serious, in secret.

CHAPTER 94 THE MAX IS A GENIUS CLUB

SHORTLY AFTER Max and Vladik's chance first meeting at the Hancock, Max was awarded an Honorary Doctorate from the Royal University of Rhizobia. The university president had been Director of SINISTER during

Max's days at NUS. There was cash to go along with the degree, of course, but more importantly, he was asked to found and operate The Frood Center for Molecular Engineering at RUR. At first, he swept the idea aside as being too impractical. How, he asked the former SINISTER Director, could he run two labs, when at least one of them, HMRI, demanded, contractually, 80 percent of his attention?

Then RUR came back with an offer to pay him a full-time salary for the remaining one fifth of his time. They told him he was a genius and they showed him a proposed budget, funding the lab with even more money than he could get from Qasima and the NIH combined. You could bribe Max, and the prestige of having a research center named after him was almost as good as having a law named after him. Even that time commitment, 20 percent, wasn't really available. He had a contract with Genormx, and he wasn't living up to it there either, thanks to his consulting for the VCs and hatching yet other launches. He signed on to the RUR proposal and resolved to worry about how to please everyone another day. After all, they were Fucking Idiots and they wanted him.

Awards are funny. You get a gold medal at the Olympics for being the fastest runner on a given day. You get a PhD for meeting certain requirements. Max got an honorary degree because some committee decided to give it him. They didn't have to. It could have been someone else. They committee had policies, but there was nothing absolute about their choice. Did it make them feel good to give it him, or was he supposed to feel good for getting it? By selecting Max, a genius, they hoped to anoint themselves with his genius-juice.

The degree from RUR put all the other similarly conceived committees on notice that Max was a capital-G Genius. The (hypothetical) committee is composed of mostly insecure people who want to feel good as a result of giving the award. Selecting an acknowledged star made the committee members feel like they had made a good and important choice, one that would bring recognition and maybe even fame to the institution that commissioned the committee.

Dear Reader, long before I was born, there was a saying that "No one ever got fired for buying IBM." It meant that you could feel secure in your job by buying the top brand, even if it sucked. Obviously, by buying IBM you were a VSP, a very serious person, and therefore above reproach.

In another one of those cicada years, before I was born, my *alma mater* gave an honorary degree to Bob Dylan. The last thing he said about it, that he was glad to get out of there alive, confirms, to me anyway, that it was about the committee and not about him.

Max's star was ascendant, and no committee wanted to be the last to give Max a prize, or even worse, the only one not to give him one. They all had to be in the Max is a Genius Club. The honorary doctorate from RUR was just the beginning of a long and accelerating series of honors bestowed on him, the emergent celebrity. If all went well, the stream of honors would culminate, but not of course end, in the awarding of the prize that cannot be named.

Are awards given because of what you've accomplished, or because you've won others, like being famous for being a celebrity? Was he, Max, getting the gold out of sympathy because of his not-leg? Who could tell? Minutes of committee meetings were rarely public.

Collecting the citations became a chore, one that made it more difficult for him to meet his commitments to the I, to Genormx, to the VCs, to RUR, and to his hatchling projects. "Why can't the Fucking Idiots," and he looked at me while I peered into his office and he stuffed papers, books, a tablet, and chargers into a backpack, readying himself for a trip halfway around the world to collect a medal, "just send a fucking check?"

Awards are weird in another way. They can destroy you.

William Shockley, whose writings about eugenics serve only to prove that expertise is narrow, won the Nobel Prize for Physics in 1956 for his co-invention of the transistor. No small feat. His 1936 MIT PhD thesis was devoted to the emerging theory of the electronic band structure of solids, a crucially important bit of physics arcana without whose understanding we would not have modern society, full stop. When a guy like Shockley immerses himself at the forefront of a mind-warping subject like band theory, he develops an intuition about how it works and how it can be applied that is unmatched for a very long time.

From MIT he went to Bell Labs, the sprawling New Jersey research center once richly funded by AT&T's monopoly profits, and there his instincts led him to the poorly understood elements called semiconductors, for example, germanium and silicon. They were fertile ground for making an all-solid, or solid-state, switch; an alternative to the bulky, finicky, power-hungry vacuum tube. He reasoned, from band theory, that the conducting properties of those semiconductors—materials that were not quite conductive metals and not quite non-conducting insulators—could be changed at will with a small, carefully applied voltage. That trick is impossible with metals and insulators. As my mother might have said, "Gold is gold and glass is glass and never the twain shall meet." Shockley guided Bell Labs' Solid-State Physics Group to put the ideas into practice, and the transistor was born in 1947.

By 1950 Shockley had codified his understanding in the monograph *Electrons and Holes in Semiconductors*, extending his influence far and wide. The National Academy of Sciences admitted him in 1951, and more awards rolled in after that. Like Max, he was inspirational and brilliant, revered as God, but abrasive and abusive. The Traitorous Eight—Noyce, Moore, Kleiner, and the five other young guys who quit Shockley Semiconductor Laboratory in 1957 to form Fairchild Semiconductor—said that receiving the Nobel Prize was the beginning of the end for Shockley. His head became too swollen by the accolades and he stopped listening. He knew better. He had won that which could not be named.

CHAPTER 95 CFDNA

THE LESS Max was around the lab, the happier we all were. When he was around, he played l'enfant terrible, frightening the students and staff with prospects, sometimes exaggerated, of getting scooped. We did get scooped sometimes. Then the whole lab felt it. Max made us feel it. We had all let each other down by not helping the one who'd gotten scooped. Balancing our own interests against those of the communities; that was a bitch. Winning, being first, that was everything. No rationale existed for anything less. If we didn't win, we'd gotten the balance wrong. Still, it was the most fun I'd ever had in a lab coat. I loved working for him, even after I'd begun working for him.

Fortunately, he had other places to be or people to be with, and we rarely saw him. He could be conferring with HMRI management in the Adminisphere, at a doctor's appointment, working from Menlo Park, at Genormx, pitching investors, in Washington, in Rhizobia, in Indonesia at some seaside idyll about which we were little informed, being honored, or giving a plenary.

And yet, for all those absences, the lab produced anyway. The people he'd brought in were individually brilliant, although brilliance had a gray scale of its own, and also broadly communitarian. Max taught, if not by example, that someone's own individual success would be determined in part by the success of the lab as a whole. They'd succeed by association. Make the enterprise better and their careers would flourish. So people shared what they knew and mentored the less experienced, the newcomer, the stuck one, the one changing disciplines.

Where Max led, where he was great, absolutely world class, was in problem selection. Not only was he plugged into a boundless network of scientists, many of them collaborators, so he knew in detail what they were doing, but he had a keen sense of what was worthy, and what could be accomplished if only the right tools and money and attention were brought to bear. HMRI's 10-year grant cycle permitted him the luxury of working on really hard problems that would take years to solve. How he set himself apart, and the lab apart, was by helping us pick deserving problems that almost no one else could afford, for reasons of time or money, to take on. The brief moments Max spent with us conveying boldness more than offset the unpleasantness of his eccentricities.

As Max had explained to me over dinner at Maître Dix, fetal diagnostics using cfDNA was a hot topic. Eventually I was scooped. It was too much to have hoped for anything else, but I had hoped. The others had too big a lead on us, even though they had started down the wrong path.

I began by learning the published protocols for extracting cfDNA from blood. I put together a list of them, along with a comparison of their details and findings they described. Then I implemented the most promising of them in the lab. Finally I added my own modifications, resulting in what I thought was best-in-class, where the notion of best included concerns of extraction yield, time, susceptibility to error, and cost.

Then I developed a sequencing protocol. The I had every kind of sequencer known to Man, any of which I could have used. But like in most things, there were fewer real choices than superficial appearances suggested. My sequencing problem was pretty easy compared to WGS, so I could live with what some people considered the worst, lowest tech, crudest sequencing solution. We said sequencing was free, but it wasn't free yet. It was still expensive, so cost did count. "The worst" only meant that it couldn't read long fragments, and mine were short. "Low tech" meant it was relatively cheap and very reliable. It also meant it had been around a while, so there were software tools I could use and wouldn't have to build myself. "Crude" was still adequate for my needs. In what other people later said was no time at all, I was sequencing cfDNA from blood. Our competitors, or to put it more accurately, the acknowledged leaders, were still using PCR at that time, or so we thought. I had a chance to beat them across the line, if only I could have gotten my hands on the right samples.

To find the fetal DNA in a pregnant mother's blood, I'd chosen a very general method. There are millions of places along the genome where two variants of a gene differ by a single base, the so-called SNP. Suppose I'm homozygous for an eye color influencing SNP called rs12913832 in the gene HERC2 on chromosome 15, and that for each of the two copies I'm carrying I have the thymine, or T-allele. The odds are that I'd be brown-eyed, and I am. When we sequence my cfDNA, we'll find that all the eyecolor SNPS are rs12913832-T. All the millions of SNPS for all the different genes together are called my genotype. Now suppose I'm pregnant, and the father is homozygous in rs12913832-C, the cytosine allele. Then the fetus, carrying one copy from each of us will be heterozygous, and we can write that as rs12913832(C;T). By exactly the same processes as my cells dump my DNA into my blood, the fetus will do the same into its blood, and then since its waste enters me through the umbilical cord, there's now a little bit of rs12913832-C in my blood, too. Sequencing my cfDNA and examining all the instances of rs12913832, if my extraction scheme and bioinformatics analysis pipeline are efficient, we must find both variants, with the cytosine form from the fetus in much lower abundance than the thymine form from me. If the father had been heterozygous, rs12913832(C;T), then the complete absence of C would tell me that the father had contributed his T copy, whereas a very small amount of C would tell me that he'd given his C copy.

I tried to build on this idea by comparing the pregnant woman's SNPS (as observed in her cfDNA) with her genotype, that is, the SNPS natively present in her genome or similarly, present in her blood before her pregnancy. It took me a long time to recognize that this was, if not a dead end, then at least not the best method.

As I have learned from painful experience, getting samples is always the bottleneck for these experiments, and part of the reason it's the bottleneck goes back to John King's adage: make a lot of mistakes quickly. Without proper samples, you can't adequately test your methods, your biases, or the state of your ignorance, and you can't make any mistakes. In this case, all of the above delayed me.

Biology being a woman's field—notwithstanding the fact that of the nearly two hundred recipients of Nobel Prize in Physiology or Medicine, you can count on your fingers the number of women who've won it, and notwithstanding the fact that men dominate the leadership positions in academia and biotechnology—there was always someone pregnant at the I. Making a simple poster that read, "Thinking of getting pregnant? Contact Lakshmi Stein to participate in a study - lstein@jbshmri.org or 650-[redacted]." I then walked the floors, pinning it up on bulletin boards, handing it out in the lunchroom, and schmoozing admins who might know someone who knew someone. I got calls from gals who were legitimately trying to get pregnant, and calls from guys whose significant other was legitimately trying to get pregnant, and calls from guys who'd been too shy to ask me out, and girls who'd been too shy to ask me out.

One of the callers politely informed me that if my goal was to get a baseline of the mother's genome before pregnancy, I needn't look any further than the nuclei of the mother's own cells, where there would be no fetal DNA at all. Duh! I retraced my steps, replacing all the signs with ones that read "Pregnant?" but were otherwise the same.

Ten months had elapsed between the time I began to solicit guinea pigs, figuratively speaking, and the time I had genotyped, sequenced, and analyzed the results from the first pregnant woman. The method worked like a charm and I could easily see the fetal SNPs!

Unfortunately, the established leaders hadn't stood still. I'd been collecting intel on the competition by attending seminars at Berkeley, the University of California at San Francisco, Stanford and UC Santa Cruz, all powerhouses in All Things G. Between the talks given by students, postdocs, faculty and visitors, and the friendships I made, and a conference or two, and flow of information coming to me from Julia and Reed back in Princeton, and rare conversations with Max during which he'd tell me about what was going on at the Fraunhofer Institute in Schmallensee, or some such place, I had a fair idea of where everyone stood. When I visited other labs and research centers, I noticed their demographics were eerily like our own. As a rule though, they were mostly straight and not as good-looking. I missed Julia.

Max got me an invitation to join him at a small meeting in San Diego around the time I got my first results. There I learned, second hand, that PCR had been abandoned in favor of sequencing at the three most important labs. I also learned that they'd developed better algorithms to transform the sequencing data into something medically significant; they'd found a practical method to detect the marker—an extra copy of chromosome 21, aka fetal aneuploidy or trisomy 21—for Down's Syndrome in maternal blood. What they had done was going to revolutionize prenatal diagnostics. I'd developed a general methodology, but not an efficient means for detecting trisomies.

As I said, I'd been scooped. I had been fast and I almost closed the gap of their eighteen-month head start. But speed alone wasn't enough. They were working smarter, pulling ideas in with a broader net(work). When the tears fell in my beer, I promised myself to get more access to doctors and to patients. The I was remote, so I'd have to improve my game.

The only stages of grief Max could experience were denial and anger. I thought he was going to break something. I may have seen smoke come from the hairs in ears. I guess he didn't yet feel he could rant in front of me, or act the animal that I would later see him become. So he seethed, teeth clenched in the back, air pulled in hard, whistling between the gaps. He didn't want to believe that this opportunity had slipped past him. He had already mentally banked an appointment at the National Academy of Sciences. Who was there to blame? His leg? Me? Those Fucking Idiots? I wished he'd been concentrating a little more about what might have gone wrong, but I couldn't put the blame anywhere. We went into this starting from behind and ill-prepared. We should have expected to get beaten.

There was no noteworthy publication to come of this. No one questioned my ability to develop new protocols in the lab and new software pipelines in the cloud. I should have run my sample collection in parallel with the protocol development, and that would have saved me four months, but it wouldn't have been enough. For me to have determined that trisomy 21 was *the* problem to work on, that seemed to me like a pretty high standard, an unfairly high standard. After all, where was Mr. Problem Selection? I wanted to be done with my thesis before I was an old maid. I appealed to Max using Delbrück's characterization of Watson's thesis, and I paraphrase, "At least Watson didn't waste much time on it." The members of my thesis committee felt sympathy or something, I don't know, but degree granting ended up being a formality, and all of a sudden I was a postdoc.

Max thought I should keep racing ahead with fetal diagnostics, at least to put us on the map there. He couldn't let go, but I thought that was a solved problem no longer worthy of our effort. I wanted to harvest all that work I'd put in on cfDNA, and I needed something to persuade him to get off my back about prenatal.

ON our dinner-that-wasn't-a-date at Maître Dix, Max had told me that he had some big idea that would remake all of medicine, not just prenatal care, but he hadn't told me what it was. After getting beat on the last one, I began badgering him to let me in on the secret. He didn't want to talk to me about it, he said, because it would distract me from thinking about how to bury the others. He denied that there was such an idea. He said he'd never told me about it. He said he'd forgotten it. He said it was lost to traumatic amnesia. He said he no longer thought it was a good one. He was teasing me, so I decided to shake him up.

I showed up for our next meeting in his office wearing my lab coat as usual. Then I closed the door, which was kind of unusual, but not that unusual. He motioned for me to sit while finishing what he was doing, watching Chatroulette, in front of an array of computer monitors that would have made a day-trader envious. I put my coat up on a hook, stepping out in only the bikini I'd been wearing when we played football on the beach, the game that led to Dixon Mock later the same night. Then he turned around, gave me a good look over from top to bottom, or head to toe anyway, and said, shaking his head, "Nice bikini! Girl, it's a shame you are wasting that on the ladies." Then he threw me a facial tic from his library of them, and for the first time, I understood the meaning; "Got me."

"I thought I'd try to jog your memory of that conversation you say you can't remember."

"Oh yeah, that conversation. Now I remember."

Would he have told me later if I hadn't used all of my wiles, or if I'd toned it down a bit and worn my dinner outfit instead? Working for Max was like working for no one else, even my limited experience told me that was true. Everything was extreme with him, and I had to take my case to extremes to get a hearing.

CHAPTER 96 EXPRESSION

DNA HOLDS the hereditary information. It's a reference library, a database, a template. Other molecules, the proteins and RNAS, do the body's work. Somehow, the information from the DNA is translated into those other molecules. That mysterious "somehow"is called gene expression. An organism, perhaps one of us, has the genes for all the hundreds of thousands of proteins, millions of them if you include the proteins of the immune system, it will ever need.

How does the organism know how or when to go to the library and look up the recipe for making hemoglobin, or insulin, or an antibody that binds to poliovirus? It's complicated, but RNA, the other nucleic acid, plays a big role in it. When certain molecular signals are given, a protein, RNA polymerase, reads the coded message of the gene and writes it in a new molecule, an RNA called mRNA, the messenger. That process is called transcription. The still coded transcript, itself a nucleic acid, is then decoded and trans*lated* into the protein prescribed by the gene. The complex machinery for this is called a ribosome, whose 1955 discovery by George Palade, in another win for the Rockefeller Institute for Medical Research, now Rockefeller University, was awarded the 1974 Nobel Prize for Physiology or Medicine.

CHAPTER 97 CFDNA -> CFRNA

MAX'S IDEA, the idea that I made real, was that gene expression could be read using my methods of cfDNA extraction and informatics. If the life cycle of a cell resulted in its DNA entering the blood, wouldn't its RNA enter the blood too? And couldn't I then extract it, transcribe it in reverse into DNA—or cDNA for any nitpickers out there in Readerland—and sequence it, or even sequence the RNA directly? Max, with his flare for underappreciation of the technical difficulties in the lab, said it would be easy. But then again, even I thought it would be easy.

The idea was stunning.

DNA is the molecule of inheritance, the genotype, but proteins are the molecules of experience, the phenotype. The expressed proteins, the ones you have now, not the proteins you might have later, determine whether and how well you can metabolize your food, absorb oxygen, or fight disease, in addition to an almost uncountable number of other tasks that make our lives possible.

Gene is to genomics as protein is to proteomics. The tyranny of the proteome is absolute! If you could determine a patient's proteome, you'd have an incredibly powerful diagnostic, one that could tell you simultaneously about kidney function, transplant rejection, or any of a host of other activities for which protein is involved, in effect, a universal diagnostic. There are tests, assays, that can tell you how much protein you have in your blood, or even how much of a particular protein you have, but there is no assay that can tell you how much of each of all the different proteins you have. Proteins, long chains of amino acids, are like transcendental numbers. They have no rule. They are also difficult to sequence. State of the art methods use digestion enzymes to chew off the amino acids on one end, then vaporize the chewed off stuff, run the vapors through a mass spectrometer to determine its chemical composition, and then employ the enzymes to chew off the next piece in the protein sequence. It's hard.

Nucleic acids, DNA and RNA, are different. A single assay, aka sequencing, can read every different nucleic acid, no matter which protein or gene it's coding for.

Gene is to genome as transcript is to transcriptome. When I pull RNA out of the blood, I'm really pulling out RNA transcripts, the transcriptome, and since that leads directly to the proteome, my assay will be a proxy for the proteome, obtained by sequencing. *Perfect*!

No respectable clinician would be seen at work without his or her stethoscope. It's an instrument from the early nineteenth century, nearly two hundred years ago. Useful, versatile, and ubiquitous, as well as reassuring to patients, Max hoped his idea would become as iconic as the stethoscope. He branded it the Molecular Stethoscope.

Once I'd jogged his memory, and with my lab coat properly cloaking me, and while he grimaced under the acoustic pressure of his worsening tinnitus, he and I scribbled on whiteboards for an hour. I took pictures of them with my phone, for posterity I hoped, and then erased what we'd written to make room for more. We wrote about moby methods, bioinformatics, translation to medicine, experiments that would have to be done, publications we'd be targeting, grants we'd apply for, how we'd reorganize the lab, and how we'd rope in collaborators at the I and elsewhere.

By then he was exhausted and asked me to leave so he could nap.

"I have to ask you about this, first. The stethoscope is the quintessential point of care device, don't you think?"

"Go on."

"What's point of care about this method?"

"You mean sequencing in the doctor's office?"

"That's what I mean, yes. We're years and years away from that."

"It will get there, Lakshmi. Give it time. For now, there's universality, ubiquity, utility. Those are the lines of analogy."

"OK, I hear the physicist talking." I wasn't convinced, but I had a bigger fish to fry. "I give up. But one more thing?"

His eyelids were heavy. He was too tired to defend himself, so he motioned with his hand that I should get on with it. It was the best time for me to get what I wanted.

Even Max knew that Molecular Stethoscope was a mouthful, so he'd come up with a contracted form to make it easier on the tongue. I cringed when he said it.

"Max, the product name?"

"MoleSt?"

He looked at me like he didn't begin to understand why that was the worst medical product name ever.

"MOST, Max, MOST!" I said.

Before the accident he had been indefatigable, and I might not have gotten through, but weakened as he was, he caved.

I spent the rest of the day and a couple of the next ones writing invention disclosures that were dated and witnessed and delivered to TTO.

We had said nothing about commercialization, spinning it out into a company. That was for the future.

I WAS surprised to find out later that my filings were the first. He'd had the idea for more than a year, and hadn't yet filed a prophetic patent application, the kind that read "and with this method so described all of immunology is solved." That was unlike Max. Maybe he really did have amnesia. I'd never know.

CHAPTER 98 NOT THE MOST

BEFORE I even got into the lab, I found that Max's dream of taking the mRNA right out of the blood was tricky to realize, if only because RNAses would be working against me. Those enzymes, whose role in life is to digest RNA, would make mince meat of it, or consume it altogether, leaving little for me to extract. Worse, the fraction of RNA left behind would be highly variable and dependent on factors I couldn't know or control. Max didn't want to hear about any of this, telling me I was procrastinating, not results oriented, listening to the naysayers, and not brave enough. He probably said some other things too.

While I was thinking about a better way to get the transcriptome and brainstorming with others about it, I decided to placate him and do it, against my reservation. I had the samples, RNA-stabilized blood samples hanging around from all the effort I'd put in on cfDNA. With the invocation of a few magic tricks befitting my new PhD, I got results right away. I could see the mRNA in the blood, a representation of the transcriptome. I say representation because I didn't know whether RNases were digesting all the different mRNAs (from all their possible sources) at an equal rate, and therefore I didn't know whether the relative proportions I observed were meaningful or not. And, just as I had proved that earlier that I could see a baby's SNPs in the material blood, so what?

We'd always believed we'd need lots of help in translation, that is translation of scientific findings into clinically meaningful results, and my early good fortune didn't change that at all. We needed MDs to help us think through the list of possibilities and decide what to do first, and to tell us their definition of the term "clinically useful." Every discipline—math, physics, biology, or medicine—has different standards because of their unique problems and methods. We knew enough about theirs, the MDs, to know that it would be too easy to do the wrong experiment. One of us was going to have to find those MDs.

Max was always secretive about matters of his health, leaving us guessing about cause. There were enough docs around and sophisticated health science types to speculate soundly that Max was suffering from severe kidney disease, with side effects bordering on dementia or psychosis when it swung out of control. And there was the tinnitus. He had just entered a period of frequent absences and erratic behavior characterized by pettiness, a temper so short it could only be measured under a microscope, and passive aggressiveness, all of which were summed up in the words of a college-age intern who'd one day seen Max unloading on a postdoc, "What's he all butthurt about?" With Max's health having gone south again, the someone to find the MDs was going to be me.

Two people had given me particularly good counsel in the time I'd been at the I. One was Rinchen, who wasn't even there anymore. As part of his "life is outreach" mode of living, he had stayed in close touch with the lab, and had swept me up into his robes. The other was Salim Jawhariyyeh, a distinguished investigator on staff who had his hands in many things.

"Stein," Salim said, in our first conversation, "you don't look Jewish."

When I answered him, "Salim, have you ever been on a Jihad?" and after he had finished chortling, he told me he knew he could expect no bullshit from me and that made me his friend.

When I went to visit him in his office next to Qasima's, proximity itself a measure of the stature he held at the I, several other staff members were standing in the hallway, heads back, eyes shut, in a singular moment of reverie. Some were peeking through the wide open door as he played his oud, accompanied by a loop machine into which he'd programmed a long multi-layered percussion track. Walking in, I took my place among a few others sitting on pillows and listening to the performance. I'm sure what he played spoke its own words to each of us, but there was a deep sense of longing and grief seeking expression in minor keys that could not have been missed. There was universality in that.

"Stein," he asked me when the room had cleared, "have you ever been to Jerusalem?"

I thought he might be ready to launch into an anti-Zionist exposition. I suppressed my instincts for retort before he had given me a tort to react to, and instead applied my Don't Know Mind to my reply. "No, Salim. I haven't. Should I want to?"

"It was a beautiful city. I like to think about it, but not to visit. I have no recommendation for you. But what brings you here today, Lakshmi, my friend."

After telling him about my pursuit of cell-free RNA, he told me to forget it. "I've wished that someone would try to take the messenger out of exosomes and characterize that."

Exosomes are tiny vesicles—bags, packets, droplets—bounded by membranes, containing expressed mRNA of the cells that made them. Salim believed that they would contain molecular markers or tags unique to the type of cell that had produced them.

Following along, I said, "Instead of going after the entire transcriptome, grab the part of it that belongs to the set of cells you care about, maybe using flow cytometry to sort by type. You can sequence that and try to establish correlations, or even causality about clotting or whatever process you're studying."

"Yes. If you try to do the whole transcriptome, you'll spend the rest of your life trying to convince reviewers that your measurements are meaningful, that is, if you don't convince yourself otherwise first. In as much as you work for Max, I know he must be thinking about the commercial potential here, and I have to say, this is a lousy idea."

I looked on and said nothing.

"Since you won't ask why, I'll tell you. It will be hard enough to convince the academics, but it will be impossible to convince the payers, the actual regulators of these businesses. They'll look to the noise, the disagreement in the literature, and they'll throw up their hands. You'll never get a product on the market."

Before I left, I asked him to join me for lunch some day. He answered with a poem.

There's a place nearby where a surfer goes,
Divine schwarma and creamy hummus flows
Banana frappes, marvelous saccharine
Rare in San Jose or the Levantine.

"You will be my guest?" he concluded.

SALIM was right. Max was already thinking about how to put this into a company. He'd said as much when I caught up with him about a month after the bikini meeting. He chided me for being negative, but I had absorbed Salim's points.

"A month in the lab can save you a week in the library," Reed, my Princeton advisor had taught me. I spent several days rummaging through the literature, trying to test what Salim had told me, and concluded he was right on. Conversations with a few others in the lab and on staff corroborated this.

I spoke with Rinchen, who warned me about Max's ability to visualize a mirage, and to mobilize millions in pursuit of it. "You make him sound like a religious warrior king," I said to him.

"I meant millions of dollars, not millions of people. But, Max is no warrior. He stays away from the front lines. He's more like civilian military." After a moment of silence during which the unspoken was supposed to suffuse into me, he also said, "If this is Max's baby, don't get in his way. He'll steamroller you if that's what it takes." He spoke like the Buddhist monk he was beneath his lab coat. I believed we had a commercial problem.

Sequencing is free. I know it's true because I hear myself saying it. But that's a catch phrase, a mantra. It's good for PR and good for strategic thinking, but not for working out next year's budget.

For any given problem, let's say pancreatic function, the amount of relevant RNA in the blood is small, so you need to sample a lot of blood, and that's bad. Then you have to sequence exhaustively, adding cost no matter what the sloganeering says, in order to find enough of the pancreatic RNA to make a statistically valid clinical finding. Of the obvious first applications Max and I had dreamt up, the expense would not justify reimbursements from Medicare and all the other insurers who follow Medicare's decisions. I'd already learned how they think. Someday, several years in the future, yes, the HER, the health economics research, would pencil out. The big question was, "How to get there from here?"

As for the big vision, one tool for many, many different diagnostic applications, well, the world of doctors and hospitals and regulators and payers wasn't going to accept a radical new solution dropped into their lap. Change had to be incremental, and we'd have to deliver that vision one application at a time. The first one would have to be so good that it paid for itself, and I'd concluded it wouldn't. Max did not want to hear this from me. I thought it was better to keep the work in academia, let the publications come out from several different labs, and build enthusiasm among investors and potential customers. "Let the government and the foundations, like HMRI, fund the early work," I said, to the wall. I had to say it to the wall because Max wasn't listening.

It wasn't easy having him be dismissive of me. He said, more than once, "I can explain it to you, but I can't make you understand." That wasn't the way Vladik and Jay had responded to my critiques of Jay's original plan for Orrigen. I needed to give him more evidence, from MDs and so-called experts in diagnostics companies. More talk with Max wasn't going to be persuasive. "Data talks and bullshit walks," was our rule for arbitrating disputes. We'd see what the data said, and whether Max believed it.

CHAPTER 99 CASELODE FITTINGS I

MAX WASN'T getting what he wanted at Genormx. He wasn't getting enough equity. He wasn't getting enough influence. He wasn't getting enough respect. Carmie and the Board were going to marginalize him, and they could because they had the votes.

On a trip to Cambridge, Max had Dykkur meet him at 12 Bow Street, a subterranean café where Joan Baez once performed, a place that might have been built for midgets. Max favored the Café Pamplona because the staff barely spoke English, and because he suspected the offices of Ph'eer, Dowd, and Sertantiy were recording everything that was said—the phones, too, and not for quality assurance and training purposes. What he wanted to discuss with Dykkur was too hot to risk a security breach.

"You have to have more equity if you're going to have the control," Dykkur said.

Over a half-eaten panini of ham, pork, muenster cheese and pickles, a bowl emptied of its black bean soup, a piece of apple cake, a cherry soda, and a Café Americano on ice, Max glared back at him. Dykkur was getting paid $800/hr out of some future company's business for this advice?

"OK, I knew you knew that. I won't bill you for it, heh?" He tried to get Max to chuckle. He failed.

"And if you raise money, you're going to have a board and somehow you'll have to control them. You probably can't. Even if you can, you'll have given away so much equity that you won't have a majority, so can't control the shareholder votes all by yourself. This is if you raise money."

Max continued to glare.

"If you don't raise money, you can own it all, but then you have two new problems." He paused, hoping against hope that Max would say something.

"You'll have to operate from revenue and not from raised capital."

Max responded. "Bootstrapping. I can do that. I can find someone who will do that."

Dykkur, relieved, said, "Bootstrapping. A fine tradition. Used to be called starting your own business. That's one problem solved. The other is that HMRI sets limits on how much of the company you can own."

"I know the rules the Fucking Idiots have set up for me, yes."

"Well, consider it a solved problem."

"No way."

"Problem solved. Way."

"Every other Principal at the Institute is gaming the system somehow and you've found a legal solution? You are worth $800/hr if you've done that. Tell me and maybe I'll believe it."

"That's my discounted rate, by the way. We'll create a holding company, call it Water Boy LLC, that takes majority ownership of the real company, NewDx, the one—

"Nice fuckin' name, Dykkur. Did you think of that one all by yourself?"

"No, one of our naming consultants came up with it. I like the ring of it. But where was I? Oh, Water Boy LLC takes majority ownership of the real company, NewDx, the one with employees, products and revenue. Water Boy's cap table will show that you are only a small minority owner of it, the bulk of it belonging to a third party who will do your bidding with a handshake. The cap table, which is as far as most due diligence will ever go, doesn't raise any suspicions. Well, it does, but let's ignore that for now."

"Let's not ignore that for now, Dykkur. What suspicions?"

"Well, you have a third party, Water Boy's majority shareholder, controlling NewDx, but there's no reason why they should, unless they've put a lot of money into NewDx, which they haven't. So that looks really bad, in fact."

"How bad?"

"It depends on who's doing the due diligence. Worst case, it will look like a steaming pile of shit with vapors emanating from you as the someone who is intentionally, overtly subverting his contract with his employer. Then they'll want to look at Water Boy's Operating Agreement and you'll be done for."

"What's damning in the Operating Agreement?"

"The Operating Agreement will give you extraordinary powers over the actions of Water Boy, even though you don't have the ownership."

"The majority shareholder is my puppet, and that will be documented in the Agreement?"

"Pretty much. Not quite that bad, but pretty much."

"That's bad. That sham is legal?"

"We call it good as gold, aggressive and untested. AU. Get it?"

"Very funny. Stick to the law. What does that mean, aggressive and untested?"

"It means no one knows. We'll beg for forgiveness in the courts if we have to, and we'll tell everyone it's watertight until then."

"For an investor doing the due diligence, it still looks bad, right?"

"Steaming pile of shit. But it should never come to that. You're always working with sympathetic investors, people who want the Frood Brand, so with some fast talking and hand waving, you can probably persuade them it was a necessary evil that will go away later."

"Your odds on that?"

"Pretty likely, and even more likely, as I said, is that no one will ever look at it."

"So. Dykkur. Let me get this straight. I start a company and give almost all of it away to some third party. Let's back up. Who am I giving it to?"

"Dyk maybe?"

"Not Dyk."

"OK, not Dyk. Can't be family, either. The code rules that out. Someone close that you can trust and is willing to look the other way or not ask questions about why you're subverting your contract with your employer."

"I've got it! Another Principal, *quid pro quo*."

"You're a genius Max. It's now a mutual transgression, a conspiracy to subvert, but still you're a genius. And you can get them to pay part of the legal fees, too."

"All of them, since it's my idea. And since there can't be any documentation of this, I'll charge the company, too."

"No documentation on that one, Max."

"Is this it? I start a company and give most of it away to one of my colleagues in an undocumented swap. If one of us gets caught by an overzealous investor—"

And here Dykkur interrupted, "Qasima will have your balls in her pocket and your head on a plate, or at least fire you, probably the next day. Depending on how publicly you're humiliated, your careers will be either diminished or ended." He finished with a smile, pleased at what he'd wrought.

"But I'm not likely to get caught. Is that right?"

"That's right."

"You know, I don't think Qasima will take it that hard. She likes having me lay all those golden eggs. Besides, I can blame it on you."

"And I can blame it on someone else. Let me see, who? Probably some other partner at the firm. I can find a fish for this one."

"This is going to be OK. This is going to be OK." Max paused to let it all sink in, and then continued, "Let's go ahead. Write it up and call the holding company Amnio LLC."

"This a fetal diagnostics company?" Dykkur asked.

"Yes."

"Then Amnio is too traceable."

"What do you mean too traceable?"

"You're hiding something. You don't want the name of the company to point to you."

"What about Mniotix?"

"You're a name factory, Max, but no. Still too informative."

"Felated Pig LLC?"

Dykkur laughed so hard he farted. "You're going to ask someone else to be the managing director of that?"

"Pigeon Productions?"

"Too suggestive."

"I'm out of gas."

"We could hire a naming consultant."

"To charge me thousands more dollars?"

"Remember, it will end up being charged to the company."

Max pulled out his Slab42, swiped a few swipes, punched the glass a few times, and then said,

"I'll get something. I'll get something. Give me a second. I can see it. I need to concentrate."

For a moment, Max and Dykkur sat in silence until Max continued, "One," tapping on the glass, "two," tapping again, and "three," the final tap. Pausing again, he looked up and said to Dykkur, "OK, I got it. Caselode Fittings LLC?"

"And why?"

"Fuck, Dykkur. You told me there's got be no reason."

"Just testing. If you're good with that, I'm good with it, too."

"And get ready to clone this, because there are going to be more of them," Max said.

"OK, I'll set it up as Caselode Fittings I LLC."

"Heh, you don't look so much like a dinosaur dick anymore."

Dykkur put his fingers onto his forehead and ran them through the thick growth of his regrown hair, ran them all the way back to the ponytail.

Volume 4

Max is Out

CHAPTER 100 THE STALKING

ARIANNA'S CLIENT flew her to Manhattan for a day of consulting and gallery shopping. On the same day, his flagship property at 85 Broad Street was the site of an intimate gathering of very high net worth individuals—mostly hedge fund and private equity managers—and a few biotech celebrities. The carried-interest tax loophole had made these otherwise normal New Yorkers rich enough to buy privilege for their heirs in perpetuity, rich enough to capture a regulatory agency, rich enough to change the legal code of the United States of America; in other words, richer than Croesus. Events like these were intended to help the fortunate spend their fortunes, perhaps wisely, perhaps not. Vladik had heard about this one from Jay, who had declined an invitation to be one of the celebrities because he didn't accept anything which didn't further his thing, whatever his thing was. Jay didn't believe in favors or karma. He believed in focus.

Finding Jay unavailable, the meeting organizers had asked Max, who had declined their original offer of $15,000 plus expenses. He accepted their second one, which was $25,000 plus expenses and transportation from California on their private jet. It did make him wonder how high they'd go, and he promised himself to hold out a little longer next time, just to see.

As a favor to Arianna, her client Yoshi Kocheryozhkin appointed Vladik as his representative, and just like that—*SNAP!*—Vladik was on the list of attendees. There are privileges to owning the building, and privileges to being an exotic woman's husband.

When Arianna and Vladik landed at the Downtown Manhattan Heliport, a black Escalade shrouded in dark glass waited to livery them to their destination two minutes away. At 85 Broad, Yoshi and his bodyguards broke through a line of protesters chanting, like some Greek chorus,

"I saw the best minds of my generation succumb to finance,
Trading mysterious paper,
Insiders selling secret tips of Board minutes,
For a single basis point."

He approached the door, shook hands with Vladik stepping out, and then slid in to take a seat beside Arianna. The driver then took Yoshi and Arianna to meet David Zwirner at his 19th street gallery, and there they would spend most of the day before heading further north to Yoshi's 9,000 square foot townhouse on East 63rd. In the manse they would oversee murals being painted or painted-over, admire new installations in plastered alcoves, and contemplate what he would have space to show off if only he could buy (and then demolish) his neighbors' apartments. Vladik would meet them afterward for dinner. All the logistics had been worked out by Arianna's assistants in Cambridge, with the unwitting participation of the client's assistants in New York, and with the aim of insuring that Max and Arianna would never cross paths.

On the key-access-only 31st floor, Vladik was directed to the meeting rooms, whose centerpiece was a Statue-of-Liberty facing, glass-enclosed corner expanse with a conference table for forty. A boom mike in a headset wrapped over her corn-blond hair, the meeting organizer presided over her staff of three facilitators and four under-employed actors acting as servers. Their quintuply-pierced ear lobes and pouty painted lips were outdone by their perfected smiles and well-informed patter on the sources of the berries and the butter in the plattered light pastries. To twenty seated men and seven women, they also offered curated fair trade coffee in made-to-order, individually pulled variations on espresso.

Of the women, five were the personal CFO's or the family office managers of invited investors. Their business suits broadcast, "We're here to support some rich sport, so no flirting please, or not much, and no vulgarity, because we are CFOs and we know how to dish it out." At least three of them could have been selected as escorts on the basis of their looks alone, but they were there for their heads.

For the banking men, this was a day off. The VSP signifiers of pinstripe suits and solid shirts had been left at home in favor of other signifiers that said, "I have a large closet and a larger budget, and time to develop taste in clothing." They wore Kiton sport coats, bespoke of course, and single-stitched Italian shirts of the most beautiful checked patterns and colors, ones that Vladik, only worth $30 million, exclusive of primary residence, would never see for sale. Never mind their watches.

The technologists and entrepreneurs, that is, The Talent, two women and five men between the ages of thirty-five and sixty, conveyed something altogether different with what they wore. "I'm working too damned hard and earn far too little to look beautiful. If I have a sense of style, it's from the ready-to-wear collection and some magazines I read while riding the commuter train. You should value me for what I have done, what I have to say, and what I can do for you, not for my glamour."

Vladik was somewhere in between. To the technologists he was a banker and to the bankers he was a technologist. His hand-made suits from the Ulya Khoslovsky days had grown fat in the lapel. Instead, he wore an off-the-rack black one, very lightweight and contemporary, a solid shirt of aubergine that Arianna had selected, and his tennies to signify that he couldn't be classified.

And then there was Max, dressed as usual in distressed khakis and faded red knit pullover, taking that message of the technologists to such an extreme he might as well have introduced himself by saying, "Go fuck yourselves."

Max winked bushy eyebrows when Vladik walked in, as if he got the joke, or was telling Vladik he was glad Vladik got the joke. Vladik, for his part, was glad to see Max communicating with him like they could be in on something together. That was the whole point of this staged coincidence, this stalking.

There was an ice-breaking intro, during which everyone was asked to offer up some interesting part of their medical history, and then seven talks of fifty-five minutes each, inclusive of Q&A, with an hour lunch break in the middle. Other than Max, the final presenter of the morning, the speakers focused on drugs. Max concentrated on diagnostics, reviewing the history of medicine and asserting that the inability to diagnose disease was the biggest obstacle to treating it. He stood out because he made a lone argument, had the best rhetoric, and wore the worst clothes. Over lunch, the investors' memory of him was fresh and they talked about him while they ate.

These were not company pitches to raise money. They were concept pitches to help the "angels" understand the critical factors when they got around to placing some bets. It was clear though that if Max had had a company to invest in, he could have flown home with checks. Vladik saw it happening, heard the conversations, felt the interest, all confirming his belief that Max was The Man. Vladik took time to go deeper with the technologists. With the bankers, he listened to their impressions and corrected their misimpressions of what was said by the technologists, reinforcing the bankers' suspicion that he was a technologist, although not The Talent, and definitely not a banker.

Vladik would meet those angels again, he was sure. He obtained business cards from Rolande Haroutunian of Madison River Capital: Stefan Aaadelman of Aaquinass Bros; Vadim Preobrazhensky of Prophetic Capital; Kay Litman, the CFO of Litman Holdings; and eventually all the others, too. To each of them he handed back in return a very simple but elegant card Arianna had designed. In letterpress on 100-pound textured cream stock, it said simply, Vladik K, in fourteen point black Didot Bold across the center. His Gmail address and phone number, right and left justified respectively, were in smaller type below his name. Perhaps it's true that the angels were daydreaming about the carpet selections on their Citations, Bombardiers, or Gulfstreams, but to Vladik they seemed to be paying attention and asking good questions.

When the talks had ended, and old burgundy from Domaine de la Romanée-Conti—selected to satisfy the needs of the preening bankers—had been poured, Vladik and Max made a date.

"I want to hear about what you've done. You should come to California. I'll show you around the lab and introduce you to my family."

"You have a family?"

"No. It's a private joke. My lab is my family."

Max did not ask Vladik about his family, and Vladik did not say, as he had planned, "Max, there's something I need to tell you." And thus he failed to reveal how they were joined through Arianna. When the bankers spirited Max away, Vladik's opportunity for disclosure, at least partial if not full, vanished.

Later that evening, after *kaiseki*, and after Arianna and Vladik attended a private performance by Anna Sophie Mutter at Yoshi's daughter's private school, they were sliding between high thread count sheets in their suite at the Mandarin Oriental.

"Did you tell him?" she asked.

"I can't even say I was about to. He intimidates me."

"I know. He sweeps you along in his, his what? His wake? He sweeps you along and you become a willing participant without knowing it."

"It's called the presumptive sale. I'm invited to California to see his setup."

"Vladi, are you sure you want to do this? I don't think you know what you're up against. He's already beat you at the first hand."

"You mean, I had something I wanted to say, and I didn't say it because he, he, umh, he suppressed my will to say it?"

"Something like that. You don't know who he is. The man you don't know is mendacious. He's salacious. *Demi-homme, demi-cochon.*" She spat out the last words with a force Vladik had never heard from her. "He's using you somehow. I don't know how." But then she eased off.

"I shouldn't speak that way of him. Maybe he's developed some empathy after his accident. What did he seem like to you?"

"If he's who you say he is, then what I'm seeing is Dr. Jekyll. He's a crowd pleaser and knows how to work those bankers. The dark side must be buried very deep, or it's gone."

"Vladi, you can hope it's gone. I'm guessing it's only buried. You're going to go to California and you're not going to tell him about us. I see that, both of those things. Maybe you can figure out what his game is before it's too late. Either way, we'll live together with it."

She had been married to Max, so Vladik couldn't argue from experience vis-à-vis knowing him, but what she said seemed impossibly at odds with what he saw. Vladik really needed to sink his teeth into something. He would be using Max as much as Max him.

"I'll let Max know I'll visit him in California," Vladik told her.

CHAPTER 101 IMMUNOGENETICS

IMMUNOLOGY IS a great mystery gradually revealed. Long before Edward Jenner noticed that milkmaids developed immunity to smallpox, keen observers and experimenters were trying to make use of the fact that smallpox survivors were immune to further attacks of the disease. Jenner's great contribution, more than two hundred years ago, was vaccination, an attempt to direct the immune system by introducing a mostly harmless foreign agent, thereby initiating an immune response conferring long-term protection on the patient, preparing him or her for the day when the real, wild, harmful foreign agent knocks on the door. Cowpox (vaccinia) confers protective immunity to smallpox (variola), for example.

It is a fact that a healthy immune system is capable of responding to a myriad of different assaults on it, and a long-standing question had been, how the heck does that happen? Some of our responses are innate—we have them irrespective of our exposure—and some are acquired in response to exposure. More often than not, our acquired immunity is called adaptive immunity. Too briefly, innate immunity is the ancient front line of defense against infection. By means of chemical signaling, it recruits some white blood cells, also known as leukocytes, to bombard foreign agents with corrosive chemicals, to poke holes in them, or to engulf and then digest the pathogens. The innate immune system (on occasion) calls in the more modern adaptive immune system that provides immunological memory after an organism is first exposed to a pathogen. What follows here is a short one-hundred-year history of discoveries about one component of the adaptive immune system.

Antibodies, and the fact that they're produced in response to antigen attack, were discovered around 1880. Then around 1920 Oswald Avery—the same Avery who discovered that DNA is the molecule of inheritance—learned that antibodies are proteins. Different diseases provoke different antibody, or Ab, responses; so the diversity of antibodies must be a *very big* number, call it N_{VB}. And yet, the ones we need, and only the ones we need, swarm when we need them. The others remain dormant. Jerne, Burnet, and Talmage first theorized the swarming, now called clonal selection, as early as 1954. Antibodies are made in a class of leukocytes called B-cells, each of which makes one and only one Ab, and the working assumption was that an Ab was a single protein.

Protein structure determination is very much a modern thing. Linus Pauling laid the foundations of the field with his 1930s' deduction that certain helical and sheet-like substructures would dominate, but it wasn't until 1958 that John Kendrew and others published the first detailed protein structure; the myoglobin of a sperm whale. Kendrew shared the 1962 Nobel Prize in Chemistry with Perutz. Within a few years, Gerald Edelman at Rockefeller and Rodney Porter working independently at Oxford had shown that an antibody was not one, but a pair of a pair of proteins, four in all, made from two different genes. Joined together, the four proteins form a Y-shape. Edelman and Porter shared the 1972 Nobel Prize in Physiology or Medicine for their discovery.

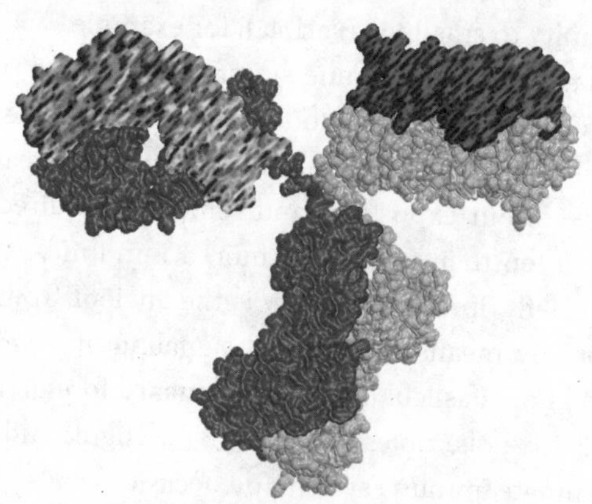

The long winding chains of an antibody's amino acids fold into a 3-dimensional configuration with one special region, the binding region, whose shape is complementary to the shape of a molecular structure, the so-called epitope, on a particular antigen. The binding region gives specificity to the Ab. Over the years, the term immunoglobulin, Ig, began to be used interchangeably with Ab. Different immunoglobulins have different binding regions. How so?

Moby's central dogma teaches that proteins have their origins in genes, so antibodies have their origins in genes. But the number of different antibodies, and therefore Ab genes that you might have, is estimated to be greater than the number of all other proteins and all other genes. Theories of N_{VB} predict it is larger than the number of B-cells, or even than all our cells of any type, trillions. That is enigmatic. Are there N_{VB} types of B-cells and are we individuals born with all the types we might ever need, almost all of them lurking around and waiting for the right antigen? Probably not, but if so, the embryologists must answer the question of how diversity arises in the first place. It is certain—because the theoretical diversity exceeds the number of cells we have—that you don't have all the possible diversity. The term "immune repertoire" was coined by Jerne in 1970 to describe the Ab inventory that you do have, and there emerged a dream that if you knew your immune repertoire, you would be able to answer the question, "How's my immune system?" The unexplained origin of Ab diversity led Susumu Tonegawa—a Japanese molecular biologist working at the Institute for Immunology in Basel where Jerne was Director—to try to determine if and how diversity might emerge from changes in B-cell genetics.

His findings were spectacular—so much so that he stood alone before the King of Sweden, as has happened only six times in the last fifty years—and yet they have been little explained outside the world of immunology. Simplifying greatly, but not so much as to lose the facts as we know them, it goes like this: There are genes that code for the two different proteins of which there are two copies of each in the Y-shaped antibody or immunoglobulin. Those genes are part of somewhat larger regions called Ig loci. Almost all of the difference between Ab proteins is confined to their specificity-conferring binding regions. The binding region is coded for in a sequence of a few hundred bases called the complementarity determining regions of the Ab gene. In these CDRs, there are three subsections called V, D and J. A B-cell is born with a library of different Vs, Ds, and Js. The cell contains wonderful molecular machinery that selects one V from the library of about fifty functional

Vs, one D from the library of about thirteen Ds, and one J from the library of about six Js, and then stitches them together into a V(D)J, after which the cell is ready to make Ab protein unique to that V(D)J. Thus we are born with the potential to make about 50*13*6=3900 different V(D)J combinations. Amazing, and large, but small compared to the diversity N_{VB}. That's Tonegawa's Nobel Prize work in a nutshell.

More diversity is added by mechanisms that alter the base sequence where V and D gene fragments come together, and ditto for D and J fragments. Each alteration tweaks the binding region, and the number of possible antibodies increases to trillions.

The next and final source of diversity kicks in when a B-cell encounters an antigen whose epitope binds, even if only weakly, to the antibody it's producing. Through another set of wondrous processes, that cell receives a signal to begin dividing, making many copies or clones or daughter cells of itself, each producing nearly the same Ab. Describing any other cell in your body, you wouldn't need the adverb "nearly." Apart from a very low likelihood of random mutation, a typical daughter cell makes the same—identically the same—proteins as the mama, thanks to the high fidelity enzymes responsible for copying DNA during cell division. B-cells making daughter cells—in response to the signaling whose explanation itself is beyond the scope of this text—are a different story.

The usual replication mechanisms which keep mutation at a very low level are confounded by an enzyme, activation-induced cytidine deaminase, that produces mutations on the Ig loci, with the result that mutation rates on antibody genes are cranked up a billion-fold. The selected mother B-cell makes daughters, each of which produces variants of the preferred Ab, changing the binding region in subtle and random ways, hoping, if we can impute anthropomorphic intent upon the program of evolution, hoping for a better fit of Ab to antigen, and producing even more signaling to increase the production of daughter cells with the preferred Ab. The hypermutating CDR produces the most monstrous Ab diversity, N_{VB}, orders of magnitude larger than the number of cells, including bacteria, inhabiting us. The measured diversity in a human is, of course, much much less, but it is the potential for diversity that makes the adaptive immune system effective. That's the explanation of the clonal theory of selection and the massive antibody diversity all rolled into one.

DNA, as you can see, is at the heart of the immune system, and people who like polysyllabic names would create a new field, immunogenetics. Others might call it molecular immunology, reflecting the very long term enclosing of all biology under the umbrella of molecular biology. Others might just call it moby.

Getting back to the immune repertoire, Jerne was thinking about the diversity of proteins. His goal of cataloging and categorizing and analyzing the distribution of all the proteins you have at a moment in time makes it a goal of proteomics, and hence thwarted by the same factors that thwart proteomics. On the other hand, the cataloguing is enabled by the fact that the proteins are coded for in nucleotides and those are easy to analyze because sequencing gets cheaper every day.

And this led Max to the immune repertoire.

CHAPTER 102 SALIM JAWHARIYYEH, OXON

SALIM JAWHARIYYEH, Oxon, MD, DPHIL, FRS was born in Jerusalem before the Six-Day War. Before that time, his family was a centuries-old fixture in politics, music, and commercial life. Afterward, well, "Things were different," Salim told me.

"My father still had his café, but I had no prospects except serving hummus and baba ganoush to wealthy Israelis, wealthier tourists, and poor East Jerusalemis. I only managed to get out because of *him*," and he pointed to a framed picture next to his oud on the wall. Standing alongside a very young Salim was a man who looked for all the world like an archetypal bearded Jewish professor from Princeton. Even in black and white, this man's eyes lit up the room.

"He was a physics professor at Hebrew University. He also had an appointment at Birzeit. He was very unhappy with the Israelis and their militarism. He resisted the draft, he didn't show up for miluim, that's what they called obligatory reserve duty in the army, and was imprisoned for it. As I said, he was very unhappy. He loved my father's café. He said we had the best hummus in all of Israel, and he was always asking for the recipe, but my mother would never share it, even later. You could count on seeing him often when he was at his worst, or, almost his worst but not in prison.

"One day, he is the only one in the café. I am maybe fourteen. There is no one else to serve, so I am playing my instrument. He says to me, 'Salim, my son is a violinist. You two should play together.' And I say back to him, 'Where can we play? We would make a very unpopular couple.' And he said,

'Just play, and then see what dice He throws.' His shoulders rose. His hands were together, but they opened up as if he was cupping something. His eyes widened, all in a very distinctive way he had, and he finished that declarative sentence as if it were question. I will never forget it, that shrug.

"Not long after, he brought his son in, with his violin. He was a year older than me maybe. Very dutifully, the boy took out his instrument, wiped it clean, said nothing to me, and began to play. He played Stefane Grapelli with hints of Middle Eastern folk music, in other words Bedouin jazz. So, this was very interesting, and I took out the oud, and began to accompany him, and then improvise, Django to his Stephane, and then he accompanied me, and it was music, real music.

"The professor found money for me to go to Hebrew University. During the summers, I traveled with the boy in Europe, busking, making good money. I had an aptitude for studies." As he said this, Salim made that same shrug he had described as unforgettable, and his voice rose, too, as if there were irony in the fact that he had an aptitude for studies. And then he said, "My parents encouraged me to live abroad."

Later, Salim cobbled together enough money with grants and generosity to make it through Oxford Medical School where Qasima spotted him. She then supported his DPhil in immunology, and after a postdoc at Rockefeller University in New York, put him on the HMRI payroll permanently. A decade later she invited him to head up the Immunology and Biomarkers Division at Lobitos Farm. His discoveries in rheumatoid arthritis and lesser autoimmune diseases led him to cofound seven different biopharma companies, three with nice exits, two plugging along, and two never to be named or discussed.

Wealthy, even by Bay Area standards, he wasn't yacht-rich, nor did he care to be. He owned a small percentage of his companies, leaving the greatest rewards and the greatest effort to the managers who took the risk and made the companies happen.

Salim was a passionate anti-Zionist. He was a public supporter and large financial contributor to Hamas. He never cheered for the suicide bombers at Sbarro's, the buses, the bus stations, Mahane Yehuda, or anywhere else, but he defended them by saying, "We're at war. You want only one side to have the weapons?" This won him few friends and made him an outcast among a certain set of people in American academia.

With his music, his politics, his history, his science, and his wealth, he would have been a remarkable person anywhere. At the I, he was also a mentor to younger staff from every department, including me, as I explained. Beyond its walls, he had devoted friends and colleagues in every leading medical science community in the world. He had brought himself to the top of his field, human immunology, and he held more disdain for intellectual poseurs than he did for Zionists. "Immunology is not for punters," he would say in public and private forums. He reserved particular contempt for over-promoted work on model organisms, and would begin his lay lectures by saying, "For you mice in the audience, I have some great news," and then gave attribution to a friend whose line he'd ripped off.

Salim was one of only three or four people in the world who had tried to understand the immune repertoire and how it could be useful in science and medicine. The recent traffic of VCs into the conference room he shared with Qasima left many of us with the impression that the first immune repertoire company was about to launch. He and Max had spoken about how to optimize the moby at the front end and the challenges of informatics at the back end and the triviality of sequencing in the middle, and it had even seemed for a while like this might be an area of collaboration or joint venture. Max wanted to try something different. Given Salim's unconventional disregard for institutional authority, Max thought he might be open to the Caselode Fittings I scam.

And so it came to pass one day that the two of them met in Salim's office beside Qasima's. He had a heavenly view to the West. Max, as discreetly as he could, explained the structure of Caselode Fittings and its legality according to Ph'eer, Dowd, and Sertantiy, all the while his face radiating tics of subliminal import. He told Salim that he shouldn't have to suffer financially just because the I had benighted ownership rules that failed to give the inventor his or her due.

"Salim, you should be really, really rich by now. Rich enough to have your own institute." Salim was a good listener, saying not a word. Then Max proposed that he and Salim support each other in hiding a majority ownership in each of their next companies.

Salim studied Max. He looked into his eyes and he thought, *Finally, I can see into his soul*. "Max," he said, voice gravelly and grave. "The Institute, you know, is my whole professional life. Qasima has been my great supporter for twenty-five years. Yet," he paused, "we disagree vehemently about almost everything except science, and especially about The Occupation and its resolution. She has held my hand while my family has been ground into the dirt. We cried together on September 11th. We lunch together every day we can."

Another pause. "You expect me to consider entering a conspiracy with you to subvert her wishes and the Institute's policies which are so clear they are published transparently on the web for all to read?"

Max was about to say something, but Salim put his finger to his mouth, indicating that he wasn't finished yet.

"Max, I'll tell you what. How about if we agree that we will end any discussion of further collaborations, and you agree never again to set foot in this office or any of my laboratories, and I will agree to forget that this conversation ever happened? OK?" Salim stood up, put out his hand for Max to shake, which he did after he got up but before he walked out the door.

What an asshole! Sameer'll do it, Max resolved.

CHAPTER 103 THE MICROBIOME

WHILE I tried to secure meetings with the MDs Max had introduced me to by email, and with those I'd met in the cafeteria at the I, and with some I'd met while pursuing fetal diagnostics, I kept up my reading and thinking. Academic or entrepreneur? Lab rat or titan? The temporary derailing of most had thrown me off.

I had long put off another experiment I'd been thinking about but had never quite found the time to begin. Yet it was so dead easy, I could do it at my desk without even putting on my lab coat. If experiment means moving stuff in and out of glass plates or tubes, then this didn't even qualify as an experiment. It was a re-analysis of my old data. All I had to do was write a few more lines of code and throw a software switch. Why hadn't I done it? I don't know. Why do we ever procrastinate?

Gene is to genome as microbe is to microbiome—that's pronounced *micro bīōm*. You carry ten times as many microbial cells in your body as you carry human cells, and between all the species of gut flora, ten times as many different genes than in your own genome. Because the bacterial genome is typically less than a thousandth the length of a human's, the microbiome has less genetic material, maybe a hundredth. Also, an individual bacterium is small, only a tenth the size of a human cell, and so about one-thousandth the weight. The virions are even smaller. I'm carrying about half a kilo of microbiota.

The DNA floating free in your blood, the cfDNA, comes from cells that have died, their contents, from centrioles to vacuoles, spilling out of the busted cells and into the bloodstream where it is metabolized and reused or excreted. Max had seen that there should be RNA there too, the detritus of the transcriptome, and so he dreamt up the MOST. I wondered whether we could see the detritus of the microbiome, too. Of course we could. I knew that. There were approved tests out there already, but these were based on PCR—so old school, so last-year. Those tests targeted one particular bug or virus. Could we use sequencing to do a much better job of finding the DNA of dead bugs in our blood?

It's no longer enough to write an article stating, simply, I did X and I found Y. The data supporting peer-reviewed publications must be submitted to publicly available archives so that others can examine it. The research groups leading the world in cfDNA research had put reams of sequence files into the archives. If they'd ever mined them for the microbiome, they'd never written about it, nor had anyone made an offhand remark to me about it. And there were the sequence files from my own testing of pregnant ladies. Signals of the microbes, both bacterial and viral, had to be buried somewhere in all those files.

An experiment like this is as much like plumbing as it is science. You must connect the pipes together before anything will flow. I connected a pipe from where we'd archived the fetal diagnostics experiments to a new storage sandbox I'd set up, and then I downloaded the sequences of almost a billion DNA fragments that had been cell-free in our patients' blood. With only a few more clicks, I added several billion more fragments from the online appendices of the papers from my competitors. Then I tapped microbiome databases that researchers from half a dozen centers had amassed in the course of stamp collecting, or possibly some more grandiose ambition.

Did the populations of those microbiome databases overlap with the bloodborne cfDNA in my samples? Software tools have been developed to compare sequences and quantify their similarity. One of them is a short-segment pattern matcher called BLAST, the Basic Local Alignment Search Tool. From a federally funded collection of bioinformatics programs, I sucked over a copy of BLAST, connected pipes to it from my store of cfDNA fragments and my store of microbiome genomes, wrote a few lines of code to BLAST each fragment against each genome, and instructed the completed software pipeline to text me if it found a particularly interesting, that is to say close, match. After a little bit of testing and debugging, I set the job to run and drove over to Menlo Park to meet Vladik for dinner.

CHAPTER 104 THE ORRIGEN EXIT

A DIVERSIFIED SUPPLIER of laboratory electronics located in the Route 128/Interstate 95 Corridor of high tech enterprises outside Boston, not far from where Vladik had worked at ITSY, paid $900 million for Orrigen. Jay had set out to develop instruments for directed evolution and to use them to find plant genes that ease the conversion of sunlight into fuel. Jay's team abandoned the fuels bit to focus exclusively on the instrument, the instrument I'd told him not to build if he was going to pursue fuels, and it still took them five years to get that right. They'd planned on three years, and that was for both the instrument and the application. Having funded Orrigen with his own money, Jay had the freedom to take the deals he wanted and none other. He was at times frighteningly focused, but he gave better than he got. He had more details at his command than any of his staff. He lived by the rule that no one will work harder than the boss, so it was up to him to set the standard.

He shaped that enterprise for sale, and sell it did. $900 million, and he owned ... well, what he owned never became public information. Rumor had it that he owned 85 percent. That couldn't have been right, I don't think. Even if it was 50 percent, his share was a king's ransom.

News of the sale came from about fourteen different sources when Max logged on at 6:40 the next morning.

Oh fuck me with a wire brush, Max cursed under his breath.

I, on the other hand, knew there had to be something in it for me, as I was a stockholder. Vladik, too.

CHAPTER 105 MOBY DICK'S

IN THE Castro District of Mountain View, at the intersection of Dana and Villa, there stands Moby Dick's, a venereal establishment, erected post-Stonewall, and dedicated to the proposition that all men are created for the pleasure of other men. Initially it was an in-your-face-mofo institution, threatening to the middle class families—mostly Indians and Chinese, hence the IC industry—which came to eat at the Castro's dizzying selection of ethnic restaurants. Then it went into retreat during the height of the AIDS epidemic. Its bathhouse closed and it became as much a Wake Bar as a Gay

Bar. Gaunt brown-spotted men sat out front dispensing leaflets and asking for signatures and donations.

At the market's very bottom, Sameer and his sister Sameera Barbozoo bought it for a song, reincorporating it as Moby Dick's LLC. Fears eased a decade later, the sound of *ka-ching!* was heard again in the land, and some peace was made with the lesbians—culturally I mean, nationwide, not something that Sameera did alone. Moby Dick's became a boisterous non-denominational LGBT hangout, a teeming mass of gay people yearning to breathe free. To accommodate the growing numbers, the old, officially idle bathhouse, which had since been used as a discreet bondage (and discipline and sadomasochism) playground for trusted friends, and which had generated a certain mystique but no revenue, was demolished to create a longer bar, more tables, and more bathrooms.

A cantilevered roof provided rain protection to the CO_2, nitrous, and propane tanks secured to the exterior wall. Interspersed among the tanks were four quarter-inch screw eyes facing outward at chest height. Through-bolted to the roof, a three-eighths-inch screw eye faced down. On the ground, two small sections of concrete had been chopped away to a depth of three inches, and at the bottom of each excavation a hole had been bored deep enough to drive a drop-in expansion anchor. In each anchor was yet another screw eye, the top of its head just flush with ground level so as not to trip up the unsuspecting. By the time Max moved to the Bay Area, that hardware was all that remained, on the premises anyway, of Sameer's strappado kit.

CHAPTER 106 THE STRAPPADO

THE ORRIGEN news came on one of those December days in California that feels like fall in New England. Newcomers to the Bay Area say we have no seasons. When the lights are out, all men look alike, too, if you get my drift, Delicate Reader. We have our seasons here, if your senses are open to noticing.

Max picked up the smell of dead leaves riding in on wet Pacific Ocean air. He heard the rustling sounds of trees shaking in the wind. It could have been Cambridge in October if the Charles River were substituted for the Pacific. Within an hour the rain came and the scent morphed to the distinctly Californian—more redwood and fir than elm and maple—but the hour had been enough to set him off, to transport him back to Harvard on the night he walked in on Jay and Joosey, and to fill him with fear and loathing.

He had been happy to leave MIT if only to avoid the once-every-year-or-so confluence of leaves and moisture and early closing-in of night that conjured those memories—memories of anticipation denied, of Joosey denied him, of his mother denied him, maybe forever, probably forever—as if he was re-living them. But even in California, his tormentor sniffed him out. *Why the smell of those leaves!* Jay's successes had only become greater than before. First he got the girl, then he rode the dotcom and genomics bubble as if he was Kelly Slater, and then, Orrigen. *Orrigen! Did Jay think he was Darwin with that fucking name!* And Arianna, too! He could not make up his mind about her. He didn't want her the way he wanted Sameer, but he wanted her anyway, even if he couldn't show it. Not since Miriam ... He wanted Arianna's love, and he missed her. *How can that be? Why can't that be?* It seemed possible that he could reunite with her, on some terms.

By the time the rain came, Max's untreated PTSD had made him a wreck. He was so agitated he feared he'd run off the road if he drove over the hill to the I. If he talked on the phone, would he spew so much trash he'd expose himself as the sociopath he suspected he might be? If he stayed inside his Menlo Park condo, he'd break something: a TV, a bone maybe, his prosthesis. He couldn't live within his mind, and he needed to get outside it.

His nearly two-million-dollar exit from Tiny was paltry. Salim and Jay were rich, rich, rich, and so different. Everyone loved Salim. Everyone respected Jay. Max needed a huge exit, a $100 million liquidity event of his own. Until then he'd have to be satisfied by oxazepam and a good flogging. He started with drugs, refined the plotting of his exit, made arrangements to meet Sameer when the bar closed, and then went walking.

A ticker runs along the bottom edge of the weather app on my Slab42. It said of conditions that day, "RAINING CATS AND DOGS." The bitter rain was driving and cold, its edge softened only by the fact that the storm had moved toward the Central Coast, and the wind was now coming from the warmer south. Max wouldn't have cared if the edge hadn't come off. The horizontal torrents lashed him, tore at his face, and made him teeter-totter in the gusts. Dozens of oak trees fell that day. Within walking distance of his condo, one caved-in the roof of a home, one killed a bicyclist, and several took out cars. Max was spared. He had no desire to kill himself, just to get outside himself, to be released for a moment from the clamor in his head, not to mention the ever-worsening railroad train of tinnitus, and the ceaseless striving for colossal financial success that drove him and eluded him. Returning home at mid-morning, he was soaked to the bone and as cold to the touch as a refrigerated steak. He showered and slept until after dark.

The storm had abated some by then. Still, it was not a fit night out for maid nor teats. If the young graduate student hung up behind Moby Dick's hadn't been mostly wound round in thirty yards of plastic food wrap, she might have been cold.

City ordinances dictated that the bars would close at eleven; it's Mountain View after all, not that *other* Castro District. Max showed up at quarter after. He was hungry and angry. Following Sameer's instructions in the morning, he'd had a butt plug in place since he emptied his bowels, and he'd only had water to drink since. He knew, too, that there'd be some antics before he was strung up. A promising ordeal of deprivation and misery played out in front of him. He stepped over yellow boxes strewn on the floor, boxes emptied of their long roll of thin polymer film.

From the top of her pink lingerie briefs to her matching bustier, Sabreena, that was the young woman's name, was wrapped in three overlapping layers of clear plastic. Each leg was covered from the ankle straps of her platform heels all the way to her crotch. Feet tied together and knees bent, her upper body leaned forward. Her arms, pulled back behind her and cinched from elbow to wrist with more wrap, were hoisted high over her head with a climbing rope threaded through a block hanging from the screw eye on the roof. Another cord was slung between her legs and over her shoulders in an ingenious tie that forced her into a trade off between stimulation in her nether spots and intense pain shooting through her arms. She verged on losing her balance. If by some fluke she fell, she'd dislocate her shoulders or worse. The sport looks dangerous, but it's safe enough if you know what you're doing. Sameera, wearing the foul-weather gear of a Caltrans workman in the still-stormy conditions, belayed Sabreena and maintained the halyard's tension just below the point it would have torn up her joints. Kitchen staff stood read to rush in and break her fall if it had come to that.

Why was Sabreena, the submissive, laughing? It was all play for her, and she was readying herself to be Max's dominant. Sameer, the master dominant, a nuanced attendee to the needs and souls of others, was just helping her along.

Sameer was dressed like he was often dressed, and "Let the weather be fucked," he said. He was a Kashmiri merchant wrapped in the deep red- and blue-dyed textiles of his tribal home, ready at any moment to sell the clothes off his back or to offer you something from his samovar, hookah, or soup pots. Oh, what Amma used to say about the Kashmiris! "So shifty wifty."

Sameer tickled Sabreena with a long-haired brush, and being blindfolded, she could only guess where the tickler would find his way next. Between her breasts? Behind her neck? Somewhere else? She strained against the rope pulling her up. She set her face into the wind and rain, smiling as all thoughts of mundane matters passed and she was left only with the experience of the moment, mindful of a drop of water touching her and the ever-so-slight sensation on her skin and the muscles beneath, and then letting go of them, releasing tension. Her muscles softened, lengthened, and stretched, all in response to one of thousands and thousands of drops of water hitting her. She shifted focus to two rivulets of water running down the mounds of her cantaloupe tits, rivulets catching in the film stretched on her belly, filling it up like a cup she could only empty by bending over more, in an act that ground the crotch knot in a most stimulating way, but pulled her arms back most excruciatingly. Sameer watched her closely, trying to help her find what she was seeking so she would be centered for Max, and able to give him what *he* needed. Sameer knew her well, anticipated her, had listened to her, and let her be alone after he had set the scene. After a few minutes more she yelled, "Quiet!" That was her safe word, the signal she'd had enough.

Sameera released pressure on the rope. Supporters with dry towels rushed in to support the girl as she regained her legs. They whisked her away to warmth. She changed into fresh clothes.

The wind had backed off and the rain had stopped. Sameer set Max up, going about his business with the same constant patter familiar to his customers at the trucks, the same congeniality with people that would have led him to a corner office in a more traditional business if he had had the chance.

Safe, sane and consensual. Those were ground rules, seminal, always met, whatever the scene may have appeared to people looking in, or as insiders called them, narrow-minded judgmental freaks on the outside. Max had a long way to go to throw the world aside that night. Sameer doubted Sabreena would be able to take him there, certainly not alone. Sameer was expecting he might have to intervene, or finish him off.

"Max, we have a new game for you. OK, my friend?"

"What is it?"

"Sabreena and Sameera and I, we wrote down some questions. Ten questions. Easy ones. Yes or no. You'll answer them, and that will chart the course for the evening. OK?"

"And what's the game?"

"We don't tell you the questions before you answer them."

"So I just give you ten yesses or nos?"

"That's it, my friend. That's it."

"Then let's make it easy, the answer to the first five is 'No' and the second five is 'Yes.'"

Sameer took that in and finished strapping Max into place. He wore his knit red shirt but had stripped off his pants. The butt plug remained in place. The stump of his amputated leg (bolted into the robotic knee) was visible to all, a rare event. A mooring line wrapped around Max' waist and was secured to one of the eyelets on the wall. Just like Sabreena had been, his arms were pulled back, lashed with food wrap, and then directed up to the roof block by means of the climbing rope. Sameera belayed.

When Sabreena came back she was a sleek ninja in a vinyl body suit, a black one that covered her hands and fingers and her head, too. The smallest of slits gave her sight, sound, and breath. For contrast, or maybe just because she was fundamentally girly, she wore lacy pink lingerie on the outside. Sameer huddled with her, telling her about Max's answers.

"Max," said Sabreena. "Shall we go over the ground rules?"

"Yes, Mistress."

"Good Max, I like that. You're all mine tonight. My toy alone. Please respect me or I will have to hurt you, OK?"

"Yes, Mistress."

"Sameer told me your answers to all the questions in our little game. Five no and five yes. Is that right, Max?"

"Yes, Mistress."

"And Sameer told me you want rrrough treatment, Max. Is that right?"

"Yes, Mistress."

"Max, I warn you. I can dish it out. Are you sure you're ready for that?"

Max nodded. Sabreena, unhappy with his casual reply, lashed him and said, "Respect, Max. Respect!"

"Yes, Mistress," Max said, grimacing.

"OK, then. The whole Megillah. When you've had enough, what's your stop codon, Max?" A Stanford graduate student in genetics, my friend Sabreena thought this was a very funny way of asking him how he'd like to end the game.

Max had thought about this, but hadn't quite decided. He paused, pondered, and said, finally, "Fish, Mistress, fish."

"OK, Max, fish it is. Tell me, is there anything you'd like me to know before we start?"

"I'm very thirsty, Mistress. Very thirsty, and hungry."

"Sameer, what do you think?"

"I think we can let him have some water, but hold back on the food. He needs to be hungry. Hungry for your love, Mistress!" and belted a big belly laugh that was seconded by the audience.

Sameera relaxed pressure on the belay. Max's head rose. Sabreena poured tea from the samovar. She tipped the cup back into Max's mouth. He craned his neck, hoping the brown liquid wouldn't run down his cheeks like drool. An evening raga, performed on guitar, sitar, and tabla, played over humble speakers. The music's simple harmonies were calming.

Sabreena nodded, and Sameera pulled hard on the belay line, jerking Max's arms up and his body down.

"Ready Max?" Sabreena asked.

"Yes, Mistress."

Reaching over by the samovar and hookah, she pulled a short whip off the table, making a loud crack on Max's fleshy ass when she hit it. A red welt rose up immediately. "What was the first question, Sameer?"

"Was that too hard?" Sameer said.

"You answered, 'No,' so I guess I need to give it a little more gusto." Then she ripped him again, hard enough that he grunted, emptying his lungs. "That's probably hard enough. It's hard enough for me," she said. Everyone, including the boys from the kitchen who had cleaned up and were now watching, everyone but Max, all laughed.

"Max, tell me," Sabreena said, "Who's the fish?"

"I don't know, Mistress"

"That's not respect, Max." Pointing to one of the kitchen boys, she said, "Tie his balls off, and make it tight." While they were doing that, and Max was groaning, she asked Sameer for the second question.

"Shall we leave the butt plug in?"

"Max, it looks like you answered 'No,' to that, too." She reached over and gently freed the plug from its home, waving the business end under Max's nose. "Get that piece of shit out of here, will you?" he said. She tossed it into a corner, scaring a rat out of hiding.

Max almost lost his balance when Sameera let some slack into the line. Sabreena caught him, mashing her best bits against him, running one hand over his hair and another between his legs. "Max, you like me Max, don't you?"

"Yes, Mistress,"

Then as seductively as she could, she asked, "Then tell me who the fish is, Max."

"I don't know Mistress. I don't."

She pulled his shirt up, exposing his back, and drew an angry streak on it with her thrash.

"Ah, Jesus Christ!"

"Next question Sameer."

And so things went. The music intensified in pace and pitch, warming the night with its building complexity. Max's "no" answers then deprived him of something to eat and of sexual release. Sabreena jerked him not quite off, and then asked him again about the fish, but he had no answer. She rubbed an amber grease on him, and when Sameera had gotten him well bent over, Sabreena put one and then two fingers in his ass, and strapping on a dick of her own and began wailing away on him, continuing because question number five was, "Have you had enough of this?"

When again he answered her question about the fish, "I don't know, Mistress," he almost squealed. She slapped his thigh hard, very hard. Her plastic dick came popping out and then he really did squeal like a pig.

Max could have said at any time, "Fish," and all would have stopped, no questions asked. He was in control of that. He didn't want it to stop. His looping thoughts were melting away. The doors of his perception were narrowing, but still too wide-open, way too wide. He would earn his escape from the worldly in the end, although he would suffer along the way. He didn't know how to get there on his own. That's what Sabreena was for, to guide him. Sameer would help. Who was the fish? What was the fish? Why fish? But even these thoughts were too much. He had been trained in the meditative methods. He knew what to do. He had to empty his mind and know, learn, experience what was right there in front of him. He asked himself, "What does it feel like to have my balls tied off like this? Can I sense the twine and the way it binds into the skin, and the skin as it pulls my scrotum? Can I relax any of that?"

From Sameer came a stream of mind-calming instructions, each a mantra on its own, a salving voice, coaxing Max through the steps of stepping outside. "Just be aware that I'm asking and then move on, and on, and on."

"Sixth question Sameer."

"Do you want my hand in your ass?" She knew the answer, and it was yes, Sabreena. "Hand me more juice, Sameer," she asked.

Getting down on her knees, Sabreena returned two lubed fingers inside him, palpating him, and then three, and then her whole black costumed arm, shiny with the silicone lube, disappeared in him while he moaned, “Uh aahh aah uuh ahh,” long and low. He would have come, but she squeezed the base of his shank and edged him off the peak.

“Who is the fish, Max?”

“I don’t know, Mistress” and he cried it at her, wanting the interrogation to stop. It wouldn’t, he knew, until he brought the whole thing to an end, at his command and control, and he wasn’t ready for that.

He said yes to sucking Sameer, condom off for his intimate partner, who soon came in a creamy shower over Max's face. He said yes to being fucked, condom on, by one of the kitchen boys. He said yes to licking his own butt plug, but Sabreena denied him. “It touched the floor. *Yuck!* That’s disgusting,” she said. Still, he couldn’t answer her question, “Who is the fish, Max?”

His mind began to clear, and that was beautiful to him. The raga had become feverish. Although it was past midnight, what he saw in his mind’s eye was a bronze glow—filmy, heavenly, and pacific. He felt the rope in his wrists, binding and pressing into skin. He relaxed his arms, and they rose higher but hurt less. The lab, Qasima, fucking Jay Orrix, his own awards and the obsequious award-givers, Carmie, and the rest of them; they all faded away.

While Sameera braced herself to pull his arms up and bend him over to his limits, Sameer put his hands on Max's hips and pounded away on his ass, answering Max’s request in the final question. Through the narrow crack that had become perception’s door, the mystifying light streamed in, and all he could see was one fish, still far away but swimming closer.

“It’s coming, Mistress” he whispered. “I can see him.”

Sabreena came close, untied his balls and began stroking him. In an acrobat’s move, she leaned back so her hands touched the floor. Raising her pink lingerie-covered twat to his crank, she dry humped him. He had become like an old piece of garden hose, thick but not hard. She flipped to her knees and prepared to suck on him, but Sameer's servicing was too vigorous.

“I can almost make out the face now,” he said to no one. The fish swam toward him. Max knew he recognized the fish, but could not place the name. Sabreena clipped two electrodes of an electrostimulator to his balls. When she flipped a switch, he snapped to attention. She gloved his shank with her hand, swabbed her tongue on his glans, and when Sameer paused for an instant, she took in the whole plum-sized head till it tickled her throat. His skin thinned as he swelled in her mouth.

She knew the moment of no return was approaching. Unsuctioning Max, ripping off the latex shield, she said, "Sameer, are you ready? It's almost time."

Sameer nodded and prepared shoot. Max shook with tension. Sameera pulled harder on his arms, driving his head down. Sabreena kept her hand on Max's joystick for the final strokes, steering it away from her, and then he, recognizing the perfect fish with perverse delight, shouted, "It's Vladik! It's Vladik. Vladik is the fish." Sameer came again. Max came, squirting a white load of tapioca into his own face. Sabreena slowed the motions of her hand, smeered his jam over his cock, and was thankful she had escaped the line of fire.

Had Max said fish? No one knew, but it was over. Max had seen the light and recognized the fish. And for a moment, at least a moment, he didn't think about Jay Orrix and his nine-figure exit.

"Who the fuck is Vladik?" asked Sameer.

Max smiled and grinned. His eyes shone like he'd seen next week's Wall Street Journal and was ready to collect his winnings already. "He's a friend I'm gonna pwn. I'll piss in his face and tell him it's raining. And he's gonna say he likes the weather. Details, Friend, another time."

Sabreena grabbed her Slab42 and Googled pwn. "It means to conquer, dominate, or humiliate," she said. "Then let's see, there's something about gamers and typos, and an example, 'Putin pwned POTUS.' I guess that's a reference to Bush 43."

Sameera and Sameer and the kitchen boys disconnected Max from the stimulator and then untied him. He went to the showers while the others joined in to clean the space. And then, only then, the seemingly endless raga stopped.

CHAPTER 107 THE PIPELINE

MORE THAN twenty years after the collapse of the Soviet Union, the girls continued to flood out, although the ones leaving today hadn't yet learned to read when Yelstin stood atop a tank. From Russia, Ukraine, Azerbaijan, Uzbekistan, Transnistria, Bulgaria, and Belarus, and the other occupied territories, the young lovelies enter the pipeline to Silicon Valley by several different paths.

Intrepid ladies made several stops along the way, in Europe, the Middle

East, and Asia, studying, marrying, interning, temping, working full-time jobs; trying legit and semi-legit means to survive. When they were on their backs, at first it was for love. If providence didn't shine on them, then later they might have gone to their backs for money. And there were veterans of the slave trade, girls who escaped and found their way to California.

The centuries-old business of mail-order marriage was a route out for girls too beautiful to hustle, and girls too poor to get across the border. Sun Microsystems hired the Russian computer scientist Boris Babayan to lead a research center for Sun in Moscow, and then Intel and others extended the idea to impoverished academic cities, or secret cities of the weapons industry. American engineers and engineering managers, mostly male of course, took long assignments in or made frequent visits to the motherland. Rumors soon made their way to Silicon Valley—a place known for its skewed population of eligible women—about girls who knew a ticket when they saw one, girls for whom California Dreamin' meant marrying wealth, or at least marrying into the stable American upper middle class. Everyone had thought that the old Beatles' tune from *The White Album* was all tongue in cheek, but soon everyone learned that John, Paul, George, and Ringo had been dead serious. Photos were mailed or hand-carried. Faxes were faster, but still faxes. Email imploring friends, in a day before browsers and digital cameras, contained messages like these, "American women are men with boobs," or, "Once you've tried Kazakh, you'll never go back." Dating agencies and printed catalogs soon followed.

Moore's Law brought us social media, and in Russia that's been VKontakte since 2006. To most of its hundreds of millions of Slavic speaking users, VK just meant "In Touch." To a few of its female customers, it meant a ticket to the place that minted more millionaires than anywhere else on earth. To American gaming nerds, for whom VK meant vaginal contact they might never get any other way, VK was the channel for the ultimate booty call.

CHAPTER 108 THE ROSEWOOD

CIVILIZATION IS the swath of territory between California Highway 101 and Interstate 280. West, or southwest anyway, of 280 are the foothills, the Santa Cruz Mountains, and the Pacific. East, or northeast anyway, is EPA, San Francisco Bay, and then, the East Bay, which is no bay at all, but the vernacular for the cities on the Bay's eastern shore. At one end of a perpendicular joining the highways was the Four Seasons Hotel, in what used to be Whiskey Gulch next to 101. At the other end of that perpendicular was a new hotel in what was paradise not many years ago.

The Rosewood, or to be precise, the Rosewood Sand Hill Hotel and Spa, may not have been pink, maybe it was closer to mauve, but it was everything that Joni Mitchell had in mind when she wrote *Big Yellow Taxi.* On the last undeveloped piece of land on civilization's side of Interstate 280, Stanford University and Rosewood Hotels and Resorts LLC built a six-star hotel complex. Driving by on Sand Hill Road, the cluster of California Ranch-style buildings with their faux shake roofs—low slung and non-descript in the spirit of 1970s-era shopping centers dotting the Peninsula—suggests nothing more than apartments built to serve the semiconductor boom of the same period. What you cannot see from the road is that the stucco'd exterior walls facing the road give way to stacked bricks of delicately varicolored tropical porphyry. Nor can you see the 5000 square foot piazza covered in four-inch square hand-hewn cobbles of pink, black, and burgundy granite. Nor can you see its central fountain suggesting perhaps the Navona in Roma, or the palm trees at its corners suggesting enormous goal posts—goal posts because if you've made it to the Rosewood, you've scored! The piazza valets watch the Lamborghinis and McLarens and Ferraris and liveried Rolls Royces and lesser exotics, as well as silver and black V-12 AMGs parked side by side as far as the eye can see, not that any of this is even hinted at from Sand Hill Road. Nor from Sand Hill Road can you see the steep hillside the hotel is built into, giving it views and grace and prominence you could never guess at.

A resort hotel, its understated opulence hides beneath an exterior of extremely well maintained modesty. Its target customer is the LP, the limited partner in a billion-dollar venture capital fund, or a fund manager from another financial capital, among whose own LPs there are many VCs on Sand Hill Road, or the titanically wealthy parents of Stanford kids, or the cashed-out entrepreneur developing new business in Silicon Valley, or the gift-bearing guests at the Bar or Bat Mitzvah of some fortunate parents' child. Around the edges of this audience are ten times as many bar and dinner guests. Some come out to visit and conduct business with the overnight guests. Others drive to the outskirts of civilization to sample the view and the ambience. Others yet are there to ogle the beauty accompanying wealth, and the celebrities. The hookers are there only for the overnight guests. If you have to ask what it costs, any of it, it's not for you.

Vladik had not let me know about his first meeting with Max. We hadn't spoken since the wedding. I would get an occasional card from him, or links to a flickr slideshow about big fish or some vacation he had taken with Ariana; always a neutered message to a long distribution list, sweet but without a hint of what he was really up to. He had sent a warm but *pro forma* note to all the early Orrigen team after resigning from the Board, reminding us of how much fun it had been, wishing us well, etcetera. That was it.

He knew that I'd gone to work for Max, but I was still in the dark about his wonderful wife's connection to Max, and that he, Vladik, had decided to draft in the wake of MDx.

When he did call me after stalking down Max at the 85 Broad Street meeting, it made me smile earring-to-earring, flashing back through the memories of an intense summer when I was so naïve. And *he* sounded excited to talk to me. We shared enough in that conversation to guess that our lives were likely to converge again, but decided to save the details for a face-to-face over dinner at the Rosewood.

My phone buzzed with text alerts by the time I pulled into the parking lot. My much-procrastinated little experiment had found the microbiome in human blood samples. *Borrelia burgdorferi, Streptococcus pyogenes, Clostridium difficile*; lots of little bugs. The news streamed in way too fast and I'd gotten the point; there was signal. I took a seat on an architectural boulder by the piazza, secured some open Wi-Fi on my laptop, logged onto HMRI's servers, paused my job, edited the alert criteria, and when I closed the laptop, found Vladik standing beside me.

"I see you have only changed for the better," he said, offering his hand, and referring, I think, to my work ethic.

"I'm getting results from this thing I just tried today. I'll tell you about it, but I shouldn't."

"I'll tell you some things I shouldn't, too."

Passing the restaurant where we'd be eating, and walking through the bar onto the terrace, I was shocked by the level of luxury on offer. I'd seen it at hotels in India with my parents, and I'd imagined Beverly Hills would have it. We—see how I self-identified?—had our own celebrities now, so I shouldn't have been surprised to see that private-jet class of service here in Silicon Valley. In the last gilded age, that class of service was called Pullman. Somehow, we had exceeded even those excesses.

From a terrace, the hillside fell away below us. Swimming pools as blue as the Caribbean lay in the developing shadows. The sun closed in on the Santa

Cruz Mountains. The girls carrying drinks and appetizers were gorgeous and not too slutty. Were their tongues as good as Julia's? Could I flirt with them while I was with Vladik? Not sure. Vladik had arrived a few hours ago, but already he knew which of them spoke Russian, and that was almost all of them.

I'd never been there before, but I knew our server. We'd spotted each other at a famous EPA hangout for lesbians called Home Depot. I wanted to flirt with her, and I was pretty sure she would flirt with me. I ordered a plate of hot olives and hummus, while Vladik ordered straight vodka for each of us. I'd need beer to back it up. From a long list of microbrews on draft, I chose a pilsner from Berkeley and Vladik chose a hefeweisen by Schwarzbier with a slice of lemon.

Fingering the dark thick curls on his face, and remembering the clean-shaven Vladik I'd first met, and the hipster Vladik I'd seen at his wedding, I asked him, "So you're out of the habit of doing it yourself?"

"I'll lose it before the summer, but I'm enjoying it now. I'm going to transform myself for the next stage."

"And what stage is that?"

"CEO of a new company with Max."

"Really. And what company is that?"

"I don't know, we haven't discussed it yet."

"I see you have a plan. When are you seeing Max, by the way?"

"I do have a plan. I'm going to seduce him with understatement. Meeting him at Buck's for breakfast tomorrow. He said something about spending the night in Menlo Park."

"Yeah, he has a place here."

"And then we'll drive to his institute, your institute."

"The I," I interjected. "We call it, simply, the I. You'll sound like a gringo if you say anything else."

"Right, the I. Tomorrow afternoon I'll come back, and he arranged to have some of his postdocs give me a briefing at Genormx."

The food and drinks came. Bill Gates walked by, talking with his hands and speaking loudly.

"I'll bet people come here just for the star gazing," I said, impressed.

"Definitely a place for the rich and powerful. Arianna's first Bay Area client is putting her up here. It's a strange story. She had Arianna buy her a house in Woodside."

"Arianna's in real estate?"

"No, but the client had something in mind and Arianna was the person to pull it off. The house is a work of art, an undiscovered masterpiece. Arianna's got this whole spiel about it. She'll tell you. They've been working on the purchase for a year. Now Arianna is buying an art collection for it. Crazy wealth involved in this. We flew out on her Gulfstream. I'm hitching a ride, as usual."

"Arianna's?"

"*Ha!* The client's. Wuang Wenqian, the wealthiest woman in the world, or maybe the weirdest woman in the world. OK, now I've told you something I shouldn't have. I just breached the terms of the non-disclosure agreement."

"The client doesn't want to be known?"

"No. Chinese something-or-other. Real estate, casinos, military, I don't know. Very secretive. I usually get to see the houses or the installations. This time, nothing. I won't even be meeting her."

"Will Arianna join us for dinner?"

"No, she's fully committed to the client's schedule, and D5 isn't telling us what that is."

"D5?"

"Wendy. The client. Her moniker. It's a two-syllable contraction. Five w's, but even double-u was too long, so just D5."

I must have given Vladik a look of disbelief, because next he said, "Heh, don't look at me that way. I didn't come up with it. That's what she's called. I would have chosen W^5."

Georgina, that girl I'd seen at Home Depot, was wrapped in silver sequins over silk that ran only halfway down her thigh. She touched my shoulder and let us know that our table was ready. Then she slinked, while Vladik and I walked, through the bar again. The setting sun streamed through the wide passageway to the terraces, and the bar evoked some tropical feeling, but different than the hot and loud Cubana of Maître Dix. Its dark marbled paneling on the walls reminded me of a fine guitar, and then I got it, of course, rosewood! I might as well have been inside a giant and ancient Martin guitar! The barroom exited onto a corridor with display cases full of Harry Winston or something and—need I say more after that? In two steps, Georgina—her curves making me hungry for something I had been missing for too long—led us to the equally sultry restaurant, the Michelin-starred Madera. Vladik didn't try to flirt with her, which was wise, because she had no eyes for him, only for me.

CHAPTER 109 MADERA

THE FIRST thing out of Vladik's mouth when we were seated and alone was, "Max was Arianna's first husband!" He leaned over and grinned hugely at me, orbs wide, eyebrows raised to the pain point.

I slapped my hand down on the table, making a sound much too loud for the busy but restrained dining room, and said, trying to whisper, "No!" and then "Does Max know?" meaning does he know of the second marriage.

Vladik shook his head and said, "No, and I'm not planning on telling him. That's got to be our secret for now."

I had only the vaguest recollection that she'd been married before. Two very remote dots connected themselves all of a sudden; specifically, Max's stay at the École and the French aroma that swirled about Arianna. But at the Rosewood dinner that night, I still knew nothing of their tribulations.

"Then why are you telling me now?"

"You mean, now instead of at our wedding, or now at all?"

"Well, now, I guess."

"I thought it would help me if you knew, and I thought I could entrust you with the secret," Vladik said to me.

"It's nothing for me to keep it, but I'd like to know why you want it kept secret."

Vladik had not thought through his answer to that question, and was still studying me while trying to find the right words, the properly politic formulation, when I threw this out. "Max is still single. Maybe he's still attached to her and would consider you an interloper."

"Remember Jay's story on the *Lucky Strike*? Max has a history of being interloped. I don't think I should say more, but I'm sure you can make up your own perfectly good narrative from there."

"The essential point being that he wouldn't want to be married, figuratively speaking here, to someone who had horned in on his love interest."

"I think we understand each other," Vladik said.

I was working for Max and I revered him even with his flaws. I had a strong allegiance to Vladik, too. After all, he had mentored me back at Origen's formation, shaping the way I thought about the business of science, or the science of business, or the confluence of science and business. Max gave me the most interesting scientific challenges, but he didn't help me think. The problem was that the secret divided my loyalties, and I knew that

I would someday have to choose sides. My calculation turned on whether Max knowing the whole truth would help or hurt him, and I concluded that it would only hurt him. If he asked, I'd be bound to tell him, so I hoped he wouldn't ask. But why would he ask me about Vladik's marriage? I'd brought up a little about my mother in that first dinner in Florida, but since then we had never talked about my family, or anyone else's for that matter. What would make him bring up Vladik's family with me? Max wanted to think of us in the lab as having no personal lives. You could be the world champion Scrabble player or a soloist with the San Francisco Symphony and he wouldn't want to know about it. He was an island, he said, and he both expected us to be islands and he knew full well that we weren't.

"I can agree to keep this to myself until Max asks," I told Vladik after a short silence. He nodded acceptance of that condition.

"But now I'm complicit, too. What am I going to say if he asks me why I didn't tell him earlier?" I continued.

Words were about to come out of Vladik's mouth, when I stopped him with a wave of my hand. "No. Don't say anything. Whatever you say will make it worse. Secrets are corrosive, don't you know?" With my elbows on the table and my thumbs on my cheekbones, I massaged my forehead with three fingers of each hand, trying to sort out how I had so quickly become a co-conspirator to a confidence.

"Max is keeping something from you, I'm sure, and you're sophisticated enough to be guessing as much," I told Vladik. "You're guessing that this gives you leverage over him."

Vladik interrupted me and wouldn't let me wave him off the second time. "No, I'm not thinking about the leverage. I want to work with Max because he's a genius, he has cred with investors, and he has, excuse the phrasing, monetizable ideas. If we tell him this, it will queer the deal. Arianna believes that and has convinced me of it. But he needs me, too, or someone like me. I know what I'm saying is self-serving, but it's also true, don't you think?"

"Why did you tell me if you want me to keep it to myself?" I asked him.

"I thought it was a harmless secret that you would enjoy knowing, knowing what you know already. I should have known that it would make you feel compromised. I'm sorry I've told you." Although much of his facial expression was hidden beneath that beard, his face looked sad and deflated.

His admission was unlike anything I had ever heard from Max. "OK, I can do it."

He perked up and then said, "Thank you. Now, can I tell you why this is important to me?"

"I know why it's important to you. You've as much as told me already. You don't meet many genius-class innovators who want you to be the CEO of their latest and greatest thing. That makes Max your date to the ball. Wait, it's better than that. He's more than your date, he's the belle of the ball, has the tickets, and has invited you to join him, or her, or whatever the right pronoun is in this gender-bent analogy."

"And with one successful, even moderately successful venture cofounded with Max, I'll have relaunched my career," Vladik slipped in. "Arianna has hers, and I need something to do. All the things I did at ITSy, and Jay's Agrigene and Orrigen, and even my summer jobs in high school? Someone else brought those ideas forward, made successes of them. I want to do that with my ideas, with our ideas, this time. A startup with Max, one in which I'm the CEO, lets me do that. I short-circuit years of ladder-climbing this way."

Our server, Lena, in sequined black silk that shimmered and slenderized her already slender body, went over the evening's specials. She had been well trained, and reviewed the elaborate offerings and their French and Spanish names without a stumble. I tried not to look at the column of prices, as Vladik had insisted that this dinner was his to pay for. The local red abalone in bacon broth with squid dumplings was a bit too chi-chi for me, along with most of the other items on the menu.

Vladik's news about Max and Arianna, no matter how much it troubled me to have been let in on it, was too delicious to ignore, and I couldn't keep it out of my head. Then, the idea that Vladik would be in California frequently, and that there would be excuses to have more dinners like this with him and maybe even Arianna someday, and to have Georgina fluttering around me; all of it put my appetite in a holding pattern.

We split two entrees of Mexican prawns with housemade cocktail and one of gnocchi with indoor locally grown basil pesto and hothouse baby tomatoes, and then the New York strip steak. I can't remember the name of every farmer who touched the food on its way to our plate, but I do know the names were on the menu. We ordered more beer, and got back to talking.

I told him how Max had opened my eyes to cfDNA, and how I'd failed to catch the other groups at the frontier of prenatal diagnostics, but I was going to bury them and everyone else with the molecular stethoscope.

Vladik had been following the news releases about prenatal and had become familiar with some of the issues. "What about cancer and organ transplantation? I thought those were up and coming."

"Meh. There's so much money in cancer that the liquid biopsy—"

"The what?" Vladik interrupted.

"The liquid biopsy. It's like biopsying the tumor with a blood test. Blood biopsy came and went already. Too yucky. Liquid biopsy is the new marketing wizardry."

"People don't care about technology, they care about function. Calling it cfDNA would draw too much attention to the technology. You think?"

"I do. But this is an NMR thing."

"Oh," Vladik got it. "The old nuclear magnetic resonance imaging became magnetic resonance imaging because nuclear was too apocalyptic, too yucky?"

"It was a name only physicists would love." We physicists, or whatever we were, paused to reflect silently on how investigations of the nuclear magnetic moment, about which chemistry cares nothing at all, had led to one of the great medical innovations of the last century, although no medical condition has anything at all to do with the nucleus.

Then I continued. "I think the liquid biopsy would be a financial windfall, but it's complicated."

"Cancer's complicated?"

"Yes, but I meant that the reasons for not doing it are complicated. My analysis of the literature says the concentration of informative mutations of the tumor is low. Not so low we can't find them, but low enough that the breakthrough in the field is going to come from the clinic, not the lab. You need to be in the middle of a cancer center. That's not us. Besides, Vogelstein's all over it like a wet rag, and Max thinks it's already too crowded."

"A field with no products and no companies in it is already too crowded?"

"The work is being done as projects within the big sequencing and PCR companies. It's not that no one is working on it. It's that the work is hidden from public view."

Vladik's face radiated pride, as if his tutelage during our summer together had helped me become what I had become. "And organ transplantation?" he asked.

"A wasteland, I think. Too few patients."

"Yeah, but the patients keep coming back, don't they?"

"Max is dead set against it."

"Max *is* dead set against it. When I push him as to why, he says—"

Interjecting, I said, "I would prefer not to?"

Vladik had not yet heard this conversation-ending refrain, and he looked at me with his face in a question mark. "No. 'They're all Fucking Idiots.' And then, winking at me, he says, 'Regenerative medicine.' I guess he means that transplantation diagnostics are a band-aid, and the better solution, one he doesn't have, is to grow new ones. I have to choose my battles. That doesn't seem like one worth fighting."

Max did have one, a solution, but I wasn't permitted to say anything about it. There was a windowless lab detached from the area where most of us worked, and in it he was growing kidneys. The sole marking on the door with the fingerprint lock was one word, Froodenstein's.

And so it went on. The table was cleared. Lena was seating a small party only two tables away from us. Venus Khlobama, Silicon Valley's best looking and most outrageous VC was there with a Donald Trump impersonator. A third place setting was unoccupied while Lena poured sparkling water from Lake Baikal. Then Al Gore, who had become a VC at one of the local firms, walked in to join them.

"Vladik, excuse me," I said.

Lena had pulled the Veep's empty seat out from the table and was helping him into it when seconds after leaving Vladik I was saying, "Hello Mr. Vice ..." and Mr. Gore said at a volume that had long shed any sense of shyness, or the possibility that not everyone within very long earshot would be interested in what he had to say, "Well hello, Lakshmi," and wrapped his arms around me. "My you have grown into a beautiful young woman."

"Thank you Mr. Vice President."

"Now call me Al, please."

"I still can't do that, Sir. But thank you. I wanted to say hello. I don't want to interrupt your dinner."

"No interruption at all. Let me introduce you to my friends. This is Venus Khlobama ..." and my eyes were fixed on her amazing and immense physical presence while the former Veep introduced the trumpish character. Within two minutes, all of the Madera's guests knew of me, of my apprenticeship to Max Frood at the Haldane Institute, and of way too much more, but I could not easily pull away from him.

"Lakshmi, may I call on you someday?" he said. "Perhaps Venus would like to join me."

"Yes, I would like that. I know Max. I know Max very well," Venus said, looking me over as skillfully as a buyer of thoroughbreds. Through my normally protective veneer and deep into my core, she appraised me and wanted what she saw. But all that took place in nothing more than a blink.

"Mr. Vice President, Ms. Khlobama, with pleasure. Shall I call your offices tomorrow to make arrangements?" After the contacts were exchanged, I escaped to Vladik's frozen look of astonishment.

It became my turn to remind *him* of another detail from Jay's tale on the *Lucky Strike*—Jay ignoring me when I mentioned that I knew Al Gore—and then I filled him in on that history, at the conclusion of which his astonishment was still frozen in place. Nor did that melt either when I gave him the details, as I knew them at the time, of LGTBQ and the accident that left Max with only one leg.

"And you know Venus, too?"

"No, just of her. In Silicon Valley, it's trendy to burnish your libertarian credentials by taking pot shots at government. She's a champion of the sport."

"In Soviet Russia, government takes pot shots at you," Vladik said.

An echo of something he said on our first day together reverberated, and then I let his remark fade away.

Like Gore, Venus Khlobama was obsessed with energy. But Gore was known as a deal maker, a lover, a soft guy, a great guy to get stoned with, and a girly guy prone to public displays of affection, whereas Venus was known as snake charming, brilliant, pioneering, and litigious. Her peculiar last name, and the fact that she looked like the President, although bigger, made her the subject of conversation among the Birthers. In the press, she waved that off as so much dross, but it kept coming back like a bad case of *Herpes labialis.*

Both Vladik and I listened with pricked ears, but overheard little, much of it very predictable. "Our democracy has been hacked!" said one, and "You're fired!" said another. A third said, "You're all so naïve." Vladik then said to me, "She's probably thinking, where I come from, your neighbor hacks you with a machete."

"I do not think that woman grew up in a village," I said.

"It's a joke."

Georgina, the silvery server from the terrace came back to flirt with me and ask about our dinner. "May I get you another drink, compliments of an admirer?"

"Not now, but how about on the decks after our dessert?" I asked, while planning to leave Vladik behind for that one. She nodded and then glided out of the dining room. Lena arrived with dessert menus. We split a wheatless chocolate cake with raspberries: always great, but verging on cliché. Then we had some espresso to go along with it.

I hesitated telling him about my new results. I had checked them while in the Ladies, and they were still streaming in. Not only the bacterials that I had seen at first, but some viral genomes, too. This method was much more likely to hit pay dirt than the MOST. When Vladik pressed me to disclose what I shouldn't have disclosed, I told him I had some new findings, but I couldn't share them with him until I'd had a chance to review them with Max. "What's your NDA status with HMRI?"

"Virgin."

"Yeah, better wait until Max says it's OK."

Vladik was not a pleader and so he let it go.

"What do you know about these other companies? He's told me there's Genormx and some others he wouldn't name. I can't find anything about Genormx except that they've raised $24 million."

"I don't know about any others. That's weird." It was weird confirmation of my hunch that Max was hiding something.

Vladik twisted his hands, showing me his empty palms, shrugged his shoulders, and opened his eyes wide. He must have done it a hundred times, yet I'd never recognized it before. And it was spookily like Salim's pantomime, too. He was saying, "Who me?" or "How could I know?" He had nothing more to report on that.

"Genormx, I've never been down there. I know the postdocs that did all the work. One of them has been a mentor to me, Rinchen. I guess you'll meet him tomorrow. It's supposed to be the up and coming thing in sequencing, you know, single-molecule, bias free, small samples, cheap reagents, super fast, and on and on. You know the list, right?" Vladik nodded, so I continued. "And going really well. Max is rarely at the I. I thought he's down there, but maybe if there are other companies, I've got that wrong. Anyway, I think it's a fucked idea, but what do I know? Let me know what you find out."

"Genormx? A fucked idea?"

"If the reagents are cheap, then the instrument has to be really expensive if you're going to make money selling it. If it's really expensive, then there are only a few labs in the whole world that have the capital budgets to buy it. How is that a business? It only works if it's part of some bigger integrated company making money on applications of sequencing."

Vladik looked at me seriously, studying me, as if to ask, "Where did you come from?" Then, in another of the Russian inversions he was struggling to insert into conversation, he said, "In America, the idea may be fucked, but in Soviet Russia, idea fucks you."

"Well, I think this is one of those ideas that's going to leave everyone feeling fucked. You're the first person to ask me about it. People around here, they don't ask enough questions. They think they have all the answers."

It was late.

"Is Arianna back yet?"

"No D5 is getting her money's worth tonight."

"Well, it's time for me to go." I didn't yawn, but I pointed to Georgina who had just poked her head into the dining room entrance.

"Let's compare notes in a couple of days." He complemented Max so well, I thought as I fist-bumped him. We'd sworn off hugging after that night on the bluffs.

Georgina sidled over and offered me a drink, but I declined, suggesting instead that she show me the grounds. Walking me to an occluded corner of the hotel's property, she suddenly pushed me hard up against an ill-lit wall, planted her lips on mine, and then ignited me with a kiss as if we were reuniting. She wove her fingers into the dense net of my pubic hair, unfolding my petals as if she was the morning sun.

CHAPTER 110 THE MERITOCRACY

IN 1923, the publisher of the Los Angeles Times put up the HOLLYWOODLAND marquee—the one that now reads HOLLYWOOD—on Mount Lee in the Santa Monica Mountains, creating a symbol of dreams and glamour. In the same year South San Francisco erected its own sign on that hill called Sign Hill, proclaiming South San Francisco as the industrial city. Eighty years later, Venus Khlobama and several other members of the Nine Figure PAC—a political action committee devoted to protecting the interests of individuals whose net worth exceeded $100 million—organized to purchase one-hundred-eighty-three acres of property on the slopes of the Santa Cruz Mountains due west of Silicon Valley Airport in San Jose. Three years later, the PAC erected on the hillside a sign that would become as iconic as those two others.

Millions of residents see it as they go about their daily business from as far south at Tully Road to as far north as Mountain View. Eleven million visitors to Norman Mineta Airport in San Jose get a spectacular view of it from the air, as did Vladik and Arianna coming in from Providence. The sign imprints us with its message both overt and subliminal. It blinks one word, MERITOCRACY, day in and day out, as if repeating it enough would make it true. And if the repetition did not actually make it true, then its omnipresence and scale would make people believe it without questioning it, and that would be enough for the members of the Nine Figure PAC.

DURING that summer of 1986 when Vladik worked at Intel, his most frequent lunch companion was not Bob Noyce, but Gordon Moore, the Gordon Moore, cofounder and then CEO of Intel. From the moment Gordon left his cubicle to head for the cafeteria, a few of the company's engineers would begin to congregate around him. The numbers grew with each step. By the time the passages between cubicles were behind him and he entered the much wider hallway corridors, there were a dozen followers and by the time the smells of food were overwhelming, the assembled were like so many puppies crowding around their mamma to get close to the source of their strength. The throng broke down as it was pushed single-file through checkout, and then reassembled at long tables where Gordon sat—black-suited in a white shirt, standing out against the field of their less formal attire—and they showered him with questions, detailed questions about material science, applied physics, device physics, product specs, manufacturing methods and the state of the industry, and they listened attentively while he answered in mild tones. Vladik sat close enough to overhear the conversation, what little of it he could follow.

Often, a supplicant wouldn't even bother to sit down; he would stand by until a momentary break in the conversation permitted him to slide a question in edgewise, and Gordon would answer it, or offer his opinion, and then the petitioner would run out. One day, Vladik overheard a question about oxides of silicon presented in this manner, and not understanding the details, he asked the man sitting next to him to explain. "The proof that Gordon is made of something different than the rest of us is that he simultaneously ran the whole company and solved the dielectric cracking problem." And of course, that required another explanation. In short, Intel had once been brought nearly to its knees by cracks in oxide layers used as insulators between metallic conductors. When his R&D staff couldn't identify and solve the problem, he stepped in and did it himself, inspecting failed parts under a microscope, collecting data, speculating on mechanism, dreaming up a fix, and formulating the chemistry changes to put the fix in place, all the while maintaining his responsibilities as chief executive. His solution became industry standard practice. Like many of Gordon's inventions, his name wasn't attached.

On another day, there were several discussions going on in parallel about lithography, the processes of transferring lines and other circuit features onto a chip. The cornerstone of the scaling that makes Moore's Law possible, lithography is the most expensive process in semiconductor manufacturing, and it garners extraordinary attention from executive management because of its cost. One conversation, one that could have formed the basis of Michael Crichton's *Rising Sun* six years later, was about the company that built the Hubble Space Telescope, another company in Boston, and others in Japan. Gordon was talking about X-rays and a company called Hampshire Instruments[1]. In a third conversation, two guys sitting next to Vladik were discussing some new instrument from IBM called Gamma Blue.

"The light is two hundred fifty something nanometres," said the first of the two guys talking about IBM.

"What kind of lamp?" Vladik heard the other say.

"High pressure mercury."

"Can't be. Mercury doesn't have any emission there."

"Does."

"Doesn't"

"Does."

"Doesn't."

And then Gordon turned to the arguers and said, "2537."

Everyone stopped in mid-syllable. Heads turned. Without so much as a smile, Gordon said, "Mercury has an emission line at 2537 angstroms, $6^3P \rightarrow 6^1S$," and that ended that.

Curious about how Gordon Moore had come to be the biblical source when his full-time engineers didn't have the detail, Vladik introduced himself to the great man and inquired as the lunch crowd dissolved and everyone returned to their offices. The Chief Engineer said, "I was a spectroscopist before there was a semiconductor industry. We had to know that stuff."

1 Hampshire Instruments failed with a whimper after receiving close to $100 million in funding from DARPA, the State of New York, Venrock, Harvard, Kleiner Perkins, and others. Kleiner's Floyd Kvamme was on the Board of Directors. The CEO Moshe Lubin committed suicide after Hampshire closed its doors, and if you believe the nutcases who think that the NSA is secretly tracking your every movement, he was murdered by a cabal from "the octopus companies" who wanted to shut him up about how they stole his company's secrets.

GORDON Moore went to San Jose State University before graduating from Cal, the University of California at Berkeley. He earned his PhD at Caltech. He was no child of privilege. Moore was a beneficiary of the once-great, once-cheap system of public education in California.

"The underclass is lumpy with talent," my father used to say.

Gordon was one of the Traitorous Eight that left Shockley Semiconductor to form Fairchild Semiconductor, and by 1959 he was its director of R&D. In a meeting with his staff on November 22, 1963, the news came through that President Kennedy had been shot. Floyd Kvamme was in the room.

GENEALOGICAL trees, or pedigrees, describe the relationships of marriage and birth across generations. In academia, the trained students of a lab director are often referred to as sons or daughters, and so on down. Thus I was Max's daughter. By analogy, Floyd was Gordon's son, and Eugene Kleiner, another member of the traitorous eight, was Gordon's brother. As in real families, much more than genes are shared between siblings or passed between generations—experience and access being prime examples.

Kleiner escaped Nazification in Austria and came to the US as a teenager. Not on the basis of privilege did he earn employment at Shockley or cofound Fairchild. Fortune, wisdom, and experience in hand, in 1972 he then cofounded one of the most important venture capital firms, the one that has become Kleiner Perkins Caufield and Byers. He amassed great wealth and his enterprises created wealth and opportunity for many others.

Floyd Kvamme worked at Apple Computer in the early 1980s before arriving at Kleiner Perkins in the mid-1980s. Figuratively speaking, Gordon's son went to work for his brother. A graduate of California's public schools—including Cal Berkeley, where tuition was about $100 annually at the time—Floyd was a first generation American and had many talents, rising later to the position of co-chair of the President's Council of Advisors on Science and Technology during George W. Bush's administration. Floyd's son Mark was another Cal graduate, and one with an interesting history as an appointee of Governor John Kasich (R. Ohio). Mark was hired at Apple while Floyd was still there. Mark left Apple, bought a share of a friend's consulting firm, and then merged it with a company founded by Joe Firmage. Joe is famous for his firsthand accounts of visits with extraterrestrials. A year later, Mark became a partner at another of the great VC firms, Sequoia Capital. Sequoia's founder had previously cofounded National Semiconductor, where

Floyd had established himself as the general manager of Semiconductor Operations. Genealogically, this is the grandfather hiring the son. Much, much later, Sequoia made a first round investment in LinkedIn, itself founded by Reid Hoffman, former COO of the fabulously successful Sequoia-funded PayPal and a member of the so-called PayPal Mafia, the group of former PayPal employees who have gone on to found or invest in several significant startups such as YouTube and Tesla.

I had just arrived in the Bay Area when I attended an evening meeting featuring several investors and entrepreneurs on a panel discussing something or other, probably molecular computing or mobile advertising. One of the panelists was a colleague of Mark's at Sequoia, and he described how Mark's son Michael had gotten an idea for the humor equivalent of an early and influential social media site called Hot or Not. Funny or Die's website declares that Michael instructed Mark to write a check and the company was formed. Details are obscured, but it's documented that Sequoia invested and so did Reid Hoffman. Mark is Chairman of the Board of Funny or Die, sits on LinkedIn's Board, and Michael has been an intern there.

You cannot make this stuff up.

ONE OF the investigators at the I is a cyclist, a specialist in the kilometre sprint on a banked wooden track. Upon returning from Europe where she had won her event in the world championship for women over 40-years-old, and after I congratulated her on her accomplishment, she said to me, "I know there's at least as much talent in the stands as there is on the field. I have the luxury of training."

A meritocracy does not dedicate itself to finding talent among the privileged, the fourth generation descendants of pioneering talent, but to finding the talent in the stands. Silicon Valley is no meritocracy, unless the figure of merit is money. The California education system, once proud, now relies on bake sales to fund such extravagances as a part-time school nurse, and tuition at Cal is over $13,000. California Dreamin' no longer means affordable world-class education. Instead, the California Dream is an anti-state utopian dream preserving the genetic rights of elites. But their utopia gives me dyspepsia.

The imprint of my father's liberal conscience tells me that when the winner-take-all windfalls and the excesses of executive pay—a kind of group grope that leaves all group members quite satisfied—combine with regressive taxation to concentrate wealth and power on a scale not seen in a century, and to buy experience and opportunity for scions instead of millions, the term to apply is not meritocracy, it's oligarchy and imminent aristocracy. As Al Gore says "The government has been hacked!" Tocqueville would see it right away. His countryman Thomas Piketty says that one man's successes in the past devour the future opportunities of the masses.

CHAPTER 111 BUCK'S

ARIANNA HAD stayed overnight on the premises of D5's new house, because D5 had told her, "One day is not enough, but one day is all we have. I want you to live in this house and feel its changing moods. When you understand it, then you will know how to fill it up for me."

Vladik woke up alone, swam a few laps in the Rosewood pool, performed his ablutions, and stepped into a taxi at eight o'clock. Rather than take the most direct eight-minute route to the venerable Buck's of Woodside, he had the Sikh driver take a four-minute detour that led him to D5's Martian Home Road.

Martian was the private road to what Orson Welles called his "getaway from Nepenthe." The old house had long ago burned down, and after these many decades, all that remained of it was the bow and bowsprit of a pulpit from which he intoned the story of Jonah on the set of the 1956 movie, *Moby-Dick*. The great actor had liked to take his starlet girlfriends there, re-enacting counter-fictional reunions with Ahab's wife.

But recently, not a decade ago, a new icon of American democracy had been erected. Within the past year it had become the property of D5, and Vladik was hoping to see this masterpiece (where his wife was probably still sleeping) if only from the road. If only.

A tasteful but imposing kiosk of redwood-framed and probably bulletproof glass guarded the bronze double gates that guarded the road. The gates were ornate sculptures of Illuminati circles and pyramidical mysterium and the third cycloptic eye. Vladik wasn't sure if Arianna's influence would extend to choices about external appearances or only the art collection. But these were intended to be art, he was sure. He pondered their meaning but came up empty. A young and well-manicured Chinese woman occupied the kiosk. Her plastic smile was the first deterrent. No doubt, he thought, armed men in camo played cards in an unseen bunker behind her quarters. He imagined her name was Mei Mei, and that the camo men would spring into action if she called on them. Vladik did not test the system. From the main road, he couldn't see even the domed roof of the house. After a moment's pause, he asked the driver to continue on.

Vladik texted Arianna, letting her know that he wouldn't be taking any calls while he was with Max.

BUCK's Restaurant in Woodside is the very model of California Ranch Style that the Rosewood elevates in the same way Ralph Lauren elevates Western Rustic. It was also ground zero of power breakfast dealmaking during the go-go years of the Internet when Hotmail, Confinity aka PayPal, and others were founded, or at least conceived there. In the world according to Jamis, when it did seem that all you needed for success was a table at Buck's, three TV crews a day showed up to document the flowering of the buds. There had been stacks of applications to fill jobs as table waiters, either from real beauties looking for a rich partner or aspiring entrepreneurs looking for a rich Partner. It became a museum of newspaper clippings, murals, and Jamis' Collection of Oddities; a whacko jungle of stuff, somewhere between Ripley's Believe It or Not and the Smithsonian, where an astronaut swings from the ceiling, rare photos of Steve Jobs hang on the walls, and Lady Liberty holds an ice cream sundae on high. Its proprietor, Jamis MacNiven, just a restaurateur, he says, who, he says, is often mistaken for an influential person, has been so frequently featured in the international press that he is recognized on the city streets of Helsinki, Shanghai, Bangalore, and Moscow, that is, in all those places where startup fever rages. Now that we've come full circle to the new normal, Buck's has returned to being what it was before, a place to eat and do deals in the shadows of the sequoias, albeit in the atmosphere of the history it helped to make.

Max was waiting at Table No. 40—where Tesla was founded—when Vladik arrived. With his kidneys failing, Max was on doctor's orders to eat less and eat better, and he didn't have the appetite he once had. Breakfast was no longer the 3-egg baguette with bacon and cheese voraciously devoured. And yet, for all the extra energy an amputee must expend just keeping up with the rest of us, Max was not exactly slimming down or wasting away. He wiped his face and hands of the blueberry muffin that was no longer there, and waved Vladik in to sit.

"Heh, quite an exit your friend Jay had," Max said, offering his hand, winking.

"Got to hand it to him."

"Ninety percent marketing and ten percent substance as usual?"

"I wasn't in the deal discussions, so I don't know what those guys think they're getting."

"What are you getting?"

"Can't say yet. Bigger than a car, smaller than a house is what I'm figuring." As Max absorbed that, Vladik changed the subject, gesturing at the collection, "Fun place."

"Epic. You could spend days going through it all."

"What's with that fish?" referring to a twenty-seven-foot-long redwood salmon parked in the front."

At that moment, Jamis walked up. "How's the wooden leg old man?" and slapped Max on the back. Max grimaced as if he would rather not be reminded of his peg. Before Max had the chance, Jamis introduced himself to Vladik as a former chauffeur now looking for real work.

"Woody is a hundred-ten-year-old labor of love. Why does anyone carve? The Tlingit had coho in their DNA. Must have been a dry year in the creek and Enoch Kadashan couldn't bear not to see 'em for a whole season so he made one that couldn't get away. Got bought up decades later by one of the local deadbeats avoiding the IRS, and when he needed to raise some cash, I was there. He didn't make it out alive, nor the sculptor either. The fish lives, vital as she ever was." And then he walked away, as if that explained anything at all.

Max projected an influence field that kept Vladik in a state of reserve. Max knew everything and knew everyone. He had started companies and had taken one of them public. He was making an epic wave. Surfing Max's wave had become Vladik's operational definition of drafting in the wake of MDx. There was no one else at the line-up, so that was cool, if actually a little strange, because if Max was so great, why was he choosing Vladik the Unknown? Still, Vladik had to be careful as he entered it, the wave, finding just the right moment so that he caught it rising up from the ocean's bottom, giving him energy, bales and bales of energy to ride and generate his own momentum. He had to be sure not to let the wave close out on him, snapping his neck as it broke, or holding him down in the swirling sand where he couldn't breathe. Vladik was still very far from confident that he could just drop-in, charge down the line, and expect anything better than a wipeout.

Breakfast was ordered, consumed, cleaned up, and paid for. Arianna had texted her love. "Free at 6, LA"

Vladik sent back, "Rosewood Lobby 7PM, LV,"

She responded, "Be careful."

That was all they would exchange until late in the day.

Vladik had told Max about his career at ITSy, consulting for Jay, living in Rhode Island, and wanting to get back into the game. Vladik was pleased that Max listened, and Max was impressed with Vladik's understatement of what he'd done. They played who do you know in the various professional societies they had in common, but the overlap was small.

"How are you getting around?"

"Taxi."

"Then we can go up together and I'll have Issahaq drive you back to Genormx later." Max nudged him with his elbow and nodded knowingly, and then continued, "How was the Rosewood? Meet any wild kitties?" and he winked again.

"Rumors abound, but no. I had dinner with Lakshmi."

"You knew her from Jay Orrix's thing? Super young woman. One of the best students I've ever had."

"Never seen a better business strategist that young. What's she like at the bench?"

"Best-in-class. The work she's been doing is going to be the basis of Moby Dx."

Vladik remembered his conversation with Jay.

"You mean molecular diagnostics?"

"No, I mean Moby Dx. Our company. The great fuckin' American diagnostics company."

This was Max's presumptive close. He'd done it with Arianna in lieu of a proposal. Here it was again, with Vladik, now that they were about to embark on something that was not quite a marriage, but a big commitment. Vladik was flattered that Max had selected him from all the other candidates. His head swelled but he couldn't see or feel it happening. *This hasn't been some fantasy*, Vladik thought.

He'd said the name himself, but had never thought of it as a company name. "Kind of irreverent for biotech, don't you think? I thought the customers want a more buttoned-down package."

Before Vladik could finish his thought, Max jumped in, "They're Fucking Idiots. We'll have the best science behind it and that's all anyone should care about. If someone wants to put $100 million into it and change the name, then I'm all for it."

"It is a terrific name. I like it. We can have it? I thought with moby and all, it wouldn't pass trademark registration."

"I got the domain name, and that's all that really counts these days. It's a Max Frood original."

Something must have passed across Vladik's face, some intimation that the name was not all that original.

Max backtracked. "Well, not completely original. It's also a Japanese pool-cleaning robot. I didn't find that out till later, but I can claim first use in English."

Vladik laughed with him. "I don't think that will upset the trademark folks here in the US. I was concerned about it being too generic for—"

Max interrupted to change the subject. He didn't give Vladik time to agree or disagree with the idea of them starting a company together, he said, "Look, we'll be late if we don't leave now. But we have to found the company here at Buck's. The symbolism is too rich, don't you think?" Max prodded him with his elbow again and nodded vigorously, caricaturing Monty Python, maybe, but if there was symbolism behind Max's tics, Vladik didn't get it. "I'll tell you about my plan for Moby Dx in the car."

Is that all there is? Vladik thought. He felt a let down by premature company formation. Had Max gotten ahead of himself, or was Vladik behind? He didn't know, but he thought that this was the moment to drop in, so he grabbed a plain white napkin, wrote Moby Dx on it, signed it, dated it, and slid it over to Max, who signed and dated it. Vladik added, Buck's of Woodside.

Max grabbed the receipt, looked at it admiringly and said to Vladik, "When I get the Delbrück Prize, I'm going to hold this up and tell everyone at the March Meeting," by which he meant the largest annual meeting of the American Physical Society, "about this momentous occasion on my path from physics to fortune." Then they shook hands and went to the car.

Vladik missed and worried about Arianna. She had anticipated that Max would seductively and presumptively sweep him into an endeavor. Max would have to be told about her, too, someday.

CHAPTER 112 THE STARSHIP I

VLADIK HAD been wowed. The foothills rolling down to the ocean were emeraldine up close, but faded into ever more airy pastels with each succeeding layer of hill and valley. There were green glens, the occasional fence for cattle or other livestock, a few brown dirt trails or fire roads, and the obligatory phone or power line. Six or seven miles into the distance, all was white, and with your retinas bleached, there was no detail in the reflections off the sea or the clouds in the marine layer. You couldn't be sure exactly what you were seeing, but the gestalt was awe-inspiring.

Vladik texted me. "What a place to work!"

The HMRI architects had created a building complex combining glass and steel modernism with the Scandinavian curves of Saarinen and Aalto, nods to local materials, and acute site sensitivity. The modules large and small seemed to have grown in place under the direction of a higher power. In this way it reminded Vladik of his own water-facing creation.

The Pore, as the main entrance was known, was capped in Yosemite granite and engraved with Haldane's words, "He has an inordinate fondness for beetles." Max and Vladik breezed through its great four-spoked revolving door, and went from there on a tour of Max's quarters, labs of other notables, and core research facilities shared by everyone. Max's staff was surprised to see Vladik receiving all of Max's attention, so much more than grant-givers usually got. "Must be a big fish," was the message circulating around. Not a specialist, not a researcher in the field, he had only passing knowledge at best of most of the topics under research. The range, in Max's lab alone, impressed him. Additive manufacturing of artificial organs, synthetic protein design, electron optics of the Beam Team, molecular immunology, molecular embryology, my cfDNA, but no Lakshmi except for my text reply to message, "Getting my oil changed. Later maybe." And, there were allusions to several external collaborations that he couldn't see. Max (or was it his lab?) was an idea factory. His management style appeared to be a mix of the authority of the sea captain who could send you to the brig or out on the yardarm in a gale or keel haul you, and of the professional guidance of a more experienced colleague who could share ideas and criticism yet never demand anything.

Vladik was taken—he later said, "Taken in." Max was selling and Vladik bought.

Vladik had fifteen minutes to meet with Director and Institute Chairman

Zipp, and then another quarter hour for TTO Director Nguyen-Berry. Qasima's office was a sweeping field of radial clerestory glass aimed west at the ocean, reminding Vladik of nothing less than the Starship Enterprise, which was how Qasima viewed it. She surprised Vladik with her opening. "Max is not only queerer than you suppose, but queerer than you can suppose."

Vladik told me, "Her Oxford English, and the way she let the phrase drop and resonate around the room, and the way she looked at me as if I was a naïf, left me wondering how many layers there were in her n-tuple entendre. Caught off guard, I let praise rain down on Max."

He was selling, because he wanted to let them know that he and Max together were going to create the kind of company that could bring TTO-licensed technology to market. Without his own track record as a biotech CEO, he needed them to visualize a glorious future rather than rely on a list of past accomplishments in the field. Qasima's enigmatic smile said that she had bought some, if not the whole story.

Ms. Nguyen-Berry's office was humble only by comparison. Ample, cozy, lit by the western sun, and hung with awards, photos of her with IP celebrities and university presidents, recognitions, and press clippings. There were too many to read, but one in particular was near the chair Vladik sat in, something about intense rains, mudslides, and flooding a year back. "Flood Threatens to Destroy Local Community," it read, but the "l" in Flood had been crossed out, and an "r" inserted in its place with a Sharpie. Ms. Nguyen-Berry's irony and intent went over his head. It being their first meeting, and he being a guest of Max Frood, she was happy Vladik didn't ask for an explanation.

On the drive up and over the ridge in Max's Outback, Max had told Vladik about the MOST. Immune to any of my reservations, Max had begun talking about it with some of his friends in Big Pharma and they'd gotten all hot about collaborating. "There are a lot of moving parts," Max said as they rolled into the breathtaking grounds of the Institute. "I'll lay more of it out for you at the end of the day."

But time at the end of the day got squeezed, so Issahaq, always there when needed, drove Vladik back to Genormx by way of a longer but faster and much less nausea-inducing route. Max had left at the handoff to Qasima. Later in the day, he texted Vladik, "Thin about it MF"

Kind of harsh language, Vladik thought at first. *Ah!* Max Frood.

CHAPTER 113 GRIGORY ALEKSANDROVICH

THERE IS so much lore and often so little fact. Lore has it that Prince Minister Governor-General Grigory Aleksandrovich Potemkin, favored lover of Tsarina Catherine the Great—of Russia, Dear Reader, of Russia—employed thousands of serfs, Jews, Cossacks, Australians, and others in his debt, to paint villagiferous facades along the banks of the Dnieper in early 1787, for the purpose of deceiving her royal highness into believing that his success at populating and enriching her southern Ukrainian and Crimean holdings was greater than the facts on the ground. What matters if this really happened? Today, the multi-talented Potemkin is two bloody centuries in his grave. The eponymous villages he may or may not have built have become a metaphor for deceit or charade, maybe large-scale and government-sponsored to boot.

CHAPTER 114 THE SITE VISIT

VLADIK HAD no business being at Genormx, and it irritated Carmie that Max would expose the company to the potential confidentiality leak—and she was unaware of what Max had been leaking at conferences—but she had been persuaded to let Vladik have a guided walk around as long as he didn't ask too many penetrating questions. He wanted to compare it to what he had remembered from Agrigene and Orrigen.

Vladik had not been given much information about what to expect at Genormx, and he found less activity than he had imagined. The sales and business development functions were in their infancy and taken care of by the Kahns. So much of the tough engineering had been outsourced; only the Beam Team and Informatics remained at the EPA office. Carmie ran a lean crew. The place was almost too quiet for Vladik's taste.

Carmie had designed a very simple two-hour agenda for him, delegating all but ten minutes of expectation-setting and ten minutes of wrap-up to various team members. She was obviously a great leader. Her team had been briefed on what they could and could not say. They were polite, forthcoming within their limits, direct in answering his questions, and wasted no words. Vladik didn't probe hard because he wasn't interested in what they were doing, especially after Lakshmi had opined that it was a zombie company that only looked like it was thriving. Their corporate objectives were emblazoned in posters along the walls, Management 101 style, along with posters they'd prepared for investors, and handwritten flip charts that were work-products of planning sessions. Large whiteboards carried rapidly developing news and messages they needed each other to bear in mind. Vladik was taking stock of the big picture, not absorbing the details, so he didn't even bother to get close enough to read the fine print, and his guides would have steered him away if he had.

What Vladik was most interested in was how the company used Max's time and talent, and about that he learned a lot. Max had been very hands-off. His work had been high level, almost architectural, and the details were all left to the Beam Team. At no time, they told him, did Max get involved in schedule or budget, and after the mid-course correction on the Alpha machine, details of which were kept from Vladik's view, he was rarely involved in strategy. Occasionally he was called upon to make an introduction to someone in academia for them, or to reach out to a powerful person in Washington, or Sacramento, or in Rhizobia, or France, or somewhere else where he'd become connected, and he always turned those around quickly and successfully. The engineering teams were satisfied with this arrangement; they were making terrific progress toward the Beta machine and were generally happy about their prospects. Carmie was reserved during the final summary discussion. She pumped Vladik for what he was up to, yet all he was able to tell her was that he was drafting in the wake of MDx, a phrase whose meaning she didn't ask him to explain. If the follow-on to the Beta served the MDx market, maybe he'd be a customer. Guessing that the Genormx CEO might be sensitive, he was careful not to say that he was going to be a drain on Max's time.

Vladik left feeling that Max would be the perfect partner for creating a new molecular diagnostics company, a Moby Dx. Max would help choose the powerful technologies, but then he'd hand it off and stay in the background. He was going to let Vladik run the company, just as he let Carmie.

She chose not to say what a pain in her ass it had been working with Max, or how much of her effort had been required to keep him in line. She didn't sense in Vladik the toughness required to keep Max under control, and wasn't prepared to offer unsolicited advice as a bleeding member of MFUG, the Max Frood User's Group.

Genormx, by the date of Vladik's visit, was Max's Potemkin startup. The Beam Team didn't know it. Carmie and Kozmo Kahn didn't know it.

The Board didn't know it and certainly Vladik didn't know it, but Max had checked out of Genormx and was using it only as a prop. When he didn't need it any more, or it became too much of a burden for him, he wouldn't even bother to blow it up. He'd just let it die a lingering death, like Potemkin did in his pneumonia.

Genormx presented well, especially with its eye-catching but serious CEO, ran well with strong, tightly managed engineering teams inside and out, and looked like it had a bright future in an area that was way hot. The structure of advisory committees was rational, and Max's role was commensurate with his abilities. That was real. The façade was that little of this was Max's doing. He wanted a very different kind of involvement with the company. He wasn't any longer putting effort into it. If you were trying to figure out what it was like to be working with Max on an early stage venture, you couldn't use Genormx as a guide.

When my mother died, as she would the following year, I learned so much about her that I'd never known I'd never known. Who can understand everything about another person? We're too complex for that, and too self-absorbed to try. Some people are easier to decode than others. Max was undecipherable, hard cryptic. Vladik thought he was transparent, but he was only looking at a façade.

While the taxi, driven by another Sikh, carried Vladik back to the Rosewood through rush-hour EPA and Palo Alto and Menlo Park, his heart fluttered like a lover anticipating his first taste of something new, just like Max's had fluttered in the moments before he walked in on Jay and Joosey. Thoughts bounced in his head like steel balls struck by a pinball wizard.

"I'll be working with Max Fuckin' Frood! The namebrand, the IP, the technical leadership, the contacts! So many problems gone, short-circuited. Co-founding with Max Fuckin' Frood! It's too good to be true, but it's true." He felt like a king, and wanted to celebrate like a king, lording over Arianna's olive-skinned body in an oily celebration. And he knew he would, soon.

The thoughts kept coming. "Danger, Danger! 'Too good to be true' means it's probably not. No, this has checked out. Quash that thought. Well, there's Arianna. She's not going to like this. And there's location, and that won't be easy. I can't do this from Block Island, or Providence, but maybe Cambridge. Silicon Valley would be better, though, much better. Will Arianna move to Cambridge with me? Worst case, I'll fly home every three or four days."

Rush hour in horrible crosstown traffic. Stop-and-go up Sand Hill all the way from the Stanford Shopping Center, and that was after stop-and-go all the way up University Avenue. By the time his taxi was about to turn left into the Rosewood it was already 7 o'clock. Being Thursday, Cougar Night, even the parking lot was jammed, with cars stacked up all the way to the road. Vladik paid the driver at the light, letting him avoid that mess, and then he walked between cars across the parking lot that Sand Hill Road had become, took a shortcut over the maze of islands and dividers, and walked into the lobby.

CHAPTER 115 MY MONTICELLO

On Wednesday morning, the Ethiopian driver had picked up Arianna and Vladik on the runway at the private aviation terminal in San Jose when D5's Gulfstream arrived with them on board. Spring had not yet come to Rhode Island, so they were delighted to feel its warmth and the fragrance of what used to be called the Valley of Heart's Delights, even if all that remained of the legendary orchards were rows of trees on divided highways. Sheba, the driver, got on I-880, merged with I-280, and then drove them through the rolling edge of the foothills for eighteen miles to the Sand Hill Road exit, dropping them off at the Rosewood. As they pulled in, D5 texted Arianna. "Pickup in two hours."

Driving the roads between the Rosewood and Buck's you'll pass by some of the most extravagantly conceived and priced properties in this great nation. One of them is a village unto itself, a Japanese village; a fifteenth century Japanese village built to twenty-first century California earthquake standards. A $200 million project, it is not the most expensive of its entrepreneur-owner's undertakings. Most of the houses are borderline-impossible to see from anywhere but the grounds and their own private roads. It was one of these that Arianna had advised D5 to purchase, and to which Sheba drove her.

Mei Mei stepped outside the kiosk and handed Sheba an entry log noting Arianna's name alongside the time, date, and the VIN. Sheba rolled down all the dark glass windows, permitting confirmation that the car was carrying only the two of them. With formalities complete, Mei Mei shook her black hair out of her face, cracked a white smile, pecked Sheba on the cheek when she got the log back, and returned to the kiosk to fire up the atomic pile that powered the gates. Kidding, Glowing Reader, just kidding about that pile. Haven't you always wondered about "atomic pile" and what the hell it means? It was Fermi's joke. The enclosure of his, the world's first, controlled fission reaction vessel was a pile of bricks. *Ergo* ...

Arianna had been beyond the gates once before, to meet the owner and walk the property with him and D5. She'd seen the gates herself, so no surprise there. She'd had the kiosk designed, so no surprise there. What did surprise her were the three armed women in a bunker behind the kiosk, uniformed in the brown on brown on brown camo of the PLA. She first noticed them when Sheba put the car in gear and pulled up the hill to the hidden manse. But Arianna's concerns were elsewhere.

D5 had a few requirements, or so she had said when she first asked Arianna to help her find the ideal property. They were few in number, but they were significant. First of all, the property had to be located within an hour's drive of Japantown in San Francisco. She would not say why. Secondly, D5's privacy and security concerns imposed severe restrictions on access to the property, and at the same time, D5 demanded that the house be the size of a small embassy. Again, she would not say why. Finally, the house on this property, "one that's there or one I'll have built," must look down on water and give her, D5, the ultimate American experience. Although she was Chinese and had made her money through real estate and construction in the PRC and casinos in Macau, all facilitated through contacts in the Party and its not-entirely-democratic institutions or processes, she vehemently expostulated the belief that American democracy should be revered, and that if she was going to move to America, to be closer to her daughter and granddaughter, she wanted to live in the most American of all houses, Thomas Jefferson's Monticello. Fortunately for all concerned with this transaction, price was no object.

Within the delimitations of D5's chosen territory, the available properties broke down neatly into two categories: ones that might be occupied immediately because they had houses on them, and those without houses on them and that might be ready for occupancy in five years or more. "What?" she asked Arianna. D5 knew that had she been doing this in China, she could have had her estate prepared, which might include building a mountain and a lake if not relocating a river, in less than four months, and the house built and ready to go in another eight. Her crews would be working one hundred sixty-eight hours a week. Arianna, who was not at all expert at these matters, even if she did have impeccable taste in art and architecture, explained as well as she could that the construction workweek was constrained by everything from union work rules to local ordinances governing noise, traffic, and such. In Woodside, for example, she showed D5 Ordinance 151.55, curbing construction to an absolute maximum of fifty-five hours, and that included Saturday.

D5 was not interested in any five-year incubation, so her choices were among ones that had ready-to-go houses on them, and of these, there was but a solitary example embodying American virtues of simplicity, proportion, and quality in sufficient measure to satisfy her. Its rotunda, inspired by an unbroken line of design from the Panthéon in Rome, through Palladio's work in Veneto, and on to Jefferson's at Monticello, was created with a mastery, Arianna said, that had not been achieved in over two hundred years. Its dual wings flying off front- and rear-facing portico'd entrees, and its pools and pond set below it, were more than homage to the third president's slave-powered estate in Virginia. It was reverence. That one house, though, was not for sale. But D5 had said, perhaps a little curtly, and certainly without ambiguity, "I want my Monticerro!"

Her security apparatus informed D5 of the owner's habits and preferences. Then she had her helicopter hover over the house on a day when the owner was known to be at home and entertaining someone other than his wife. Arianna, D5, and a large Chinese man carrying a satchel full of legal documents, a degree from Harvard, and what appeared to be a man-sized shipping case that would survive being dropped from a great height onto a surface which was not soft, were all three then lowered onto the property near its southeast facing portico, and from where it was a simple matter of banging the knocker on the door. There was some confusion while gardeners alerted the maids, the maids alerted the Master's Man, and the Man alerted the Master, after which they, including the Mistress who was not the Wife, were all served tea in the Rotunda, light cascading in through its high curved windows, and at floor level below each window, a Buddha or Buddha-inspired sculpture on a pedestal.

D5 explained that she had an insatiable urge to own this property. Not wanting to be unreasonable, she offered two times what she thought the market price would be. That did seem to get the attention of the Master, who being in this compromising position was expecting quite the lowball offer. He countered with a number twice as large, she offered the average, and he held out his hand to seal the deal at something north of $117 million, making it the most expensive private home sale recorded in American history. Arianna's law school classmate, the large Chinese man, opened the case and from it withdrew a museum quality Bodhisattva—seated, of porcelain with bluish white glaze, with provenance dating back to its arrival in Macau in 1558, and with an estimated date of manufacture in the early fourteenth century. D5 offered it as a gift. The Mistress begged to be excused. The Master took his guests on a minutely detailed tour of the house and the grounds. There was lively talk of landscaping, facilities infrastructure, the broken-down US Congress, and how Jefferson might react if he saw what had become of his country. There were some papers to sign, too, but that was a formality. One hundred and twenty days later, the gentleman, his family, and his staff had vacated and emptied the premises, and D5 delightedly took possession. She felt she had gotten quite the deal, as the sculpture was only a contemporary copy, recently manufactured and distressed in Singapore.

For those one hundred twenty days since first choppering in, Arianna had been disengaging as much as possible from all but her most important client visits, had stopped taking on new ones, and was focusing more and more attention on (1) identifying the art that should be installed at Martian Home Road, the art that would make My Monticello as American as Jefferson's Monticello, and (2), finding a way to purchase it. D5's rough instructions were to buy it, commission it, steal it, or have it remanufactured until the original could be acquired. Arianna, being who she was, could not condone theft, so she limited herself to finding sellers and constructing legal frameworks for tax-advantaged transfers, and to commissioning original artworks. For difficult cases, D5 had someone who knew someone who knew someone, maybe a painter or a sculptor in Xiamen, maybe an artist of a different kind elsewhere, either of whom could do what was necessary to fill the spot on the wall, the alcove, or the designated landscape placement. Arianna didn't want to know more than that.

On the days of her West Coast trip with Vladik, she walked the house and the grounds, absorbing sunlight's changing effects on this room or that. She carried with her a mental catalogue of all the painting and sculpture she'd ever seen, and for where memory failed, there was her Slab97 linking to public and private online databases, and for where both fell short, she was accompanied by a large Chinese man rolling a case of books and catalogues of important and obscure collections and exhibitions she thought might be helpful. He also had with him a set of property maps and blueprints, and a portable writing table and folding chair. Sitting on this chair and at this table, and referring to her neural, electronic, and paper records that comprised an almost satisfactory inventory of all the art that ever was, she made notes on the maps and blueprints of what should go where.

By the middle of the afternoon on the second day, when she had texted

Vladik, "Free at 6, LA," she felt like she hadn't begun. There was too much to decide about too many spaces with too many moods in flux, all inter-dependent upon each other as My Monticello filled up. And there'd be the installations she'd have to supervise and the commissioned murals she'd want to watch as they were painted and the frescoes as they were hand-spread and the mosaics as they were laid in place. She had not wanted to think about it before, the gnawing sense that she'd have to unplug from Block Island. That afternoon she couldn't avoid it and she acknowledged to herself that she'd have to live in Silicon Valley if she were ever to complete this project, maybe even live at My Monticello.

CHAPTER 116 THE NIGHT OF THE COUGAR

On my twentieth birthday, a one-hundred-eight-pound mountain lion terrorizing the local elementary school was treed and shot dead in Palo Alto. The big cat's population in California has grown ten-fold while its habitat has shrunk. Darwin reminds us that our livelihood is most threatened by our own species more than any other, so why should we be surprised that the cougars are moving out and looking for squirrels, dogs, or younger humans? I wasn't in Palo Alto on the day that police helicopters searched the neighborhood and felled the tawny lady, but stories of lithesome predators moving out of the Santa Cruz Mountains and into the residential areas to the east are more widely told than ever, and nowhere with more excitement than at the Rosewood.

Arianna was waiting outside on the piazza when Vladik arrived. The bar crowd—the Cougar Night crowd—flowed over every surface inside and out.

"Let's just see, shall we?" they said to each other, holding hands as they walked inside, pushing through dense mingling masses of the young, the not so young, and the desperate. Bits of disjoint conversation penetrated the blooming, buzzing confusion.

There were beefy men of all colors and blond females and perfectly coifed Southeast Asians with equally perfectly toned bodies. Holding their drinks and mixing as fast they could, the women were on average one just-noticeable difference older than the men. The men dressed to exude the cool of wealth, not cool itself. The ladies were done up to reveal flesh and style.

"... are ostrich [something something] money for a fashion company."

"I'm Safonda Tang!" one Chinese girl shouted.

"... holding his dick in his pocket?"

A woman in her forties flew, after being flung, over a table of drinks. She needn't have had a fear of flying, as more than enough hands reached up to catch her and land her in a willing lap.

"... great happy hour and people-watching."

"... Ina..."

" ... Rina ..."

"... recovering from a divorce, can you believe ..."

" ... Irina ..."

" ... Arjun ..."

"... Master's Degree in Higher Education, from Ukraine."

A girl discouraged a groper's grope while keeping up her end of the dialog and making no attempt to escape.

"... Anand ..."

The bartenders were so busy no one could get a drink, or at least our two visitors couldn't. Vladik nodded to Georgina who was on the job again, carrying a tray of Cosmos and Manhattans. Manhattans! Vladik told me he hadn't seen one of those in decades.

"... Kristin ..."

"... pretty dead tonight, don't you think?"

"Heh, little lady, can I buy you a drink?" someone said to Arianna, who only smiled politely and moved on, pulling Vladik up close.

On the terrace, a dozen propane-heated sculptures flamed near tables and sofas arranged for lounging. Dates were made, olives pitted, hookups planned, appetizers served, and Slab42 phones checked to see if any better prospects were available. A group of thirty, keeping to themselves, celebrated together, and the dregs of their cake waited to be removed.

Our two circled back inside, toward stairs leading to their room. Conversation was more serious, more extended, mostly with Indian and Chinese girls and younger professionals. At a large round table, there was a demonstration, a product demo of some kind, with glowing paddles of red lights strapped to one guest's hands and another to her shoulder. Model-beautiful Chinese girls stood in line, smiling rows of eight white teeth. Were they waiting or helping? One petite and one tall. One with perfect English and one with little to none. One with her Indian husband, and one with her Caucasian boyfriend. One in tiger and one in snake.

Arianna and Vladik were both exhausted. Too tired to compete for server attention in the crush of the cougars and their prey. Too tired to go out into the maw of traffic. They retired to their room and ordered in.

"I'm going to need to be here," she said to him, lying in bed, silk robe wrapped around her.

"Me, too." He explained that he and Max had made a pact to create Moby Dx. He pulled out the napkin, pressed like a leaf in his notebook to show her, trying to organize his thoughts into a straight line for her, all of them leading to the conclusion that he really should be here, at the epicenter.

She would have put up some resistance to the venture, but she knew he needed something big, and she had her own work that would be completely absorbing, so instead she said, "We'll be bicoastal together, I guess. And I'll be here when you figure out what Max is really up to."

"Thanks," he said, not believing there was subterfuge, and not wanting to argue the point. "Shall we look at some places while we're here?"

"D5 might prefer to have me living at My Monticello. I might prefer to live at My Monticello."

"Both of us?"

"There's tons of unused space for us now."

"The company will have its own offices and lab."

"So let's not look at some places while we're here?"

"Right."

"I'll text D5 and have her ready the jet for tomorrow morning."

"I'm going to miss home."

"But it will be nice to be on the mainland for a while, don't you think?"

"Four years. Both of our projects are four-year projects. Four years is an infinity. Who knows where we'll want to live when we're done? We'll have the bluffs if we want them."

Arianna texted D5 about the plane.

She responded with an implied demand, "Where are u going to live?"

"Here! With my husband ;)."

"Ok. And dogs?"

"No dogs."

"Kk! Sheba get u at 7"

"Kk A"

She threw her arm around Vladik and pulled herself close to him. "We're in."

"That was easy," he said as he finished up his own conversation with Max.

"Max. I'm in. Back in a couple of weeks."

"Beautiful! MF" which seemed to be his way of saying the conversation was over.

"Talk to you later, VK"

He returned his attention to Arianna.

"She loves me," she said, then paused, and then finished, "like a daughter."

The next afternoon they were back on Block Island, planning a long but temporary relocation.

CHAPTER 117 LETTING GO

ARIANNA AND Vladik were having long dinners with friends, saying their goodbyes until who knew when. She was spending time with her colleagues in Cambridge and thinking about how few things she really needed, for now, in California. It was a short list consisting almost exclusively of clothes, plus laptop, Slab42, and Slab97. My Monticello would be her own private hotel, chef included, with maid service of course. She could expense another set of makeup and hair products, and anything else; absolutely anything else she wanted. "I'd look pretty good in a Cayman, but the 911 is so much more practical," she thought. She was ready to go, and the jet would bring them back when she needed a dose.

Vladik, being a guy, his list was longer. He couldn't live without cameras and scanners and dive gear and a hideous assortment of other stuff. "Try without it," she told him.

"Simplify and simplify again," he told himself. "Many round trips yet to come," and he concluded, "Spartan, but not monastic."

A friend was going to live out on the bluff house, taking care of the dogs, maintaining what needed maintaining, and being a presence to ward off the unwanted. There was nothing that kept them from leaving now.

She was running the dogs, absorbing as much BIRI as she could. The daffodils were out and a few lilacs, too. It was going to be a late spring. She'd hoped to see the shad blossoms and the quince, but it wasn't to be. She knew departure needed nothing more than a spark, and then they'd be gone.

While she was out, Max texted Vladik, asking when they could talk.

"Skype?" Vladik replied.

"Better ftf"

"I'll get back to you later."

He didn't want to tell Max he had to confer with his ex-wife. They had not yet had a single conversation about their personal lives, and Vladik was hoping to keep it that way.

When Arianna returned, he showed her the texts.

"Do you think we're going to need two cars?" she asked.

"I thought you'd have a driver."

"I want a little more independence than that."

"Three then, it's California."

"*Ha!* When do you want to be there?"

"Three days, max."

Arianna texted a request for the plane to retrieve them in Providence.

Vladik texted Max, "Will arrive tomo+1. See you tomo+2. Where?"

"Rossottis 4pm"

"The law firm?"

"That's Rosatis. Food and beer joint. Zotts in pv"

"I'll find it"

"Alpine rd"

"Really looking forward to this"

"Yes going to be great"

And then he said to Arianna, "He's kind of terse."

"He can go either way. *Demi homme, demi cochon*," she said. He wished she wouldn't say that.

The next day, just before their final dinner on island, as the sun was setting, Arianna shaved Vladik down to beardless beauty and cut off most of his long hair. She coiffed him into her best imitation of a Silicon Valley executive: neither hipster, nor hippy, but younger and hipper than he'd been for years.

CHAPTER 118 THE PETIT PARTHÉNON

My Monticello, both the house and property, were a masterwork, as Vladik knew they would be, but to see them for the first time awed him. D5 was away. Arianna gave him a little tour. The pool house, which would be their home, was no rectangular prism of unfinished concrete blocks and pumps and a filtration system. The architect, modeling the house at the owner's request on the archetype of the architecture of democracy, Jefferson's Monticello, argued that it should be accompanied by the transcendent symbol of democracy, Athena's Temple, the Parthenon. And thus arose the Petit Parthénon, its façade a scale-accurate replica of the original on the Acropolis, and its interiors, although not so spacious, almost as extravagant as the assonantly named Petit Trianon, the playhouse of Marie Antoinette. A magnificent sculpture of the Goddess of War (and Law and Justice and much else) had once stood in the ancient monument. In one big, hairy, audacious touch, the artist rendered the 2500-year-old work of art, but in relief on the bottom of the pool. Arianna later told me that a full-scale standing replica would have violated the city of Woodside's building codes.

Vladik disabled the video cameras in their magnificent pool house rooms, an act which in turn provoked a visit from Jie Jie, the head of the Security Team. Then there followed a flurry of texts between D5 and Arianna. Jie Jie departed and the cameras remained disabled. The Security Team knew that soon enough they would be collecting keystrokes on Vladik's and Arianna's phones, and transmitting them to APT operations on the sixteenth floor of 525 University Avenue.

The two lovers swam along the pool bottom, inspecting the high relief of fine mosaic that mixed images of the ancient Parthenon's original sculpture of Athena with the fantasies of My Monticello's original owner. The temple goddess in her golden-armored gown stretched out to the full forty feet of Phidias' fifth-century masterpiece. In her left hand she held Medusa's head by the limp snakes of the monster's hair, its lifeless head rolling, or seeming to roll on the pool bottom in which it was embedded. In her right hand, she held a single snake, a giant constrictor. Athena's relieved head rested on the floor, canted to her right. Goddess of Wisdom, she wore a self-satisfied smile of self-knowledge on her ivory face. Her hips were positioned on the ledge where the floor dropped away to greater depth. Her legs dangled: knees open; gown unbuttoned and nary a fig leaf in sight; her divine temple exposed and realized in exhaustive minutia by the artist. Her hand was loose around the snake's body as it slithered down and over one leg, changing course and heading up the column of her thighs to the vertex of her legs. He—one presumes the snake was a he—spread apart the inner labia of Athena's pussy and wrapped a forked tongue around her clitoris. Even if she remained a virgin, at least she could be released. Every wise woman knows that. Vladik and Arianna ran their hands over the face of Athena's vagina, patted the boa's head, and then surfaced.

"Fuck Athena," Vladik said. "You're my goddess." He slipped his hand beneath her suit and she pressed tight against him. The whine of D5's becamera'd drones ruined the mood. Arianna would try to do something about those, too, but another time.

"Let's get out of here," she said. They slithered over the pool's edge, dried off, and disappeared into their private quarters.

With unexpected verve, she threw Vladik onto the floor and stood above him, pausing, as if not sure what would come next. She bent down, touched a finger to his lips, silencing him just as he was about to speak, and then she stepped aside to pull her Slab42 from her purse. Moments later, out came the tinny sounds of some jazz pianist they favored.

"I can hook that up to—" Vladik began, but she gave the sign with fingers over her lips again. He wriggled out of his swim trunks. She didn't complain, but she remained in her suit as she stood over him again.

Arms akimbo, Arianna closed her eyes and let her hips find the rhythms of the throbbing melodies. Vladik propped himself up—arms straight behind him, his neck arched back—and observed his wife in new wonder. "Fuck Athena. This is my temple," she muttered, shaking off inhibitions one layer at time. She pulled his face into her and made him nibble at her temple through the spandex, and then she stepped back.

"I need a joint," she said, releasing him.

Vladik walked naked to his pile of bags. After a moment of rummaging, he pulled a ziplock of buds from his toilet kit. "One of the pleasures of flying private," he said, smiling as he waved the turquoise flowers at her. "Can we smoke in here?"

"Fuck Athena. This is my temple."

"It was D5 I had in—"

She put her finger to her lips again, and slipped out of her suit. Just at that moment, the pianist let out a groan of his own. The accelerating chords rippled through Arianna's frame and shook her like Scheherazade. Vladik, overloaded, couldn't watch, roll, listen, kiss, and touch all at once. "Here. You roll." He handed her the bag.

He looked around, found speakers and where they were connected, jacked in the Slab, and the two of them were enveloped in sound. Arianna, her body alive with the musician's improvising, vamping, repetitions, variations, and his grunting accompaniment, touched the joint to her tongue to seal it up.

"Start it from the beginning will you?" she asked.

Five minutes later they coughed as they finished the joint, and laughed as they felt its first effects; a subtle lifting of all seriousness, a subtle focusing of all attention on the moment, a subtle new appreciation of the music's melodies, and of each other's charms. Five minutes later, Vladik was on top of her on the bed, their mouths locked together. He touched the tip of his cock between her legs, felt her fur against him, and with a slurp she sucked him up and in, before whispering, "Now snake me."

From the low-scoring outer reaches of the dartboard that was Arianna's body, Vladik spiraled his way into her bullseye, leaving behind her mouth, taking her breasts one by one, two at a time, by hand and by mouth. Her torso. Her upper thighs. A navel. Kissing her softly all along the way, humming titillating vibrations, letting her know how much he loved her. A broad flat wet tongue gently finding its way over her outer lips, she and the pianist moaning together, and finally he found his way to her clit. "Bullseye. Oh, glorious tongue," she exhaled.

"Fuck Athena. This is my temple."

While Vladik was able to enshroud her clit like a little wurst in his bun of a tongue, and while he ring-popped it, and while he sucked it as if she was the last drink he would ever have, and while she came in multiple shuddering shakes, each time crying out, "Fuck Athena. This is my temple," Vladik's tongue wasn't serpentine enough to wrap twice around Arianna's clitoris like the artist's snake had Athena's.

She wriggled from beneath him and looked for the remains of their joint. Finding nothing but charred paper, she encouraged Vladik onto his back and against the headboard. She looked at his bursting penis. "Oh, you poor thing. Close your eyes." And before he could, she swallowed him whole and then gradually pulled away, her mouth suctioned tight around him for the seven-inch traverse that seemed like twelve.

"Now let's show Athena how it's done." She straddled him, knees on the bed, and plunged down. Rocking her pubic bone into his, she fell forward on her outstretched arms against the wall. Her breasts swung in Vladik's face, as Joosey's had in Jay's. Something incomprehensible swept across Vladik's mind while his wife thumped on him, mashed her breasts on him, and (between hungry kisses) cried, "Fuck Athena. This is my temple."

What was that incomprehensible thing? He was fucking his partner's wife, or ex-wife. He was a player in a reenactment of the scene that had blown his partner's mind. His wife was his goddess and her split mound his temple, and this house of theirs was her temple. Was she Athena, and if so, what did that mean and who cared? He pushed away an unwelcome image of Max and Arianna together, something she had never spoken of. He was too stoned to make sense of it, and the thoughts were there only because he was so stoned.

The music built to its final chords. Vladik and Arianna came, finally and together in a gusher of hot lava and one more simultaneous shout of "Fuck Athena. This is our temple."

CHAPTER 119 ZOTT'S

ALPINE ROAD runs from Stanford's golf course in Palo Alto, through Ladera and into Portola Valley. I-280 splits it, and on the far side, the west side, the foothills side, if there's not a traffic jam because a driver has run over a bicyclist, it is a fast moving two-lane, gradually curving blacktop with decent shoulders, lined by soccer fields, horse farms, foot paths, a tennis and swim club, a school, and a ranch-style shopping center, becoming more and more rural, leaving you in steeper, curvier, thickly wooded horse properties and estates hidden from view, before it dead ends at trails leading all the way to the crest. That's in PV, Portola Valley.

Among the last businesses you'll pass on your way up the hill is the Alpine Inn, formerly Rossotti's, aka Zott's; a legendary beer garden and déclassé eatery. Tucked in under old California Live Oaks, the dirt and gravel parking lot is filled with bicycles and bikers and non-descript cars and luxury SUVs and maybe a horse. When the barometer is particularly high, that is when the barometer known as Ferrari Silicon Valley in Redwood City is high, Zott's parking lot may be marked by low-slung red and yellow cars sporting Ferrari's prancing horse. Any old day it's a place to show off your gleaming tricked out Harley. It's a place to start drinking when it opens half an hour before noon, or to bring kids on Sunday or coworkers on a rough Friday. It's a place to listen to live music beside Los Trancos Creek out back. It's a place to end a long hot bike ride. It's a place to begin a tryst, the Internet, or a venture.

Even though it wasn't on the most direct route between the I and his condo in Menlo Park, or between the I anywhere Max frequented for that matter, Max had been a regular before calamity struck—halcyon days when he hadn't had to worry about his animal protein intake. Being cheap when he was paying, he liked the high fat-to-dollar ratio. Since then he went there rarely, as a special treat alone, or to introduce friends to the "local cultcha," he would say, clipping the r, imitating someone imitating someone from New York City or Chinatown. At four o'clock on a weekday afternoon it promised to be quiet. It would still be warm enough to sit outside, and he and Vladik could get a couple of picnic tables by themselves and talk expansively in private, in public.

Vladik in his rented Subaru found Zott's; the yellow shack that been dried and bleached pale in the sun. Max was already there. They shook hands warmly. To Vladik, Max looked haggard, his face gray and sagging. He appeared to have aged even in the weeks since Buck's. Vladik wondered if the aging had something to do with his leg, and if so, how could that be? "There must be something else going on," he told Arianna later.

Still, Max was smiling. He was happy about where their little adventure was going, and he held open the spring-loaded front door, inviting Vladik to enter a too dark barroom with picnic tables as elaborately carved as a Pacific Island harpooner.

After ordering a "boat" of fries, a pitcher of Fat Tire Ale, and some cheeseburgers, and after Max had paid, as a gesture of his generosity, they retired to the back, a setting that could have been in the rolling hills of Austin or rural California; either way, it felt very far away from their Silicon Valley.

Max began. "Nice beard."

"Yeah, I thought it was time. After that meeting in New York, I decided the money men would prefer no beard and less hair."

"They're a conservative bunch. You never know. Maybe they want Seiji Ozawa, maybe they want Peter Thiel."

"And who is Peter Thiel?

Max winked at Vladik. "Got me. Good one."

"Max?" Vladik appealed. "Good what? Who is Peter Thiel?"

"Really?" Max paused and threw Vladik another wink whose meaning escaped him. "He's a local Randian hero. Plays John Galt in his own real life drama about himself."

"So this libertarian thing really has the valley by its balls?"

"Not by its balls. That would be coercion. This is co-option. People embrace it with open legs, hoping they'll be able to freely fuck the next guy in the name of meritocracy."

"Christ. Outside of New Hampshire, I thought they were fringe. I didn't realize they'd had that kind of penetration."

"We're up to our eyeballs in their voodoo economics and social theories. Liberty and equality don't commute."

Careful Reader, that's not a typo. Max meant commute. To commute is to travel back and forth, so we say that addition is commutative because the simple algebraic expression 3+10 is the same as 10+3. But Max was alluding to the fact that the root of the Heisenberg Uncertainty Principle, the fact that it's impossible to know the absolute position and momentum of a particle simultaneously, lies in the non-commutative algebra of quantum mechanics. And worse than not being able to know them simultaneously, if you nail down one really precisely, you can't know the other one at all. Of course, Vladik knew the physics, but hadn't pondered its application to social theory.

"So, there's an uncertainty relation between liberty and equality?"

"Yes. The two exist in a delicate balance. Let liberty go to the limit, and you get zero equality. The libertarians, pursuing personal freedom with a vengeance, have willfully forgotten the other half of the promise. Jefferson's promise. Lincoln's promise. Equality. Let liberty go to the limit, and you get zero equality."

Vladik gushed, "I didn't realize you were so poetic."

"I had to read Tocqueville, in the French. Where these clowns are headed is a utopia for them in which equality is utterly forsaken, thrown to the winds like, ..." Max paused, couldn't find the simile, and came around with a general attack instead. "And like all utopias it violates some commutation relation of a social science whose Hamiltonian we don't know."

Again, an obscure term. I can't help it. That's their way. The Hamilitonian Max referred to is not some construct of that founding father, but is instead a bit of mathematical physics essential to quantum mechanics, and beyond the scope of this history to explain further.

"And it will fail," he continued, more excited than ever, "or destroy this country in the process of succeeding. But being provably idiotic and ill-fated doesn't make it dead. It's alive and well, like some zombie of an idea that keeps coming back, because it serves some special interests very well. They're techno-utopians without a heart. And the full-blown egalitarians? They're just Fucking Idiots."

When much later Vladik told me about the conversation, he said, "Dumbstruck! I was dumbstruck. Max said what I and so many others had been thinking, but had never put into words. And it was so far afield of what he was famous for, I knew I was in the presence of a genius. It made me love him. I could understand Arianna's passion for him, just to get close to that fevered intellect. If I couldn't have that kind of intimacy with him, at least I could surf his breaking wave. In my mind, he had become my long time friend, and I reflected on all the good times we would have in the future as if they had already happened. And looking back now, I think that moment was the peak."

Max went on. "Russia was the natural home for communism? Silicon Valley is the natural home for libertarianism."

"That worked out well. And Hollywood for the Scientologists?"

"They're kind of the same, aren't they? Mid-century kooks with followings in the millions. Then there's another guy who wants to split California into six smaller states—"

Vladik interrupted him, "So the State of Silicon Valley can lower its taxes because it won't have to bear the burden of Mexicans needing health care, or farm workers on disability, or the unemployed detritus of the aircraft industry?"

"Of course, and in the name of efficient government. Peter Thiel, you know, makes long pronouncements about the nature of *things*. Says that freedom and democracy are incompatible."

"And he's writing a book called *The End of Fukuyama*?"

Max twisted his face to signal that he didn't follow.

Vladik explained. "Francis Fukuyama wrote in *The End of History* that liberal democracy is the end state of the evolution of government. So if your Thiel character says, freedom and dem—

"Yeah, I got it." Max was quick enough to connect those dots. "The non-commutation of liberty and equality is the end of liberal democracy." With that, the steam went out of him. "Anyway, he's a handsome boy with a smooth face and short hair."

Vladik still didn't understand Max's point about the long-haired conductor Ozawa and Thiel.

"So, do the VCs have a preference about politics or about hair?"

"About flair, Vladik, *flair*. Ozawa is a dynamic performer and Thiel is kind of flat. Some like it hot, some not. But leave your politics at the door."

In the ensuing pause they devoured their cheeseburgers and gulped at their beers.

Vladik got up to pee, and when he came back, Max picked up the conversation right away.

"Anyway, are you settled?"

“Settled is hardly the word. I arrived yesterday. I’ve got a cottage behind a friend’s house. It’s all I need for now.”

“Great. Let me tell you what I have in mind.”

Max wolfed down the fries like a recovering alcoholic who's decided it's time for a drink.

"I've been giving some talks about the work we've done, and the attendance has been SRO." Vladik tried not to be like the eager postdoc, always ready to please. He cracked a small smile on the surface of a blunted affect.

Max continued. "From the questions, I could tell they'd been anticipating results like these, and they all wanted to work with me."

"Have you published something?"

"No. With the fetal stuff getting press, ideas like this have been in the air, and people have known this was going to be coming from somewhere. You know the likely suspects now, right?"

"Yeah, I do. And what about the patent filings? Are they in?"

"Lakshmi and I have been hard at work on that. We won't have any problems. The provisional applications have been filed so we have the earliest priority date and the international coverage."

"Do you know what the others have filed?"

"No. The provisionals aren't public, so we'll have to wait until they file applications, and then those only become public eighteen months after their own priority date. If they haven't filed, well, it's going to take some reconnaissance to figure out what they're doing. I'll get the inside stories there. But don't worry about that. The I's got decent lawyers, and I work with absolutely the best lawyers, so we'll get our claims in and it won't matter what the other fuckers have done."

Vladik understood from this that the patents weren't filed and Max didn't know what his competitors were doing, and that Max didn't want him, Vladik, the putative CEO, to worry about it, because he, Max, The Talent, had it under control, even if he very explicitly didn't. Agitation began to make itself felt, but he told himself to be listening, and not to fall into interrogation mode too soon.

"OK. I got it."

"I don't think we're going to need to raise money here. We can bootstrap our way into the future. Are you up for that?"

Vladik was surprised at this. He knew bootstrapping. He loved bootstrapping. "Yeah, they used to call it starting a business. Best way to go if you can."

"Yeah. Best way to go if you can. I think we can get contracts from Hitachi, Abbott, and iUDx. Maybe some other pharma guys too."

"Who is iUDx?"

"Unified Diagnostics. Misnamed. They're a VC-funded rollup of a bunch of smaller pharma and MDx companies with a kickass central research group. South San Francisco."

"And the i?"

"What's the i for in iPad? Marketing. Misnamed."

"Or someone's pun that got past the suits."

"Maybe."

"And pharma's interested because?"

"They want to use it for PD and PGx studies, guiding trials, selecting patients, CDx."

"I got pharmacodynamics because they want to track efficacy of the drugs by watching protein markers. I got pharmacogenomics because they want to see if the drug efficacy is correlated with genomic markers. And they can use it to select patients in trials, figuring out in advance who is likely to respond, so that the trial will show a terrific Kaplan-Meier or receiver operating characteristic. But CDx, I don't got."

"So much jargon. So little time. Can't help it. Companion diagnostics. It's a slice of individualized medicine. You test a patient to see how they'll respond to a drug, and then you prescribe the drug only for ones that test positive. For them, the efficacy should be very, very high, ditto the safety, and ditto the price pharma can charge. It's a big, big deal. The new, new thing. And you can charge pharma a fortune for these tests because they leverage so much drug revenue."

"So what exactly are we going to sell them?"

"Sublicenses and research collaborations."

"Sublicenses to?"

"The technology the company will license from the I, through TTO. These—"

Vladik cut him off. "Why don't they license it directly from the I and hire you as a consultant? That's got to look better to TTO, and be better for the someone like Abbott."

"Whose side are you on?" Max said, stinging Vladik. Then Max laughed to break the tension and continued. "For something early like this, they need me, and I won't help them on those terms. Anyway, they're not there yet. They want access to the technology. They think they can throw some money at the I and then we can collaborate. I'll let them know that I'm spinning this into the company early, and that all future development of it will take place there. I'll introduce you as the CEO and you can negotiate the deal."

"Sublicenses I can do on my own from Zott's or Buck's, but if we're talking research collaborations, we need some people and a lab."

"Sublicensing revenue and upfront payments on the contract research will pay for all that. We won't need to spend much on capital because we'll outsource the sequencing."

"And my salary will come out of these streams, too."

"And I usually get a consulting fee of $150 to $175,000 annually, too."

Vladik tried not to flinch when he heard that. He'd managed the early finances at Orrigen. Consultants were paid $1,000 or $2,000 a day, twelve days a year. You couldn't make use of a consultant more than that. That meant $24,000 or less. Vladik hadn't read the I's policies, but he knew the University of California's, MIT's, Stanford's, Caltech's, and some others, and they'd permit roughly 20 percent consulting, or a day a week. At the outside, at the absolutely never-to-be-achieved extreme, that would mean fifty-two times $2,000 or $104,000.

Max continued without acknowledging a flinch, if there'd been one. "The first year contracts should be $500,000 each, and you should be able to close three of them. Second year, we can crank those up and add a new one, so maybe $5 million. I think we can do this very, very lean, like a software company. We can pay some decent salaries."

"Somehow the sub-licensing and contracts are rolled into one, right?"

"Right. Heh, we killed these fries and the beer. I'm going to take a pee in the river and then get some more. For two?"

"You're kidding."

"There's nobody here but us girls." Max poked Vladik with his elbow and gave him a quick nod. They looked around. They were alone.

They both peed, gleefully like boys, on a tree trunk which smelled as pristine and urine-free as any in the woods, while Max said, "And we'll fund our own internal research and development with what's left over." Then Max made his almost-imperceptible limp back to the grill, returning with a tray carrying another boat of fries, a pitcher of ale, and a second cheeseburger for himself.

Vladik had done some woefully naïve arithmetic in his head. If they took in $1.5 million from the internal organ division of iUDx and others in the first year and paid out $400,000 for their salaries, benefits and taxes, and if their costs to support the individual contracts were about $200,000 each, then they'd have $500,000 left over for IR&D. With that they could hire two people. The crux would be getting that first contract. Without that, there'd be nothing in the bank and they wouldn't even be able to pay for wireless access at Peet's.

"How sure are you about iUDx?"

"Those guys are salivating. And they'll be glad not to be dealing with TTO. I think we're just a call away."

"Really?" Not having to raise venture money would be too good to be true. Bootstrapping was a tack that was too scary for many people, mostly because they didn't have the cushion of cash needed to support them while they were getting going. Vladik had his cushion and Max had a job and an exit, so they didn't need an income, although if Vladik was going to be working full-time he wanted one. He thought, too naively, that the company would only burn cash after the contracts were signed and he hired people to do the contractually obligated stuff. He knew of the time-honored tradition of working for stock options in the early days of a startup, so he wondered if he could find some moby guys in between jobs, willing to sweat for equity until the contracts came along.

"Yes, really. And I'm close with the VP of Research there, so I can goose the process if it's going slow."

The other great thing about bootstrapping, Vladik knew, was that you owned it all. There would be no pesky investors to meddle, listen to, or share the proceeds with.

"Sounds great," Vladik said, and then he grabbed a napkin and wrote this short list on it:

(1) Incorporate Moby Dx LLC
(2) Negotiate licenses/contracts
(3) Hire IR&D staff

Max then wrote one more line below the others.

(4) $100 million exit in 36 months.

"That's a sweet exit," Vladik said, with enough hint of irony to suggest that he doubted it was possible.

"Companies without products are worth more," Max said.

"Only as long as someone believes you're going to have a product."

Changing the direction of the conversation, Max said, "If that cunt Ariana can make $300 million, then we can sell this for $100 million."

Vladik flinched. *What did Max know?* Meanwhile, Max crossed out $100 million and wrote $300 million.

"Max?" Vladik asked.

"If that Merkington can sell someone else's blog posts for $300 million, then that should be our number. Just make sure we don't have a product."

Vladik breathed relief when he was convinced that Max was not talking about the hypotenuse of their love triangle, but rather a pioneer in online news aggregation.

They stared at the savory creation for a moment. Max believed it. Vladik believed Max knew what he was talking about even if it sometimes made no sense; geniuses think different and all that. He also had the conviction that he could figure out the right thing to do with Max's brilliance.

To a scientist, the breathtaking leap from staffing-up to 9-figure exit evoked an old cartoon. To anyone under the age of twenty, it evoked the Internet PROFIT meme,

(1) Step one
(2) Step two
(3) ????
(4) Profit!!!

"And what about Lakshmi?" Vladik asked.

"She's working on some other thing. She's either got to be in or out. She shouldn't straddle the fence; it's bad for her research career and not good for the company. Besides, there are rules." Then, getting excited, he shouted as if declaiming a manifesto, "There are rules for everything!"

Aware that he'd gone overboard, Max quieted down and said nothing for an uncomfortably long time. Then he broke the silence, calmly, "For now, she wants to sit this one out."

"I thought this was her baby."

"Our baby, yes, but still, she's working on something else, bigger she thinks. Think about how to turn Moby Dx into an incubator and then maybe we can license in her next stuff when it's ready."

"And the tech transfer, who will be responsible for that?"

"Lakshmi will be able to do that under the terms of the license."

"And the pie?"

"Yes, the pie. Typically, the CEO would get about 8 percent, on a four year vesting schedule."

By no scenario that Vladik could conceive would his contribution deserve 8 percent. Five times that if bootstrapped, maybe three times that if venture-funded. He had missed the moment, and regretted it, to clear the air with Max about Arianna, and he knew he would have only one chance to make his case with Max on this.

"Max," Vladik said, standing up, "There are a lot of things not typical here. I think we have a fundamental misunderstanding and this doesn't make sense for me. I'm calling it a night and will fly home tomorrow. If you want to sleep on it and find some better terms for me, then call me in the morning, will you?" He pushed away from the table, offering his hand to shake with Max, giving every indication that the evening was over, and the deal along with it.

The bluff fooled Max, who did not want Vladik to be his fish that got away. "Vladik, Vladik. Slow down. Don't be so hot off the collar."

Vladik dropped his hand, as it was clear to him that Max was not going to shake it, and began to move across the garden and toward Zott's back door.

"Vladik, listen. Just tell me your concerns. What were you thinking?"

"Max, we're too far apart." At that moment, Vladik's resolve broke, and instead of playing his hand all the way through to the final card, he showed weakness. He said, "I'll sleep on it and maybe feel differently in the morning."

Max must have sensed the change because according to Vladik's telling later, Max put on the assured and reassuring voice of the fully robed and bedecked scholar, and he began to reel Vladik in. "I think we should try to get it done now. You're probably thinking that with my commitments to Genormx, I don't have that much time to deliver to this, but I don't think you're seeing that clearly. I'm going to be winding that down. This is going to be the focus of my consulting."

"That's surprising. They communicated something different to me."

"They want to preserve appearances, and they don't see the whole picture, either."

"OK, 8 percent for a CEO is typical after he's been brought in by investors and a founding team after a Series A or B financing. It's not typical if he is cofounder and there is no outside money in."

"Those research collaborations are really about me personally. Even with the licenses, they wouldn't happen without me. I've done this five times already, so my name goes a long way."

Vladik knew only of Tiny Machines and Genormx, making two, not five. He thought it was hyperbole and let it go.

"I'll be working hard closing those deals, so you should think of that as money I've brought in. It's just not my own cash."

It was an audacious proposition, but if it panned out, then there was something to what he said.

"And there's grant money. There's tons of NIH money available. We could be pulling in a million dollars a year."

Vladik, never having applied for an NIH grant, but aware that they were very time-consuming to write and that competition for them was fierce, said, "And who's going to write those?"

"You are, but I'll do the hard part, and I'm a great grant writer. You pull the pieces together and I'll write the Specific Aims."

"The what?

"Specific Aims. It's what they call the main body of the grant application."

"And your consulting contract? That fee's a very big drain on a fledgling company."

"Just make it a percentage of revenue. If the deals don't materialize, I don't get paid."

This appealed to Vladik, although it wasn't until later that he realized that Max's gargantuan claim on the pie wasn't going to be linked in the same way. In retrospect he ... oh in retrospect, oh woe in retrospect.

"How about this?" Vladik offered. "My salary will be 10 percent of revenue, no limits. Your fee will be the same, but it will only kick in after the first $500,000 and it will be capped at $150,000. There should be enough margin in these deals to support that."

"Look, because there's no dilution here, if we cash out with $100 million in three years, you'll be taking home $8 million, and a $500,000 annual salary. That's pretty sweet, don't you think?"

"Max, there will be dilution. We have to give equity to the team."

"How much do you think they'll need?"

"It depends on what we try to do, and how many people we have to add. But suppose we get Lakshmi, she's got to be 5 percent or more, and then we'd need a medical director, and it goes on. We have to cut out at least 20 percent for them. We may not use it all, but we have to set it aside."

"You're going to have to be tougher than that with Lakshmi. I penciled her in at 1 percent."

"I don't mind being tough, but I don't think 1 percent is right. And there will be consultants and board members. Really, it goes on." Vladik wanted to add: *Don't you know that?*

"HMRI doesn't permit its investigators to be on boards."

"So you mean you won't be on the board?"

"I mean we won't have a board."

"I'm fine with that. Governance will just be you and me."

"Right."

"And if we're deadlocked, we're deadlocked?"

"Right."

If Max and Vladik constituted the non-board, and their votes were equal, then Max couldn't overrule him with his super-majority ownership. That would go a long way toward blunting the equity inequity. Vladik said, "Look at this," and he drew another pie. "Let's set 25 percent aside for team and consultants. I'll take 25 percent and you will get 50 percent."

Max paused and gave Vladik a look. To hear Vladik tell it, you'd think he was being assayed for auction.

"You're right," he said to Vladik. "We're too far apart," and Max began to get up.

If he was expecting Vladik to beg, it didn't happen. Vladik knew that he'd given in too early once that night. He believed, based on an evening's worth of tics and vocal inflections, that Max wanted a deal as much as he did, if for reasons Vladik didn't yet get. There would be a deal before the night was out. While the terms would stink in so many ways, the outcome would still be great for Vladik. He would have to learn to hold his nose when thinking about the noxious parts. The longer he equivocated at this critical point in the negotiation; the better off he'd be later.

"Max, we tried. I'm sorry it didn't work out," and he held out his hand again.

Max took it and offered, "Twenty-three, twelve, and sixty-five."

"Deal!" Vladik said, with too much relief and enthusiasm. And then he remembered vesting schedules. "Three year vesting."

"I'll give you three year vesting, but mine will be a grant, no vesting."

Zott's was closed and the staff had gone home, leaving the two of them outside, undisturbed. It had been dark for a while. Vladik needed to pee. He was tired. He was very tired. He didn't want to enter a minefield over vesting schedules. Max was in this. It would be the focus of his consulting. Vladik had looked into his eyes and gotten a sense of his soul. Vladik didn't have to worry about a vesting schedule for Max. "Deal!"

They'd agreed on some of the main terms of a contract, and those terms strongly favored Max. But there was a deal, and that's what Vladik needed for the next stage of his career. In the days ahead, many other terms would be discussed before they signed a formal written contract.

CHAPTER 120

GENORMX INC. - SCENE IV OF V

THE ALPHA had met its targets for performance, but these were far short of what was needed for launch. Accuracy had to be improved from 96 percent to 99 percent, and overall speed had to be increased three hundred times. The consultants and the engineering team examined each sub-system, evaluated the individual improvement opportunities, and hoped to find an overall gain of thirty when all were combined together. Another factor of ten would come from a ten-fold increase in the number of pores on a chip.

The fact that no more than 10 percent of the pores could be filled with DNA fragments—and the team's decision to increase the number of pores on a chip so that 10 percent fill factor was sufficient to meet their performance targets—had created a boatload of new problems whose solutions came with their own unwelcome consequences. The SEM and the system electronics were forced to run ten times faster, pushing the technology into, or at least very near a realm where components were exotic and expensive. Then there was the unacceptably long time that it took to load the chip. Reading a chip whose DNA fragments were hundreds of bases long would take only a few seconds, but washing it and loading it with new fragments took twenty minutes. In factory-speak, the system had low utilization. They would need to learn to wash and reload faster; improving the system utilization little by little as they came to understand what it was they had built. There were opportunities to increase fragment length too, but these were limited by counterproductive reductions in the fill fraction. There were systems engineering choices, such as whether to separate the loading stage from the reading stage, but these too came with complexity that drove up the system price. In short, choices were few and prospects dim.

The CEO kept everyone optimistic. The team met intermediate milestone after intermediate milestone. Genormx Beta took shape. The company planned to make ten of them, delivering one to the I, five to genome centers, and keeping the other four on site in EPA for development and customer demonstrations.

Max was largely absent.

At meetings of the Engineering Advisory Committee, where his presence was required but his talents not needed, he usually called in on a conference line in order to meet the conflicting obligations of speaking engagements, awards receptions, and his growing number of consulting contracts. Then too, owing to his very real, serious, deteriorating physical condition, and to his growing disillusionment with Genormx, he often called in sick.

The company needed Max to sell the story to the genome centers in Cambridge, Bethesda, San Diego, Houston, St. Louis, Seattle, Walnut Creek, Santa Cruz, and elsewhere. Genormx needed them as partners because those centers had the experimental staff, the samples, and the ideas necessary to exploit a breakthrough instrument like Beta. With peer-reviewed papers from the centers describing how Beta was used to obtain results unobtainable by any other means, Genormx would receive the recognition it needed to secure its next round of funding, future sales, or a buyout. Carmie and Kozmo, each with sales, marketing, and business development experience, did all the groundwork for these deals, but neither of them was the scientific visionary whose gravity would pull the centers in. Max's name, his person, his handshake; his commitment of mindshare was essential to get the centers to take an instrument. It wasn't even enough for a center to buy one. They had to use it, and that was a bigger commitment because staff was always over-stretched. Only Max had the cred to get those deals done.

The entire Genormx enterprise—from the ten-hour a week janitors who kept the building tidy, to the office staff who answered phones, kept schedules, and made sure there were pencils and paper clips on site when they were needed, to the engineers and contractors whose sixty or more hours per week was responsible for bringing Beta to life, and finally to the executives, consultants and investors—depended on Max to bring these deals home. In some cases, success would only mean an upgrade in luxury, but in other cases it meant the paycheck that paid for music lessons, soccer jerseys, and dinner out once-a-week, and in others, success would be the bulwark between having health insurance or not, or between home and homelessness.

Max questioned what he'd brought to life. He concluded that with all the compromises and competition, Genormx was going to be a commercial (and maybe a technical) flop. If he continued to support it and it failed, he'd look bad. If he did nothing, he could plausibly deny responsibility and blame the bad result on management. Consciously or otherwise, Max made it impossible to schedule the meetings with center directors that were so critical to the future of Genormx.

To Kozmo's credit and everyone's surprise, engineering, including bioinformatics, was ahead of schedule and under budget. But the instruments would be all dressed up and have nowhere to go if Max didn't make every effort to place them at the centers.

The Board was furious, livid, apoplectic, incredulous. Were there other words to describe the slow dawning of awareness that Max had screwed them?

This was not a pleading board. They called him in to talk to him, not to bargain with him. He gave excuses about his health. He told them they should hire a deal guy. He told them he didn't want to do that kind of work. He told them it wasn't in his contract to travel for that purpose, and that it might even be prohibited by his HMRI contract—to which he said he had to give first priority— to make such deals, and to lend his name to the company's products. He distributed copies of the HMRI contract, yellow highlighter circling paragraphs that were explicit about the consulting services he could provide and the prohibitions against his endorsing the company's products or being its agent. "I prefer not to," was his final remark.

The letter had been prepared in advance, just in case. When Galena Radgloom handed him his notice of termination letter for non-performance, he told them, with the eyes of a killer and the detachment of a banker, that his medical condition invoked a clause in his contract prohibiting them from reclaiming the unvested 5 percent ownership he had in the company. Then he left.

Even though the Board had anticipated this confrontation and had made all the necessary preparations, they were shocked at what it had come to.

"I still want his head in a jar of formaldehyde," said Roberta.

"He's a technology pimp, if you'll excuse the phrasing, Ladies," said Armen.

Galena opined, "All these academic and institution guys, they think they're Jim Clark and want the Jim Clark equity premium."

"You mean the Michael Lewis premium."

"Don't talk to me about him. It's a decade after that damned book and the damage he did to the ecosystem is still rippling through."

"The Michael Lewis premium?"

"Yeah. *The New New Thing* is the Great Man Theory. He accepted, lock, stock, and barrel, Jim's argument that Great Men are underappreciated, and wrote about it during the peak moments of dotcom inflation when people were ready to believe it. So, Jim ends up on a pedestal. Ever since, guys with grand ideas and no ability to execute, sometimes not even the desire to execute, want that equity premium, too, because they are Great Men."

"Jim put up $3 million to fund Netscape. Money talks. He got the premium because of the money."

"That's an inconvenient truth most Great Men don't want to acknowledge."

"Max is one of those guys. He wants to be a broker and get paid for steering the IP, not for making it real. I don't think that's why these institutions have 501(c)(3) status, to be platforms for these arrogant sons of bitches."

"His students are not his indentured servants for him to rent-seek in perpetuity, but you'd never know it the way he talks about what he is owed for bringing them here."

"The I owns the technology we licensed. There's a huge conflict of interest in him having a say in where it goes, when where it goes is someplace in which he's got a big chunk of ownership, or when he gets a chunk of ownership for exerting influence on the decision process. It's a kickback. What else would you call it?"

"I don't think it's the COI policy that's flawed. It's the fact that he didn't deliver. We'd all have been happy enough with his 10 percent if he'd actually done what he said he'd do."

"I'm not going to name names here, but there are guys in positions like his who get 20 percent, but they deliver."

"That much?"

"Before or after funding?"

"Whoever's doing those deals must be desperate."

"Ladies! Ladies! Gentlemen!" Carmie said, with impatience, banging a book on the table to get their attention, having failed to do it with more gentle interventions. "It's done. Max is out. Unless it's our plan to file a complaint with HMRI, I think we should put this ugliness behind us and move on."

In a moment, or a little more than a moment, the other Board members had collected themselves and the CEO continued with the afternoon's business.

CHAPTER 121
MAX AND RINCHEN AT PING-PONG

RINCHEN CORNERED Max as he skirted the ping-pong table on his way out the door. "Max. Does it have to be like this? You're our leader." Max had long since ceased to be their leader, but Rinchen felt the cosmos creaking, and he wanted to buoy his erstwhile advisor.

"You're all fools. Can't you see it's over?"

"It's only over because you say it's over. The world is only what you say it is, Max. You have that power to transform."

"Don't bullshit me, Rinchen. You've built a mediocrity and the world has moved on. I won't have anything to do with it any more."

Rinchen marshaled all his diplomacy, "Max. Remember the first days when we planned this instrument? We had that hope, as if she was our child, our responsibility and honor to bring into the world? Max, we can go back there. The journey has been a long one, but it will be over soon with only the slightest bit of help from you. Don't abandon ship now."

"Abandon it. They've fucking fired me! I don't give a rat's ass what happens next. That Board, they've ruined my fun. This machine is everything to you. But it's nothing to me, nothing to me but a stain about to happen. The investors? They're all nothing to me."

"And the team, Max. The team? Your beamers? Max, what about us?" Rinchen waved his hands around the room, pointing here and there. "Nothing to you?"

"Nothing to me," and he stormed out, brushing Nico and others who had been standing by in silence.

CHAPTER 121 THE AFTERMATH

ALONG WITH Carmie's quarterly report to investors and shareholders on company progress and important events, including Max's termination for cause, Max received the notice that the company had reclaimed his unvested shares. Dyk Schmalis, acting as Max's attorney, sent the Board a draft of the lawsuit he threatened to initiate if they did not reinstate the shares within thirty days. Armen smelled a bluff. Max's ambitions could not withstand the public scrutiny of a lawsuit, and he wasn't about to sacrifice his ambitions. The Board did not respond and Dyk did not sue.

CHAPTER 122 THE CORPORATE COUNSEL

MAX'S RESPONSE to Vladik's summary of the conversation at Zott's was an email message. "By way of this email I make these introductions. Vladik K is the new CEO of Moby Dx and Dykkur Ph'eer is an experienced attorney I'd like to represent us."

Vladik called Max. "Do we need such a high priced firm?"

"Dykkur and I have worked together for years, since Tiny Machines, and I've always found the advice worth paying for. They have a great IP practice, too, so we'll save on costs there."

"And they're kind of far away, too."

"Just think of it as having a company-paid-for excuse to visit the East Coast. It will be up to you to decide, though."

Vladik liked the sound of that. "OK, will you get on that introduction to iUDx? Unless they want to meet us tomorrow, we'll have time to make a deck."

"I'm not sure we'll need a deck."

"We'll always need a deck."

"Alright. I'll get on it."

Vladik set up a meeting with Dykkur a few days later.

"How's the video, can you see me?"

"Yes. Spring yet in Boston?"

"Getting there." And there followed introductions, during which Dykkur was blessedly brief, and they played a few rounds of "Do you know?" too. Vladik sang Max's praises, and it became clear that Dykkur was at least as big a fan.

Then, "Heh. Let's take care of the client services agreement first, shall we? Did you get the draft I sent you?"

"Yes, I read through that. I'd like to see all fees deferred until we have revenue of a million dollars in a twelve month period."

"Max told me you had a natural sense of humor."

"*Ha!* No, really, that's what I'm hearing is par from the big firms here. The little ones, it's all cash all the time, but they're half your rate. Less."

"We can defer the first $100,000 in fees, but then we'll have to get paid."

And so it went, negotiating every term with parry and thrust, thrust and parry, until there was a deal. Still, Vladik had not decided Dykkur was worth it, even at a 15 percent discount to his normal rate.

"Let's work from these terms, shall we?"

"OK. You're corporate counsel for now. Will you take care of incorporation or shall I?"

"In that capacity, we'll want to have copies of all the agreements. I think it's easier for us to do this."

"OK, go ahead with that then. And Max told me you've already started the discussion with TTO about licensing the patent?"

"Patent applications, yes. I'll send the correspondence to you and you can get in touch with TTO. I've had my associate working with Louisa ben Dayore in that office. Do you want us to finish that negotiation or do you want to do it yourself?"

"I need to get familiar with it, so I'll do it myself. You can review the license before I sign it."

"Did Max mention to you that we're actually writing the patent filing itself? He thinks the I's patent attorneys, are, uh, um—"

"Fucking Idiots?"

"Yes, I believe that was his exact wording. So we write them, and then TTO approves them. They have rules which require all that."

"Isn't that a very expensive way to do things, having two sets of attorneys touch all the documents?"

"Yes, but it's only for the patents you're licensing. The company's own patents won't have to go through the I."

Dear Reader, Are you bored yet? The minutia would erase your soul, unless you're a lawyer. You thought a startup was exciting, full of zest and thrill. Alas, not all of it. Before the miracles and shagging, it's all just slogging.

"Has Max explained Caselode Fittings to you yet?"

"No. What is it? Your docket manager?

"No, it's a procedural thing for the I. Ask him to tell you about it."

Vladik made a note of that and ended the call.

VLADIK called him back right away. "Dykkur, one more thing. You can't incorporate until we've decided whether this is an LLC or C-Corp?"

"I thought you were headed to LLC. Did you and Max decide something else?"

"No, we haven't discussed it. What do you think?"

"Well, it depends on what you want to do with the company. C-Corp is vanilla. The legal structures are very well defined, state-by-state, and the documents, you know the bylaws and the articles of incorporation all the other stuff, are formulaic and cheap to produce, but you have to live within what the C-Corp legal code says. LLC is made to order. You can make an LLC be almost anything you want, so the formation documents, that is the operating agreement and everything around it, are bespoke."

"Why wouldn't we want to go the easy way?"

"LLC is a pass-through tax entity. The members pay taxes, the LLC doesn't."

"And the members are the shareholders?"

"Right. The members pay taxes on the profits, or write off its losses in proportion to their ownership in the LLC. You'll get a K-1 instead of a W2."

"And why is that better for me?"

"You avoid double taxation. If you're a C-Corp, the company will pay taxes on the profits. If the company pays you a dividend, which comes from the company's profits, you'll pay taxes on that, too."

"And not everyone does this why?"

"For you, the most important reason is that the venture guys can't invest in LLCs. They'd have to give up their carried interest tax benefits if they did, because the LLCs already have a tax benefit compared to C-Corps."

"No, we can't ask them to do that," Vladik said, letting down his guard so that sarcasm dripped onto the floor. "If we're going to need VC investment, we'll need to be a C-Corp. Our bootstrapping model doesn't call for venture funding, so I guess that means LLC. What do the documents cost?"

"We can set you up with the C-Corp for under $5,000. But the LLC, that takes time. Even if I have my associate do it, and she bills at probably $535 an hour instead of my ..." and his voice trailed off, "and then I have to check it. It could easily be $20,000."

"Your $5,000 is high to begin with. I can get that done with docs from Nolo Press for, Dykkur, hmm, let me see, you don't want to know what it costs." The line went silent for a moment. "I just checked their website and I can get the LLC done for $99."

"Look, Vladik. You're hoping there's going be piles of money made, and that's going to invite scrutiny, so you want to get it done right at the beginning. That's why people hire us. We're the best."

"That's what I'm hearing, but only from people who have an interest in saying so," and he laughed at his own joke. Dykkur wasn't laughing.

Vladik went on. "I'm going to have to think about this. Hold off on the incorporation and I'll get back to you. I'm leaning toward C-Corp because I just don't see real advantage and it's a big difference in expense."

"A big difference you won't be paying because of the fee deferral."

"We'll pay it eventually."

"LLC is very popular right now for incubators. You should know that. If you're thinking that licensing revenue from multiple products is going to be important, then that revenue can get locked in a C-Corp and you can't return it to shareholders until the company is sold. With an LLC, since it's a pass through entity, you can distribute the licensing revenue to the members without having to wait for an exit."

"Oy. Licensing revenue is definitely the key for us, but we haven't talked about multiple products."

"It's not just multiple products. It's licensing deals that mature at different times, maybe with the same products."

"You're lobbying pretty hard for this," Vladik said.

Dykkur said nothing. The tension built up as the silence ticked away.

Finally, Vladik said, "I give up. *Ka-ching!* You win. Moby Dx LLC."

"Vladik. One more thing."

"Does it have a price tag?"

"No."

"I'm listening."

"Delaware?"

"Of course. Don't their license plates say 'The Company-Friendly State'?"

"No, I think it says 'The First State.'"

"Joku, Dykkur-san, Joku."

Dykkur paused for a moment, and then said, "OK Vladik, let me know when you have had that conversation with Max about Caselode Fittings."

CHAPTER 123 OFFICE MANEUVERINGS

VLADIK HAD made the call to Dykkur from home, aka the Petit Parthénon. Arianna was in and out of the house all day, and in and out of the property sometimes for days, with Sheba in the Escalade or alone in her midnight blue 911. The little Parthenon provided all the privacy he needed. When he had to meet someone, he went to them, or they met at neutral ground in cafés from San Jose to San Francisco. He couldn't have meetings at My Monticello, as he was really only one step up from being a couch surfer.

He soon, very soon, tired of being itinerant all day. Caffe del Doge, Peet's, University Café, Peet's, Douce France, The Woodside Bakery, Buck's, The Mayfield, another Peet's, Café Borrone, Il Fornaio, not to mention about twenty different Starbucks. The hero spotting—Whit Diffie at Coupa, Dave McClure at Mayfield, Jim Breyer at Il Fornaio, Sandberg and Zuckerberg before Facebook moved out of downtown—lost its allure after a few weeks. There was too much time wasted coming and going, setting up and taking down, trying to find a quiet place or a private spot, and then repairing to his car if he had to make a phone call—and there was the feeling of homelessness all that engendered. And driving back and forth to Woodside several times a day, eight miles each way? That simply didn't work.

Arianna tired of the 911 at the same time. Great as she looked in it, as she'd guessed she would, it was a crummy art car and a worse client car: too small to transport artwork that wasn't in a cardboard tube; too noisy for phone calls; and too hard for her business partners to get in and out of. It became Vladik's hand-me-down. She bought a red Avant, folded the rear seats down, and looked pretty good in that, too. Sports car or not, Vladik still needed an office.

Vladik had money to rent an office anywhere he wanted. That wasn't the problem. The problem was that he and Max had made no mechanism to bring money into the company other than through research contracts, and there wasn't so much as a date for that. He, Vladik, had moved across the country—OK, he probably would have moved anyway, seeing as Arianna was wound up in My Monticello—and was putting in a full-time effort for Moby Dx, and as nearly as he could see nothing was happening on Max's end, so if he was going to put cash into it, he wanted Max to put in the same.

"Got a few?" Vladik texted.

"Yes."

Vladik called him. "We need a little cash for operations, you know, office, travel, etc. And there will be more. I think we should each write checks for $100,000."

"$50,000."

"Max, I need $100,000 from you. If I thought $50,000 would do, I'd have asked for it."

"Don't get your hackles up. Everyone's positioning. I was dialing you in."

"Then $100,000?"

"Done. I gotta go."

"One more thing, Max."

"Yeah."

"iUDx?"

"No word. What's the deal with the license?"

"I've decided to go for an option instead of the full license. It will be cheaper."

"Whatever. Just get it done. We want to have that ready when we meet with those guys. Heh, I gotta go."

"What about opening the doors with Abbott and Hitachi?"

"No, I want to put it in front of iUDx, first. I gotta go, really." Click.

Vladik did wonder what was taking so long, and why Max didn't want to pursue several fronts in parallel. With Max having all the contacts, he was the bottleneck and things could only move as fast as he wanted to move.

After a bit of housekeeping, Vladik opened at Silicon Valley Bank in the name of Moby Dx LLC, deposited two checks for $100,000 each.

Commercial real estate had come out of the doldrums of the Little Depression and was booming again. There were no bargains anymore, especially for one- or two-person offices. What Vladik really wanted was a place with lab space to grow into. University Avenue in Palo Alto wasn't the place for that. Other convenient districts—like Stanford Research Park stretching from California Avenue (where Facebook had moved when they left downtown) all the way to the Veterans Administration Hospital where two wars worth of the young and the wounded recovered—had the right kind of facilities, but there he would have to lease thousands of square feet and make a commitment of three years. Worse, the owners would probably want to see a few million dollars in his bank account. All of which is to say, that wasn't happening either.

D5 was reviewing Arianna's recommendations for a mural under the rotunda's dome when Vladik arrived at My Monticello. He had worn himself out talking to real estate agents and driving around to see what the spaces actually looked like. He liked to think of himself as being inured to defeat, but to Arianna, and to D5 on that day, he showed some fissures. "He so hansom. Why face so rong?" she asked Arianna. Arianna explained after recovering from D5's impersonations.

Two days later Vladik moved into an unoccupied suite with two offices, one with a window view overlooking the plain of Palo Alto and the foothills to the southeast, an open seating area suitable for a receptionist, and the most elaborate Wi-Fi sign-on procedure he'd ever encountered. All of this was situated on the sixteenth floor of 525 University Avenue, where D5's APT was headquartered. The glass entry to the space was lettered with the words, Asia Pacific Trust Incorporated.

CHAPTER 124 THE LOGO

THE PRINTING of business cards is a major milestone in the history of every enterprise, from your first venture into selling snocones on the sidewalk to your first venture-funded startup. In the critical path of that task is designing the company logo. Max had picked out the name and it was up to Vladik to do the rest.

Vladik didn't so much design it as run the process of having it designed. He asked several friends and went online to reach some commercial artists. On a lark, he asked the artsy daughters of his mobster cousins. He tried to include Max in the design process, but Max said, "Do what you want." Then Arianna decided for them.

The design guide Vladik had provided explained the big ideas that went into the company. "The company's business, diagnostics, invokes the ubiquitous stethoscope. The stethoscope invites thoughts of professionalism and of the friendly family physician. Moby, a bonding of molecular and biology, first suggests thoughts of Melville's whale. The message of the whale has become a chameleon. As friendly as a baby beluga or malign like an angry beast, its power as the leviathan is universally acknowledged."

Arianna made comments on all the original submissions, received second submissions from some, and then selected a drawing by Gili Kakitelashvili; Vladik's second cousin once removed, whom he thought of as his niece. Her black ink drawing was of a massive whale. Dense lines at its flukes gave way to whiteness at its head—white symbolizing health and virtue, so important in Moby Dx's markets. The whale breached, nearly vertical, flukes out, cleansing water pouring off. A simple stethoscope hung from its ears. The binaural tube, curved upwards, left the impression of a benign smile. The chest piece swung to one side conveying motion. The cetacean's flippers stretched long and down, appearing as arms.

The company needed something simpler for a logo, so Arianna trimmed down Gili's idea, and *voilà*.

CHAPTER 125 TTO

VLADIK LEARNED a few things during his first meeting with TTO. Some of them he wished he hadn't.

Assistant Technology Transfer Officer Louisa ben Dayore, or LBD as she was sometimes called, was barely a snatch over five feet tall, trim, tight, and fair skinned. She wore a near-shoulder-length blond pageboy that might have come out of a *Cosmo* ad. Louisa graduated from Stanford with a degree in biology around the time HMRI moved into Lobitos Farm. More important than continuing her education was staying in the area with her girlfriend, Pabla Mirabella, then a first year medical student at Stanford. When she saw the job listing from TTO Director Nathalia Nguyen-Berry's office, she applied and got the job.

In the years that followed, the commute wore her down. Nathalia didn't allow her staff any telecommuting except on an *ad hoc* basis. Louisa bought a small place near the I. Pabla had become a nephrology resident and was nearly resident at Stanford Hospital, so LBD was both missing nothing by being away and missing everything by Pabla's absence. She and I had become friends.

Louisa had been assigned the Frood portfolio, and this most recent addition, the MOST filing, was to her just another in a pile of gold. She hadn't always been responsible for Max's IP. Associate Technology Transfer Officer Zlata Slutzkaya had once managed it, but Zlata had a dustup with Max.

At the I, Principals are The Talent, and as such, are treated with deference and even reverence. Everyone in TTO was instructed to address the Principals as Dr. This and Dr. That, unless given explicit permission by the Principal to do otherwise. I think there could be a better way. Does anyone ask me? Max was Dr. Frood.

Zlata had been taking a first pass at another invention disclosure Max had submitted with one of the I's renowned pharmacochemists. It was unusual, for Max, in that the disclosure was devoted exclusively to the design of a new molecule, a new molecular structure. According the USPTO, an inventor is someone who has conceived the invention. If they have not conceived the invention, they are not the inventor. Case law, e.g., Townsend v. Smith, 36 F.2d 292, 295, 4 USPQ 269, 271 (CCPA 1930), defines conception as "the complete performance of the mental part of the inventive act."

Much as she respected Dr. Frood, and had been trained to show it too,

Zlata thought it her duty to inquire how it had come about that someone with exactly no history of work in molecular structure was a named inventor, that is, had participated in the complete performance of the mental part of the inventive act on this patent application. After the kicking and screaming and denials and self-justifications, and after his patient explanations that he was a genius and an auto-didact, and after assertions that Zlata was not showing the called-for respect and after *ad hominem* assaults on Ms. Slutzkaya's character—Fair Reader, Zlata's last name reflected only that her family had long stayed in Belarus—Dr. Frood backed down and agreed to have his name removed from the application. Both he and Zlata appealed to Director Nguyen-Berry that she, Zlata, no longer be responsible for the Frood portfolio. After this incident he would occasionally be referred to within TTO as Dr. Fraud, and Louisa was assigned the portfolio.

Louisa and Vladik exchanged pleasantries. He reviewed his history, giving more emphasis than he thought warranted, but as much as he'd learned was appreciated, to his time advising Jay. Those successes counted for a lot with people who wanted to believe a good story. He explained how he'd known of Max and how they'd met and found common cause, and on and on, continuing with how great it was to be working with him, his history being so illustrious, his circle of colleagues so brilliant, the opportunities so rich, and on and on; a well-oiled script. He neglected to mention, of course, that he was married to Max's former wife and that between what he he'd heard from her and from his college roommate Jay, he probably knew more juicy bits about Max than anyone alive.

And with Louisa, because it was the I, he did mention that he'd known the co-inventor, me, even longer than he'd known Max. When he said several complimentary things about me, Louisa smiled and turned around a small, framed photo on her desktop. It was of Louisa and her lover, me, so entwined, lounging in mid-summer heat on the deck of a houseboat on Lake Shasta; big black sunglasses, stupid grins, both of us looking like twenty-six going on fourteen. We're holding vodkas laced with fruity something, a paper umbrella sticking out, and I'm sitting across her lap, cowgirl sidesaddle, you might say. A slim, nice looking young man is poking his head in from the side. "Nice bikinis," Vladik said. He later asked me if she was in my stable, too. "Girls will be girls," I told him.

From there the conversation veered to TTO's business processes, how they had to market the technology to other interested parties, take bids, compare them, respond to the bids, etc. Then there was some discussion of the non-trivial schedule for all of that. And a discussion of typical licensing terms, and TTO's philosophy on this matter—based on industry best practices reviewed at the annual meeting of the Technology Transfer Society—which was to take a tax, that is a licensing fee, at every possible toll, but to be in the middle of the range of accepted rates. There were annual fees, fees for milestones such as the patent being granted, fees for entering clinical testing, fees for completing clinical testing, royalties on sales, fees for sales exceeding mutually agreed upon milestones, fees for sub-licensing deals the company executed, and fees for extending the licensing agreement beyond its initial ten year term. And there were sliding scales for all of these, based on meeting other performance milestones. And, of course, the licensee was obliged to pay for all the legal fees incurred filing and prosecuting the patent. All of this, all this universe of fees, they believed from long experience, guaranteed that no revenue opportunity passed them by, but didn't impose any undue burdens on the licensee.

Dear Reader? Still awake? If you're going to be CEO, you have to love these details, or at least be willing to master them. Otherwise, find another job. Find another book if you must. This is the way the sausage is made. Live with it.

Vladik mastered them with graceful displeasure, and for a variety of reasons—including that he was mentoring me and that the first licenses were based on patents with my name on them—I was let in on many of the details. In her office, he was under spell, in the daydream she suffused. Louisa was distractingly beautiful to everyone, I think, exuding health and virtue, looking like the perfect lemon vanilla cupcake that she was, all the way down to her follicles. And through the fogginess of that dream, he was surprised to hear her say, "I guess Max told you about the filing date problem on this one?"

"Uh, no, I can't say he has. I'm sorry. I must have been distracted for a second." He laughed and said, "It's all so fascinating."

She laughed and projected a warm smile to him, passing back to him the knowledge that she knew that he knew that she knew that what they were doing was a necessary evil, and they had to bring humor and professionalism to it, otherwise it would grind them down. "So fascinating, yes." I think she may have been thinking of me, or Pabla, as Vladik was at that moment thinking of Arianna and his faraway home on the ocean.

"The patent application was only filed after the first publication. So while the patent will remain valid in the US, we can't obtain any international protections for it."

"There's a publication already?"

"Max showed some slides about it and they were published in a conference proceedings. We hadn't filed the provisional patent application yet."

"Well, that's—" and he checked himself.

"A fuckup," she finished, flashing a gleaming mouthful of whitened teeth at him, laughing again.

"Yes. I was going to say so if I'd been in coarser company."

"You know Lakshmi so I thought you could take it."

"I can take it. How did that happen?"

"I really don't want to say, especially as I am on one side of a dispute and Dr. Frood is on the other, none of which I'm at liberty to discuss. Shall we just call it a failure to communicate?"

"I guess. I think I'm shot for the day. What would you like from me next?

"A proposal. A bid. We have a template. Given the early stage of your company, we'll need a business plan, too."

"As long as we're clear about what a business plan is, then I can do that. For me, for us, at this stage, a business plan is a two-page text with a few figures. If I'm sloppy, three pages. It is not a twenty-page document with fold out spreadsheets showing five-year financials. OK?"

"Yes, that is fine. Vladik," she said, extending her hand, "it was really a pleasure."

"Yes, indeed, a pleasure."

He called me on his drive home. I explained Zlata's discovery and how in Max's anger over that, he had failed to give TTO instructions on when to file the provisional for the MOST IP. And I also told him that Louisa was as blond as she looked.

CHAPTER 126 VLADIK, MEET SAMEER

"MEET me for lunch today?" Max said over the phone.

"Later is better for me," Vladik said.

"Me, too. One o'clock, 3000 Sand Hill Road."

"Restaurant 3000?" Vladik had heard stories of celebrity sightings there and was keen to go.

"No. Outside. You'll see me by the trucks."

Vladik parked near Max's car. At that late hour, the frenzied cluster of people buying and selling had dissipated, so the scene only hinted at what he had missed. The caravan of trucks left as he arrived. A few of them still in place were shuttering their windows. Only Sameer's Samosas and Truckin' Sweet, serving desserts exclusively, were still open for business. Max stood in front of Sameer's, leaning on a cane.

"Looks like you're a regular."

"Kinda. Sameer here is my friend. Vladik, meet Sameer."

Sameer, recognizing the name he'd heard Max utter at Moby Dick's, stuck his fat hand through the truck window. "We meet at last," he said, leaving Vladik confused.

"Sameer, very nice to meet you. What's your recommendation?"

"My friend, my recommendation is to get an umbrella! *Ha*! No, my recommendation is to eat what I serve you, because I'm out of everything else," and he laughed a big bass belly laugh, making the whole truck shake as he slammed his hand down on the counter, convinced of his own hilarity.

Through the portal, Sameer passed their lunches. Each paper plate held two exotic samosas. One was of potatoes, peas, and wild mushrooms, spiced with garlic, Sameera's masala du jour, and a dollop of mango dip. The other was of sweet potatoes, jalapeno, spinach, fennel and ginger, and Sameer's mint chutney. A mound of saffron biryani with a sprinkling of lamb lay beside the samosas. Sameer slid across some napkins and plastics forks, and finally, bottles of addictively sweet 2Sweet iced tea.

"Only two, my friend?" Max asked.

"All out, my friend. All out," in an apologetic tone. "Business was too good today. You are the sucker today."

Max thanked him, handed him three ten-dollar bills, waved the change away, and said to Vladik, "I'll get it this time. Let's go here," pointing to Truckin' Sweet, "before we sit there," pointing to the grass. "They have the best chocolate-dipped baklava."

Once situated, Vladik said, "I didn't expect this. Fantastic."

"Best food in the valley, these trucks. Like street food in old Singapore."

"Never been, but I like street food where I can get it."

"And Russia?"

Vladik thought that was weird. Max never, never ever brought up private matters.

"I left when I was five. Russia was no foodie place in those days. I haven't been back."

Max let that conversation die out and then started on a new thread. "So, you met with Dykkur?"

"Yeah. What's up with his hair? Is he shooting for Honorable Mention in a Brad Pitt impersonation contest?"

"He had LAD and lost all his hair in the chemo. He's enjoying the new growth and says he's never cutting it again."

"Lateral Amyotrophic something? I thought that was ALS?"

"Close, Lance Armstrong Disease."

"Sociopathic lying and conspiracy to commit fraud?"

Max's reply missed a beat. He threw some incomprehensible facial tics in Vladik's direction. "No, HGH-induced testicular cancer. The schmuck had three balls before he had one."

"Lance?"

"No, Dykkur."

Then Max changed the subject quickly. "Heh, did Dykkur tell you about Caselode Fittings?"

"He told me to talk to you about it. Is that what this is about?"

"Yeah. The I has benighted rules about how much stock I can own in my companies. Period. Full stop. Let me spell it out for you: b-e-nighted. They're going to lose a bunch of us entrepreneurial types if they don't come around. We're all pushing the envelope as much as we can, some openly cheating and hoping not to get caught. Dykkur has found a legal way to get around their rules. Period. Full stop."

Vladik, listening, said nothing. His thoughts surfaced in staccato bytes. *OK. I've seen this before. Entrepreneurial? Maybe. Cheating? Bad. Legal? Good. Dykkur? Still withholding judgment.*

Max continued, "Dykkur has created a separate entity, we call it Caselode Fittings I, that will hold my share in the LLC. Sameer will hold the majority interest in it, and the arithmetic will work out so I'm HMRI -compliant. Sameer will be it's managing member, but he'll vote however I tell him to. The whole thing is Halal, OK?"

"Sameer?"

"Sameer looks like an old kitchen boy, I know, but he's a savvy businessman and he's become a close friend. You'll get to like him, and he can probably be helpful to us."

"And why Caselode Fittings I?"

"Dykkur said to come up with something meaningless, so I did." And then Max drifted onto a tangent. "Dykkur's smart, and that's why we pay him what we do. I had wanted to name it Mniotix, back in the day when we thought were going to do fetal diagnostics, but before we got scooped. Dykkur—"

Vladik interrupted him, "You mean scooped by—"

And then Max cut him off before Vladik even could utter their names. "No, don't say it! I can't even bear to hear their names anymore." He put his hands over his ears. "They beat us last time. We'll crush them this time. And now I hate that market anyway. It's too crowded. They'll race to the bottom of their investors' pockets. I'm glad we lost."

Each sentence was punctuated with an exclamation point and a crescendo. It was the second time Vladik had seen Max explode without warning. He changed the subject. "Legal?"

"Yeah. Dykkur says it's legal. Designed to be HMRI-compliant. You'll see more of that shit in the operating agreement, too. Read up on the HMRI policies. They're all online."

They got up and threw their plates away, covering a few more business items as they walked to their cars, Max moving slowly.

"You're looking a little tired. Everything OK?"

"Nothing's really been OK since my accident. I had to go in today for some testing. It wears me out."

"The testing?"

"Yeah, the testing, and the follow-up. My kidneys are not what they used to be and not what they should be."

"Dialysis? Transplant? I hear transplants are a true miracle."

"I don't want to think about it."

Max changed the subject again. "Did you get an office yet?"

"Yes, I know someone who knows someone. I could put a couple more people there, and we have a view."

"In Palo Alto, a view of what, entitled kids?"

"Entitled ants maybe. We're on the sixteenth floor. Come and see it sometime."

"Where is there a sixteenth floor anywhere in that shallow shithole?" Max asked rhetorically, and then he was silent for moment. "And what about the license?"

"It's coming along. I had a nice meeting with Louisa. She's like a doll, you know. A toy. So fine, so fair? Not real somehow."

Max interrupted, "You should go for it."

"I think she plays for the other team."

"Really?"

"Really. A distractingly beautiful lesbian—" Vladik cut himself off before mentioning that he was already committed, or describing the Lake Shasta photo LBD had shown him. "Anyway, there's a long process, as you know, with the marketing and bids and whatnot in front of us."

"They're Fucking Idiots. I'll tell Nathalia to short circuit a lot of that."

Vladik didn't think that was going to help.

"It's not like we even have it in the bag. I'm writing an executive summary and calling it a business plan."

"Run that by me before you send it to them, will you?

"Of course." He paused. "I heard about the filing date fiasco, too." Vladik looked carefully at Max, hoping for some sign of contrition, but there was none.

"The company will file its own patents that will have foreign coverage. Don't worry about it. Just get this license."

"I'll negotiate the terms down because the patent is worth less without the foreign coverage."

"Good luck with that."

"And what about iUDx? Any more word?"

"Yes, actually. We have a date. I'll send you some introductions."

"That's great. And we can go over the deck."

"Yep. Just connect with the people on the distribution list."

While seated in his car, Max sent out three letters of introduction from his Slab97. One was to Vladik and Serena Fraguglia, his long time Italian elder, now the Director of Biomarkers at iUDx. One was to Vladik and Sameer. And then there was one more.

CHAPTER 127 AND THEN THERE WAS DYK

THE FINAL one of those three email introductions was this: "By this email I introduce Dyk Schmalis, former Director of Genormx, and Vladik K, CEO of Moby Dx. Vladik, I think you'll find Dyk very helpful to our cause. Please get together. MF"

When they did meet, Vladik's first impression was that Dyk was a nineteenth century banker from New York City. Missing only the monocle, he came with beard, vest, pocket watch, gold chain, and paunch and a half. He came looking for paid work and Vladik soon discerned that Dyk was a member of that regrettably-not-rare or even unique-to-Silicon-Valley species called *Mentorus self-proclaimed.*

"I was an o-chem undergrad, tried biochem in grad school but was going nowhere, so I switched to law school," Dyk said. Then there followed a forgettable tale, much embroidered and not at all to the point, about the ins and outs and whys and wherefores of his arc, landing him in biotech in mid-career. He became a consultant, closing deals, maybe, building his Rolodex, and sitting on boards. "I think I can make myself useful, let's say one day a week, with commensurate pay, maybe sixty thousand a year."

Vladik had immediately taken a strong dislike to him, if only for the existential threat he posed. While Dyk bloviated—those are Vladik's words—Vladik had prepared his response. "Max spoke very highly of you, but I think you misheard him if you think there's a board position open right now. There isn't. Max and I make the decisions by consensus." Vladik let that sink in. Dyk twitched.

"However, I definitely need help opening doors and closing deals. How about if we take a few minutes and I show you the deck I'm preparing for iUDx?"

It wasn't a few minutes. "I pitched MOST from DNA in blood to the most naïve experiments you'd done," Vladik told me, "and then all the way to some vision of point-of-care delivery with bedside sequencing which turned it into a realization of Star Trek's tricorder.

"Dyk asked questions that purported to test my understanding and be revelatory for him, but in fact they were off the mark. They were show-off questions. I'd learned, years ago I'd learned at ITSy, not to waste everyone else's time behaving that way. Also, he wouldn't let go of things. He seemed not to have heard the expression, 'Well, let's take that up offline.' He tried to wear me down, and I could see that some day he would. He would be difficult company in meetings. It was clear why he was a consultant. His employers wanted to have day-to-day control of whether he'd be on the job or even in the room. He was a caricature of himself. *Ridykurous*," Vladik said, invoking one of the Seinfeld episodes we'd seen so many times our first summer together in New Hampshire.

"Still," Vladik continued to me, "my deck took forty-five minutes and I had promised something short. So I gave him my *mea culpa*. Dyk replied, 'No, it was great. Max told me you were a physicist, so I was expecting something quite different. You have the passion of the entrepreneur and the understanding of the business context I wasn't expecting.'"

After politely acknowledging Dyk's compliment, Vladik explained to him,

"What the company needs is business development, but we can't pay for it. Those guys are expensive and used to getting paid." Hoping that Dyk would turn him down, he added, "If you can close some deals we can give you a piece of each one. If you're willing to work that way, let's talk about where to start."

That did not end their relationship as he thought it might. Dyk invited himself to the upcoming meeting with iUDx. Vladik, caught off guard, didn't push back and deny him, as he had every right to do.

"Max will introduce everyone and say a few words. I'll give the pitch, and you can do the follow-up and close the deal," Vladik told Dyk.

Vladik reported back to Max, "I tried to like him, but I found that he wasted my time, taking the conversation in not very fruitful directions. He tried to impress me with his technical insights, but they were all superficial."

"Yeah, that's not his strongpoint. He's a great negotiator. Really understands contracts and makes sure we have the right terms."

"If that's not his strongpoint, why did we spend so much time on it?"

"Heh. Let it go. I think you did the right thing asking for his help closing iUDx."

Dyk reported back to Max, "He's going to have to go. You're not going to be able to control him, Old Man. He treated me like a kid."

"*Ha!* So he called you on your bullshit. Good for him. He's not going yet. Hang in there."

CHAPTER 128 FOUR BETTER ANGELS

MAX HAD bypassed any need or desire for Salim to participate in Caselode Fittings, but Max had not let up on the immune repertoire. The idea factory that was Max still needed Salim.

As part of the restless networking that is the life of the big Principal Investigator, Max had learned that among the tens of millions of people who had been exposed to the Human Immunodeficiency Virus—almost all of whom were either in the grave, steadily on their way there, or in a holding pattern fueled by drugs developed by what was once known as the War on Cancer—a very small sub-population progressed much more slowly than the whole. Something made them fight off the virus more effectively. Immunologists hoped that these few were the modern equivalent of Jenner's milkmaids, holding the secret to an AIDS vaccine.

The gp120 surface protein of HIV is essential to the virus's ability to enter a CD4 cell of the human immune system, commandeer the cell's machinery, multiply within it, and then kill it. Within gp120 there is a region, CD4BS that binds to CD4, enabling the entry that leads to death. In its effort to evade antibody attack, gp120 has evolved two strategies. First, it throws up a plethora of fast-mutating scaffolds and decoys around CD4BS. Antibodies that have evolved to neutralize one scaffold configuration, and therefore one variant of the virus, are not effective against variants carrying mutated gp120. And, the mutations around CD4BS do not (generally) compromise functionality of the binding site. Second, gp120 enlists the Golgi apparatus—organelles of the invaded cell—to coat the entire protein with short sugary molecular fragments, oligosaccharides. Like ivy hiding a college beneath it, the coating further occludes CD4BS from antibody attack. The putative milkmaids, Max and others surmised, were carrying some special "broadly neutralizing" antibodies that were effective against not just one scaffold variant, but against all or almost all that the virus could throw at the patient.

Max knocked on Salim's door and poked his head in.

"I smell sulphur," Salim said.

"Salim, I realize our last conversation did not go so well. Can we talk science, just science?"

"Ground rules, Max. First, ground rules."

Max nodded.

"I will file the invention disclosures," said Salim, "and I will be the contact investigator of record for TTO. Negotiations will go through me."

Max nodded.

"Publications and announcements will go through me."

"Let me guess, the grants will be my responsibility to write."

"That's it, Max. You are a fast learner!"

"Anything else?"

"No poaching of my students."

"Anything else?"

"No, I think that's it. What do you have Max?"

"Three points. First, the broadly neutralizing antibodies—"

"Ah, it's the Nobel Prize juice you're after. *Help!*" Salim said with disdain.

Max continued, halting only momentarily at the recognition that Salim now believed every one of Max's moves was motivated by money, power, or glory, "are what we want our immune systems to produce, and clearly—"

"Max. Clearly is one of those words you use when you don't know what you're talking about. Did you learn that at MIT?"

Refusing the bait again, Max continued. "It seems to me that in almost everyone, those good antibodies are not being produced. In the lucky few, thanks to some accident of inheritance or nature, the evolution of antibodies results in these, umh, really special molecules. Second, with sequencing that's free, we should be able to follow the pathway of their evolution ..."

Max had by then gained Salim's attention, but he lost his train of thought, and he paused. He couldn't finish the sentence or make his third point. He looked at the floor. He looked at the ceiling. He had no scribbles on stickies to help him out. Max hadn't yet concluded that he needed to make notes to keep himself on track. The pause had become long. He stumbled, reiterating what he'd already said as if getting a running start would help him over the ravine of his memory, but it didn't work.

With a leap of intuition about where Max was going, and a little bit of pathos for his flawed—but he could now see also ailing—colleague, Salim offered "and third, use directed evolution to design a multi-stage vaccine that tricks the immune system into doing the right thing."

"If you think that's a claim you think we should make in the invention disclosure, which we'll license to Maxyvax, then who am I to say no?"

"Not Maxyvax, Max." Whether Salim's suggestion was what Max had been thinking, or there was yet another plan of attack that Max had forgotten, Salim never learned.

Name or not, thus Max found a collaborator.

ONCE every month or two, Max visited an elementary or middle school classroom somewhere in Silicon Valley, in Half Moon Bay, or in Santa Cruz. He explained basic concepts of energy, the cosmos, and life. He held the normally jittery kids spell-bound with deftly timed insertions of magic tricks and pyrotechnics. When Max felt that he had refined his presentation of a particular topic, a film crew captured it, a team of illustrators transcribed it, and Max reviewed it before a hundred thousand copies of the thin single-topic book were released under the Maxbooks imprint half a year later.

Max described what he was doing as the Feynman Method.

IF Max had cornered the market on implantable artificial kidneys, the recognition might have been enough to close the open wound that was Jay's very existence, but all he sought was a solution for his own failing organs.

After the chance meeting with DARPA Director Duncan in the late 1980s, and the summer internship spent 3-D printing at the Naval Research Lab, Max watched the field from a distance, dabbling when he could, and contemplating its utility for him. I'd seen the product of some of his hobbyist initiatives. Flesh-toned plastic renderings of hyperrealistic sex organs, male and female, human and otherwise, to scale and larger than life, lined the bookshelves of his office. Where he got the data files, I never inquired. But those sculptures were just playthings for him. It was in the locked lab labeled Froodenstein that his team advanced regenerative medicine.

He once gave an I's Only colloquium on the subject. Such talks were closed-door meetings for staff and staff only, intended to share a glimpse of the hottest research at the Institute. The rules stipulated that there be no computers, no slabs, no cameras, no microphones, and no handouts, and that handwritten notes would not leave Lobitos Farm.

Max credited Linda Griffith and Bob Langer of MIT as being his inspiration. "She was interested in my droplets for her own work on bioreactors, so we got to know each other." Max did not mention that he'd been thrown out of the microsystems technology lab. He described her work in 3-D printed bone, and how she had introduced him to Anthony Atala at Harvard. "Atala's 1999 work was a milestone. He grew a bladder from epithelial cells on a shaped scaffold of biodegradable polymer, and then implanted it in a dog. Just like a dog," Max said. I'm not sure how many in the audience got his Kafka reference, but there was muffled laughter.

"Cambridge incubated amazing results in tissue engineering when I was there. I hadn't known anything about it before I arrived, and I was busy with other things, but I sat in on some of Langer's courses because I was a 3-D printer and a MEMS specialist. Someday, I figured, I might get lucky and have an epiphany at their crossroads. Bob taught me about patronage," and here Max paused to smile and connect with his audience.

[Enduring Reader, Max had gone very far off script, and his words need a little explanation. Robert Langer has had a long career at MIT in the fields of tissue engineering and biomaterials for drug delivery. He presides over the world's largest bioengineering lab at the David H. Koch Institute for Integrative Cancer Research. Engineer, inventor, and entrepreneur, he has filed for hundreds of patents through TLO, and participated in the founding of more than two dozen companies. He is the very model for many enterprising academic entrepreneurs.]

Someone shouted, "He sure did," and someone else, "You're no Langer." Several people out there guffawed and coughed before he continued, although the smile had left his face, "But it was Linda, though, who was my guide."

He told us all to read her "very accessible 2002 SCIENCE paper," and he shook a copy of the magazine in the air. The cover image, projected on the screen behind him, was of a skeletal figure sheathed in a blue glow, and on its left leg, an above-the-knee prosthetic just like his own.

"Then this happened," and he tapped his robotic leg. "Lose a leg. Lose a kidney. Look at diabetics. And it's not just them. All of sudden, the subject of transplantation and regenerative medicine became very personal for me."

Max went on to describe the three pillars of the field: biomaterials, scaffolds, and vasculature. "Atala's early work proved that we are in control of the first two, and there's been abundant progress since. But vasculature," and he paused, "vasculature is still in its infancy. I don't think I can tell you the how of this, because the IP hasn't been filed yet," and his face erupted in a welter of tics that made Louisa squirm as she sat next to me. "But I would like to show you another dog." Then Qasima came in from the wings, walking a toy Schnauzer; not some Sony Aibo but a real live dog.

"Two months ago, in a procedure performed by friends of ours at Stanford, this patient was implanted with an artificial kidney grown here at the I. It may be a decade before such a kidney finds its way into a human, maybe less, but we are on our way." Loud applause. Then, without slides, he went on to tell us what he said he couldn't tell us.

"Lost wax casting has been used for millennia to create complicated shapes in difficult to work with materials. What we have done in the Frood Lab, Froodenstein's we call it." He paused for chuckles to subside. "What we have done in the Frood Lab is use those old ideas in a new way. On a fractal scaffold mimicking the dense branching vasculature of a natural kidney, we cast a synthetic organ using the latest in imaging and printing technologies, most of them developed elsewhere. Then we lose the scaffold like the proverbial wax, and voilà." Nathalia and Louisa got up and left in disgust, followed by Zlata Slutskaya at their request.

Because the meeting was I's Only and we were all under NDA, TTO was able to contain the damage, but only after the ladies had returned to the auditorium with their slabs bearing an electronic addendum to the NDA, specific to what we'd just heard; and we'd heard many fine details of the material science and manufacturing methods that I haven't revealed here. Hundreds of us stood in line for as much as two hours, making for a bittersweet afternoon, as we waited to sign the slabs and get past the gatekeepers of the I's intellectual property.

ONE of the figures visiting Paris in Max's years there was a pioneer in lymphocyte regulation. Those white blood cells, key components of the adaptive immune system, might be turned off, leaving you immunocompromised, turned on too high, leaving you with autoimmune disease, or dialed-in just right where you wanted them. Pierre Golstein was then like a man with his hair on fire as he tried to get people to listen to him about how cancer treatment would change if only we were the masters of T-cell regulation, and not the subjects of it.

Max, in those days almost deaf to such specialized topics, slept through Golstein's talks or simply didn't go to them. But he absorbed something about their significance, something that resurfaced decades later as he came to grok how sequencing could improve our grip on immunology.

He called me one night. I was with Georgina.

"Hi, Max."

"Tell me about CTLA-4," he said.

"Hi, Max."

A few seconds of silence passed.

"Let's see," I continued. "Cytotoxic lymphocyte antigen 4. An on-off switch for the immune system. Maybe it gets stuck off and you get cancer. Your pharma friends are developing anti-CTLA-4 antibodies to modulate it, to activate it and fight cancer. Hmm. I think that's all I know."

"And what do you think?"

"I think it's a delicate balance. I'm not sure they'll know how to dose it right."

"Turn it on too much and you give someone autoimmune disease?"

"How's that for a gift that keeps on giving?"

"And the solution?"

"I have a band-aid in mind, but no solution."

Again, I heard only silence, so went on. "The band-aid is to find the T-cell immune repertoire by sequencing, and use that to dial in the dose to where you want it. But it's not a solution because we don't know enough about how those systems works, or what a normal immune repertoire looks like, except superficially, and that means there's too much we don't know, and we don't know whether we can reverse an overactive immune system once we've turned it on."

"If medicine was engineering, what we don't know would matter a lot."

While I was flattered that Max had called me to discuss this interesting topic, I knew the conversation he was starting could go on a long time. This could wait.

"Max, I've got company."

Again. Silence.

"I'd like you to start working on a grant proposal for this," he said at last.

"Can I tell you all the reasons why it will not get funded if you and I are the only investigators?"

More silence, and then, "Have a nice night."

"Good night, Max."

Max never did get back to me on that one, but he did find a collaborator who wrote a grant application to NIH. It got a good score and would have been funded had it not been for sequestration.

CHAPTER 129 THE OPERATING AGREEMENT

PRESSURE ON Vladik to get documents out was relentless. The Operating Agreement needed completion before the money could come in from iUDx or any other client, and the money needed to come in before TTO would license the patents to Moby Dx. It was going to take months to get the money and the licensing agreements, but Max insisted that Vladik get the Operating Agreement out of the way before first meeting with iUDx.

The Operating Agreement locked in place many, but by no means all, of the verbal and hand written agreements Max and Vladik had been using since the meeting at Zott's. Its most important elements were self-governance and the pie.

About self-governance: the Operating Agreement named a full-time Managing Member, Vladik, and it created a non-governing Council, consisting initially of Max and Vladik. Normally there would be a board of directors or governors. The board is the CEO's boss, and sometimes more. Its chairman, not infrequently the CEO, manages the process of setting corporate goals. In its meetings, the board reviews the CEO's progress against those goals, advises the CEO about changes that should be made, and replaces the CEO if necessary by majority vote. The CEO likes to have and must cultivate allies on the board in order to stay in power. In addition to the CEO, the board appoints other officers, let's say a treasurer or a secretary, who together with the CEO are responsible for all the day-to-day activities of the company. The board will periodically review activities and operating procedures, to ensure that they are compliant with company bylaws.

HMRI didn't want its Principals having that kind of decisive management role in a company. It wanted its Principals investigating. So, it prohibited its Principals from sitting on boards. Max had felt cut out, and *had been* cut out of important decisions at Genormx because he wasn't on its board. His proxy, Dyk, had been tossed. Max wanted to be there, on the Moby Dx's governing board, but he had to appear to HMRI as if he wasn't. *Ergo*, the Council, the non-board. Dykkur wrote the Operating Agreement so that the Council was HMRI-compliant.

To understand the role of the Council, you must understand the role of the Managing Member. The Operating Agreement endowed the Managing Member, Vladik, with extraordinary powers. He did not need the Council's approval for anything, although the Operating Agreement suggested that it would be a good idea to review operations with the Council from time to time. The Council did not by itself have the power to remove the Managing Member, because if it were so endowed, it would have been a board, not a non-board. The Operating Agreement stated that the condition for removing the Managing Member was a vote of the majority of the shareholders of Moby Dx LLC, and a vote of the majority of the members of the Council. Max controlled Caselode Fittings I, he said, by a handshake with Sameer, making him the defacto majority shareholder in the LLC. All by himself he could decide on behalf of the shareholders to remove Vladik as Managing Member. The Council, comprised exclusively of Max and Vladik, would be deadlocked on this matter. Vladik retained absolute power over the LLC so long as only the two of them sat on the Council. If an ally of Max, let's say Dyk, was appointed to the Council, an appointment which, according to the Operating Agreement, would also require Vladik's consent, then the balance of power would shift, and Max would have absolute power, exercisable in an HMRI-compliant fashion through the alchemy of Caselode Fittings and the non-board Council Max wanted Dyk to sit on the Council so that he could fire Vladik whenever he felt like it.

Vladik was supposed to have been wowed and maybe cowed by Dyk, and to have agreed to have him appointed to the Council. But Vladik's strong allergic reaction to Dyk was the end of that plan, at least for the time being, thwarting Max's plottings.

Vladik knew, though, that even with all the power he had, he'd be exercising it in a vacuum if he and Max weren't in agreement. Max's reputation and commitment to the enterprise were essential to its advancement. Max could walk away from the company and still own all the stock because he'd gotten it in a grant without a vesting schedule; Vladik hadn't had the balls to put the kibosh on that in the final moments of their long, long negotiation at Zott's. He needed Max's support to get the deals that would bootstrap Moby Dx into the future. Formally though, he didn't need Max's votes. All of this meant he couldn't go around like a big swinging dick, acting independently of Max's wishes. He needed to run the company by himself and run the Council by consensus, and that's what he did.

About the pie, it was as they had agreed at Rossotti's; Vladik would take 12 percent, there'd be an option pool of 23 percent, and Max would take the balance of 65 percent, although by way of Dykkur's wizardry and CFI, it would look like he owned only a few percent of the company.

There was one other important element of the Operating Agreement, a statement that it superseded all other agreements. The only other agreement they'd had was one about how their salaries would be paid from revenue. In as much as the Operating Agreement was silent on this matter, and there were no new circumstances that would lead him to reconsider the wisdom of that agreement, and Vladik didn't need the Council's approval to make salary decisions, he planned to pay their salaries as they had previously agreed.

The Operating Agreement of course allowed for the appointment of various officers, but in a company with one employee, Vladik, it wasn't time to add any additional officers.

The Moby Dx LLC Operating Agreement was signed and dated by the members. Max Frood and Vladik K signed on behalf of themselves. Sameer (of the samosas) Barbozoo, Managing Member and 93 percent owner of Caselode Fittings I, signed on behalf of CFI. They put a valuation of $77 on the company. Although Max and Vladik had dreams of a $100 million or $300 million exit a few years into the future, $77 was a reasonable valuation at the time the Operating Agreement was signed because the company had no IP, no contracts, no revenue, and no other assets. It was a hollow shell weighted down by the $100k debt owed to the two cofounders. In exchange for their Membership interests, and in light of that valuation, the members wrote checks to the company in the amounts of $2, $12, and $63 respectively. The members completed their Internal Revenue Code Section 83(b) elections, and Vladik submitted the paperwork for all three to the IRS within the permitted thirty-day window, thereby starting their long-term capital gains clocks, so should it come to pass that their interests became liquid a year or more into the future, any appreciation would be taxed at the lowest possible rates. Vladik signed a three-year vesting agreement. Copies were made and distributed to all parties, plus a fourth one for Ph'eer, Dowd, and Sertantiy, Corporate Counsel to Moby Dx LLC.

CHAPTER 130 THE CALIBRATION

MAX, VLADIK, and Dyk, showed up at iUDx headquarters the next day. They were all in uniform; Max in his tattered red shirt, khakis, and tennies, Dyk in his fat-banker's rig, and Vladik in black suit sans tie, cotton button-down shirt open at the top, and black shoes.

The lobby screamed success, like an office high up in the Transamerica Pyramid. On one of the tastefully orange walls were Chuck Close inspired prints of the company's founders. Vladik looked at them more carefully and found not only were they Close-inspired, they were Close originals; oil-on canvas-paintings in his grid-over-photograph style. *Incredible. If they had money to burn on those, then our proposal is mouse nuts.* The receptionist, a would-be gallerina if the lobby had been in Manhattan, told them that Serena Fraguglia's associate Sapphonda would soon arrive and escort them to the conference room.

Max had insisted on several revisions of the deck. All Dyk had to say was, "Yeah, that's great." After some late night and early morning tweaks it was ready. Vladik had laid out a coarse script for the two of them to follow. He told Dyk, "Let's listen, and let's respect the twin sisters of brevity and clarity. We only need to ask questions if the answers will help us get the deal."

Sapphonda Koch, PhD, used her electronic badge to buzz them through the glass wall and walked them up two flights of stairs and into a kitchenette where they were offered water, coffee, 2Sweet sodas and iced teas loaded with iUDx's proprietary fat-burning sweetener, granola bars, and an opportunity to whack at the remains of a slab of birthday cake. From there she walked them through corridors where signs announced the St. Moritz Telepresence Room and Heaven's Doerr Auditorium, and past walls in blackboard and whiteboard paint and fresh scribblings of molecular structures.

"Excuse this," Sapphonda said, as she led them single-file beside workmen in white overalls who were undoing someone's vandalism to the entrance of the Kleiner Perkins Music Listening Room. The lettering in gold paint had been scratched through, as if with fingernails clawing for life, and new words had been scrawled on the door in what looked like blood. "We like to take things seriously here, but these guys overdid it a little," Sapphonda said. The vandals had written, Eine Kleine Perkins Kristallnacht Music.

Then they brushed by laminated posters describing cellular- and federal-regulatory processes, and iUDx org-charts, and posted announcements of scientific meetings long gone and yet to come, and 30"x40" technical posters already presented, and Investor-Relations-approved versions of the Corporate Goals. They got a few peeks into offices where the disease pathway posters on the walls and the content on the whiteboards revealed that staff had been doing real science. But they walked past not a single lab, because their route had been designed to avoid exactly that. Eventually they were escorted in to a conference room called Biomarkers.

"Serena asked me to ping her as soon as we're in. She'll be here in a sec."

Max and Serena greeted each other as professional colleagues. Serena and Vladik signed two copies of the NDA whose terms they'd agreed to by email. Then they all did introductions. Serena explained how Biomarker Group drove research in regulatory pathways that suggested new ways to quantify disease. If what they found was interesting enough, then it got passed off to Development Group, and from there into Trials Group and ultimately into Production Group. Sometimes, she said, Biomarkers had a chance to collaborate directly with Trials, and it was one particular trial then in progress that sparked her interest in Max's talk.

Vladik pondered this. Serena had put very narrow boundaries around the collaboration before their conversation had even begun. Their meeting was about this one thing and only this one thing, not because of a broad interest in the possibility of using cfRNA as a diagnostic.

Sapphonda said a few words too. A lovely Spanish woman, she had trained in Barcelona, done one postdoc at UCSF, then a second one at iUDx. She wore a simple gold band on her ring finger. A very disciplined woman, Vladik couldn't tell how much she'd open up without her boss in the room.

Then it was the team from Moby Dx's turn. Max said not more than ten words, and Vladik, thirty. Dyk took five minutes, saying too much about too little. Vladik shut him off when he ignited the projector and put up his first slide, his agenda, on which a live clock floated, transparent over the background; a hint if there ever was one.

Serena and Sapphonda asked some questions during the five-page presentation, a deck that began with a review of cfDNA history and concluded with my recent results. Sapphonda said she'd been waiting for years for a solution like this to emerge. What she was after couldn't be measured with specificity any other way. Serena wanted to know why I wasn't in the room with the men. Max reminded them that I was completing my postdoc and would consider joining the company later. Vladik asserted that the process would be transferred under the terms of the technology license, and that I would be involved as necessary.

Vladik put up a slide showing his proposal. He knew in advance it couldn't be right on the mark because he didn't know what they wanted, but he had to take a chance and present something. He proposed a two-step plan with the first one taking six months and costing about half a million dollars, and the second one eighteen months and two million dollars. He had included estimates of the number of samples to be run in each phase. There were suggestions about how the IP would be divided, based on what he believed they needed and wanted. There was a start date of six weeks in the future.

"It will take me a year to get authorization for $500,000," Serena said, and with that one sentence, with that one fact that might have been ... well, forget the might-have-beens. Vladik knew then and there, and maybe Max and Dyk knew, too, that the entire bootstrapping scheme was a phantasm.

In the parking lot, Max didn't want to take the time to distill down what had transpired. Hobbling into his car, he texted Vladik from the driver's seat, "Will talk later, MF."

Vladik instructed Dyk to write up a quote based on the reduced expectations Serena had given them and to have it out to him by email for review by close of business the next day.

What he got in his inbox was an email message with, more or less, Vladik's exact words. Did Dyk not know what a quote was? This was not some green kid out of business school. This was a very experienced guy expecting a big salary. Where were the terms for how long the quote was valid? Where was the company letterhead? Where were the representations and warranties and the terms of indemnification and reference to the NDA? In short, where was the quote?

Ten months later, after too much effort on our part, a contract for a $100,000 project of thirteen weeks duration was signed. There was no discussion of more later. I was on the team by then, and we were hopeful, because why not be hopeful? Our great work would lead them to start another larger project with us. That's what we wanted to believe, so we believed it.

Dyk had been relieved any responsibilities by then because he hadn't done anything useful. That was an easy matter procedurally because he'd never been hired, but it caused some friction with Max. Max, in fact, talked about Dyk as if he was one of the company's advisors. Vladik had written contracts with all the company advisors and he knew who they were. Dyk wasn't one of them. If he was giving Max advice, that was Max's problem. Max wanted Dyk rehabilitated in Vladik's mind. I knew Vladik's mind and there would be no rehabilitation.

CHAPTER 131 THE PIVOT

MAX CALLED Vladik later the same day.

"Heh."

"Change of plans, eh?"

"Short or long term?"

"Kinda both."

"Meaning?"

"There's no $100 million exit in three years if we don't have value. Clearly, we are not valuable today. How much value can we build if we can only get money to do development in dribs and drabs?"

"So your thinking is?"

"Gotta go to the well to build our own IR&D program, or go home."

"Ye of little faith."

"Max, my faith is strong, but faith is not a currency. It won't cut it if all we have is an idea, no results, and we can't get funded."

"Let's go to the well, then."

"And let's be clear about this. We'll put together our research program, fund it with money we'll raise, and we'll put an end to trying to be a contract research shop, you know."

"No. Do both."

"Is there in history an example of a company that succeeded in doing both?"

"No. Do both."

"You're kidding. There's so much precedent against it and only so many hours."

“That’s why you get paid the big bucks.”

“I don’t get paid, not without a revenue stream.”

“Take your salary and my fee out of the capital we raise. About those deals, do your best. Use Dyk.”

“Oy, Dyk,” and Vladik paused, waiting for Max, who didn’t bite. “I need an IR&D plan from you. We’ll crank out some grants. I’ll get a team together, starting with Lakshmi.”

“I’m not so sure.”

“I can’t think of anyone better.”

“You’re in love.”

“*Ha!*”

“I agree. She’s super fast in the lab. Just not sure she’s right for this one. She seems to want to work on something else.”

“Then we both have to work on her.”

Volume 5

N_{max}

CHAPTER 132 A POI

THE NSA, the CIA, and the FBI should all have picked up D5 as a POI, person of interest, but they missed her. They missed her because she was a spy, and one with better spy craft than they had. She played a very long game, a game that evolved so slowly no one saw it happening.

ALL those twenty-five years that D5 spent hosting English-speaking tourists in Macau and selling real estate to English-speaking customers in Shanghai left her with nearly perfect American English. Like Vladik, she could return to the sounds and accents of the native tongue on command. She did it to manipulate the conversation, make someone feel smart or stupid, or just bring on laughter.

One day not long after Arianna and Vladik had moved into the pool house, Arianna and D5 were working alone in the Rotunda. D5 said to her, impersonating the person-of-little-English she'd put on when she first met Max, "I see Vradik is wooking with Doctol Flaud."

Arianna laughed, yet didn't know how much she was being put on. "It's Frood, Wendy, Frood, not Fraud."

"That's wha I say. Doctol Flaud."

"Wendy? How do you know that?"

"News travers," she said. Then she got down on all fours and began romping and twerking, squealing and rooting like a pig, laughing and imitating a porcine sniffer. Arianna looked on, about to bust a gut with laughter. D5 rose up, and with her hands grasping an imaginary something in front of her, pumped her hips and her pelvis suggestively until Arianna begged her to stop.

"There were tapes." She winked, and Arianna did not ask for an explanation.

UNWITTING new owners of each Slabloid product assumed their handsome toy was as secure as Slab's advertising and product warranties claimed. For the most part, they were right; the Slab security team and the team working in secret at APT in Shanghai had engineered a tough-to-crack communicator. But Roxy Bird's code, the firmalware she had secreted on each and every device, was a security backdoor opened upon the decoding of a specially prepared image file.

When activated, the device became a secret slave to computer servers running APT's Snupy surveillance software on the sixteenth floor of 525 University Avenue. The enslaved slab could be instructed to log keystrokes, extract cookies, take screenshots, turn on cameras or microphones, or record phone calls or chat sessions, and provide time, date, and GPS stamps for each and every slug of data. First stored in a portion of the device's temporary memory where it hid in plain sight so obscurely as to be securely invisible even to curious folks with root access, the data was then cut up into very small chunks, inconspicuously sent out on top of other traffic as unlogged phone calls and email messages to Snupy, and then deleted. Reconstructed and encrypted within the servers, the messages were then stored on USB memory sticks, placed in a messenger bag, and in a well-rehearsed dance of operational security involving the exchange of pre-configured Rubik's cubes, the bag was swapped with an identical one over lunch with an actual messenger at Pluto's, or Gyro's, or Sprout, or Miyaki, or the Creamery, or Janta, or Darbar, or Jing-Jing, or Mango Caribbean, or another of downtown Palo Alto's dozens of dining establishments.

This low-tech, air-gapped, data transfer over sneaker-net made tracking transmissions to China all the more difficult for the agencies that should have been following this but were not. The messenger then traveled north to the Chinese Consulate in San Francisco's Japantown, and over a secure network the data was transmitted to a twelve-story white building in Pudong, the headquarters of Army Agency Tao 61398.

A few days of surveillance was often enough to capture credentials sufficient to access to email accounts and corporate databases, in which case instructions were sent back to APT and Snupy, and then to the compromised slab, and the collections and transmissions were discontinued. In other cases, in which information gleaned from the phone or tablet was considered of continuing value, collection went on for months, or even years.

HOSTING eclectic dinner parties at My Monticello, like those of her Shanghai Shalong, had been one of D5's dreams. An A-list event from the start, with the Jefferson-inspired setting, her remarkable personal story, and her locavorian catering, D5 soon had both print and online media anointing her as Queen of the Confucian Chow Fête. From there, the Martian Road Salon soon went elite-list.

Its sixty or so guests were as celestial as the name MRS implied, including local heroes like Joan Baez, political figures like George Schultz, and financial titans like Venus Khlobama and Bill Gates, not to mention already-made and up-and-coming CEOs, ballerinas, opera singers, sculptors, academicians, dissidents, and journalists of note; although what transpired at MRS was strictly off the record. While the salon was held at D5's home and its Chinese progenitor was held at a hotel, the format of new was the same as the old. Each month there was a special topic. A luminary spoke for a few minutes, perhaps taking the time to introduce extra special guests, and for the next two hours there was ceaseless milling, networking, eating, drinking, Arianna's guided tours of D5's collections, and of course discussion of the salon topic. At the two-hour mark, order was called and D5 announced details of the next event. Although few in attendance would be invited to the one that followed, guests were keen to know anyway. Part of D5's plan was to keep the crowd fresh and increase the reach of her network, so back-to-back repeat invitations were rare.

Befitting such a special event, D5 always set up a small photo studio, sometimes inside, sometimes out, depending on the weather. Outfitted with slaved strobes on umbrella'd tripods, an array of backdrops to create different moods, and with the latest in lenses and camera gadgetry, the studio was run by her comely photographer, Avedonis. Alone, with D5, with other guests, with props or without, Avedonis created exhibition-grade mementos for her guests. As subjects left studio, one of Avedonis' assistants, and he had several, handed each guest a business card with the web address of a flickr account devoted to the MRS and a unique password for getting into it.

Two years after D5 had taken possession of the property, the MRS had become the "It" event of the Northern California elite. The photographs, in which Avedonis so tellingly and forgivingly revealed character, and flatteringly projected grace, went a long way to making it so.

FOR the busy people who attended these functions, it was easy enough to forget to log on to flickr to view photos. But we are a vain species and Avedonis' images were remarkable. And where vanity wasn't enough, Avedonis' assistants sent reminders and promises of gifts of framed prints by email, SMS, and private messaging services, and these usually sufficed to entice the guest to log on to the website. Without the password, they'd find thumbnails of the public images of the event. With the password, they'd gain access to private images the photographer had curated specifically for the guest.

By convention of the joint photographic experts group, or JPEG, such image files usually begin with a short slug of data providing details on how the bulk of the data is organized. That slug is called the header. Private images from the MRS contained an encrypted payload within the header. If the device being used was a laptop, then the image opened normally. If the device happened to be a Slab42 or Slab97, as was increasingly likely given their market dominance, then Roxy Bird's firmalware decrypted the payload, activating the Snupy client in the slab. Thus, the device's owner became an unwitting agent of the People's Liberation Army. At that point, the only safe place for a victim to hide his or her data from D5's team was in a wheel of stinky cheese.

There was some slop in this system; not every guest owning a Slab was ensnared right away. The reluctant received phone calls from D5's minions, following up with surveys, invitations to other events, and inquiries as to whether the guest had seen his or her most flattering portrait. The system was conceived to elude detection at all costs, not to achieve 100 percent capture at any cost.

CHAPTER 133 G'S SPOT

WHEN HAD I started calling Georgina G? It was before she had moved out of her depressing cellblock of a studio apartment in Mountain View and into the cottage behind what we called the Big House in Palo Alto.

I had been a frequent visitor, first at the cellblock and then at the cottage, but only a visitor. I continued to maintain my own residence, a remodeled shed on a decaying horse property not far from Lobitos Farm. That place was close enough to work that Louisa and I were able to take a nooner there sometimes. Other than proximity, there was little else to recommend it for a city girl like me.

The Big House was a rambling one-story home, its exterior painted in the faded lime green of 1970s interiors, and its interior in whatever colors inspired the itinerant tenants. The neighborhood was full of the clank and whine of demolition and construction, projects of a magnitude that could only be properly appreciated by flying over them. Small quadcopters with cameras filled that need, and construction workers would occasionally shoot them down with gas-powered rifles to protect an owner's privacy.

G's spot in the back was sheltered from much of the street noise, and had the advantage of being self-contained. She shared no bathroom with barely-potty-trained undergraduates and no kitchen with kids who had never learned to wash a dish.

"Nice spot," I told her on the first morning after. I lounged in a tattered but comfortable chair while she laid spread eagled on the bed in the morning sunshine.

"It's cheap because I'm renting month-to-month," she explained.

"Cheap in Palo Alto is still not cheap when you're waiting tables."

"It's closer to work, though," G said.

"It's kind of boring, though, if you don't have kids, don't you think?"

"I like boring, for now," she said, summoning me again to her bed. I hoped her remark was no reflection on me.

BRONZE hair in long luscious tresses rained down on her shoulders to frame her pale rouged face. Her eyes shown like the blue corals of Gili Trawangan. Georgina had a serious look about her, with lips usually closed, even if her mouth was spread wide with pleasure. Occasionally, she'd show me her teeth, and while they were good by standards of the former Soviet republics, she was insecure about them in Silicon Valley where the latest in orthodontia is a prerequisite. In that sequined dress she wore when I met her, or in glorious red satin one with a wide-open neck that revealed the uncontainable upward heave of her breasts, she was a breathtaking beauty. Without a line on that classic Russian face, G could have passed for someone five years her junior, someone my age.

She had two master's degrees, one in cybernetics and one in international relations, both from the Taras Shevchenko National University of Kyiv. She fled for Silicon Valley on an internship with a company that turned out to be a front for slave traders. After escaping their clutches, and as a person seeking asylum, she secured a green card from Citizen and Immigration Services. She was enterprising, trying to find a way to parlay her post-graduate degrees, her fluency in four languages, and her KGB agent's agility into prosperity. She didn't seek riches necessarily, but prosperity, the American dream. The job application process wasn't going well.

"Thirty is the new fifty here."

"I thought it was the other way around," I said.

"With all the software companies hiring like mad, you'd think that I could find a job worthy of my degree." She paused before correcting herself, "Degrees. They look at me like I'm over the hill because I'm thirty-one and I don't have six years of experience with NOSQL, or whatever."

I let it pass that I had never heard of NOSQL.

"The hiring managers will never say it, but if you're over thirty and unemployed for more than two weeks, unless you've invented RSS, in which case they interpret the extended break as a lifestyle choice, you'll never get hired again as a developer, or at least not at a living wage."

I did know something about RSS. "So you're talking about age discrimination?"

"That's what I *said*. Thirty is the new fifty. A new vector of youth obsession. All these schemes to make you seem young," she said, exasperated.

I began listing them. "Died hair, hair removal, hair implants, Botox, breast lifts, face lifts, Spanx, testosterone injections."

"That's just the physical side. The kids are so fast, so agile with code, you need a video game tutor to get through the new job interviews, and you'd better be profiling your declining mental acuity—."

"Declining? You're barely thirty."

"I'm telling you, it's noticeable in the coding world. There's an app for that."

"And then another app to close the gaps?"

"Another app? Another coach! Half the boom in Silicon Valley must be in coaches for the few who have real jobs."

"Or their kids?"

"Not my sphere," Georgina said. "I don't see what's going on there. But we're way beyond personal crossfit trainers. There's a whole industry built around coaching people just for Burning Man. Costume coaches. Playa outfitters to prepare your camp for you, build your playa art for you—"

"I didn't guess you're a burner."

"I'm not. How could I afford that? But you hear so much about it from the hiring managers at these places I interview. It's one more thing I need on my resume."

Burning Man attendance on your resume. I let that sink in.

G went on. "The second tier salaries here, for the part-time work, the grunty stuff, I could live on those salaries in Kyiv. But they don't pay those wages in Ukraine. And maybe they wouldn't hire me there, either. There's no shortage of hungry engineers in Kyiv. Anyway, I'm not going back."

"Bioinformatics?" I suggested.

"Another specialization for me to learn? I don't think so. I can't afford it. So many of the girls at the Rosewood are cougars or hookers, the men over tip me because I am what I seem. I may be pumping them for a job idea, but not for money or a ring." Then she told me more about the Pipeline.

"There are these girls from the FSR who came just to get divorced," she explained. "They allowed themselves to be found on Vlagalishe Kontacte,"—

"That's the V in VKontacte?"

"No. It's obscene slang, mat. It's the V," and she grabbed her crotch, "the cunt hounds trolling VK are after." After a moment's pause, she went on, "So, these women have been reading blogs about how to fish for, date, and marry an American. They allowed themselves to be found on VK by some *mudák*—"

Here I didn't interrupt her, but waited until later to learn that a *mudák is a* castrated piglet according to Wikipedia, but I think she intended it to mean schlub.

"—no self-respecting Bulgarian girl would even talk to at home. Meanwhile, he's been following blogs about how to fish for, date, and marry a tall beautiful girl who'd be utterly dependent on him. They marry. He's plotting containment from the start, and she's plotting upward mobility. It's not a fair contest.

"Once she's here, she finds the kind of guy she's really after in the first place. The first guy, her husband, she washes the floor with him and his pathetic jealousies and insecurities. The second one, the eligible Silicon Valley millionaire, the guy she meets at the Rosewood? She milks him for as much as and as long as she wants. Single or married, he's happy to have an affair without commitment, he thinks, until she shows him what a Ukrainian girl—or a Latvian, a Romanian, an Estonian, and forget a Georgian—is made of."

The look she shot me made my knickers wet.

"Once he's learned that American women are men with boobs, or at least the straight ones are, all resistance is futile, and she marries up."

G could have married one of those guys. She'd have been a good wife, too, but she was hungry for women, and that would, she told me, be the wedge issue. For the moment, she was fine being single.

Eventually we were roomies at G's spot, lovers but never a couple.

CHAPTER 134 MY CALL

IT WAS still dark when I called my mother from bed.

"Hi, Rani. How are you, Dearheart?"

"I'm fine Ammaji, and you?"

"We just finished dinner, your Appa and me."

"I miss you Amma. I wanted you to know that I love you."

"Something sounds off, Rani. You are always the upbeat one. Now you sound like you need me to help you. Tell me, Rani. What is it?"

"Melancholia, Amma."

Silence. She knew to wait for me.

"My work is stuck. Max doesn't really believe in what I'm doing."

"Your new assay?"

"Yes, for infectious disease. I think it's important for so many people, I can't let it go."

More silence. More patient listening from her.

"He wants me to join his company, but I don't believe in what they're doing."

She knew that if she gave me another chance, I would break the spell on my own. She said nothing, still. Seeing her brown sweet face smiling back at me on the little screen was all I really wanted from that call.

"Maybe the clouds will lift later. That's what it feels like. The clouds seem to lift and then the world is different."

"Chellam, you need a husband and something to eat."

I laughed.

"Amma. I don't need a husband, but maybe you are right, I need something to eat. Tell me about my sister."

"Oh, she's as busy as a little ant, and as troublesome, too. Why don't you talk to her yourself? She *is* your sister, Rani!"

"I do talk to her, Amma. I just wanted to hear it from you."

"Dhaya and I have been out shopping all day. The trade union strikes, the bandhs, you know. There will be another one tomorrow, nationwide, a bharat bandh. The BMTC is shutting down. The trades want us all off the roads. We will just stay in and watch cricket if we don't lose power."

"Do you have enough food Amma?"

"Rani, you talk to me like I live in some third world city. What do you think this is, New Orleans?" Mamma loved to say this to me. We both laughed. She thought it was funny, genuinely funny, and for me it was like eating comfort food, you know, curd rice or something. "Of course we have plenty of food."

I was about to tell her that I would get up and have some breakfast when she said, "Rani, there is a delivery. Your sister says she is too important to take it. May I go and then call you back later?"

"Amma, yes. That's fine. We'll talk in a day or two. I love you. Give my love to Appa, too."

"Bye-bye, Pattu. Feel better, Rani. I love you, too, Rani."

We waved to sign off and then we clicked that little red icon.

CHAPTER 135 APPA'S CALL

THE NEXT morning, while I was still asleep and it was still dark, my little Slab42 rang. Caller id read Home. Nobody ever called me from Home. It was my father.

"Hello?" I said.

"Rani?" my father's voice cracked.

"Daddy! What's wrong? Something's wrong."

"Mamma," and he broke down sobbing as I'd never ever heard him sob.

"Daddy! You're scaring me. What's happened?"

He passed the phone to Dhaya, my little sister, and she told me the story in one stream, interrupted only by choking sorrow.

"Although she probably hadn't said anything to you, Amma's stomach had been upset all day before you called her. Dinner only made it worse. By nine o'clock she was on the floor in her bathroom, on some blankets, vomiting and sleeping. She wouldn't let Appa sit with her, but he went in to check on her every hour or so. At four in the morning he was sleeping when she called to him. It was a voice we'd never heard from her; possessed, terrified. 'Izzie!'

"I woke up. The servants woke up. It was scary. I thought I was hearing the voice of death. We bundled her into the car, even though we weren't supposed to be on the roads because of the bandh, and we took her to RxDx, the little clinic nearby, you know what I'm talking about? The strikers, and their hateful urchin children threw stones at us like we were criminals. We were taking a dying woman to the hospital for God's sake!"

"Dying! What are you saying, Rani?" We called each other Rani in our most unguarded moments together."

Dhaya continued. "She looked terrible, first hot, then cold, like she had malaria or something. At RxDx, they said she was in shock and they couldn't treat her properly there. Shock! Why would she be in shock? Rani. *We* were in shock! And we had to get her to Manipal Hospital right away. I called six ambulances before one of them, Yashawini, finally agreed to come. And by the time Amma was loaded in on a stretcher, the strike was in full force and the roads were blocked.

"Appa was in the ambulance with her. The med techs didn't want him there, until he shoved five hundred rupees at them and they changed their minds. We were in our car behind them. The ambulance had its siren on, but the trade unionists and the beggars were pummeling us. To them it must have felt like Diwali or something. It was stop-and-go, driving like five kilometres per hour. We kept texting back and forth until the phone network went down at ten o'clock. The ambulance driver leaned his head out of the car and shouted at the crowd, 'A woman is dying. A mother. A wife. Get out of the way you fleas, you ratbags, you *thevidiya pundai vervai'la molacha kaalaan*.' Too awful, the things he said. He did his job Lakshmi. He did his job. We were so scared, and all crying, so powerless. It made me hate India. I am sorry, but it did.

"We didn't dare get out to talk to Dad, to find out what was happening. The crowds were too scary. We thought we'd get separated, or worse. We made a little progress after that, and then it was more of the same. The ambulance driver shouted the same, or better, again. And then more again. Again, more of the same. The phones came back on. Dad texted that Mamma's blood pressure was ominously low. At noon, the ambulance driver turned off his siren. He and Dad got out of the ambulance and walked over to us."

Dhaya couldn't talk. I couldn't ask. The line was silent for a minute, before she continued.

"Mamma's dead! Septic shock, they said, whatever that means. Then we turned the cars around and drove home, if you can call that driving." She could not finish the words she started, "I'm so sorry, Lakshmi."

CHAPTER 136 ALL-IN

WHATEVER I was going to say had been said. Whatever I'd held back, it was too late. Naija Ramachandran Stein had had one last chance to be Amma, and she did it. She was very good at it. Where was the air I used to breathe?

There was nothing I could do except go home, or where my parents had been living. It had been home for her, but her parents were gone, too, and her siblings dispersed. It wasn't home, but it's where I had to go.

I made flight arrangements before breakfast, but I couldn't eat anyway. Then I called my closest friends; Louisa, Georgina, Vladik, Max. I tried to drain all the emotion out of my voice, not that this was some matter-of-fact conversation, but just to help me get through it. It only worked for Max, whom I couldn't reach. The girls told me they loved me and wanted to see me if I had time before I left. They were kind and sweet and tearful, too, but couldn't find much to say. Vladik made me come over to their pool house immediately. I'd never seen it. Arianna wept with me and stroked my hair. She knew exactly what to say: very, very little. What was there to say? That she didn't suffer long? Should that be a consolation?

Vladik made me lunch and then walked me around the grounds. I told him some of the things I had told my mother the day before, if what seemed impossibly out of reach could have been only the day before, about being frustrated at work. He explained what they'd learned at iUDx, and that plans were changing at Moby Dx. Bootstrapping was out and they were going to need to set up a lab as soon as possible. "There's not going to be anyone better than you for this."

"It's flattering that you think that and can say that to me. At the same time, you know how I feel about it. I think you're going to crash and iUDx is just the first shot over your bow."

"You mean the fact that they want to give us money makes you think we're going to fail?"

"I think if the world's most sophisticated diagnostics company thinks that the application is very narrow, you're going to need heaps of time and money to prove otherwise. Unless you have both, you're going to run out of one of them before the world believes you. That's what I think."

Before I left to go up and over the hill to get ready for the next day's flight, Arianna told me she'd have her driver take me to the airport, and pick me up whenever I returned. That would be one less thing to worry about.

I met Max in his office at the I. He was actually a little consoling. When I broke down, it made him very uncomfortable and all he could do was politely hand me some tissues, hoping, I guess, that I would stop crying soon.

We talked about careers and their defining moments. He gave me his full attention and put on the unabridged professorial manner. My work in infectious disease couldn't save my mother, but if I really believed in it, he said, I should put myself behind it in a company. "A broad spectrum diagnostic for infectious disease would be a breakthrough in medicine." And then he gave the concept a name, and an owner. "No one is going to make BroadID real faster than you, because you're you and because it's yours." He winked and let that sink in. The wink's meaning was almost clear.

"I know I haven't been terribly enthusiastic about the commercial potential of your project. Maybe there's a way to fold it into Moby Dx and we can scratch each other's back. We have to run some material and strengthen the business case. Vladik's got to get a lab up. He has already asked me to help persuade you to join us. How about if Moby Dx takes a license to our ID portfolio and you can work on both? You're in a unique position. It's rare to get one chance in a lifetime to take an idea from invention all the way to market. You'll be able to do that with two inventions if you jump in with us."

My mother—the thought stopped there. Even to myself I could say so little. My head hung. I felt weak. I couldn't cry in front of Max again, and I didn't think it would pay to sit on this decision while I was in Bangalore. "I'm all in," I told Max. "Start the paperwork, will you?"

While I was gone, I had only one email exchange with him. I felt bad, as in guilty, being concerned with such things when I had so many real life concerns at home, but this floated to consciousness and wouldn't go away.

"Max," I wrote, "we haven't talked at all about the terms of my employment. What's the process for that?"

"We'll take care of it later, after the company's formation documents are in order."

CHAPTER 137 ALL-IN-ONE

A SOCIAL MEDIA start-up or a company making slab apps can launch and thrive for months in a café. You need a laptop and that's about it. The list of things you no longer need is amazingly long. Most importantly, you don't need racks of servers or a rich uncle. Who needs real servers when you can have virtual machines? What you need is energy, chutzpah, Internet access, and the coding and design brilliance that leads you to a unique and appealing mix of features in a field where a dozen or more teams of kids—thirty is the new fifty, after all—are already trying to do the same thing. You can make this happen in a café whose Wi-Fi connects to cloudspace where your slices of server sit. You can try out an idea, modify it, abandon it if it stinks, or advance it if there's traction. When you need more permanent resources, or you need more bandwidth, or some privacy, you can rent a few cubicles at an incubator or accelerator like Plug And Play, KickLabs, Rocket, or SOMAcentral. As long as you and your staff can work for free, you need very little capital to get started or keep going.

On the other hand, if you're a life sciences startup and you need centrifuges, autoclaves, -80 °C freezers, fume hoods, chemical resistant lab benches, chemical safety management, and waste removal, sinks, and distilled water supplies—to make a short list—then you're in meatspace where few of the startup options don't begin with assembling a pile of cash. One of them is to outsource all the moby and sequencing to a CRO, a contract research organization, and try to make it as a data and ideas company. For Moby Dx, a company committed to assaying blood, that wouldn't work. It needed stuff, or at least that's what I was told when I got back from Bangalore, and the company needed a place to house and operate all that stuff, and of course, staff to operate it too.

Vladik's earlier attempt to find office space had led him to a unique property near Genormx on the other side of Highway 101. It was a life sciences incubator space the owner called All-In-One. Its occupants called it All-In. At the time Vladik didn't need that kind of space, but his needs had changed.

In the Bay Area there are only three biotech incubators I know of, so, including the ones I don't know of, there's a small handful at most. There is no template for space like that, and each is different. All-In's business model grew out of former fashion model and Russian Academician Paula Allinakova's observation, made in the early 1990s, that the almost inevitable demise of most life sciences companies meant that the millions of dollars they'd invested in equipment would come onto the market for something between free and pennies on the dollar. She reasoned that if she could collect enough of the free equipment in one place to make it attractive to other life sciences companies, she could sublease parcels of the outfitted space at a rate that worked for tenants and paid for her own research. Even a very high monthly rate would work for many of the life sciences startups because they wouldn't have to lay out wads of cash for the benches and all the other stuff.

When Vladik had first visited, there were fifteen companies performing all sorts of work, the scope of which Paula asked me not to discuss here, so I won't, especially not ██████.

CHAPTER 138 THE BUDGET

MOBY Dx also needed staff, paid staff, in addition to stuff. Biotechies, unlike software engineers, are not used to working for free for very long. If they're any good, they've got offers at big life sciences companies. But isn't it true that software engineers have offers at, well, a dozen places from Akamai to Zynga? I think it's a cultural difference, and with the demand for software engineers having risen to new heights thanks to the successes of Google, Facebook, and others, working for free may be a thing of the past.

Vladik tried to figure out what positions the company needed to fill. He drew an org-chart that had the effect of making his scribblings look official. At first it would be simple. In addition to me, we'd need a tech so I could be more productive, and a bioinformatician to handle whatever CS and IT problems I couldn't handle myself. Figuring dirtbag salaries for the four of us, we'd need $35,000 per month. Add 20 percent for taxes and healthcare, and that made $42,000.

Our lab and office space at All-In would be crazy expensive at $8500, so we needed $50,000 per month to cover staff and space. Then we'd need to pay advisors, buy reagents and supplies, book some airline tickets and conference passes, etc., and in a flash, the monthly burn rate ran up to $80,000, or $1M per year.

Vladik called Max.

"I sketched out the expenses."

"Let me guess. A million dollars a year."

"That's the basic unit, eh?"

"Always."

"We should raise $2.5 million. What do you think?"

"Two years with a little runway."

"And upside from grants and some contracts."

"Heh, can you give me a second?" Max put Vladik on hold to take a call from somewhere, than came back a minute later.

"OK, where were we? Oh, right, grants and contracts. Yeah."

"Debt or equity?"

"Debt if we can get it. We should try that first."

"I'm going back to those bankers we met in New York City."

"You do that. I've got friends here. Go talk to Dykkur about writing up terms for a convertible note."

CHAPTER 139 THE NOTE

WHEN YOU raise money for a startup company, you can borrow it, that's debt, or you can sell part of the company in exchange for it, that's equity. From the founders' point of view, debt is good because they don't have to give up ownership. Giving up ownership at the beginning stinks because when you're just starting out, it's not apparent you're worth very much, so you have to serve up large portions of equity for relatively small amounts of cash. On the other hand, with debt, you have to pay it back, so that's bad, especially if you don't have the revenue, and startups most often don't have it. From the investor's point of view, equity is preferred because it allows you to share in the long-term value the company creates with the money you've invested. On the other hand, equity investors go bust with the company if it fails, whereas debt investors would be first in line to get the company's remaining assets, if there were any. A hybrid is the convertible note, a debt that converts to equity in the future if certain milestones are met. There is no right and wrong, but I think convertible notes are for suckers.

Imagine your goal is to invest the first $2.5 million in Moby Dx in exchange for some equity ownership. At the time of the investment, the company has two founders, one of whom works full-time and the other, a certifiable genius, is an advisor, whatever that means. The company is in the process of licensing some patent applications the genius has assigned to his or her parent institution, and it has grand commercialization plans. The company also plans to hire a full-time technologist who trained with the genius and who has her name on the patent applications. How much is the company worth?

My rule of thumb, Lakshmi's Law, is that, absent any more information, the company is worth twice what it can raise. For example, if the founders can raise $1 million, then their company is worth $2 million before the money is invested, and $3 million afterward. If the founders have a great track record, or if the market they're targeting is very hot and they have a great story to tell about that market and about the team they'll soon be hiring, then the company might be worth three times or even four times the money raised. If, on the other hand, the founders have a so-so track record, or the market they're going after isn't faddish, or the economy is in the tank, then the company might be worth only as much as it's raising, or (God forbid!) even less.

Let's suppose that Lakshmi's Law applied to Moby Dx. With $2.5 million raised, the company is valued at $5 million before or $7.5 million after the money went in. The investors would own a third of it for their trouble.

One third for only $2.5 million! "Highway robbery," say the entrepreneurs. "Dude, it's too early to put a value on the company. How about if you lend us the $2.5 million at slightly above market rates of interest, and we'll get working? We're going to need to raise more money later, and when we do, you can convert your debt into equity on slightly better terms than the new investors. What a bargain for you!"

"Whoa, Dude! What kind of a fool do you think I am?" replies the investor. "I'm offering to put $2.5 million into an enterprise I think is worth $5 million, and one I expect to be worth $15 million in two years as a result of that $2.5 million having been put to good use by you. You want me to put it in today at a slight discount to a $15 million valuation, so maybe $12 million? You can't get to the future without me, but you want me pay for my slice as if you've already done the work. As I say, what kind of fool do you take me for?"

If it's so clear-cut that convertible notes are for fools, why are they so very widely used? The answer is that investors, like lovers, can get carried away and will make investments that are not, on the face of it, rational. Perhaps there is some star status in the founder and the investor hopes it will rub off on him. Perhaps the founder is a friend and the investor will accept less than market returns just because. Or perhaps the founder is family and, sharing many more genes than two unrelated parties, the investor sees the below market rate investment as a means to propagate those genes. These, Dear Reader, are among the reasons convertible notes are in use.

So, Vladik talked to Dykkur Ph'eer about a term sheet, that is, a short, plain English document that conveyed the intent of the sought-after terms to prospective investors. The two men discussed interest rates, discount rates, expiration of the investment, when the investment period would close, limits on funds raised, defaults, automatic and optional conversions, and caps, a cap being an investor-friendly term placing a maximum valuation on the conversion. Eventually, many hours and many dollars in deferred fees later, they had a term sheet to show Max, who accepted it without edits.

CHAPTER 140 MY SLICE OF THE PIE

On the day before Venus Khlobama's annual event called the Night of the Luminosities, the paperwork suspending my appointment at the I came through. Max summoned me to his office.

He slid the papers in front of me.

Then he handed me a plain cream envelope worthy of a wedding. In it was an iridescent invitation to Venus' party.

Max was going, of course.

"Would you like to join me?"

"Laks and Max? Our second date!" I said.

"No, as my professional colleague and business partner, now that you're an employee of Moby Dx?"

"I'm not an employee yet."

"Let's not go there, now. Venus called me and says she knows you. She instructed me, *instructed me,* to bring you along. How the hell do you know Venus?" he asked me.

"I met her at the Rosewood. She was with my old friend, Al Gore. Max—"

"How the hell do you know Gore?"

"It's nothing. An accident. But Max, asking me if I wanted to go, without first telling me that she'd called to invite me, that's obtuse, even for you."

Max ignored my accusation. "Well, whatever you said or did at the Rosewood, she wants more of it."

I wasn't a Moby Dx employee yet. I still had two more weeks to clean up my work at Lobitos Farm. There was no employment offer letter and no equity agreement. Max had been in Rhizobia, and he told me to work out the arrangements with Vladik.

Vladik was improvising.

"We're trying to raise money, I guess you know, that. The company is incorporated, but stock hasn't been issued. The founding documents are still being written. So, whatever agreement we have, it will be based on a handshake."

"Greaaat," I said with as much exaggeration as I could summon. "I can't quit my job at the I and then not have a salary. Are you expecting me to go without pay until you raise money?"

"No, I'm not. What's your salary at the I?"

"Twenty-nine hundred a month."

"You're joking."

Silence.

"I guess you're not. An entry level position in biopharma for someone like you would be about $12,000—"

I cut him off. "$13,000 at least because of my informatics background. I checked salary.com"

"OK, $13,000. We can offer you $8,000. That's still $5,000 more than you're making now."

"$10,000 and ten percent bonus if—"

"—if we raise the full $2.5 million," Vladik finished my sentence for me.

"And equity?"

"Max and I would like to offer you 1 percent of the company."

"Now you're joking, right?"

"We could go to 1.5 percent."

"You're still joking. The whole company is based on my work, and I'm going to be the one making it happen. The BroadID technology isn't something Max even wanted, and it really should be in a separate company."

"Backup. What is BroadID?"

"Max didn't discuss this with you?"

"Didn't discuss what with me?"

My head hung down in exasperation, my forehead on my right hand. I was too young, I thought, to have wrinkles forming there.

"I agreed to join when Max said we'd license in my infectious disease portfolio, and I'd, somehow, work on both at once. I should be getting at least 10 percent."

"Max and I never talked about it." Vladik massaged his forehead with this right hand, too. "This is—"

"—fucked in so many ways," I finished.

"Shall we count them?"

"One: Max made and acted on a strategic decision without talking to you, cofounder and full-time CEO."

"Two: Your 10 percent share, which seems fair, would eat up almost half of all the available equity in the company."

"Now I'm guessing, three: your $2.5 million budget was for one IR&D program not two."

"Of course, and four: a startup with two programs is a startup that hasn't decided what it wants to be. These are both great ideas, but two at once is too much. Anyone looking at it from the outside would say its crazy."

"Yes, this is crazy. I just quit my job for something crazy."

"We can pay your salary, so that's not a problem. It's the equity that's a problem."

"How did you and Max divide it up?"

"Max gets 65 percent and I get 12 percent. The rest is set aside for options."

"No."

"Yes."

"That's just wrong. Why did you agree to it?"

"I get something else out of it other than equity. I get to surf Max's breaking wave. When I ride it out, I'll have a successful enterprise behind me, and I can build off of that forever, serial entrepreneur and all that. I thought that was worth more than fighting him to the point he might walk away."

"I see that. But doesn't it bug you?"

"It bothers me more that he's making these decisions behind my back."

"That's bad. And I'll tell you what. It's also par. But here's something good. Now we have one good technology in the company. If we ignore MOST, maybe it will go away."

"I'm not there yet."

"You'll get there. Just wait."

"I can start paying you right away. That's real. The equity, that won't become real until we have an option plan, so can we agree on best effort north of 5 percent? I can't promise to deliver ten but I can promise five."

"I'll get used to it."

"You're going to Khlobama's party tonight?"

"Yes. Venus asked for me, through Max. I guess it was the Rosewood. You?"

"No way. I'm nothing to someone like her. D5 is going and she asked that Arianna and I join her, but we want to avoid any contact with Max. You should dress to the nines and raise some money tonight."

"Should I wear my brainy glasses, too, or my contacts?"

"You've already seduced her, so emphasize brains and make sure she knows you're The Talent. It will make a difference."

CHAPTER 141 VENUS MAXIMUS

I HAD ASKED Max, when he had asked me to join him, what it was I was joining him at, this Night of the Luminosities, and all he would say was, "Venus Maximus? If there were words, they would be 'multivalent performing arts circus,' but there are no words. Dress to kill."

It was not quite dusk when I arrived at a guarded gate. A very tall, perfectly complected South Asian of ambiguous gender and strong mellifluous voice, checked my credentials, and indicated to someone that she should park my car. The eunuch introduced himself as Marlowe. "How luminous you look tonight. I see this is your first visit to the Luminosities. Welcome home!" He lifted me up in a bear hug to end all bear hugs, crushing me against the white flokati overcoat he wore over nothing at all, and then he put me back on the ground. "Your date is already here—"

"Date?"

"I mean Venus!" and he bent over laughing. Before I could get his attention. "Just kidding. Venus is everyone's date tonight. Your friend Max is here, but he's not your type, is he?" Then he doubled over again, sending huge volumes of high soprano laughter into the sky the way only a eunuch can do. "I'll be your guide for as long as you need me, and can escort you to him whenever."

Then he signaled for me to follow him to a vintage fighter plane sitting atop a mutant golf cart. The smoke belching from its faux gas engines was born of medicinal grade Mendocino Madness.

Half a mile up the hill we disembarked in front of a sculpture of a runner that could only have been Venus in *her* prime. Forty-feet or more from ankle to forehead, a slowly changing light show illuminating her lightweight wire mesh skin from within. The anatomically correct woman bolted out of starting blocks in a position that could not possibly balance, and yet it did. She was brazenly naked: shamelessly, proudly naked. The force of her acceleration, revealed in defined muscles, blew her hair back, flying. Venus Maximus reminded me of David, Michelangelo's David, a giant beauty of a man, deep in concentration and ready for a fight, with nothing between him and nature. Standing there, Marlowe beside me, I began to absorb the scene.

Venus Khlobama's house in the town of Portola Valley looked down into the actual valley whose west side was Windy Hill, the popular public park with footpaths leading to Skyline Boulevard. Her fifty-three acres backed up against a land preserve protected by the State of California. Traffic nearby was sparse. The hilltop estate was serenity augmented by $51 million of construction. There was a 48,000 square foot sprawl of simultaneously acclaimed and derided Internationalist School architecture in eighteen individual buildings and another 20,000 square feet of rusting warehouse called The Incubator. Who knew how much more had gone into the art collection? It all continued to grow out, up, and down below ground.

Venus stayed there all alone, but for her live-in crew of nineteen, as she allowed herself one additional staff member for every building, and an always changing community of twenty or so young men and women between the ages of eighteen and thirty-two whom she called her sherpas.

Sherpas? When asked, she laughed and said only this, "My private joke. Even someone like me is owed a little privacy, don't you think? Would you rather I call them my harem? Then you'd think you know what that meant, but you wouldn't. I prefer to keep it my private joke," and then she invariably broke into near hysterical laughter until one of them came over to share her amusement and calm her down.

The sherpas weren't really staff, as they seemed to have lives independent of her property. They were, how should I say it? Entertainers? Pets? Most of them were dancers, musicians, circus types, and DIYers. A few were fine artists and actors, and all of them, universally, were eye candy. When she had guests, as she did most evenings, one or two from the harem would perform, maybe, either as ambience or with the full attention of Venus and entourage.

And why was this night, her Night of the Luminosities, different from all other nights? The sherpas and dozens of their friends were out in force, shticking[1], mixing, dipping, or even double-dipping with Venus, the staff, and the guests, in the amphitheater, on portable outdoor stages, permanent indoor stages, in the fountains, on the grass, and in strange—there is no other word for it—exotically lit, music-blasting, fire-belching, roving sculptures everyone referred to as Art Cars.

The guest list was Venus' handpicked selection of venture capital celebrities. Some had IPO'd. Some were IPO'ing, they hoped. Some were her investor friends. Some were the bankers. There was a lawyer or two who'd helped key deals go through. There were advisors, influential consultants and writers on energy and healthcare, academics, and politicians. Some were old (hands) and some were new (comers). Unlike the actual world they inhabited, the guests were men and women in equal numbers.

1 Even a full blooded Tamilian can learn a few Yiddishisms if her father's name is Isador Stein.

The sherpas showed more flesh than anyone else dared, but experienced guests strived to arrive in something more provocative than their everyday attire, and everyone, once they were so well lubricated as to be frictionless, took advantage of a costumerie on the premises. National celebrities dropped their evening gowns to the grass, and in their underthings they rummaged through racks and mounds of leopard-print tights, tutus, see-through vests, or long overcoats of white wool or black leather to be worn over not much beneath.

I did not recognize Max at first. For the only time other than our beach football game in Florida, he was not wearing Max Frood regulation colors. Only because Marlowe Sherpa pointed him out, "There's Max," and steered us toward him, did I notice that the bronze-skinned fedora-wearing peg-leg in a pea coat was my boss. Now that I worked for Moby Dx, was Max still my boss? Hmm. I would ponder that another time.

"Max, I'm stunned."

"Yeah, there's nothing like it anywhere, is there?"

"I meant I'm stunned at the way you look."

"When in Rome, do as the Romanians. Well, you look luminous yourself, good enough to live here." He leaned on a cane and admired all of me without reserve.

I was wearing Georgina's silver sequined silk dress. The moving lights made me shimmer and change color moment by moment. Marlowe had placed some orange LEDs beneath the uppermost layers of my hair, arranging them so that one not-so-small part of my head glowed like a radioactive flower. From what I could pick up in the reflecting pool, I didn't need the excuse of being a Luminosities virgin.

"Can you walk with that thing?" I asked, pointing to his nineteenth century prosthesis.

"*Magna cum difficulte*, but yes. Someone would carry me if I asked."

"And the Art Cars ..." I said, letting the thought trail off. I tried to release Marlowe, but he insisted that he stay with us until he handed me, personally handed me off to Venus. She was standing nearby, talking to Bill Gates and two very prominent and elegant it-girl executives of Silicon Valley holding hands. One was dark-haired and one fair-haired. They later asked that I not use their names here.

Marlowe started us moving toward them, and without him saying so much as a word, when Venus saw me, it was she who interrupted her own conversation. "Oh my dear, you look so luminous, you must come and live with us. Darling, who are you, really?"

Her question confused me. We had met at the Rosewood. She remembered enough of me to extend a personal invitation through Max. What did she mean, "Who are you?" I wore Georgina's dress, but did that throw her off? Or was she asking some kind of deeper question about what made me tick? Before I could begin to answer, Marlowe started to sing "Is That All There Is?" in a eunuch's amplified imitation of Peggy Lee. He attracted a crowd.

Venus imposed on us, loomed over us. She had been an Olympic heptathlete for Kenya in 1980, '84, and '88. I guessed she was nearly six three. Her shapely legs ran all the way up to her thighs and beyond. Twenty-five years out of peak fitness, her still-proportioned frame supported at least two hundred pounds. And even if you didn't see her, you'd know she was nearby because her voice was loud and lilting, quickly changing the song it sang with her moving moods.

Max had told me to dress to kill. Vladik had told me to seduce her with braininess. But it was she, in her own forward-off-the-blocks way, who was trying to seduce me.

She picked up the conversation where we'd left off—at the beginning. "Lakshmi, are you Max's date tonight or are you his talent?"

I had to go along with her obliquity. "I'm his talent, but I'd like to be your date," I laughed, faking sincerity with all my heart. I put my arm around her waist and pulled her in tight against me. Everything goes at the Luminosities. After I gave her all that skin and I felt her sumptuous heat against me, there was no more need for fakery.

"Oh Max, I do like this girl very much." She laughed too, looking around to make sure others heard her and saw us. She surprised me with a sudden squeeze, and my face mooshed into her breast. That was awkward, but she threw me a bone. "If you're with Max, there must be a company. Tell me about it." The genuine article of sincerity glowed within when I recited the words Vladik had taught me.

"Medicine has always been limited by how well doctors can see inside patients. The stethoscope they all carry was invented to solve exactly that problem. And so were the imaging tools like X-rays and ultrasound and NMR that has had such a huge impact in the last century. Moby Dx is a platform for the next generations of tools—molecular stethoscopes combining molecular specificity with the locality of imaging methods. We will give doctors better diagnostics tools than they've ever had." That may have been too much already, so I shut myself off.

"And your timetable?"

"Less than three years before doctors are using our tests in their practice," I improvised.

"And what about funding?"

"We're raising a $2.5 million seed round now, followed by a Series A within two years. $10 million or so. Details TBD."

"Come and see me after the fireworks." Then she leaned down and frenched me! Close to my ear, she said, "I'll write you a check," before walking off with a snake charmer.

CHAPTER 142 THE BUFFING

THOUSANDS OF candles flickered in the darkness while LEDs, electroluminescent wire, and neon of every hue gleamed and pulsed and even waved to the beat permeating the hillside. Blue-green lasers shot off into the night, scanning to the same rhythms. Halogens and stage lights flooded where they must. Did I say fire, too? Bare-breasted fire dancers, mixing light, motion, danger, and the erotic popped up unexpectedly, performing for a few moments and then disappearing back into the night. They left behind only arousal and the smells of burnt Sterno. Behind glowing translucent scrims, screams and cries of joy rose above the grinding hum of power tools. And topping the scrims, two words blinked in neon, "Buff City."

Max said to me, about my little speech to Venus, "That was masterful," and then, "I need to sit down."

And we both said, "I need to eat something."

No longer refusing the circulating food, drink, and smoke, we tanked up and were soon strolling again. Everywhere cavorting and groping, the sherpas encouraged the guests to shed their armor. I wanted to jump in, all in, and lose myself. The sex-charged truffles of the night didn't seem to move Max. The intoxicants had their effect though, loosening his speech and his thoughts.

"Get Vladik up here."

"Can I?"

"You're Venus' chosen. You can do whatever you want. Just tell your boy genie Marlowe and it will happen."

It was already eleven o'clock when I called Vladik.

"You're giving me live reporting?"

"No. We're having an all-hands meeting."

"Good. We need to talk about this two-product nightmare. When?"

"Now.

"Very funny. When?

"Now. Get yourself up here."

"No way."

"Way."

"Then it's not that kind of meeting is it? And it's OK with Venus?"

"No it's not, and yes it is. She's in."

"Already?"

"Rounding error."

He paused. "What do I wear?"

"Something that will be easy to take off."

"What?"

"Don't worry, they'll give you a costume when you arrive."

Then I found Sherpa Marlowe. He was being stroked with palm fronds by scheherazades almost certainly of legal age. After some difficulty getting his attention, I informed him that there'd be someone else joining us and he'd be in need of a costume. "Will you please bring him to Max when he arrives? I'll find them."

"Any guidance?"

"Pair him with Max. Not too embarrassing. He's unusually square."

Then I returned to Max, he had become the center of attention of a small group of sword fighters and maidens in tight bodices and spiky chokers, all feigning distress and finding his costume piratically stimulating. "Do you mind if I go off on my own until Vladik shows?" Max barely acknowledged me with a nod, leaving me free to get my massage.

I pulled apart the scrim curtains below the illuminated "Buff City" sign and walked in on piles of shed costumes. On each of a half-dozen tables was an amused, ecstatic, or post-orgasmic female covered with a soft thin blanket. Tousled hair, maybe a glowing face, hands drooping over the table, and bare feet were all that was exposed.

At work was a masseuse—a trained professional licensed by the Silicon Valley Chapter of the Society of Female Manipulators—and an assistant, either a friend of the lady or a complete stranger. Her hand held a buzzing beast of a power tool, its orange cord reaching out to a snake pit of extension cords on the floor. Like a finishing sander, its butt end was palm-sized, but instead of an abrasive on its business end, the tool held a soft, fast-orbiting pad. The intended use was polishing cars, but I'd heard that buffing had become the latest greatest route to a girl's mechanically assisted happy ending.

A pleasure conductor spotted me wide-eyed. "Hi. My name is Bacchus and I'll be your buffer tonight."

"Paine?"

"Yes, have we met?"

"No, but I've read your books. I'm a fan." Bacchus Paine, a local legend, was a gender theorist and cunnilingus trainer. Georgina would be green when I told her.

Bacchus, smiled, but had her hands full, and squirming flesh called. "Would you like to assist?" she asked, offering me a position as one of the complete strangers. How could I refuse?

She handed me a tool, and with her eyes and shrug said, "Follow me." She worked her way up and down the back and shoulders belonging to a pile of walnut hair, and then said, "Her legs are yours." I was cautious at first, following their full length to her feet, and back again to her behind. When she turned her head in my direction, and I saw I was operating on the dark-haired it-girl, I must have shown something like fealty. She was almost royalty! She gave my hand a squeeze and told me to forget it while Mistress Paine advised me on pressure, how long to stay on each muscle group, and how fast to cycle between them.

The blond was on the table beside us. If they were so inseparable, why wasn't one playing doctor?

Anyway, *la machina*'s energy released stored tension, and the masseuse's chatter and light conversation accelerated its flow outward. My lady and other buffees said the most amazing and intimate things, indifferent to the inhibitions of normal Silicon Valley life, or civilized life anywhere. I scanned the room to watch as one buff artist worked over glutes and thighs, easing apart the large muscle groups, preparing to sweep the instrument over the most tender flesh most maddeningly. I followed form. My charge, long limbered by hours of lotus-sitting, flopped her legs open like pages of a well-bound and well-read book.

Around me, assistants roved hands and fingers. One was deployed on kissing duty while the fun doctor adjusted other parts. Digits disappeared under the covers, grasping for the *raison d'être*. I saw one assistant whose foot had disappeared beneath the blanket, and judging by the length of her other leg, she was socketed all the way to the ankle. My queen, whose rump was by now raised well off the table and whose knees were spread to its full width, invited me to open her fur coat.

For each and every woman on the table, there came a moment when her chatter ceased, only to be replaced by a series of familiar sounds in familiar patterns, loud fist-pounding on the steel frames of the massage tables, energetic squirming that threatened to overturn them, encouragement from onlookers and assistants, envy in the eyes of those waiting, and all of it coming to a conclusion in straining cries of "*lean fucking in!*" or heroic shouts, laughter or tears, or tears and laughter together. Buffing was better than Botox for removing those nasty wrinkles.

A line of girls stood and sat, waiting their turn. They'd stripped down to undies, covering themselves in plush terrycloth robes of a pale pink. Each was emblazoned with a plump and anatomically correct vagina embroidered on the left breast, and a voluptuous red V beside it, the logo of Venus NV. Some repeat customers didn't even bother to put their robes back on. Having done my civic duty as sous masseuse, I was worked up and ready to go when I finally stripped down and got horizontal. Bacchus, my maestro, along with the help of an able-bodied male assistant, polished me to a fine shine.

The oxytocin coursed through my brain, helping me bond with my new BFF the buffer. A server popped her head through the scrim offering, "Pot, mushrooms, acid, E?" Not for me. But she woke me from my reverie. It was time to dress and look for my buddies.

CHAPTER 143

THE PACT AT THE LUMINOSITIES

MAX HAD not moved from the scene that had precipitated around him. Marlowe stood there with Vladik, having clad him neck to ankle in a muscle-printed leotard worthy of Grey's Anatomy, the textbook, and a peacoat like Max's to keep away the cold still settling in. We exchanged glances of disbelief and mock horror, absorbing what was happening around us. "Did we have to do this?" was all he said to me.

Several boats, Art Cars really, had rolled up. Docked by the stage, which had come to resemble a wharf more than anything else, the mutant craft had transported new partiers to the developing spectacle. Max strutted around on the keelless hull of a schooner secured to a flatbed truck. Fixed to its bow was a queer carved and painted figurehead, a dimpled smiling cartoonish merman, curly headed on top, fish tailed on the bottom from fluke to waist, a finely detailed 8-pack in the middle. At his waist, his fish self unzipped in a V, trouser like, revealing only curly short hairs that felt to me like real hairs glued in place. His cucumber cock's bulge strained at the confinement but was locked forever in its wooden prison.

Stagehands moved lights and microphones into position as more sherpas joined in the production. Max was yelling to a part of the crowd, one of many voices there, one of many sights to see there, when he grabbed a portable mic. He wobbled. Marlowe climbed up to him for support. Then Max flipped the switch on the mic. Its electrostatic crackle snapped everyone to attention.

Like someone opening a well-oiled performance he said calmly, "Someone bring me a bottle, a full bottle of clear truth. And three glasses." Staff ran off to oblige him.

Then he boomed, "Who wants to be a billionaire?"

Movement stopped. Sound stopped. And then a responsive roar rose up, "I do!"

He'd become, or maybe he'd always been, Mesmer.

"How much?" he cried into the mic.

"Real bad, Captain! Real bad!" they shouted.

"You have the great ideas, do you?"

"Yes we do, Captain!" they boomed back at him.

Dancers handspringed through empty hogsheads of real fire beside him. Green and blue lasers swept across the sky, so close to our heads I thought I could smell the burnt protein of the tallest among us.

"Then who's holding you back, lassies?"

"No one! No one! No one!" the crowd chanted.

Over them he yelled. "Take your chances when they come. There won't be many. Don't let fortune pass you by. Seize it. Seize it. Seize it," he shouted into the mic. Marlowe kept him upright. Then the crowd picked up the rhythm, "Seize it! Seize it! Seize it!"

Max looked straight at me and motioned for us to climb on up to him. With no more sense than puppies, we followed our master's directions. Marlowe handed the glasses to us while Max held the bottle over his head. "See, see this bottle of aqua vitae! It makes you feel alive, like a new man! Now drink it all down will ya! Whatever you're drinking, whatever your smoking, take it deep down with you and feel the new man rise up in ya!"

All of us, all of the guests and staff and sherpas within hearing, took our drinks and tokes in far greater measure than usual, and we let it breathe promethean fire into us.

"Let me hear it from you. Are you a new man, now? Are you a new man?"

"I'm a new man. I'm a new man. I'm a new man," we all yelled back, our response to his call.

"Then give the new man a drink!" and Max poured us another round and made us take it all in a single gulp. I thought I might lose it, and would certainly be too drunk to drive home. Vladik could hold it. The crowd roared with laughter and got higher.

What was in that stuff? I felt a wild buzzing in my ears and then my visual field filled with blue and yellow blocks.

"Now someone find me three swords," Max cried. Under these circumstances, that was not a hard request to fulfill. Sherpas appeared with the props. Sword in hand, painted muscle-tights rippling, Vladik looked like nothing less than a swashbuckling harpooner. I was completely out of place in my sequins. Captain Max called the shots. All doubt about that was thrown overboard.

The crowd rollicked. Music had crept back in. Makers in fire breathing exoskeletons stalked around. Stilters stilted and jugglers juggled. Each of the colored blocks of my hallucinations grew a trumpet that reached into my ear and played a unique note, yet one harmonious with the others. The blocks grew in size, or did they shrink, or both? What was in that food? *Venus, you snake!* Or was it the aqua vitae? I thought I might jump out of my skin.

"All of you. Find your mates and cross your swords as you can." He pointed his straight down into the deck and leaned on it. Then he urged us to press ours against his. Pointing to the one spot where they all crossed, he recognized he had better hand the mic to Marlowe who then positioned it for him while he cried "Now grab the cross and squeeze until you feel the bite and your hands are slick with blood." For us, the lunacy of the moment was not at all lessened by the fact that these were plastic props and *my blood,* at least, remained in my skin.

"Make your pact with your mates now. Swear to the Luminosities that you're in it together. Whatever your dream, let the heavens hear you chase it." At first, the dozens of small groups yelled their own dreams upwards in a chaotic din. But we were amplified, and as we three shouted, "Moby Dx! Moby Dx! Moby Dx!" our private dream was transferred to the public, and they joined us. So ferocious was the feeling—fueled by everything that had come before and that was around us—that if Vladik had told me the plastic swords had taken a bite of our hands and our blood had run out and pooled together, I might have believed him.

This was the moment that the fire crews let loose, drawing attention away from the primal shouting, leading it to the heat and light. Makers ignited their wooden sculptures and spinning bonfires. Fireworks screamed across the sky, streaking Vs every time. After the final thunderous climax, Vladik and I lowered our skyward gaze. The sculptures soon became fields of red embers. Small crowds encircled fifty-five-gallon oil drums, emptied and rusting, red hot with firewood and scrap lumber. We huddled close for the heat.

I'd come off my buzz, thank God. Had it come from the food? Max and Marlowe were nowhere to be seen and Venus was by my side with her arm around me.

"I'm Venus," she said to Vladik. "You look luminous. Is there anything I can help you with? Anything?"

Vladik had a few things on his mind, but nothing Venus could help him with. One of them was closing the gap with Max on his insane two-program plan, and another was being with his wife at that place he had (almost) become used to calling home.

"You are the most luminous of all, Venus, thank you. Your happening is happening. I was forewarned but not prepared. I will never forget it. I'm Vladik K, the CEO of Moby Dx. Lakshmi," nodding in my direction, "told me that you've already spoken. Let me leave you in her able hands, and when I'm needed, she knows where to find me."

Venus frenched him before he could say "*Nyet*!" That girl would do anything.

D5 and her photographer appeared with auspicious timing. Avedonis arranged us together with some other celebrities, popped the shot, handed out his special business cards, and promised to send everyone copies. "You need a ride home, Vladi?" D5 asked.

I laughed out loud while he looked at me, helplessly embarrassed. His eyes spoke, "Please never use that diminutive in public." She must have picked it up from Arianna, because no one called him Vladi.

CHAPTER 144 THE CHECK

Dawn light, real dawn light—not the dawn light I might have perceived under the influence of the already-metabolized psychotomimetic snacks—and rosy fingers crept over the East Bay hills. I'd never been awake in Silicon Valley at this hour, or at least had not been outdoors on a lone hilltop with everything at my feet. The fires died down and the mutant vehicles went back into hiding. Crews began to disassemble stages. Some guests were escorted to their cars, but most of them headed indoors for another something. I didn't ask what.

The Luminosities was a no holds barred event, and it was hers to set the tone, but IMHO, Venus could have used a little more discretion vis-à-vis public sex. I'm kind of girly and need a little seduction and a little privacy. She, it is often said, could be mistaken for a guy. That said, it's not like couples were doing the wheelbarrow on stage.

Venus led me to her private residence, a V-shaped Norman Foster design of seven rooms, the bedroom at the apex. Sure, I wanted to have sex with her, but the tying of it to a check for Moby Dx was creepy.

"Do you have some drugs?" I asked.

"What about molly?" she asked while putting her hand between my legs.

"Oh, my favorite! And some more aqua vitae? And some water or a beer chaser? Please?"

It was all too fast. I was grateful to be free of her for at least a minute while she gathered the goods. We were alone. There were no sherpas or staff to watch over us. God only knew what surveillance there was. I tried not to think about it. When she returned, she wore one of her signature robes, like I'd seen in Buff City.

"I have this made for me," handing me a celadon bowl, probably 500 years old, containing what looked like fifty grams of pure crystal MDMA. "It's the only way to guarantee quality," she said. I couldn't have agreed more.

I took a big shot of aqua vitae with my first dip into the bowl. It was crazy bitter, like eating dandelions. Excellent! I hoped something would kick in quickly. I didn't know how long I could hold her off. I couldn't spoof like this for long.

After a little kiss to placate her, I used the bathroom to slip out of my clothes and into a robe like hers. On the wall hung a triumphantly displayed diorama of life-size ceramic vaginas, apparently the model for the embroidery on the robes. Otherwise, there were original paintings by Georgia O'Keeffe, a Klimt masturbator, and, inexplicably, Brian Josephson's 1973 Nobel medal under Lucite.

When I returned, I noticed that the bedroom walls were similarly adorned. I sprawled onto a large lounging sofa beside Venus. The molly was within reach of both of us. This was a night like no other. Why not dip twice?

I wasn't yet in the moment, the mood, the groove, not ready to have her all over me, so I took control. She may have been a billionaire, but I had youth, and I counted on that to give me authority. The biggest challenge was her size. My arms weren't long enough to get where they needed to go. I propped myself up with some pillows and had her lie back against me.

"Women will get you through times of no molly, but molly won't get you through times of no women," I said in *non sequitor.* Then I slipped my hand inside her robe and began to explore.

"Oh, I couldn't agree more," she said.

Then she was mine, utterly a girl.

Jesus, I hope I have breasts like that when I'm fifty. Venus must have been on a proprietary regenerative drug-something her companies were testing; her flesh had the same taut tone as mine. I was learning she was forgetful and crazy, too, sometimes completely out of her mind. I didn't know if the symptoms were related.

The alcohol had kicked in. I was already rolling when I licked my little finger and shoved it in deep, working it around and around, mindfully feeling every corner and crack of flesh, making sure it was fully covered with the fine white crystals before I extracted it, and sucked it, quietly, clean. This was my third dip into the molly, but who was counting? I certainly wasn't counting hers. She was softening, becoming less aggressive, more sensitive. Her muscles lengthened. Her joints opened. Her breathing slowed.

I still needed time.

"Venus," I whispered, "tell me about your brother."

"Lakshmi! Not you, too?"

"What do you mean? Your tales of being Barack Obama's sister are all over the press."

"Yes, and I've disavowed all of them."

She had taken so much flak after the 2007 interview that she sued the writer for libel rather than stick by her story. As we kneaded each other in silence, a thought came to me in a flash, "Brian Josephson brought the V_{jj} to physics."

"I will tell you something, Luminous Lakshmi, if you consider, simply consider taking up residence here."

I elbowed her in the affirmative.

"My mother was the daughter of a Dutch mining engineer and an alcoholic Jewish Kenyan Princess, if you can believe there are enough of them to warrant a classification of their own. There are. There are even jokes about them."

She waited for me to say something, but instead I slapped her left breast. Bad cop. She gasped before I dashed in to lap at her lollipop nipple. Good cop.

"Ah, Likshmi." She said nothing else for a while.

Then, "Do you know how a Jewish Kenyan Princess eats a banana, Lukshmi?"

She turned to me so I could see her as she freed her hands from her own beautiful knobs. She'd been stroking them after my slap while I'd been at work in her beavoire. She mimed peeling a banana, slowly, first one and then another quarter of the skin peeled back, until at last she had brought to mind a banana ready-to-eat in her left hand. Then, swiftly and forcefully she put her right hand behind her own head and forced it down onto the imagined phallic fruit, gagging, eyes bulging, and a crazy grin all over her face. We both broke out into disentangling laughter. She could have been a comic, that girl. So many talents. I had fully warmed to her.

She fell back onto the bed, draping her legs over the side, and I positioned myself between those African twin towers. I could just barely reach her tits. "Comfortable?" I asked.

"Very. Well, my mother, Lisa Loufbourrow, had an affair with Barack Obama, Senior in the late 1950s. In a secret ceremony, they were married and she became pregnant by him in 1960—"

"What about Ann Dunham and Kezia?"

"Affairs of the heart won't leave lovers apart, my dear." She paused to let her hips widen another click. "Do you really want to hear this? It must bore you."

"Bore me? Are you kidding? I've never heard anything like it. Keep going."

"You keep going, and I'll keep going."

She must have been on some proprietary hormones too. Her vagina was as loose and sweet as a big ole jelly roll, but not so sticky. She was my harp and I played on as she told the tale.

"Within a few days of each other, Ann had the boy and my mom had me and my runty twin brother. He does look exactly like—"

I interrupted her again, "But your last names. If Loufbourrow married Barack Obama, Senior and took his name, why are you Khlobama?"

She then began to sing to me, "You say tomato and I say tomahto, you say potato and I say potahto." Really, she could do a good imitation of Louis, and I'll bet that eunuch Marlowe could have done a pretty amazing Ella. She had made her point, though she wasn't finished. "Or better yet, what about Peking and Beijing, Bombay and Mumbai, Mombasa and Manbasa. All bets are off transliterating a foreign language with its alien pronunciations. Look, even the Jews can't figure out whether its mishpo'khe or mishpucha'. In Dad's tribal Luo, they'd be written the same way."

I was torn between wanting her to fuck me and wanting to follow the rabbit of this craziness into its own hole. Like all the other birthers, she'd produce a new twist and new evidence to advance the adventure, even into a mirror world if necessary.

I was torn, too, because I wanted to get paid, I mean I wanted the company to get funded, and had to be careful not to show too much disbelief, and certainly no contempt. I knew, I just knew, I could never put an end to the rabbit's journey.

"You were saying something, that he looks exactly ..."

"The President, he looks like my brother."

"Venus, you do look like him, too, but not so runty," I teased her.

"Of course I do. He is my brother. There was a swap. Ann's boy was really runty. Anyway, Lakshmi, it used to be hard, but now it's easy. We could settle this," and she snapped her fingers while licking her lips, "so easily if he'd just spit in a cup and send it off to 23andMe. I think there's Stimulus Dollars for that, don't you? They have an app for measuring similarity, don't they?"

"Relative Finder," I said.

"If he turned on Relative Finder, he'd discover he shared more DNA with me than he possibly could with anyone who wasn't his brother or sister."

A long tale worthy of Ayn Rand followed, with enough material to fill a fifty-minute TV episode, but the truth was that I had heard enough, and didn't want to learn how Stasi, Putin, and the NAACP, and Ebola had played a part in her brother's life and her own path from Kenya to Peru to Oxford and the Olympics, and eventually to the top of that hill in Portola Valley. I gave up listening and yielded to the moments of emotional technicolor brought on by her ecstasy. She had had an uncanny ability to stay calm, but I was giving her the rubdown of a lifetime and in time, resistance proved futile. She drifted off into speechlessness.

I flopped around so that while her legs hung over the edge of the bed, I looked deep into the Y, and she looked straight up into me, great differences in our height notwithstanding. With a power tool in my left hand, applying gentle pressure and vibration to her belly and pubic bone from above, I had three fingers inside her and pushed up from below on that blood-filled pussile organ, the one that a thick or upturned cock might, just might be able to stimulate if everybody cooperated, but which fingers were so much better adapted to find and follow and stay on. Squeezing, and imagining myself when she returned the favor later, I became her. "Likshmi Lucky. Fuckshmi Lickme." Then she had no more words at all, just sounds, calling out "gee … gee … gee," each syllable separated by a short breath in. At first I thought she meant it as a compliment, that I was good, giving, and game, but the G's kept on coming, in some kind of onomatopoeia, increasing in volume and frequency, and decreasing in pitch, and sounding less like human utterances, until it all let go inside her, a great galloping orgasm of an extended "gee spahh ahh ahh ahh ahh ahh ahh ahh ahht," and an Olympian golden shower, too. I was thrilled to see what I had wrought, and identically glad to have ducked the stream as it came pouring out so fountainously.

"Quality is its own variety," I whispered in her ear.

Venus was GGG herself. Two hours of pussy riot later I was a sweaty, exhausted, and much, much satisfied girl. On the floor, chaotically flung everywhere were plastic toys, electric toys, eighteen-volt power tools and their depleted lithium batteries, leather toys, empty bowls, empty bottles, empty glasses, healthy snacks, a boa—a feather boa—and more clothes than either of us had been wearing when we started, and of course, a buffer. I was expecting to see a live tiger, too, but I didn't: just one hot bitch.

WHEN I awoke, I was alone in bed and it was mid-afternoon. I checked my slab and found texts from Georgina, Louisa, my father, Vladik, and Max. None were urgent. Max was still on the premises, I gathered. His message read, "Ur just a bauble."

Her V-ness sensed motion and called to me from the next room over, an office. "There's food and coffee in here. Towels in the bath."

I poked my head in and smiled. I wanted to get professional as soon as possible, and hoped she was feeling the same way. I showered, used the unopened toothbrush she'd left out for me, and dressed before giving her a proper greeting. Georgina's dress felt about one monolayer thick, so even clothed, it's not like I had a lot of armor on. Still, it was better than nothing.

"Lakshmi," she said. "I didn't want to run off and leave you feeling like a slut, so I've been working here as well as I could. It would be better for me if I left, so please don't be offended if I dash."

There is a God.

"No, Venus, please. Thank you for everything. Last night was unique. And you are delicious, amazing. I should go too. Experiments never sleep. I have to get back to them."

"Such a committed girl. Your hands in the lab are as masterful as they are on me?"

"It's not for me to say. I get results. I can say that."

"And I can say that, too!" She grinned, but did not pull me in to her and try to initiate more sex.

"About that check," I said.

"Yes, of course. Is the entity an Inc or an LLC?"

"LLC."

"OK, here, let me fill in this line here," and she slipped me a check in the amount of one million dollars made out to Moby Dx LLC.

"But you haven't even seen a term sheet. Don't you want to wait until the papers are done?"

"Honey, you're not going to screw me, are you?"

"No, of course not."

"Nor Max, nor your friend Vladi."

"I think he'll die if you call him that. But no, of course not."

"So, what do I have to worry about? Nothing. I could still screw you, papers or not," and she laughed the laugh of a billionaire with money to sue.

"So, I'll just deposit this check and when we have papers you'll sign them?"

"Well, I'd prefer that we had at least a semblance of negotiation about terms."

"But you've lost all your leverage by paying me first."

"But you said you're not going to screw me. So you'll do me the decency of at least listening to my concerns. If you ignore me, I'll be a very difficult investor. If you listen to me, well, you've seen how compliant I can be."

There was not much to say about that, so I did exactly what every girl does when another one hands them a million dollar check, I hugged her gratefully tit to tit, kissed her on each cheek, and said thank you.

"What's your email address so I can put my attorney in touch with you about the terms?"

"lakshmi@mobydx.com"

"Wonderful. And you'll hear from me about making an extended visit here sometime, ok? I have to be in two other places this very minute, so think of me as already gone. Leave on your own schedule. Someone will help you down the hill when you're ready." And then she was actually gone.

I texted the girls first, "I'm fine. Fill you in later, OK?" I texted Vladik, "Holding a check." He called back right away for details. Then I texted Max, "Got it," leaving it ambiguous as to whether I meant I got his message that I was just a bauble or whether I'd gotten the check. He didn't respond at all. My father, half way around the world, would have been asleep, so I didn't call him.

Picking up my purse, I walked out of the V and onto the estate grounds, by then as tidy as an English garden where there had not been 200 partiers the night before. I cringed when I saw Max with a sherpa locked on him in a wheelbarrow embrace. He crawled away from me, and so I don't think he saw me before I ducked into the Incubator, left by another exit, and was soon off the premises.

CHAPTER 145 NO MAX!

WITH OUR $1.2 million in the bank, we could have started building and gotten some work done. Unfortunately, our founders had a major disagreement over the strategic plan. Until we untangled that, we didn't know what work should be done. For some reason, that uncertainty was getting resolved very slowly, and the reason was that Max was unavailable. Not unseen. Unavailable. After a few weeks, Vladik capitulated to my way of thinking, which was that we should stop fighting Max over what to do because most would die on its own accord. Sure, it would have been cheaper and better to abandon it early, but parents don't easily abandon their children. Although Max had done approximately nothing on most, he still thought of it as his baby.

Vladik gave me responsibility for moving us into All-In and getting the experimental program under way. He took responsibility for rounding up the rest of the money, negotiating the contracts and company formation documents, kicking off the academic collaborations, finding and working with the advisors, developing the strategic plan, preventing Dyk from doing something destructive, and dealing with Max, but everything else we did together until it made sense that one or the other of us should be doing it alone.

He, Vladik, wanted to complete the financing and have it behind us. On the other hand, he couldn't afford to postpone work on the collaborations because those would take a long time to evolve into something useful. Every day of delay only delayed the moment when we would have demonstrable results in hand. All our activities had to proceed in parallel, or as they say in the engineering world, concurrently.

On a Monday, Vladik took a look at the business cards he'd collected and the notes he'd made at the 85 Broad meeting where he'd stalked down Max. Then he started dialing. He got through to Bloated Bay Trust and Yellow Stream Advisors, and Madison River Advantage Partners, too, but only to a receptionist who promised to deliver a verbal request for a meeting. Then, he made some progress.

"Good afternoon, Prophetic Capital. How may I place your call?" said a twenty-something female with a voice like a glass bell and a beluga-smooth Russian accent.

"Vladimir Preobrazhensky, please."

Explanations followed wherein Vladik described where they'd met, and Xenia, that was the name behind the voice, said, "Dimi," and then she corrected herself, "Vadim, is unavailable." She failed to suppress a giggle. There were sounds of shuffling chairs, laughing, muffled Russian speech Vladik couldn't quite hear, and then she said, "until 4 p.m." Vadim being on EST, and Vladik being on PST, that meant "in two hours," or ample time for those two to finish whatever they were up to.

WHEN Vadim Skyped Vladik two hours later, the former looked relaxed, even knackered, with his tie off and his Berluschetti shirt unbuttoned at the neck. He was a handsome fifty-something with very thick, mostly black hair, a Greco-Roman nose, and the smile of the gregarious. He greeted Vladik with unexpected familiarity, as if their day together in a New York City office building had been his most enchanting and warmly remembered experience in months, and that Vladik had been central to it. "How can I be of service to you, Vladik?"

"You remember Dr. Frood, I guess."

Vadim launched into lilting praise, as exaggerated by design as his exuberance over reconnecting with Vladik.

He smiled, nodding acknowledgment and confirmation of Max's status as super-special genius boy, and when finally there was silence, he said, "Max and I have formed a company, we call it Moby Dx LLC, to commercialize those ideas he discussed. We're raising money in a convertible note and we wanted to know if you were interested in taking a slice."

"Yes, of course I'm interested. Anything with Max in it, I'm interested. I have a meeting with Gates and Buffett tomorrow." He didn't mute the call when he shouted in Russian, "Xenia, can we squeeze Vladik in at TAC Air tomorrow?"

"Maybe on the return," she said. "Dimi, we have reservations at Nobu at 8:30," and there was a pleading anticipation in her voice, in Russian.

Vadim returned to Vladik.

"Vladik. Xenia will send you the details, but I'm expecting you and Max to meet me at TAC Air in Omaha, 2:30 p.m. local time. We're going to be wheels-up at 3:00."

"Vadim, so sorry about the misunderstanding. I'll be bringing my Chief Scientist with me," making up my title on the fly, "but I can't get Max on this short notice."

"Is he in the company or what?"

"Yes, he's in, but not day-to-day."

"Already, I'm not liking it." Everything about his demeanor had changed. He wanted Max, The Talent. "I'll have thirty minutes. See you then?"

Vladik texted me "We're going on a road trip," and then Max, too, on the off chance Max would join us. "Money is on the line. Need you in OMA tomorrow. Pack your pro kit."

"OMA! NFW. Washing my hair tomorrow."

Vladik called him.

"Vadim's decision could be all about whether or not you're there."

"I've got a board meeting in South San Francisco. You know you can tell the story better than I can, and Lakshmi did the science. You've got everything you need."

"That won't matter if it's you they want. And what company are you on the boards of? I thought HMRI —"

Max cut him off. "Heh I gotta go. Text me when know something more."

Then Vladik called me and explained, none too happy about Max's recalcitrance. "Is Max on the board of some company in South San Francisco?" he asked. In the time squeeze, that topic was forgotten.

Vladik had checked the connections and they were awful. The only flight the next day was 6:15 morning flight from Monterey, and that would have us at Eppley in Nebraska with only forty minutes to spare. The meeting was too important and too short to risk being late for it. By the end of our call, it was 1:40 and too late for the 4 o'clock departure from SFO. That left only the 8:05 flight, a horrible prospect, but there were no better ones. SFO -> LAX, then a three-hour layover. LAX -> DFW arriving at 5 a.m., and an 8:40 departure to OMA, arriving at 10:25. The only good news was that it required the violation of no laws of physics. We'd get the 6:15 p.m. return through DFW, touching down at SFO at 11:35.

"We're gonna miss The Max?"

"The what?"

"Best dance club in the," I paused, trying to figure out how to finish that thought, "the Great Plains."

"Gay or non-denominational."

"Non-denominational."

"Well, maybe we'll plow through and take a morning flight out Wednesday."

"No sleep?"

"Catch as catch can."

"Business class?" I asked optimistically.

"After the IPO, maybe. Wear something you can sleep in and bring a change of clothes that will make him want to work with you even though you're not Max."

"I'll see what I have stashed at G's spot. Where and when?"

"How about if I pick you up at her place at 5:45? We could get stuck in rush hour traffic."

"We'll be in the commuter lane. No checked baggage. How about 6:15?"

"6:15 at 525 University."

"6:00 at her place."

"See you there."

CHAPTER 146 PROPHETIC CAPITAL

I WANTED TO wear footy pajamas but didn't have the courage. Instead, I wore sweatpants and a sweatshirt with a tank top underneath in case it got too warm, and my tennies. I hated looking so shapeless. In my shoulder bag I had pillow, earplugs, eye mask, Slab42 and Slab97, USB charger and cables, external battery pack, headphones, spares, laptop, charger, charger extension cord, RJ-45 dongle, six-foot Ethernet cable, VGA dongle, six-foot VGA cable, USB memory stick, and my Moby Dx LLC business cards with the soon-to-be-obsolete 525 University Avenue address. Then, in a separate bag I had my personal kit and the much-deliberated-over clothes.

Traffic was light. We could have left at 6:15. We called in and ordered some sandwiches to pick up at Max's Opera Café in Burlingame; the irony was too sweet to miss. We valet-parked the 911 at a lot just down the street from Max's. A shuttle took us to our terminal. Once we got past security at 7:00 p.m., we talked non-stop—except for a few interruptions attending to the women in our lives—about the deck. At 12:40, when we took off down the LAX runway for DFW, we fell asleep before the wheels were up.

All told, between the long flights and layovers, and the four hours waiting in Omaha, we probably got six hours of sleep that night, which wasn't really so bad. We both showered, separately, at the FBO. The staff was very polite to us, as we were paying customers, or at least guests of paying customers.

Georgina had decided on a look for me which we called STEMster, trying to convey some of Max's disregard for formality while at the same time expressing—it's too immodest to say, but I'll do it anyway—my intelligence and sophisticated style. I wore a black jumpsuit exposing my shoulders and not too much cleavage, a wasabi cardigan to keep me warm and provide me with complete control of discretion, and red mesh wedge sneakers for hipness, choosing those over my pointy black pumps which would have been more glamorous and less comfortable, although, how much did comfort really matter for a thirty minute meeting we'd be taking sitting down? I bunned up my hair for that Marion the Librarian look, and chose my black hipster glasses. Vladik wore exactly what he had worn that day he met Vadim in New York City.

The TAC Air waiting room would have seated twenty. We were there alone. The building was quiet, airy, elegant but not opulent, away from the bustle of airports, and yet, still an airport. While we rehearsed the pitch, the co-pilot came over and told us that Vadim was running a few minutes late. Did we mind having the meeting on the plane itself? He walked us through the hangar whose floor was cleaner than a dinner table. The parked cars inside were all washed and sparkling. Our Citation X was outside, but inside this hangar there were two other planes, G450s. They waited, like sleeping dogs, for the owners. If they'd been bought to generate income, there'd be a service crew or a flight crew around or on them all the time, moving them in or out, tearing them down or readying them for the next flight. Not here. Here all was calm, spotless, hygienic, low-utilization luxury.

Venus probably had a toy like this. I knew D5 did. As baubles go, private jets rate high on the list. This was my first time near one.

The appointed hour came and went while we were offered access to all the plane's treats. At 2:55 Vadim and Xenia boarded. "I'm glad we're not late. If we're going to talk, you're going to have to go to New York. Do you mind?" At 3:00 sharp, we were wheels up for LGA.

Xenia, OMG, Xenia. She was completely het, but I could not stop staring. Her distracting blue eyes were as pale as the waters of the Caribbean. Rouged cheeks, and lips so bunny-pink I thought they might hop off her mouth, itself so petite I didn't know how I could even slide a tongue in it, were there the opportunity. Her light hair, not brown, not blond, maybe golden, straight-parted in the middle, framing luminous pale skin. Was she Vadim's plaything or something else? We would see.

Vadim showed off his memory. "Vladik, have you changed your clothes since I saw you?"

But he was charming, so was Xenia, too. Drinks, snacks, chitchat, and finally we got down to the business. Vladik and I worked with two laptops. One I shared with Xenia on the sofa, and the other Vladik and Vadim shared on a carbon fiber table set up between their two truffle-white leather chairs.

While I breathed in Xenia's scent and felt a few of her loose hairs against my cheek, Vladik gave the umbrella overview, the three-minute version of what I'd told Venus in twenty seconds. I explained and claimed credit for all the scientific results, and gave Vladik credit for pulling together the strategic and operating plan. Vladik went over the schedule and budget. Max we mentioned as having conceived the initial vision.

Xenia said, most respectfully, like a little girl asking her parents when they've contradicted themselves, "Your two programs want more money than you're raising, don't you think?"

And then Vadim, "Yes, exactly. Maybe with one program, $2.5 million. With two, you need at least $5 million. Even that's thin."

"I agree," Vladik said, "that we could use more. Max is pretty clear about wanting to keep things lean, use other people's money, you know, grants and contracts, wherever we can. In two years we should have another $2 million in revenue from grants alone."

"Who wears the pants here?" Vadim said, a little agitated. "If Max wants to get those grants himself, fine, but it's a lot of work, writing them and reporting on them, if your only reason for doing it is to save some dilution."

"Well, that's not the only reason. We don't have $5 million being offered."

Xenia, quite obviously not Vadim's toy, said, "I think Dimi's telling you that you do."

"Of course you do. We're offering. $2.5 million is too little. I'll take the entire $5 million, or that minus what you've raised already. But I won't put in a kopek if all you're going to raise is $2.5 million."

We were all silent for a few seconds, and then Xenia said, sweetly, "Why don't you two think about it and get back to us in a few days."

"I have to nap," Vadim said.

He and I changed seats, leaving him leaning against my infatuation. From across the aisle, I talked to her for a few minutes. She praised my getup and I hers. I asked to see her rock. Very impressive, but not garish; a 4.5 carat fancy vivid yellow diamond with two white baguettes beside it, all set in platinum. I managed to touch her hand when I returned it, and from the brief brush, I concluded she was not 100 percent het.

Sexuality is fluid and mysterious. Ask why I'm attracted to women, and I answer: Why is anyone straight? OK, we're programmed to be straight for breeding purposes, sexual selection driving the maximum possible diversity in the gene pool while preserving the ability to reproduce. But we're so much more than binary breeders. We are analog in an analog world of biomolecules. Uncountable genetic interactions, regulation pathways, copy number variations, and epigenomic accidents contribute to our actual phenotypic being. Add molecular noise to the mix, and the expression of hormones that combine to create gender—as if gender is a real thing rather than a convenient and sometimes inconvenient abstraction—is not only continuous, but stochastic, too. How could sexuality be binary in an analog world?

Same-same sex is at least ancient. We know that from the written record. It must be older than the ancients. The middle ground of the ambisexual might be and might have been suppressed, as territory too difficult to inhabit, but that doesn't mean the impulses aren't there. Of course Xenia wasn't 100 percent het!

Vladik logged onto the plane's Wi-Fi. Then he arranged his laptop for me to watch as he began an email exchange with Max, explaining what was on offer from Prophetic Capital.

"We should feed the ducks while they're quacking," Vladik wrote.

"Stick with our plan. Don't set expectations too high."

"But the plan has changed. Now there's BroadID in the mix, and we have to talk about that, too."

Max's reply? "I'd prefer not to."

Max did not respond to Vladik's next message, "When's going to be a good time then?" Instead, Vladik got this message from an autoresponder, "Dr. Frood will be away from the office until Dec 15."

I'd seen the flippant Max, so I took it in stride, but that message really pissed off Vladik. Max would be going away to Southeast Asia for several weeks, combining his obligations in Rhizobia with a long vacation in Indonesia. He wasn't due to depart until Sunday, five days away, so something local was taking precedence over what was supposed to be "the focus of my consulting effort."

Vladik and I knew the protocol for getting Max's attention while he was away, so it's not like he would be gone gone. Still, it was annoying to both of us. His secrets were corroding our trust, and the huge slice of the pie on his plate was looking increasingly difficult to justify. My eyes were closed and I was nodding off when Vladik said to me, "Labor disputes never start over money. They always start over mismanagement, and then they devolve to the only thing you can quantify, money."

Vladik could not sleep after that. On the way to LaGuardia, while the rest of us dozed, he got in touch with some old friends.

CHAPTER 147 THE MANDARIN ORIENTAL

XENIA TOLD us that Air Preobrazhensky would be flying to California three days hence. She'd fly us home then or we could go commercial and send her an expense report. Vladik said, "We have a little thinking to do first. How about if we get back to you on that?"

Vladik and Vadim shook hands, very manly, while Xenia and I brushed cheeks, very Euro. She whispered to me, "Dimi's only jealous of other men," and slipped me her business card. Then she and Vadim were chauffeured off to Nobu. Vladik and I were left holding two laptops, a backpack with my traveling clothes, and little else.

"What are you up for?" Vladik asked me. He was the CEO but he did not boss me around. Sometimes he was pedagogic, sometimes reverential, and sometimes he treated me like his peer. Sometimes he let me lead.

"Sleep and room service in a really nice place."

"OK, your call tonight, but tomorrow, I have plans for us."

"We're laying over till they go back, or Xenia goes back?"

"We have work to do tomorrow. It will be different. By the time we've decompressed, we'll be on her plane."

"Can I buy some clothes on the company?"

"Be prudent, but yes."

Vladik called the Mandarin. "Do you mind a suite?" he asked me.

"Is that prudent?"

"Prudent enough. Suites are nicer. Yes or no?"

"Suites are nicer. Yes, a suite."

Vladik secured a Central Park View Suite for us and then we took a cab to midtown.

"I'm nothing if not prudent," I said, picking up the conversation.

"So I've seen."

"What goes on at the Luminosities, stays at the Luminosities."

"That's fair."

"And more prudent than Max."

"Meaning?"

"What goes on at the Luminosities, stays at the Luminosities."

"You're teasing me."

"Yes, I'm teasing you. Give me some time to be alone with Xenia and I'll tell you."

Arriving at the Mandarin Oriental, the bellmen remembered Vladik and greeted him courteously as Dr. K. If they wondered why he was sharing a suite with a twenty-something brainy STEMster rather than the elegant art lady he'd previously identified as his wife, they didn't let on.

As we were checking in, Vladik got a text. He turned to me and said, "The room's yours. I'm going to stay with my cousins in Brooklyn. Take the B or the Q to Brighton Beach, and meet me at Tatiana at 1 p.m. tomorrow. Just head down Brighton 6th for the Boardwalk. It's a couple of minutes' walk."

"Really?"

"You'll owe me the blow-by-blow."

"Dress code?"

"Something more conservative than this get up," gesturing in my direction. "Not-too-bright solid jeans with a loose fitting black top. Non-descript shoes. Buy yourself a coat to cover it all up. It's going to be cold, remember?"

I hugged him for the first time since that night on the bluffs.

"Oh. And don't eat lunch first. We'll feed you." And then he was gone.

CHAPTER 148 THE BROTHERS K

When the B left the caverns of Columbus Circle at 11:31 a.m. the next morning, I was on it, standing. Mostly, I kept to myself, but New Yorkers are so friendly I couldn't help but get engaged in conversation, especially with older men who wanted to know which of New York's specialized high schools I was going to at this late hour of the morning. We came above ground to cross the East River on the Manhattan Bridge, dropped down into the underworld again, re-emerged into the sunny November cold at Prospect Park, and then got elevated above the roadway at Newkirk Avenue. Eight stops later, I was at Brighton Beach, still standing. A wall clock read 12:15.

With our meeting set for 1:00, I had at least half an hour to explore. I walked along Brighton Beach Avenue, on street level in the shadow of the El.

First thing you should know; the subterranean hipster bars of Brooklyn are somewhere else. Brighton Beach is a Russian neighborhood; a Russian neighborhood like Bangalore is for Indians. Actually, there's more English on the storefronts of Bangalore than there is on the storefronts of Brighton Beach. Starbucks is reliably Starbucks though, so it was there that I headed first to get something to warm me up. The Northeast's cold had never been easy for me. Three years in California had killed my appetite for it.

With chai in a paper cup between my hands, I headed away from the El and Brighton 6th, crossing Coney Island Avenue into the sun and picking up whatever radiant heat there was. Every place was crowded. A line of ardent shoppers led into The Holy Mackerel Emporium on the corner, where the boxes of fruits, trucked a thousand miles or more, were piled high outside, and the smell of coiled challahs and smoked fish wafted through the door.

The Kefir Shoppe a few establishments down was devoted to—drum roll, please—kefir, in all its varieties. Outside, a Russian dude imitating a black dude juggled a large cardboard arrow painted with the single word "KEFIR," while he danced and sang to a popular melody:

Get you to the Kefir Shoppe,
We got the juice that will make you plop,
Special bugs that will chew on,
What's in your big and your small colon.

Low-fat and non-fat, whole milk, sheep's milk kefir from local sources, and gourmet seasonal elk's milk kefir flown in from Jackson Hole. Cranberry, boysenberry, blueberry, dingleberry, coffee, and plain; half a dozen brands of each, all in square or round quarts, and with label artistry worthy of a chateau in Bordeaux, most of them in Cyrillic, too. In a locked refrigerated glass case were several containers free of any writing at all. Instead, there were only drawings, each different, of a black-haired Jewess Madonna and a suckling child. I wanted to ask, but I didn't want to know.

Besides kefir, all they sold was toilet paper.

Down the street, a bakery. Rolls and the loaves filled the shelves. Rugelach in four flavors, three shapes, and two sizes were stacked to the ceiling in bushel baskets. In a refrigerated display cabinet with no obstruction to the buyer's inspection or sampling, was the greatest collection of many-layered cakes and *gateaux Napoleon* I have ever seen. A riotous collection, chaotic and inviting. Maybe it was the Russians' special love for the little emperor, or maybe just their love for dessert, I don't know. On four shelves, each wider than my wingspan, there were cakes on platters, cakes in cardboard boxes, and cakes in plastic boxes. Most would be sold intact, but many had been sliced by a customer using the broad steel cleaver hanging nearby, and paid for by the pound. Others had been pre-cut and would be sold by the piece. There were cakes of fifteen layers, each a few millimetres high, white cream oozing out. There were cakes with shaved chocolate on the top, cakes with chocolate poured on ganache-like and dripping down its sides, cakes with Orthodox onion-domed dollops of white icing sprinkled with edible gold, and cakes with fillings so thick you could barely see the cake. There were éclairs with white cream and chocolate cream and no cream fillings, and small specialty cakes coated top to bottom in chocolate glaze, or in unnaturally pink glaze of impossible-to-guess flavor. But I'd been instructed to arrive hungry, so all I did was look.

Before the Kashkar Café where I turned around, I dropped into a delicatessen whose narrow entrance belied the range of food for sale. First, there were buckets upon deep buckets of individually wrapped Russian candies, whose milkmaid graphics of the Soviet era brought back memories for Brighton Beach's transplanted citizens. And then, an exhibit of individual pastries, elegant and formal behind a curved glass enclosure, God forbid you might touch one of them, like something Max and I would see at Draeger's Market in Menlo Park where I sometimes helped him shop. A refrigerated cabinet held cooked and processed meats to be sliced and sold by the pound.

Eighty different varieties! I counted. From light tans to deep browns. From three-inch diameter to nearly a foot. Head cheeses and turkeys and long pipes of salami, each with handwritten Russian labels and the only English in sight being the letters "lb." I was running out of time and could only glance at the trays of raw linked sausages and the counters overflowing with prepared stews and cooked vegetables and salads and rice plain and rice spiced, and every few yards, thirteen-inch blinis in a stack so high that you had to climb a ladder to take ten off the top. And at the back, the very back, in a display case guarded by leather-wearing men I fingered for armed former inmates, there were authentic black sturgeon caviars from the Caspian Sea, red salmon caviars from California and Alaska, fifty shades of grayling roe, sliced smoked fishes labeled in Russian, and canned truffles. All I could do was glance before I bolted.

Last stop was the Kashkar Cafe, whose very existence in Brooklyn reminded me of the ambitions of the Soviet Empire. Central Asian ikats, dyed in rich primary colors hung in the windows. Inside, yellow flames of an open fire leapt up, while Muslim gentlemen in white pajamas and skullcaps sat and talked over coffee. I would have liked to sit and talk too, but time had run out.

I crossed the street and headed back toward Brighton 6th. Under the El again, I soon made a left toward the beach, only to collide with a four-foot Chassidic kid on a three-wheeled scooter as he was chased by a five-foot kid on a longboard. Collecting myself, I walked down the canyons of six-story brick apartment buildings. A nails salon called "Lucky Style"—my lucky day, it was named after me—staffed as always by the Vietnamese ladies, its clientele made up of orange-haired and white-haired and black-haired locals. Exhausted sinks and toilets and bathtubs were repurposed as planters in small outdoor gardens. Babushka ladies and older gentleman in wheelchairs and the lucky still-walking ones in aluminum lawn chairs, sat outside their apartments, accompanied by the even-more-fortunate who remained motivated to stand, all wrapped in overcoats and sometimes blankets, catching what was left of autumn. Missing from the original tableau in Russia were the tables of matryoshka dolls for sale and maybe a small fire of burning furniture; but of course, it was colder there. Incongruously colored signs for "Day Care," "Dentistry," and "DIVORCE! $399 (plus court fee) Spouse's Signature <u>NOT</u> Needed."

And then, semi-infinite light from the sky over the semi-infinite ocean poured in. Having crossed Brightwater Court, the dark red bricks gave way to higher albedo beach-bright stucco and then the buildings yielded to the boardwalk and the beach itself beyond. Tatiana and Vladik were waiting for me there when I arrived at 12:59.

The signature blue awnings of Tatiana, the restaurant, covered its outdoor seating. Although, they had a 371-item menu, not including drinks, and I was by then starving, we did not take a seat indoors or out. Straw-blonde and barely five-feet-tall, Tatiana walked us into the main dining room, and there I was introduced to the family.

Vladik's father's older sister Tatiana—no relation to the restaurant's namesake—survived her deceased husband Oleg, as did the three boys, Boris, Morris, and Lev Kakitelashvili. Bo, Mo, and Tatiana occupied the same apartments above the restaurant since they'd arrived in Brighton Beach in 1970. Like his father the boxer, Lev had chosen the ring, making a national name for himself as a judo coach, but he had moved a thousand yards east to a single-family house in ocean-facing Manhattan Beach. The K's who had stayed owned the building, and had come to occupy much of its top two floors. Circumstances had been modest during the few years that Vladik, still known in these parts as Vova, had lived there. Circumstances were no longer modest.

What their business was, I never wanted to know, I never asked, and I was never told. What I gleaned, eventually, is that it generated cash that needed cleaning. What our business was, exactly, they'd already learned enough from Vladik.

On Vladik's word, they'd invest $1.3 million of dirty money in Moby Dx, more if Max would let us take it. We would return it fresh as a daisy; preferably more of it than we'd taken it, but laundered would be good enough. From me, all they wanted to know was that I was loyal to him. Stamina and willingness to go along with whatever they threw at me would be a mark of loyalty. Complaints and impatience would be a mark of disloyalty. Disloyalty was a punishable offense. Before we'd taken the money, the punishment would be no money. After we'd taken the money, punishment would be … Vladik hinted I didn't want to think about what the punishment would be. Following the pleasantries, we made our way into the private residence.

We walked through what looked more like a design showroom than someone's house. The diverse and contemporary furniture, and the large rooms whose reconfigured and blown out walls were covered in birch veneers and fabric wallpaper, were at odds with the earthy and scrappy character of the neighborhood. But why not? They had the dough with no place to go, and no plans to move out, and the beach light beaming and filtering in complemented the airy modern spaces.

In a two-story dining room we sat down to a buffet of everything I'd just seen on the street. Iced bottles of vodka, the omnipresent Russian God, were always within arm's reach. Beer was available on demand, and plain water, too, but wine was "a lousy drink," for sissies, and unavailable.

And so we ate and talked. Mostly, they did the talking. Part of my ordeal was to show that I knew my place, never complaining, always listening, answering the odd true-or-false question, graduating to multiple choice as the sun set. Streams of family and associates walked through, grabbing plates and piling them high, working the piles down, and then refilling them. Dining staff came and went, and came and went. Vladik—long lost Vova—was the main attraction, but the visitors wanted a glimpse of me, too. I met them all and made lists, mental lists of who was who. A couple of girls came through, maybe sixteen years old, the red-haired daughters of Morris and Borris, one of whom had done the artwork for the Moby Dx logo. They looked me over.

"You're kinda fetch for this building," one commented.

"Nasty Gal?" the other asked, referring, I guess, to their favorite online emporium.

"Nope. Bought 'em this morning just for you," I said.

"Are you sure you're really with him?" the first said, pointing to Vladik.

"With, and not with. Business partners."

"You're nerdier than you look then?"

Reaching, I said, "Hella ratchet nerdy."

"Not bad."

"Nice try," and they both laughed with me and at me, and then their nympholicious selves disappeared, probably, I thought, to go make some boys die of *Hardonia simplex*.

Lunch—*that was lunch?*—was cleared and we were swept out of the banquet hall so it could be set up for dinner. "You'll go to the banya," was all that I was told as we walked to the staffed private gym on the premises. Handed towels, gym clothes, and a tank suit, all of the right size, I found the girls again in the locker room, getting ready to work out at something.

"Do you even lift?" one taunted.

"Be nice," the other said to her. "You can do our routine with us if you want."

"There's a trainer here, too, and she can help if you'd rather go your own way."

"But you should do the banya before you leave."

"It's best if you've already worked off lunch. Wear yourself out if you can."

"Do you know what's coming up for me?" I asked.

"I think more eating and drinking. They'll want you to talk about yourself in complete sentences sooner or later. We've seen this before. It's not that hard to pass. They won't pull your fingernails out or anything like that," one said.

"No, not a friend of Uncle Vova's," the other laughed.

"I can barely tell you apart now that you're not wearing clothes, I mean, street clothes. Are you really only cousins?"

"Just cousins."

Once upon a time I could have followed their workout. As I had once been, these girls were athletes in training. They were too fit for me. I had made the choice.

They were pushing big weights and I was on a stationary bike when a call came in from Max. Putting the slab on speaker and leaning it up against the trainer's screen so I could keep my hands on the bars, I said hello, but only heard road noise and Max humming. "Max, Max!" I said, loud enough to draw the girls' attention my way. If it was a bump call, I thought maybe he'd figure it out and we would talk. I prepared to explain the inexplicable and happily relay how close we were to completing the financing when Max's voice came through, not loud and clear, but loud and clear enough. He recited poetry, working out lines to something only a Pynchon fan like Max could have written.

Stiffer than the wood on a Castro queen,
Stiffer than extrusions of an engineer's dream,
Stiffer than a foot thick block of glass,
Stiffer than Sameer's cock stuffin ...

And then, "Shit!" and dial tone.

One of the indistinguishable teens almost dropped a barbell on her cousin. "Tell me that's not someone you know," the other one said to me, after wiping away the tears of laughter.

"I can't."

"He burnt for that."

That's when we began to bond, I guess.

An hour later we were in the Ladies Banya, an authentic replica of a Siberian sauna, or so said my hostettes. It didn't seem that much different from other saunas I'd been in, until the steam from water poured on hot rocks hit my nostrils and filled them with the smell of berries and menthol, and until the girls picked up fronds of eucalyptus and birch and began beating each other with them, their naked selves exposed head to toe when their towels fell to the ground in some Russian equivalent of a pillow fight, sans pillow.

"Want some?" I was asked.

It seemed impolite, or even unwise from a funding perspective, to decline. I got up, towel still wrapped tightly around me, and joined the three way massage-cum-beating-cum-food fight, sans food. I could see that with the right partners, this could be a special experience. My towel dropped off and I was as naked as they were. The number of social conventions I would have had to break to really let go were absolutely too numerous, and the twin cousins weren't taking any unusual liberties with each other or inviting them from me, so I kept it platonic, that is, until, how did he say it? Gentlemen of the jury, it was they who seduced me. And I quite suddenly found all my lips opened and penetrated by two aggressively probing tongues. They were young, so I gave them slack for lack of subtlety, but they were skilled, I will say that, and willing, and in youthful bloom, too. I gave as good as I got, if sights and sounds and their responses trembling up through my fingertips don't lie.

When we did finally make it out of the sauna and the gym, the girls accompanied me back to the banquet room where Vladik was surrounded by even more old friends and family than he had been earlier. When he saw me, he signaled to his watch and gave me a look of disbelief that I'd been away so long. He was still free of suspicion of the real cause of the delay, but he doubted that I might have been working for the good of Moby Dx. The girls paid their respects to him. To their parents, they whispered something, and then I heard them say they couldn't join us for dinner because they had homework still to do. Following that, they went their way with so little acknowledgment of me that I might have been hurt if they hadn't turned about abruptly and silently mouthed the words, "You passed," before smiling and returning to their schoolwork obligations.

Everyone but the immediate family dispersed, and in the flurry of activity, Vladik got me alone and asked, "Four hours?"

"It was all work. Your nieces have their hands in everything. It was a penetrating investigation. They made me really open up. Girls will be girls. I had to take a nap afterward."

Vladik just looked at me in disbelief.

"I don't think they're going to sue for statutory rape if that's what you're worried about," I let him know.

Only Morris and Boris, Tatiana, Vladik, and I were left in the gigantic banquet hall. Borschts and stews of rabbit and lamb and beef, but no pork—out of respect for me and the possibility I might be a Mohammedan—with potatoes and carrots, and little raviolis they called *pelmeni*, and dumplings they called *vareniki*, a round of black bread, beer, the Russian God, and champagne, too. But the main event was me. They wanted to know about me, about my family, and how I knew Vladik. I charmed them with my birth story, and I guess I did so too when I talked more about my mother, and my voice kept cracking. "May her memory be a blessing," Tati said as I took time to collect myself.

MORE than twelve hours after I had arrived by train, in the wee hours of Thursday, Vladik and I walked in texting silence toward the El.

Vladik to Max: "The Note is full up!"

Me to Georgina: "Still busy. See you Friday night."

Vladik to Arianna: "Got it all."

Me to Louisa: "Still busy. I'll call you later."

Me to Venus: "In NYC now ;) Not this weekend."

Max to Vladik: "Great! Breakfast tomo?"

Vladik to Max: "Still in NYC. Saturday?"

Max to Vladik: "To Indonesia Sunday. See when I'm back."

Before Vladik dropped me off, he asked, "Have you confirmed our flight with Xenia?"

"Not yet."

In this city where nobody sleeps, I texted her: "Is your offer still good?"

I asked Vladik, "Did we pass?" knowing that I already had two votes, but not sure how many there were.

"Flying colors," and we hugged again, for the third time, then high-fived, fist-bumped, and hugged again. Unprofessional? Maybe. Adulterous? No.

Xenia's incoming text, "Yes. Madame Wong's at 11?" made me feel all warm and fuzzy.

"She says yes," I told Vladik. "I'll shoot you the departure time later."

When turned to go back to the Brothers, I cabbed on over to 57th Street, sleeping most of the way. Before I closed my eyes, I had a few more exchanges with Xenia. We decided to have our own private *tête-à-tête* at the Mandarin Oriental before connecting at Madame Wong's pop-up club with Vadim later.

CHAPTER 149 THE CLAIRVOYANT

PROPHETIC CAPITAL'S Citation X took off from LGA at 6:07 p.m. with an ETA at SJC of 8:01 PST. Vladik texted Arianna and asked her to have Sheba pick us up.

The flight back to California was like a meeting with Tiresias the Clairvoyant, although Vadim was anything but blind.

We told Xenia and Vadim that we couldn't accept their offer, and why, or sort of why. Vadim had wanted to invest because he thought Max was a genius, because I was special, and because Vladik could straighten out the bullshit and get things done. Xenia wanted to invest because she liked the premise, because Vadim spoke so highly of Max, and because she wanted to see more of me. She could do the last of those anyway, but it would be harder without board meetings as the mechanism for rendezvous. That Max's obstinacy was bringing the whole thing down, that Max would not bend—not only to Vadim's wishes but also to what was obviously the right thing to do—released Vadim from any obligation to be politic.

"If you don't have the power to make this decision in the right way, the power structure is broken. What does the cap table look like?"

Vladik explained it.

"No, no, no! That is all wrong."

"Dimi, calm down, please," Xenia said, putting her hand on his. "The plane is too small for your voice." Hers was honeyed.

"I'm sorry, but that is wrong." We paused, and we waited. "He doesn't come to the necessary meetings, he doesn't put in the time, and he craters a critical decision. What reason did he give you?"

"Really, he offered his reasons. Let's leave it at that, shall we?"

"No, we shall not. I demand to know what he offered. You need me to know. Believe me, you need me, you need Xenia to know."

"Dimi, please," Xenia tried again.

Vladik did want to tell them, and Vadim's imprecations to stop defending Max gave him the privilege.

"He said, 'I would prefer not to.'"

After that, the only sound was the hum of the Rolls Royce engines.

"I would prefer not to. I would prefer not to!" Vadim shouted louder each time, his tone turning it into a question. "*Bozhe moi.* What kind of an answer is that? It's the answer of a child, or a sociopath. It's not the answer of a businessman."

"Really, that's harsh. I, or Lakshmi and I will be able to control him. We have enough money, $2.5 million, for now. We'll get the rest. It may be harder than it should be, but we'll get it."

"No, I am afraid not. He will bring the company to its knees someday. Look at what he's told you. Bootstrapping? Failed. MOST? Shit—at least according to your Chief Scientist the inventor. Time commitment? Does not meet it. What else do you need, man? What else do you need? There's going to come a day when he's going to tell you you've been sacked."

"Dimi, you must stop." Xenia stood up and glowered at him. "This is just your speculation, and it's too much."

"Yes, it is my speculation. But no, it is not too much. I'm trying to protect these people. They're too naïve. This is a trap and they don't see it. As our guests, we owe them an opening of their eyes."

"He can't fire me," Vladik said.

"If he has the shares, he can fire you."

"He has the contract with HMRI that prevents him from exercising that kind of control. He won't violate that contract. They'll fire him."

"Vladik. He's a narcissist." He paused for a second, changed his tone, and proceeded with complete calm. "I know, I know. Narcissism is good. It makes the world go 'round. We're all narcissists. I know all that." Then he reverted to adamance. "Max, though, he's of a different stripe. He has a disorder, a psychopathy. He's classifiable. He's alexithymic or something. No remorse. No empathy. He doesn't care, or maybe even acknowledge that you exist. Plain as day, he doesn't care an iota about you, or maybe even you," pointing to me, throwing his finger at me. I winced as if he had hit me.

"So far, Max has been very careful about playing by HMRI rules, so I don't think ..." and then Vladik stopped. The others waited for him to continue. He was lost in thought. Max had been as overt in sidestepping the rules with Caselode Fittings I and the Council as he had been overt in obeying them otherwise. He made his own rules, and he'd change them when it was convenient. Vladik hadn't told our two hosts about the holding company and he wasn't about to, either. Vadim and Xenia would never invest under the terms of that operating agreement. Never.

"Let's suppose you're right. What do you suggest we do?"

"Fold 'em."

"Just quit?"

"That's right. You're only losing more every day. You're on a voyage with him that's going to end badly. He's a monomaniac, seeking his own goal. Power and money, certainly. Fame, probably. Doesn't seem to be about women or sex. Somehow he's made you take on his goals. I can see that. I can even see why."

Xenia had given up trying to calm him down. I was cowering.

"I myself said he was a genius, and I'm sure I'm not the first, and we're all probably right. What the hell difference does that make? That doesn't make it any more likely to turn out well. He's not a genius about these matters. Xenia's a genius of the right kind for this. Vladik, you could make this work. But Max, he's bent on absolute control, and he holds too many cards. This is going to implode. I've seen it before." And then, parenthetically, Vadim said, "Although I'll admit, this is one for the record books."

He looked to each of us, but we had nothing to say. After a long silence he continued. "But it's not like some ship where you're stuck. You can get off, and the sooner the better. For you," looking straight at Vladik, "and your lovely friend here. She's more than your employee. She's your friend. These things are not difficult to see."

Vadim was spent after his soliloquy. We were all spent. He slept for the final hour before we touched down. Xenia and I sat close together. Vladik wondered whether he could unwind Moby Dx. What would Venus think? He hadn't taken any money from the Brothers K, yet. Better not to start.

"It's the worst pun," she said to me.

I looked at her, quizzical.

"I'll be Xenia?"

"Yes, you'll be Xenia. Will I be Xenia, too?"

"I'll leave that to you."

I followed her off the plane, admiring her figure and her composure, which I'd only seen drop at the Mandarin Oriental. I wondered what she was like in bed with Vadim.

When we landed in San Jose, Sheba was on the runway in the Escalade. She dropped me off at Georgina's before taking Vladik aka Vova to get his car, still parked near SFO. Then he drove back in solitude to his wife at the hundred million dollar house.

CHAPTER 150 THE MISSIONS

VADIM'S MESSAGE reverberated over the weekend. Vladik told Arianna about Max's "I would prefer not to." She wept with remembered pain. He hid from her the specifics of Vadim's oratory. I was silent about the founders' strains, maintaining an upbeat posture on the premise that we'd raised all the money we were after. Neither of us was about to quit. Time worked its magic, the echoes damped out, and we got on with the business of Moby Dx LLC. There was a lot of it, beginning with the creation of a more detailed plan than we'd ever had.

Our first morning back at 525, we shut ourselves in *sans* Max and covered whiteboards with dry erase markers until we had something. Our unstated mission, the one we kept secret from Max, became one of proving that MOST was a dead end while at the same time appearing to be giving it all our soul. In parallel, and at lower profile, we would get some results, grants and publications on BroadID, all of which would be the foundation of the company. We'd hire aggressively for MOST and cautiously for the other, moving the MOST staff to BroadID when the former was pronounced dead. We'd play Max by leaning on him to find the collaborators for MOST and involve him in the data analysis. If he couldn't or didn't deliver the collaborators, there'd be no data. Data talks, bullshit walks. It would be a quick fail. When the infectious disease results were confirmed, he'd come around. That's what I'd seen in the Frood Group many times before. And with the results in hand, we could get the money or partnerships we needed to take them forward and to market.

We erased all our damning, conspiratorial notes from the whiteboards and then wrote a Max-appropriate version of this mission. From that flowed an eighteen-month plan with milestones, staffing, and budget, all on a single piece of paper. We'd hire three professionals and a tech, move into All-In-One, set up the payroll and benefits infrastructure, keep everyone aligned on the stated mission but not the shadow mission, get the real work done, and generate revenue or raise more money. Always, raise more money.

Max had a different plan in mind, but we didn't hear about that for a while.

CHAPTER 151 THE FIVE HORSEMEN

SOCIAL MEDIA was all the rage, and in our company's first year or so, LinkedIn, Facebook, Zynga, Groupon, and Twitter were the darlings of private investors because, well, because of FOMO if nothing else. Remember when Yahoo went public? I don't. I was 12. Its story has become part of Silicon Valley lore, told and retold. Investors had to have a piece of the Internet, and there weren't many pieces to buy, so the money flowed in to the few available properties, Yahoo among them. The same thing was happening with social media, along with some aggressive and untested methods of income reporting.

What was different in the social media boom was that the private investors, meaning the early venture investors and the later stage private equity investors, believed that by going public later when the company story had developed further, they would capture more of the upside, and would have to share less of it with later stage investors, that is, public investors. This raises the question not to be answered here: Why would public investors buy the stocks if the private investors had already taken the upside? One consequence of the hanging on was that company employees had to wait a particularly long time to get cash for the stock they'd earned. There were buyers who were willing to buy that stock. Secondary markets developed to link up both sides. One was called Second Market. There were others.

I heard about these markets, and being an avid consumer of social media, I checked one of them online to see about buying some FB. Yup. As long as I could pony up $17 million, I could buy a block of one million shares. That was before Goldman Sachs had driven the share price to $25. Smaller blocks were not available.

Tolerant Reader, while what I am writing here may seem like some grand digression whose sole purpose is to add a whiff of verisimilitude, it is far more than that. I'm writing about a central, could-only-happen-here development in the crashing bromance of Max and Vladik. Patience, please, Dear Reader, patience.

One player in the secondary market consisted of corporations, usually LLCs, set up expressly for the purpose of taking investments from smaller fry who wanted to buy a slice of one of those larger blocks he or she couldn't afford on their own. Pooled together, those smaller investments bought the larger block, and when the company—let's say FB—went public, LLC would distribute the FB certificates to the small fry to sell or hold.

Artie "Pupa" Branzino set up such an LLC, Social Media Fish, and through several well-known private investor groups who will remain nameless, he offered the small blocks of FB that were unavailable from any other source. I won't even bother to tell you the terms, or get into the subject of transparency. They're embarrassing evidence of the power of scarcity and greed. The terms don't matter. Branzino found so much interest for the pre-IPO shares that he then set up Social Media Fish II, III, IV, and V for LinkedIn, Zynga, Groupon, and Twitter, respectively. The same or similar investors snapped these up, too. Vladik was like me, an avid social media user. But unlike me, he had money to invest. He heard about Branzino through Jay.

When Jay acquired a large venue for live music in Portsmouth, he become friendly with some celebrities who performed there. To Vladik, Jay sent an excerpt of an email message from Boky. Yes, that Boky.

"... We tried to get the shares through Second Market, but we're priced out, or they're sold out. Can't tell which. Anyway, several of us in the band are in on that Branzino deal I mentioned backstage. We already bought Facebook shares from him. You might still be able to get in on that. He can get us LinkedIn shares, too. Would you have an interest in this and, if so, what would be the tentative dollar amount of your purchase? ..."

Such stilted language from an Icelandic rocker like Boky? You would see from a font change that the tail end of his message copied and pasted from one Pupa Branzino's much more formal messages to prospective investors. After a short exchange between Jay and Vladik, my boss had printed out the subscription forms for the suite of Social Media Fish offerings.

Vladik had not fully absorbed Arianna's message, "*Demi homme, demi cochon*." He and Max continued to act like friendly cofounders. True, Vladik was conspiring with me to execute the shadow mission, and true, Max had defaulted on all his responsibilities to the company with no apparent penalty, but they continued to act like they were friends. They drank beer in Mountain View at Moby Dick's where Max was heralded, and wine in Palo Alto at Vin, Vino, Wine where he was recognized but not a regular. They went to nice restaurants. They talked about science and medicine and politics. They played cards. They gossiped about the rise and fall of valley celebrities and their companies. Social media came up. The five horsemen of social media—Facebook, LinkedIn, Zynga, Groupon, and Twitter—came up. There was so much interest in them, if you owned them early, before the IPO, how could you lose money?

"Max, I hesitate to mention this to you, but I've just seen an offer to buy these through the secondary markets. Do you want to see the documents?"

Max went over them, boned up on the latest critical analyses in *Business Week* and *Seeking Alpha,* and ran the numbers through his left-brain odds calculator. "Look at the revenue Groupon is putting up," he said to Vladik. "They're printing it."

"That's what worries me."

"Fuck. Have you seen the list of lawyers who are in this deal?"

"Trial lawyers, not securities lawyers."

"Anal all. Makes me feel safe. And Zynga! Wow. Farmville? One hit after another."

"Why are people paying for virtual goods?"

"Millennials. Ours is not to reason why. Ours is but to hold or buy. And I'm fuckin' in. The investment profile is so different from Moby Dx, we can write checks for this and offset the other's illiquidity within a year."

"The more you get excited about it, the worse I feel about it."

"You make your decision for yourself. Don't come running back to me if you put money in and then it doesn't work out," Max told him.

"Don't worry. This will be my decision. Win, lose or draw, I'm on my own. Same with you, right?"

"Sure. Of course! I'm a gambler. I know there are risks. But this is going to work out. Public companies with earnings. Pre-IPO pricing? How can we lose?"

Vladik told me later, "Jay was less enthusiastic, but he thought Boky had done the due diligence, so Jay was going along for the fun of it. For him, the money was chump change. But Max, said, 'When the fish is on the line, pull it fuckin' in.' He was very proud of his financial analysis. Right around that time, Boky had become a partner at Escalation Ventures. The press was all over the news, and Max liked being associated with a Boky deal. He had told a few of his local poker friends, and they had told a few of theirs—not all of them nice people—that the genius Max Frood was backing up the truck to invest in Social Media Fish, and everyone thought Boky had done the due diligence on Branzino."

After submitting the paperwork and wiring their money, Branzino sent email to all prospective buyers that they would be getting their shares at the Goldman Sachs price of $25 per share, not the $21 per share stated on the prospectus.

"I'm out," Jay texted Vladik.

"Max, I think we should bail," Vladik texted.

"Patience," Max replied.

Then there was a flurry of email between Branzino and individuals on the long mailing list. Demands were made. Branzino promised to return cash to anyone who, like Jay, wanted to get out. Parties reported receiving their cash back. Branzino said that he'd guarantee the original price anyway.

Max called Vladik, who was driving at the time, after the final message came through. "See, it's all cool. I'm in." In his voice though was a peculiar sound, like a dog panting, near exhaustion. There was fear in it.

"I don't know. Either he had the price or he didn't. Seems fishy." Vladik paused. There was more panting on the line. "Max, are you alright? Sounds like you dodged a bullet."

Another pause. More panting. Finally, Max said, "*Ha!*" Then he changed the subject. "How's the license coming along?"

Vladik said, "Slow as usual. I—"

Max interrupted, "Are you in that fucking Porsche?"

"Yes. Can you hear me OK?"

"The road noise and this tinnitus are killing me. I gotta go," he said, and hung up.

Max went on to invest in all five LLCs.

The first of the companies went public. Then others. Some rose, some fell. I remember seeing Max, halfway out the building and finishing a conversation with Vladik. "I'm feeling pretty fucking smart right now," he said, and then let the glass door close behind him.

I was still unaware of any of these goings-on at the time, and his words meant nothing out of context. "What was that about," I asked Vladik. He told me about Pupa, and explained that one of those five horsemen had IPO'd and doubled on its first day, quadrupling the price at which Max had bought it.

The shares, as is typical in these situations, were subject to a 180-day lockup intended to prevent them from entering the market too soon after the IPO. Although Max could have bought a McLaren like Jay's on his paper gains, he was happy driving his Outback. Still, Max began his 180-day countdown.

Vladik had accepted Pupa's offer to withdraw his investment in Social Media Fish I after the re-repricing fiasco, and had not participated in the others. "I still haven't told Max because I couldn't stand to watch him gloat over my timidity," he told me.

CHAPTER 152 THE BIG WINNERS

THE BIG winners were not, of course Social Media Fish's investors, but the children of the five horsemen's VCs, private equity investors, bankers, founders, and the few early employees who owned tenths of a percent of the companies. Their tens, hundreds, or even thousands of millions of dollars would, in the hands of a clever tax accountant, provide the financial foundations of a lifetime, or maybe a dynasty.

The VCs and private equity investors don't put much of their own money at risk in these deals. [N.B., of course, Careful Reader, there are exceptions, but they are rare, very rare, so don't be snowed on this by their raised cries.] They raise funds, hundreds of millions and even billions, from private and institutional investors, invest it for them, take an annual fee of a few percent to run their offices and pay their salaries, and then take twenty, thirty, or even thirty-five percent of the return when the investments become liquid with an IPO or a sale. That final piece is their bonus, or their carried interest. Now, if you or I were working at General Electric, or Genentech, or Intel, whether on the shop floor or in an executive suite, and one of us received a performance bonus, the IRS would tax it as regular income. And if we were at the top of the tax rate pyramid, as is every venture capitalist worth his salt, that rate would be about 40 percent. But, thanks to the carried interest loophole, the VCs and private equity investor taking home millions in bonus is taxed at 15 percent.

That, Appalled Reader, is called regressive taxation, and it's only one of many dodges and ruses that the winners use to hang on to a disproportionate share of their unearned income. I use that term advisedly. Unearned income is what we used to call investment income, much as citizen is the old term for someone we now call a taxpayer.

Other dodges and ruses include grantor retained annuity trusts, generation skipping trusts, dynasty trusts, not to mention cleverly and even fraudulently obtained valuation of assets, and more. It's now old news that a presidential candidate put undervalued paper assets in an Individual Retirement Account—a vehicle intended to allow tax-free appreciation of retirement savings for the middle class, in amounts of a few thousand dollars per year—and those assets appreciated at a rate approaching that of cosmic inflation, leaving him with an IRA worth over a hundred million dollars. There being no chance whatsoever that those assets will be needed by the candidate, the principal will only grow, and will grow faster than society as a whole. When he dies, the IRA will go to his beneficiaries. Those scions can live off the millions in annual distributions, or pass it to their own heirs who can let it grow tax-free for even longer, employing the magic of time and compound interest to defer and defer the day until the taxman is paid. And what is a dynasty but a big bundle of assets—or, Forgiving Reader, in the Newspeak of the moment, a bundle of merit, *Ha!*—growing faster than the demands on it, and which is then passed on? Thus a dynasty is made, largely tax free, legally, although with a deft valuation of the account's seed gift, and with the helping hand of the tax code.

There is insufficient space here—nor do I have the energy, nor do I think you have the patience if I did—to explain all the nuances upon variations, especially the gifts to oneself or one's heirs under the name of philanthropy. Nevertheless, this is your meritocracy at work. Drink the Kool-Aid, or don't drink the Kool-Aid. You, Taxpaying Reader, decide for yourself.

CHAPTER 153

MEANWHILE, BACK AT THE FARM

QASIMA PUT something like the Great Wall of China between the I's IP and the rest of the world. The only way across was through the TTO. I's technology licensing agreements were designed to shut down a widely used exploit called pipelining. Suppose a Principal signaled to TTO that he or she wanted a patent or technology portfolio licensed to his or her company, and that in turn a licensing agreement was put in place. New results on related matters, valuable to the company, obtained by the Principal at the I, using the I's resources, did not automatically flow to the company. They had not been licensed to the company; only the original results had been. A new licensing agreement would have to be negotiated for the new results. Circumventing that process and incorporating the new technology into the company without going through TTO? That's pipelining. Qasima frowned on it with extreme prejudice.

Max adhered to the pipelining guidelines assiduously. He discouraged his group from talking to staff at Tiny, Genormx, Moby Dx, or the other companies whose names we had not yet heard, and limited the information he gave to CEOs and key technologists. In addition to keeping Qasima happy, his compliance had other benefits. If his companies were in the dark about what went on at the I, he could compete with them when it suited his purposes. He advanced certain ideas inside the I and others outside, making the choice based on his card-playing-refined abilities to estimate which outcome would provide him—not the company and not the I—the greatest return. And, in the name of avoiding pipelining, hid his activity with other companies, activity which might lead someone like Vladik to ask, "Where in the world is Max Frood and why is he not at Moby Dx?"

Vladik knew he was not getting the commitment Max had promised, but other troubling issues were only very slowly emerging from the shadows.

In one meeting with Dykkur, Vladik asked general questions about how the Genormx deal had come to together, and what he, Dykkur, thought had made it possible to raise $24 million, or ten times what Moby Dx had raised. Of course, circumstances were different, because Genormx had years of development at the I and very clear objectives for the instrument being built. You can't raise $24 million unless you need it, and Moby Dx couldn't yet prove it needed it.

Dykkur's answer was a revelation. "Max and [another Principal] are in the middle of raising a $40 million round for Mongocyte. I don't even think they have as much filed IP as you do. What was key there was the relationship between [the other Principal] and ..." The rest of what Dykkur said remains confidential, but it's not essential for the point I'm making.

Vladik, describing his thoughts to me later that day said, "How can Max have a $40 million deal in the works? What happened to 'This will be the focus of my consulting?' and how is it possible that I've never even heard about it?" Pulling his hair and grimacing, he continued, "What else is going on that I don't know about?"

Plenty, as it turned out.

Genomax Inc. was Max's company dedicated to mining his own genome. He expected whole-genome sequencing and proprietary informatics to uncover the secrets of his IQ, his memory, his energy, his sexual prowess, and his hoped-for longevity. "If fucking SCOTUS doesn't get in my way, I'm going to license these genes to every pharma and Dx company there is," he told Dykkur. Dykkur acquired the URLS, did the trademark searches, and incorporated Maxiq, Memax, Dynomax, Orgasmx, and Maxilife on Max's behalf in anticipation of great findings, *ka-ching!* He reserved Xenomax for the possibility of inserting Max's extraordinary genes into animals, and someday creating the first talking dog.

The tag line for Think Shake LLC was "Digest your food for thought." Max observed that the number of letters in the English alphabet is not too different from the number of amino acids in human protein. Just as with mapping the sixty-four three-base codons to the twenty-something individual amino acids, it would be possible to map the same codons to the twenty-six individual letters of the alphabet. Max wanted to encode text, you know, like *Moby-Dick*, or *Wintrobe's Clinical Hematology*, into single stranded DNA fragments aka oligonucleotides, using the methods of in vitro gene synthesis. Sweetened and flavored with berries and bananas, or Fruct2 in a premium product, thickened up with lipidicious vanilla ice cream, and blended smooth with ice, the result would be ideas ready-to-drink. He wrote in an invention disclosure that if you slurped such a smoothie while reading the text, your body would learn the code, and pretty soon you'd be able to consume your news, books, and blogs through a straw, but at a rate a thousand times higher than reading. Think Shake promised, he told some FOMOing at the mouth investors, to transform learning globally. Those, like Max, who had early access to it, would become supermen compared to everyone else. "The singularity in human intelligence is around the corner," he pitched. The thesis was completely untested of course, and its cost-effectiveness depended on being able to write oligonucleotide fragments a thousand times more cheaply than had yet been demonstrated. Max formed a small team to work on core technology for, as he called it, the OligoMaker.

There was a parallel company too, Think Meat LLC. To its investors he sold the belief that only if the target text was encoded in protein would there be conversion from food to thought. Think Meat aimed to apply additive manufacturing to the production of text-encoded burgers and steaks.

And there were companies founded by his staff. Max had little involvement in those, but for the use of his name and as the gatekeeper for TTO licenses, he took what became known as the Max Tax, or 20 percent of the founding equity.

Max devoted more time and effort to hiding all of this from his partners than he did on any single project, even ones which were the focus of his commitment.

CHAPTER 154 MISSED MESSAGES

BUSINESS MEETINGS I had with people outside the company were of two kinds. The first were all dedicated to bringing up our lab at All-In. They were mundane, transactional meetings about things like the price of reagents, equipment, and service contracts, or discussions with other researchers about their published protocols and the pros and cons of choices they'd made. Vladik wouldn't have known what to say even if I'd included him, so I didn't. Meetings of the second kind were of a higher level, and he arranged those. The topics were science and medicine, occasionally strategy, and almost never technology and operations. If the other parties had something delicate to say, they'd say it in private to the guy in the suit, the CEO, Vladik, and not to some over-confident cinnamon girl, me. My point is to say that much of what follows I heard from Vladik.

"Looking back, I missed several early signals. Vadim, OK, it's not like we missed that memo. He put me on guard. And Arianna's message, I didn't know how to parse it. There was so much marital acrimony," by which Vladik meant between him and Max, "clouding things that I under-valued the import of what she said; the import for me, for all of us.

"But the other signals, they came from different directions, impugning the quality of his work, work I still thought was beyond reproach. I sloughed off what I was hearing as sour grapes from people who weren't good enough to hang in his company, or from people with thin skin. I was with the prettiest girl at the ball. Don't tell me she's syphilitic, please."

Then Vladik told me about three conversations. Forgiving Reader, I've replaced the actual names with meaningful but untraceable descriptions.

"[One of his scientific peers] said to me, 'Everyone of his papers reads like a company prospectus, so I've stopped reading them.'

"I had flown to San Diego and spent a few hours with [a pundit in the employ of one of our prospective collaborators], telling him about both research projects. He said to me, 'The molecular stethoscope is, uh, fraught with problems. I like what you're doing with BroadID. But the guys in my group were burned when they worked with Max at Tiny. I don't think we'll have any internal support to fund you.'

"I got a meeting with [one of the most prominent health sciences investors], just to talk to about the merits of our pitch, a conversation that was explicitly not about raising money from her. She said, 'Vladik, the questions any VC is going to ask you to answer are: (1) Why would I invest in you, a first time CEO? And, (2) Why would I invest in Max whose attention jumps around so much he's not a real contributor?'"

CHAPTER 155 INCONTROVERTIBLE ILLOGIC

I KNOW, SUFFERING Reader, that much as I've tried to remain neutral in my presentation of the facts, Max may appear as the anti-hero of this tale. It may not therefore come as a surprise to you that Max claimed credit for all the money we raised. It did come as a surprise to me and it did to Vladik. We still had things to learn.

The Night of the Luminosities was beyond rational. As Max and everyone else said, "If Venus had given us only the Sherpas, Dayenu." For me, the anointed, it was transcendental. I'm grateful that my association with Max helped get me there, but let's not forget that I became the apple of Venus' eye when I spied Al Gore at Madera, and without any introduction from Max. And, about the Moby Dx, Max didn't say a word to her. He didn't know the pitch. And he didn't have his fist in her up to his elbow, either. I'm not saying that was work, but if that's what it took to close the deal, he couldn't have done it. And based on my last sighting of him with a hunky Sherpa in a tantric wheelbarrow, I'm not sure he would have wanted to. So where did he get off claiming credit?

"I introduced you," he said.

"Max, I met her at the Rosewood while having dinner with Vladik."

"You were trading on my name. She wanted Frood Brand. They all do."

Now suppose that she hadn't come up with the money. Would he take that to mean that his name was no good? No. I think he'd say, "No, you screwed the pooch, or the pitch, or something." He takes the credit and you get the blame.

Vadim and Xenia, Prophetic Capital? We did not get the money from them, but we can say for sure that we did not get the money precisely because of Max. Going into the meeting, Max would have been the deciding factor for investing. By the end of the meeting, I don't think, based on Vadim's harangue, they'd have invested if Max had any association with it at all. That's pure speculation on my part. If we hadn't gotten the money from Vladik's cousins, we'd have had to have a discussion with Max about why we couldn't get Prophetic to put in $1.3 million. We would have repeated what Vadim had told us. And Max? He would have said we were [EXPLETIVE DELETED] closers. And if we had gotten the money, it would have been the same argument he made about Venus. "I introduced you. You were trading on my name. They want the Frood brand." And as before, it wasn't true that Max introduced us. Vladik met Vadim on the same day. Max would have finessed that by saying that Vadim was only there because of Max, and not at all because of Vladik. It is true, we, mostly Vladik, traded on Max's name, but that doesn't mean Max deserves all 100 percent of the credit. The name is part of the package and deserves part of the credit or the blame, but never the entirety of either. For Max, it was invariably all of the former and never any of the latter.

Now, about the Brothers Kakitelashvili, whom Max had yet to meet even over the phone, and whom he had never heard of until we had the deal done. Again he took the credit. He said, "Without me, you wouldn't have a company." The counterargument, "Without us, you wouldn't have a company," seemed to carry no weight. We were Lego, interchangeable commodity parts, and he was The Talent.

Tinnitus put Max on edge and had him grinding his teeth around the clock. Mild vestibulopathy left him wobbly once in a while. Kidney disease cut down his endurance, always, and on occasion sent him into dementia. His robotic leg was a bright spot in his new life, but missing a leg took one more tax on his stamina. If with his failing health and his unrequited ambitions it could ever be said that he was happy, he was happy to have $2.3M of new money, and not a dime more, in Moby Dx. Max wanted to pull out his $100k contribution.

"You can do the same," he told Vladik.

"I don't think it works that way. The investors will want us to have skin in the game."

"You think Venus is going to get her tits up about our hundred grand? It's not even noise to her."

"It's what it means to us that counts to her. She knows it's a meaningful amount to us."

"Let them go fuck themselves. We're giving them all our time."

"Max, you're playing with fire. Let me go have some conversations with them before I make a decision on this."

"What do you mean, you will make a decision on this?"

Vladik remained silent on the other end of the line. With only two members on the Council, they either agreed or they were deadlocked. Since the money was in the bank account already, and Vladik had sole signature authority there, a deadlock meant the money stayed in place. Max had stated his preference, so the decision was Vladik's. He didn't want to rub Max's face in that, though, so he said, "I mean, I'll make a decision for myself."

He could hear Max's heavy breathing. After an uncomfortable silence, Vladik continued. "I'll let you know."

"OK," and then Max hung up.

Vladik didn't even bother to call his cousins or Venus. He came straight to me.

"Bad idea," I said.

"It's a show of bad faith,"

"It's common knowledge that investors want the entrepreneurs to have skin in the game."

"How can he not know this?" Vladik asked.

"He knows this, and thinks he can break the unwritten rules."

"I'm going to tell him Mo says the money stays."

"Don't even bring it up with Venus."

"And if he asks?"

"Tell him Mo said he'd send your teenage nieces to rip his fingernails off, and then laugh like it's a joke."

Vladik looked at me with another of his, "What planet did you come from?" looks.

"MAX, I spoke to Mo," Vladik told Max a few days later at Douce France, a café next to Max's physical therapy clinic.

"So you've made your decision?" Max said, mocking and sarcastic.

"No, Mo made it for me."

Max was silent.

"He said they wanted to us to have skin in the game, so if you wanted to take your money out, he'd send teenage girls to rip your fingernails off." Vladik tried to laugh, but he couldn't; his desire to watch Max squirm was too great.

After a moment of waiting, he went on. "It was a joke," Max.

"And what did Venus say?" Max was deadpan.

"I didn't bother to ask. It's non-negotiable with them."

Max finished his crêpe and his cake, changed the subject, and then left without saying another word about the money.

Chapter 156 Convertible Negotiations

All that remained in the realm of financing was for Vladik to negotiate the final terms of the Convertible Note with Venus and with his cousins, and then go through the same tedious drill he had done with the Operating Agreement. Venus designated her lawyer as the negotiator on behalf of Venus NV. Mo Kakitelashvili worked directly with Vladik on behalf of their investing entity, Kashonli LLC.

Venus's concerns, as relayed by the lawyer Kenda, squeezed on the very company-friendly terms that Vladik and Dykkur had forwarded to her. Kenda asked for higher interest rates, higher discount rates, and a lower cap. Translated into English she wanted (i) to earn 8 percent interest (instead of the 5 percent we offered) on her $1M, (ii) to pay 30 percent less than follow-on investors (instead of 15 percent we offered) when the Note converted to equity in the future, and (iii) under no circumstances did she want her $1M to be worth less than 10 percent of the company, whereas the company had her offered 8 percent.

Venus, through Kenda, also wanted the Noteholders to have veto power over major financial transactions like a corporate sale, and over amendments to the Operating Agreement.

Venus had one other concern, which she took up herself, and that was that Moby Dx be *the* thing that Max was committed to. She spoke to him over the phone. "Maxi, I hope you had a good time at the Luminosities. I saw you helping with the gardening the next afternoon," gently hinting that she expected him to keep his ribald escapades out of public view.

"Venus, fantastic as always! I gather Lakshmi found it entrancing, too," trying to score by pointing out Venus's own libertine excesses.

"Yes, wonderful girl." She paused. "Maxi, the reason I'm calling, now, is that before I go ahead with these note documents," and then she wandered off in a grand parenthesis, "and of course, you know I've already given you the money—"

"Yes, thank you so much. I know you're going to be proud to be associated with this venture."

"Yes, Maxi. I know. Before I go ahead with these Note documents, I just want to make sure that you are in this, that this is your thing for the next several years."

"Oh, absolutely—"

"Maxi," she cut him off. "Don't try to play me."

"Venus. Seriously, this is the main focus of my consulting effort. You know, my commitments to Tiny Machines and to Genormx are winding down, and I think what we're doing in this new company is going to transform medicine and make us a fortune. I'm very excited. Vladik is terrific. I'm so happy we met. He is an acquired taste, really. He's not flamboyant, but he does the right things. A lot of people just talk, but he does the things he says he's—"

Venus cut him off again. "Maxi. You. I am asking about you. Are you in this?"

"Venus, yes, of course. The focus of my consulting effort. I'll be there every week, or involved—

"There for them to feed you lunch, or there to work, lead the research program, fly to godforsaken places, press the flesh with the team and visitors?"

"Two full days a month. And mired in the details by phone several times a week."

"OK, Maxi. Thank you. That's all." And then, just dial tone.

Max called her back right away. "Venus, there's something I'd like to ask of you."

"No, Maxi, I don't do amputees!" And she laughed uproariously, taking a full minute to calm down. Max was silent. "What is it Max?"

"I'd like to see an amendment to the Operating Agreement, and Vladik is being quite difficult about it. If *you* asked, I think he couldn't say no."

"What sort of an amendment?"

"Very minor technicality, but important to me. As the Operating Agreement is written, Vladik has consolidated rather too much power because the Council is just the two of us. I'd like to see an amendment that precludes him from voting on the Council on matters of his employment."

"Giving you absolute power over that decision."

"Well, the members must vote and I control only a few percent of Caselode Fittings I."

The sarcasm dripped from Max's cell phone when she said, "Yes, and your samosa man is a well-qualified independent actor on these matters?"

"Venus, this is very important to the long term health of the company. It's not about me."

"Maxi, stop. You are transparently insincere. That said, I'm of two minds. I recall that, ummh, what's his name?" She delayed for a moment, searching, giving up, and then going on. "He wanted to be the CEO of ... uhhh ... oh Max, you know when these nootropics wear off I can't remember anything anymore, but you know the company I'm talking about, right?"

"Yeah, yeah, yeah, of course," Max said, not knowing.

"I thought the position should go to the scientific founder, not that anyone cared what *I* thought," she giggled ironically. "Well, you know ... ummh ... Max, this is embarrassing, what *is* his name?"

"Fred, John, Jim, Mike, Marc, Ron—

"Not Ron, Don. Don Giore. It was Don Giore."

"Venus, there's no one named Don Giore. What about Brook, Bryan, Mark, Peter, Josh, Bill, Brian, Nu—?"

"Yes, yes, yes. He didn't like it at the time, but he made a fortune, a *fortune*, on the deal, so he didn't come out too bad. That says I should agree to your green eyeshade maneuver. On the other hand, this is not your day job. In no way can you be compared to a scientific founder who has demonstrated focus for a decade, is a terrific manager, and doesn't think everyone is a Fucking Idiot. He can wear a suit, too."

"Where do you come out, then?"

"I'm not sure. What's it worth to you?"

"How about a piece of one my other companies?"

"You mean one of the other companies you're not going to be focusing on?"

"Yes, one of those."

"I'll think about it." Then she hung up.

CHAPTER 157 MO NEGOTIATIONS

Mo DIDN'T care about any of those financial terms or Max's commitment. He wanted to dribble the money in slowly, and he was willing to pay more for less in exchange for the privilege. Vladik sent him to Dykkur, whose rule-skirting work with Caselode Fittings seemed to qualify him for concocting a solution to Mo's challenge. He and Dykkur came up with a scheme whereby Kashonli LLC would become the payments processor for all Moby Dx expenses other than payroll. The company terminated its relationship with the extant, above board, fully transparent payments processor that had been receiving electronic invoices for us at mobydx@bill.com. That company logged them, facilitated their approval by me or Vladik, and triggered payment by the bank. Instead, paper invoices were sent to me at All-In-One. I reviewed them and approved them, or pushed them to Vladik for approval. Twice a month I put the approved ones in an envelope and sent the packet to Kashonli's Brooklyn address where it was opened and the invoices were paid by handwritten check. The monthly lease at All-In-One, supplies, capital, travel, and such; the payments were credited against Kashonli's $1.3 million commitment. Interest was calculated based on the date of spending. No one on the receiving side of these transactions ever complained that the money they got wasn't green, nor for that matter, that it was late.

Max did care a good deal about those financial terms, as did Vladik who was subjected to Max's rants about "Venus' outrageous demands." I was kept out of it until Vladik had reached an impasse with Kenda while trying to satisfy Max. Then Vladik asked me to find a middle ground with Venus directly. Again, it wasn't what I would call work, but no one else could have done it. I agreed to maintain a *pied-à-terre* on her property until the Note converted.

CHAPTER 158 THE POINTILLISM

AT THE risk of digression, let me say that the pointillism of the Milky Way on the moonless night sky in Portola Valley was reason enough to go out there. Looking up, the heavenly painting made me wonder if we'd ever wander among the planets of our star's sisters. Georgina and Xenia and I—yes sometimes as a threesome, a wholesome threesome, Licentious-minded Reader—spent many nights beneath that black canopy thanks to Venus' largesse.

On one such evening, Venus joined us too. Our body heat steamed up the windows of my one room house. Xenia and Georgina left to walk on the bald hilltop, for moments together conversing in their mother tongue. After preliminaries, Venus asked me for an update on the company.

"Max tells me how much time he's devoting to Moby Dx."

"Oh, brother. Max is a genius, I know, but he should give it a rest."

"Give what a rest, Dear? Oh, touch my breast, here," and she put my right hand to work.

"He's trying to convince you that whatever progress we're making, its because of him. Right?"

"That was implied. Yes."

"He's not with us much, and that overstates it. I don't see how he can take so much credit, or any credit, for progress. And people who don't know any better believe him. It's soul killing."

"People like me?"

"Without fear or favor?"

"Yes."

"Then yes, people like you. You," I said.

"Darling, coming from you, I can't tell if this is a comment about Max, or—"

I had to interrupt her to share an epiphany. "His demand for all the credit is a form of regressive taxation."

"Oh, Lakshmi, you're harshing my mellow. Can we ever get off that? You might as well say nigger as taxes if you don't want to be loved in this world. Anyway, regressive taxation is good."

"*Ha!* The myth of the deserving rich. No. This is good," and I palmed the face of her always-wet vagina. I had come to learn that this was the best way to get her to listen to me.

"I'm channeling my father now," I said.

"Your father is good, for a man. Do you think he wants to fuck me?"

"Channeling my father's lessons on tax policy and democracy."

For someone so rich and powerful, Venus was easily manipulated. You couldn't call it anything else. I used the optimal degree of stimulation to open her up to me, to all that I am, but without losing her completely to ecstasy.

"So, are you ready?"

"Just don't stop, will you plee ee ee ease?"

"Winner-take-all-economics favors windfalls. There's no dispute about that. The dispute is about what the winners get to keep. They want everyone to believe that they won on their merits alone. Never mind that the winners are often as not the ones who break the law without getting caught, or who lie, obscure, or tell partial truths to their peers, their partners, their clients, and their bosses. And even to themselves to preserve that all-important sense of invincibility. That's merit of a very special kind, don't you think?"

I expected her to come back at me with some derisive critique of my overly broad characterization, but instead, she said, "I'm mollified, or is that just mollied? Feel my thighs, will you? They're super warm."

Indeed they were, and still firm. "But anyway, the bigger the pot, the more meritorious they feel, and the more they feel deserving of the right to keep it all."

"Lakshmi, is this your John Galt speech?"

I was going to answer, "Who is John Galt?" but I wasn't sure she would appreciate my sarcasm.

"Good Ganesha, no. That was what, thirty something thousand words?"

"Thirty-three, I think. We did a word count at the annual reading—"

"You do an annual reading of John Galt's speech?"

"Yes, before the Luminosities. If I had thought it was your kind of thing, I would have invited you."

"Thanks, I'll pass."

"So, is this an Emmanuel Goldstein? Maybe he's more your style."

"That was eleven thousand. This is five hundred, six hundred max."

"I'm yours, Baby, do me, but do me while you're doing me."

So, I began. "I think all the losers contribute to the success of the winners, making him or her better, so the losers are deserving of some of the rewards."

"As we were all a team. Right, a little to the right ... and up ... ahhhhh."

"A team, yes, a tighter or looser confederation. And is our country not a loose confederation of citizens?"

"Taxpayers, Lakshmi, taxpayers."

I was surprised she fought me with transparent Newspeak while I had her in such a vulnerable position. She had reserves of strength worthy of an Olympian, of course. I couldn't go down that path and keep to my six-hundred-word promise, so I tacked back.

"The winners see the coins coming out of the slot machine, each one with his or her own name on it. When some get diverted to the tax man, they don't like it. 'Heh, that coin had my name on it. It's mine, mine I tell you, all mine!'"

I had her on the edge, in a state of incipient convulsion. I could move her on or off the precipice, and I threatened, she knew, to move her off if she stopped listening and let herself go too far into full-blown frenzy.

"And being the winners," I went on, "and seeing their businesses or whatever prosper, they believe, in the great tradition of conflict of interest—Upton Sinclair and all that—that everyone else is a loser. They believe their good fortune is merit, and having converted luck into lucre, they want, naturally enough, to hang on to the actual fortune, all of it. They believe, and I know you believe this, too, because I hear you say it, that they are the job creators; the makers in a world of moochers. Therefore, your class believes that if, after all, taxation is as unavoidable as it is execrable, then at least the winners should be paying less on a percentage basis because, you're the ones who create the jobs for everyone else."

"Yes, yes, yes ... Oh, Sweetheart, bring me home, bring me ho oo oo oome."

"And you call it a meritocracy. You want everyone to call it a meritocracy because the winners rule."

"Yes, yes … uh uh uh. Don't stop. Don't stop. Don't stop."

"By what political science does the skillset of winning at business translate into the skillset of supporting the public interest? Organization management, maybe, but the organizations have very different objectives, even diametrically opposed ones. A CEO exploits opportunities for rent extraction; market ones that support high profit margins and organizational ones that support his—"

"Or her. Or her. Oh sweetness," she purred.

"—high salary. That's not what a government, whether you like it big or small, is about."

Venus panted like a dog and ground her pubic mound into my palm, but all she said was, somewhat dreamily and very incongruously for her, "I like it big." I didn't ask for clarification.

"Take you, for example."

"Yes, take me, take me."

"You're an Olympian! Blind to your own faults so they don't get in the way of your success. You're the envy of all. But would you want you running the show, unless your job was dismantling the show? Robber, listen to the words, barons. The crooks running the show."

As if through a haze, she whispered, "I am not a crook."

"No. Of course. Not you."

We went to silence, both focused on her pleasure. After some shifting around, I had my right hand on her controls and my left stroking her hair. "My tits are tingling. Can you feel them?" she asked.

I was out of hands, so I rubbed my cheek against one and then another youthful breast of my fifty-something companion. A faint tremor possessed her entire body, and it made me tingle, too.

Picking up one of the threads, I continued, "And having the winners take all leads to corrosive levels of inequality."

She emerged from the clouds of reverie just long enough to ask, "What's so corrosive about inequality?" before returning to orgasm management. "Please don't stop. Right, right, right, no too far."

"What's so corrosive? It corrodes the democratic process when so much legislative power can be bought by a few. It corrodes the American dream when almost everyone knows that mobility is stalled, and that the system is rigged in favor of the children of the rich."

"All your dreams can come true if you have the courage to pursue them."

"Venus. Now you're quoting Walt Disney? There's a cartoon vision of America if I ever saw one. All your dreams can come true if you have the do re mi to do so. That's my point."

"Woody Guthrie?

"Precisely."

"Too far left. Too far left. You're losing me."

"My politics?"

"No, your fingers."

I adjusted. "The vast majority of citizens have no impact at all on policy. There's no meritocracy in that. All the talent is in the stands instead of on the podium."

"Too far now, just a little left, a little left, a little more, ahh, ahh, ahh."

"The great fortunes that have been built? We're talking dynastic wealth now. One of those fortunes reverts to the mean over ten or fifteen generations. That's forever in the history of the US. Talent, whatever that means, corrected for the beneficial effects of privilege, reverts to the mean after what, one generation? Two?"

"Lakshmi," she panted. "Did you get that from some academic scribbler?"

"Venus. It's evolutionary biology. Darwin." I plugged in a vibrator and then inched her back to bliss' edge.

"So," I continued, "we have these inheritors of wealth ruling our country because of some lucky circumstance of their forbears. It begs the question, can society, our unique, exceptional American society survive the consequences of levels of inequality no one has seen since Louis the Sun King?"

Venus' mouth hung open. She breathed in slowly and exhaled forcefully, but uttered nothing. She was almost too far gone. I backed off with the toy. "Are you with me, Venus, my Venus?" I performed a quick trick on her Skene's glands, one I'd learned at some O'Reilly conference from sex and technology polymath Violet Blue. She gasped. If she hadn't been so tall, I might have been able to see her eyes pop wide, but alas, not.

"Yes, you've got me. Still here. Finish please. I'm dying. Finish me please."

"Max may be smarter than me, or have more merit than me, but how much? Twice, thrice, five times? Thirteen times? Sixty-five? A hundred? You know that's crazy. How can you even measure the merit of a life that way? And how does that translate into worth measured in dollars? Plato opined on it and came up with a small integer number as the range. I have this simple model—"

"Oh, Lakshmi, not the whiteboard. I beg you. Not the whiteboard now, you geeky bitch. I am your slave. But not the whiteboard, please." I thought she might cry.

Indeed, Venus had me pegged. I had used my feet to pull my whiteboard—on its aluminum A-frame—to within a few feet, and I was about to free one hand from her to draw on it.

"OK, Venus. No whiteboard. I'm close. It's a simple model, you'll picture it in your head."

"Now? Please, no. I promise you, later, I'll listen later."

"It has to be now, Venus. Now is the time. Now's the time, my volcano lover." I tormented her on the sharp precipice of flight into O-O-land.

"Then fucking get fucking on with it, will you fucking please?" She almost blew the roof off.

"A life is worth $a+c \times m$ where a is the baseline owed to everyone just for being born, m, a positive integer, is your merit in jnds, and c is the factor that converts merit to financial worth."

"So the argument," she interjected, with surprising coherence, "is over a and c. But Lakshmi, you should really do this in dimensionless units and make $a=1$, then we would have only c to contend with."

"Venus, yes, we could do that. Your merit has risen by one just-noticeable difference in my estimation. We could even get rid of the 1 and refer everything to zero, but that introduces infinities later. And, there's also the question about whether c is a constant or $c=c(m)$, but yes."

"Then give me my O, will you? I know what you're saying. I got it. The winners want c to be very large, superlinear, maybe even doubly exponential in m, so it overwhelms the constant term, and you and your populist pinko friends think it should be small, and maybe even sublinear in m, maybe even logarithmic in m, because otherwise the promise of the Constitution, and the country as described by Tocqueville, and the sacrifices of the Civil War, and the middle class triumphs of the last century will be lost. I got it. I don't agree, but I got it. Next you're going to tell me we need an annual wealth tax."

"A wealth tax isn't a bad idea. As long as the returns on capital, r, are greater than the growth in the economy, g, we'll need a mechanism to temper their difference which drives the accumulation of wealth and inheritance."

"Inherited wealth is good, my dear."

"We're going in circles," I said, petulant. Then, recovering, "But, my mind is a slate. Please tell me why inherited wealth is good."

"It saves the children of the very wealthy from the shock of being like everyone else. It's intergenerational consumption smoothing motivated by your Darwinian altruism."

"I know they might print that stuff in the *Wall Street Journal*, or even the *New York Times* in a misguided spirit of balance, but it's a lot of self-justifying blather. If I said it you, you'd laugh me out of the room. There is something unalterably good about inherited wealth, though. A little bit is essential to getting a start in life. But you don't need a hundred million dollars for that."

"I can't argue from this compromising position, but I can tell you we'll buy out Congress before we allow them to pass a wealth tax."

"And who is we?"

"My PAC. My friends. You know, people with something to lose. Organized Money."

"Case closed." I had never heard the term before, and I let it bounce in my head for a few seconds. How was Organized Money any different from Organized Crime, the target of the Racketeering Influenced and Corrupt Organizations Act of 1970? Rackeetering is the pertetuation of fraudulent solutions to problems that exist only because of the racketeers. The entire premise of the No Taxation movement, the Starve the Beast movement, is fraudulent, and provably. But its perps are immune to prosecution because they bought the legislators who made the laws that make it legal to do so. Maybe Max, with his lightning-fast dot connector could have plotted a strategy to undo Organized Money while being serviced by Sameer, but I couldn't figure it out while servicing our mutual benefactor. So, I continued.

"A hundred years ago, Venus, the prospect of a progressive income tax was just as remote, and look, we have one now. It's broken, hobbled, and skeletal, but it's there. And way back when, Andrew Carnegie seemed to think that half a percent tax on assets wasn't confiscatory, so why not two percent for the POP, and then steeply progressive from there? It's obviously about the price, not the principle."

"What's the POP?"

"The point one percent."

"And that makes me the shit?"

"The what?"

"The POOP. The point oh one percent."

"Yes, but no, my sweet. Anyway, see? Not even six hundred words," I whispered. With two hands and two lips I propelled her over the cliff of satisfaction. At first she shuddered. Like a thousand women in synchronous climax, she erupted in a vesuvian wail that blasted through the open windows and echoed off Windy Hill.

I hoped I had another hundred words in her bank of good will, so I continued even as she quaked, confident she was listening as the neuromodulating hormones of intimacy bathed her brain and kept her bonded to me. "And don't you, who speak always about motivation as being the be-all and end-all of success or climbing out of poverty, think that passing your wealth on to the next generation just demotivates them? Wouldn't it be better, if in fact your spawn are the great and merit-worthy, to give them the chance to succeed by removing the disincentive of inheritance? And taking it one step further, as Ayn Rand always, *always* does, doesn't your own wealth make you slothy, and wouldn't it be better to redistribute, or even bury it, Keynes style, so as to galvanize you?" That was a hundred words, exactly, so I had to stop.

"Lakshmi, I have to admit, that's new. That's new. Uncle."

Although to my ears Venus's ululations were joyful, Georgina and Xenia came running in, breathless, and fearing some catastrophe. My giant still quavered, but when my Slavic girlfriends saw Venus' just-fucked luminosity, they knew she was fine. Then they piled onto the bed and smothered her magnificent frame with more kisses and caresses.

CHAPTER 159 THE CLOSING

AT THE last minute, I am serious, the very last, when everyone in the Note negotiations was so exhausted that saying anything but yes would have meant an end to the deal, Venus dropped in her request that the Operating Agreement be amended to exclude the Managing Member from a vote by the Council on his or her removal. Vladik took that hard. To deny Venus would invite her wrath, and who knew how she'd deliver it?

Accepting it wouldn't give Max control on exactly the terms he wanted, because exercising his power would have violated HMRI rules and might have provoked Qasima's wrath. But the amendment would bring Max one step closer to absolute control, and that was threatening.

Vladik assumed that Venus's request had been the result of some backroom dealing—although it wasn't until Venus told me later that I knew he was right. To Vladik, the action signaled that Max was headed, someday, exactly where the oracular Vadim had foretold.

Thus Venus got her terms and the Brothers K invested their money in a way that worked for them. The Brothers' arrangement never raised any suspicions with Venus because she never asked, and she never asked because she didn't care to know that kind of detail about the company's operations.

Like one domino tripping the next, the First Amendment to the Operating Agreement was written by Dykkur, reviewed by all parties, verbal agreement was obtained, and the Council, being Max and Vladik, approved it in writing, fulfilling yet another necessary formality. Max, Vladik, and Sameer signed the papers. The Council approved issuing the Note. The Notes were signed and dated by Max, Vladik, Venus, and Mo Kakitelashvili. Multiple copies were made and sent to the signatories, and finally, one more copy was sent to Corporate Counsel Dykkur Ph'eer.

CHAPTER 160 THE TAB

MAX HAD paid cash for his condo in Mountain View, depleting most of his hoard from the Tiny IPO. His plans to seed company after company, seeking VC support only after results were promising enough to secure a good valuation and leave him with a big slice of the pie, ran aground when Vladik told him he couldn't get his $100,000 out of Moby Dx. Max had been banking on using the same $100,000 for each company. The news that his brand wasn't as strong as he thought meant he needed hundreds of thousands more dollars than he had, or had liquid. Then there was Social Media Fish, into which he poured another $250,000.

From the moment he moved to California, Max had been running a tab with Vera. She was a shrewd accountant. Investments in her business kept it slightly ahead of growth on the island. She funded most of that with cash flow, leaving Murray's hash cash in the mattress for Maxime or the business in the future. It would be enough for a lifetime, she figured, so when Max came to her with requests for $50,000 here and another $100,000 there, and promises of 8 percent interest, she let him launder the money for her. He had wanted her to invest, rather than loan him the money, but she was not that kind of woman. Eventually, the tab grew to half a million dollars, not including the interest she kept track of on a 5x7 spiral-bound flip notebook with pale green paper, of which there was no copy.

CHAPTER 161 THE TEDIUM

DEVOTED READER, in order to be absolutely certain that you appreciate the torturous and tedious activities that consume large parts of the day of the CEO and large parts of the budget of small companies with strong legal teams, I offer you two morsels.

THE Operating Agreement didn't provide a mechanism for issuing additional membership interests, or equivalently, stock, in the LLC. It only provided that there shall be a mechanism. Thus such a mechanism had to be created if I, Dorani Lakshmi Stein, or anyone else were going to get even a nibble of the 23 percent equity slice that had been set aside for employees and advisors. And such a mechanism was created, but it had to be done in a very special way because we were an LLC. If we'd be an Inc., it would have been easy.

On the day the Operating Agreement became effective and Membership Interests were sold to Max, Vladik and Caselode Fittings I, the company was valued at $77. When $1 million from Venus, $1.3 million from Vladik's cousins, and $0.1 million from each of Vladik and Max was taken into the company through the magic of the Note, Moby Dx was worth, arguably, at least $2.5 million. If you believe Lakshmi's Law, that a startup is worth three times what it has just raised, then Moby Dx was worth $7.5 million.

Now suppose that Moby Dx wanted to issue me a 5 percent interest in the company, that being Vladik's minimum commitment to me. For purposes of illustration, let me assert that the company *is* worth $7.5 million and that my 5 percent interest is worth $375,000. Since the company has just given that to me, the IRS wants to tax it as if it's regular income, therefore at the highest possible rate. Having received from the company a piece of paper that is more than likely worth nothing, based on startup odds, it is a real and tangible problem for me that the IRS wants a third, more or less, of $375,000, and the State of California wants something too.

There's a workaround called restricted membership interests. The restricted interests, worth nothing (at issuance) while the company is valued at $7.5 million, appreciate as the company increases in value. They would become indistinguishable from membership interests when someday the company had the nine-figure exit we all hoped for. Being worthless on the day they're issued, the IRS doesn't try to tax them, and the real and tangible problem of owing the IRS over $100,000 goes away. The method is not dissimilar to setting an option strike price for common stock in a C-corp.

After discussing at mind-numbing length the nuances of such plans, and the valuation methods acceptable to the IRS, and how the valuation would change over time, and the algorithm used to ensure that the value of the two different types of interest would become almost indistinguishable in the future, a Moby Dx LLC Restricted Membership Interest Plan was agreed to and signed off by all parties, Note holders included. Following that, the company could issue me stock, and we could talk about how to distribute stock to our new employees who were already at work, and who had been promised stock options.

Vladik delivered on his commitment of 5 percent but couldn't get me any closer to the 10 percent we said he'd strive toward. The price he would have had to pay to give me more without Max's consent was, in Vladik's words, "unbearable."

SEVEN months had transpired since Vladik first met with Louisa at TTO. He had given her a business plan. TTO had completed its long process of marketing the most technology portfolio, and had found there was no non-trivial interest other than from Moby Dx. The two parties had negotiated many of the terms of the agreement. Max had been playing both sides of the negotiation, as he had with MIT and Tiny Machines. Exclusivity, normally the most difficult term to get, was granted because there was no other interest.

As a condition to issuing the license, TTO demanded, albeit politely and with the greatest tact, as the demand came from Louisa whose will was iron but whose manner was kid leather, that Moby Dx had the financing to advance the technology. With the Note now done, Vladik made another trip up to Lobitos Farm.

Louisa and I were having difficulties. I was astride her in bed one night, feeling the extra stiffness of her nipples against the tender mounding of her half-melon breasts. My back and neck arched as I rode hard. My head was pointed up when I said, "You know, Love, the ceiling needs painting," and without missing a beat she said, "Pink." That's when I knew the fire had gone out.

I was overloaded and not giving her the attention she needed. She was more the monogamous type anyway, and while she tried to be accommodating of me, that is monogamish, it didn't suit her.

Vladik, ignorant of these strains, told her about how much time he spent with me, how, in his words I "was growing beyond all expectations," and he asked what the two of us, Louisa and I, had been doing recently. A look of sadness flashed across her face—something quite different from the sparkle of joy he'd seen during that first meeting, he told me later—and she directed the conversation to concluding the license.

Previously, Vladik had driven the royalty rates down as far as TTO would go, 4 percent. He was surprised to see them take a hard stand at such a high number. Hervé Lebret at the École Polytechnique Fédérale de Lausanne had done a survey of licensing-royalty rates at major American universities. Vladik's reading of that told him there should have been room to move the rate down to 3 or even 2 percent. We later found out that Max himself had set the 4 percent limit for TTO because it served his interests as co-inventor.

On the day of the meeting, Louisa surprised Vladik with an offer of downward movement in exchange for equity in the company. TTO wanted 2 percent in Moby Dx equity for every 1 percent drop in royalty. Vladik raised his flukes at that because the patent wasn't going to have international protection, owing to Max's failure to communicate filing instructions. A two-for-one swap was too rich for Vladik's blood. Also, through my influence, he was expecting MOST to fail, so he had much less interest in the license than he had had earlier. If indeed it did fail, and Moby Dx didn't generate MOST revenue, it wouldn't owe royalties to TTO. On the other hand, if Moby Dx gave up equity for the license, there'd be no way to get it back if MOST failed later. Even one-for-one was too much, given our skepticism about the value of the IP. So, Vladik passed on the offer. TTO was disappointed, and even Max was disappointed, as it revealed how little value Vladik attached to MOST. Vladik would have preferred to walk away from the license entirely. Doing so would have broadcast in plain text his true feelings about MOST—feelings he hid from Max—and led Max to suspect that Vladik managed the company to a shadow mission instead of the stated mission. Also, Max was due fees and royalties from the MOST licensing agreement, so to abandon it would be taking money out of his pocket. In other words, Vladik thought that walking away from the portfolio would upset the applecart of his relationship with Max. I thought so, too.

The only task that lingered as Vladik and TTO Director Nathalia Nguyen-Berry prepared to put ink on the signature pages was for Max to complete the COI disclosure. This was Max's written commitment to the I that his ownership in Moby Dx was compliant with HMRI rules on conflict of interest. The COI was between Max and HMRI only. Vladik never saw it. While that was in process, and it was done without fanfare, Vladik had Ph'eer, Dowd, and Sertantiy review the licensing contract, *ka-ching!*

TTO-10/0137, the HMRI-Moby Dx licensing agreement for the Molecular Stethoscope co-invented by Max Frood, PhD and Dorani Lakshmi Stein, PhD was signed by Vladik K, PhD, CEO of Moby Dx LLC, and Nathalia Nguyen-Berry, PhD, Director of the HMRI Technology Transfer Office. Copies were made, including one for the lawyers. Then HMRI invoiced Moby Dx for all expenses accrued in writing the patents and filing the patent applications, and for the licensing fees due on completion. Vladik approved those invoices, I sent them to Kashonli LLC, and HMRI was paid.

But that was only for the MOST IP. There was also the infectious disease IP. Yes, Dispirited Reader, it never stops. TTO had begun marketing that IP months after the original MOST portfolio, so the ID license process was initially behind. There was some interest in the ID portfolio from the sequencing companies and large diagnostics companies, too. Vladik and Max came up with a thinly supported argument that MOST and BROADID went together like dogs and ponies, and therefore should be licensed to a single company because they relied on the same moby and used very similar software pipelines. Technology Transfer Officer Dayore smirked when she heard that, but did not tell Dr. Frood—to whom she was required to show deference no matter what, or risk termination—that it was specious and self-serving. *That,* she told *me.*

At first, TTO offered only non-exclusivity. That would allow them to license the patents to some of the other interested parties. But Max had a conniption, pointing to numerous startups whose failure he attributed to divided or weak IP. I think if I hadn't been involved with Moby Dx, Louisa might have asked to be transferred off the case. She probably should have done that anyway because our relationship gave her a potential conflict of interest. Instead, she stuck it out as an unrequested favor to me. On the verge of telling Max to shove it, and she was within her rights to claim the Moby Dx did not have the wherewithal to bring the two technologies to market with its $2.5 million in the bank, and therefore was undeserving of the license, she bit her lip and worked with Vladik on a compromise. They came up with a license whose period of exclusivity was particularly short, but which included a mechanism for buying more of it later if Moby Dx was inclined. Otherwise, using the MOST license as a template, everything else went quickly from there.

Again, Max completed a COI, our lawyers reviewed the license, their cash registers went *ka-ching!*, documents were signed, and the company had its second license from HMRI. Invoices were sent to Moby Dx, forwarded to Kashonli, and HMRI was paid. With luck, those two licenses would be all Moby Dx needed from the I.

CHAPTER 162 THE NIGHTMARE

AS FODDER for a how-to manual for startups, Moby Dx's experience navigating a Kafkaesque world in pursuit of healthcare insurance for its employees—first Vladik and me, and then Hermina, Marina, Malvina, and Martina—is no longer relevant, thanks to the Affordable Care Act of 2010, or as posterity will know it, Obamacare. Those experiences, and the long nightmare of American history leading to them, may be found in this book's supplemental material.

CHAPTER 163 THE CONSULTING CONTRACT

EVERYBODY MUST get paid. Dykkur sent over some employment contracts for us; generic ones we could have downloaded from the Internet, but ones we paid for through the nose thanks to Dykkur having touched them. I showed mine to Xenia.

"These are not very employee-friendly," she said. She trusted Dykkur even less than I did. "You should hire an independent employment lawyer to write them."

"It's Vladik's call," I told her.

"He listens to you."

"Not on this one."

"He could have another layer of protection against Max if he put a decent contract in place."

"He's not listening."

"And why?"

"He feels that if he's writing employee-friendly contracts, he's not protecting the interests of his investors," I told her.

"I think he's doing the opposite. All he protects with these contracts is the interests of Max."

"There's more. He still wants to believe that Max wouldn't try to fire him. And he's sick of paying lawyers. And, he thinks Max would flip if he found out. If I pushed him, I think he'd come up with another justification for the same conclusion."

"There's no information in his response then."

"In Shannon's sense. No entropy. Yes."

"Now *that* is not listening. And you don't care because you *know* Vladik isn't going to mistreat you."

"Of course."

"Did he give you the equity that you deserve?"

Pause. "Touché."

Another pause. "He wanted to do the right thing, but couldn't. Short of folding, which is what Dimi says you should do, Vladik couldn't go any further," she said.

"So as long as Vladik is not protected, I'm not protected?"

"That's my point."

Armed with Xenia's insight, I went back to Vladik once again. That was enough. We soon had California-compliant employment contracts with parachutes—little ones, not golden ones—to discourage arbitrary firings and capricious management changes. Vladik, exercising his power as Managing Member, signed the paperwork and didn't bother to tell Max or Dykkur.

Then we hooked up our bank accounts to the company's by means of a payroll processor, ADP I think it was, and we started getting checks twice a month. For me it was a big deal. For Vladik, it was the principle.

That left Max and the other consultants we'd bring on board someday. How did they or would they get paid? Each one of them needed a contract.

According to a whiteboard's contents and a handshake deemed null and void by the Operating Agreement, and yet remaining in full force as far as Vladik was concerned, Max was to get a consulting fee equal to 10 percent of revenue after the first $500,000, capped at $150,000 annually. Thinking of the Note as revenue accruing over two years, Vladik interpreted the agreement to mean an annual salary of $100,000.

True, that seemed like a lot considering what Max was doing for the company, but not a lot considering what he *said* he'd be doing for the company, that is, as we heard repeatedly, "I'm making it the focus of my consulting effort." Vladik presented those numbers to Max, who nodded approval, and that led him to begin work on Max's consulting contract.

Vladik had already been written contracts for medical, regulatory, biostatistical, marketing, and scientific consultants whom he had pulled in to help us develop our experimental and commercialization programs. For these, Vladik used the Ph'eer, Dowd, and Sertantiy boilerplate to get started, and modified them to meet the specific needs of Moby Dx or the consultants. Max, though, had different, very special considerations.

One of the mechanisms that Qasima Zipp had devised to keep her Principals investigating on HMRI's behalf was to include in their employment contracts a most unusual clause. It stated that their external consulting services would be contracted through HMRI, not with the Principal directly. This ensured, she thought, that all parties would comply with HMRI rules and regulations, end of story. Thus, for Max to be a paid consultant to Moby Dx, Moby Dx would have to enter into a contract with HMRI. A three-way contract written by HMRI's estimable lawyers spelled out those rules and regulations in numbing detail, and made representations and warranties that Moby Dx and Max would adhere to the most up-to-date version of those rules as posted on the I's website, http://bit.ly/19RrNEE.

Up until that point, the company had not signed any agreements with HMRI that read implicitly or otherwise on Caselode Fittings I, nor had Vladik been aware that he'd have to. The three-way with HMRI changed all that. When in due time Vladik got around to signing the papers, he'd be legally obligated to ensure that Max, who was skirting HMRI rules as creatively as anyone ever had, was in fact HMRI-compliant.

The word Vladik used when he later described to me how he felt about this was "*OUTRAGE!*"—shouting font, punctuation, and italics, all his. He was glad he had D&O insurance to protect directors and company officers from the ill effects of lawsuits, and he was glad that Dykkur Ph'eer's firm had dreamt up and drafted Caselode Fittings and told him it was kosher, because Vladik was going to put the blame on Dykkur if it turned out otherwise. He'd begun assembling the paper trail to prove it, too.

Dear Reader, am I getting my point across? Vladik said it to me this way, while his hands waved over his head, yanked at his hair, clenched into fists, and made long strong motions suggesting penetration: "Max led me to the altar, carried me across the threshold of the bridal suite where he fucked me so good I wanted more, and then withdrew until I agreed be a co-conspirator against HMRI."

Originally, Caselode Fittings I was a matter for Max and his employer, full stop. With the consulting contract, it had become a matter for the company and for Vladik too. Vladik could walk away, giving up everything he'd invested in time, money, and, last but not least, self. He could refuse, which he believed would lead Max to walk away. Either outcome would have been fatal for the company and, this being Max's doing, with unpleasant ramifications for Max at the hands of the Kakitelashvilis; not that Vladik cared any longer for Max's well being. The third alternative was to hope that no one ever looked at the contract. There was good reason to hope for this. Who ever looks at such agreements? No one. Well, no one who wasn't buying the company or making an investment in it.

There was one very small upside for Vladik in this chess game. Once Max signed the consulting contract, he'd be entering into a commitment with the company to obey HMRI rules for Principals, effectively nullifying the First Amendment to the Operating Agreement he'd asked Venus to demand as a condition to her investment. Not that it mattered much, because what Vladik really needed was Max's cooperation and participation.

There was another item in Max's contract, though, that generated even more "*OUTRAGE!*"

HMRI measures its Principals' consulting in days per year and tracks it using a primitive database called the Consulting Master Spreadsheet. At Zott's, Max had said he'd make Moby Dx the focus of his non-HMRI effort. Based on the day-a-week rule applicable at most major academic institutions, Vladik assumed Moby Dx would get not less than two-thirds of those, or thirty-five days, from Max. Later, Vladik learned that HMRI permitted forty-eight consulting days annually, just like the University of California, so thirty-five might have been a skooch high, and he dialed back his expectations by a couple of days.

On a blank space in the section of the consulting contract whose heading read "HMRI Compliance," Company and Principal were to specify the number of days each year Principal would consult for Company. Back at HMRI, elves or trolls extracted said number of days from said space and entered it in any empty cell (in the Consulting Master Spreadsheet) in the forty-eight columns E through BZ of the row belonging to the investigator—row 1729 in Max's case. Columns A and B contained the investigator's last and first names. Column C was his or her identifying employee number. Column D was the sum of contents from columns E through BZ. If its value exceeded forty-eight, conditional formatting rules turned the font red instead of black and the trolls were instructed to chop off Principal's head.

Ha! Ha! Ha! No, they would do no such thing, but Qasima would be informed and she would have a very serious talk with the Principal, at least.

Dear Reader, when Max returned the draft contract to Vladik with an entry in the previously blank space provided for Company and Principal to specify how many days per year Principal would devote to Company activities, do you think the number he wrote there was (a) 33 to 39, (b) 25 to 32, (c) 17 to 24, or (d) less than 17?

The answer, Friend, was (d). And not only that, it was a single digit number. A single digit! His vaunted contribution to the company for which he was receiving 65 percent of its equity, was going to be delivered in fewer than ten days per year. That made his daily consulting rate was more than $11,000 per day. I cannot even bring myself to tell you what that single digit number was, so I'll write it like this, N_{max}. I will tell you though that this was no accident. This was premeditated.

I was working full-time, was co-inventor of both IP portfolios, and was driving all the scientific effort. For all that, I was receiving about $120,000 in salary and 5 percent of the equity, but the equity vested only if I stayed for four years. Compare that to Max and what he was getting for his contribution. Let me not spell it out for you in any greater detail; Max was fucking us all, and Vladik was a fool not to have clarified many of these things at the outset. But he was deceived, and I would probably have been deceived too. Dr. Fraud lived up to his name.

When Vladik pressed Max on this, and he did press him on it, Max backed down and said he wouldn't invoice the company for his consulting time. But where were his other thirty-nine or more days going and why wasn't Moby Dx getting more of them? What in the world was Max Frood doing with his consulting time?

"Rhizobia," Max said. Remember Rhizobia, and that honorary degree and the lab there and the full-time salary they paid him for a 20 percent effort? Rhizobia ate up fifteen of the days. His 20 percent effort was delivered in fifteen days per year. Did that include travel time? Rhizobians worked like crazy to turn the ancient volcanic kingdom—without roads prior to 1949—into a modern Southeast Asian Switzerland. What self-respecting Rhizobian would call a work year seventy-five days? We'd always thought his work there was part and parcel of his work at the I.

And the other twenty-four or more days? "I'm an advisor to Pernicious Planet Absolute Return Partnership. I give them three days."

"Max, can I ask you what they pay your for that?" Vladik asked.

"$50,000."

"Nice work if you can get it. What else?"

"What what else?"

"Where do the other days go and why aren't we getting them?"

"Heh, back off. I'm not feeling the love, Vladik, not feeling it at all."

And he was right. The love was gone.

He stared, expressionless, winkless at Vladik. "I work more than enough days and hours that are not captured in that number," referring to N_{max}. "You should be satisfied."

The war between the two founders was on.

Dykkur reviewed the contract (*ka-ching!*) and then Max and Vladik and HMRI's counsel signed three originals, one of which was held by HMRI, one by Max, and one was sent to Dykkur for filing (*ka-ching!*).

CHAPTER 164 THE WAR PLANS

WITH A war on, each party revisited its plans. For Max, the thinking was very simple; stay the course. He bet Vladik wouldn't walk away, having put so much in already, so Max had him as some kind of indentured servant. He thought highly of Vladik's work, but for one deficiency; insufficient appreciation of all that Max had done for him. There was no urgency to remove Vladik. In the shadows, Max would line up other investors. He would advise them that Vladik was no more essential than an old razor blade, and when the pieces were in place, he'd fire him. If the new investors didn't like Dyk, maybe they'd bring in their own CEO. In the meantime, Max would keep on keeping on; running the lab at the I, meddling with the inner workings of his various companies, starting new ones, collecting awards wherever they were bestowed, traveling to Rhizobia to be present for fifteen days a year, gambling in Macau if he got routed through Hong Kong, taking extended breaks in Indonesia, mentoring Maxime, hanging at Moby Dick's with Sameer, eating like it was his last supper, and trying to manage his ever declining health. He'd even put in an appearance or two at Moby Dx if they asked.

Vladik needed a different sort of plan. He knew Max knew he knew he had been lied to and cheated, and that his days were numbered. His employee-friendly employment contract, the little parachute, would inflict some pain on Max, but Vladik needed a plan that would make his own firing an act of suicide for his cofounder, and therefore, by the logic of mutually assured destruction, save him from the fire.

Our mission remained unchanged. We would create new molecular diagnostic products based on clever interpretation of cell-free DNA or RNA measurements. Much as Vladik, or more precisely, Vladik and I would have like to drop MOST, we couldn't, because that would have raised the hackles on Max's neck and probably shortened Vladik's career at Moby Dx. We worked by the principle that you should never piss anyone off unintentionally, and it wasn't yet time to piss off Max. So we had to keep everything going as it had been before. What was different was how he thought about funding beyond the Note.

All the funding scenarios we'd considered up to that moment had put Max's growing reputation front and center. If we continued in that vein, a wink from Max would end the investor's confidence in Vladik, and any new investment would be conditional on Vladik's exit. In the aftermath of declared war, we had to strike a deal with investors who didn't value Max. A shareholder vote and a Council vote would be needed to approve any investment, meaning we'd need Max's consent. Would the narcissistic Dr. Frood vote against his own interests and turn down new money if there was none else available? We thought not. Short of walking away, this was the only option for us.

As we got results, publications, grants, and maybe even research contracts, on our own and without Max's participation, and as we approached investors through Vladik's networks rather than through Max's, we stood an ever increasing chance of finding money that didn't care about Max. Of course, we already knew of one investor who didn't much value Max, Prophetic Capital. Vadim wouldn't invest without rewriting the cap table, and Max would only agree to that if he were tied down and flogged. Nevertheless, Vladik began to develop a long-term relationship with Vadim, and I had already begun mine with Xenia.

CHAPTER 165 GENORMX INC. – SCENE V OF V

BETA, THE second generation sequencing instrument, was a marvel. Error rates were still too high and throughput too low for production, but for Beta, both were fine. Max's abandonment of the project had gone largely unnoticed by the engineering team. Actually, they had all noticed and were only relieved.

Carmie, Kozmo, and the Board had never found another evangelist to win over the various genomics center directors who were key to the advancement of any new sequencing platform. The technology vision, a radical departure from everything in the marketplace, was Max's. If he was no longer behind it, that itself was a red flag to the center directors. There were always unknowns with something so new. Without the luminary's name, the brand name, Max's name, associated with it, the platform would languish, fail to thrive, and die.

Despite everyone's best efforts, Beta had no home, except for one instrument at the I's core lab where it had been promised as part of the license agreement with TTO. Forty-eight months and $24 million after initial funding, Carmie announced at an All Hands Meeting that Genormx would cease operations. The little money remaining in the bank would be used to sue or threaten to sue the three sequencing incumbents in the event that those behemoths ever did anything in pore sequencing. Maybe Genormx would get a settlement and return some cash to the investors. It would have snowed in hell before any settlement generated cash for the other stockholders, Max included. Win, lose or draw, the lawyers would make money on the suits.

The technology or the leadership? That is the question that circulates around the rotting corpse of any venture. Partly blame game, partly case study, the debates about which was responsible for any failure are as long and intense in Silicon Valley as debates about the Red Sox pitching rotation are in Boston.

In this case, it was both. With so little known, in fact with nothing known about the extensibility of the technology, and no prize-winning scientist ready to put his or her reputation behind it, the center directors thought that the rewards were too few for the risk involved.

In private, Max was unremitting in his criticism of the leadership, calling them incompetent, greedy, and of course, Fucking Idiots. He claimed plausible deniability for himself because he had no operating role. His technology had worked. They couldn't sell it, QED. To the outside world, Max looked like the technical genius foiled by weak execution. His public reputation, the kind that was written about in the Grey Lady, was untarnished.

As a star in the VC community, he was no longer ascending. He had demanded very tough terms from investors, promised the moon, and then hadn't delivered on his commitments. He had taken the most literal and technical interpretation of contracts when it favored him, but demanded the most lax interpretation when it favored the investors. There was no reciprocity with Max. It was Max, all Max, all the time.

He had burned the last bridge he would ever burn with Armen. Guzman and Intuition, two of Silicon Valley's leading life science investors, would never invest in Max again. Ask his opinion? Sure, to have his opinion. Want to know what he was doing? Sure, it's always good to have intel. Invest in a company where he was a principal? Never. Word got around, but you had to be deep inside to hear it. And when you did hear it, if you were used to getting your news from print media, or from people who knew Max or Max's work only at a distance, or from sycophants, you thought you were hearing something else: thin skin, sour grapes, and incompetence.

The investors were only the easiest to identify of those hurt by Max's behavior, and they were, of course, the ones most able to absorb the hit. As a group, it's the non-executive team that is always whacked hardest by failure. While they wanted to believe they were in the World Series with a fifty-fifty chance of eternal glory and a big exit, or even higher owing to the brand name investors and entrepreneur who had launched it, in fact, they had bought a lottery ticket. A well-trained CFO had harangued them at every opportunity to keep spending down, to accept reduced salaries because success was right around the corner, and to work longer days. When it was over, Carmie's little girl or Francisquita's grandchildren would continue visiting the Stanford Shopping Center and walk away with well-laden logo-rich carrying bags of stiff glossy paper with string handles, yet some of the non-execs would begin visiting Goodwill Industries and collecting food stamps as they slipped out of the middle class. In the damp climate of the Great Recession, finding another paycheck to replace the lost one was a lottery in and of itself.

Nico, the Shanghainese beauty, had put her own (correct) interpretation on the cause of Max's uncharacteristically light touch in months leading up to his firing, and so she had shopped her résumé in Shanghai. She came to the US seeking a Frood stamp on her union card. As a postdoc she had led development on what became venture-funded Genormx, and there she solved every technical problem before her. Beta was a marvel, and no one would fault her if the executives had chosen the wrong goals. Her association with Max Frood and the four years of Silicon Valley experience was career-making for her in Shanghai. Within days of shuttering the doors, she'd be on her way home to her family with a position as Vice President of R&D at the Shanghai Bioengineering Institute, a privately funded incubator.

Of all those affected, the former postdoc, my inspirational friend Rinchen took it the hardest. He had put in six, nearly seven years of work, the fruits of which Max claimed credit for. So many years of sacrifice, dead-ended because Max would prefer not to attend a few meetings or make a few sales pitches. Rinchen felt so deeply aggrieved by Max's betraying disavowal that on Genormx' final day, when the doors shut for the final time two weeks after Carmie's announcement, he showed up for work in the robes of a Tibetan monk. It was, he said, a form of silent protest.

And when he exited the building and the doors closed behind him, he left EPA on foot, walking due south on University Avenue. Private homes were protected from thunderous traffic noise by grape stakes. His mind jumped, as it had it never jumped before, to the Deep South and the Great Depression and the paper thin exteriors of sharecropper houses in Walker Evans' photographs in James Agee's *Let us Now Praise Famous Men*. Those grape stakes were about as effective in shielding out the noise as those clapboard houses were in shielding their inhabitants from the winter cold. What was the connection? The dispossessed, the disenfranchised, servitude.

Only a few trees provided relief from the sunlight beating down hard on his maroon robes, the asphalt, and the sidewalks. He passed by La Estrallita and Las Adelitas Market and Restaurant, and empty lots of tall grasses bounded by chain-link fences, and two bedroom one-story houses with rolled composite roofing; scrapers they'd call them on the other side of the highway. A tacqueria. A church. EPA's mix of Vietnamese mani-pedi and Mexican beauty salons, and their Indian, Fijian, Tongan, and Samoan grocery stores. A gas station.

He took the freeway overpass for the last time, looking down to his right at the crush of traffic, and across to the curved mirrored wall of the Four Seasons Hotel in its sophisticated elegance built on the ruins of the old Whiskey Gulch. Spandexed cyclists whizzed by almost as fast the cars, their street clothes in their backpacks.

The sun still pummeled, and no trees gave relief as Rinchen waited with the cars and the cyclists at the traffic light of demarcation separating EPA from PA. Only a few yards away hung a four-inch-thick wheel of wood, engraved in gold with letters that read, "WELCOME TO PALO ALTO," and painted with an image of the tall green *Sequoia sempervirens* known as El Palo Alto. But he could hardly see it through thick growth of roadside trees.

No more grape stakes, either. High overhead, the stucco'd concrete sound- and sight- and security-barriers did the job as intended. Powered gates of wrought iron gave only a glimpse of the two-story, many-bedroomed manses with raised or columned entrances, and made way for the owners' three or four cars. And there was no more composite roofing, only ceramic tiles, or slate, or thick cedar shakes, or maybe solar panels.

He entered the neighborhood called Crescent Park, and then made a left on Lincoln Avenue. Where the street was just a little narrower than University, the drooping boughs of palms did reach all the way across and touch, and the sun trickled through, no longer throbbing at street level. Ferrari, BMW, Porsche, BMW, Mercedes, Audi, Mercedes, Tesla, Lexus, BMW, and then another Tesla shrouded in a space-age fabric car cover. Rinchen felt the difference between EPA and PA as he had never felt it. Before, he had thought he belonged in PA, one of the chosen, the special, let's say it out loud, the privileged. Now, with this dream and his effort crushed, dismissed, tossed away by what seemed to him one man's arbitrary stubbornness, he felt as disenfranchised as those in EPA. Why should Max have so much? What had Tom Wolfe said? "A liberal is a conservative who has been arrested." Max had thwarted if not exactly arrested Rinchen in his assent of Silicon Valley's ladder to fame, employability, and shelter. Unlike besotted Jacob, who could throw off Laban's deceit after seven years and put in another seven to attain his beloved Rachel, Rinchen had decided it was time to speak up.

At Channing, he jogged left and continued on Melville, walking through Professorville to Melville's bitter end where it petered out at Bryant Street. Crossing Embarcadero Road into Old Palo Alto, passing the Castilleja School, noticing a gaunt Steve Jobs and Laurene Powell Jobs making one of their now famous circuits, he then turned right at Churchill Avenue. Two blocks up, he waited for the long light at Alma Street, crossed it, and then waited again by the swinging yellow fence at the Southgate tracks while Caltrain's 5:12 Baby Bullet sped southbound to Sunnyvale. Spryly, while the red lights flashed warnings, and while drivers listened to *All Things Considered*, or read their email, or browsed on a Slab97, and while Paly High School students waited to continue their walk or their bike ride home after track or Physics Olympiad practice, while they texted and talked, self-absorbed in their all-engrossing lives, and while the glorious California sun shone down, drenching everyone in warmth and beauty, Rinchen leapt over that yellow gate and met the oncoming train. There his journey ended with a speechlessly quick chaotic binding of himself to Eternity, contributing one more entry to the roster of Caltrain fatalities that grows longer at the rate of about one a month.

CHAPTER 166 RINCHEN'S NOTE

RINCHEN PROBABLY expected the note he carried in the pockets of his robe to survive, but the train's devastation was nearly complete, and only a few fragments survived. He'd sent a copy to Carmie and to the New York Times. That launched an investigation, much mud slinging, the turning of one reporter against a longtime go to source, and a scathing two-part piece on abuses of Bayh-Dole titled *The Rise and Fall of Genormx*. Neither Carmie nor the Times ever published Rinchen's note, but everyone guessed it must have been a big *j'accuse!*

WAFTING down from the sky, red with sticky blood, the largest remnant of the note attached itself to a pair of panties dangling from power lines. The words on it read, "... before I came to work for you, and that's why I came to work for you. They say things like, 'Brilliant people think differently, that's why they are brilliant.' But they miss the point. Being brilliant and thinking different comes with the same cautions as being normal when it involves other people. You may be forgiven some harm, but only if you do good. Why are you exempt from a code of decency, Western or Eastern? Brilliance is not a license to destroy more than you build. If all you do is destroy, then what are ..."

Another piece was found not much above eye level on a telephone pole. "... a snake in the grass, unseen and leth[al]."

"... self-immolating protest has worked be[fore]..."

MAX stuck to his position of plausible deniability about Genormx. About Rinchen he said, "He took it too personal," and that's all.

CAUSE and effect are not always easy to establish. We do know that the date of Max's last award notification preceded the date of Rinchen's suicide by one day. We also know that Max had been shortlisted for the 2013 Max Delbrück Prize in Biological Physics, but the Prize Committee withdrew his name from consideration without explanation. The Max is a Genius Club appeared to have shut its doors when news got out that the suicide was a protest. If the whole purpose of awards is to bring honor onto the institution bestowing the award, then giving it to someone with shit on their clothes, warranted or not, didn't serve it.

CHAPTER 167 THE DAILY GRIND

EVERY DAY is different and yet the same. Vladik explained. "How do you climb a Himalayan peak? A step at a time. When you're on its lower glaciers, the mountain has a particular character and your progress is made up of thousands of identical steps. You slow down to probe suspect ice, working yourself around a crevasse if you find it. Days of this. And then the terrain changes, getting steeper, and your technique adapts, or else. Now each step is an ankle-articulated placement of crampons onto blue ice, with an eye to the life-saving rope and the other climbers on it. Hours of this, maybe even days of this, broken only by the labor of melting snow for drinking water, or chopping a platform to make camp, and then more glacier slogging and route finding, until the next life-threatening exposure. And then it gets hard because the mountain has become so steep and the wind so abrasive that you are now climbing on a loose matrix of rock and ice, so tenuously held together that you are worrying about knocking it loose onto your mate below, and you're wearing a helmet in case your mate above does the same, and God help you if kicking some rocks loose leaves you off-balance and you fall, at which point you've put your friends at greater risk and become even more dependent on their abilities to withstand the shocks. Your retinas may be hemorrhaging. There's almost no air to breathe. You're worried about every unusual sound from your lungs or your companions' lungs, sounds that presage life-threatening or expedition-threatening edemas. Your feet, forget your feet. No one wants to hear complaints about your feet, and you're not hearing any others because you're all living by the No Whiners Code of Conduct. And, you celebrate, if only a little, in the tent every night, because you made progress and you're still alive, and the tent is holding up against the storm. You're thinking, if you're lucky, you won't have to go out into the storm and dig an ice cave. And you're thinking, we should have done that earlier before the storm was this bad, but if we had, we wouldn't have made as much progress up the hill, and that's the choice we made. And we're trying not to get on each other about that decision, because we're living by the No Douchebags Code of Conduct, too. When you wake at 3 a.m.—which you're doing because it takes hours to melt enough snow to make the water you'll all need for a day in the near-zero humidity of the near-space high mountains, and you need to use all the daylight that's available—what was once moisture in your breath, yesterday's snow melt, is now crystallized onto sleeping bags and tent walls, falling on you at the slightest movement. You brush it aside where it can't melt, and can't compromise the warming, life-giving insulation of your bag. With what you need for the summit on your back, you start out in the pre-dawn. You look around, and everyone else, almost everyone else, those other teams that started out when you did, they're nowhere to be seen. Did the challenge overwhelm them, or is the summit a death trap you've just been too stupid or stubborn to quit? Up high, you can radio back to base-camp and get some advice, and that's all. No one else can carry the load or carry out the decisions you make or make the decisions for you, nor can they save you. You ask yourself, how much are you sacrificing for this peak, and how much are you asking others to sacrifice for you? Is it too much? Then you realize that thoughts like that have to be banished because they subvert your summit orientation. So you take the next step and go on. You try to appreciate the rarified environment, the purity of your mission, polluted only by the details of having to squat with your butt exposed to the -30 °C air, -30 if you're lucky, and other similarly mundane tasks. Reflecting on it, you admit there are an awful lot of those details, and they do, most of the time, keep you from seeing the crystalline goal, but if the sun is shining, you can look up, and see the goal."

Vladik would pause here.

"And that's why we have our mission statement plastered all over the freakin' place! For those moments when you can't look up and see the summit!" And so went another of the All Hands Meetings, or beer and bitch sessions, or one-on-ones, or lunches that were supposed to, and usually did, keep us or bring us back on track.

A largely thankless grind it was, and much longer than any mountaineering expedition. Even the shortest startup is rarely shorter than Magellan's circumnavigation of the sphere, and he died before he got around. You do it, maybe against the advice of your closest friends or blood relatives or your psychiatrist, because as more than one extremely competent gal whom you would think could do and be successful at anything, absolutely anything, put in front of her has said, "I'm not fit to do anything else."

The startup world was once the province of eccentrics: iconoclasts who refused to fit in, visionaries, missionaries, and risk takers with plans. In boom times, and we have seen boom times lately, cool kids have entered the fray, as the social-acceptability of a billion dollar payout is unquestioned in the meritocracy where money is the figure of merit. But will they endure when the boom is off the growth?

Why do true startup types do startups? That's the equivalent of asking why is there life in the universe. We observers are alive in a universe whose laws admit life, and so we observe life. If our universe did not admit life, we would not be here to observe it and ask why not. The weak anthropic principle of startups is this: You only observe me doing startups because it's not really me if you see me doing something else.

The laws of the social universe called France don't admit the existence of startups, whereas the laws of the universe called Silicon Valley do, and we attract those unfortunates, those retards, those half-broken, half-functional monomaniacs who can do nothing else, would be happy nowhere else, and will be seen as freaks almost everywhere else. As satisfying or not as Mallory's explanation of why he climbed the peak he never returned from, "Because it's there," or Descartes' explanation of what confirmed his own existence, "*Cogito ergo sum*," ours is that we make because we're makers. We grind because we're grinders.

CHAPTER 168 THREESOMES

WE DIDN'T need the great combinatorist Gian-Carlo Rota to tell us that there were C(10,3) or a hundred and twenty threesomes to be found among Xenia, Vadim, Lakshmi, Venus, Georgina, Max, Sameer, Vladik, Arianna, and Louisa. Ruling out Arianna and Vladik as being hopelessly monogamous, and Max and Sameer the same, and Louisa as being hopelessly dead in bed, that left C(5,3) and of those 10, only the following three merit writing about: Xenia, Vadim, and me; Xenia and Georgina (and me); Venus and Georgina (and me, again). Then there was Отредактированное.

DOUCE France in the Town and Country Village is my favorite café in all of Palo Alto. It is low key, and you don't go there for celebrity spotting. Town and Country is too dowdy and staid for that, and it's not close to the offices of the coolest of startups or social media powerhouses. But the crêpes are perfect, the staff remembers you after months of absence, and you can always, *always* get a seat and a table. So what if you're surrounded by PTA moms, or grandparents eating breakfast with their kid's kid at Stanford? Also, it's close to where I work out.

Xenia, who had the looks of a supermodel and made her own cool, was happy to meet me there late one Saturday afternoon. Heads turned, the seas parted, and conversation stopped when she walked through the glass doors, cut in line to stand beside me, put her nose into my just-drying hair, and whispered, "I love you when you're like this."

I always felt great after practice, and I know it showed. It always had. My parents said it. My high school boyfriend said it, although he was jealous that I loved practice more than I loved him. And Julia said it, too, although she caught me during the least serious phase of my career.

As I turned to look at Xenia, I recognized the person standing behind me, behind us. He was someone of real wealth and fame, someone I knew, but didn't know I knew.

"I didn't place you with your clothes on." Then he held out his hand and said, "Отредактированное," by way of introduction.

Without his clothes on, he was just anybody.

"Same here. Call me Lakshmi."

Then with an ease that bespoke some ancient familiarity, he leaned in to Xenia and bumped cheeks with her before she could utter her own name.

"Ксения," she said.

Maybe out of deference to me, he continued in English.

"Yes, I know," he said, his eyes going all googly as he took in her beauty. "That *Times* photo of you at the opening of the ballet season? Hard to forget."

"Yes, I know," I said, affirming the truth about her.

To me, he said, "Christ, you're good."

"Division I recruit. But I didn't stick with it. Rusty."

"Hardly. You're the best one out there."

"It's true," Xenia said. "She coulda been a contender."

"Do you think that's his greatest line?" he asked her.

"I do, but some prefer '*Stell-aaaa*!'" Xenia shouted and shocked, I mean *shocked*, everyone in the little café into silence. Maybe in Los Angeles, maybe in Manhattan, maybe in Mumbai, but not in that buttoned up little shopping center did you expect that kind of theater. After a moment, I laughed and kissed her on the lips, and the other guests laughed and clapped at the performance.

Not much later, Отредактированное induced us to visit his little mansion, where we learned the nature of his game and then blew his mind. When his marriage splintered, Xenia and I were not surprised.

CHAPTER 169 VLAB

When Max got up to introduce the panel of speakers at VLAB, a monthly symposium of the Bay Area Chapter of the MIT Enterprise Forum, the space was SRO. Over 300 people had taken seats in the auditorium of the Knight Management Center at Stanford's Graduate School of Business. They had just spent an hour schmoozing and networking, if there's a difference, over drinks and South Asian delicacies provided by Sameer. Those still filing in stood along the amphitheater stairs or the back wall. The meeting organizer asked that everyone settle down, and that the doors to the outside be closed to cut down the ambient noise. Finally calm prevailed and Max himself was introduced. They'd come to hear Max, The Talent, open this monthly forum of business school students, engineering students, entrepreneurs, technologists, lawyers, publicists, investors, and life-long learners. The evening's topic was DNA and Diagnostics: What Next After the Genome? Max's assignment was to give everybody context about the important issues in the field. Then he'd ask the two CEOs, the lawyer, and the investor on the panel to introduce themselves, briefly. Following that, he'd lead a discussion with the four panelists. After ninety minutes, there'd be a few questions from the guests. Most of the audience would file out into the cool, dark Palo Alto evening and head homeward, but dozens would stay to ask more questions of the speakers, to say hello to an old friend, or to introduce himself or herself and ask for a meeting some other time.

Max wished he had never agreed to it. He felt like he was going to collapse. He couldn't suppress his mental chatter about all the moving parts of his rock-star scientist life. If he'd been healthy, he'd quiet all that noise and do what needed doing. As it was, every little thought, even the best of them, distracted him like a song he couldn't get out of his head. Lack of sleep broke his powers of concentration, and his kidney problems ensured lack of sleep thanks to frequent nighttime urination punctuating the little rest he got. He was caught in a maddening cycle and woke up tired, drained of energy every day. In the mirror, he hardly recognized himself, especially with the puffy eyes and the strange paleness he'd acquired. His right foot and ankle had swelled up, and he looked like an old lady out of her support hose. Then, too, he was always hungry. His doctors warned him not to eat too much protein, salt, or sugar, and their definition of too much was his of too little.

The numbers were clear. His kidneys were on their way out, slowly, and probably not reversibly. "Sequellae of ischemic acute tubular necrosis" is what Pabla Mirabella labeled it, but that was just an umbrella covering many routes to end-stage kidney disease. The septic shock following his accident, the nephrotoxic antibiotics, his taxing diet, and probably some novelties of bad luck thrown in, all conspired to set him on this course. Pabla's entreaties to Max and medications for his ailments had not sufficed to turn them around. "You're transplant bound," she told him. "I don't know when, but I think that's what you have to prepare for."

At VLAB, what he felt wasn't just the usual fatigue. Something in his lungs wore him down, too. Nighttime coughing had reduced further the sleep he desperately needed. He'd have to go see Pabla again. *So many damned visits. I can't get any real work done!* The chatter had ramped up to a new level, and so distracted him that he missed his cue after VLAB President Naveena Singh-Cohen's introduction. It was just a second, but a second that everyone noticed. When he recovered, he knew where he was, but he wished he'd made notes when he'd prepared his thoughts and questions on the drive over the hill. His powers of recall had always, *always* sufficed. They failed him then. He stood in front of nearly 400 people and didn't know where to start. If he'd had his mental edge, being the worst dressed person among them would have given him power. But the edge had dulled, and he felt naked before them. Little shoots of panic sprouted, and his mind clouded over. The silence embarrassed everyone.

"What about Rinchen?" someone shouted from the audience.

What? Max heard it as the *j'accuse!* it was. Max had never been asked about Rinchen. He'd never been heckled, and he'd suppressed the thought that someday he would be. He hadn't suppressed thoughts about Rinchen, though, and they were an important part of the chatter that left him sleepless. Rinchen reached from the grave and made Max feel like Raskolnikov. *Damn him!*

Thirty seconds of silence in this setting was too long. Naveena got up and moved over to help him. He saw fear in her eyes, fear that there was something really wrong with him, and fear that her evening was about to collapse on itself because of him. Full blown panic took root. His breaths shortened. Then they became hard to draw. That forced his mind further inward and away from what he was doing there on stage.

The stage and the audience became nebulae of nothingness. He could think now only about getting more air into his lungs. He asked Naveena for something. I saw her reaching to help him balance, but he pulled his hand to his chest, made a high-pitched gasp as he tried to draw air through his constricting airway, and then he collapsed.

CHAPTER 170 THE CLOT

THE EMERGENCY Room at Stanford Hospital and Clinics is only slightly more than half a mile from GSB. The EKG on board the ambulance had already established that Max was not having a heart attack. But even with oxygen he was very short of breath. The residents thought this was a textbook deep vein thrombosis thrown off to his lung. Pabla Mirabella had been deeply engaged with Louisa ben Dayore when she got the call that her patient had been admitted to the ER on suspicion of a pulmonary embolism. That left her rushing in from her condo in Menlo Park and promising her old girlfriend she'd be back as soon as possible to pick up where they'd left off.

Wilhelm Conrad Röntgen's 1895 discovery of X-rays and the photograph he made of bones in his wife's hand, for which he was awarded the first-ever Nobel Prize in Physics, was the beginning of a revolution in medical imaging. X-rays are strongly absorbed in the dense calcium of bone and only weakly in our watery, fleshy tissues. That difference provides the physical basis for the high contrast image we think of as an X-ray. A blood clot on a background of lung would hardly register on film at all. Over the decades, doctors learned to selectively insert strong X-ray absorbers like barium and iodine, so-called contrast agents, into certain tissues, thereby providing good images of the body's interior. Every traditional X-ray, even one with a well-administered contrast agent, is a projection of the body onto a single plane. If the image is shot from the wrong angle, the physician can miss the detail he or she is seeking.

In the 1956, Allan McLeod Cormack, a South African particle physicist and crystallographer, conceived computed tomography, or CT. His new system would shoot X-rays from many angles, detect them electronically after they passed through the subject, and then use computers to reconstruct a three-dimensional image. That last piece was devilishly difficult, and with computers in their infancy, the idea was impractical. At the Indian

Institute of Science in Bangalore, my maternal grandfather C.V. Ramachandran—who along with Francis Crick learned crystallography at the Cavendish in the late 1940s—and his student A.V. Lakshminarayanan developed an algorithm, the Laks filter, which greatly eased the computational burden. Moore's Law goes a long way, but algorithm innovation has always been an important and little appreciated component of computing improvements. Godfrey Hounsfield, an English engineer working without knowledge of Cormack's invention developed the first CT system in London in 1971. In 1979, Cormack and Hounsfield were awarded the Nobel Prize in Medicine or Physiology for their contributions, an advance amounting to a three-dimensional X-ray viewable from any angle, and one not prone to the "wrong angle" problem.

What Max needed that evening at VLAB was a CT scan with contrast, but the contrast agent was nephrotoxic and could worsen the already delicate condition of his failing kidneys. Max was alert and calming down, although pissed at the world. Dr. Mirabella discussed the case with the other nephrologists and hematologists and pulmonologists on duty, ruling out all other possible courses of action, weighing contingencies while waiting for the lab results. His serum creatinine came back at 2.5 mg/dl, near the low end of the range it had been for two years. Such a value would have been devastating news for a healthy male of his age, and even worse for an AK amputee whose levels should have been even lower. But for Max, it was encouraging, and all he could have hoped for. She reviewed the possibilities with him.

"If you've got a clot in your lungs, you're an RCH from a stroke. If it gets loose, *yuk!*"

"Could you put it any more plainly, Pabla?"

Glad to see that he was following, she continued, "You have two bad choices. You can take the risk of throwing a clot—with an unknown but guaranteed bad outcome that might include stroking out—or we can do this CT scan. The contrast media could send your kidneys off—"

Max interrupted. "Yeah, why's that?"

"Not well understood. Many mechanisms. Different for everyone. If you have problems with it, mostly likely the agent is directly acting on your tubules and killing them, and then maybe you'll be suffering from dysregulation of the renal dynamics, a subject of contemporary research. We can hope that because your kidneys have been stable in spite of all the abuse they've taken, they'll do OK here. If they do go really bad, at least we can do something about it."

"I'm not feeling lucky tonight, and I'm not going back to dialysis."

"I think we should get you on the transplant list *now*. You'd be eligible. You might be on the machine for only a little while if your kidneys hold up."

"What are the chances of that?"

"I thought you were the brilliant stats guy. The numbers are a jumble. You know as well as I do that they're all about distributions and not you as an individual, so it's just a guess. A guess. Do you have any family members who might want to give you a kidney?

Max grimaced and shook his head, saying, "I'm not going there."

Pabla continued. "If your HLA-type is common in the population on the donor list, and your kidneys hold up for a while, then I stand by what I said: the wait might be short. If it goes the other way ..." and she let her facial expression carry the message.

"Yes?"

"I'm a nephrologist. I think kidney transplants are great, and no big deal. You'll be better off with a new kidney than you are now. We should have been preparing for it already. Today, I'm sorry I haven't pushed you in that direction before."

"So you're saying that I should get that CT scan, get on the transplant list, and hope I get a donor before my own kidneys crash."

"That's what I'm saying."

"What else?"

"There's nothing else. If we had time, we could reduce the chances of problems with the agent by putting you on prophylactic dialysis now."

"Just get me that scan, will you?"

By then, it was 6 a.m., the morning after VLAB. LBD and Pabla hadn't gotten back to the their *c-something interruptus*.

The scan exposed a small pneumonia in one lung, but no clot. Antibiotics cleared up the pneumonia. The contrast agent was too toxic for Max's kidneys and his creatinine was soon 6 mg/dl.

"That's ominous, Max, ominous," Pabla told him when she saw the lab tests after a checkup two months later.

CHAPTER 171 MAX'S DOG

In a worsening gyre, Max had too little time for any of his too many commitments. I was grateful that he kept away. We, the team I'll describe soon enough, accomplished a great deal in his absence.

Vladik and I stayed close to Prophetic Capital. Vadim and Xenia were our best source of advice. Vadim was relentless in his insistence that we should purge Max or walk.

"This is going to end badly," Vadim told me over lunch. We were somewhere over the Great Basin at 45,000 feet, enroute to Wyoming. Xenia had routed the Citation to pick me up in San Jose so I could join them for a weekend fracking conference. Vadim's remark had broken my train of consciousness, one focused on an evening alone with Xenia.

"Vladik isn't Max's business partner," he continued. "He's his dog. And a master expects his dog to crawl into his kennel, barking with pleasure all the way. End this delusion now, will you? We'll all find something else to do with your talents. This is just going to end badly, and only worse if you delay."

CHAPTER 172 SHE WOULDN'T BE MY GIRL

On a personal note, my infatuation with Xenia, triggered within her sleek fuselage en route from Omaha—when my arm brushed hers, oh Lewd-Minded Reader—had become not quite unrequited love. Whether it was fingering Snap-ons at Home Depot, stretching our mental limbs at the Churchill Club, or dancing our bottoms off at Rackspace—formerly the renowned Mabel's Dyke Bar in Redwood City, but renamed in the '90s as the scene became more inclusive—my heart sang,

She was the girl I always went to,
The girl my knee was bent to,
The girl nude dreams were sent to,
The girl that Tashkent lent to,
The girl I would cement to me.

I wanted to marry her, and while that had become possible, she remained bound to Vadim. I was just an accessory, a beloved, respected, well-treated accessory. I couldn't really have her the way I wanted, as an equal partner. So our "thing", whatever that thing was, had its limits. LBD felt the same way about me, that is, that we had reached our limits. She realigned with Pabla. I put more energy into my "thing" with Georgina.

Volume 6

Maxed Out

CHAPTER 173 PUPA BRANZINO

FIVE MONTHS had passed since LinkedIn went public as LNKD, and investors in Social Media Fish II held their breaths, counting down the final thirty days until the shares became liquid.

Vera told Max that the breakneck appreciation of real estate in the Gilis, and some unexpected opportunities to buy puzzle pieces of the empire she was building had put new demands on her finances. She needed the capital she'd lent him immediately or sooner.

He texted her. "What's left in the mattress?"

"All gone"

"Fuck"

"You have half of it, and the rest is in the business"

"Fuck. I'll see what I can do"

"Please. There are a lot of wet dreams ☺ riding on this," she wrote.

A hoarder more than a spender, and an investor when he did spend, the one-sided economic recovery from the depths of the Great Recession had put Max on top of a pile of stocks worth more than enough to return his loan to Vera. Max decided, instead, to empty his low yielding money market accounts and borrow against his portfolio rather than liquidate any of it, confident as he was that LNKD would soon return him what he owed her, ignoring the interest of more than a hundred thousand dollars.

A week after their last exchange, he texted her again. "Did the wire come through?"

"Yes. Just now. Thank you, Love"

"So we're square again, finally?"

"There's interest, but yes. Do you want to know what I'm buying?"

"No. You run the business. Good luck with it."

LATER that same day, Pupa Branzino sent e-mail to all the Bay Area members of Social Media Fish II, informing them of a breakfast meeting at the Rosewood when the six-month lockup ended. The meeting would be informational and celebrational.

Vladik had reclaimed his Facebook money from Branzino and had never even considered investing in the other funds, but Branzino had kept him on the distribution list. Vladik thought it was only to tweak him-of-little-faith.

The message reminded him of the chance he'd missed. It irked him, and he considered asking Pupa to take him off the list so he wouldn't have to see more consequences of his own hesitation. But picking at the scab of that wound was too tempting, and he didn't want to have to ask Max.

The message also reminded him of his first to the Rosewood with Arianna. He had been so optimistic about Moby Dx at that time, and so trusting in Max. He felt remorse of ten different kinds, and just plain sadness that those sunny feelings were gone. He could hardly believe he'd been such a sucker. What kind of due diligence had he done, after all? He'd learned of Max's work through the startup of Orrigen. That was evidence. Max was every journalist's go to guy for incisive commentary on MEMS developments. That was evidence. And then, too, Vladik had called one of his boyhood friends who had since become a Harvard Medical School professor, and asked him what he knew of Max. "Never met him, but he's the best in the world in his field." Max's public persona was clean.

But Vladik had ignored all the non-public messages, among the first was self-generated. "Too good to be true," was what he'd said to me at the Rosewood. And when did it ever turn out that what's too good to be true actually turns out to be true? His own wife (*his own wife!*) had told him that Max was a remorseless liar. That was specific. She worried that Max would hurt them, without specifics. Vadim had seen in an instant that Max's unwillingness to attend an important investor meeting signaled worrisome problems to come; although Vadim said Max would fire Vladik, and that hadn't happened, so maybe Vadim's analysis was flawed. And then, going back to the beginning, there was Jay's story of Max unhinged, and its dovetailing with Arianna's account. If he'd been digging for specific dirt, he might have found it, but only maybe. He hadn't wanted to find it. What was there in front of him, he ignored. Vladik gave himself a fail, an epic fucking fail, on the due diligence.

The Rosewood would always remain something special to him, and to everyone who went there, because of its setting and its feel of casual ultra luxury. Vladik even contemplated going to Pupa's meeting, seduced as he was by remembrances of things past, and the idea of watching the morning fog burn off the eastish-facing slopes of the foothills.

"Pupa," Vladik said on the phone. "Congratulations on LinkedIn. Do you mind if I come to your meeting? I heard about it."

"No, of course not. Please do. There's still time to invest in some of these others, too."

“Yeah, I know that. I’ll consider it. See you there?”

“Vladik, glad to hear from you. Yes, see you there.”

The gathering was in a small banquet room below the bar and terraces. Social Media Fish LLC hoodies, black with the silver fish logo, were stacked high at the entrance. Like victorious team members, all the guests wore them as they sipped made-to-order espressos or locally sourced mimosas, or as they sampled the Rosewood’s signature breakfast buffet of French pastries and curated fruit. Pupa, and everyone else, Max and Vladik included, felt the return of those great late ’90s days when money grew on trees. Other than Max, Vladik knew no one, but he recognized a few names from the e-mail distribution list. Max knew several people, but did not introduce them to Vladik. Pupa came up to introduce himself, putting down his croissant-laden German porcelain plate and a cup of yogurt with blackberries to shake Vladik’s hand and pass him off to other LLC members.

“Oh, ██████. Pleased to meet you. I’ve been a great admirer of your work. I didn’t realize you were in on this,” Vladik said to one of Silicon Valley's most accomplished inventors.

“Got in at the last minute. When I heard Boky had *escalated* his buy, I went all in.”

Vladik understood by her verbal wink that she thought Boky’s investment had something to do with Escalation Partners. “Why would Escalation need Pupa Branzino?” Vladik asked, knowing he should have let it go. She gave him a real wink in return, conveying that she knew, but couldn’t say. He moved on, exchanging business cards in a networking ritual as common as the cold in Silicon Valley.

Max and Vladik may have been at war, but it was a cold war. And on the morning of that celebratory if minor social event, one heralding that all was good in the world, there was little need to talk. Max would be taking home a pile, and he thought Vladik would be, too, and the other IPOs were still yet to come.

After forty-five minutes, Pupa called the session to order, thanked everyone, informed the audience that interests were still available in Twitter, and then explained the Social Media Fish II LLC Interest Liquidation Process. Those in attendance, mostly members of the LLC, held interests, that is, shares of LNKD. Pupa told them that any member could sell half or all of their interest on the last day of the upcoming calendar quarter.

That rankled. As of that morning, the lockup had expired. In the minds of the members, the shares, their shares, were liquid. The stock price had already shown great volatility, increasing to more than four times what the members had paid for them, and then falling by nearly half, all within six months. The members didn't want, and couldn't see any reason to accept restrictions that would prevent them from getting out at the most opportune moment. They wanted to place sell orders on the shares whenever they damn pleased.

The questions and complaints came fast and furious. Pupa, who had been so affable during the greeting, shut down emotionally, appearing to several of those who exchanged mail about it later, "like a turtle with his head withdrawn." Some guests tried to talk to Pupa with the sweet voice of reason, suggesting that there were alternatives. Pupa answered that these would be too expensive to implement. Guests complained that Social Media Fish's management fees should have been ample to provide a more customer-friendly liquidation process. He responded in a terse, affectless voice, "I would prefer not to." That sent several guests leaving the room in frustration, Max included.

After Max climbed the stairs to the main level, he stopped for a moment to text Vladik. "You got me into this. You better get me out whole."

Vladik, feeling good about having pulled his investment at the very beginning, left the room, too, and walked to his car. Max, whose stamina had taken another hit after VLAB, hadn't reached his own yet. Vladik caught up with him.

"I got your text."

"Fuckin' A you did."

"Branzino was unbelievable. Have you seen anyone so unresponsive to his customers?"

"Fuck that. If this thing goes under, I'm holding you responsible."

"What are you talking about, going under? And anyway, you made this decision on your own."

"Are you kidding? The guy is a reptile. Something bad is going on. I don't know what. I can guess what, but for now, I'm not saying. And if it goes bad, you're going to find a way to make me good."

"Max. Don't threaten me. Pupa sucked this morning. But if there's a problem, it's his and yours to solve, not mine."

"We'll see," and Max turned to get into his car.

Many e-mail messages shot back and forth over the next few weeks. Pupa sent notices of a new and much-improved liquidation process. According to the revision, members were able to sell half or all their interest at any time by completing and returning a scanned copy of a form Pupa had attached to the notice. Pupa would sell the shares and inform the member of the execution price. Within five business days, proceeds would be wired using instructions the member had provided on the form.

Payment was prompt for the first executions, resulting in joyful emails to the distribution list, reassuring others that their fears were unfounded. Members who sold later reported receiving only partial payment, along with unmet commitments to send the balance in five, then ten, then twenty days. Max, and others like him, had believed in the company, LinkedIn itself, and had gambled that the stock would climb out of its doldrums. He, and they, never received anything more than the notice of sale.

Two such gamblers were poker friends of Max's poker friends. They had put five times as much money into Social Media Fish funds as Max had, and they let him know that he was on the hook for whatever they could not recover from Pupa Branzino. They had no more claim on Max than Max had on Vladik, but they scared him.

"Should I be scared?" Max asked his poker friend.

"They're mob," his friend told him.

Max's financial life only got more complicated. He had agreed to test a cockamamie new protein sequencer, and in the expectation that the fledgling company's stock would fly after he wrote a glowing paper-that-looked-like-a-business-plan about its utility, Max had, in violation of conflict-of-interest rules, sunk a big slug of money into their stock. The sequencer was a dog, there was no paper, and the stock tanked. There was a margin call he couldn't meet because he was already margined to the max in anticipation of a LNKD payout that hadn't happened. Max was in a panic. The looming threat of physical violence from goons he'd never met left him short of breath and looking over his shoulder. There was no timetable for whatever they were going to do. For the margin call, however, the timetable was clear. He had five days before some broker would begin liquidating his equity portfolio.

Under the best of circumstances, Pupa couldn't get cash to Max fast enough to meet the margin call. Max could have tapped his equity portfolio, but he had other plans for those, something imminent. His other assets were illiquid. Venus might have been willing to help him out, or Sameer, but pulling teeth would have more pleasant for thin-skinned Max than enduring the humiliating daily jibes he'd take in exchange, not to mention the exorbitant price in dollars.

It had been only a few months since he'd repaid Vera, but he saw no option to going back to her for another loan. Late that night he called her.

"Baby, I need you."

"Max, that's not like you. What do you need?"

"I'm fucked. I'm being fucked. I need cash again."

"Max, it's spent."

"Already?"

"Everything was queued up. Had been for months. I got a great price! You should be happy."

"Hard to be right now."

"What I have left in the mattress is my backstop."

"I thought that was all gone."

"We all have secrets, Max."

"What are your terms?"

"Twenty cents on the dollar. I'll liquidate our partnership and your interest owed."

"A sale, not a loan?"

"A sale, not a loan."

"That's harsh."

"It's just business, Max. Don't take it personally. I'm sorry it's come to this."

"You can't loan it to me for sixty days while I straighten out this motherfucker?"

"A sale, not a loan, and that's that. See, I still remember your Lady Chatterley." She paused, waiting for him.

"That gardener. What's his name?"

"Oliver," she said. "The game-keeper."

"Oliver. Remember when the two of them are in the cottage, on their coats by the fire, and he roasts some of his garden carrots and slips them inside her and then they—"

"Max! Stop. I'm sorry I brought it up. Whatever you're talking about, it's not D. H. Lawrence."

As Vera told me this, she broke out of her almost-hypnotic absorption to say, "He was not himself. He'd gotten himself into financial trouble and the stress showed itself in unexpected ways."

"Maybe it was his kidney disease, too. Memory loss is a symptom for some," I said.

"His memory had always been perfect, and from the moment he said 'gardener,' I knew something was wrong. Then the vulgar fantasy." She shivered in recollection. "Was that some subliminal desire of his that he accidentally projected onto the text, or was it like a dream, a quilt of random thoughts?"

We sat, silent for a minute. I summoned Max's erratic behavior of those days, and Vera appeared lost in her own thoughts. Then she returned to telling me about the phone call and how she steered the conversation back to the transaction.

"I've done this many times. It's too much effort. We should make a clean break on the business. It's just the business. Don't take it so personally, " Vera pleaded. "If we were married, it would be different. If you were here it would be different."

"You know that won't work."

"I know that won't work," she said.

"Where are the Snowdens of yesteryear?"

"I know, Max."

"You know how to wire me the money, then."

"We love you, Max."

"I know, Vera."

THANKS to Vera, Max escaped the margin call. Then he began a regular exchange of text, email, and phone calls with Branzino, hoping (against hope) to collect his LNKD payout. Pupa would text him in the morning, "Expecting good news Monday. I'll call you 4 pm pst" Max would take the call, only to be told that there'd been a screw up, and it might take a couple of more days. Then Pupa would go silent for too many days, and then reappear with the message, "My wife had to go in for breast cancer surgery," and he would cry on the phone. Then he'd blame it on an unnamed partner who actually held the shares, and then on an unnamed trader who traded the shares held by the unnamed partner. After that it was bureaucrats in the Caymans.

"The Caymans!" Max shouted at Pupa, "What the fuck does this have to do with the Caymans?"

When Max, or any other member caught in the same trap, asked for documentation of any of this, Pupa refused. "I would prefer not to."

Whether he was in Menlo Park or at his house near Lobitos Farm, Max was sleepless, anticipating a knock on the door from his poker friend's friends. He received several calls from Unknown Called ID. There was only breathing, breathing, and more breathing in response to his, "Hello, MF?" "Hello?" "Hell mother fucking o!" He cursed Vladik.

Then one day, Max received a phone call from the SEC. An agent, Ms. Emmanuela Kunta, inquired about his investments in various Social Media Fish entities. Was he aware that Pupa had been charged with millions of dollars of debt fraud in Louisiana but had moved out of state to protect his assets from seizure? Fuck no, he wasn't aware. There were other, less troubling questions, although the whole call served only to convince him that Social Media Fish was a Ponzi scheme and he was on the wrong end of it. When Max asked about the scope or charges of the investigation, Ms. Kunta said only, "I am not permitted to discuss ongoing investigations." Max vowed that he'd make Vladik pay for his own losses, if not those of the goons who'd terrified him.

Within days of the SEC call, its pattern repeated itself with other members of the LLC, and the news of those calls circulated within the distribution list. Then someone shot across a link to some business news web page, describing the SEC investigation, naming Pupa and another partner, stating that other partner had loaned himself more than ten million of dollars from the Social Media Fish account, had forged the original share purchase agreement onto the letterhead of a lawyer they had not retained, and more.

Vladik, still on the distribution list, was having a schadenfroodian moment when Max called him. "I'm patching you into a call with Branzino."

"These are unproven and baseless," Pupa said. "Our lawyers are working very hard to go after the people who made these allegations. In the meantime, everyone will be paid up by the end of the quarter."

"The stock has fucking doubled since you told me I'd be paid in twenty days. I want the new price. The old one is stale."

"Not doubled, but yes, we can do that. Send us a new Intent-to-Exercise."

"And I'll get paid when?" Max said.

"Ten business days after we receive it."

"Send me that in writing."

"What in writing?"

"Your commitment to pay me within business ten days after receiving my Intent," said Max.

"I'm doing that now. Look in your inbox."

"Vladik, do you have anything to say?" Max asked.

"Only that I'm glad I never invested with you, you scheming *gonef*, Pupa."

"We have to talk about that later," Max finished, and then there were two clicks, and Vladik hung up, too.

Intent to Exercise or not, ten day promise or not, Social Media Fish LLC didn't pay Max or any of its members what it owed them.

Veiled threats from the mob guys never materialized as visits in the night with baseball bats and chainsaws. The breathing-only phone calls stopped. Gradually, Max caught his own breath and began to groom Dyk for taking over as CEO once he shitcanned Vladik.

CHAPTER 174 THE LETTER

I RESORTED TO writing when she could no longer pick up the phone. I wrote to hear her voice. The mere act of putting the words down conjured her up, a miracle of the mind, of consciousness, of our uncanny ability to defeat our own destiny as selfish genetic machines. The autoresponder on her Gmail sent one and only one notice of her passing, a notice I had crafted, and that was that.

To: naijastein@gmail.com
From: callmelakshmi@gmail.com

Dear Ammaji,

Ahhmmmmaaahhh!

Can you hear me crying Amma?

I don't feel like your Rani any more, Ammaji. How can I when you're not there for me to talk to every day. How can I keep our pact intact this way every day? Forgive me, Amma. I know you do.

First, the unhappy news. Max and Vladik are near killing each other. There would be blood if they were in the same room, but we don't see Max. See? We? I gave it away already. We is me and Vladik, and when you left, we was still Laks and Max. You remember all those calls and how I loved him. How he plucked me from the east and replanted me in the west. And watered my flowering self, and how I thrilled to him and his genius. The thrill is gone Amma. So much for my mentor *shmentor*. For some others, though, it's been worse. You don't want to know, Amma. Now it's time for *me* to spare *you* the details. Eh?

You would have wished that I stayed optimistic. I know. I remember. I've tried. Without success. Makes me mad, and sad.

Max's health is terrible. He's going to need dialysis or a kidney transplant. How can I not be sad for him. I can hear you say, "Oh, Rani, a kidney transplant, a triumph of immunology. How wonderful." Yes, wonderful for him. I hope he's better for it, and better for all of us. See, I'm still optimistic!

Next, the good news. With our cofounder AWOL, Vladik has run the ship straight, and I can hear you finishing my sentence, "not straight into the rocks I hope." No. Straight to where we wanted it to go. We plan. He delegates. I execute. I have free rein. You can imagine how much I like that. "Oh, my headstrong girl, I can imagine," I can imagine you saying.

I have a fancy title. Chief Scientist. But there is no one to call me Rani. Dhaya sometimes. Dad sometimes. But not every day. No way. Maybe I should change my email address to callmerani@gmail.com, and then ... Ha! I miss your sweet laugh, too, and your rhyming timing. I laugh every time I write that, rhyming timing. A little joke, our joke, just the two of us, momma Amma.

We've hired a staff. After the money came in, oh, about a year ago, we could finally. Two biologists, a computer scientist, and a tech. Such a big pain, hiring. Though not so bad as firing. I know you know. The computer jocks are almost impossible to find, what with Facebook and LinkedIn and all those mobile and cloud startups. Mom, here's where I expect you to interrupt and ask me "Why a startup in the clouds, Rani?" I hope you know what I'm talking about. You're in the clouds, after all. Anyway, I got lucky. Maybe because you gave me the lucky name, Lucky Lakshmi. I've been lucky since the night I was born.

The Valley churns companies and people, Amma. Big ones come and small ones go, and vice versa. Just for you Amma. So much silliness. Only with you can I feel child-like again. Where are the snows of yesteryear? Oh, hiring. Yes. Industries come and go, too. Roche closed up its Palo Alto site after forty years. Three thousand people set in fluxion.

Remember the quints from Sevastopol? Taxovich? They were all there, at Roche. I hired four of them: Hermina, Marina, Malvina, and the bearded transexual, too, Martina. Christina, the youngest, is burnt out. She said something about opening a borscht boutique, I think.

But the ones working for us at Moby Dx, they are a franchise all by themselves! And I barely need to train them. They're why we're moving ahead so fast. Manuscripts in preparation. Maybe some patents too.

They are disappointed with Max, though. When they interviewed, we dropped his name without making a big deal about his role. But he is so famous, even the hint of him left them thinking his golden glow would make them shine, too. Now they mock him.

Remember *Take the Money and Run*, Amma? You and Appa bought the VHS for us and we watched it night after night for a week? There's an epilogue, and Louise Lasser is interviewed about Virgil, the *schlemiel*, the Woody Allen character? "I actually believed that he was an idiot, and I wasn't the only one ... you've never met such a nothing," she says, circling her finger by her head. Marina, Lasser-like does the same, and says, "I can't believe it, that there was a mind working in there." The first time, I laughed so hard, I thought I would *plotz*, and I remembered you, and home, and the things I would never appreciate without you, Amma. And then I cried. Pathetic, I know. In front of the others. Would you have cried, too, Amma? I think so.

The lab is wonderful. Simple, but wonderful. There are tall windows and we are bathed in light. Martina described the space as "the chaa chaa chaappiest I've ever seen." They grew up sixteen miles from Petaluma, but it's a family joke with them, imitating their parents Boris and Natasha.

There are a few walled offices here, I'm writing from the lab now, Amma, but mostly it's all open space with rows of benches and storage racks. A few are ours, and the rest are shared or used by the other companies in the incubator. They're all young and small like ours, each with three or maybe eight employees. There are babies here some days, and older children off early from school while their moms, or even dads, get a whole day's work in. Sometimes we share lunches, or have barbecues in the parking lot when the days are long. It would be lonely, I think, to be small and by ourselves with only the walls. This way, someone from another company is always there, and it makes us feel like we're part of something bigger.

Vladik spends most of his time pitching, searching for collaborators and more money. He says it's like digging a tunnel through bedrock with a spoon. I go with him sometimes, and I help him make the presentation when the visitors come to us.

Did Dhaya tell you that we are all going to join Appa in Baltimore for Thanksgiving? I will leave it to her to fill you in more.

I can't describe how much I miss you.

Love, your Rani.

P.S. Amma, one more thing. I've been meaning to tell you this for so long. I wanted to tell you in person, but I missed my chance. I didn't know the clock was ticking.

I am a woman who loves women, Amma. That's it. That's all I really want to do, to tell that to you. I'm not ashamed. That's not why I didn't tell you.

I'm not like Max. He hates himself. He makes every one hate him, even bait him, too.

I didn't tell you, tell you about me, Amma, because I thought you would be embarrassed, or maybe ashamed. But you were so wise. Maybe you knew.

This is the way I am, Amma. I couldn't change even if I wanted to. People love me as I am. Men. Women. I hope you will still love me as I am.

We have time, only time.

Love, again, your Rani.

CHAPTER 175 SCENES FROM A STARTUP

SCENE I: MAX'S JINGLE

AFTER HIRING the Taxovich clan, we built infrastructure. Those girls, and Martina, too, all with young kids, were very disciplined, maybe because they had young kids. Why, after Roche, they wanted to take on the maker mentality of the startup I don't know. Probably it was for the autonomy. Everyone wants autonomy. I gave them as much rope as Vladik gave me. They trusted us, and pitied Vladik, who had no support for the five jobs he did, but they trusted us, and that brought out the best, I guess.

I had begun the process of designing the lab, so they picked it up from there. Still, there's a long way to go from writing "PCR" in a rectangle representing a lab bench on a PowerPoint slide to making an experiment happen using PCR on an actual lab bench.

It's so tedious. I can't bear to write it. Yet, it's the stuff of life of a startup.

Ordering supplies, which couldn't be done until we'd made comparisons to determine which of the several competing vendors would give us the best combination of price, service and support, and how much we were willing to inconvenience ourselves in the name of price, because "Cash is King!" we reminded ourselves all the time. Ordering supplies, which couldn't be done until we'd established credit with the providers. At least we had a proper shipping and receiving department, thanks to the rent we paid to All-In, so the suppliers shipped to a real place they were already familiar with and they didn't have to impose another dose of delay while they determined whether we were a fraudulent operation intent on taking delivery and going out of business before we paid.

Organizing ourselves, calibrating instruments, being cheap because Cash is King, validating our processes, writing and validating data analysis software, tracking samples through the lab, reviewing data among ourselves, gradually discovering where All-In's resources were inadequate and finding means to supplement them with our own, keeping our lab notebooks up to date— ensuring each page signed and witnessed by someone else—for the purposes of documenting what we'd done and establishing priority dates for future patent filings, *ad infinitum,* or *ad nauseam,* or both.

Group meetings. We were so tiny; we ran the company's operations from a whiteboard in my office. Every day the five of us crammed in there after kids were dropped off in the morning and we reviewed the progress of samples; samples collected, samples on their way through the lab, and samples analyzed. Occasionally we'd get a call from Max, a pocket dial, an accidental call full of road noise, radio static, bits of conversation he was having with someone else, music, running water, or what we could only imagine was the sound of animals being sodomized. One day we heard him singing, presumably alone in the shower,

Who is the world's greatest inventor,
And how did I get that way?
Who made me the genius so clever, prolific,
So wise and insightful, call me Señor Terrific

Then more sound of water and humming, then no water and more humming, then "Shit!" and then dial tone.

Scene II: A Phone Call with Max

When our own shortcomings didn't produce enough bumps in the road, Max was ready to supply more, usually by trying to change the business model. He'd call Vladik and say, "Heh, I just met with Blofield," or Gasbagh or Chick Creek or d'Anconia Gnotch, "and I think they want to invest.

"What do they want to invest in?"

"Immunotherapy." On a different day, in a conversation about a different investor, Max might have mentioned autoimmunity, or diabetes, or xenografts.

"We're not a drug discovery company."

"Yeah, but we can position the molecular stethoscope to help pharma in their trials. We can titrate dose, or monitor for overactive immune response, or for patient selection."

"All very nice. Here's what I've learned. These discovery stage companies want to put all, and I mean *all*, of their risk on the drugs their trialing, and none of it in systems they use for any of the things you just mentioned. Bringing in MOST, for which there is not a single publication showing its usefulness, is something they will never do. It's a non-starter. We won't get their attention."

"I just told you, Blofeld wants to talk to you. You've got her attention."

"I thought it was Blofield." Vladik waited for a second. "She's is an investor, not a customer."

"I thought we were running this company with a lot of leeway to move, to be flexible, to be nimble, to be quick. All I'm hearing from you is *no*."

"I'll say yes to something that's within the parameters of what we're doing, but I won't pitch something I think is a bad idea, even if I can raise money for it." Then Vladik paused, "Well, if I could raise a bundle, and only spend part of it on the *fakakta* scheme, then maybe I would make that pitch."

"Well, that's what I'm saying. Bait and switch."

It comforted Vladik to hear Max admit to this. "You are the master baiter, Max, I'll give you that one."

"Acknowledged."

"What have you told her you want?"

"Another million, and on the terms of the existing convertible note."

"That's not enough. We need north of three. You need to stop telling investors about deals and terms before you clear it with me. You start me off in a hole."

"Yeah, yeah."

"I can probably handle my cousins, but do you think Venus will agree to let in new money without her getting some additional preference?"

"She'll get her preference through other channels."

"I don't know what that means."

"I'll give her stock in one of my other companies."

"What other companies, Max? I thought this was the focus of your consulting effort."

"I can't hear you, Vladik. What did you say?"

"I said, what other companies? I thought this ..."

Max interrupted. "Look, the connection has gotten really bad ..."

"I don't know, I can hear you fine."

"... have Lakshmi do the research on applications in immunotherapy. Make up a deck for Blofeld. I'll send you the introduction and you can schedule. I have to go now."

Then there was only dial tone.

Scene III: Group Meeting with Max

On the rare day when we did have a formal group meeting, meaning lunch and a review of programs, and Max didn't have a better offer somewhere else, we may as well have had fireworks, too.

He loved to look at data. Like a good physicist, he could explain anything. Whether the explanations had predictive power, that was something else. The potency and range of his logic never failed to startle. Presented with a problem that held up the flow of experiments, Max would instantly, I mean instantly, unwind the conundrum and suggest workarounds. Vladik, who wasn't a bench scientist and had only a superficial understanding of the moby, was easily convinced. The Taxovichim, who'd seen everything, were never convinced. While Max winked, they rolled their eyes. Then the fun would begin.

Max: I think the errors are systematic and you can subtract them out.

Hermina: Roche would never have accepted that, and we're trying to sell to Roche, or their equivalents, so we can't expect them to accept it from us.

Max: You're having problems because you've deviated from the protocol we developed at the Institute.

Hermina: I think that protocol wasn't tested on a broad enough sample population for a production test, and we're collecting that data now. These are just startup transients.

Max: If it were all diversity, you'd see less noise because you wouldn't have the diversity in the sample set to drive the variation you're seeing.

Hermina: Our technical replicates are proving that it's not that kind of noise.

Malvina: We think that the I's method is a good first start but not production ready because, well, we've been through this already. Lakshmi?

Here I had to duck the fact that the experiments were intended to expose the weaknesses in MOST.

Me: Max, that protocol from the I is my protocol, right? I know its flaws better than anyone. It was designed to get us results right away, but the problem here is that we need to show results that customers want to pay for, hundreds of thousands of dollars per experiment. The improvements we've got going here are intended to expose the real facts of the matter and eliminate any doubts they might have about the interpretation, or our ability to move this test into production. If we can't do all that, they'll just say, "You're too early. Why don't you call us in six months and let us know about your progress?"

Vladik: I think we've heard the same thing from the VCs.

Max: What do I have to do to get a drink around here? God I'm thirsty. Do you have Dyk along with you at these meetings?

Vladik: I haven't heard from Dyk for six months. More maybe. He is not helpful.

Max: Dyk is a great negotiator; you should really have him along. Is someone going to get me something to drink?

Vladik: Max, first, we're not at the negotiation stage with these customers. Second, let's take this up outside this meeting. It's not a good use of our staff's time.

Max: Let's wrap up. I have to be somewhere else in thirty minutes.

Max's presence had the effect of drawing the staff closer together, but against him, The Legend. It left us exhausted and wondering how or when the time bomb of internal strife at the executive level would detonate.

And while he did little but irritate us at Moby Dx, somehow he continued to advance the frontier back at Lobitos Farm, to impress peer reviewers, journalists, and schoolgirls. He could not be stopped, except maybe by himself.

Scene IV: An Afternoon in the Park with Max

In an effort to break the monotony and build solidarity, the team got out of the lab together as often as possible, sometimes during work hours, sometimes after. Sometimes it was with kids, and sometimes not. Always it was with food. If we'd told Max, we might have been able to get him to join us, but every occasion seemed more likely than the next to be incendiary, so Vladik and I chose to invite advisors, as they were more fun, appreciative, and helpful. Occasionally though, we did invite Max, and occasionally-squared, that is, very infrequently, he graced us with his company.

One such event placed all of Moby Dx LLC and All-In's Paula Allinakova at the Baylands Nature Preserve, a sprawling marshland only a long stone's throw from All-In, at just around noon. Max had been in Menlo Park in the morning, lashed to his bed perhaps, and something, I can't recall what, possessed us to ask him to join us. We did, however, learn what possessed him to accept.

Issahaq, Sameer's brother, dropped Max off by the Nature Center and asked us to have him ready for a 1:15 p.m. pickup. From there, Issahaq would shuttle him to SFO for a 4:45 p.m. international departure, details of which Max kept unusually secret. He looked worse than we'd ever seen him, bent, hobbling, holding his ear as if doing so could contain the blasting whistles of tinnitus going off in his head.

There is, at the Baylands, a boardwalk raised above the protected marshes. Waist high fences line it on both sides as it runs 830 feet north northeast from the park's office building and museum, terminating at a small seating area, also surrounded by fences. If your desire were to get down to the muck or native plants, you'd have to hop the fence. Put differently, it was safe even for a wobbly walker like Max. As we strolled leisurely and he struggled, the Taxovich Ensemble and Max walked in no particular order, talked about nothing of importance, and enjoyed the noonday weather. Max did drag, unbearably for the rest of us, relying on the fence for support with one arm while working his cane with the other.

At the terminus, we looked out on the mudflats only a few yards away and at shorebirds picking goodies from the marshlands; and beyond that the southernmost part of San Francisco Bay, four miles wide, its gray waters never glassy, but not yet whipped up in rolling whitecaps that would attract wind surfers and kite surfers later that same afternoon; and still beyond that, we saw Newark, and Fremont, and the East Bay Hills, their covering grasses dead and yellowed in the months since they'd last seen a drop of rain.

Paula's sycophantic lover owned and operated one of the mobile food emporia serving our business park. The camo-clad former general manager, of we never learned what, generously provided us with a lunch of Bosnian and Iraqi delicacies and 2Sweet drinks. We ate it out on the point of the pier.

From there we worked our way back. Paula and the Taxovich clan returned as one, leaving only me, Vladik, and The Legend. We moved so slowly that a ranger ran up to us and unfolded a wheelchair to ease Max's suffering for the final hundred feet. We were not able to contain our laughter when he offered, "Let me try to help your father here."

Vladik pushed Max as if he *was* the old man. Ailments aside, he hadn't let go at all of what he thought was his grip on the company's direction, and possibly even our willingness to hear about it.

"I have some other things to discuss, so keep going with this chair, will you?" Max said.

"I'll take us over to the jetty," Vladik said, referring to a floating dock at the bottom of a ramp on the other side of the parking lot. There the estuarine waters of the marshes made their entrance into the bay. Kayakers and windsurfers use the dock to make their own entrance into the water.

"I had dinner with Blofield again last night."

If looks could kill, Vladik's would have put an end to Max's quite obvious misery, about which he, Max, seemed remarkably indifferent.

"I know they're not really interested in what we're doing, but they want to fund us anyway," Max said.

"Yeah, but only without me as CEO."

"They're among the anti-Vladniks, I know. But still, there's a way to thread this needle."

"There are more anti-Vladniks?"

"They're not alone, let's say."

"Max, you're poisoning me with them. You don't even know what the company is anymore, and you're poisoning my relationships with our potential investors."

"Listen, we can thread this needle."

Vladik tried to find the words, but couldn't, coming up only with, "..."

"All they want is the team, minus you of course, so they'll invest if you can arrange a sale of the assets, and then you can exit holding your vested shares, and we'll redirect Moby Dx to execute their plan."

"Max, you'll have to take another tack if that's your plan."

And then turning to me, Vladik said, "Lakshmi, I'll see you back at the lab." Taking my cue, I left.

Vladik had by this time arrived at the wooden pier. Its aluminum ramp dropped sharply, sharply enough to induce vertigo, down to the six-foot-wide dock that floated in a foot or two of water over six feet of mud. It was midday, a weekday, and nearing low tide.

The men were alone. If Vladik were to slip and Max were to slide away and down, there would be no fences to protect him as the wheelchair hit the dock and he launched into space. Vladik guessed Max would hit the water face first, plunge into the mud, and be pinned in place by his own weight and the weight of the chair. Then he'd thrash and suffocate before Vladik, even if he wanted to, could trudge out far enough to try to pull him out.

Vladik stopped just a step below the top of the ramp and tilted the chair forward, encouraging his rider to put the death grip on its arms. "Where are you going on this trip, Max?"

"First stop Dubai. Kind of a tour. Sabbatical."

"Really. So nice of you to tell us. How long will you be gone?"

"Put me down you fucker. I thought you were my friend."

"I could say the same thing. But you didn't tell us how long you'll be gone."

"A month or so in Asia. Six months total."

Vladik increased the pitch on the chair.

"Let me down you fucker, and pull this death trap back up to where I'm safe," Max commanded.

"That's a nice long break, Max. Are we going to see you, or are you expecting me to sell the assets without your participation and then hand over the keys?"

"You'll see me soon enough. When are you letting me down?"

"You know, if I slipped, just a little, then you'd slide ..."

"I know, you fucker!" He was shouting now. "That's why I want you to get me off this fucking ramp."

"Max, you know, I think you should take your sabbatical and clear your head. Forget about the sale. The company's future is my hands right now. Do you know what I mean?"

Max said nothing.

Vladik jerked the chair hard enough to loosen Max's grip. He told me later that he felt like he was channeling his cousins when he whispered into Max's ear, "Do you know what I mean?"

Max said, affectless, "Yes, I know what you mean."

Rather than back up the ramp to the safety of the pier, Vladik wheeled him down to the dock. "Have a nice flight and a great sabbatical. You look worn out and could use a long break. Shall I carry the chair back up the ramp for you?"

"You fucker."

"Get up. I'm taking the chair back."

Max sat.

"Max. You're going to have an accident if you don't get out of that chair."

When Max stood up, leaning on his cane, Vladik said, "It's 1:15. You'll make your flight. I'll tell Issahaq to drive over and meet you here at the pier." Then Vladik folded the chair and carried it up the ramp while Max yelled at him.

"You fucking fuckhead of a fucker."

CHAPTER 176 THE ORGAN BAZAAR

AFTER VLAB and the CT scan, Dr. Mirabella began the work of getting Max on the kidney transplant waiting list. He had his extensive physical, confirming that he had no cancers or infections lurking, that he had decent cardiovascular function, and that his GI tract was OK. He was blood-typed and found to be O. He was seronegative for human immunodeficiency, Epstein-Barr virus, cytomegalovirus, and the alphabet soup of hepatitises. Results of "panel reactive antibody" testing were promising, informing the parties that his immune system was quiet and wouldn't reject many donor candidates. He was HLA-typed, too, providing the transplant team with a piece of information that would later be used to determine whether a given donor organ was a particularly good match for him. A good match would have some influence on the long-term survivability of the graft, where graft is a fancy name for transplanted organ.

The only unusual medical finding turned up in his colonoscopy, and well, HIPPA prevents me from disclosing that.

He had the financial means to pay for the transplant and the immunosuppressants that would keep his immune system at bay in the years after the surgery, not that it mattered. The Social Security Amendments of 1972, what President Nixon called "landmark legislation," extended Medicare protection to all Americans (irrespective of age) if they needed hemodialysis or a kidney transplant. Driven by the epidemic of obesity and diabetes, the demand for services had increased six-fold in the previous twenty years. In 2010, Medicare paid out $33 billion for the care of nearly half a million patients with ESKD. Transplants, expensive as they are at the outset, are cheap to maintain compared to dialysis; $88k annually for dialysis and $33k annually for transplants, per person per year in 2010. Generous Reader, think about donating your kidneys on your way out.

Max met all the necessary criteria and his name was entered on the lists maintained by the Organ Procurement and Transplantation Network and the United Network for Organ Sharing, UNOS, in compliance with National Organ Transplant Act of 1984. If there'd been a willing living donor, he could have had the transplant any time, but as there was not, he had to get in line behind 95,000 others waiting for the right cadaverous opportunity. The wait could easily be five years, maybe ten.

Given that his creatinine was 6 mg/dl, he was functioning OK. That meant he continued visiting his labs at Lobitos Farm and his companies more or less as usual, and he did not yet have to go on dialysis. He believed his kidneys would fail within two years. The prospect of being on dialysis for months, much less years, was too awful, too restricting, too imprisoning for him to contemplate. He needed a different plan, and its name was Sameer.

Sameer knew a guy who knew a gal who knew a guy who could get Max a kidney in the organ bazaar known as Rawalpindi—that's in Pakistan, across the street from the capital, Islamabad. In fact, all those guys and gals were family, even the surgeon at ████████ Hospital in Pindi. Sameer had a big family.

In the eyes of the entrepreneuring bazaarist, the state hospitals with their thousands of poor and uneducated patients in Pindi and Islamabad are monetizable pools of prospective kidney donors. Here's how a kidney would find its way from the pool to Max's belly.

Alongside every prospective donor there is a medical chart. Reading that chart, an educated individual, let's say a staff nurse, would learn the donor's blood type and compare against Max's O. If not O, the nurse would move on to next prospective donor. If O, she would continue to the next step.

Although not necessarily called for by the donor's condition, said nurse could easily draw a few ten-millilitre tubes of blood from said Type O prospective donor and spirit the tubes out of the hospital to a private laboratory, call it Privlab Pindi. If in the course of events the nurse was caught or questioned, a little baksheesh would go a long way, particularly if said baksheesh was in the green currency of the United States, notwithstanding widespread Pakistani ambivalence or outright hostility toward American hegemony, hypocrisy, blasphemy, etc.

The blood samples would be tested for HIV, EBV, CMV, and various flavors of hepatitis. They would be HLA-typed, and finally, tested for donor-specific antibody-mediated reactions, or crossmatch. Crossmatch is a measure of cytotoxicity, or cell-killing potential that would predict hyperacute rejection of the donated kidney. Some of the recipient's, Max's, blood serum would be mixed with the donor's white blood cells. If the mixture is unreactive, the crossmatch is negative, and this being one of those situations where bad is good, that's good. A negative crossmatch is good, indicating donor/recipient compatibility. If the HLA-types of Max and compatible donor are close, so much the better. If the crossmatch is positive, that's bad. The nurse or nurses would be instructed to find other Type O prospective donors from the near-infinite pool.

That process of finding an acceptably matched donor might take a few weeks, but not years like in the US, for two important reasons, the first being that in Pindi, 95,000 others are not in line in front of Max. In Pindi, he *is* the line. The second reason has to do with informed consent, a troublesome matter—troublesome for the organ broker and a cornerstone of medical ethics for the rest of us—requiring that the patient understands a procedure and its ramifications, and agrees without coercion to have it performed. Informed consent to give up a kidney to a complete stranger? Fuggetaboutit. Almost never gonna happen. Not gonna happen anywhere *you* would want to go for treatment. That reality greatly diminishes the availability of and increases the wait time for well-matched donor organs. In the organ bazaar, there is no informed consent. Every unsuspecting unfortunate possessing two kidneys is in the pool, so if the match were good, it would be time to remove one of them.

Said nurse, with the help of more baksheesh in larger denominations, and with the help of some other medically trained members of Sameer's extended family, would anaesthetize the donor, remove the sought-after five ounces of kidney and put it on a bed of ice in a stainless steel bowl. Then they'd eliminate the possibility of clots by flushing any remaining blood out the kidney through the renal artery, double bag it, drop it in the ice-filled 16 quart Coleman Excursion cooler Max had been instructed to bring with him from the US of A, and ship it thereafter across town or from Islamabad to the private ████████ Hospital in Pindi where Max would be waiting in an operating room. As for the donor, he or she would be closed up, and later it would be explained that he or she lost a kidney—so sorry, it couldn't be helped.

And why was the ice necessary? Among the many accomplishments of Svante Arrhenius, the Swedish savant and Cassandra of climate change, was the prediction and explanation for why life's metabolisms proceed at a rate proportional to the exponential of negative inverse absolute temperature, *T*, that is,

$$e^{-\frac{E_A}{T}}$$

where E_A is a measure of how much energy is required to initiate a reaction. With the kidney on ice, the rate of natural degradations decreases by ten-fold or more, with all important consequences if the jitney ferrying the goods were to get stuck in the city's infamous, infernal, and all-too-frequent traffic jams. Max knew this, of course.

"You're Yenta the Matchmaker, Sameer."

"Sameer's Surgery at your service, Boss."

"The fees, please?"

"$250,000"

"That's rich."

"For just anyone, it might be $200,000. For you, $250,000"

"Why the generosity?"

"Just anyone is a rich Saudi, and we don't care whether he lives or dies. You, we're going to make you live well. So, we take more time and get a better match. We'll actually do the viral testing instead of only reporting that it's done. The daughter of the sister of my third-cousin-once-removed's husband will do the surgery."

"I'm touched."

"For just anyone, the rejection rates and the flat out fatalities are three times as high as you'll get here in the States. When we take care of our friends, the results are just like home, I mean here."

"And I should believe that?"

"Should I be offended by your sarcasm?"

"It's a lot of money, even before the surcharge."

"What we are doing is punishable by death. While the Human Organ Transplant Authority looks away, we're safe. If they start making inquiries, Sameer's Surgery is out of business. We have to make it pay while we can."

"Like professional athletes."

"Or seasonal tourist spots!" And they cracked up laughing. Sameer was Max's only true friend. Sameer loved him like, well, a wife, or a little sister.

"Half in cash and half in Moby Dx Common?"

"I don't need any more shares of Moby Dx. I have Caseload Fittings, Max, remember?"

"Bastard."

"Thank you. You should go soon. Don't wait until you need dialysis because then you won't be able to sit tight in Pindi while they're finding you your kidney."

"You'll take care of my visa?"

"It's included in the fee."

CHAPTER 177 PINDI

THREE MONTHS later, on the day following his bimonthly checkup with Dr. Mirabella, Max began a six-month sabbatical. The first two months would be devoted to his transplant and recovery, about which no one knew zip of course, and the following four would be used to regroup, think about big new initiatives in the lab, put new management in place at Moby Dx, and start some new companies. New, new, new. That's what the sabbatical was all about. A new filter, that is, a new kidney, and a new life, or his old one back again, minus a leg, but he didn't really miss that any more. He didn't even tell Pabla he was going away. He'd be back in a month or so and she probably wouldn't notice he was gone. She could always find out later. He didn't think it very likely he would get a call from UNOS, and if he did, he'd pass. The money had been delivered in one big bolus to Sameer and the harvesting network had been activated.

Following a morning of shopping to pick up supplies Sameer had instructed Max to bring along, including the cooler he found at REI, and fishing line and other surgical supplies that would serve to restock the Surgery, and following an upsetting picnic by the Baylands with the team, Issahaq drove Max to SFO. There he helped Max check in for Emirates 226/614, departing for Dubai at 4:45 p.m. It would continue on to Islamabad. Well, the flight was supposed to land in ISB at 1 a.m., but it landed in Lahore instead.

A tall Pakistani woman seated near Max, in red salwar kameez and speaking perfect British English, informed him of the changes. "Leave the plane with me, and we'll walk across the tarmac to the terminal." She looked at Max's bare arms. Reaching into her purse, she pulled out an extra scarf. "Cover up with this if you're at all concerned about malaria."

"Should I be?"

She looked him over, seemed to decide he wasn't well, and said, "Yes. The monsoon was strong. You should be."

Max let her wrap the scarf around his head and arms before they stepped outside.

The wait in Lahore was two hours, then three, then six, and then they were airborne again.

Members of Sameer's family greeted Max when he arrived in Islamabad. They brought him a plain brown salwar kameez. Against his strenuous objections they forced him to change out of his preferred uniform into theirs, so as to attract as little attention as possible to his obvious American citizenship. With his luggage already in a jeep, they drove him to Flashman's Hotel on Haider Road in Rawalpindi. After the operation he would be recovering in fancier digs, but since he might be waiting as much as a month, it made sense to Sameer to put him up in a twenty-dollar-a-night hotel. Sameer would have preferred a hotel owned by his own family, but they hadn't yet broken into the lodging business in Pindi. Maybe by the time the next paying customer came along.

Jarred is the only word to describe what Max must have felt upon first entering the medieval melee of trucks elaborately painted in bright yellows and deep siennas, with images of friendly tigers, opulent peacocks, and grand mountains; of motor scooters transporting whole families; of bicycle rickshaws carrying an entire grocery store, or so it seemed; and of men dropping their pants to shit in the streets, all in the service of this immunological miracle of transplantation that promised to give Max a new life. But so it was.

Later that same day, he visited the ████████ Hospital, and had blood drawn at PrivLab Pindi, fainting dead away as he did every time. He was introduced to the lab director, a handsome and serious and slender third cousin; a very professional and polished scientist, even if his lab operation didn't have the money to do things "right" by American standards.

Each evening for a week Max was a guest at the private residence of some relative or another. He met the surgeon, trained in Singapore, and the anesthesiologist, trained in Korea. Both of these women had been to conferences and continuing education programs in the US, and both spoke of America as if it were the Holy Land. Others were less kind. Max read during the day, when he wasn't shepherded around to Raja Bazaar, and Saddar Bazaar, and the Pakistani Army Museum, and monuments and, at his insistence, sites of bombings in Islamabad. They made the now-obligatory trip to Abbottabad to see where the Imam bin Laden hid out, and then on to Muzzafarabad to see the ruins of earthquakes.

Two weeks had passed, and they had done all the day trips. Then it became just a waiting game. He sang to someone faceless and nameless in defiance of the rampant anti-Americanism.

I don't want to hegemonize you,
Blasphemize or hypocrisize you,
I am really glad that you grew,
The kidney I'm takin from you.

The hotel was festive, wrapped in decorative lights in observance of no holiday. Twice a week the large banquet hall was decorated for an Islamic wedding, taking place amid the terror, and the horror, and the hope for better times. Afterward, the hall was cleaned, and then redecorated according to the preferences of the next bride.

Max discovered the oeuvre of George MacDonald Fraser, for whose Sir Harry Paget Flashman VC KCB KCIE Max's hotel was named.

Sameer arranged an overnight trip to Muffinassabad, just to break the monotony after ten more days of nothing. A convoy of five jeeps left before dawn so they could make it to that city near the frontier with a few hours of daylight. Max turned a spit roasting a goat when a drone strike successfully took out the parked convoy. Apparently, one of the jeep drivers was the brother of an Al Qaeda operative, and carrying the brother's phone, the driver had become a target. Max was knocked over but unhurt by the blast, although he did have to change his clothes.

The overnight stretched into a few days as it took that long to replenish the jeep and jeep driver supply, and by the time they were back home at Flashman's Hotel, Max had finished the twelve Flashman novels. He'd been in country for more than four weeks, had lost weight, and felt better.

CHAPTER 178 SAMEER'S SURGERY

ON THE thirtieth day the match was made. Max's doctors, and his armed bodyguard, and his driver—also armed—said it was a match made in Paradise, worth waiting for, and worth paying for. Max asked for no further detail. After a final battery of tests, he was admitted, put to sleep, and skillfully sliced open on his right side. Sameer's distant relation the surgeon cut away connective tissue in Max's abdomen, sucking up excess fluids as she went. Within two hours she was ready for the renal vein anastomosis, the attachment of veins from the donor to Max's own. Then there was the lumbar vein, and then finishing up the major plumbing with a joining of the trafficked donor organ's artery to Max's iliac artery. The surgeon attached the new ureter to Max's bladder and left his original equipment in place where it would do no harm and might even help. She closed him up and he was making urine on the table in the OR, all in less than three hours. They would have been proud if such surgery had been done at Stanford.

Max was released from the hospital with a creatinine of 1.8 mg/dl five days later. He spent another seven days recuperating in luxury at the Pearl Hotel in Islamabad. He almost missed the earthy Spartan digs of Flashman's, but only almost. He was seen daily and had blood drawn twice—fainting both times—to check his kidney function and monitor the metabolizing of the immunosuppressants. He left a message on Pabla's answering machine, saying he wanted to see her right away, two weeks ahead of his scheduled appointment.

After six weeks in Punjab, and with his creatinine now down to 1.6 mg/dl, Max flew home on Emirates 615/225, ISB->DXB-> SFO, feeling better than he had since he'd lost his leg.

When he walked into Dr. Mirabella's office the next day, she said, "Max! You're grinning. What's wrong?"

Max lifted his shirt to show her the scar, and with a smile of someone who felt like he was winning he said, "I'm going to need some help monitoring this." Then he handed her a sheaf of histocompatibility data, lab results, and surgical notes. They were all laser-printed in Courier on paper without letterhead that Max had brought with him. There were no identifying marks printed on the pages, and the handwritten notes were in a neat cursive that could have come from anywhere in the English-speaking world.

"Max! I don't want to know the details. I don't even want to know the broad outlines of it. I'm probably committing a crime by not reporting you, and I'd be violating my Hippocratic Oath if I didn't treat you. But *wow*, creatinine of 1.6, you must feel good. "

"Just great. Like a new man. It's a cliché, I know, but that's the way I feel."

"You are lucky, lucky," and she shook her head in disbelief. "You know how many of these vended transplants come out like yours?" She didn't leave him time to answer the rhetorical question.

"None," she said. "I've never even heard of something like the treatment you got. You can live twenty years on this kidney if you take care of yourself."

CHAPTER 179 ROBERTS MARKET

ALONGSIDE THE glass display cases filled with grass-fed ground beef, $7.95 per pound, and ground gourmet dog food $2.49, Mediterranean lamb burger $6.98, and warmwater lobster tail, $35.98, and oxtail $6.98, Vladik and Arianna bumped lovingly against each other, preparing to order some sandwiches. She put her hand on his shoulder, tracing the line of it with her finger, laying her head against it, smiling the smile of the shagged. He too had his hands on her, lightly around her waist, pulling her closer when he sensed she might have moved a hair's breadth away.

Monday morning, 11 o'clock. Late for lunch and early for breakfast. But it was a lazy November morning, and they had spent it together, first with vigor and then with languor in their poolside house on Martian Home Road. Then they had walked hand in hand down the private drive of the residence, chatted briefly with Mei Mei at the kiosk, told Sheba that, no, they preferred to walk, and then turned left, winding along Mountain Home Road until they arrived at Roberts Market. The sky was gray and leaves that would fall had fallen. The air smelled of them.

A most unusual day they were having. Had they ever been there at that hour? They couldn't remember. If they had, they might have known that on Mondays it was Max Frood's habit to stop by on his way from Menlo Park to the I. Ready and waiting for him at the sandwich counter would be a ciabatta filled with prosciutto, provolone, and portobello, and topped with the works. He'd grab a 2Sweet Iced Tea, hobble to his Outback parked head-in in front of the corner store, and drive the winding road up and then down to Lobitos Farm.

As anyone who frequents Roberts knows, the gourmet dog food is opposite the coffee bar and the display cases of meats and cheeses from which sandwiches are prepared. The two lovers turned around to inspect those choices, including the cakes, brownies, and tartes, and then thought better of it, turning back to the gourmet dog food, roasted eggplant, Thai noodles, spinach salad with pine nuts, meatballs, penne with pesto, and other deli'ish delights. Imagining how they'd enjoy them, eating outside, sitting on a stone wall, dangling their legs like kids, they made some selections and had them handed back in pint-size clear plastic tubs which they then placed in a plastic basket. Then they walked past self-serve thermoses of coffee, racks of wine, and all the way to back of the market where open refrigerated cases were stacked floor to ceiling with choice after choice of bottled and canned milk, juice, tea, coffee, soda, and water, possibly colored, possibly vitamin-enriched.

When Max walked in through sliding glass doors, he kept the magazine rack to his right and the cashiers to his left. He loped around the large curved glass display case with cakes and other pastries, and sidled up to the sandwich counter to claim his order. A sunny-bright girl, her name might have been Amanda, or Heather—a girl he'd seen a hundred times—said, "I have it right here for you, Max." He tried to smile while thanking her, before heading past the coffees and wines to the cold drinks. That is where he bumped into Arianna.

She turned around, and although *he* did not immediately comprehend whom it was he was seeing as the two of them faced each other for the first time in almost a decade, *she* did. "Maaxi!" she said in a combination of French and Farsi inflections that he had never heard from anyone else on Earth.

Vladik held his basket in his left hand and Arianna's hand in his right, was horrified as the foreseen scene developed. He broke away from the selections of Mango Cha-Cha, Harlem Shake, and 2Sweet Iced Tea. Then he turned around to face his business partner. Max registered Arianna's face and then Vladik's with its still post-coital softness about it. He saw the held hands, and the gold band on her left ring finger. "Hi, Max," Vladik said, as blandly as he could.

THE transplant had had a wonderful effect on Max. Most symptoms of ESKD had gone away, from the ceaseless itching to the swelling in his face and extremities. He was rarely nauseated any longer, and the constant thirst had abated, although he still consumed litres of carbonated drinks daily. He was left with his tinnitus and impaired balance—the vestibulopathy being a permanent consequence of the gentamicin that saved his life—but the irritability, the anxiety, the lack of ability to concentrate—that ability so essential to his scientific productivity—were in the past. And so too, for the most part, were the episodes of being dazed and confused, episodes which verged on delusional during upwards excursions of his creatinine.

But the PTSD of his youth—triggered when the leaves fell, the humidity changed, and smells reminding him of autumn in New England lit up his limbic system like the esplanade at Burning Man—remained untreated. November had done its trick, and the interior Max had turned turbulent already.

The scene before him—his former wife whom he still thought of, as she had conjectured, as his merely estranged wife; his business partner with whom he was in a kabuki-slow dance for control of their company; those two in apparently happy matrimony—detonated all the emotional charge he held within, transporting him back to childhood and adolescent and adult humiliations.

"YOU'RE FUCKING my wife," Max spat. And then shouting, "You are fucking my wife!"

Vladik mastered himself and let the impotent, ill-informed insult go unanswered. Then he paused and said, "Max, you outrage me, and it's not the first time. Beware of yourself, Max. Beware of yourself, old man. You don't understand what you're unleashing." Then he stepped backed and unclenched his fist.

"Max, beware of Max! *Ha!* You're not wise or brave." He shook his cane at Vladik.

Arianna jumped in. "*Cochon*!" she grunted, and used both hands to push Max hard against the drinks. He lost his cane and his balance, falling backwards as hundreds of bottles toppled off their shelves, banging on him, breaking on him and on the floor. Vladik watched, speechless, as Arianna grabbed Max by the collar of his soaking wet shirt, standing him up and saying in a hushed voice, "I am not your wife, you pig." Then shouting, "Now get out of here," and she pushed Max down the aisle of black powder-coated steel racks filled with baby crackers, snacks, boxed and canned soups, cookies, candy, and coffee. She grabbed a box of English crackers and beat him on the head with it as he stumbled from one side of the aisle to other. Racks, boxes, and cans, and then more bottles, crashed on and around him. "*Cochon! Cochon! Je pensais que tu étais moitié homme et moitié cochon, mais maintenant je vois que tu es tous cochon*."[1]

Max tried to gather himself against the magazines, facing her and Vladik, too, who had walked behind Arianna as she swung and crushed cracker after cracker against Max's balding head. His mind swam with the indignities he'd suffered at Vladik's hand. Vladik had never acknowledged all he'd done for Moby Dx. Look at how he dissed Dyk? And that fucking, ponziferous Social Media Fish, too! It was time.

---

1 Pig! Pig! I had thought you were half man and half pig, but now I see you are all pig.

"And you!" he hissed, pointing to Vladik, "You're fired!"

The long anticipated day had come.

CHAPTER 180 THE ALL HANDS MEETING

Of course, no Taxovich had any idea that events like those at Roberts were in the making. Vladik and I, forewarned by Vadim, and working hard to forestall firing, hadn't anticipated it was imminent. The whole company was caught off guard. To say that Moby Dx went off the rails doesn't begin to describe it.

Dykkur, the architect of the scheme that empowered Max to fire Vladik, moved swiftly. He prepared Vladik's severance documents, and others naming Dyk as the new CEO and Managing Member, and had them signed by Sameer and Max. Then late that same day Dykkur sent out email informing us of an All Hands Meeting to be held the following morning at nine o'clock. There was no agenda, but Vladik had called me after he left Roberts Market, so I knew, more or less, what had happened.

Dyk, whom none of the others had ever met, along with Max, whom we hardly ever saw, showed up at All-In the next morning. Max told us that Vladik had been removed at the request of the Council, and that Dyk was the new CEO effective immediately. He handed out copies of documents on the letterhead of Ph'eer, Dowd, and Sertantiy, and the job was done.

"Have any of you ever been involved in a company in litigation?" Max asked. He received only blank stares.

When Malvina asked why Vladik had been cashiered, she was told, "That's not on the agenda of this meeting."

"Then what is the agenda of this meeting?" asked Marina.

"It's to inform you that Vladik has been let go and introduce you to the new CEO," said Max.

"OK, then are we done?" said Martina, who had already risen.

"Get back in your chair, you cunt," said Dyk. Martina had not been called a cunt for a very long time and didn't much care for it. He started to leave the room, but decided instead to watch the spectacle from the open doorway.

Max tried to make amends. He had planned for nothing except adoration at having removed the execrable Vladik. "Let's all calm down. Why don't we go to lunch and have a few beers? We can all get to know each other a little bit."

"It's 9:15 in the morning," said Marina.

"Four of us came out of the same, how shall I say it … cunt? We know each other pretty well," said Malina.

I had to suppress my cackles. I should have been crying.

Dyk had said enough, so Max tried to wrap up the meeting. "Dyk is here to help get this company on track. He's an experienced hand in the biotech industry." Max glossed over the fact that Dyk didn't have a single day of operating experience on his résumé. "He and Lakshmi and I will be writing a new business plan for the company and showing it to you two weeks from Friday. Then we can all go out for beer and get to know each other."

"What is wrong with the business plan we have now?" asked Marina. She went on to explain the company's two-pronged approach, dividing time between MOST and BROADID.

"I think the plan you're talking about is something that exists only in your head," piped in Dyk.

Martina, shouted in from the doorway. "You fat fuck. It's not in her head. It's right here on the ground, in front of your eyes to see."

"I think we should adjourn this meeting. Shall we?" Max said. Everyone agreed that it was best adjourned immediately, and they all fled, including me.

Max caught me on the way out.

"Heh, I'm going to need your leadership here to get this mess shipshape."

"Max, if I exercised leadership right now, it would be to lead everyone out the front door."

"What? You're with Vladik! You …"

But I interrupted him. That was leadership. I knew if he said what he was going to say I would go out that door and never come back, and whether I led them or not, the four Taxovich quints would be gone too.

"Max. Don't say it." And I waited for him to collect himself. "I'll give you thirty days to have Vladik back in here on terms he likes. Get Dyk out of here and never bring him back. Otherwise, you'll have my resignation. In the meantime, I'll try to get some work done." I went to my office, gathered up the others, and we left to get some beers. It was 9:30.

CHAPTER 181 ZIPPLESSNESS

LATER THAT same day I went over to the Petit Parthénon. Arianna and Vladik gave me the blow by blow, and I did the same, all through a shower of laughter and tears. Arianna needed as much consolation as any of us. She wanted to get as far away as possible, and to her that meant Block Island or Paris.

She persuaded Vladik that he could do whatever he needed to do from either place, because what he needed to do was nothing. "Vladi, it's over. It's not that you've been outsmarted. You've been out connived. That's not a shameful thing, to be fired by a bad man. Pig!" And then she laughed some more. They would leave in a few days, if not the next morning as Arianna preferred.

Before I headed for Georgina's that evening, I made it clear to Vladik about the thirty-day deadline I'd cooked up on the spur of the moment with Max—I was serious. What the team would do, I could only guess.

Vladik knew it was pointless to talk to Dykkur, whose conflict of interest ran so deep it needed a bathysphere. I was still only a bauble to Venus; however potent our intimacies, I had no card to play there. Vladik wanted to avoid calling his cousins. Matters would be entirely out of his hands once he did. That left him one person: Qasima Zipp.

After a few days, he managed to reach to some lower level functionary in the I's Office of Contractual Relations. It was the least they could do. After all, he, as CEO of Moby Dx, had signed a contract with the I to secure services from one of their Principals, and not just any of their investigators, but Dr. Max Frood. Vladik explained the situation, said that actions had been taken in violation of the three-way contract, with potentially tragic ramifications for the company and for HMRI, and he wanted their help enforcing it.

And what did he hear back from the OCR or Qasima? Zip. Nothing. Nada. Niente. Niets. Nihil. Zero. The goose egg. HMRI had circled the wagons to protect its own, I guess.

CHAPTER 182 THINGS FALL APART

THE THIRTY days following the All Hands Meeting were interesting. It was that kind of time.

A company's lab notebooks are rarely kept up-to-date, and when there's a lull in the normally frenetic pace of development, the technical staff tries to catch up. The lull was upon us. We spent many afternoons completing notebook entries, reading those of others, and dating and countersigning them. I tried (unsuccessfully) to keep to a minimum any speculation about what had happened and what each of us would do in the event the bottom fell out.

When the alarm on the -80 °C freezer holding most of our samples went off in the middle of the night, sending out notifications of the imminent crisis by SMS, all of us except Vladik were drowning our sorrows in over-priced vodka and absinthe at the DNA Lounge, south of Market Street in San Francisco. We had driven up together in Hermina's Suburban, and when we got the call, we all piled back in to do the right thing. On the way home, an overturned truck on 101 blocked traffic in all lanes for five hours. We called Paula Allinakova, and gracious as she was, from a speakerphone she described being wrapped in generally compromising positions from which she preferred not to disengage. Vladik had already gone back East by then, so never mind that Dyk had disabled his electronic access key as part of an executive order. Why didn't we call Dyk and ask him to do it? Dyk couldn't be counted on for anything more than insults. Max? He didn't answer our texts. Eventually we did get through to one of our colleagues from another of All-In's client companies, and she averted catastrophe by driving in from Redwood City in her pink PJ's and throwing a circuit breaker that revived power to the freezer before dawn. We arrived back at the lab on 8 a.m. on Sunday, got into our own cars, and drove to our respective homes.

Martina and I were driving to lunch when his car was totaled. The offending black Cayenne bore the license plate 6DWA454. Its driver was of such gender and race and cellphone-using habits that if I were to mention them here I'd be subjecting myself to claims of racism and sexism. Having made an illegal left hand turn at the intersection of University and Runnymede, the Porsche's driver went through the windshield. Martina and I could have been killed, but neither of us was hurt. Then I got food poisoning from some BBQ and spent the next twenty-four hours on the bathroom floor at G's spot.

A sequencing run went bad at one of our service providers and it set us back three weeks, which was tantamount to infinity. A network server went down and we lost access to shared files for twelve hours. Marina hurt her hand in a bicycling accident and couldn't use a pipette for more than a week. Martina started having anxiety attacks and suffered spontaneous blindness for three or four hours at a time. Everyone caught the flu. Our dogs ate our notebooks.

It was that kind of time.

CHAPTER 183 THE MONARCH DEPOSED

AFTER A weeklong trip to Block Island, Vladik and Arianna returned to California. Arianna was at a stage of her work where she could come or go as pleased. Living on-site at D5's Monticello wasn't really necessary for her anymore. She would have stayed away, but Vladik wanted to come back and meet with Max one more time.

Max had sounded reasonable, even recovered, on the phone when he asked Vladik to come up to his office at Lobitos Farm and clear the air. Like in old times, they met again.

"Vladik, you did a really poor job and you needed to be replaced."

"This is clearing the air? Max, what you're doing is suicidal."

"Stop attacking me. I've talked to lots of people who thought you'd done a really poor job and needed to be replaced. *Mea maxima culpa*. I should have fired you long ago."

"Max, you're an absentee landlord, a rentier who's been sucking the life out of the company."

"Sameer, who owns the controlling interest in the company, wants you gone. It's not up to me, you know. I only have a few percent of the voting stock."

"There are too many crazy ideas in that sentence for me to respond to it. It's not even wrong. The samosa man! The samosa man is deciding my fate in this company and the fate of the company?"

"And what's wrong with that?"

"Before I enumerate them for you—" and then Vladik stopped himself.

"Max, you know what? I'll feel worse if I tell you what I think. I've already said too much. But you have to understand this. You can't disappoint investors and expect not to have a comeuppance. What you're doing is suicidal.

Call me when you are ready to listen." Vladik turned to leave the office.

Although Max had deposed Vladik, Max was like the monarch deposed, in disbelief that the love of his subjects could have fled. "You're destroying this company! You may be the CEO, but I'm the SEO, the Supreme Executive Officer!" Max yelled at him, catching the attention of the half dozen people within earshot. "You were a mediocre CEO anyway! And your mother wears army boots!"

Just kidding, Mother Loving Reader, just kidding about the last one. Max loved his mother and would never have said anything mean about someone else's. But he did continue with a string of curses of such diversity and ferocity, and pitched at such a volume that one of the passers by called in Lobitos Farm Security. When escorted into the site-nurse's office, Max fainted away as she pulled fifty milligrams of Thorazine into a syringe.

Thirty days came and went. I submitted my resignation, and without my having suggested anything to the others, they did the same. Moby Dx, the would-be leviathan, was beached. Chinua Achebe could not have predicted this rapid decline, but every experienced entrepreneur or investor in Silicon Valley could have.

A CHICKEN doesn't stop walking after its head is chopped off. Max and Dyk tried—I don't know if tried hard is accurate, but they tried—to bring the company back to life with the nearly $1 million left in the bank, the NIH grants coming, and follow-on to the iUDx contracts.

Vladik had no alternative but to inform his cousins in Brighton Beach.

CHAPTER 184 PARADISE DREAMS

THE PRESSURES that Max felt after seeing Arianna again: after the embarrassing—even for him—psychotic breakdown meeting with Vladik at the I; after Qasima's grilling about Caselode Fittings I, II, III, IV, and V; after the he-hoped-still-temporary-shuttering of Moby Dx; the pressures were like none he had felt since his son died and Arianna left him. As he put it to Vera, "They made me feel like a submarine about to implode." And yet, what he wanted more than anything, the one hope he had for relief was to get back into the deep water of the Gilis. Aforementioned traumas aside, he felt so strong after the transplant that he was sure he'd finally be able to follow

Putu into the homes of pelagic fish where he'd shoot them, if only with a GoPro. Max knew, too, that if all he did was drink strawberry margaritas while sitting on the deck of Wet Dreams' Bungalow Zero and swishing his feet in the shallow pool water with his nearly twenty-year-old daughter Maxime, that would bring relief, too.

CHAPTER 185 FULL DISCLOSURE

VLADIK COULDN'T use the phone to inform his cousins about their investment. He had to see them in person. There were reasons: loyalty, the possibility of wiretapping, and honor. Even Russian mobster money launderers have honor.

As it was, they had smelled a change. Kashonli LLC, the payments processor for Moby Dx, had stopped receiving my biweekly shipment of invoices. That mightn't have been so surprising if all of Kashonli's $1.3 million commitment had been called, but it hadn't. Why had invoices stopped? Work must have stopped. Why had work stopped? They didn't know. Vladik would report soon enough and tell them.

About three months after Vladik was terminated, he called in as expected and arranged to meet Morris and Boris Kakitelashvili at Tatiana's on that same afternoon.

"He did what?"

"Vova, how stupid is he?"

"Does he understand?"

The questions came in rapid fire with no time for Vladik to answer.

"He fired me and the team quit a month later because they hated working for him. He is enraged more than stupid. He's so used to being told he's a genius, he's incapable of listening to what needs listening to. No, I don't think he understands. I don't think he'll be capable of understanding until it's too late."

"That disloyal SOB. If we put you back in, you know, as boss, Vova, that would fix it?"

"We'd lose a year, just because of momentum, rehiring, morale. It's not only about getting rid of Max. The lawyer is in the way, too. So you'd have to convince Max, not eliminate Max. I couldn't do that. Max is a force of nature, immovable by Man."

"Yeah, so is a mudslide."

"A lightning strike."

"An avalanche."

"A tornado."

"A forest fire."

"Flood."

"Asteroid impact."

"Tsunami."

"Locusts."

There was a pause.

"Anything else?"

"Supernova?"

Silence.

"сила природы[2]! We'll see, Vova. Maybe he's movable by Woman. It's out of your hands now. Where is he?"

"In California right now, but headed for his Frood Center in Rhizobia in three days."

Bo and Mo's emissaries for the job of talking sense to Max were the banya girls; Vladik's near-twin, red-haired, improbably-virgin (in the heterosexual sense), American-born first-cousins-once-removed, Rani and Gili Kakitelashvili. Hebrew names had become common in Brighton Beach, that Russian immigrant community turning increasingly toward Judaism, perhaps as a reaction to having been denied it for seventy years, or perhaps from the gravitational pull of Chasidic communities overspilling the boundaries of nearby Williamsburg.

Just turned nineteen and recently graduated from the Fiorello H. LaGuardia High School of Music & Art and Performing Arts, they were in the middle of a gap year before heading to Bard College, whose illustrious, long time, *wunce wunderkinder* president was also a graduate of Music & Art. They divided their time between: too much cable or streaming TV; designing and painting a mural on the seven-story brick façade of a building their families owned; dance and drama classes; some standup; and a post-modern Hamlet in which Gili, the Drama Studio graduate, played the leading role, and Rani, the Tech Theatre Studio graduate, did the set design. They also dated and disrupted the dreams of horny boys and did some odd jobs for their parents.

This job was bigger by far than any they'd ever taken on, and their parents

2 Russian, meaning a force of nature. Transliteration is cila prirody..

were reluctant to entrust it to them, but Mo and Bo were almost as susceptible to the girls' charms as the young men they seduced and left hanging high and dry.

Encouraging independence, the only instructions their dads had given them were, (i) "Change his mind or leave him there," and (ii) "Use cash wherever you can, but show us your receipts for everything over fifty dollars." Boris handed them half a dozen clean GSM phones, $2500 each in Ulysses S. Grants, airline tickets, and forged passports with matching Visa and Amex cards in the names of Chana and Chava Bush.

The real and original Chana and Chava Bushinsky were twins from the neighborhood who had succumbed to Tay-Sachs as infants. Born in the same spring season as Rani and Gili, their identities were kept alive for purposes such as these, and their names legally Anglicized long before George W. Bush had become a national figure.

Morris then added, "He's already a gimp, so you shouldn't have a hard time chasing him down."

Bo said, "You're leaving in two days. You'll have to book the hotels yourself."

And Mo again, "The return is in ten. Be back then, will you please?" That final request was delivered with the whine of a parent insinuating past offenses.

Boris, the protective one, getting the last word, finished with the not very helpful, "And don't talk to strangers."

Anticipating something like a weeklong trip that would feature daytime highs in the mid-80s, they packed light. If they discovered in the field that they'd left something at home—they were going to Singapore after all, they could *get* anything—the receipts would speak for themselves. They deliberated over whether to bring a stealthy trench coat, but then decided to wait until Singapore to figure out how to blend in. They brought anonymized slabs in two formats, and mp3 players, electronic devices that would be left on the other side of the world. Everything that could be linked to their real identities would be left in Brooklyn. Paper books were good and e-book readers with Kindle account credentials were not.

For research, they talked to some other relatives about methods of persuasion, ones that wouldn't require too many pulleys or big wheels and stretching tables. They knew too little of Max, and so decided to plan for changing circumstances instead of a specific course of action until they knew more. Just in case, they took some tools and supplies from Mo's workshop: a five-pound sledge hammer; a fourteen-inch dozuki; a set of chicken shears; a matched set of needle nose pliers, electricians pliers, and dykes; one four-section telescoping leg from a Gitzo aluminum tripod; one six-inch length of three-quarter-inch diameter maple dowel; one six-inch length of one-quarter-inch dowel; one five-inch square of one-hundred-twenty-grit sandpaper; a pocket knife with a locking blade; a whetstone; a one-ounce bottle of bicycle chain lube; two rolls of duct tape; a roll of paper towels; and some fast setting liquid adhesives.

They also had to find Max. Spoofing a Rhizobian landline and leaving no traceable number on caller ID, Gili called the I at Lobitos Farm and was transferred to Max's admin, Kenneth. In a very weak impersonation of a Rhizobian office worker, she asked for Dr. Frood's flight number. Her premise was that her boss wanted to meet Max at the airport and drive him over the long causeway into Rhizobia, and thence to his hotel. Kenneth not only provided the requested detail, but also gave her the dates, times, and flight numbers for the six-day excursion to Bali. Effervescent Kenneth informed Gili that Max would spend his first night at the Bali Rani Hotel in Kuta. Rani Googled her namesake hotel and discovered it was only a few miles from the airport. Kenneth then gave her details of Max's return flight to the US. He didn't provide any information about the other five days in Bali. Gili thanked him and hung up.

Max's plan, they learned, was to disembark Singapore Airlines SQ 1 at 11:45 at Changi Airport and connect for Bali on KLM 835 at 17:30. The girls would arrive at Changi on SQ 25 at 06:50. Somehow, and they hadn't quite imagined how, they'd find a way to kill most of eleven hours before maneuvering themselves into the line next to him as he boarded KLM 835. Getting off that flight, they'd follow him again, act ditzy and ask for his help to pay twenty-five dollars for their Visa on Arrival from the Republic of Indonesia, before casually discovering that they're booked into the same hotel. All that was easy.

What they couldn't figure out was where Max was going after his one-night stay in the Bali Rani. It sounded like the kind of place he might be spending all week, but why book it for only one night? They reasoned that he had another excursion planned, but to where, and with whom? If they'd asked Vladik, he might have been able to give them some hints based on his fragmentary knowledge of his wife's honeymoon with her former husband, but they didn't ask.

They bought the KLM tickets to match his, made a reservation for one night at the Bali Rani, added more clothes that would mark them as goofy American tourists, continued their exploration of how to get Max to yes, discussed who would be the bait to distract him, and made their final preparations before shuttling off to JFK for their 21:10 departure.

CHAPTER 186 PARADISE BOUND

RANI, TRAVELING as Chana, reread Ivo Andric's Nobel Prize winning novel, *The Bridge on the Drina,* on the twenty-one-hour flight—layover in Frankfurt included. Gili, traveling as Chava, read *Influence: Science and Practice.* Both girls hoped to find some tips or insights for the work ahead. The girls used the five hours before Max arrived to get some sleep, a massage, and a shower. Then they ate noodles at Ramen Champion and went clothes shopping for what they guessed they might be doing in Bali, which was going to beaches.

They watched Max sturdily enter the transit area on hybrid legs, wearing, as expected, his uniform of expired red shirt, khakis and tennies. He used the men's room and then made his way to the Hard Rock Café where the girls, unobserved, observed him consume a 1750 calorie lunch (as noted on the menu) consisting of a ten ounce bacon cheeseburger and fries with a pint of beer. Dragging a backpack with rollers, he walked to the Skytrain for transport to Terminal 1. From there he delivered himself to the gate of the KLM flight, took a seat nearby, checked his Slab97 for news, and napped. The girls, right behind him the whole way, as invisible as two red-headed gym rats in the absolute bloom of youthful beauty could be, rolled their own bags up to KLM. As they assured that fate would appear to have it, they found themselves in the boarding line precisely in front of Max. Changing acting modes, they removed their cloaks of invisibility and began giggling, gum-chewing, and chatting, seemingly oblivious of the attention they attracted.

Chava gave Chana a carefully scripted shove in mock jest, causing Chana to feign losing her balance and fall backwards into Max's arms. There she made sure to rub as much breast and breathe as much sweet, fruit-scented air-of-nymph as she could, while Chava chortled, exclaimed "Oh, watch out," grabbed Chana as she fell, and fumbled more before the three of them fell together to the ground, whereupon both girls took the opportunity to give Max a fine feel of their nineteen-year-old juiciness. With overwrought atonement, they explained a little about their limited travel experience and how they were going to Bali without a plan, "except to *party, party* in Kuta!" they sang in unison. Then they peppered him with questions about beaches and bars, cities to visit in Bali, all of which he answered only reticently.

On the plane, Chana walked over to Max's seat and offered to buy him a drink as reparation. He declined. Then she returned to Chava and their chatter.

Arriving in Ngurah Rai International Airport south of Denpasar, if there had been any doubt up to that point that they were headed for paradise, the doubts were dispelled by twelve-foot high paintings on the walls, all of them announcing that they had arrived in Paradise. The near-sisters placed themselves next to Max in the long line for short term Visas on Arrival. There were hundreds of other passengers from several other planes; Dutch, German, Finnish, Columbian, Argentinian, French, Kiwi, and Tasmanian, all in their twenties and thirties, and almost no Americans, all waiting. The girls singled out Max and asked him for help. He reviewed the simple procedures of submitting immigration cards and cash payments for the visa, picking up their luggage, and then passing through customs. There they penetrated Max's consciousness, prying it open just enough to reach in and get a firm grip he couldn't escape.

Max used a cart as he retrieved his two pieces of checked baggage; one a non-descript roller and the other a long hard case the size and shape you might use for a rocket-powered grenade launcher or a machine gun, but holding and protecting only a custom dive fin and some accessories; unique in all creation, but just a dive fin. Kuta bombings or not, customs was as refreshingly easy as it had been when, as student in France in the '90s, he went over the border into Germany for dinner. On the far side, a driver waited with a sign that read Dr. Frood, and Max was spirited away before the girls could wish him well. They scrambled for a taxi. Encouraging their driver to go like hell, they got ahead of Max's car and then (surprise!) were unloading from it just as Max arrived at the Bali Rani Hotel.

"It's you again."

"It's fated."

"I'm famished. I want to go to the Hard Rock," Chana said.

Max said nothing but did register a little shock when he heard the name called out. He threw off a tic that did not go unnoticed by the girls. They'd come within a cunnycurl of showing Max their hand.

"I heard it's a short walk from the hotel," Chava chimed in.

"We could do it together," Chana said.

"Yeah, two of us together would be just right for you," Chava, hinting at something lascivious, "I mean age wise." That in fact was nearly true, but the years of ESKD had made him look three times their age.

Max hadn't gotten a word in yet. "I don't know. I'm tired." Max hadn't been with a woman in years and wasn't sure he wanted one, much less those two nymphiferous ones.

"But we're on vacation, and you know the place. You can show us around. We don't know what to do."

"We'll come to your room and we can order in. How's that?"

"No, we should take a drive or a walk and see something. We've come too far to stay in a hotel, I'm all hot to trot."

Max was defenseless against their onslaught, and began warming up to the idea that the fine specimens of American youth might be his together for the taking.

Max had a peculiar logic. He thought he remained faithful to his wives, Vera and Arianna, neither of whom he was married to, if he had sex only with nameless girls, and to Sameer also, if only with nameless boys. Sameer was OK with that. Vera and Arianna were beyond caring.

"OK, give me thirty minutes after I check in, then meet me in my room. If you still feel like going out then, I'll go out. Otherwise, we'll order in and I'll tell you what I know about Bali."

At twenty minutes, the freshened and more-luscious-than-ever girls banged on his door.

"I need ten more!"

"We'll turn away if we have to. Let us in, pleeease?"

Max let them in, and immediately received a big hug from each. He was wrapped in his light-as-air, cool-as-a-breeze hotel robe with its tumescent pink love-heart embroidered over his right breast. The twins were giggly, chattery, and lewd, hopping around, brushing their taut bosoms against him at every opportunity, saturating his olfactory bulb with their naturally pheromoned scents. He encouraged them to sit and be patient while he finished his ablutions in the bathroom. Chana riffled through his papers and found what she came looking for, the missing part of his itinerary. She scanned it on her small Slab. From the look of it, they were going on a boat ride.

When he emerged, the girls were decidedly less forward and provocative. He wanted a reprise of their meaty squeezes, but they kept him at arm's length. He must have been thinking *WTF!* From seductress to tristesse, or was it? His hunger for them rose, if the increased bloodflow in his groin was any indication. The aching awareness that Arianna was lost forever was a bit less acute than it had been. A piece of strange twat might be half good enough, and if one were half, then maybe two would be the whole thing. Still, they were about as old as his daughter. Lusty as Max could be, Prurient Reader, he was no pederast.

From the girls' point of view, he was nibbling the bait. Setting the hook would be purely a matter of time. What they do once it was set? Well, that was still TBD.

As the night wore on, his fantasies of lithe teenage escorts and theirs of him began to deepen and converge, if only superficially. At 11 o'clock, they finally left the hotel and walked along the Jalan Kartika Plaza. They ate rice cakes steamed in coconut leaves and coated with sticky peanut sauce, and fried peanuts in a sweet sesame sauce, and they drank orange Fanta. The girls bought woven bracelets and silver earrings from street vendors. Max bought them matching swimsuits at Blue Glue Bikini. He began to drop hints about threesomes while the twins steered the conversation to how to spend their week's vakay. He spilled the beans about his own plans, to which they exclaimed as if it was news, "Oh, that sounds so great." And then, "Can we come? Can we come, too?" like a couple of puppies yelping for the bitch's teat.

Something feral in him loosened. Even while they were withholding, they were taunting. When he said, "There's nothing to stop you from going. There may be other places, if Vera is full up," Chana countered, "Oh, we don't want to tie you down."

"Well, maybe we do." There followed Chava's snorts, a poke in Chana's ribs, and a pair of sly looks at Max; looks as undecipherable as his own winks.

"And maybe I do, too," and he tried to poke Chava in the same way. But she was too quick, and pulled her slender abs away.

While his fantasies ran to bondage and submissive sex, theirs ran to bondage and whatever devices would bring around, bring him to his senses.

The girls feigned exhaustion, thwarted all advances, refused all offers, and separated at the hotel elevator. "Goodnight you Chava Bush," he said, trying to get a smile or something from her, but she'd gone flat on him.

"7:30 in the lobby, Max," they said, and were off.

He had to jerk himself off in the bathroom mirror when he got back to the room. His head brimmed with desire for girls in a way he hadn't experienced in years, maybe, no, definitely in decades, if decades means ten years and a day. *Damn them,* he said. *She chava bush, all right. I'll be sniffing their red cunt hairs soon enough.* His wet dreams of easy pussy, the strange, the young, and the bad further lifted the lid—in a word, depression—that had been keeping him down.

Max waited for Chana and Chava Bush in the hotel lobby the next morning, but they didn't show. He called their room. They had checked out. "Those teasing cunts!" Seeing that he was running out of time, he grabbed a taxi and was the last one to board his boat.

The girls had left the hotel at 7:15 and gone ahead to the docks at Serangan. A taxi drove them from the modern nightclubs of Kuta into the third world. Past the canals, past the goats and oxen feeding on trash, past the burning heaps of what was left after the animals were done with it, around the harbor, and to the piers and beaches, high-powered catamarans awaited them. Max would be on the Green Machine to Gili Trawangan, so the girls took the Narooma.

Already at 9:00 o'clock the sun and dead air made for a hot mixture, so the girls were mostly out of their clothes, clad only in new bikinis on the upper deck of their boat. One pier away, they observed Max board his boat, and then abruptly leave it as its number two engine exploded in flames. Moments later, the Narooma pulled away from the floating dock, passing him and his smoking boat. He heard his name called out. He looked up and waved instinctively. Arms high overhead, the girls' breasts waved side to side, although out of phase, in arcs that brought back memories of Joosey. *Fucking Jay!*

"See you there, Max!" And the cranking drone of the their boat's three 250-horsepower engines drowned out whatever he said in reply.

The Narooma moved at first slowly beside local fishing boats, cruise boats, and world-cruising sail and powerboats at anchor. Then it accelerated through unusually flat water, hitting top speed of thirty-something knots as it headed out into the Bali Sea. Towards the shore, waves rose up over coral reefs, thinned near their peaks, and turned to aquamarine before they became only spray. Big ships—ransacked for every last scrap of value after their captains had misjudged the coral—remained grounded, rusted skeletal reminders to others. In twenty minutes the Narooma passed north of Nusa Lembongan, then was in open water, and at 11:15 a.m. was pulling in stern-first to Gili Trawangan.

The girls had been the youngest guests on the Narooma, and were deluged with attention because of it, not that their native attractiveness wouldn't have been enough. Explaining to the captain, a puckish Lombok local eager to help, that they had not yet booked accommodations, he called ahead and placed them at Yasgawati's Farm, the most remote hostel on the island. The faux twins counted on their disappearance to increase Max's frustration and accompanying judgment-bending, blinding lust. They would find him when they wanted.

Yasgawati's Farm was owned by a restaurateur from Denpasar and his Finnish girlfriend in a partnership as typical as Vera's and her stoner-, diver-, Australian-, deceased-, and former-boyfriend Murray's; local talent meets foreign money. Each of the hostel's tile-roofed huts was named for a 1960's musician—the girls stayed in the Richie Havens—and were kept meticulously clean by always smiling staff. Beer, fried eggs, frozen margaritas, blended mudslides, coconuts; all were served day and night, delivered to the bungalow or by the pool. Puck had done well, proximity to the mosque notwithstanding.

CHAPTER 187 PARADISE FOUND AND LOST

THE FIRE on the Green Machine turned out to be minor, as life-threatening shipboard fires go, and most of the passengers coaxed themselves back onto the bomb-waiting-to-happen. All arrived safely about an hour and a half late, not that anyone keeps time in Paradise.

Over more than twenty years, Max had been surprised by the island's changes each time he arrived. With this visit, he was beyond surprise. He was shocked and disappointed to see that the growth had only accelerated. The boat traffic close to shore had become dangerous. Men had been hired, like pilots of old, to relieve congestion and improve safety. They collected a toll, too. Piles of pony shit were everywhere. Bags of ready-mix concrete were stacked head high, and there were crowds. There had never before been crowds. As he took this in, he was almost knocked over by the amplified call to prayer from the island's new mosque, out of sight, but not out of mind.

When his boat beached, Vera was there, wearing a just-picked poppy against the jet-black background of her hair—now flecked for the first time with a few strands of gray—and matching gold poppy earrings Max had brought her long ago. She had thickened and lost the splendorous beauty of her springtime, but not a bit of her drive. Her thick rouged lips around her petite mouth opened as always to show the most inviting of smiles. If he could have transferred to her his newfound obsession with those salacious twins, and renewed with her the passion he had once shared with her, he might have had something. He knew that, and he knew he couldn't.

"Max, you look so strong. Stronger and healthier, such nice color in your cheeks. Better than since your accident. I'm so glad you've made it back." She didn't let on that she saw something was eating at him.

With genuine emotion, emotion that we at the I had never seen, that Arianna had probably never seen, he said, "I am glad to be here. I had my doubts. This is where I want to be forever, Vera." They hugged again, and then he heard another unfamiliar sound. The wop wop wop of helicopter blades was near. Looking up, he saw it over the tops of the palms before it disappeared into them.

"One of my new businesses," Vera said.

"What about No Motorized Transport?" Max asked, referring to the law, or policy, or whatever it was that kept cars, motorcycles and scooters off the island.

"Long conversation, Max. You'll like it. We'll take a ride tomorrow when Maxime arrives."

Max said nothing, a sure sign to Vera that he had changed. In the old days, he wouldn't have let the conversation be put off to a later date when it might be forgotten. She told me that he looked great, yes, much better than since his dismemberment, but sadder than she'd seen. "The fire in him was extinguished. The force of nature, vanished. I hoped the water would revitalize him and we could restore him to life, but I never believed we, or he could recover all that was lost," she said.

"Well, Bungalow Zero is ready, Max," Vera continued. "And, some girl called a few minutes ago. Chava? She said she was sorry for the screw-up, but she and her sister would come by later."

Vera saw Max light up like a Chinese lantern. She couldn't see his hose engorging with blood. She guessed it had.

All was forgiven of those little bitches, he thought.

"Did she say when?"

"No. Just, "later." Look, let's get you settled. I have a cidomo waiting for us."

"We're the liveried class, here." He paused. "I'm glad. I'm tired."

"I know, Max. I know."

"I'm maxed out, Vera. But the water. The water is what I need. Maybe the water will be enough." Then Max began to cry.

With her arm around him, she gave him the comfort he never would have asked for from Sameer—although Sameer would have given it, even in the light of day in front of the crowd at 3000 Sand Hill Road. Vera said only "You'll fight back, I know," and that reassured him.

THE girls guessed that Max had picked Chava, if only because of his oft-repeated, "You Chava Bush." Its capitalization-defying Russian accent was so lame they almost puked. Chava was the lure and Chana was the hook, or at least the hammer. Not that he'll ever get close to it, Chava was thinking while she taunted with a smile. "There's nary a slip twixt bush and lip, Max."

They spent a lazy contemplative afternoon, imagining how they'd work Max into a position from which he couldn't refuse them. Chava lay back in bed and as her slab shuffled through her music collection. Chana worked on her project.

At home she had packed all her artisan's tools into a multi-pocketed white canvas artisan's bag. She carried photos of some of her set constructions. If someone at Immigration had asked her why she was transporting all those sharp tools, the professionalism and the photos would, she hoped, carry the day.

She removed all the supplies from the workman's bag and laid them out neatly in one of the clothes drawers. Examining them, she took the four-part tube of tripod leg, the dowels, and the knife, and got to work. The leg she disassembled completely, cleaned all its parts, and in particular the surfaces where the telescoping pieces fit together. She made certain that the three knurled rings, each controlling the junction of two sections, could be screwed down so tightly that even a hammer blow wouldn't loosen them.

Then she popped the plastic foot off the free end of the smallest diameter tube. Holding the three-quarter-inch dowel in her hand, she imagined whittling it down so that one end fit snugly within the tube, and half of it remained without, tapering conically to a very sharp point. After a few quick pencil strokes to guide her, she patiently (and remarkably quickly, thanks to all those hours spent in set construction and model building in her Stagecraft classes at LaGuardia High School) reduced the dowel to a nose cone. Obtaining a near perfect fit using sandpaper, she then mixed a quarter teaspoon of epoxy, slathered it on the wood, inserted it into the tube's end, rotated it once to ensure that the two-part adhesive coated both the wood and the aluminum, wiped the excess from the outside, and put it down to set. The joint would achieve full working strength twenty-four hours later.

She stretched her legs. Chava had fallen asleep and stayed that way through ear-shattering blast after unholy blast of public service announcement, news, or prayer from the Masjid's speakers. Chana removed the headphones from her cousin's ears, put them back after she thought better of it considering how they might have made all the difference in her ability to sleep through the noise, and covered her with a light blanket. They were almost sisters. Born only a day apart, they were almost twin sisters.

Chana left the Richie Havens and walked around Yasgawati's property, enjoying the feel of a light breeze on her skin, finally taking a seat beneath the shade with some other guests by the wading pool.

"You look young to have finished college," one bearded German hipster said.

"But not too old not to have started, I hope," she answered.

"No, not too old for that, but too young for your act, I mean, for the way you act."

"I'm nineteen, but I act twenty-one," she said with a smile that drew out his laughter.

A Russian translated for her boyfriend. Chana elaborated in their native tongue.

A French girl, in English, said, "That makes you three years younger than me, and everyone else I've met is older than that."

Chana replied in French that actors develop presence they carry with them off the stage. What she didn't say is that she was Brighton Beach royalty, and as is common in royal families, or families of the ultra rich, the children are uncatchably far ahead of the hoi polloi, an example of privilege reinforced through the generations, often said to be the result of meritocracy, but in fact, the result of a regressive tax system.

RETURNING to their room, her workshop, Chana held the other free end of largest diameter tube in her left hand and the one-and-one-quarter-inch dowel in her right, and visualized, not a nose cone, but a flat plug, a solid butt end she could hammer away at with the sledge. In about half an hour she was done, mixing more epoxy and fitting her plug into its new home. Then she took a nap.

When Chana woke, the sun was low as Chava flipped through pages of a medical textbook on surgical amputations. The girls were hungry and so decided to look for Max. Over black bikinis, in the manner of Gili girls, they donned short white-hot tank tops and batik sarongs of dusty rose secured at the hip, just below exposed belly buttons. They were not too flirty and nasty, but suggestive of flirty and nasty, and nearly indistinguishable from each other. Then they walked to the beach and Wet Dreams. Max was out.

MAX was out on the hotel's glass bottom boat with Vera's girl Putu. As she often did in the afternoon, Putu guided a group of guests into the waters shallow and not-so-shallow between Gili Trawangan and Gili Meno. With masks, snorkels, fins, and even light wetsuits rented from the hotel dive desk, some of them went overboard with her. Some stayed dry and watched through the hull.

Gili Meno had the better viewing. Consensus had it that two degree ocean warming in the El Niño of 1997 and '98 had done in the coral, but why it grew back more vigorously on Gili Meno was a topic of ceaseless debate. The most widely accepted explanation for that island's richer population of fish, turtles, and sea snakes was that the rapid development on Gili T brought with it disruptive traffic of all kinds, and that put pressure on the fragile emergent corals and the mobile species that lived among them.

In the water, Putu was alone with Max. They saw some turtles near the Meno Wall, the steep drop-off that began a couple of hundred yards from shore at a depth of about fifteen feet. Putu reminded Max of the freediving basics.

"Loosen up your diaphragm, Max, and then breathe deeply into it, from the bottom, filling it up. Let your blood fill up with oxygen, then take one more breath and go down. You'll be able to reach the top of the wall."

He challenged his cardio-vascular system, dialed in his head-mounted GoPro video camera, and field-tested his fin. To most people, the fin was more interesting than Genormx Beta.

The patent pending invention of Dr. Max Frood, assigned to Frood Plastics Inc. of which he was the sole shareholder, was a fluke, a thirty-inch-wide carbon fiber monofin in the shape of whale's fluke. One of its two attach points a typical dive-fin foot pocket. The other was a spring-loaded, titanium quick-disconnecting mate for a special prosthetic. Thin-walled, internally reinforced, and sealed at both ends to prevent water leaking in, Max's single purpose, anatomically correct dive leg gave him buoyancy and gave his wetsuit a proper shape. Where his left knee had been, there was a flexure. Swathed in black neoprene, inserted into his fluke, and swimming in the clear blue soup, Max was half man, half-cetacean; as much a merman as there ever was. It took some getting used to, coordinating his legs together in the dolphin kick, but had he figured that out in Silicon Valley pools.

One problem remained. He was neutrally buoyant. Even with the air in the volume of his fake leg, even with the thick layers of body fat he had accumulated, the dense plastic of his fluky contraption left him barely floating at the surface. He and Putu would have preferred positive buoyance for safety. He had a solution for that, too, but only in his notebooks. Unless he used a SCUBA diver's inflatable vest, and an air tank to go with it, he'd have to live with neutral.

A turtle near the surface bolted for the edge of the Meno Wall and Max followed it down. Putu went after him, monitoring his depth with her dive watch. Both he and the turtle descended to the edge and continued on down. Max forced air into his sinuses and through his Eustachian tubes to his middle ear, equalizing the pressure frequently, warding off painful squeeze and dangerous barotrauma. When necessary, he pushed air through his nose into his mask, relieving the pressure as it squeezed on his face. Well below any depth he thought he would have reached, he let the turtle go its own way and began flicking back toward the bright surface. He locked eyes with Putu and could see her smiling, holding her thumbs up.

Breaking through into the air, stale gases escaped Max's his lungs and he inhaled forcefully, repeating the process several times. "Fuckin' 'Donesia Putu, that was great!" Then he put his snorkel back on.

Putu, who had never completely forgiven Max for imposing himself on Vera in their failed attempt to re-unite not long before he lost his leg, said, "Did you have trouble with your buoyancy coming up?"

"No, I was fine."

"Terrific, Max, that was a good dive. You should be proud. You can go to twice that depth, I'm sure."

"How deep was I?"

"Ten metres."

"I thought I was going to die."

"You weren't close to it. That dive was only thirty-five seconds. You can go three minutes without worrying about dying, if you can train your mind to trust your body."

"That's optimistic."

"I'm not saying you need to do a three-minute breath hold. You can dive to twenty metres, maybe even twenty-five, look around, and be back to the surface in less than a minute twenty."

The driver motored around, pointing out brain coral, schools of fish, more turtles, moon jellies, and much more to the other guests. Putu and Max practiced yogic breathing exercises and efficient duck dives.

The water had the effect Max had hoped for. Warm, saline, full of life; it revitalized him. As if re-wombed, he was being reborn.

"I'll take you hunting tomorrow morning, and you can see what's out there," Putu said to him as they climbed into the boat and headed back to Gili Trawangan in the final light of day.

THE girls had come and gone, leaving only a message slid under his door that he was to meet them at Tir Na Nog at eleven that night, Tir Na Nog being an Irish bar known for outlandish parties. That left him less than four hours to clean up, eat, and clear the air with Vera.

Max ached with fatigue. He had fallen asleep on the twenty-minute drive to Serangan and on the two-hour fast boat to the Gilis. He had taken a nap before going out with Putu, and he had even dozed for a few minutes as the glass bottom boat motored the final few hundred yards across the channel.

He explained to Vera over dinner, "I'm either recharging or dying. I don't know which."

"Max, don't talk like that. Maxime is going to be here tomorrow. She needs you."

Maxime was the one person in the world he both cared about and had not fucked over at least once, intentionally or otherwise. He was determined to keep it that way.

"Which reminds me," he said to Vera, I have these papers for you." He handed her the Maxime Katawijaya Trust Agreement naming Vera as Trustee and requiring her witnessed signature. He also brought with him a properly notarized copy of his Last Will and Testament naming Sameer as executor of his estate. Its sole beneficiary was Maxime's trust.

"That's too generous. What's it worth, Max?"

"There's a condo in Menlo Park and a small house with a view of the Pacific Ocean on a good day. Some mortgages on those. Got a brokerage account with a million or so in stocks and bonds, and there's a safe deposit box with certificates that are either memorabilia suitable for framing or worth a fortune, I don't know which. The other Max may have known. I don't know."

"Max, you'll find your mojo. It scares me to hear you talk this way. What are you going to tell Maxime?"

"She doesn't need to know the details. That I'll be there for her, financially, no matter what." He paused, searching for words, "I don't know exactly how else to be there for her. That's partly up to her."

"That's beautiful, Max. It's all a beautiful gesture."

VERA showed Max what she had built and was building. The first six condos still stood, and then the next ten behind them, and the new resort and spa with a hundred rooms, each capable of sleeping four. The structure was built around an archipelago of small swimming pools and an Olympian one. Its prize-winning Uruguayan architect had designed many seaside resorts and homes for oligarchs on difficult cliffs in magnificent spots.

"You can fly in on the helicopter, hang out by the pools, and never touch the sea the whole time you're here," Max said.

"Yes! Isn't that wonderful? So many of our guests are going to do just that."

The back of the New Wet Dreams Spa and Resort, as it was called, was not the servants' entrance. It was a grand second entrance. Vera had bought the land and clear cut the trees all the way to the west side of the island, giving her guests an unobstructed view of the sunset from the east side; a triumph of engineering. And at her road's western terminus, there was her heliport on one side, and her dance bar on the other. Fleets of charged Segways stood ready to shuttle guests from one end of her private strip to the other.

"The moon will be full in two days, Max. It's going to be *wild*." Her brown eyes grew wide. "There will be a thousand people buying vodka at ten times what I've paid for it. More even."

"What's happened to you, Vera?"

She didn't answer.

"How can the island support what you are doing to it? The fish, the fuel, the food, the labor; they've been imported for a long time. The drinking water is a bright spot, sort of, now that you're desalinating on island, but that only takes more fuel."

"Like you said, Max, it's never been able to support our guests. How could this little island system provide food for a few hundred hungry westerners intent on tasting, no, gorging on the local offerings? With our little fishing fleet? No way. And we're at thousands now, not hundreds. It's just the business, Max. If I don't grow, someone is going to grow on top of me and destroy me."

"I got that, but the growth seems to be destroying what we came here to enjoy in the first place.

"It was paradise for you because it wasn't like America. It was paradise for me because it was like America. It's more like that every day."

"You've built a sunset strip, haven't you?"

"You're the first to get it, as usual Max, yes. When I'm done it's going to be our private shopping mall end-to-end. And that dance bar, it was the brainchild of one of my guests. He develops them for Steve Wynn in Las Vegas. It's a cash machine already. We can't keep it going every night like he does, but it spews cash."

"OK, but what about the entropy?"

"The trash? It's a problem."

"It's a problem? You put your brick pavers over paradise and put up a third world slum. Every front yard or storefront has been swept clean of the sand and the pony shit, but the backyards pile up with garbage."

"That's true."

"There are parts of this island that make Pindi look like a metropolis. It's Kathmandhu, exactly like Kathmandu, with the rich tourists and the beggars living only yards apart, with the first being barely aware of the second."

"I haven't seen any beggars."

"I haven't either, but I've seen the skinny brown kids playing naked in the dirt, and nothing about the scene reminded me of Gili Trawangan."

"Max. Look around you. Everyone is having fun, having a great time. If they want to get lost in yogaland or yogurtland, they can do that. If they want to rave, they can do that. If you want to be able to roam the island and have your particular version of paradise everywhere, you can't do that, and you never could. There was a time, and I saw it, and you saw it, and Maxime was born of it. Remember, Max?"

"Yes, I remember, Vera. You made me see stars."

"There *were* stars, Max. Anyway, there was a time when one version of paradise was everywhere, and that's gone. But in those days, there was nothing else, so most people would have been unhappy. This is better."

"I'm not so sure. What was here was something unique. What you've built is not that much different from Kuta, or the Canaries, or the Caribbean. Gili T is like a species that's gone extinct."

"The developers are going to keep building until there's nowhere left to build, and then they'll scrape and build more."

"Vera, you talk like the developers are the other, but they are you."

She acknowledged him with barely more than a nod. "We have to encourage more sense of pride in the island. I know that. I'm sick of people throwing their cigarette butts on the ground like it was one big ashtray. But unless some money comes in to bid for land against us, we'll keep building until we're maxed out, and the smell of trash turns off our guests."

"Yeah, particularly your guests who just want to drop in from heaven above, sample, and get the hell out without ever experiencing it. They want an antiseptic experience. Bhutan, not Nepal."

"Max, what happened to you? I wonder if you'd be having this conversation with me if you still owned part of the cash machine."

"Ah, ye olde problem of the conflict of interest. I don't know. How can I know? Nobody would say they have a conflict, because if they had one, they'd say they didn't, and if they didn't, they'd also say they didn't. You can't learn anything, in an information theoretic sense, from someone's statements about his or her own conflicts of interest. No. I take that back. If they say they have a conflict of interest, you can learn they're crazy, but that's it."

"Max. It's the old Max, channeling *Catch-22*. You're back!"

"I don't know, Vera. It's not the same."

Max looked at his watch. He wouldn't be able to walk to Tir Na Nog in time to meet the twins at 11.

"Can you get me a cidomo?"

"Max, are you going to see those girls?" There was a hint of shaming mixed with a hint of longing in her question.

He didn't answer, but the expression on his face told her.

"Max, I was thinking, maybe, you know, just for old times' sake?"

"Vera, Putu would kill me!"

Vera laughed. "She might even kill me."

"Yes, she might. See, it's too dangerous. Our love could kill us, so we can't love each other."

"Not that way."

"No, not that way."

"But those girls, Max, they're Maxime's age."

"They're not children, whatever they seem like to you. They're murderous," and he grinned, as if there could be a good way to be murderous. "Can you get me a cidomo?"

CHAPTER 188 TIR NA NOGGIN'

At Tir Na Nog, the hottest Sisters of Lesbos and the buffest boys on Gili Trawangan surrounded the two cousins-parading-as-sisters. When Max appeared, Chana and Chava dropped everything and gave him their all, beginning with a full contact hug and all of Chana's trimmings. An hour later, a disappointed Max was back at Bungalow Zero.

It happened this way. Chana began. "Heh, we're sorry about this morning. We didn't want to cramp you, so we went by ourselves." She kissed his neck and ran her hand down his shoulder. "Maxi. So sexy, Maxi." Chava, the bait luring him to senselessness, kept her distance.

They told partial truths about their day and talked of staying up till dawn. Max did not have the stamina for a night of partying that led to a 5 a.m. fuck on the beach. His plan called for a rapid scoring drive and a decent night's rest before going into deep water with Putu. He tried to steer the conversation back to sex whenever he could. Chana indulged him. Chava was hot and cold. The reggae music came in on the wind:

my life like Mr. Obama,
be happy, be happy on Gili T,
come and let's go dancing la la la la,
you're in paradise in rastafaria

The killer twins got up and danced together, bumping and swaying seductively, and then came back to him, "Oh Maxi, dance with us." He did, and then excused himself to use the loo. While he was gone, they left too, without a note. Chava had feigned bad nausea, so the kids nearby told Max that one girl escorted the other doubled up in pain.

Walking back to Wet Dreams, he cursed them and his swollen cock and the way they'd pulled him out of his insularity only to leave him alone. He needed to get laid or get off. Back at Wet Dreams, he might have asked Vera, but she would have been insulted to be second on his list, if she'd been serious in the first place, but all he really wanted was to do those girls and no one else. Before he could even jerk off, he fell asleep and dreamt of them.

They had him tied to a table on his belly. His arms hung down and his wrists were secured to its legs. His legs were pulled apart—a taught rope yanking on each ankle. He was naked on a filthy sheet. Chava—that red-cunt

Chava drive driving him nuts!—was in a bikini, black—no, white, virginal, white—a white bikini in front of him, dancing like she had with her twin, but alone, rubbing herself and mouthing "sexy Maxi" to the music, whatever the music was. First one nipple and then another peeked out from her tit cups. Her hand disappeared under the white patch of bikini and she sighed while he watched the nylon stretch. He saw the outline of the back of her hand as her fingers played out of sight. The noises she made, were they fake or real? Who cared? They made *him* juicy. She turned and mooned him, then pulled the bikini bottom up before facing him again. Chava whacked him hard on the buttocks and thighs, slapping his scrotum with something, maybe a snorkel, but it hurt, whatever it was. "If you're good Maxi, sexy Maxi, maybe you can get a taste of something red and wet. Can you be good Maxi?" she said, in his dream. He woke up to the sound of himself shouting, "I can be good! I can be good!" and struggling against restraints that weren't there.

The clamor woke Putu. She cracked open the unlocked door to make sure he was OK, and saw that he was awake, eyes wide and teeth gritted. He was covered in sweat, and getting nowhere jerking off beneath the sheet. Without a word, the incubus climbed onto the bed, dropping down onto his face. He kept up the stroking until she reached back, pinning his hands. His legs waved when she half-suffocated him in that revenge face fuck. Easing off until he calmed down and caught his breath, she then smothered him again, cycling him through air and no air in a way that might have violated the Geneva Convention. She grew tired of the joyless game, slipped off his head and onto his cock. She rode him till he cried in agony and she demanded that he give her more. When he fell asleep beneath her, she poked him hard in the ribs and hissed at him, "Stay away from Vera." Then she unsaddled herself and left the room.

Max was dazed. It didn't make sense that Putu had come in and fucked him raw. Those twins were fucking with his mind. What was it about them? They were young and they were wild. They were Miriam's age in his earliest memories of her. They were prime specimens. Was that it? Had they drugged him at Tir Na Nog? Then he lapsed back into sleep.

Putu woke him at 6:30 a.m.

"May I bring your breakfast in, Max? We have to leave in thirty."

He remembered his plan to accompany her on a deep-water fishing expedition. His mouth felt disgusting, like the bottom of birdcage, but he tried to smile graciously at her generosity—the new Max.

"No, please put it on the table by the pool. I'll be there ... I'll be there ..."

and his words trailed off as he tried to make sense of the night.

She turned to leave when he asked, "Putu, was I yelling last night? Did you come in to check on me?"

She was out of the room, placing the tray of scrambled eggs and bacon beside the pool when she called back, tittering, "No, Boss. You slept like a baby."

She paused and he called out, "OK, then. I'll see you at the front desk as soon as I'm done."

Max passed a painful half-pint of yellow piss. Then he sat down to eat his breakfast, at the end of which he found two short curly hairs; one on his plate and its twin between two of his teeth.

CHAPTER 189 REVENGE

NO ONE likes to be deceived, especially deceivers. Before the SEC could complete their investigation, two representatives, Radius and Billy, of Max's poker friend's friends—not-so-easy-to-please fish among Social Media Fish's fish, and professional deceivers both—made a surprise visit to Pupa's Ft. Lauderdale home one morning. They intercepted him and his partner—and it was never clear to me whether that meant business partner or significant other—on their way to wherever white-collar, overt, repeat criminals go at 9:00 a.m. With only a threatening look, Radius and Billy persuaded Branzino and his partner to re-enter the house. At first Pupa said he had nothing to give them. After Billy reached into a briefcase fat enough for a Philadelphia litigator and pulled out a blackjack with which he shattered Branzino's right knee, the new cripple led his guests to a wall safe behind a velvet painting in his bedroom, which upon opening disgorged bills equivalent to about half of the original investment of the syndicate represented by the goons—but nothing like the bounty they'd have received had the money actually been used to purchase pre-IPO shares as promised. The opportunity cost was in the millions.

"Is that it?" asked Radius.

"Yes, that's everything. I swear."

"Half?"

"Yeah, about half."

"Everything?"

"Yes, I swear. It's everything," he said from the floor where he was nothing more than a simpering sack of broken sobs.

"OK," Radius said. And then with military precision, Billy choked Branzino's friend until he passed out while Radius stuffed a stifling sock in Pupa's silently screaming mouth. Billy dragged the limp guy and Radius prodded Branzino on hands and knees into the kitchen. The two toughs duct-taped Pupa, backside down, to a table. Radius then tore off his victim's shirt. Using the baton, he fashioned a tourniquet high on his thigh, patiently twisting and tightening until he was certain he had cut off circulation. Billy plopped the gradually-coming-to partner into a chair, securing his hands behind his back with the same versatile gray tape. Then he turned the chair so the partner would have a fine view of what was to come.

Radius reached into the briefcase, this time pulling out a 10 1/4" circular saw; red plastic and steel, its brand name, Victor, screen printed in white on one side, and its model name, The Inflictor, screen printed on the other. He plugged it in and fired it up, filling the room with the shrill transverse vibrations of the big metal blade before they damped out and were overwhelmed by the motor's whining thrum. He asked one more time, "Is that it? Half?"

He definitely had Branzino's attention now. Branzino rocked his head forward and back, cracking his skull on the table top with each signaling of the affirmative. Then he shook his head side to side, maybe signaling that there was more, somewhere, or something else. Every muscle, every bone, every sinew and tendon and ligament tugged and strained and flailed and jerked at their restraints. Other than the fact that he was seventy, he had the look of a baby squirming in the doctor's office, but a lot more scared. The smell of his shit, and the other one's shit, made the kitchen rank. Pools of his pee ran off the tabletop. Branzino's eyes bulged, protruding and huge. Even with the sock in his mouth he made sounds, but they couldn't be heard over Victor. Radius no longer cared what Pupa had to tell. He'd crossed the line, Branzino had, with his cheating, and he'd crossed the line, Radius had, with his desire to let blood.

Branzino's partner, strapped to his chair, shook up and down, thumping the floor, grunting, trying to be heard. Maybe he had something to say about where to find the money he'd secreted away, and maybe he'd decided, finally to speak up about it. Radius would speak to him after Victor had spoken.

"Half?" Radius tilted his head toward the compression bandage. "This one is shot anyway, so no point in hanging on to it." *Zip!* Pink mist shot in every direction. He took Branzino's right leg off above the knee, the tourniquet being all that prevented him from bleeding out. If the partner had had something to say, it was too late now; he'd gone into cardiac arrest before Radius shut off his tool.

DRIVING away, they called 911 from a burner, directed the EMT toward Branzino's home, and tossed the unwanted phone down a sewer drain.

CHAPTER 190 THE LESSON

BLUE WATER hunting is different from coastal fishing. Never mind that you might never see a fish in a day in the blue water, but the ones you're going after are big and strong. Shoot a twenty-pound bass near shore and you can wrestle it to submission. Shoot a hundred-and-fifty-pound tuna, especially a dogtooth tuna, eighty feet down, and you'd die trying to subdue it the same way. In the shallows, you attach your spear to your gun with a short line, tethering you to the fish as soon as it's hit. When you shoot big pelagic fish, if the spear were attached to the gun, either you'd lose it or get the final Nantucket sleighride of your life, or both. In the deeps, you set up your spear so it flies free of the gun but is attached to a very long line floating to the surface, and there it is attached to large buoys. They provide the drag that fights the fish. You, the diver, after surfacing, hang on to the floats and, eventually, pull the exhausted fish to rest. Sometimes, if the fish is large enough, it will swim away, triumphant with all the gear.

In that environment, Putu was a killer, the most productive spearer working on the island, and one of the best that'd ever hunted there. Although she had begun fishing for Vera's restaurant before it was Maxime's and when there were only six bungalows on the property, she never adjusted the size of her catch to the relentless growth of Wet Dreams. "Let them eat cake," she told Vera. "I'm not killing fish to feed them all." One fish over twenty kilos, or two under; that's all she'd take on any day. Scarcity made Putu's catch more and more prized and highly priced at Vera's Maxime's. The hundreds of other guests, those who didn't win the lottery seat at the table, ate net-caught, mostly imported fish.

Tommy was the boat driver. It was he who later told me, "Boss, if I'd known ..." referring to the growth that had transformed the island. He brought with him, on Putu's recommendation, another American dive client who would be Max's buddy while she worked. When they approached the hunting grounds in the Apnean Sea, Max pulled his wetsuit on. He spat into his dive mask and rubbed the saliva in a circular motion over the glass lens, and then pulled it and the snorkel over his head. "Shall we have our lesson now?" Putu asked Max. "Herman, jump in, too, so we're all square on the safety procedures."

Max popped the fluke's quick-connect onto his dive leg, inserted his foot into the rubber pocket on the fluke, wriggled himself onto the gunwale, pulled the mask over his face, pulled the GoPro in its mount over his head, put the snorkel in his mouth, and let himself fall backwards into the water.

"Fuckin' 'Donesia, Putu. I'm a fish with this thing!" He turned to face the other client, an older but fittish and black-bearded gentleman, "Heh," trying to offer his hand, "it's Max. From California. Menlo Park. Sorry, what's your name again?"

Yes, Observant Reader, Max said he was sorry.

"Herman," the other fellow said. "Massachusetts. Pittsfield."

Putu trained them both in breathing techniques, concentrating first on filling the lower lungs, then expanding the ribcage to fill the uppers, and finally, the neck. "Three, no more than four deep breaths, nice and slow. It's the oxygen in your blood that's gonna give you hold time. Go easy. Let your system take it up. Then your biggest and final one. The sea is calm. We're lucky. It's that much easier."

She reviewed relaxation techniques, and equalization, and rescue, too, the hardest, most important, and most often ignored aspect of diving; ignored as if a catastrophe couldn't happen to any one. Of course, there was no one to rescue Putu if she got in trouble in deep water.

"Hold on longer, Max," she said after he came up for air. "You have to conquer your own fear."

"Are you trying to kill me?" he joked.

"No, Max. I'm not trying to kill you." With Putu, you never knew. "You have two minutes before you're maxed out. If you've done your prep right, you have more than two minutes, easy peasy. So when you're panicked at forty-five seconds, it's panic, not hazard. You have to find a way to still your beating heart."

"But last night's dreams are freaking me out."

"Don't worry about those dreams, Max. They're only in your head."

"How does that help?"

Putu laughed.

"Leave those back in the boat, Max. This is not the time. Imagine you're in a world without words, a time before you had words, and all that's in your head is what's in front of your eyes and coming to you through your other senses. Let your dive reflex take over, and you'll hold on much longer than you ever thought you could. You'll be safe. Don't worry."

They were less than two miles out, in three hundred feet of water. Tommy called over to them. "The fish finders just picked up schools of king mackerel over the crack, Boss."

"It's time. Max, Herman. You two stay together, and Tommy will watch out for me." She left them with a bright yellow buoy, something they could hang on to and something easy to see. A regulation dive flag on a two-foot mast made it even easier to see. The ocean currents were strong, a couple of feet per second, over the rocky notch they called the crack, and especially so in the build up to the full moon. The boat and divers drifted together, but Putu swam up-current where the schooling would be better, and in a few minutes, she and the boat were a hundred yards away from the two men. She found wahoo and tuna at depths of less than a hundred feet. When she was among them she saw sharks, as she always did, swimming deep, scarfing down what fell from the surface, and ready to swim for it if it didn't fall on its own. When Putu drifted beyond the crack, she pulled her hundred and ten pounds of brown-black Balinese perfection into the boat, and Tommy motored downstream to the others. Then they headed back to top of the crack for another drift.

"What did you see, Max?"

"Only sharks. Lots of sharks, very deep."

"You must have done a good dive if you saw them at all. It was twenty metres, I'd guess, before I picked them up below me. Saw one fat mackerel. Couldn't get a shot."

Max breathed hard, and Herman sat stonelike, as if he'd seen it all before. He looked old enough to have seen it all before, but he was lean and hard, an odd sight with his thick black beard, thick with water like moss beside a waterfall.

Putu asked, "Did you feel the downdrafts? If there are doggies, they'll follow the downdrafts. Gotta watch that."

"They'll swim you right into the sharks?" Max asked.

"I wouldn't worry about the sharks unless you're bleeding. These sharks don't attack humans very often. Humans carrying food, maybe."

Max pushed those cunty twins out of mind, along with his crazy dreams of rape and Putu, fucking Vladik, Moby Dx, Joosey, fucking Jay, the work he had to do on Rhizobia in less than a week, Arianna, Vera's proposition, and even his anticipation of seeing Maxime in a few hours—all out of his mind.

And it worked. He'd never before, even when whole, been swimming and diving out in the deep waters. He felt like he was home, where he should be; so relaxed. Blue everywhere. Visibility maybe seventy-five feet or more. More than fear would let him go.

He cleared his mask, settled himself, took three deep breaths and held the last, then swam down as far as he could to where he could see just blue and blue and only blue, an infinity of blue. There was no bottom, only sharks below. He had gone beyond fear, and there he saw a fish, a silvery pelagic fish with stiff short spines and a crescent tail. Mackerel. *Some kind of mackerel! Ten, twelve, maybe only fifteen feet away, and twenty kilos, maybe more. A prize fish.* That was enough, and he felt strong as he calmly finned to the surface, bright like the sky. When he broke through, he felt great. He wasn't on-the-rivet the way he had been on the first dive. He was coming back. Then the cacophony began to rush in. The girls. Soon, he'd get them, or at least Chava Bush. Then, next time in the water, he'd bring a gun and shoot a fish.

Putu had brought back a nice king mackerel like the one Max had seen. Herman said he saw a doggie. Maybe Putu would get a shot at one next time. Maybe Max would, too.

CHAPTER 191 NINETEEN IS PRIME

CHANA AND Chava spent the same morning planning the next couple of days. They would give Max a little taste of something that night, and promise him the whole cheese-dripping, hot chile relleno the night after. The island was small and they'd already been seen with him. There was no escaping the fact that if Max disappeared, they'd be suspects with no place to hide. If they were going to end Max, they had better be off the island before anyone noticed. All of which led them to choose Yasgawati's Farm over Wet Dreams for the final act of their play. Everyone living nearby the Farm had become accustomed to wearing earplugs in an effort to shield out the mosque's broadcasts, so Max's screams, muffled as they would be by socks and duct tape, would go unnoticed. And they could bury him only a hundred yards away, if it came to that, in a banana grove that had become the island's defacto cemetery.

The coming night would be a dress rehearsal, minus the violence. They'd get him tied down at his place and then release him, proving to him that he was safe. Out of control, but in control. That's the way he wanted it. And then the following night, they'd tie him down at the Farm and turn up the intensity by a few points on a log scale.

Chava hated him. Chana just felt sorry for him, partly for who he was, and partly for what she was going to do to him. Who knew? Maybe he'd say yes right away. Or maybe he'd only say yes after they'd had to crush some of his fingers, or cut off his other leg, or drive the nose cone of that improvised javelin into his scrotum and all the way through his body cavity until it came out near his neck. Neither of them thought he'd be saying yes if things got that far along. They had some of the script worked out, but this would be improv. They'd been trained in improv. There was lots of time yet.

The girls walked south along the esplanade, checking out the restaurants and their Internet connections. Small island, and they were picky, and in no hurry. They walked halfway around, previewing the bars where they'd later drag Max. The Beach House on the west side had decent Internet, so they put their feet up, jacked in and sent news back to Brooklyn.

MAXIME had left the Royal School for Girls and was on her way home. She drove across the causeway to Changi, took the evening KLM flight to Ngurah Rai, spent the night in the same Bali Rani Hotel. She departed Bali at 11 a.m. the next day, arriving at her mother's heliport on Gili T at 11:42 a.m. Max was on a Segway, letting his thinned hair dry in the breeze, when he saw her jet-powered bird touch down.

"Vera, you can argue all you want about how these don't violate the No Motorized Transport rule because they're not actually transporting anything on the island and therefore are no different from boats which have been motorized since the beginning of time, but *I* think they're different. The boats operate off the island, below the public mean high water line—"

Vera cut him off. "Max, I am so happy that you really are back. Now let's go see our daughter."

Maxime had at times wondered why Max was always there, wherever there was. More than any other westerner, he had been a constant in her life. Her mother told her that her father was someone she had once loved, but Vera hadn't hinted that it was Max. After she had begun boarding school, she learned what a big cheese he was in the world outside, and in particular in Rhizobia. He had nurtured her with "learning moments" which he, more than anyone she had met, seemed to deliver with perfect timing when she was most receptive. Twice she and Vera had visited him in the US, once in

California and once on the East Coast in the winter. By the time of the second visit, she developed the silent conviction that he was her father. When the moment was right, she would bring it up.

Until that East Coast tour, she had never seen snow. Although Max had told her that she was naturally a West Coast girl, with its better weather and year round beaches, she decided on that trip she was an East Coast girl, or would be for those four years when she went to college. He had pictured her at in San Diego, but if she wanted east, he would get her east.

In record-breaking, city-disabling, infrastructure-collapsing snowfall, they visited Columbia, Barnard, and NYU, and then in the days following, Yale and Princeton. Max used all his leverage and arranged for Maxime to talk to brand name professors everywhere. Botstein wasn't in town, but over the phone he listened carefully to the story and then suggested that they go visit Bard College—a hundred miles north of New York City on the Hudson River—where his brother had been president for nearly thirty years and had quietly, or fairly quietly, turned it into a world-class institution. He arranged a meeting.

A year and a half later, she applied there for early admission, and in the coming fall she would be a freshman. She planned to major in marine biology, a field in which she already published original research completed at the Frood Center for Molecular Engineering in Rhizobia.

And yet, they were not easy together. Max was a great, and this is no exaggeration, a great pedagogue. Remember, at first I did it for love. She felt, she told me, that he was a different species.

"It's not that he was uncool, but he was so remote, like the Dog Star. He's encyclopedic about so many things. He knew everything and he knew everyone. I had a lot of respect for him, but I couldn't relax with him. And he treated me too gently, like a fragile flower he might accidentally rip apart. Most of the time, when we were together, we were sitting quietly over food at a restaurant, doing nothing, waiting for the other to say something. That trip to New York. That was different. He opened up like he never had, and later I missed it."

Max had not expected to be pursuing a pair of titillating twins of the same generation as his Eurasian daughter, and while in the company of that daughter. If she saw him with Chana and Chava, he might blow this one last chance he had of never disappointing someone he loved. *I'll have to spear them where they live,* he thought, *and out of sight of Wet Dreams.*

He and Maxime walked clockwise around the island. They had been at work on two long-term field studies. The first one explored the changing microbiota of Gili T's waters, and for that she collected water samples she would systematically categorize under a microscope in her room. The second one investigated tidal extremes as a proxy for climate change, and for that she measured the high water mark on the beach against some stakes she and Max had driven into higher ground more than a decade earlier. Breaking a long period of silence, she asked him, trying to evoke that more boisterous trip to NY, "Where are the snow days of yesteryear?" Then he told her about huge snowy winters in Pittsburgh when he was a boy.

Returning to Wet Dreams, they lunched at Maxime's, the restaurant, on Putu's mackerel and then ran out of things to say.

MIRIAM Frood is nineteen years old in Max's first memory of her and in the only memory of his father.

THE cousins arrived at Wet Dreams again in the late afternoon. Max napped. Other than his bottomless and uncharacteristic frustration over those two pieces of ass, he felt great. He had seen Maxime and had not yet fucked it up. He had dived, and had gone deeper than ever before. He'd seen the silvery beasts and been close enough to shoot one of them. Putu had the gun and floats for him, as she had told him a long time before. He'd go the next day, to the doggies, maybe. And the girls had arrived to make him happy.

Chana leaned over him as he slept, putting a hand on his back and whispering in his ear, brushing her lips against him, but not quite kissing him. He woke to see her close. She was sweet, and so red it did make him happy. He rolled over on his back, covered up, smiled, and said, simply, "Hi." The new Max.

"Chava got so sick last night, we had to run out. It seems like we're always running out on you, doesn't it?" She left no time for him to answer. "Promise. Not tonight. Not tonight, OK?" She slipped a hand under the light blanket and rubbed his chest.

Chava sat in a chair, acting a little weak. "I'm OK now. Must have been food poisoning or something. Getting better by the minute."

"OK, OK. You're here now. That's enough. Let me tell you about—" and he stopped himself in a panic when an image of Maxime walking in on them popped into his head.

"This place makes me claustrophobic," he said. "Let's get out of here." Then Max hung his head. It was bad enough that Maxime might have seen the twins walk into his room. He couldn't risk being seeing them with him, on the premises or off. *I'm on Gili Trawangan and worried about surveillance? Vera's right. It's just like America.*

"Where are you staying? Can we go there?"

Max inviting himself to a trial run on their turf was almost too good to be true, and not what they expected. "Do you have a map?" Chana asked.

She traced the route for him. They would exit Bungalow Zero through the staff entrance in the rear and then follow a trail into the island interior where Maxime was very unlikely to travel.

Not much later, they were waltzing arm and arm over paths and past businesses he'd never seen in decades of visits. This was where the hippie tourists of yore still hung out, driven away from the more expensive waterfront properties, growing ganja on the ground and psilocybin mushrooms in the shadows, distilling methanol enriched moonshine, getting high on kombucha. "It could be Portland," Max said.

"Or Brooklyn," Chana and Chava said in unison.

Max was torn between his desire to get wasted with these girls and to get a good night's sleep and be ready for the next morning when he'd need all his strength and wit if he was going to land a game fish. He tried to keep them moving to the Farm, and the redheads wanted to stop at every smoke shop, bar, and dance floor they saw. It's no exaggeration to say that Chana and Chava livened up every one of them with their teasing and flirting, nubile flesh flashing, and suggestive talk. Only hours later did they finally made it to the Richie Havens bungalow at Yasgawati's Farm.

"Maxi, sexy Maxi," Chana said, "How come a nice man like you isn't tied down?" Chava meanwhile appeared to be on her own drugs, dancing to her own playlist with her earbuds in, shedding a light shawl and exposing nymphy shoulders and muscled arms.

Max, putting his hands on Chana's waist and dancing around the room, said, "I've been tied down. Maybe it's the right time again. Do you want to tie me down?"

"Oh I do Maxi, I do. We both want to. That's the way we like it best. Don't you think so Chavileh?"

"Oh I do. Maxi, do you want to watch us? Would you like that?"

Max was swollen and breathless with desire to put his hand on Chava's bush.

"If you're good Maxi, if you're very, very good Maxi, we'll give you a taste of something fresh. What do you say Maxi, can you be very, very good?"

Chava removed her sarong, revealing a white bikini bottom, and sending Max reeling in a profound sense of déjà vu. He was so compliant and dazed that Chana could have castrated him and he wouldn't have uttered a word, but all she set out to do was strip him naked and secure him to the bed with the duct tape and ropes she'd carried from home. Although not as easy as it might have been, she did finally succeed. Then Chana stripped down to match Chava, and they cavorted like naughty virgins safely out of his reach, beating him with a snorkel now and then, scratching him hard but not drawing blood, and hinting that there might be something there for him, if he was very, very good.

The closest he got was not very close when Chava said, "You know Max, it's not late," it was 1 a.m., "but you have to be up early for diving. You don't want to be maxed out before you do it to the doggies tomorrow, I mean this morning. Do you?"

Chana threw more cold water on the night by agreeing. The show had ended and the actors were sending their guests home. Chana cut the duct tape and untied the rope, rousing him and encouraging him to get dressed through chatter meant to keep his hopes up. "Max, tomorrow. Tomorrow. No time limit tomorrow."

"Full moon tomo, Max. The whole island will be out."

"DJs. Cidomos lit up and blasting music. All night party."

"I can taste that Moscow Mule."

"Sex on the Beach."

"We'll get you there, tomorrow. Good luck with those fish, eh?"

He reached out suddenly and grabbed Chava's crotch, a move that she countered with a wicked slap to his face. That snapped his head and left red impressions of three fingers on his cheek.

"Sorry, Max," Chana said. You caught her by surprise. We thought the fun was over for tonight.

"You hurt me," he said, feeling his cheek.

"We have rules, Max. Tonight, the kitchen is closed. Tomorrow, it's all you can eat. Promise."

They helped him through the front door and then shoved him out the front gate and into a cidomo, with instructions on where to take him. Then they turned their attentions to each other.

"He's going to shit when we tell him what this is all about."

"He almost shit with that slap."

"I don't want him touching me."

"He has such a hard guy rep, it doesn't all make sense. Other than that grab, he's been as docile as an old dog."

"Maybe it's this place."

"I guess we'll see tomorrow night. I hope he has some sense in him."

"He's a schmuck," said Chava.

Max was so tired that he didn't have the energy to curse them for leaving him unsatisfied one more time. And that slap *hurt*. He fell asleep in the cidomo and the driver helped him into Bungalow Zero. His wet dream of Sameer was interrupted when Putu brought in breakfast half an hour before she would leave for her morning dive.

"Coming, Max?"

CHAPTER 192 SHALLOW IN THE DEEP WATER

CHAVA'S SLAP on Max's cheek had raised three purple welts, and they hadn't lost their sting. He brushed his hand over them, fingering the raised flesh, as if knowing them by touch would hasten their healing.

"Neptune's trident has marked you, man," Herman observed.

"I think he is having the full Gili experience this go around," said Putu.

Max said nothing.

BY 8:30 a.m. their boat had already made one drift. Max and Herman did their best to sort the spearing gear. There were too many new bits for Max to manage easily. The combination of the previous day's exertions and too little sleep left him feeling weaker than he had been. The gun Putu had loaned them was perfect for the conditions, but much longer and heavier and unwieldy than he was used to. Just pushing its fifty-seven-inch bulk through the water was an effort, and he couldn't load it himself. Max might have been able to dive to twenty metres again, and might even have been able to hang there and get off a clean shot, but after that he would be too knackered to bring a big catch to rest. Herman would be more than Max's safety buddy, he would be his assistant, his finisher. Graciously, even grandiloquently, Herman offered to be the one who dragged on the float, hauled in the line, and stove a Froodblade into the head of Max's catch.

That first drift left Max so beat he couldn't even swim alongside the buoy to second Herman. A little positive buoyancy would have helped him, no doubt. After Tommy eased him over the gunwale and into the boat, Max lay down on the seats and was asleep before Herman could hoist Max's gun over the railing. Answering Putu's querying look Herman said, "Been there. Done that. Leaving only bubbles and taking only video this time." The second drift was Herman's alone—and the third drift too.

Tommy nudged Max. "Doggies, Max. Doggies." He had heard reports of them swimming in twos and threes nearby, big ones, more than forty kilos. Size was hard to judge in the water with no points of reference. You had to study the eyes to tell. Fisheyes don't grow much after maturity, no matter how gargantuan the fish. The experienced spearer gauges the eye and head together, judging only then how big the beast really is. Putu saw nothing worth wasting a shot on.

The nap made the difference. Refreshed, Max fell back in the water. He thanked Herman for his efforts.

"Neptune would not grace me with the luck of the diverish, old man."

Max did not like being called old man. He recoiled, and said nothing.

Herman continued. "I've taken a score and five trips to the lockers and every time the silvery flukers have kept their distance. Are you the anointed one today, or will you be just another failed seeker like me?"

"With the wide angle lens on that GoPro, if you're not less than four feet away, every fish looks like a guppy. I don't need to get that close," Max replied, and then put his snorkel back in his mouth. He wanted to string the bands on his own, but gave up after a struggle.

Herman drew back on the stiff rubber tubes, cocking the gun. "You look a bit gray about the gills. The measure of a man is not how many fish he kills, so think again before you tear a hole in the thin fabric of your existence in that pursuit. Dive without the gun and see what's there."

"No, I'll be fine. I just need to settle down." Max's mind was only half there in the water. The other half was in conversation with almost every person he'd ever known; from Miriam in New Orleans, to Arianna in Cambridge and Woodside, to Qasima, Sameer, Vladik, Dyk and Dykkur and Dix, and his daughter only two miles away, and to Chana and Chava Bush. Did Chava give a rat's ass about his fish? No. Who did he want to spear more, that fish or that bitch?

Herman saw Max throw his head back, as if in exasperation, and in doing so his snorkel went in the water. Max tried to draw air, got the sea instead, and nearly choked. "You can calm down, Man. Breathe. Be here. You can do this. Forget everything, even that fish," Herman counseled him.

He did calm down. Then he checked his gear. His mask was clear and free of water. His snorkel was set back behind his head, aimed straight up. The quarter-inch stainless steel spear was in its groove, held in place by twenty feet of nearly unbreakable monofilament wrapped around the gun. That mono was clipped to a hundred feet of soft black rubber sleeve surrounding more mono. His Froodblade was strapped to the ankle of his good leg. Those knives were the best, and even though thinking of his father left the taste of battery acid in his mouth, he wanted its well-balanced and improbably tough blade nearby. The float line, slack in the water, was clipped on its other end to a high volume buoy, one even a beasty fish would have trouble dragging down and away. Herman hung on it. The air was still and so was the sea.

Everything looked good. Max readied himself, took his preparatory breaths, trying to slow his heart, calming his feverish self, and then was distracted again by the sound and the sight of Tommy motoring up to them. If Max was going to get a dive in on this drift, he had only one moment to get under way. Seeing the gray outline of fish in the deeps, he dove for them. He freed the snorkel from his mouth, pointed the gun straight down and made himself streamlined, thinking about descending and trying to block the fish from his mind. A koanic thought calmed him further: only when you're not looking will you find them.

As he went deeper, equalizing like a pro, his wide fluke worked in a dolphin kick. The depths squeezed him, compressing his wet suit and his chest. He became denser, negatively buoyant, and fell slowly but surely as gravity gravitated. Two king mackerel, four or five feet long swam lazily at fifteen or twenty metres, as deep as Max had been the day before. He needed to go a little deeper to get a good angle on them. A few seconds. Barely a kick. And he was there, level with them. Fifteen feet away and they hadn't noticed him. He slowed. He swung his gun into position just a touch too quickly. A sound, a pressure wave, motion, something registered in their pelagic brains and they fluke fluke fluked away. He pulled the trigger. *Zzing*! The big gun slammed into him, surprising him with the force of its recoil. The spear hit only blue water as the monofilament ran free, took up the slack of the float line, eventually slowed, and fell. Max flicked his fluke and zipped to the surface while Herman pulled the lines in.

Max swam over to him, exhilarated. "I was close," breathing heavily, "but I spooked them." Even with all this gear, he felt in tune with nature. "Mackerel. Good ones, I think."

"Spooks? The white ghost of some past failing, Captain?"

Herman's mystical phrasing left Max cold, so he said nothing and channeled all his energy into recovery.

"The penultimate dive? Or has it bested you? There's no shame in letting the gods have their fun instead of your skin," Herman omened.

"Not even penultimate. I've got a few more good dives in me." His breath had slowed again. He handed Herman his gun when Putu, now close in the boat, shouted to them.

"We're too far off the crack. There's doggies at the upper end of it. We'll go up there for one more drift. But you have to be careful. The current is kicking in and really strong today. Full moon."

WHEN they all went in the water again, Putu warned them. "There's downdraft in this current. Lots of it. You'll have trouble fighting it to the surface."

Herman passed. "It's all your pertinacious pursuit, Man. What goes around comes around. Will the old fish be pursuing you next?

"I'll get it this time. I just have to be a little more patient, just have to calm down more."

He heard a shout and turned to see Tommy on the gunwale, pulling a monster doggie by the tailfin. Putu was still in the water gathering gear. He would have two dives at most before they made him head back home.

With the loaded gun back in his hand, Max swam away a few yards away from Herman to tread water, center himself, and be in the moment in Fuckin' 'Donesia! He couldn't help but laugh at his own joke. And then other thoughts, thoughts not about the here and now distracted him again, thoughts of pawing over the Bushies' bushes, and having them fluff him up to bursting, and fingering … he had to get that shit out of his mind.

"Gather yourself, Man," Herman yelled to him. "This will be your last."

"Yeah, yeah. But there'll be time for two. Just trying to get everything together." His conversation turned inward. *Guess I've been taking a long time. More breathing exercises. OK, calmer now. Mind in the water. Eyes in the water. Fish. Fish! Deep breaths now, slow, slow down, slow. And one last one, all the way to the bottom of the lungs. Expand the upper chest all the way, and then into the neck and upper airways for good measure. I can do it. I can do it.*

With GoPro recording, he dove, pulled his snorkel from his mouth, streamlined, equalized, and finned firmly but slowly. Caught in the downdraft, he equalized harder and more frequently, just to keep up with the fast pace of descent. Four dogfish tuna came into view, one big and fat. *Lucky day. Lucky day!* If he got into them, close enough to shoot, he wouldn't pick between them, he'd take the best shot. *Any of them would be a prize.* Denser than water, he sank into the fish, deeper than he'd ever been, and stayed calm. He leveled his gun ever so slowly, now kicking to stay up in them as they circled. He was still. Suffused with calm, he observed as he never had before. His float line hung in the water near him. He had never held his breath so long. His lungs had compressed to half of their normal volume and forced more oxygen into his blood. His spleen pumped out bright red oxygenated blood cells. Time slowed and he saw everything. Only the worry that he didn't have enough buoyancy pricked the perfection of his bubble. Did he have another ten seconds, maybe twenty before he had to surface? That would be it. No more after that. His chest felt like it would explode, but of course, it wouldn't. *Overcome fear. Wait. Look around. Sharks below. Always sharks below. Ignore them.* The doggies, though, they were coming into range. Fifteen feet. He could shoot, but they were still closing. The biggest of them, huge, fifty kilos for sure, swam straight at him, and then as if inviting attack, turned its flank toward Max at less than ten feet away.

Zzing! High-pitched vibrating modes of spear rang their metallic twang in all directions. *Hot damn! Wow, deep into the gill plate. Not bad, Max. Not bad!*

In an instant, all the fish scattered. The lines flew free of his gun. The big tuna bolted straight for the bottom, pulling the float line before Max's eyes. He still had air. He grabbed the line to feel the force of his fish. *Sweet Jesus! What a beast!* On the surface, Herman lost control of the float as the fish pulled it away from him. Max yanked on the line and tried to rein in his catch, horsing it back toward the surface. The fish was too strong, though, and as Max held the line, he was pulled along, down.

Inexplicably, suddenly, the fish stopped. Max obeyed Newton's first law. He was an object in motion, so he remained in motion until acted upon by an outside force, and so he continued on, slowed only by the frictional drag of water. He obeyed Newton's second law, and accelerated downwards under the force of gravity corrected for his negative buoyancy—a factor equal to the difference between his density and that of the surrounding water. The float line, taut only seconds before, curled up in tangles as he rushed over it. Having had enough fun, and no longer confident he had enough air, he gathered himself and kicked toward the surface. *Shit, that's seventy-five feet up, at least.* Progress was slow. Fighting the downdrafts and gravity was far harder than he had imagined. *It's all your pertinacious pursuit, Man. What the fuck did that old man mean? My pertinacious pursuit will get me to air.*

He kicked and rose, and he knew he would make it to the surface when, as inexplicably and as suddenly as it had stopped, his catch took off again. The fast-moving tangles ensnared Max's left wrist and with a *jerk!* that shook the gun out of his hand, he went flying down again toward the sharks.

In fright he'd known only once—when he saw his father's head cracked and gushing blood—he almost gasped, but his reflexes saved him and he kept his mouth shut. The pressure of speed ripped his mask off and away. Max was almost blind. The force of the leviathan pulled him stiff and board-straight. His free right hand could not reach down to the chromed and serrated Froodblade dive knife in its calfboard scabbard. With all the strength he had to live he stretched and bent and finally retrieved it. Hacking and whacking at the line, he cut it and was free. *Thank you, fucking Dad*! But he had slashed his hand, too. He watched as his left index finger floated away. Blood gushed out, life-giving oxygen with it, and he felt faint, as he always did at the sight of blood, and in the knowledge that he was maxed out, already a dead man.

Can't see much without a dive mask
It's been ripped from my old face at last
My eardrums are frighteningly bowed
And my lungs like they're gonna explode
The blood in my veins that has flowed
Drained of the O_2 *my cortex was owed*
Leave my legs freakin' limp as a toad
Monofilament wraps, the forefinger taps, and the pain
Of these visions of Arianna and that boy still remain.

Free at last, he kicked toward light and life. He focused as he had not done in a long time, and rose in a futile race with the oxygen-binding curve of hemoglobin. His lungs, rapidly expanding in the decreasing pressure ten metres from the surface, drew oxygen from the metalloprotein, the molecular lung, according to established principles of physiology he knew well. He was latent hypoxemic. His thoughts began to wander to the white tip reef sharks and the spiny dogfish sharks approaching from below. His mind roamed over Miriam. *Fire of my loins!* It meandered to his father, to fucking Jay and Joosey, to a little boy who died before his second year, and other scores that could not be settled. He dropped his Froodblade. His kicks became irregular and ineffective. He stopped ascending a few feet from the life-promising surface, shallow in the deep water. Latency gave way to actuality and Max blacked out, hypercapnic.

The high CO_2 levels in his blood triggered the urge to breathe he had suppressed while conscious. He gasped and gulped. Sinking in a trail of blood, the hypertonic seawater in his lungs drew fluid from his circulation by osmosis. His blood thickened. Max died from cardiac arrest a few minutes later. With his left wrist still snared in the float line leading to the buoy, he came to rest dangling fifty feet below the surface. The curious cartilaginists sniffed him, tasted the blood, and swam off.

Herman, more than a hundred yards away from the buoy, knew only the direction in which trouble must have occurred. He waved frantically for Tommy and Putu in the boat. Tommy was the first to spot Max's blood on the surface. Putu swam down for rescue, and Tommy pulled Max in like a game fish that had died on the hook.

From the memory card in the camera, Vera reconstructed the sequences of events.

CHANA and Chava called home when the twelve-hour time difference permitted it, informing their fathers that Max had found his own unique way to sleep with the fishes. Mo called Vladik. Vladik called me.

FULL moon parties swung into gear that night. In keeping with the spirit of exclusivity, aka scarcity, that preserved the revelers' willingness to pay an entry fee, an attention-getting table fee, and exorbitant prices for food and drinks, Vera's bouncers at the Blue Bikini, her new dance club by the beach, turned away about half the men and a few of the women. Vera imagined a day when the demand increased, and a long line of wannabees, all of them ready to pay the price for premium triple-distilled ethanol. The lucky partiers propped themselves up with platters of seafood from the grill only a few feet away, and with big bottles of vodka, fresh fruit juices, Bintani on draft, and the other accoutrements you might expect where there was no police presence.

Max's death had already become common knowledge across Gili T. A funeral pyre consumed him at sunset, and like some surreal big brother, the masjid speakers blasted the news for all to hear. Soon, he was competing for airtime. Just before midnight, one tourist and one Indonesian resident succumbed to methanol poisoning from local bootleg.

Two red-haired American teenagers calling themselves Rani and Gili met a young Indonesian with cinnamon skin and distinctly European features who called herself Maxime. The cousins used their real names either in a lapse of protocol or the premonition that this one other girl should know their real names, and only their real names. When Maxime blurted out that she was bound for Bard College, the three discovered that they had plenty to share.

On the dance floor, one DJ after another, most of them flown in from Kuta only hours before, pumped up the thousand-strong crowd with EDM and propane flame-throwers. Vera's cash register *ka-ching*'d with abandon, slowing down but not stopping as the full moon set.

Epilogue

A STARTUP IS a journey, an adventure, an expedition. As in any expedition, divided leadership is doom. In the case of Moby Dx, the enterprise and half the leadership met dismal fates. The rest of us? A startup is like a family, and its demise is like a death in the family. Ours slipped away with the inexorability of Alzheimer's, forcing us all through the wringer of protracted grief. Like a martini, some were shaken, some only stirred, and some were altogether shattered on the floor.

Dyk was shattered. No longer able to feed at the trough of Max's technology pimping machine, he was out of work and living off his assets—a very difficult business with interest rates depressed almost to zero—and then on Social Security, although he denied ever having accepted benefits from any government program. He was last seen pushing shopping carts and selling pencils on the lower Manhattan street corners he said he hailed from.

Vladik was shaken. After they moved back to Block Island, he wrote a book, *Spooky Action at a Distance*; an awful, turgid murder mystery; a *roman à clef* based on the Einstein-Podolsky-Rosen paradox, its clues entangled in anagrams of the first characters of the chapter titles; an unreadable book full of bitterness; a book violating David Foster Wallace's dictum that above all else a novel must be fun. It was a book whose only virtue was that it was shorter than *Infinite Jest*. Fewer than N_{Max} people had read it when he burned the files, lock, stock, and thumb drive, on the night Arianna delivered the triplets Nympha, Nadezhda, and Vida, girls who have focused his mind ever since.

Arianna stayed closer to home than she had before, but continued advising the rich and the richer on matters of taste and on art-centric tax code exploits.

Rani and Gili would soon be seniors at Bard. One was a performance sculptor, one a painter. There had been sequels but no equal to their Indonesian affair. They remained crazily seductive gold star lesbians leaving young men full of ideas and driving them insane, to paraphrase the Bard. When the boys begged to know why or why not, their answer, predictably, was "we'd prefer not to." And like Vladik, they weren't carriers, of Tay-Sachs.

Their classmate Maxime Katawijaya was voted Most Exotic Girl on Campus as a freshman. She shared a dorm room with Lucy Orrix. As I had been rebooted by Ginger Mascarpone, Lucy's brother Jason, up from Columbia on a weekend visit, was transfixed by Maxime. She was unimpressed by yachts and inherited wealth, and she made him eat shit for months before he convinced her he was serious and they became an item. Not only for her beauty was she a standout, though. During a sophomore semester at Rockefeller University in Manhattan, she discovered that repetitions of a short DNA fragment in the gene for coral growth factor strongly increased the organism's survivability at temperatures three degrees Celsius above normal. Her report on the promise of a vaccine against the widespread die offs was recognized as the Best Undergraduate Poster at the International Congress of Conservation Biology.

Vera missed Max's eccentricities and the mentorship he might have provided for Maxime, but she had a busy and full life. As Gili Trawangan deteriorated, or improved, depending on your perspective, she inaugurated prostitution on the island. There were guests, extremely well-heeled guests, who wanted it, "So why not give it to them?" she asked.

She began operating offshore on the *Fuckin' 'Donesia*—an old Dutch galleon that had been dismasted and fitted with diesels, worn out again and eventually left to be torn apart for scrap, when two ... [Excuse me, Exhausted Reader. The Editor insists that I stop. Here. Now. "Open up no more storylines, and bring this to a conclusion," she says, "on pain of revoking your poetic license." She adds, as if that were not enough, "These threads will take over your life and your book. Stop!"].

She began operating offshore on the *Fuckin' 'Donesia*, believing that soon enough the practice would be allowed on land, just as the ban on motorized transport was lifted when the prices offered for the concession were so high that the island's business-owners could no longer refuse.

D5's art collection at My Monticello filled all her available display spaces, and monthly meetings of the Martian Road Salon continued to be a public relations and a recruiting hit. She needed fewer services from Arianna, but the two women had become like mother and daughter. During the pregnancy, D5 helicoptered from New York over to Block Island. Laden with gifts, when she greeted the triplet-bearing Arianna, she exclaimed, "Why you so fat?" before kvelling over the coming miracle.

Around the same time that the lingering Lesser Depression in America threatened the economy in China, D5 and her daughter and granddaughter were called back to Shanghai for a long visit. Then the PRC dropped the hammer and leaked the story of Slab's security breach to investigative reporter Laura Poitras. The effect of her article was a short but profound paralysis of communications in the United States. No one who was anyone in the meritocracy could use his or her phone or tablet without fear that it was tapped, and so for a few days, no one did. Life was as terrifying and bucolic as in those days after 9/11, and then everything returned to normal. What did it matter whose government was tapping your phones?

Slab issued a statement that it had never worked with the Chinese government or any other agency to create a backdoor in any of its products. It also said, "Whenever we hear about attempts to undermine Slab's industry-leading security, we thoroughly investigate and take appropriate steps to protect our customers." Slab went under and Samsung bought its patent portfolio.

War proved again to be the greatest stimulus. Like brass cartridge casings on the floor of the jungle, Slab's glass tabloids had become worthless manufactured objects needing replacement, and in a hurry. President Christie promised to dismantle the NSA, winning the Tea Party Republicans support. He rushed $2 trillion stimulus through Congress, accelerating infrastructure and factory construction to deliver new phones to the freaked-out citizenry. Businesses emerged to collect old slabs, and others to reclaim their precious metals and rare earth elements. Restaurants and gas stations sprung up to serve the people working to satisfying the demand. A tsunami of new devices offering pretty good privacy arrived on shore. New stores popped up to sell them, and mortgage offices opened for the benefit of those employed in the stores. According to the meta-analysis of the econoblogosphere, the GDP rose by $1.91 for every $1 of stimulus. The economy recovered here and in China. It was all good, and all according to the script of the neo-Keynesians in Beijing.

I've seen D5 and her family in Shanghai, but we have a Snowden's chance in hell of seeing her back on the dunes, or in Woodside. D5's Monticello was at first a crime scene, invaded by every acronymic agency in Justice and Defense. Then State got involved, and argued—they're so soft—that it should become a museum. The Mountain Home Road Residents Committee blanched at the possibility of people—regular people who might have bought cars on Yahoo! or Craigslist—driving, or God forbid, parking in their idyllic neighborhood. Enlisting local support, they handed out gold-plated lapel pins at town council meetings all over the peninsula. The solidarity pins carried the Committee's campaign message, NIMBY, or Not in My Billionaire's Yard. And they fought that idea in Washington with the catchy slogan, "Billionaires deserve their privacy, too." The FBI cast the decisive vote. Still-living members of the team that had surveyed the bugged US Embassy in Moscow in the 1980s surveyed My Monticello and deemed it hopelessly compromised. And so the place, or should I say palace, was quarantined indefinitely, until better surveillance detection schemes had emerged to make it safe for Americans.

MAX, it seems likely, would have been shattered soon enough even if he hadn't run out of gas in the Gilis. One of his companies, Genomax, in the process of sequencing his genome at the time he met his end, uncovered nothing very promising to sell. On the negative side, they found a predisposition to thoracic aortic aneurysm. A Yale cardiologist speculated that given his genetics and the ravaging wrought by kidney disease on his vascular system, and absent early detection and surgical intervention, a high blood pressure event such as a serene deep dive or one of Max's "Fuck me with a wire brush" rants, or simply the unfortunate confluence of circadian and diurnal rhythms would have resulted in aortic rupture, shock, and prompt death before he was fifty. The geneticists also found that he had the markers for alexithymia, but did not have the variant of DRD4 associated with adventure and risk-taking. Maybe that's why he was never an entrepreneur.

JAY was not even stirred. Nor was Venus. Nor was Dykkur, although he doesn't deserve to be mentioned in the same sentence as those other two. There was no Froodgate. Dykkur was involved in no scandal. His rain-making friend Max, on the other coast when he was at home and much further when he was on vacation, lost a company and his life. "Shit happens," Dykkur said to me. Max was only a small part of Dykkur's fee-generation machine. Dykkur missed scraping money from Max's businesses, but what did they contribute to his bottom line? Ten percent? Not even, and not close after figuring in his profits as named partner in the firm. Dykkur emphasized his plausible deniability when he philosophized, "You can lead a horse to water but you can't make him appreciate the view." And who was there to nay say that? All the records were confidential.

Venus's investment in Moby Dx was just Monopoly money for her, skimming a little cream off the top of her sizeable capital gains. At first she threatened to sue Vladik for everything he was worth and more. I talked her out of that and revealed a little of Max's dark side. I don't mean his sexual predilections—morally neutral territory for both of us—but his wheeling and dealing, double dealing, and double dipping. Venus, who then revealed that she'd already been party to some of that, said to me, "For someone so clever, you are extraordinarily naïve. That's par, Lakshmi, *par*."

She had watched Max and his hapless Dyk make a muddle of things at Moby Dx. After Max died, she interceded, first by firing Dyk. Then she paid off the Kakitelashivili's. In exchange for the company's assets and Caselode Fittings I, she gave Sameer a long-term contract to service her staff and pets. … Service them with his food trucks, Salacious-minded Reader, with *his food trucks*.

The Luminosities had to be scaled back because of fire hazard in the drying climate, and Venus had already lost enthusiasm for making a spectacle (of herself) through the promulgation of her birther theory. When billionaires become such spectacles that they're shunned or ignored, and their well-honed sense of being deified, their habit of 'making 'em jump' as Tom Wolfe said, is blunted, they can develop a bitterness about the great mass of humanity. Venus had been desperately close to that condition before she abandoned the birther crowd at the suggestion of her public relations team. She made a few bucks, tens of millions actually, from asteroid mining interests by selling them forecasts of platinum-group metal content derived from high resolution images captured on a privately owned and operated space telescope. She limited her public self to bashing government for being irrelevant to her needs, although as I recall, there'd be no space-engineering infrastructure of any kind without some very substantial government investments spanning more than sixty years.

One summer after Max's demise, Jay, no longer slumming on his parents' boat, brought his own to Block Island. Vladik looked at the yacht's nameplate, and then chided his friend. "*The New Normal*? The new normal for whom? This thing would make Roman Abramovich swoon."

"No, Roman's boat, and Larry's boat, they're in another class, like their wealth. This is about the best a billion dollar fortune can buy you, two hundred feet."

"How did you end up with a billion dollars? You made, what, three hundred, four hundred million on Orrigen? And after taxes? How does that make a billion?"

"Vladik. Taxes are for little people. I've borrowed the money for this boat. The banks think I'm rich, so they lend me money. I find ways to service the debt. The assets from Orrigen, now [redacted], are tucked away in the Orrix Dynasty Trust. That's the new normal, dynastic power."

Vladik wanted to interrupt, but he was *verblüffen* and couldn't marshal a response. So Jay went on.

"I put them in the trust the day after we incorporated, when they were worthless paper. My CFO will make sure it generates a little income for the toys, like this," and he spread his arms to encompass the splendor, "or for the kids after I'm gone. But the unrealized capital gains just sit there, appreciating, tax-free. Then those ... you know, I have my accountants take care of it. It's not my thing. I just know I have a boat better than anyone else in the world with a $1 billion net worth."

Vladik found the words. "You've described a coup."

"Vladik, since when did we start with the class warfare?"

"Since when is it class warfare to engage in a discussion of the facts?"

"Well, it just seems like extreme language, even for you, don't you think?"

"Hardly. The world's greatest democracy, or something like that, replaced by an aristocracy powered by a regressive tax system of its own design? It's not violent, but that doesn't make it not a coup. That's a *coup d'états unis!*"

And then the conversation whirled away, as it always had and always would, ranging from irreconcilable economic and political viewpoints, to details of boat hardware and design, to their exploits, and to their children.

Jay said out loud what everyone who knew him knew about him. "I've made my family my mission, and I don't think about anything that's not furthering that somehow." By implication he said, "I'm not interested in what you have to say. If you're interested in what I have to say, then we have something to talk about." It was narcissism, but constructive narcissism, because he had made the world a better place.

"I'm glad you've made an exception for me," Vladik said.

"You *are* family. I love you like a brother."

"And I am interested in what you have to say."

"True enough," Jay said.

He then went on to tell Vladik about the next company on his drawing board, Selfish Genomics.

"I want to know why some people live to be a hundred and fifteen, and why some are so smart, and some are so successful in business. I want to find the root of exceptionalism in the genome. What makes a few of us singular?"

Vladik had no trouble finding the rejoinder for that one. "This is Perlegen redux. It's GWAS for EI, IQ, and cupidity, I mean longevity. You're going to find a lot of small effects with questionable statistics."

"I hear you channeling Lakshmi now. Dr. No."

"I hear you channeling Shockley. But OK, then. What are you going to do if you find something? Publish some interesting papers?"

"We're not going to publish anything. We're going to sell assortative mating services to strengthen the gene pool for the POP."

"So Marc Andreessen can find Laura Arrillaga? I thought they did that without your help."

"Not everyone finds their mate next door, and all they did was concentrate wealth. We're going to use genome editing to concentrate wealth *and* talent, at the embryo. We have fortunes, *fortunes*, to drop on the promise of keeping our dynasties alive, and we will. They will. That's just *The Selfish Gene* at work."

From their perch on the third deck of *The New Normal*, they looked across Great Salt Pond, over Corn Neck Road, out onto the Atlantic Ocean, and finally to the glowing horizon. Moments later, the brilliant upper limb of the sun broke through, blinding them, and forcing a pause in their discussion of altruism, Darwin, Dawkins, and regression.

Lucy and Jason Orrix, and Maxime Katawijaya, and Rani and Gili Kakitelashvili, still wet from an early morning swim, paraded their youthful beauty through the cabin. Placing a plate of pond-harvested, fresh fried clams in front of the two men, Lucy said, "Shellfish genes, Dad," and then, with a nod to her father's long time friend, she uttered an affectionate and untested term of endearment she had learned from the Brooklyners, "Uncle Vova."

GEORGINA moved to a $10,500 per month, two-bedroom apartment in the Mission District of San Francisco; some people's idea of the next Silicon Valley and other people's idea of the next Silicon Valley exurb. "I don't like boring any more," she explained. After the Summer of Snowden, she had removed every removable scrap of her Internet presence. She wore sunglasses to baffle face recognition systems in their relentless effort to get a grip on her. She believed in Slab's published policy statements, with their descriptions of one hundred percent commitment to preserving customers' privacy, and she took a marketing job there, where her package of languages and software and interpersonal skills were appreciated. Some weeks she spent commuting on the white bus down to Palo Alto, and others she spent in Russia. While promoting Slab's brand in St. Petersburg and Moscow by organizing salons for the rich and the connected, she became an unwitting agent of the Chinese. And when Slab went under, she was hired days later by TPC, a contender for the brass ring Slab left behind.

The owners dismantled G's spot, the little cottage in Palo Alto, stick by stick, like the Big House in front of it, and donated the debris to Whole House Building and Supply & Salvage in EPA. When the concrete in the old perimeter foundation was removed, no Komatsu basement excavator or Putzmeister concrete pumper with long, folding shnoz appeared to make a new one. Then the landscape architects came in, made sketches, and on the combined acreage of several neighboring properties, whose houses had also been taken down stick by stick, a moat of parkland arose around the one remaining home, creating for its billionaire owner the isolation he felt he needed, and proving to some that privacy had ceased to be a right and had become a privilege.

ME? I was shaken. At first I did moby for love, then I did it for a friend, and then for money. I wasn't doing anything at all when it ended in darkness and blood. Working for Max Frood, being in his sphere, there was no other word for it than love. Then I began to help my friend Vladik, and that led to a business, or a business idea really, but one with money in it. Along the way, the love hit its sell-by date and there was blood. All that's left of Max is this story.

When Venus asked me to restart the company with my own handpicked team, a proper investment, and a sensible cap table that included something for Maxime, I asked for and got a rain check. The molecular stethoscope was shit and we shut it down. BroadID would have been ready for some markets, but for the big one, sepsis, what was needed was fast-turnaround sequencing, and that wasn't something we could advance. The backlash against Myriad damped investors' enthusiasm for private genomics databases, and after a year, I put what I'd learned into the public domain and walked away from it. The rain check, to be used for anything I wanted, had no expiration date—a benefit of working with someone for whom money is no object.

I gave up a bench science career after planning for it my entire youth. Vadim and Xenia offered me a position as AIW, Anything I Wanted, at Prophetic Capital. I was Xenia's kept companion until Vadim succumbed to a glioblastoma. Before he died, the sperm of the prophet was *splürtten* on our wombic walls. He was happy to see to our bulging bellies, but he did not live to meet the half-siblings we carried to term. Now she and I are Partners.

I'm Rani or Queen Lakshmi to the triplets. My Naija is their "cousin" and so is her brother, Vadim. Sometimes when they're with me on the bluffs on a particular kind of November day, I feel an ancient insatiable restlessness so well described by others, but I know that my little anchors will hold me no matter how hard, no matter which way the weather blows in.

PREMISED on distinguished American engineering professor Henry Petroski's observation that the best way of achieving lasting success is by more fully understanding failure, the K Institute of Entrepreneurship in George Town—that's in the Caymans—will publish the findings of its Failure Project next Spring. A multiyear effort to identify and ultimately avoid sources of failure in early stage companies, the Failure Project will feed its results back to the community through education and marketing channels, and will establish a Hall of Shame of the worst, most spectacularly epic fails of all time. The K will define (and you can consider this an authorized pre-announcement, warts and all) their Failure Quotient [sic]:

$$FQ = log_{10}(BurntCapital) \times \textit{STAIN}$$

Scale, always an important consideration in these matters, is made explicit through the leading term, but taking the logarithm of the burnt capital, in USD, damps its effect. Like medications, every new venture has side effects on the lives of stakeholders. *STAIN*—a number between 1 (lily-white) and 10 (rorschachingly black)—is an acronym for Societal Toll And Inethical [*sic*] Norms. It assesses the economic and psychological damage to those lives, using sentiment analysis and quantitative factors involving the number of employees, womb-to-tomb duration, ethical practices of management, opportunity cost, customer satisfaction, and morbidity and mortality rates. Based on extensive interviews with principals and online surveys of over 10,000 members of the NVCA, an organization of investors, the Funded, an organization of entrepreneurs, the VFW, an association of writers focusing on venture funding, and the other TLA, the Trial Lawyers Association, the K is in the process of estimating *STAIN* and computing the Failure Quotient for over one thousand companies dating back to 1995. As of this writing, Moby Dx LLC with its *FQ* of 51 is second only to █████.

GLOSSARY

23andMe

Silicon Valley pioneer in the field of direct-to-consumer genetics. The company has its tit in a wringer as the entire premise of DTC is challenged by the Food and Drug Administration and the Federal Trade Commission. 23andMe was founded by Ann Wojcicki and Linda Avey. Ms. Wojcicki is the wife of Google cofounder Sergey Brin. Relative Finder is one of the software tools the company provides to its users.

AAAS

American Association for the Advancement of Science

Aalto, Alvar (d. 1976)

Finish architect and designer

Abragam, Anatole (d. 2011)

French physicist renowned for work in nuclear magnetism at the College de France and elsewhere

Abramovich, Roman

Russian billionaire, and owner of the world's second largest yacht, *Eclipse.*

ADP

Automatic Data Processing, a publicly traded automatic data processing company

AK

Above the knee, as in an amputation

Allen, Woody

American film maker and author.

Alexithymia

A personality trait marked by abnormally low (i) emotional awareness and (ii) empathy.

ALS

Amyotrophic Lateral Sclerosis, a neurodegenerative disease. Also known as Lou Gehrig's Disease

AMG

Aufrecht Melcher Gro√üaspach, a high performance luxury brand of Mercedes-Benz

AMP

American Molecular Pathologists, the plaintiff in *AMP v. Myriad.*

ANA

Anti-nuclear Antibodies

Andreessen, Marc

American engineer, serial entrepreneur, investor, and SVB. Co-author of the first Internet browser, MOSAIC, and cofounder of Netscape, the first Internet browser company. Andreessen is married to Laura Arrillaga, daughter of real estate developer and SVB John Arrillaga.

APGAR

Appearance, Pulse, Grimace, Activity, Respiration, the backronym of anaesthesiologist Virginia Apgar, MD, (1909-1974). Also known as the American Pediatric Gross Assessment Record. One of the most well-known clinimetrics.

APT

Advanced Persistent Threat

Arrhenius, Svante (d. 1927)

Swedish physicist and chemist. Received Nobel Prize in Chemistry in 1903, then became Director of the Nobel Institute. Major contributions to physical chemistry, immunochemistry, and more. In 1896 he elucidated the greenhouse effect and its influence on climate.

Atala, Anthony

Peruvian-born American physician and pioneer in regenerative medicine.

Avery, Oswald (d. 1955)

Canadian-born American physician and microbiologist. His experiments at Rockefeller in 1944 demonstrated that DNA is the molecule of inheritance.

AWOL

Absent without official leave, a term from the US military, equivalant to playing hookie

Bateson, William (d. 1926)

Late nineteenth and early twentieth century Engish geneticist who coined the word genetics and popularized the ideas of Gregor Mendel

Berra, Lawrence Peter "Yogi"

American philospher

Berg, Paul

1980 Nobel Prize in Chemistry for his fundamental studies of the biochemistry of nucleic acids, with particular regard to recombinant-DNA

Bienvenue à Deauville

French, Welcome to Deauville

BFF

Best Friend Forever

BIRI

Block Island, Rhode Island

BLAST

Basic Local Alignment Search Tool, an algorithm for comparing primary sequence developed by Altschul et al. and first published in 1990.

BMTC

Bangalore Metropolitan Transport Corporation

Bohr, Niels Hendrik David Bohr (d. 1962)

1922 Nobel Prize in Physics for his services in the investigations of the structure of atoms and the radiation emanating from them.

Born, Max (d. 1970)

German theoretical physicist from Göttingen. Nobel Prize in Physics. Made seminal contributions to quantum mechanics, chemical physics, and trained or assisted in the training of an astonishing array of the early 20th century's most famous names, Delbrück, Oppenheimer, Weisskopf, Fermi, Heisenberg, Pauli, and Wigner among them.

Botstein, David

Distinguished American geneticist. In 2013 he was among the first crop of 11 scientists awarded the Breakthrough Prize in Life Science. Variously affiliated with Harvard, MIT, Stanford, Princeton, Genentech, and Calico, a Google-owned company devoted to life extension.

Boyer, Herbert

American molecular biologist. Co-inventor of recombinant DNA methods in The Patent. Also, cofounder of Genentech

Bozhe moi

Russian, Oh my God, or similar.

Brenner, Sydney

South African biologist. Codiscoverer of the triplet code in 1961, and winner of the 2002 Nobel Prize in Physiology or Medicine for discoveries concerning genetic regulation or organ development and programmed cell death.

BSCA

Blue Shield of California, a large health insurer

Burnet, Frank MacFarlane (d. 1985)

Australian virologist and immunologist. 1960 Nobel Prize in Physiology and Medicine for the discovery of acquired immunological tolerance.

C-section
Caesarean section. Delivery from above.

Caveat emptor
Latin, buyer beware

CDR
Complementarity Determining Region,

CEO
Cash Extraction Officer, or alternately Chief Executive Officer

CFI
Caseload Fittings I

CFNM
Clothed Female, Nude Male

Clark, Jim
American electrical engineer, inventor, entrpreneur, and Stanford Professor. Cofounded Silicon Graphics, Netscape, Healtheon, myCFO, and others

CMV
Cytomegalovirus. A human herpesvirus.

COI
Conflict of Interest, or Conflict of Interest disclosure

Cormack, Allan MacLeod (d. 1998)
American physicist. 1979 Nobel Prize in Physiology or Medicine for the development of computer assisted tomography.

CS
Computer Science

CT
Computer assisted tomography

COBOL
COmmon Business Oriented Language, an early and important computer language heavily influenced by the mathematician and computer scientist Rear Admiral Grace Hopper, who also coined the word "debug".

Courant, Richard (d. 1972)
German mathematician, expatriated to the USA in the 1930s. The institute of mathematics that he nurtured at NYU now bears his name. He was a student of David Hilbert.

CPR
Cardiopulmonary Resuscitation

Creatinine
A metabolic product whose concentration in the blood is a measure of kidney or renal health. Measured in units of mg/dl or milligrams per decilitre, the normal range for men is 0.5 to 1.0, and somewhat higher for women.

Crick, Francis (d. 2004)
1962 Nobel Prize in Medicine and Physiology for the discovery of the molecular structure of DNA

Curie, Marie (d. 1934)
Polish physicist and chemist. Nobel Prize in Physics, 1903, Studies in Radiation Physics, and Nobel Prize in Chemistry, 1911, Discovery of Radium and Polonium

CVS
A chain of drugstores in the US, formerly a subsidiary of the Melville Corporation. The acronym may mean Customers, Value, and Service, or Chocolate, Vanilla, and Strawberry

D&O
Directors and Officers liability insurance

DARPA
Defense Advanced Research Projects Agency. The Internet was invented under its guidance.

Darwin, Charles (d. 1882)
Author of *The Origin of Species*

DC
District of Columbia

de Gennes, Pierre-Gilles (d. 2007)
1991 Nobel Prize in Physics for studies of order in complex systems

Delbruck, Max (d. 1981)
1969 Nobel Prize in Physiology or Medicine for work on the replication mechanisms and genetic structures of viruses

DFW
Dallas-Fort Worth Airport

DIY
Do It Yourself. A movement away from utter dependence on manufactured, often closed systems. May involve hacking of physical systems. Sometimes known as the maker movement.

DNA
Deoxyribonucleic Acid, the molecule of inheritance

Domestique
A term from professional bicycle racing, meaning a team rider whose job it is to defend the team leader and advance the team, not to win the race for him or herself.

DRAM
Dynamic Random Access Memory

DRD4
A gene that encodes the dopamine receptor. Certain polymorphisms, specifically DRD4 -521C/T have been associated with novelty seeking traits.

DUI
A traffic citation for driving under the influence of alcohol or other intoxicants

Dunham, Ann (d. 1995)
President Barack Obama's mother

Dx
Diagnostics or diagnosis. Many life science companies use the abbreviation, e.g., Archer Dx and XDx.

DXB
Dubai International Airport

EBV
Epstein-Barr Virus, a common virus of the herpes family.

EDM
Electronic Dance Music

EECS
Electrical Engineering and Computer Science

Einstein, Albert (d. 1955)
German theoretical physicist and inventor. 1921 Nobel Prize in Physics, for his services to theoretical physics.

Einstein-Podolsky-Rosen Paradox
EPR (1935) was a challenge to Bohr's so-called Copenhagen interpretation of quantum mechanics, involving notions such as quantum entanglement and (spooky) action at distance. Subsequently, it has been experimentally proven that EPR's assumptions are invalid, thus invalidating its challenge.

EIR
Entrepreneur-in-Residence

EKG
Electrocardiography. Instruments and methods for non-invasive determination of heart condition by electrical measurements of the skin.

Ellison, Larry

American entrepreneur and SVB. Founder of Oracle, a software company. Owner of one of the world's largest yachts, *Musashi*.

EMT

Emergency Medical Team, Technician, or Training

ENS

École Normale Supérieure, an elite university in Paris

EPA

East Palo Alto or Enviromental Protection Agency

EPROM

Electrically Programmable Read Only Memory

EI

Emotional Intelligence. The title of a book by Daniel Goleman. The abilities to monitor, discriminate between, and use emotions to navigate the (social) world.

ESKD

End Stage Kidney Disease. Also, ESRD for Renal Disease

EST

Eastern Standard Time, GMT-5

ETA

Estimated Time of Arrival

EVP

Executive Vice President

fakakta

Yiddish, hare-brained

FBI

Federal Bureau of Investigation

FBO

Fixed-base operator. A private business providing services such as fueling and hangaring at a public-use airport.

FDA

Food and Drug Administration

FDR

Franklin Delano Roosevelt, the 32nd President of the United States

Fermat, Pierre (d. 1665)

Seventeenth-century French mathematician, who wrote about a tricky problem in number theory, "I have discovered a truly remarkable proof which this margin is too narrow to contain." The theorem was not proved for another 300 years.

Fermi, Enrico (d. 1954)

One of the great of the great. Was awarded the 1938 Nobel Prize in Physics for some of his work in nuclear physics, but it could have been for his work in solid state physics, in thermodynamics, or ... He left Rome that same year and went to Chicago with his Jewish wife.

FET

Field Effect Transistor

Feynman, Richard P. (d. 1988)

1965 Nobel Prize in Physics for his work in quantum electrodynamics. He was the son of Lucille and Melville Feynman.

FOMO

Fear of Missing Out

Foster, Norman

English architect. Winner of the Pritzker Prize in 1999.

FRS

Fellow of the Royal Society of London, founded 1660

FSR
The former Soviet Republics of the Union of Soviet Socialist Republics. Examples include Russia, Ukraine, and Kyrgyzstan.

FTF
Face-to-Face

FUD
Fear, Uncertainty, and Doubt

Fukuyama, Francis
American political scientist and author, best known for his 1992 book, *The End of History and the Last Man*. Fukuyama is a Senior Fellow at the Stanford University Center on Democracy, Development and the Rule of Law

FVL
Factor V Leiden. A variant of the gene that codes for Factor V.

Galt, John
Hero of Ayn Rand's *Atlas Shrugged*. He is shrouded in mystery as the book asks "Who is John Galt?" and before he gives a famously long radio address.

GATTACA
A movie of the same name about eugenics. Also an oligonucleotide

GGG
Good, Giving, and Game. An ideal for sexual partners set forward by Dan Savage.

Glaser, Donald (d. 2013)
1960 Nobel Prize in Physics for the invention of the bubble chamber. Cofounder of Cetus Corp in 1971.

GMO
Genetically modified organism

Goldstein, Emmanuel
Fictional hero of George Orwell's *1984*. Like John Galt, he is known for a famously long manifesto.

Gonef
Yiddish, thief

GoPro
a small, waterproof video camera, often head-mounted, popular among skin-, sky-, and SCUBA divers.

Gould, Stephen Jay (d. 2002)
American paleontologist, MacArthur Fellow, National Book Award for non-fiction

GPS
Global Positioning System

Griffith, Linda
MacArthur Fellow, MIT Professor of Bioengineering focusing on biomaterials and tissue engineering for regenerative medicine. Also, Director of the Center for Gynepathology Research.

GSB
Stanford Graduate School of Business

GSM
Global System for Mobile communications. An international standard for digital cellular networks.

GUI
Graphical User Interface

Guthrie, Woody (d. 1967)
Mid-twentieth century American singer, songwriter, and political activist.

GWAS
Genome-wide Association Studies

Hadoop
An open-source framework for handling large datasets on large computer networks

Haldane, John Burdon Sanderson (d. 1964)
Mid twentieth-century British geneticist and evolutionary biologist

Helmholtz, Herman Ludwig Ferdinand (d. 1894)
German physicist and physiologist . Made important contributions to the physics of sensory systems.

Heisenberg, Werner (d. 1976)
German physicist. 1932 Nobel Prize in Physics for "the creation of quantum mechanics." Author of the Uncertainty Principle, which states that the simultaneous measurement of position and momentum is impossible without fundamental limits on precision.

Hemoglobin
The iron-containing protein in red blood cells that is responsible for transporting O_2 from lungs to tissues.

HER
Health Economic Research

HGH
Human Growth Hormone

HGP
Human Genome Project

HIPAA
Health Information Portability and Accountability Act of 1996

HIV
Human Immunodeficiency Virus responsible for AIDS, Acquired Ammunodeficiency Syndrome

HLA
Human Leukocyte Antigen. A part of the immune system that is important in recognizing self from non-self.

HMRI
Haldane Medical Research Institute

HKD
Hong Kong Dollars

HMO
Health Maintenance Organization

Hoff, Ted
American engineer, best known for his invention of the microprocessor with Federico Faggin at Intel. As a graduate student at Stanford, he invented and applied early neural network, aka machine learning, devices.

Holdren, John
American physicist, MacArthur Fellow, advisor to President Obama on science and policy

Hounsfield, Godfrey FRS (d. 2004)
English electrical engineer. 1979 Nobel Prize in Physiology or Medicine for the development of computer assisted tomography.

HP
Hewlett-Packard, the Palo Alto company founded by David Packard and William Hewlett in 1939 and that has become one of the most important technology companies.

HTML
Hypertext Markup Language, the language of most web pages. First described by the physics-trained Sir Tim Berners-Lee, inventor of the world-wide web.

HVAC
Heating, Ventilation and Air Conditioning

Hypercapnic
Having abnormally high blood CO2. Leads, normally, to increased breathing.

Hypertonic
Excessively salty, or hypertonic solutions draw water from less salty solutions by osmosis.

Hypoxemic
Having abnormally low arterial blood oxygen. If not corrected, unconsciousness and death follow shortly.

IBM
International Business Machines

ICU
Intensive Care Unit

IMHO
In my humble opinion

IP
Intellectual property, an umbrella term referring to copyright, trademarks, patents, and tradesecrets.

IPO
Initial Public Offering

IRA
Individual Retirement Account, or Individual Retirement Arrangment. Congressionally authorized accounts or part of a plan permitting individuals tax-free appreciation of certain assets set aside for retirement.

IR&D
Internal Research and Development

IRS
Internal Revenue Service, the tax collecting agency of the federal government of the United States of America

IT
Information Technology

IPO
Initial Public Offering

ISB
Benazir Bhutto International Airport in Islamabad, Pakistan

ITSy
International Technology Systems Corp.

Jacob, Francois (d. 2013)
Nobel Prize in Physiology or Medicine, 1965, for his discoveries concerning the role played by the chromosome in heredity

Jenner, Edward (d. 1823)
English physician scientist. The father of immunology and pioneer of the smallpox vaccine.

Jerne, Niels K. (d. 1994)
Danish immunologist. Nobel Prize in Physiology and Medicine, 1984, for theories concerning the specificity in development and control of the immune system and the discovery of the principle for production of monoclonal antibodies.

JFK
John Fitzerald Kennedy, the 35th President of the United States. Also, an international airport in New York City.

Jie Jie
Chinese name meaning Big Sister

JND
Just-Noticeable Difference, a term from sensory psychophysics meaning the smallest difference a sensory system can perceive

Josephson, Brian
Welsh physicist, and winner of the 1973 Nobel Prize for his theoretical predictions of the properties of supercurrents through a tunnel barrier

Judson, Horace Freeland (d. 2011)

Author of the *The Eighth Day of Creation*, a masterpiece of journalism about the history of molecular biology

Kasevich, Mark

American physicist at Stanford developing cold-atom interferrometry and its applications.

KCB

Knight's Chivalrous Order of the Bath

KCIE

Knight's Chivalrous Order of the Indian Empire

KGB

Komitet Gosudarstvennoy Bezopasnosti, the Committee for State Security in the former Soviet Union

Kezia Obama

Barack Obama Sr's first wife.

King, John G.

American physicist and MIT professor.

KLM

Royal Dutch Airways

Kornberg, Arthur (d. 2007)

American biochemist. 1959 Nobel Prize in Physiology or Medicine for co-discovery of mechanisms of the biological synthesis of DNA

Kvelling

Yiddish, expressing great pleasure or pride

La méthode

French, René Descartes' *Discourse on Method*, 1637 treatise on the philosophy and the scientific method, among other things, and the source of his famous phrase, I think therefore I am.

Lakshminarayanan, A. V.

Co-developer with G. N. Ramachandran of convolution filters for image reconstruction in computed tomography.

Langer, Robert

American engineer, inventor, entrepreneur, and MIT professor presiding over the world's largest bioengineering laboratory at the David H. Koch Institute for Integrative Cancer Research. He has filed for hundreds of patents through TLO, and participated in the founding of more than two dozen companies. The magnitude of the Langer Tax has never been disclosed. He is the model for many enterprising academic entrepreneurs.

Lasser, Louise

American actress, best known for her role as the lead character in the TV series, *Mary Hartman, Mary Hartman.*

LAX

Los Angeles International Airport

LBD

Louisa ben Dayore. Also, little black dress and lesbian bed death.

LED

Light Emitting Diode

Le loup americain

French, the wolf from America

Le marché de mer

French, open air fish market

Levée du voile

French, a lifting of the veil, a revelation

Lewis, Gilbert N. (d. 1946)

Great American chemist (d. 1946). He discovered the covalent bond, conceived of electron pairing, and coined the word "photon."

Lewis, Michael
American author of *Liar's Poker, The New New Thing, Moneyball*, and others

LCD
Liquid Crystal Display

LGA
Fiorello LaGuardia Airport in Queens, New York City

LISP
LISt Processor, an early high-level computer language developed by computer scientist extraordinaire, John McCarthy in 1959. He also coined the word "artificial intelligence".

LLC
Limited Liability Company

LNKD
Stock symbol for the American social network company LinkedIn

LOC
Lab-on-a-chip

Louganis, Greg
Sullivan Award-winning springboard and tower diver. Swept Olympic golds in 1984 and 1988.

LSAT
Law School Admissions Test

Lupus
Systemic lupus erythematosus or SLE. An autoimmune disease often accompanied by a large rash, the butterfly rash, on both cheeks. Mostly affects women.

Luria, Salvatore (d. 1991)
1969 Nobel Prize in Physiology and Medicine, for work on the replication mechanisms and genetic structure of viruses

M&A
Merger and Acquisition

Maillot jaune
French, the yellow jersey worn by the overall leader in the world's greatest bicycle race.

Maharajkumari
Daughter of the maharaja and maharani

Mat
an obscene, profane, ostracized, and widely used form of Russian slang

Maxwell, James Clerk (d. 1879)
Immortal Scottish mathematical physicist who formulated the integrated theory of electricity and magnetism.

MBA
Master's Degree in Business Administration

MDMA
3,4-methylenedioxy-N-methamphetamine, aka ecstasy, E, or X, an empathogenic amphetamine

Mea maxima culpa
Latin, by my own most grievous error

Mead, Carver
American computer scientist. Pioneered modern semiconductor device design, both analog and digital. May have coined the term Moore's Law.

Mei Mei
Chinese name meaning Little Sister.

Meitner, Lise (d. 1968)
Austrian physicist. Should have been a co-winner of the 1944 Nobel Prize in Physics for the 1938 discovery of nuclear fission. Her collaborator was the Nobelist Otto Hahn.

MEMS
Microelectromechanical Systems

Mendel, Gregor (d. 1884)
Austrian, German monk and botanist (d. 1884). Founder of genetics.

MILF
Mother I'd Like to Fuck

MIT
Massachusetts Institute of Technology

Molly
Highly purified MDMA

Monod, Jacques (d. 1976)
Nobel Prize in Physiology or Medicine, 1965, for his discoveries concerning the role played by the chromosome in heredity

MOOC
Massive Open Online Courseware

Moore, Gordon
American engineer, inventor, and entrepreneur. Best known for the observation, now known as Moore's Law, that the number of transistors on an integrated circuit increases exponentially with time.

Morgan, Thomas Hunt (d. 1945)
1933 Nobel Prize in Physiology or Medicine, for his discoveries concerning the role played by the chromosome in heredity

MRS
Martian Road Salon of D5

MTL
Microsystems Technology Laboratory at MIT

Muller, Hermann (d. 1967)
American geneticist. Awarded the 1946 Nobel Prize in Physiology or Medicine for the discovery of the production of mutations by the means of X-ray irradiation.

Mullis, Kary
1983 Nobel Prize in Chemistry for the invention of PCR

NAACP
National Association for the Advancement of Colored People, founded 1909. Headquarted in Baltimore, MD.

Napster
An Internet service that pioneered peer-to-peer file sharing of music. Founded by Sean Parker and the Fanning brothers.

NASDAQ
National Association of Stockmarket Dealers Automatic Quotations, one of the two major stock markets in the US

NDA
Non-disclosure Agreement

NGM
Next-generation MEMS

NGO
Non-governmental Organization

NIH
National Institutes of Health . Also, Not Invented Here

NMR
Nuclear Magnetic Resonance. A technique developed by Rabi, Bloch, and Purcell (Nobel Prize, Physics 1944 and 1952) to probe the magnetism of the atomic nucleus. 2002 Nobel Prize in Chemistry to Wuthrich for NMR Studies of Structure and Function of Biological Macromolecules), and 2003 Nobel Prize in Physiology or Medicine to Lauterberg and Mansfield for the development of magnetic resonance imaging, or MRI.

Normalienne

French, a female student of the École Normale Supérieure

Noether, Emmy (d. 1935)

Distinguished German Jewish mathematician and physicist who fled Germany in 1934.

NoSQL

Not Only Structured Query Language, a database architecture gaining popularity with the rise of big data. May be pronounced nosequel.

Noyce, Robert N. (d. 1990)

American engineer, inventor, and entrepreneur. Best known as an inventor of the integrated circuit. A Nobel Prize in Physics was awarded to Jack Kilby for a related invention a decade after Noyce's premature death.

NSA

National Security Agency, the signal intelligence agency

NSF

National Science Foundation

NSFW

Not safe for the workplace

NUS

National University of Singapore

NYU

New York University, a private university in lower Manhattan, New York City. Its Courant Institute of Mathematical Sciences bears the name of Richard Courant, who fled the Nazis and landed at NYU in 1936.

OB/GYN

Obstetrics and Gynecology

OCR

The Office of Contractual Relations at HMRI

OMA

Eppley Airfield, Omaha Airport Authority

Oppenheimer, J. Robert (d. 1967)

American physicist. Influential educator, contributor to astrophysics and quantum mechanics, and manager of the Manhattan Project at Los Alamos during WWII. He advocated restraint on the development of the hydrogen bomb, but was pushed aside by the inventor of Star Wars, Edward Teller.

O'Reilly Technology Conference

A diverse series of software and technology conferences produced globally by O'Reilly Media, a company founded by author and software activist Tim O'Reilly. Mr. O'Reilly is usually credited with coining the term "Web 2.0."

OTL

Office of Technology Licensing, Stanford University

Отредактированное

Russian, meaning redacted, pronounced otredaktirovannoye.

Oxazepam

A slow onset, short-acting benzodiazepine with anxietolytic properties, helpful for people with PTSD.

Oxon.

Oxonian, an alumnus or alumna of Oxford University

Ozawa, Seiji

Renowed Japanese conductor

PAC

Political Action Committee

PAMF

Palo Alto Medical Foundation

Pauli, Wolfgang (d. 1958)
Austrian physicist. Nobel Prize in Physics 1945, for discovery of the Exclusion Principle, one consequence of which is the electronic valence structure of atoms.

Pauling, Linus (d. 1994)
American scientist. Wrote the canon on the application of quantum mechanics to chemistry, *The Nature of the Chemical Bond* (1939) and won the 1954 Nobel Prize in Chemistry for related work. Crick called him the father of molecular biology. Was awarded the 1962 Nobel Peace Prize for his work on disarmament.

PARC
Xerox Palo Alto Research Center where the modern computer user interface was born

Parrish, Maxfield (d. 1966)
Influential American painter and illustrator known for his luminous palette.

Pattu
A Tamilian endearment implying the comforting feeling of silk or velvet

PCR
Polymerase Chain Reaction. The Nobel Prize winning invention of Kary Mullis. PCR is widely used to make multiple identical copies of short nucleic acids.

Perutz, Max (d. 2002)
Austrian-born molecular biologist. 1962 Nobel Prize in Chemistry, for his studies of the structures of globular proteins, and hemoglobin in particular.

Petroski, Henry
American engineer and author specializing in failure analysis.

PHP
PHP: Hypertext Processor. A recursive backronym referring to a scripting language widely used for web development. Facebook was written in PHP.

Piketty, Thomas
French neo-Keynesian economist, graduate of the École Normale Supérieure, and author of *Capital in the 21st Century*

PLA
People's Liberation Army of the PRC.

Planck, Max Karl Ernst Ludwig (d. 1947)
German physicist. 1918 Nobel Prize in Physics for discovery of the quantum of action and the quantization of energy.

Plotz
Yiddish, to fall down or collapse

POOP
The point-oh-one-percent wealthiest Americans.

POP
The point-one-percent wealthiest Americans.

POR
Plan of Record

POTUS
The President of the United States

PRC
People's Republic of China

PST
Pacific Standard Time, GMT-8

PTA
Parent Teacher Association, a national not-for-profit organization with local chapters providing services to public schools. Its ranks are dominated by mothers of children in the schools.

PTSD
Post-traumatic Stress Disorder

Putin, Vladimir
President of Russia. Exemplar of Homo sovieticus. Along with Donald Rumsfeld and Pervez Musharaff, Vlad is one of the three most accomplished martial artists among living alumni of the global C-suite.

Pwn
Internet slang, possibly pronounced as if it were spelled pone, meaning to dominate or humiliate.

PYT
Pretty Young Thing

QED
Latin, *Quod erat demonstratum,* Latin phrase used at the end of a mathematical proof, meaning that what was set out to be proved has been proved.

R
A programming language for bioinformatics

R&R
Rest and Recreation.

raison d'être
French, the reason or justification for existence

Ramachandran, G. N. (d. 2001)
Founder of the Molecular Biophysics Unit at the Indian Institute of Science in Bangalore. He was a doctoral student of the Nobelist, C. V. Raman.

Rand, Ayn (d. 1982)
Russian-born American novelist and political theorist, known as the founder of objectivism and its variants also known as libertarianism. Her ideas center around the notion that individual freedom to enforce pre-existing property rights shall not be bridged except at the point of a gun.

Rearden, Henry
Steel-making hero of Ayn Rand's *Atlas Shrugged*

RIB
Rigid Inflatable Boat

RING
Really Interesting New Gene

RLE
Research Laboratory of Electronics at MIT.

Rothberg, Jonathan
American genomics entrepreneur

RSS
Rich Site Summary or Really Simple Syndication is a document format and web protocol that enables really simple syndication of content from frequently updated sites such as blogs and news services.

RUR
Royal University of Rhizobia

Rutherford, Ernest FRS (d. 1937)
New Zealand-born British physicist. Discovered the atomic nucleus. 1908 Nobel Prize in Chemistry for his investigations into the disintegration of the elements and the chemistry of radioactive substances

Sais pas. Mais, pourquoi utiliser huit lorsque deux suffit?
I don't know. But why use 8 [syllables] when two will do?

Sandberg, Sheryl
Silicon Valley billionaire, COO of Facebook

Sanger, Frederick (d. 2013)
1980 Nobel Prize in Chemistry for Sequencing, 1958 Nobel Prize in Chemistry for Structure of Insulin

Saarinen, Eero (d. 1961)
Finnish American architect and designer.

Schrodinger, Erwin (d. 1961)
1933 Nobel Prize Physics, for the wave theory of quantum mechanics

Schlemiel
Yiddish, a habitual bungler

Schlub
Yiddish, an unattractive and worthless person

SCOTUS
The Supreme Court of the United States

SCUBA
Self-Contained Underwater Breathing Apparatus

Selfish Gene
In *The Selfish Gene* (1976), Richard Dawkins makes the unrefuted case—little appreciated outside the field of genetics—that the gene's sole purpose in life is to replicate itself. Therefore, the expression "survival of the fittest" applies not at the species level, but at the level of genes themselves. We humans exist to further the genes, not the other way around.

SEC
Securities and Exchange Commission

SFO
San Francisco International Airport

Shannon, Claude Elwood (d. 2001)
The father of information theory

Shockley, William (d. 1989)
American physicist and inventor raised in Palo Alto. 1956 Nobel Prize in Physics for co-invention of the transistor. Author of the influential, *Electrons and Holes in Semiconductors.* Founder of Shockley Semiconductor. It is difficult to imagine Silicon Valley as we know it without Shockley.

SIN
Changi International Airport, Singapore

Sinclair, Upton (d. 1968)
American author of *The Jungle* and nearly one hundred other books. Nobel Prize for Literature, 1930. On conflict of interest he wrote,"It is difficult to get a man to understand something when his salary depends upon his not understanding it."

SJC
San Jose International or Norman Mineta International Airport

Skolnick, Mark
American geneticist, was the first to clone BRCA1

Slater, Kelly
American professional surfer, and many time world champion.

SMS
Short Message Service, aka text messaging

SNP
Single Nucleotide Polymorphism

SOB
Son of a bitch

Souk
Arabic, a market, specifically an open-air market. Prounounced *shouk* in Hebrew.

Splürtten
A faux German neologism. Rhymes with hürtin'

SRO
Standing Room Only

Stasi

The East German Ministry for State Security. The repressive secret police and intelligence organization of the Soviet Era. See the film *The Lives of Others* by Florian Henckel von Donnersmarck.

STEM

Science, Technology, Engineering, and Math. A term often used in discussion about American public education policy.

SVB

Silicon Valley Billionaire. Also, Silicon Valley Bank

Szilárd, Leó (d. 1964)

Hungarian physicist and inventor, emigrated to Great Britain and then the USA prior to WWII.

TAC Air

A division of the Truman Arnold Companies, TAC Air operates private aviation facilities in thirteen cities including Omaha, NE

Talmage, David (d. 2014)

American immunologist who made significant contributions to the clonal theory of selection.

Thevidiya pundai vervai'la molacha kaalaan

a Tamilian insult

Thiel, Peter

American social theorist, investor and entrepreneur. Cofounder of Confinity, later to become PayPal, in the (failed) hope that it would break the US government's lock on currency. Is pioneering a movement discouraging young adults to attend college. In 2009 he wrote, "Most importantly, I no longer believe that freedom and democracy are compatible."

TLA

Three Letter Acronym or Abbreviation. Also, Trial Lawyers Association

TLO

Pioneering Technology Licensing Office of MIT

Tonegawa, Susumu

1987 Nobel Prize in Physiology or Medicine for his discovery of the genetic principle of antibody diversity

Tor

A message routing protocol designed to provide anonymity. Rapidly gaining popularity since the Summer of Snowden

TPC

The Phone Company. Also, a vast information gathering organization in the 1967 movie, *The President's Analyst.*

TRO

Temporary Restraining Order

TRS-80

Tandy/Radio Shack microcomputer of the late 1970s, contained Zilog's Z-80. Zilog was founded by Federico Faggin, co-inventor of the microprocessor during his years at Intel.

TTO

Technology Transfer Office of HMRI

Turing, Alan Mathison (d. 1954)

Great British computer scientist and logician who committed suicide after being subjected to chemical castration for the crime of being a homosexual.

TTYL

Talk To You Later

USB

Universal Serial Bus. A communications protocol.

USD

United States Dollars

UCSF

University of California at San Francisco

UNOS

United Network for Organ Sharing

URL

Uniform or Universal Resource Locator. The address of a page on the World Wide Web

USPTO

United States Patent and Trademark Office

Verblüffen

German, nonplussed

VC

Venture Capital, Venture Capitalist, or Victoria Cross

Verilog

An early hardware description language widely used for modeling of electronic systems.

VHF

Very High Frequency. A radio band widely used in marine communications.

VIN

Vehicle Identification Number

VK or VKontakte

A social network in Russia founded (2010) and led by Pavel Durov until he was displaced by figures close to V Putin early in 2014.

VLAB

Venture Lab, the Bay Area chapter of the MIT Enterprise Forum

Vogelstein, Bert, MD

Distinguished American oncologist at Johns Hopkins. In 2013 he was among the first crop of 11 scientists awarded the Breakthrough Prize in Life Science.

VSP

Very Serious Person. A derisive term used exclusively in sarcasm.

WASP

White Anglo-Saxon Protestant

Watson, James Dewey

1962 Nobel Prize in Medicine and Physiology, for the discovery of the molecular structure of DNA

Weaver, Warren (d. 1978)

American scientist and administrator. Director of Natural Sciences at Rockeller where he coined the term "molecular biology" and funded programs to make it real. Father of machine-based human language translation. Co-authored with Claude Shannon of the seminal *A Mathematical Theory of Communication*.

WGS

Whole Genome Sequencing

Winston, Harry (d. 1978)

American jeweler by Marilyn Monroe in the song *Diamonds are a Girl's Best Friend*.

WPA

Works Progress Administration, a Depression-era agency that employed millions in the construction and maintenance of public works.

WTVF

A television station in Nashville, TN

Wynn, Steve

Billionaire casino owner in Las Vegas, Macau, and elsewhere. Once accidentally put his elbow through his own magnificent Picasso just prior to closing its sale for $139 million.

Yelstin, Boris (d. 1999)

First President of the Russian Federation, the first post-Soviet Russian state. On August 18, 1991 he stood atop a tank to thwart a coup against Prime Minister Gorbachev's government.

Zacharias, Jerrold (d 1986)

Renowned MIT atomic physicist and educator. Was instrumental in developing practical radar for the military during WWII. Invented the modern atomic clock. Major contributor to the growth of MIT's atomic and nuclear physics research program. Reformed US high school physics education and was a target of Senator Joseph McCarthy.

Zwirner, David

Swiss-born art gallerist

About the Author

Dan Seligson studied physics at MIT (BSc) and UC Berkeley (PhD) before starting a 30-year career in Silicon Valley. He worked at Intel and held executive positions at, has been advisor to, and founded or co-founded several tech and biotech startups. He has 8 US Patents and others pending in fields as diverse as analog circuit design and immunology-based diagnostics. This is his first novel.

Here are some ways to connect with him.

Send email: melvilleanpress@gmail.com.

Follow on twitter: @mlvlvr.

Like the facebook page: facebook.com/mobydx.

Follow on Pinterest: http://www.pinterest.com/mlvlvr/all-things-melvillean/

Write a review at your favorite online retailer, send it to us and we'll post it on the Silicon Valley Novel blog, blog.mobydx.com.

ABOUT THE AUTHOR